HUSH

by
M.D. Selig

MDSelig.com

Amazon.com/author/MDSelig

Patreon.com/MDSelig

ISBN's

979-8-9928199-6-0 Hard back-Full Color bound to hard board, Dust Jacket
979-8-9928199-5-3 Hard back-Blue Cloth bound to hard board, Dust Jacket
979-8-9928199-0-8 Hard back-Color bound to hard board, no dust jacket
979-8-9928199-2-2 Paperback-Color, no dust jacket
979-8-9928199-4-6 Ebook

Going Dark

Kuala Lumpur International Airport
March 8th, 2014

O n March 8th, 2014, at precisely 12:40:38 a.m., Fariq Hamid, the co-pilot of MH370, made his final reply to Tower Control in his heavily Asian-accented call, confirming Malaysian 370 was cleared for takeoff.

"32 Right, cleared for takeoff, Malaysian three-seven-zero. Thank you, bye."

His voice would not be heard again.

Just over a minute later—the jet was airborne and climbing—making its first call to Departure Control. Except, Hamid's voice didn't make the call.

Instead, the heavily American-accented call to Departure—was made by Benjamin R. Waters. And Ben was not used to saying—*Malaysian three-seven-zero*—hence his hesitation and stutter on the callsign of the jet.

"Departure—Malaysian—uh, three-seven-zero?"

But you couldn't blame Ben, as he was in a rush. You had to give Ben a break... as he was a little anxious.

You see, Ben—was a CIA hijacker.

Having to hastily slide into the pilot's seat immediately after the two Malaysian pilots were executed, and make the call quickly, as if everything with the flight was completely normal.

And it all had to happen in less than a two-minute timeframe—as Departure Control was expecting the jet to check in on departure frequency—just after liftoff.

But Ben knew that Departure was not privy to the earlier Asian-accented call to Tower Control, only a minute before. So, his American-accented voice on departure frequency—just after liftoff—wouldn't raise any flags.

The drastic change in voice and accent, were not noticed by Departure Control. Ben knew he'd be *good to go*, as he was a consummate pro.

Even when Ben stuttered on the callsign during his reply—almost saying, *Malaysian one-seven-zero,* but then catching himself, and saying, *three-seven-zero.*

"Malaysian—one—uh... three-seven-zero!"

You had to give Ben a break... after all... it was his first hijacking. Working with a small team of highly trained CIA operatives, who had just taken over MH370.

So, it made perfect sense that Ben stumbled on the callsign when he replied. And his first dialog on the radio was only a slight blunder.

The one thing you *could* say about Ben is that he was consistent... and he would continue to stutter on the callsign for the rest of the radio transmissions. Until his final one... at 35,000 feet, roughly forty-minutes later. His final transmission came only moments before the jet went dark—vanishing from all radar screens—forever.

No... it wasn't an Asian voice that made so many across the world cry for so many years on that dramatic final transmission. That last goodbye, representing 239 loved ones... men, women and children from across the globe.

It was not the copilot Fariq Hamid saying goodbye for all of them.

It was Benjamin R. Waters—in his relaxed, clearly American, CIA-hijacker confidence, as he uttered that

forever... final call... from the void.

"Uh—goodnight, Malaysian, uh—three-seven-zero."

Praise for M.D. Selig *and HUSH*

"In a world where silence has been weaponized and truth buried beneath layers of engineered reality, *Hush* dares to dig deep. Michael Selig pulls back the curtain on the hidden agendas of the Deep State with clarity, courage and brings to light what is both unsettling and essential. This book is not just a revelation—it's a call to awaken, to question, and to reclaim the narratives that have been stolen from us. At a time when discernment is a revolutionary act, *Hush* is a vital companion for those willing to explore the darker corridors of control in order to find the light of sovereignty on the other side."

—LAURA EISENHOWER, AUTHOR & PUBLIC SPEAKER

"BRAVO for M.D. SELIG! He dares to give us humans well hidden truths that we should know about the existence of ETs living in space and on earth, UFOs, top secret programs to cover them up, and their extraordinary lethal efforts to deny these realities. In an engaging 'up close and personal' way, this well-researched material rivets our attention with its heightened state of suspense. *The truth is stranger than fiction!* This is groundbreaking material, which we should know."

—BARBARA LAMB, PSYCHOTHERAPIST, AUTHOR, LECTURER

"With 'Hush,' M.D. Selig delivers a masterfully crafted story that pulls readers into a world brimming with suspense, emotion, and unforgettable characters. Selig's cinematic storytelling and nuanced understanding of human nature shine on every page, making this a must-read for anyone who loves fiction that both thrills and resonates. 'Hush' is a testament to Selig's talent as a storyteller—riveting, thought-provoking, and impossible to put down."

—DEBBI DACHINGER, BESTSELLING AUTHOR AND AWARD-WINNING PODCASTER

"This book marks an important step toward full disclosure! Author M.D. Selig weaves a gripping tale that takes us deep into the covert world of the deep state cabal. From DUMBs deep under the Earth to competing E.T. agendas and the hidden forces that shape our world, you will gain insights that only a true insider can reveal. Extraterrestrials have played an important role in the affairs of our human world since time immemorial. As the world starts to reckon with the extent of these hidden powers, the time has come for their deepest secrets to be revealed as humanity is liberated from the machinations of the Cabal."

—KAEDRICH OLSEN, AUTHOR OF RUNES FOR TRANSFORMATION

FOREWORD

The American CIA is not autonomous.

It acts only when it's told do so. So, what entity ordered the CIA to hijack a Malaysian airliner full of innocent civilians? Who calls the shots at the worldwide level of power and control? The answer lies in understanding alien-traded technologies and the covert group that wields them.

The *Administrative Elite,* as they like to imagine themselves, is a small group of extremely wealthy individuals who for over seventy years have manipulated world events, far beyond presidential or congressional control. Fortunately for us, their takeover of the American government can be traced to a solitary event that solidified their rise to power.

An iron-fisted public execution of a deeply beloved... American patriot.

Prologue – May, 1949

A SPECTER RISING

The horror was upon him.

The American government would eventually name an aircraft carrier in his honor. And buildings, too.

When the CIA kill team threw him out the sixteenth-floor window of the Bethesda Naval Hospital, they knew the former U.S. Secretary of Defense, James Forrestal, was not dead.

His bathrobe sash was knotted tightly around his neck so that he couldn't scream, because suicides never screamed. And this kill team's specialty was *death by suicide.*

The other end of the sash around his neck was tied below the window to a steel radiator-style heater, which abruptly stopped his fall only five feet below the windowsill, hanging him by the neck. But James Forrestal was a fighter, if any man ever was one—a true patriot—who fought against that sash and attempted to pull himself up, kicking the exterior wall of the hospital, flailing and wheezing, looking up towards the dark windowsill.

The hit team had left the kitchen dark so no one on the ground, sixteen floors below, would notice four men hurling another man out the window with a bathrobe sash knotted tightly around his neck.

The leader of the covert kill squad, the CIA containment team, was Damon Slepher—a brilliant former O.S.S. man whose ruthless but efficient manner of assassination—saw him rise quickly through the counter-intelligence circles during the war. He was still a young thirty-eight with slicked-back hair, and though fluent in German and Russian, he brandished a hint of childhood Jersey, mafioso accent. He leaned out the window and lit a cigarette, watching as James Forrestal kicked against the building, trying to pull himself back up the sash, but he barely could get air to climb—almost dead, but still fighting, as he had been a tenacious boxer in college and was not someone to quit.

Slepher exhaled smoke through his nose, watching in the dark night as Forrestal struggled. Slepher leaned down and whispered to the dying man.

"Hey, Secretary Forrestal, what are your kids gonna think when you commit suicide?"

This pissed off James, and he fought to pull himself up, air or no air, while Slepher sucked his teeth and continued in a whisper.

"Will be awful for them, but I guess you don't have to worry, because either way, everyone's gonna read the news of your suicide and see you as a hero—you know—one who just lost his way at the very end."

James was only inches away, reaching his hand up to the sill, when Slepher lowered his switchblade and calmly sawed the sash just above James' hand.

"Well, James, loose lips sink ships—and we can't have that."

The switchblade cut the final strand, and James' body dropped, flipping end over end as he plunged, gaining speed. And in those extreme seconds, there was, unbelievably, time to think.

The spring night—so refreshing at the end of his wild ride to the highest office in the history of the U.S. Navy. He had everything just two months ago. His amazing family, his two boys, and Jo, his faithful wife, and he was at the top of his game. And as the night wind came to a standstill, just a second before impact—that moment in time where people always say, when they are in extremis, that time seems to stand still—and it did for James Forrestal.

As he fell, he knew his only mistake was that he wanted to tell the truth. He felt it was his patriotic duty to let the public know about the new alien presence. He had discussed this in secret meetings with his friend and new senator from Massachusetts, John F. Kennedy. And James had also mentioned it to members of the opposition party. And now, in the split-second before death, James had the thought that he mistakenly believed he was above the Majestic-12 group—that he had helped create only two years before—in 1947.

President Harry Truman had asked James to form an above-top-secret team to handle the new alien phenomenon—a matter of National Security because the aliens were invading America's airspace like never before, and the U.S. military had no way to stop them. So much so that several alien ships had crashed near America's only nuclear base at Roswell, and those crash events had been quickly sterilized and aggressively hidden from public view. Truman and his administration figured the public would riot if they understood that America was not in control of the skies above them, and Harry was determined not to let chaos ensue, especially on the heels of The Great Depression.

Since the first alien saucer recovery off the South Sea island of Saipan in 1941 and the subsequent Cape Girardeau, Missouri crash, several individuals who wanted to tell the public what they saw had committed suicide. Some were self-inflicted gunshot wounds, and some had hung themselves. A few had industrial accidents or drove their cars off bridges. So many sudden suicides in the little town of Cape Girardeau, Missouri, that the local population began to whisper about military involvement, as many of the suicides were upstanding citizens who had no reason to kill themselves.

These strange deaths had continued wherever an alien crash-recovery took place, including the 1947 Roswell saucer recoveries, where several civilians had seen live aliens and then began to whisper about the military conspiracy to hide the truth just before their odd deaths and disappearances. In those early crash retrieval events, James was briefed on all *unfortunate but necessary* erasures that had taken place. The covert death squads were embedded in the newly created Interplanetary-Phenomenon Units (IPU teams), which were 200-man units specifically set up to locate and recover crashed alien ships. The IPU teams consisted of a scientific team, a recovery team, and a counter-intelligence team, which included the covert containment and laundry squads. They ensured that any civilians who had witnessed the crashed alien ships were interrogated with warnings, and if those stern actions didn't do the trick, the individuals were deemed untrustworthy and terminated.

And though James was uncomfortable with those erasures in the early crash events, James had agreed with Truman that the phenomenon needed to remain secret until America figured out what the hell the aliens wanted, as the U.S. certainly did not have the technology to stop them. Yet only months later, the Aztec, Mexico, crash of 1948, brought with it a human-looking alien survivor named Setimus, who became the first covert Truman-sanctioned Alien Ambassador to the U.S.

Kept in a secluded top-secret army base in Vermont, Setimus met with Truman, Forrestal, Eisenhower, and a few other select military officials. James Forrestal, being a religious man, was really thrown while contemplating Setimus' claims that aliens had actually been coming to Earth before the dawn of Homo sapiens. And for James, it quickly became apparent that all the Christian origin stories he had memorized as a kid and believed in were just that—stories—and nothing more. And that was a lot for a man of such devout faith.

But unlike the others in the grave already for wanting to expose the new alien presence, James was Secretary of Defense. In his new religious turmoil, he somehow forgot his position and decided to let Harry Truman know that the public should be informed about the new alien phenomenon, as if James were the president himself. But James wasn't the president—Harry was. And Harry was hard as a goddamn stone and had dropped two atomic bombs, incinerating 225,000 innocent Japanese civilians. James Forrestal was not about to survive his sudden intention to inform the world that America was now beginning diplomatic communications with various alien races.

On March 28th, 1949, James was removed from office and given a send-off by Harry Truman with a formal reception where he was hailed as *A loyal fellow*. James departed the send-off in a limousine, accompanied by the new Secretary of the Air Force, Stuart Symington, who informed Forrestal that he was under house arrest for his intentions to inform the public of the alien presence.

"James, we will keep your arrest a secret, Symington said in his southern drawl, "and the public will never know, but any moves to further your agenda of informing the public will result in your ultimate demise."

James was escorted the next day to see his wife in Florida and then forcibly taken north to Bethesda on April 2nd, against his will, under the false pretense of suddenly becoming suicidal and needing psychological care. He attempted to depart the vehicle while it was in motion on the way to Bethesda, sensing the darkness in store for him.

The incarceration was the brainchild of the CIA's rising madman, Allen Dulles, who worked with Frank Wisner and James Angleton to assemble the covert kill team. Their idea was to isolate Forrestal away from any possibility of communication with the press or the outside world. A simple plan, and it came with the perfect deniability that allowed the CIA to keep its hands clean while spoon-feeding the press the exact headlines America would read:

"Forrestal had become suicidal after being fired and had to be admitted for his own safety."

It was illegal as hell, but in 1949, the press didn't question the CIA or President Truman about matters involving staff or senior administration officials. Truman and his most trusted advisor, Sidney Sours, even tried to reason with James during his house arrest inside Bethesda Hospital, advising him to let go of his desire to tell the public. But Forrestal wouldn't listen. Truman then sent Lyndon Baines Johnson, an imposing Texas congressman, to physically threaten James. But James showed political antipathy toward each visitor, knowing his brother Henry had secured his release and he would be free in only a few more hours. He had been held seven long weeks against his will, and the courts had ruled in his favor.

The kill team, upon arriving at James' room at 1:45 a.m., found him sleeping peacefully. The team positioned themselves around Forrestal, and on Slepher's signal, four of them held one limb apiece. The moment James awoke—he raised his head—and was immediately strangled by his own sash at the hands of Slepher... while all of Forrestal's limbs were held tightly. But he kicked as he squirmed. To James' credit, he managed to free one leg and kick the table with his glass of water, sending it into the air.

The glass shattered upon impact with the bed and floor. The watch nurse, around the corner, stood when she heard the sound but was immediately confronted by the new orderly, Harrison, who was also a member of the kill team.

"Nurse, you shouldn't go around the corner."

She stared back, then realized this new orderly, Robert Wayne Harrison—had the eyes of a killer—not a Naval Corpsman. She sat, horrified, listening to the commotion around the corner as they carried the struggling Forrestal out of his room and across the hall to the open kitchen window. The sash was secured to the heater, and on cue, all four men holding James shoved him out feet-first so that the last thing to go out was his head.

Tied tightly to the heater, with the sash knotted around his neck, James quickly reached the end of his leash. His body slammed with a whomp, as hanging bodies do. But James was quick, and since his hands and legs were free for his suicide fall, he was able to fight against his own body weight. Then Slepher said what he said and cut James' sash.

Now, in his absolute final moment, James Forrestal realized that his sons and wife would never know that he had not committed suicide, and that he loved them beyond words, and he would kill the fuckers who had just killed him, if he had the chance, and then, he impacted.

His body slammed with a building-shaking smack into the concrete roof of the third-floor extension, then bounced several feet, spraying blood and viscera before it came back down with a final thud. Someone inside the hospital on the third floor screamed, but nobody knew what had happened—not yet, anyway.

Within seconds, the lower kill team members, the laundry team, who had been waiting to ensure Forrestal was dead, raced out into the darkness to the bloody, twisted body. And still, somehow, in his mangled, face-down impact crater, James' broken torso still had a pulse.

The leader of the laundry team made quick work of the final blow, and they calmly walked away. Moments later, at 1:50 a.m., hospital staff came out a service door onto the dark rooftop. Female nurses and male orderlies saw a form—and then blood—and the screams began.

Rising in those screams for James Forrestal was *The Majestic-12.* An elitist group of American men who had taken their power seat above the President, whose office had just been bypassed with the assassination of James Forrestal.

Hidden from public view but with an absolute stranglehold on every administration moving forward, this power-hungry group would forever change the destiny of the planet without any public oversight, and far beyond presidential or congressional control. In one fell swoop, the Majestic-12 had become the true power in America and would award alien technology to private military contractors worldwide in exchange for absolute obedience and secrecy. They were the American wing of an elusive Cabal that controlled the planet.

They were the *Deep-State.*

PREFACE

U ncovering our hidden past has revealed how incredible the Deep-State is at what they do—covert operations—hiding in plain sight.

The Deep-State is now generally called *the Cabal*, and I will, from here forward, refer to the Deep-State as such.

Some backstory on creating this covert historical series.

I graduated from college in 1985 with a history degree and joined the United States Marines as a second lieutenant on my way to flight school. I became an attack pilot and intelligence officer for my Marine Intruder squadron. Shortly thereafter, in 1991, the squadron was deployed for Operation Desert Storm.

The intensity of my jet training and subsequent combat experience, combined with countless hours reading top-secret intelligence documents, taught me much about the military and its intelligence dissemination—what was meant to be seen by the public and what was forbidden. However, certain top-secret files I was privy to hinted at alien interactions possibly occurring at military installations around the globe. These whispers of a hidden realm ate at me. Like many, I am a complete skeptic by nature, especially of all things alien related. But something told me back then to follow my gut, realizing that there were far too many oblique signs of a covert world—operating parallel to my squadron's activities.

But how, I asked myself, *if aliens were real, would I have known about it? Or not?*

My first in-person hint of something amiss came while I was flying for the U.S. Marines prior to Operation Desert Storm.

In early January of 1991, on my way to the Persian Gulf conflict, my squadron of ten A-6E Intruder attack jets landed at Diego Garcia, a top-secret U.S. Navy base smack in the middle of the Indian Ocean. While the U.K. retains sovereignty of the tiny island, the United States controls the island's military base through a 1966 lease agreement, and the majority of the personnel on the base are U.S. Navy.

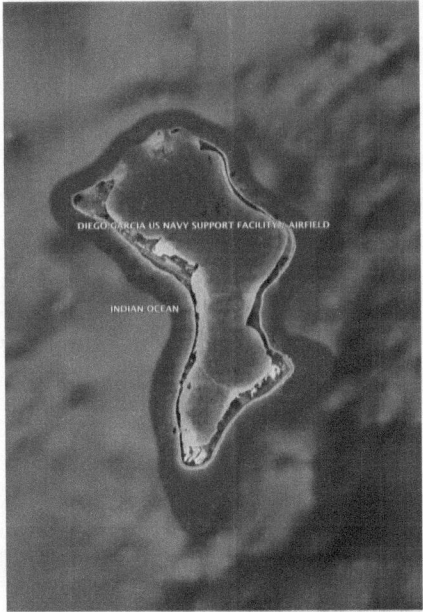

Diego Garcia Top Secret U.S. Navy Base. Indian Ocean.

I had already been briefed that no outside press was ever allowed at Diego. That immediately put my radar on high alert, wondering what I would find there. But after an uneventful landing, I was completely perplexed. There was nothing there. Nothing I could see—which, of course, only heightened my curiosity.

Having read enough top-secret intelligence briefs, I knew you didn't place a single-runway airfield on a *No Press,* top-secret status, unless something at that location required a stringent security veil.

The U.S. Naval Support Facility at Diego Garcia is a tiny airfield, with a few hangars along the main runway. Nothing more. Or at least that is the only visual I was presented with. While refueling my jet, I was intrigued by a huge construction crane working nearby—with its main cable going down—deep into the ocean. I assumed it was being used to set concrete far down in the depths for future surface structures. I had no idea, standing on that tarmac in 1991, that only a few hundred feet below me was an active, colossal spaceport for the German Dark Fleet and the American Black Navy.

For those unfamiliar with military secret protocols, think: Deep-Black Ops = U.S. Black Navy.

The U.S. Black Navy is an above-top-secret unit that supports ongoing space operations at the Diego Deep Underground Military Base, (D.U.M.B.) The multi-level Deep Underground Military Base was identified by whistleblower Tony Rodrigues as the same port his German space-freighter, the *Max Von Laue*, used as a hub for transporting materials, to-and-from various planets in our solar system.

The spaceport and DUMB at Diego Garcia were also confirmed by a former *Black Navy Assassin* during online interviews.

The Assassin's years working in the DUMB and spaceport at Diego corroborate in both time and description with Rodrigues' supply runs aboard the *Max Von Laue* at the Diego complex.

Tragically, Diego Garcia was also the final destination for Malaysian Flight 370 and its passengers and crew. This was confirmed not only by an SOS sent from the Diego airfield by Philip Wood, a former IBM executive on the ill-fated flight, but also verified by the Navy Assassin, who witnessed the hasty disassembly of that jet on the tarmac at Diego Garcia.

In addition, top-secret *National Reconnaissance Office* (NRO) videos, leaked online by a former Navy Lieutenant Commander only days after the flight, showed Malaysian 370 being tracked by two black-ops U.S. Reaper drones, moments before its disappearance.

To make this clear and simple for the non-military reader, America's top intelligence services would not order the U.S. Air Force to track a civilian, Boeing 777 commercial jet, with two, ultra-top-secret surveillance platforms, on its final flight, unless they wanted someone or something on that jet. Period.

On the flight, were twenty American engineers of Chinese descent, working for Freescale Corporation, a Texas-based semiconductor firm. All had been coerced by the Chinese government to defect. Those employees carried American technology with them and were on their final leg to Beijing when the Cabal struck.

Assisted by America's top intelligence services, the Cabal hijacked the flight, ensuring that all the defectors, their American technology, and the innocent passengers and crew were returned to the U.S. Navy base at Diego Garcia.

In late 2014, when the MH370 cockpit voice transmissions had gone viral... I sat perplexed at home, listening... over and over. Being a former combat-decorated jet pilot, I was shocked that no investigators were calling out—what was to me—a clear switch in the cockpit voice just after liftoff.

The deep Asian accent of copilot Hamid was suddenly no more—and the new voice that replaced it—was undeniably American in accent and delivery. And the man stuttered on the callsign of MH370 for the rest of the flight... yet nobody was noticing it?

I knew then... without a doubt, the jet had been taken. That covert work had been completed, and the post-investigation was being controlled.

To this day, you can listen to them online. Benjamin R. Water's clearly American-accented radio calls are first heard at 12:42:05 a.m., just after liftoff, and continue for the rest of the flight. And those transmissions intrigued me... for years... until Ben was identified by tech experts investigating encrypted pings that somehow had never been decrypted.

The hijacking and takeover of Flight 370 by a Cabal hijacking crew began during initial taxi and culminated with both Asian pilots being executed only seconds after liftoff by CIA operative and pilot, Benjamin R. Waters.

The CIA ensured Ben's name was absent from the plane's manifest as well as absent from any early media coverage after the disappearance.

His name was only flagged later after an international passenger audit cross-referenced travel manifests with known personnel in US defense databases. According to the ticket logs, Ben booked his seat less than twelve hours before takeoff using an internal travel portal typically reserved for military contractors on discretionary assignments.

Ben boarded using a fake Ukrainian passport. But the flaw in the Cabal's plan came from their assumption that the satellite-connected technology Ben wielded would be impossible to intercept. Ben's communications would remain encrypted.

But, fortunately for all of us... Ben's communications from the jet had now been identified and decrypted. Even when MH-370 had no active Wi-Fi and no satellite uplink accessible to passengers, and the jet was presumed well beyond communication range—Ben's communications had pinged a nearby satellite—and were recorded.

Those burst-style data packets sent up flags during the post-disappearance investigation with tech experts across the globe. At first disregarded as satellite noise... until experts realized, under scrutiny of the signal, that they were actual burst transmissions from an individual on the flight.

The data transmissions attributed to Benjamin R. Waters were unlike anything expected from a commercial aircraft in a total blackout. Not formatted like casual data logs or cached GPS information. Instead, Ben's transmissions were multi-art files—split into six fragments—with each fragment encrypted.

Ben was sending out bursts via satellite that cybersecurity experts identified as *nested Shaw 3 hashing*—a level of encryption consistent with military grade systems—and all of this was discovered just as Ben's background check came through as a known CIA sub-contractor and operative.

Ben, it turns out, was *interlinked*—think of technology embedded in the brain—and then you're getting the picture.

Ben was controlled by handlers—via satellite link—all the way from Virginia. His movements and communication had been deciphered, and corroborated precisely in time and burst location with his American-accented voice... as the only person transmitting from the cockpit of MH370 once the flight became airborne.

The Cabal's CIA contracted pilot was now seen, not only on boarding videos and identified on satellite investigation logs... but Ben had now gone viral with his recorded cockpit transmissions... capturing his most famous, final line in his perfect American accent:

"Uh... goodnight... uh... Malaysian three seven zero."

The horrific sequence of events during the hijacking and the tragic ending for all those families, defectors, and their loved ones at the Diego Garcia U.S. Navy base will be revealed in the story.

But unlike other infamous hijackings, this one revealed an alien-traded technology the Cabal has been employing in secret since the early 1960s. That of plasmoid teleportation. Fortunately for all of us, a courageous former Navy Lt. Commander, outraged at the Cabal's treachery, leaked the footage of that teleportation... showing Malaysian 370 vanishing... only to re-appear north of Diego Garcia, where the jet was safely landed... by Benjamin R. Waters.

The two NRO leaked videos, which can be viewed on my website, show MH 370 flying just south of Great Nicobar Island from two separate angles, before suddenly vanishing during that plasma-ball teleportation event.

Above: U.S. Air Force MQ-9 "Reaper" drone thermal imagery of MH370 moments before vanishing during this planned teleportation event. Plasma orbs circle the jet and are creating an electromagnetic vortex, which essentially sucks the jet into the wormhole. The jet will then reappear out of the wormhole, 1500 miles southwest over the Maldives Islands, and be flown south for its final landing at Diego Garcia, U.S. Navy Base.

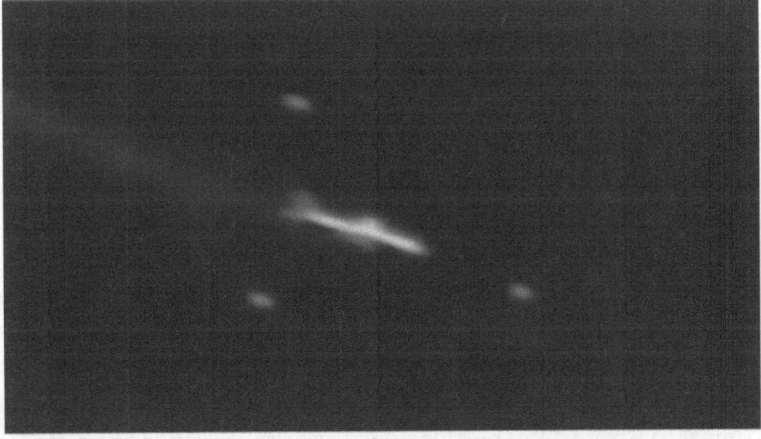

Above: MH370 being filmed from the opposite angle by a second MQ-9 "Reaper" drone, just before vanishing. This is Gorgon Stare footage at six frames per second and is not thermal imagery, instead regular video, shot on the early morning of March 8th, 2014, for the U.S. National Reconnaissance Office. The NRO satellite allowed U.S. intelligence agencies to observe the teleportation in real time. This footage was uploaded directly from the "Reaper" drones to the NROL-22 satellite. Both videos are live-stamped with the NROL-22 satellite identifier seen on the website videos on the bottom left.

The teleportation of that commercial jet—while in flight and on fire—will hopefully give the viewer a taste of the technologies the Cabal and the U.S. intelligence network have been receiving in covert transactions with malevolent alien groups for decades. Yes, *decades*.

Space-faring whistleblowers including Jason Rice, Morgan Johnson, Rebecca Rose, Corey Goode, Niara Isley, Randy Cramer, Jean-Charles Moyen, Tony Rodrigues and Penny Bradley, among others, have stepped forward confirming a decades-long hidden world of citizens operating in space, and the faulty *Mind-Wipe* technology that has now allowed them to remember their years working in the covert *Programs*.

Several of them experienced the Diego Garcia Spaceport, and more whistleblowers are coming forward worldwide as this is being written.

These advanced Cabal technologies, such as *Mind-Wipe*—happen to be rife with glitches—especially when amalgamated with the human biological system. Those glitches are now revealing an *alternate existence* to many stepping forward—from every country across the planet. Individual whistleblowers, speaking out on numerous online platforms, are now regaining detailed memories of a cloned period of their lives.

Memories that align perfectly with others across the globe who experienced the same space-faring ships and spaceports, the same alien races, and the same DUMBs and technologies being used throughout our solar system. All of these space-faring whistleblowers spent years in the Secret Space Programs, which are still active today in and around our planet—an ongoing, above-top-secret realm that is not covered in media, yet is absolutely factual. Also factual are the alien-traded technologies currently in use by the Cabal—most of which have been in use for decades.

Mind-Wipe, Cloning, Teleportation and *Space Travel* are daily occurrences in and around our planet, as well as throughout our galaxy, by the Cabal. But those technologies have been aggressively hidden for decades. The reasons for this covert agenda will be revealed in the story as well.

For those skeptics like me, who need to see a live alien before they can make the leap into our actual reality, I'm posting on my website the verified first-contact event that occurred at 1700 hours on Monday, July 7, 1947, in hangar P3 on the Roswell Army Airfield.

The never-before-seen 16mm footage, will show the viewer the exact moment that five aliens from a crash recovery, thirty-five miles north of Roswell, were covertly delivered to base commander Colonel William Blanchard and his staff for viewing during that world-changing moment seventy-eight years ago.

The original 16mm footage shows five stretchers being carried in, containing four dead aliens, and one live alien. The live one, which was severely injured during the crash event, can be seen moving its six-fingered hand and leg while being comforted by a medical attendant, as the bewildered officers and MPs stand confounded.

In the footage, all present are clearly shocked that actual otherworldly beings, dead and alive, are being placed in front of them. For a God-fearing group of American military men in 1947, the footage documents the confusion and obvious fear for those present during that world-altering moment.

Corroborating the first contact film on the website will be the alien autopsy footage, showing the exact six-fingered alien from hangar P3 being autopsied the next morning at the Roswell base hospital.

In addition, the testimonies of four individuals who were present in hangar P3 during that first contact event will accompany the videos.

Like all of you, I had always been led to believe that Roswell never happened. But fortunately for us, the vintage films are impossible to fake, and now allow our actual history to step forward.

After viewing the footage and realizing it was seventy-eight years old, I began to understand how incredible the deception of the Cabal has been to hide that earth-altering event. With that understanding, two questions stepped forward.

The first obviously is, why would any group hide that first contact event from the general populace? And the second was, if the Cabal was already in contact with alien races beginning in the late 40s... what is today's status of the Cabal's current interactions with off-world races, over seven decades later?

Those answers are ahead for you in the story, but as a hint, it boils down to power and control of the planet, which the Cabal already wielded in 1947. But for those of us who have endured that hoodwink for our lifetimes, there is good news; the Cabal's deception is finally being revealed, and with that disclosure will come an amazing future just ahead for all of us.

Knowing our actual past.

The covert history presented in this series is told from the fictional viewpoints of historical characters participating in those actual covert events.

Simply put, that is my storytelling style and allows the reader to experience those individuals confronting the unbelievable events happening to them in real-time—for which they were wholly unprepared—alien events that, from the get-go, were deadly.

From the Cabal assassinating Secretary of Defense James Forrestal in 1949, fearing he would tell the world the truth of the new alien presence, all the way to Phil Schneider, a Deep Underground Military Base engineer and whistleblower who attempted to tell the world of the covert DUMBs being created across the U.S. as far back as the 1970s.

Schneider... while helping to expand the Deep Underground Military Base at Dulce, New Mexico, below the Archuleta Mesa in 1979, mistakenly surprised a malevolent alien group that the Cabal was already in contractual obligations with. The violent encounter left him with critical injuries and many others dead. Phil waited a few years to heal, and then heroically stepped forward onto the speaking circuit at UFO conferences across the U.S.

Only months after publicly stating that *"he would most likely be assassinated for speaking about D.U.M.B.S,"* Schneider's body was found amidst clear evidence of a violent execution. Strangled with his own catheter tube, wrapped many times around his neck and knotted tightly, *with Extreme Prejudice*—a well-known execution style used on many who have attempted to expose the Cabal.

My hope is that through understanding covert historical events, the reader will gain a more accurate picture of what has occurred in our eighty-plus years of humans and aliens signing agreements.

At this moment, the Cabal still holds sway and remains in contractual obligations with dark factions of the Draco, Maytre, and other off-world races.

Rest assured, there are many benevolent alien races with their hands out to us, but it's up to us... to take that step forward into our incredible future.

Humans are now rising from across the globe to meet the Cabal and malevolent aliens head-on, and I say,

"Go, Humanity!"

You have love—and the malevolent ones, Cabal and alien—will never have that. *Love is all there is.*

M.D. Selig, September 11th, 2025.

Finally, this series is not meant to be disrespectful to the families of the missing, the assassinated, and those affected by these events. My goal is to honor them by uncovering the truth so that their loved ones' ordeals were not in vain.

We don't get answers to questions we don't ask.

Chapter One

MARCH 2014

Five hundred and fifty feet below the surface of the Earth, Vyla Kells
was staring at the data showing that subatomic particles had vanished
during her latest test.

The two atoms she smashed together had been accelerated over the
twenty-seven-mile loop at the Large Hadron Collider in Geneva, Switzerland, and
impacted at a velocity just under the speed of light. The atoms, like two race cars,
had slammed together, and the collision was captured on the Large Hadron Collider
camera a nanosecond after impact. The image on the massive video screen in front
of her showed only a total energy value of 1.98. But she knew that each of the two
atoms just before impact had held an exact quantitative value of one. She considered
herself a hack for a particle scientist because math had never been her strong suit,
but the last time she checked, the sum of one-plus-one should equal two. She stared
at the screen and scanned it for the missing energy. This post-collision sum could
only be possible if 0.2 percent of the total energy had been destroyed. She sucked
her lip, knowing *The First Law of Thermodynamics* proved energy could move or
change—but never be destroyed.

"Whoopsie," she whispered, like a forgiving mother to a spilt-milk child.

1

Except this wasn't milk. This was energy, and it had just disappeared before her eyes. Not there anymore. Gone. *Vanished.* But to where?

"One smashed into one should be a total of two," Dr. Yen Jee mused, standing a few feet away.

Her brown eyes focused on the screen as she slowly wagged her head, contemplating the missing matter. At forty-nine, she was fit and youthful-looking, with silky smooth skin. Vyla watched her, marveling that the top physics mind on the planet was only a few feet from her.

What the hell am I doing here? she thought as she watched Yen decipher the screen.

There were rock stars in every academic field, and Yen was a bona fide rock star among all particle physicists. Her papers, books, and videos were used worldwide by top universities as an imperative course curriculum. Vyla had even referenced Yen's theories when writing her thesis on plasmoid technology, but had never entertained the thought that she would ever be in the same room with her.

"Just vanished from radar," Vyla said, forcing herself to say something around this woman she so admired—then immediately regretted her nervousness.

She was tired, and lack of sleep tended to amplify her claustrophobia, which knowing she was five-hundred-feet below ground, had raised its ugly head. She tried to calm herself, but there it was, that relentless ego voice deep down, with its *less-than* whisper. Yen looked at her curiously as she sat, pulling her briefcase closer.

"Funny you should say that," Yen said.

What did I say? Vyla thought, wondering if she had blurted out *fuck* or something worse.

Yen rifled through her briefcase.

"Vanished from radar... that's what they're saying about that Malaysian flight. The one that disappeared two weeks ago. I have family members in Hong Kong who are passengers on that flight."

"Oh, I'm sorry," Vyla whispered.

Yen didn't seem too fazed or perhaps was compartmentalizing as she searched her briefcase. Vyla noticed sparkles coming off Yen's diamond watchband. It appeared to be the real deal.

Damn, that's a lot of diamonds, she thought, contemplating Yen, having read all about her growing empire.

Yen's corporation had become a conglomerate overnight. A massive military contractor rumored to have attained several top-secret projects. Jee Research and Development (JRAD) had quickly risen among military contractors and was now the second-largest R&D conglomerate next to Lockheed-Martin. Yen had hired her as part of a team researching the possibilities of other dimensions and the feasibility of time travel. In the three weeks she had been working with Yen in Geneva, she had not met the other team members, as they were stateside. Yen's company headquarters was based inside the Nellis test range in southern Nevada, but known by most as the mysterious Area 51. Yen had carte blanche access to LHC facilities as well as Livermore and various other top labs, not to mention JRAD operations in and around Groom Lake and Kirtland Air Force Base.

"I have something for you," Yen said, pulling a file and placing it next to the coffeemaker.

She poured herself a cup.

"You're the only pilot on my team. I read where you used to do aerobatics with your granddad or something, right?"

Vyla was amazed that Dr. Jee had paid that much attention to her resume.

"Yeah, my papa had a biplane and taught me aerobatics growing up."

Yen nodded, taking a sip.

"And you performed at airshows or something like that, right?"

"Yeah, just around our local area," Vyla replied.

Yen subtly caressed the folder, which Vyla could now see was sealed with a dark red strap.

"I got a call from the White House late last night, right after this arrived," Yen said.

Only Yen could say shit like that, Vyla thought.

"Yeah, cool," Vyla replied with as much casual aplomb as she could fake. Yen took a slow sip of coffee and gently placed the folder in her lap. Vyla's radar went up. A sensory thing.

Damn, she's right here, and she smells like really good cocoa butter. I bet she spends a fortune on skincare. Concentrate, you stupid goon!

Since she was a kid, Vyla sometimes felt herself to be a sensory scientist of sorts—but had to control her urge not to get carried away. An odd thing she knew about herself—but secretly liked. She could now see the red strap below Yen's fingers had *Top-Secret Majestic* written continuously around it, in little white letters. Yen had informed her that some of their work would be National Security related, but Vyla had never considered plasma technology or alternate dimensions as a national security consideration, since she knew those realms were still lifetimes away from becoming feasible. She had seen Yen carry such folders before but had never been close enough to read the important little words on the red friggin' strap.

Okay, settle down. Breathe. Cross your legs or something, her anxious mind whispered.

Yen tapped the folder.

"That's why I think this might be a perfect little junket for you," Yen said.

"A junket?" Vyla asked.

Yen gestured up to the LHC screen, showing the missing energy.

"What's happening right here in our test might have some relevance to what happened yesterday afternoon over the ocean near San Diego," she said, placing the folder in front of Vyla.

"The White House wants us to interview these fighter pilots, and I've got to get back to Nellis, so off you go."

Vyla stared down at the folder.

"I'm going to interview fighter pilots?"

Yen swiveled her chair.

"You're the only one on my team that has any flying experience," she said, tapping the folder.

"Yesterday, the White House received a call from the Gerald R. Ford carrier strike group. They had encountered several UAPs."

Vyla stared, perplexed.

"UAPs?"

Yen nodded.

"UFOs, essentially. The government now refers to them as Unidentified Aerial Phenomena, or UAPs for short. But..."

She patted the top-secret strap.

"The two F-18 pilots who engaged the UAP said it simply vanished in front of them. It then reappeared on radar one second later—over sixty miles away. That would be..."

Yen did a slow calculation in midair with her finger.

"Exactly 216,000 miles per hour."

"Damn," Vyla blurted out, astonished. Then, thinking out loud,

"That kind of acceleration would crush a human being."

Yen watched her, amused, and nodded ever so slightly.

"Hence the call from the White House. They want our team to investigate the possibility that these UAPs are operating in more than just our dimension."

Vyla nodded and slowly reached for the folder. Yen placed her hand on it, stopping her.

"You'll have to swing by the Naval Attaché's office in downtown Geneva to have your clearance level upgraded."

Vyla stared inquisitively.

"But I was sworn in at top-secret when you first brought me here?"

Yen nodded and yawned.

"Well, it doesn't happen often, but there are levels well above top-secret."

She gave Vyla a quick, tight-lipped smile and began placing the folder into her briefcase. Vyla attempted to appear unfazed, but was reeling inside.

What in the fuck is happening here? she wondered.

An unspoken bigger picture that Yen was withholding. And then, her nasty, *less-than* voice.

Don't even try to pretend you knew there was shit above top-secret, you goon!

"Right," she finally whispered aloud, wondering if she sounded legit.

She watched Yen walk toward the exit.

"After your clearance upgrade, don't forget to swing by the secure room and read this brief before you depart. You'll need to know its contents before you arrive on the carrier, and these documents can't leave the building."

"Of course," Vyla managed. "But, I mean... it's a UFO... or UAP... or whatever, but rare, isn't it? Don't you want to go?"

Yen smiled slightly.

"It's happened before."

Vyla watched her depart. When the door closed, her mouth was still open. A quick thought passed through her mind.

Do I look as stupid as I feel? Yen had made this seem so... common. A sighting of something from another planet?

Vyla was bewildered.

What have I been missing? Are these UAP things in the news all the time, and I just don't know about them?

Then, a hint of clarity. A hunch. When Yen said, "It's happened before," Vyla had noticed a slight darkness about Yen that hadn't been there before. An entire world of knowledge that Vyla was not privy to.

But I would have read about these things if they were that prevalent? she asked herself.

Then again, she had never been much of a UFO devotee, like her Papa. But still, a message had been sent. She was certain of that.

Shit. Maybe Yen's just stressed? she thought, realizing she had a brand new dream job.

And here I am... already looking the gift horse in the mouth!

But she couldn't deny it... something unspoken lingered in the air that she couldn't pinpoint. *Not yet, anyway.* She looked around and whispered to her anxious body.

"Settle down."

She exhaled and checked the room. Then, pulled a tiny flask from her shoulder bag, pouring a nip into her lukewarm coffee. She stirred it with her finger and noticed her reflection amidst the particles on the video screen. Slowly raising the cup, she spoke to her reflection.

"I have a job."

She then toasted herself and gulped, closing her eyes, savoring the warm concoction going down. She lowered the cup, gazing at herself.

"I'm going to interview friggin' fighter pilots," she said aloud. Then she shrugged confidently and felt it. *Sassy.*

"Of course, this is what I fuckin' do!"

Then she slapped her forehead. Hard. Exhaled. Slapped it again. That time, it stung. She watched herself grimace on the screen.

"Ow... shit!"

Chapter Two

Kuala Lumpur International Airport
March 8th, 2014

B enjamin R. Waters felt scattered as he approached the security screening at gate C-1 with all the voices in his head.

As a heavily controlled individual—that was odd to him. He never felt this anxious. Something was amiss, but he couldn't put his finger on it, and that was not like him.

Some would say the physically fit, middle-aged CIA operative's hair was light brown on the boarding videos and some would say blond, but either way—his lime green shirt and Caucasian skin, set him apart—on a flight full of Asians with only a handful of other races mixed in.

Ben had gotten used to the voices... the ones telling him what to do as each minute passed going through airport security. But he still despised them... as those voices were not his own—but instead were human handlers from far away—his controllers at *the CIA farm* in Williamsburg, Virginia. A covert cadre of CIA brass who employed Benjamin for missions anywhere on the planet—you see, Benjamin—was *Interlinked.*

Meaning he had technology embedded in his brain—think Jason Bourne but the real article—as in Benjamin received communications via satellite, and was a highly-trained CIA operative and pilot. A very unique one at that—as he was not the regular pilot scheduled to fly MH370 on the upcoming flight.

Ben—was a hijacker.

He placed his carry-on onto the scanning cart and walked through the metal detector. His weapon had already been placed under his seat by Cabal operatives hours before the crew boarded. Ben knew that. Ben knew everything that was about to happen on the upcoming flight.

When the CIA sent him to his pre-hijack mission brief, Ben knew he was dealing with the Cabal. A covert administrative elite who ran the planet outside of presidential and congressional control. They controlled all of America's top intelligence agencies, and the CIA was their operative wing, which provided assassins and spies for anything the Cabal wanted.

The Cabal brief had been a standard one for Ben at Diego Garcia, the secret U.S. Navy base controlled by the CIA for the Cabal.

The briefers had described to Benjamin and the other hijackers how they would be doing America a great service in hijacking the Beijing-bound jet as the Chinese government was attempting to steal American technology.

Benjamin and the others listened as the briefer said that critical American semiconductor technology was being carried in the luggage of twenty American engineers of Chinese descent—engineers who had been convinced by Beijing to defect back to China—with their technology in tow.

Benjamin had no problem with the brief. He didn't need a reason to do missions. He had done missions for the CIA all his life, and this was just another one. He always counted on the Cabal briefers to give him every bit of information to make his mission completion... a sure thing.

The brief had been very thorough—except for some things the Cabal briefers somehow forgot to mention.

Like the five-hundred-pounds of lithium-ion-batteries in the forward cargo hold that would ignite a few minutes into the flight—so the Chinese government could watch their prized possession go up in flames—with Ben in the cockpit, flying the burning, hijacked airliner. Oh... and they also forgot to mention the plasmoid teleportation planned for the jet. While it was in flight and on fire—as the Cabal's final *fuck-you* to the Chinese—since the Chinese would be watching the jet, via satellite, only to see it vanish before their eyes. And last but not least, the final detail covering the fact that—once Ben landed the jet safely, all the hijackers would be executed. Somehow the mission briefers forgot to tell Ben and the other hijackers those little details.

The Cabal was rude that way.

HUSH

Fifty-two-year-old Captain Zaharie Shah, from Penang, was ready to start his engines at gate C-1 at Kuala Lumpur.

Flight MH370, the Boeing triple-seven airliner he was captain of, was loaded and ready for departure on a flight bound for Beijing. Shah was a family man and veteran pilot with Malaysia Airlines and was assisted in the cockpit by twenty-seven-year-old copilot Fariq Hamid. Shah and Hamid had become friends in the short time Hamid had been with the airline, and the red-eye flight to China was a standard route both had flown.

Malaysian pilots and air-traffic controllers were required to be fluent in Chinese and English, and Hamid handled all the radio calls for MH370. His heavy Asian accent was easily identifiable on all the cockpit transmissions to the different ground control agencies on that early morning.

At 12:27 a.m., Ground Control replied with a standard response.

"Malaysian three-seven-zero, Lumpur Ground, morning, pushback and start approved, runway 32 Right, exit via sierra four."

That transmission told Shah and Hamid that they were approved to start their engines and push back from the gate and were cleared to taxiway S4 on their way to runway 32 Right.

Hamid responded immediately, repeating the instructions from Ground Control and confirming that there were 239 souls on board the aircraft. Captain Shah fired up the two Rolls-Royce engines as the instrument panel in the cockpit relayed vital signs of temperature, fuel and pressure. After the pushback, Shah slid the throttles forward slightly, and their taxi to runway 32 right was underway in the darkness of that March 8th, 2014, early morning.

Shah and Hamid looked out their cockpit windows and continued their preflight checklist while following the multi-colored taxiway lights. And in those busy moments, neither pilot had any idea—that just behind them in the dim light of the main cabin—several cabin crew and passengers had already been executed.

Benjamin R. Waters stood next to the closed cockpit door as the plane taxied in moonlight.

Upon first turning onto the taxiway, Benjamin and a small team of hijackers stood, and began their takeover of MH370, while the two Malaysian pilots were distracted with preflight checks and taxi instructions.

9

Benjamin monitored the cockpit transmissions—coming through the technology in his brain—because he could do that... from anywhere. And Ben could do so much more. In fact, he was also tapped into the Chinese satellite watching the flight since before engine start.

Benjamin and the other hijackers knew the dimly lit main cabin would be unseen by any maintenance types working near the taxiways. And none would be able to see gun-wielding operatives moving about the cabin as the jet rolled by on its way to the active runway.

The hijackers, just prior to the takeover, had pulled off their outer clothing to reveal black full military-style outfits. As they all stood on a signal, each brandished silencer-equipped pistols, which were immediately employed to execute the stewards and stewardesses throughout the main cabin.

Any passengers who cried out in terror were pulled from their seats, ordered to kneel and shot once in the forehead. The compressed air *PPFFT!* of the bullet exiting the barrel would not be heard in the cockpit. But the remaining passengers were certainly privy to up-close and personal views of blood gushing from limp bodies as they cascaded to the cabin floor.

Within seconds, the remaining terrified passengers were quietly being blindfolded as the plane taxied in the pitch-black toward runway 32R.

The small handful of black-clad Cabal operatives included an Israeli woman with blond hair and a shawl, wearing sunglasses, wielding two small pistols. She watched her pre-arranged section of passengers with a cold stare as those facing her had just witnessed her execute two of the cabin crew upon her rising to begin the takeover.

Minutes later at 12:40:38 a.m., the jet was cleared for takeoff by Tower Control, and Hamid responded immediately with what would be the last words of his short life.

"32 Right, cleared for takeoff, Malaysian three-seven-zero. Thank you, bye."

His heavily Asian-accented radio transmissions would not be heard again.

Captain Shah pushed the throttles rapidly forward as the jet took the active runway 32 Right, and immediately Shah went to full power as the jet gained momentum, racing down the runway. His rotation for takeoff was smooth as the jet became airborne. He raised his landing gear and flaps, adjusting the aircraft trim so the jet would climb on its own.

At that moment, the cockpit door behind them opened abruptly. Something that had never happened before on climb-out. Both turned in shock... to see a gun barrel pointed at them and a Caucasian man wearing a black tactical outfit with an earpiece in his right ear.

"Headsets off! Get up!" The American-accented operative ordered.

Both pilots hastily followed orders as the jet continued to climb smoothly on its own. Shah and Hamid exited the cockpit to be greeted by another gun-wielding, black-clad operative, and they could see several dead crew members on the floor as the cockpit door behind them was closed.

"On your knees!" the operative shouted.

The two well-loved pilots fell to their knees—and as they did so—the bullets to their foreheads came in rapid succession.

B enjamin R. Waters locked the cockpit door behind him and quickly eased into Captain Shah's pilot seat, hastily donning the headset and double-checking he was on Departure Control frequency... as the 777 continued its climb through three-thousand feet.

At 12:42:05, less than two minutes since Hamid made his final call to tower, Benjamin made his first transmission... calling Departure Control to let them know that MH370 was airborne and climbing, awaiting further instructions.

Ben, though, would stutter on his first transmission—as he attempted to remember the callsign of the jet was *Malaysian 370.*

Ben's unique American accent would be the only voice for the rest of the flight, and he would stutter each time—on the callsign of *Malaysian 370.*

"Departure—Malaysian—uh... three-seven-zero?"

Departure Control replied with standard climb information, and Ben repeated back the information but again stuttered on the callsign—initially starting with the number *one*, before catching himself.

"Malaysian—one—uh...three-seven-zero."

The Cabal had planned the hijacking and disappearance of MH370 with meticulous precision, and the execution of that mission was now underway with Ben at the controls.

He sat back as the jet rose. Ben was the jet... as he was controlling everything in the jet via his interlink. He sensed something was not on the level, and even though he was getting groggy during the climb... he was aware enough that something had been withheld—and he was pissed—while fighting the sudden sleepy, dizzy feeling.

The lithium-ion batteries that created halogen gas when they burned, which in-turn created bromine gas—the little details the Cabal neglected to tell Ben—were starting to smoulder just below and behind him in the cargo hold.

Bromine gas fumes were seeping into his cockpit and back into the main cabin—and would not explode—until Ben reached thirty five-thousand feet.

Chapter Three

M arine Captain Frank *"Knife"* Jacobs grunted through a 6-G steady turn in an F/A-18 strike-fighter off the California coast near Catalina Island.

The new Super Hornet was far superior to the originals, and his squadron had been lucky enough to acquire the new birds for this deployment. Frank had learned through the years just how much strain he needed on his abdomen and legs to make high-G turns efficiently, ensuring enough blood stayed in his brain for clear thought. Like a pro athlete, he had become nuanced in his execution of each maneuver, so when many high-G turns were required during a dogfight, he could stay focused on winning the fight. It was all about keeping blood in your brain. Six Gs were normal. Seven to nine Gs were sometimes required, but sustaining nine Gs for more than a moment would cause most pilots to pass out.

Now, as he reached his final approach heading, he smoothly rolled the Hornet out of the turn and saw the boat ahead. *Home sweet home.* The "boat" was pilot-speak for the aircraft carrier USS Gerald R. Ford, currently steaming at a steady thirty knots to receive her chicks back aboard. All the fighters that had just finished their Combat Air Patrol were coming home to roost. They all needed fuel, and the scuttlebutt around the ship was that a special guest, sent by the White House, was arriving soon.

Frank had heard the rumors and knew what it was about. And what it was about spooked him. The hearsay about his dogfight yesterday had permeated the entire strike group before he even landed. And *dogfight* didn't cover it.

Right now, though, he needed to concentrate on coming aboard safely, and all thoughts of yesterday he compartmentalized. He set his throttles for a descent of five-hundred-feet per minute and heard the landing signal officer over the cockpit radio.

"Blaze 56, paddles, call the ball."

Frank had rolled into the groove with a green ball in the center of the Fresnel lens aboard the ship.

"Roger ball," he responded, locking his harness so he wouldn't face-plant his helmet into the dashboard when he caught a wire coming aboard... a mistake he'd made as a second lieutenant and never told anyone. Procedures, he had learned the hard way, were critical to good endings. Focus... while flying a high-performance weapons platform in a carrier environment was paramount to staying alive. And now, in the midst of concentrating on holding the glide-slope, adjusting throttles minutely, and checking his alignment, he felt momentarily out of whack. A singular thought was weaseling its way through.

Normally, the many functions and physical prowess required to hold a steady green ball all the way down the glide-slope were all his brain could handle. But in this instance, he knew an investigator was coming to interview him onboard the ship. He had seen something during yesterday's intercept that terrified him more than he wanted to admit. As his jet slammed onto the deck at 150 knots, catching a three-wire and pulling it taut at full power, Frank had another thought.

Should he go into detail *about what notions had come to him regarding the encounter? Or just confirm what had been recorded through his cockpit heads-up display, and call it good?*

What he felt now, and since yesterday's events, were beyond description. He knew a change in himself had occurred. *Was occurring.* That much he would never say.

An hour after slamming onto the deck, Frank, still in his flight suit, kicked off his boots and sat heavily on his bunk. He was relieved to find that his little refrigerator had been restocked with fruit juice and snacks during his combat air patrol. The enlisted mess often did CAP pilots the favor of restocking their refrigerators while on patrol. This courtesy alleviated the need for a tired aviator to wait for food after a long CAP. His stateroom mate was off flying another CAP, so for the next few hours at least, Frank could enjoy the solitude.

He rummaged through the small dresser where he stashed booze amidst his socks and produced a miniature plastic airline vodka bottle. It had been a full day since yesterday's encounter, and this was the second shot he badly needed. He grabbed a plastic cup from the counter, some orange juice, and ice from the fridge and mixed a screwdriver. He smelled the cocktail, then slowly slid back onto his bunk, kicking his feet up. He exhaled a big sigh and felt the slow roll of the ship as he sipped. The dull vibration of the huge engines somewhere far below had a calming effect. He could get used to drinking and sailing.

He knew that tomorrow morning, he would meet the investigator. It was supposedly a woman, and this made Frank think about his wife, Kelly, back in San Diego and how he would give anything right now to have her near. Just to vent about the crazy shit now happening. But he also remembered that he rarely told Kelly anything, and he admitted to himself that he had not been the best partner over the years.

A soft knock. He looked at the door.

"Come in!" he yelled and watched the handle slowly turn as the door cracked open.

"Captain Jacobs, sir, it's Petty Officer Day, from the Princeton," the familiar voice said.

"Come in, Chief!" Frank said in his most welcoming voice.

Day was a man Frank had learned to respect over several years after their two paths crossed. Day had been the base radar officer at Frank's first duty station, and the two had leapfrogged career paths to this moment. The Chief had clearly just taken a helo flight over from the USS Princeton, sailing just a few hundred meters away from the carrier. And that rarely happened, but since *the incident*, everything seemed upside-down. Frank was glad to see him, no matter the circumstances. They had spent many good days together, and Frank admired the man immensely. At one point, Frank's softball team on base had dueled Chief Day's team for the base title, and Day's team had prevailed. But Frank didn't care. He considered a man like Chief Day the best the military had to offer. If you had to lose a damn softball title, well, who better to lose to than Chief Day?

Day was tall and unassuming, with a salt-and-pepper mustache and a deep West Texas accent. He had that unique, venerable wisdom that senior enlisted men carried, which somehow exalted them above all officers onboard. But the wildest thing about Chief Day, in Frank's mind, was that the Chief was a total sleeper, meaning—badass, and you would never know it.

His other life as a martial arts master was only known to a few. The Chief never talked about it, but had apparently trained for years with a Korean master while stationed there. Years later, he opened a dojo just off the base in San Diego, and his trainees included trophy winners in several types of martial arts and even a few UFC fighters. Most of his softball team had been recruited through the dojo, and Frank was glad their on-field arguments had never come to blows. Frank's team would have been massacred. Chief Day closed the door quickly behind him, and though he feigned a good-natured smile, Frank sensed a heaviness. He pointed at the cocktail in his hand.

"You need a screwdriver, Chief?"

Without hesitation, Chief Day looked at him.

"I might have more than one, sir."

Frank stifled a laugh as he nodded his head. He patted the end of the bed, motioning for Chief Day to sit, and quickly mixed him a drink. Frank caught glimpses of the Chief as he sat unsettled, and began folding his hat in his hands, remaining silent. Frank mixed him a double shot without asking, and the two silently toasted. Frank lowered himself onto the other end of the bed, staring at his drink and letting himself breathe. Sometimes, it was best to let a room air out. Talk was overrated, especially when the circumstances were so complicated.

After the incident yesterday, Frank knew that for Chief Petty Officer Day, the consequences of calling for an intercept were going to be thoroughly scrutinized. Day had instigated the entire thing, as he was the top dog on the most advanced radar in the world. It had been his Texas drawl, blaring across every speaker throughout the strike group, that a flight of fighters was being scrambled to intercept an incoming threat. One second later, the general quarters alarm sounded throughout the strike group. The eerie shrill of alarms on all vessels echoed between ships as each slammed their throttles forward, lurching and crashing through heavy seas on that windy day to reach thirty knots combat speed. Destroyers and guided missile cruisers began weaving in anti-submarine maneuvers as the strike-group men and women scurried through hatches and across decks, manning battle stations. Headsets were adjusted, guns readied, torpedo tubes flooded, missile and anti-missile batteries spun, and multiple aircraft on various ships readied for launch. Silent flag signals fluttered between the strike group as the ballet of war became fully engaged, and radio silence held the tension.

Before their deployment, Chief Day held a top-secret briefing for all pilots deploying with the carrier strike group. The briefing was an upbeat affair held in a large base theater. The topic was the unique capabilities of the brand-new SPY-3 radar aboard the USS Princeton, sailing with the carrier strike group. The SPY-3 would be the strike group's eyes and ears, known as *"The shield of the fleet."*

The high-powered, six-megawatt radar was capable of performing search, tracking, missile guidance, and air traffic control, with a capacity to track over one hundred targets simultaneously. This super-advanced radar would serve as the heart of the command center for all aircraft and ships within one hundred nautical miles of the strike group. Frank remembered Chief Day showing a video of the SPY-3 in operation. Five huge screens displayed sharply defined blips, with tracking and transponder identification of all moving targets. Day then stared at everyone and prepped them for his big reveal. Wielding a red laser pointer, he directed his tiny red beam at the large radar screen. The laser dot circled a set of blips entering from the top of the screen, as Day described in real-time what they were watching.

"The SPY-3, unbeknownst to our enemies, can even track U.S. stealth fighters, which no other radar to our knowledge can yet see."

Audible gasps erupted in the room. The pilots in the theater watched, drop-jawed, as the video showed U.S. Air Force stealth fighters, Navy and Marine stealth fighters, Army helicopters, gunships, and various fighters from different NATO members. The SPY-3 could see not only every jet but also every surface ship of all sizes, with or without engines or any heat signature whatsoever. Frank remembered hearing a stealth-fighter pilot near him whisper,

"Well, so much for spending billions on my super-invisible jet."

"And yes..." Chief Day had continued, circling the laser dot over a submarine blip well below the surface.

"The Princeton has the latest SQS-53B active sonar, which allows us to see what's lurking below us. And I mean damn far below. That sub is a thousand feet down."

Frank remembered many in the room were stunned at the Princeton's capabilities. But now, in this moment, Chief Petty Officer Day looked defeated, and Frank had a very strong hunch why. He saw Day take a big gulp as he stared at the wall ahead, searching for a handhold. Their friendship was solid enough that Frank felt no need to inject small talk. He knew Day would speak when all was calm. Frank knew another unspoken truth: the stigma associated with extraterrestrials had never sat well within military circles.

In yesterday's incident, once Day notified the carrier skipper of a threat to the strike group from "Multiple Anomalous Aerial Vehicles," the Commanding Officer had no choice but to follow threat protocols and issue the intercept. When Frank's two-plane sortie was scrambled, Frank was still confused about what he was being scrambled for.

How could there be a threat only a few days' sail from San Diego? he questioned. *An enemy submarine running surface, perhaps?*

When Frank inquired about the threat, Chief Day came back with a radio blast Frank had never heard.

"Blaze flight, you will be intercepting an as-yet unknown enemy, bearing 240 degrees, twenty miles, angels low."

At that moment, Frank felt his jet locked and loaded in the catapult. He slammed the throttles to full afterburner and saluted the deck shooter, Lieutenant Commander "Buzz" Orlando. Buzz returned the salute, touched the deck, and pointed toward the bow. A split second later, Frank was flattened against his ejection seat as the linear induction catapult slingshotted his Hornet off the front of the ship. Zero to 150 knots in one-point-eight seconds, and Frank was hell-bent for who-the-fuck-knew!

He felt the jet leave the grip of the catapult, and he pulled back slightly on the stick, simultaneously raising his landing gear handle and flaps while still in full burner. As his bird's hydraulic pistons slid into clean configuration, he keyed his radio.

"Roger, Prince, Blaze 56, copy all, bogey 240 degrees, twenty miles, angels low."

The profundity of the moment hit Frank during the turn to his intercept azimuth. He had just been officially scrambled to intercept a UFO.

What the hell? he thought.

An intercept was also embedded with the knowledge that his two-plane flight was cleared for lethal force.

But there are no Russian or Chinese aircraft carriers near the mainland!? he wondered.

His mind was swimming. He waited a moment for his wingman and buddy, Captain Jackie "Crazy" Caruso, to launch off the far cat. Frank was glad it was her. Not only were they close friends, but Crazy was combat-decorated from two tours in Afghanistan and had won top honors in the strike group's Top-Gun competition. If you had to have a wingman to back you up, there was no pilot aboard that could out-fly Crazy. Even for Crazy, Frank could tell that she was perplexed about their mission. Her voice came across their jet-to-jet squadron frequency—a frequency shared only between squadron mates.

"Okay, Knife, what the hell is this?"

Frank had no answer as he watched her Hornet race out in full burner to create their one-mile combat-spread formation. He armed his Sidewinders.

"Your guess is as good as mine," he said. "Arm it all, Crazy. You're clear six."

She responded immediately.

"Locked and loaded, Knife. You're clear six."

It took Frank a moment to parse the unbelievable events happening in real time. He was suddenly leading a flight to potentially shoot down a UFO. As far as he knew, this intercept was the first time the Navy had ever acknowledged that a UAP even existed. The skipper had to be worried about something significant in making the decision to scramble fighters. Chief Day radioed the flight again, informing them that the SPY-3 onboard the Princeton was picking up electromagnetic pulses (EMPs), which were wafting over the strike group, effectively garnering information for whatever was flying that UAP.

Frank leveled the flight off at 10,000 feet and double-checked his FLIR, forward-looking infrared targeting radar. His system showed one mile to contact.

Moments later, the two fighter pilots got their first glimpse of the UAP when their attention was pulled to the surface of the ocean, where a wall of white seawater shot up from the sea!

Like a Bellagio fountain show in Vegas, they both watched, perplexed, as they saw an oval-shaped alien craft, roughly fifty-feet long by twenty-feet wide, racing just above the surface of the rough ocean, at what appeared to be Mach speeds. It was slicing back and forth like it was having fun! The damn thing was displacing seawater or somehow pulling it vertically behind it, like a jet boat kicking up a wake. The water skyrocketed behind the alien craft and was reaching over one hundred feet high!

Frank heard Crazy on the squadron frequency.

"What the hell is that?!"

"Yeah, and what the fuck is it doing?!" he responded.

A moment later, he watched, astonished, as the UAP descended—below the water—and continued at the same speed! The seawater soared skyward wherever the craft raced below it, apparently unaffected by submersion. The ship then popped right back up and effortlessly raced across the blue surface!

Impossible. Not feasible. Can't be! he thought, just as Crazy came across the squadron's frequency.

"Are you seeing this?!" she radioed.

Frank rolled his jet upside-down and simultaneously pulled his nose straight down, pointing it toward the suddenly rising UAP.

"Close formation and cover me!" Frank hastily replied. "I'm going down to take a look."

But Frank had barely put any G on the airframe when Crazy called out again, this time with a hint of terror in her transmission.

"Knife, it's ascending! It's—it's coming up for us!"

Frank could now see it, too. The UAP was rising at above Mach speed, and one second later, it was at their flight level, just as Frank had rolled wings-level and Crazy was there too, having pulled her fighter into close formation off Frank's right wing as he leveled off.

And there it was, hovering in front of them as they raced ahead. It was literally flying formation on them—backwards!—as they raced forward. Yet it remained effortlessly just ahead, teasing them—like it was playing a game!

Frank could see that Crazy was now only two hundred yards off his wing, and both were face-to-face with an otherworldly craft.

"Holy shit!" he blurted, terrified.

Frank could see no windows, ports, or breaks in the surface of the super-smooth-looking craft.

Crazy was just as spooked.

"I can't see a fucking control surface or any means of thrust! My FLIR can't lock. There's no heat signature. Can you lock it up?"

Frank adjusted his FLIR targeting system. Then, suddenly, as if reading Frank's hostile intent, the alien ship began a maneuver that would imprint both pilots for the rest of their days. Frank would later tell investigators,

"It was as if someone had taken a ping-pong ball and placed it in an empty jar and then began shaking the jar violently."

The alien ship began moving up, down, sideways, disappearing and reappearing—all while hovering in front of them. As if to say,

"Good luck with targeting me."

The ship's movements were so fast and violent that both pilots would later say all they could do was hold still, mesmerized. And when the gravity-defying movements ended, the craft suddenly pulled ahead of them, roughly five hundred yards, and slowed. A split second later, it spun on a dime and came directly at Crazy, forcing her into an evasive maneuver. It then turned at a right angle again, forcing Frank to pull up to avoid collision. As he rolled back to wings-level, he looked out to see the vessel just off his wing, between himself and Crazy. Now it was flying in perfect formation in-between the two F-18s!

What the fuck! Frank thought.

An instant later, the craft circled both jets twice, at over Mach speed, while cloaking itself in and out of visible space, and then—vanished!

Radio silence as both pilots looked everywhere, their hearts in their throats, terrified gasps on the radio.

"Where is it?" Crazy yelled.

"I don't know!" Frank said, reefing his head all around.

Suddenly, Chief Day's Texas drawl cut the tension.

"Blaze flight, your bogey has reappeared at your CAP rendezvous point."

Frank stared at the radio, his heart beating out of his chest, and then heard Crazy.

"That's fucking sixty miles away, Knife!—in less than two seconds!"

Frank was attempting to right himself.

"Yeah, I know," he managed.

The fear in Crazy's next transmission was evident.

"Knife—do you—do you think that thing is waiting for us out there?"

In that tense moment, Chief Day's voice came across the strike frequency.

"Blaze flight, you are ordered RTS. Repeat, you are ordered *Return-To-Ship*."

Frank had never felt so much relief at a radio transmission.

"Oh, thank God!" Frank heard himself say on the squadron frequency.

"I'm right with you," Crazy replied. "Get me the fuck outta here!"

19

Frank took a breath and responded to Chief Day's call.

"Copy, Prince. Blaze Flight is RTS."

And with that, Frank turned toward home. He felt completely disoriented.

"Let me know if I'm not pointing toward the ship," he said to Crazy.

She seemed to feel the same sense of overwhelming confusion.

"Loose form, okay, Knife?" She radioed.

Frank looked at her bird, just off his wingtip. He knew she was equally unnerved, that she felt shaky, and flying in tight formation back to the ship was risky.

"Yeah, whatever is safe is good with me," he radioed.

He watched her take a loose form, sliding her jet away from his. He realized his jet was bobbing up and down due to his shaking arm.

No, he thought. *It's not just my arm—it's my entire fucking body!*

He looked over and noticed Crazy's jet doing the same subtle dolphin motion. And then *he felt it.* Never in a million years would he have thought this could ever happen to him. He had pissed himself in the cockpit! The unmistakable warmth soaked his groin area. He hoped none of it leaked through his G-suit to stink up the jet for whatever poor sucker would take it for the next sortie. He was tense everywhere, knowing there would be a shit-ton of explaining during his debrief with skipper Schrader. Right now, though, he had witnessed what nobody would ever believe, and if his cockpit stunk like a piss-pot dumped on a concrete slab, he just didn't give a goddamn shit. *He was alive. He was fucking alive.* And before he knew it, he blurted out what he must have felt but didn't know he needed to voice in a loud whisper:

"Oh, my God! Fuck! Fuck!"

"Can I ask you something?"

Chief Petty Officer Day said, bringing Frank back to the moment in his stateroom. Day was staring at the wall at the end of Frank's bunk, slowly rocking his plastic cup with what ice remained of his cocktail.

"Sure, anything, Chief," Frank said softly.

The chief turned slowly.

"I just want to verify that the shit I saw that thing do on my radar was completely impossible."

Frank stared at his cup and slowly nodded.

"I don't even know where to start," he said.

The Chief took a deep breath and stood, still staring at Frank.

"Thank you, sir," Day whispered, grabbing the door handle. "If you ever need to speak to someone who will believe everything you saw, call me."

They shared a silent stare, and then the chief departed. Frank watched the door close quietly. He thought about Crazy and wondered if she, too, was losing sleep about tomorrow. When she came out of her debrief with the skipper, she looked withered. They'd shared a moment then, and he saw a tear well up before she caught herself. She shook her head and silently walked away. He hadn't seen her since.

Tomorrow, they would both be doing the same debrief, but for a representative from the White House. Who knew where this was leading, but Frank could think of nothing good to come. He threw back the rest of his cocktail, gulping it, and then, holding the plastic cup, squeezed it so fast that the ice exploded.

He had controlled everything so well up to this moment in his life. A compartmentalized, smooth career of flying and rising through the ranks. He squeezed, disbelieving that this unwanted turn of events was happening to him. He now saw his self-deception, the cold slap of this new awareness.

How truly small he was in the universe. Just a tiny, tiny pawn in somebody else's big, big game.

Chapter Four

Vyla had just settled into the thought that momentarily she would be landing on an aircraft carrier off the coast of San Diego.

Wow, I'm really doing this, she thought.

A split second later, her head was thrown violently backward as the C-2 Greyhound ungracefully slammed aboard the ship. She had been seated backwards and was staring out the window at the rough blue ocean. It happened so fast. There had been a snapshot glimpse of the back end of the carrier, with a row of fighters parked on the edge, and then the impact. She was thrown again by the salute and handshake of Captain Scott Schrader, the commanding officer of the Gerald R. Ford. He shouted above the wind.

"Welcome aboard, Dr. Kells. I'm Captain Scott Schrader. Follow me!"

And with that, she followed him into the superstructure through a hatchway that had saluting guards on both sides in their finest Navy blues. As she ducked through the hatchway, she felt her claustrophobia tapping at her emotions.

Fuck off! she told it.

As if that would make it disappear—or that she could eventually beat it, but in this case, she was determined to at least manage it. She knew the worst was when she vomited in tiny spaces.

HUSH

This is a huge fucking ship! She told herself. *You're fine. Thousands of people live on this ship—you'll be okay.*

Something about the pep talk helped, and she focused on other things as Captain Schrader led her into an elevator.

She recalled being sworn up to Majestic level—the next step in her clearance—back in Geneva. How the four-hour-long interrogation by a *Man-in-Black* had disturbed her. His callous way of informing her that, with her current top-secret clearance, she could be arrested and put on trial for passing classified materials. But by moving up to the Majestic level, she was signing away her right to any privacy whatsoever.

She was now agreeing to be filmed, bugged, and monitored without her knowledge in the interest of national security. He had then asked specifically about her outside hobbies, who her friends were, and her interests outside of physics. She recalled how, after his verbal onslaught, he had barely said two words while watching her complete another two hours of paperwork. She had to provide detailed information on family, friends, and acquaintances. Addresses, phone numbers, emails, occupations, hobbies, and languages each spoke. At one point, she had the notion to just get up and leave. But she fought it.

What the fuck was all this about? she wondered.

It was all happening too fast, and she didn't have a moment to consider any of it. She reminded herself this was the only job she had been offered. Four hours had passed when she finally put the pen down. A guard standing near the Man-In-Black took the paperwork and escorted the two of them into an office where a cocky Marine major stared at her with a disbelief that said,

I'm going to read this young scientist up to Majestic? Who the fuck is she? Does she even understand what that means?

She stared at the major, realizing she had a plane to catch and didn't give a fuck about what he thought.

"You okay?" she demanded, breaking his spell.

"Uh, yes, Ma'am," he stuttered, catching himself.

The swearing-in was finished minutes later. She knew this was only the first of many hassles she was going to face in the coming investigation. Her undergraduate work had forged a distaste for the egomania environment of academia, and her friends who had gone into the armed forces said the military was the same—huge egos, lots of nasty jockeying among officers for promotions.

She thought of her best friends back at Stanford, completing their graduate work: Charlotte Hagens, a Public Policy thesis student from Norway, and Marten Lohgsroth, a psychology Ph.D. from Amsterdam. They simply would not believe the changes in Vyla's turnaround. From unemployed Ph.D. to White House

Investigator... and neither could she.

But having a non-normal existence seemed to be her path for as long as she could remember. Her parents and older brother had been killed in an auto accident on the day she was born. And though her surrogate mother had been as loving a parent as any kid could want, not having her biological family was a constant reminder that she was not like others. And with that family thought, being on this huge carrier, walking behind its skipper, she was reminded of Papa and his days in the military.

Papa, as she called him, was not related to her by blood, but he had played a huge role in her life. Having been a close friend of her parents, Papa had stepped in like a surrogate father and been there for her until his passing when she was thirteen. They had been super close, as only a father-daughter dynamic can sometimes provide. He had been a lifelong military pilot and had taken her flying in *Gloria*, his vintage Stearman biplane, starting on her seventh birthday and every year after that. She often felt that the best moments of her life were those with her Papa as a little girl. It was enough to be with him. It was everything.

As she grew up, Papa gave her more backstory on her parents. Both had come out of orphanages and did not have any extended family. They had met while doing volunteer work at the local orphanage and had fallen in love. When they were killed in the car wreck, with her older brother, Vyla, in the womb, was the only survivor. There was no extended family to contact. She was born into the world completely alone. Papa had been a volunteer at the orphanage and was on call that night when the emergency room doctor phoned. Papa had raced to the hospital only to find out that a baby was the sole survivor of the car crash involving her family.

Now, in this new moment, she suddenly had a new job, and somehow, she knew Papa was with her.

I love you, Papa, she thought as Schrader led her from the elevator.

She watched the skipper ahead of her as sailors on both sides of the hallway immediately came to attention with each new passage they entered. When he had greeted her, stepping off the COD with a salute, handshake, and smile, she knew one thing for certain: for the next seventy-two hours, she would be the most important person on this ship. That did not bode well with her. She knew a thing or two about this environment, as it was much like academia. Investigations could kill a career. She was not wanted here.

Well, fuck it, she thought. *This is going to happen. So, I'll get what I can, and damn the torpedoes!*

Captain Schrader escorted her directly into the ready room of the only Marine Fighter Squadron on the ship. The *Hawks* of VMA-533 was an F-18 squadron based out of Beaufort, South Carolina.

"Attention on deck!" was shouted.

She watched as all the pilots in the ready room snapped to attention. Schrader called out,

"At ease, everyone... please give us the ready room."

All at attention relaxed as the TV in the corner, showing news of the missing Malaysian jet, was switched off. Everyone departed except for two. She knew that military pilots had call signs stitched on their flight suits. Before her stood two Marine fighter pilots: Captain Frank "Knife" Jacobs and Captain Jackie "Crazy" Caruso. Schrader nodded to both pilots and motioned to Vyla.

"This is Dr. Vyla Kells, and she's here on behalf of the White House, so treat her right."

"Yes, sir!" They responded.

He then turned to her.

"Dr. Kells, Knife and Crazy here will tell you anything you want to know. They're two of the best and brightest. Good luck!"

With that, he gave one last look to his two pilots and departed. Immediately, Jacobs commanded,

"Attention on deck!" as he and Crazy came to attention.

Vyla watched the skipper depart, fascinated by the theatrics at play.

If you only listened to his words, she thought, *you would think everything was on the level. But visually watching Schrader, the slight tick in his dimple, his stern half-smile to the two pilots, his message was a silent shout:*

"Keep your friggin' mouths shut *and get that civilian-bitch off my ship!"*

Both pilots held attention until the skipper was gone.

"At ease," Jacobs commanded softly, and both relaxed. They turned and smiled at Vyla.

"It's not often we get introduced by our own skipper," Crazy said.

Vyla nodded.

"Well, it's a first for me, too," she replied.

Both pilots looked fit in their dark green flight suits with squadron patches and insignia. She had read that both were in their late thirties, with Knife being tall and wiry. Crazy was a sharp-featured brunette with deep-set blue eyes and a ponytail held back with a simple black hair tie. Vyla was glad to finally meet these two, who were central to her brief.

She may have been a hack scientist, but she knew a thing or two about military pilots, at least in a general way. Papa had flown fighters during Vietnam. She loved to hear his stories about his F-100 Super Sabre squadron during the Tet Offensive. He had tons of photos, and she would thumb through them with endless fascination, mainly because she loved his anecdotes about life within the squadron and what it was like to fly in combat.

He started giving her flying lessons in Gloria when she was only seven. She rode in the front cockpit of the vintage Stearman biplane during local airshows, ghost-flying the stick and throttle through loops, rolls, and hammerhead stalls. She showed so much enthusiasm flying Gloria that Papa, having retired as a colonel, began giving her lessons three times a week. And even though she was too short to reach the rudder pedals, she was hyper-focused on the stick and throttle, demanding them as much as he would let her.

After only a few flights, she started to get actual stick time, where he would allow her to do basic maneuvers, letting her control the stick and throttle while he worked the rudder pedals. During airshows, he would talk her through each step while performing the maneuvers, yelling to overcome the windblast of the open cockpits.

"There's 80 knots! Nose straight up! Now hold it! Hold it!"

Into the hammerhead stall, they would go, roaring straight up, climbing, but then Gloria's upward velocity slowed, and Vyla could feel Gloria start to shudder at full power. Finally, at zero airspeed, Gloria would begin falling backward through their own smoke!

"Kicking right rudder now!"

Papa yelled as Gloria's right wing dropped, and they would careen to the side until pointed straight down.

"Okay, there's two thousand—and smooth pull!"

She held the stick as it came back toward her, suddenly heavy in her seat, the G-forces pressing her down as Gloria pitched up, and he slid her straight into a wingover. The exhilarating rush of air and thrill of movement as they rolled upside down on a whim made her feel as if she herself had wings and could dance with the sky.

At every airshow, Papa pushed her to perform the entire maneuver with the stick and throttle. She still could not reach the rudders, but she was determined to put that stick in the right place using all her might. She quickly became more efficient at tightening her gut and leg muscles as she initiated a loop to keep the blood in her head throughout. As she learned, she could feel Papa's slight corrections on the stick when he would adjust her technique.

Finally, when she was ten and already tall for her age, she could reach the rudders. Within two flights, she had the hang of them and at the very next airshow, she realized that Papa had been silent in the back, not touching the stick or rudders the entire flight! On final approach, he yelled,

"She's all yours! Be smooth!"

The intensity of bringing Gloria down, front wheels first, was tough, and she simultaneously had to keep the rear wheel just off the runway until the lumbering bird was slow enough to let the tail wheel hit—without ground-looping her. Over the next three years, at countless airshows, she was no longer just flying the routine;

she was pilot-in-command from start to shut down.

On a glorious spring day, after she had completely owned an airshow audience with her thrilling performance, Papa gave her and her mom a huge hug and departed on a leisure RV trip in a new Winnebago he had just purchased. That goodbye was the last time she ever saw him. She was only thirteen.

Six months after he departed on his vacation, her mom pulled her out of school and informed her that he had died in a hospital in Arizona from brain cancer. She explained through tears that Papa most likely knew he had cancer for some time and didn't want his two favorites to suffer through his quickly deteriorating health. Hence, his sudden RV trip.

They did a road trip together to pick up his ashes in Arizona, and they supported each other through tears and laughter the whole way back to California. She told her mom she wanted to honor Papa by continuing lessons in the Stearman, and within a week of their return, she was working with Roland Soltanz, Papa's former student who had gone on to become the best aerobatic pilot in the state.

Roland pushed her hard, realizing that she was far beyond any other pilots at her age and had even more potential. He was shocked at her mastery of each maneuver and generally only gave her alternative methods to try out for airshows. They became fast friends, and by the time she was seventeen, Roland told her that she was well beyond any further teaching he had to offer. But she insisted they keep flying together. They traded maneuvers, challenging each other to perform aerial tricks with their eyes closed—relying only on feel and intuition—while the other played safety pilot. Several shows later, Roland watched in utter amazement as she yelled,

"Eyes closed!"

Then, without hesitation, she guided Gloria through an entire sequence, using only feel and timing, counting aloud the seconds she held between each stick-and-rudder throw.

"Eyes open!" she finally yelled. "She's all yours!"

At that moment, Roland knew he was the best in the state—but the seventeen-year-old girl in the front cockpit—she was far beyond him, beyond any pilot he had ever known.

Vyla was always the only female aerobatic pilot at the shows, and together, she and Roland became a local sensation. Families flocked to the airshows to watch her thrilling performances. She loved pulling Gloria into their grass parking spot beside the runway and shutting down the R-670 radial engine; surrounded by inquisitive girls and boys who stared at her like an alien.

When she stepped down from the cockpit, with her blonde hair escaping from her WWII-style leather helmet and goggles, the kids stood, struck dumb. She signed their airshow brochures, never tiring of their wide-eyed excitement as she helped them into the cockpit—where they had to stand just to see out.

Now, in the ready room, she found herself staring at a female fighter pilot with the same admiration those airshow kids once had for her. She had read the brief about how Crazy was a decorated combat veteran and a highly regarded air-combat tactician.

"Can we get you anything, Dr. Kells?" Knife asked, snapping her out of her reverie.

She took a breath.

"Can you point the way to the head?"

The two pilots snickered and gestured toward the rear hatch.

"Thank you. That was a long COD flight," she said as she slowly walked away. Then, over her shoulder, "Captain Jacobs, perhaps I can start with you? And Crazy, you'll go second?"

"Yes, ma'am." Crazy replied as Vyla closed the door to the head.

Her fingers suddenly went into an uncontrollable shake as she struggled with the door latch—and knew it was coming. One second later, the fire hose vomit shot through her.

She lurched for the toilet, yanking the chain as she went, hoping the flushing would drown out the sound of her claustrophobic purge. She was grateful for the steel walls and prayed the two pilots couldn't hear her. It all ended with a cold-water face wash and a huge exhale. She leaned her head against the metal door as she peed a river, reveling in the release.

God! Nobody ever gives enough credit for a good pee, she thought. Then,

I'm so odd to even think that!

And then,

I'm a White House investigator on a friggin' aircraft carrier! What the hell?! And this is a tiny friggin' head. And—fuck off, claustrophobia!

She exhaled, finally sitting up, and liked the thought that, despite all this *faking-it* business, she still felt somewhat confident.

Dammit all, she thought. *Why not me?*

She caught her own reflection in the tiny, round vanity mirror and hesitated, staring at herself. Slowly, she brushed back her blonde curls and retied her ponytail.

Inhale. Exhale. Let's roll.

She knew the next couple of hours were going to be cat-and-mouse for both sides. She had earned her private pilot's license on her sixteenth birthday and had been working toward an instrument rating when college coursework became too demanding. But her fascination with anything flight-related had continued.

But a UAP?

As she made her way back to the ready room, she tried to keep calm. She was about to get her first look at a verified UAP. And—being the investigator—she was supposedly the expert. But her mind was racing, her body anxious. She had been prepping for this moment since reading the brief in Geneva. Soon, she would see footage of a UAP from the heads-up displays of two different jets.

Why was this freaking her out so much?

Then it hit her.

Papa.

When she was growing up, Papa had always been fascinated with UFOs. So much so that he built little models and flew them around her on the couch when she was little. She had loved the game, as much for the plastic silver UFOs as for the direct attention of her adoring Papa. But she had also overheard his pilot friends chuckling at the UFO models during barbecues, dismissing them as *pure nonsense.*

Papa would then share a knowing wink with her, and she knew they had their own little secret. He bit his tongue because, as he told her, his friends were commercial pilots. If they ever claimed to see a flying saucer, their jobs would be in jeopardy.

She had seen pictures of Papa with his old military squadron. Her mother once told her that he had endured military life only because it furthered his love of flying. He was never a war-monger type. He had become a military pilot because flying meant freedom. It nurtured the hopeless romantic in him—the one who loved wringing out every capability of an aircraft as if it were part of him.

She had seen it firsthand. Papa had an almost supernatural sense of spatial orientation. He knew the limits of an aircraft's performance envelope better than anyone. Even on Roland's best maneuvers, she had known—Papa was a step beyond his best student.

And now, thinking back, everything was starting to make sense. Papa had retired as a colonel. That's when he had acquired Gloria. And in all their time together, she realized, she had never truly believed in UFOs. Skepticism had always been her nature.

After Papa's passing, when they collected his ashes, her mother had given her his flight journal—annotated from his military days. It was filled with fun notes from his many years in service. But two entries had always stood out.

Twice while flying in Vietnam, he had written something strange. Both read almost identically.

Saucer at 10 o'clock, one-half mile. Angels high. Crazy maneuvers. Vanished!

Then, a break in the writing, as if he had hesitated.

Crazy feeling inside as that thing raced around. Like they knew I was watching. And they were communicating... and... damn!

Followed by a final line about the encounter.

If I tell the squadron what I just saw—and understood from them—I will be fired for being crazy.

She now remembered Papa's secret wink to her as a little girl, and for the first time, she understood. He had tried to tell her back then, in his gentle way, what she—nor anyone else—would have ever believed.

He had seen them.

She stepped through the ready room hatch, where Knife was seated in front of a large digital screen on the front wall. As he turned, she took the seat next to him.

"Ma'am, I thought I'd play you the heads-up display and start with that?"

"Great," she replied.

The next ten minutes of jaw-dropping footage nearly shattered her practiced calm. Watching what Knife had experienced—and listening to the radio calls between him and Crazy—was beyond shocking. As Knife started the video, it showed his catapult launch off the carrier, which in itself got her heart racing. He then walked her through each phase of the intercept, detailing what they were seeing on his heads-up display.

Initially, there were only clouds ahead, but the radio calls between Knife and Crazy—regarding arming up for a possible shootdown—were full of anxiety. She watched with bated breath as the moment of intercept approached, her pulse rising with the intensity of the radio calls. Then she saw it.

Whoa!

The oval-shaped craft climbed at what appeared to be well beyond Mach speed, spiraling effortlessly up as it approached Knife's jet. Its ascent—from the ocean's surface to 10,000 feet—had taken less than two seconds. Not to mention the crazy turns and shifts that it made along that vertical rise. As if it was evading all forms of possible enemy fire, the oval craft swung from side-to-side effortlessly, zipping one way and then cutting obliquely, all while rising at such a speed that gravity clearly wasn't a factor.

Holy shit! was all her mind could muster. Beside her, Knife suddenly went silent. No more narration. It was as if he had disappeared into the moment—reliving the encounter from days ago. His eyes were transfixed on the ship. And she understood exactly why.

Upon seeing the craft, she felt her heart leap into her throat. She knew the flight capabilities of every top fighter jet in the world—she kept up on them out of her love for aviation. *But this? This wasn't flight.* She couldn't even define it as flight.

Damn—what in the hell was it doing?!

It had just risen from sea level to 10,000 feet in a manner and velocity her brain couldn't resolve. And a second later—hovered in front of two fast-moving F-18s—like they were standing still!

It was too much to comprehend. Her mind raced. Her snapshot told her that if a gravity envelope was being generated around the ship, then spacetime and light could be twisted as well. But who the hell knew?!

She quickly pulled herself back into the room, stealing a glance at Knife. He stared at the screen—frozen—deer in the headlights. The footage played on, showing the craft hovering, then suddenly shooting forward and encircling the two fighters at Mach speed. And then—shot diagonally upward and vanished! That's when it hit her. The flash in Knife's eyes as he relived the moment.

Terror. Sheer and unadulterated.

She had felt that same terror before—hurtling toward the runway in Gloria—fearing she would crash before Papa grabbed the controls and saved them. But Knife's terror—she knew it wasn't about that.

His terror was *vulnerability...* over-matched on every level. The insane capability of the alien ship confronting him that effortlessly bounced and toyed with him. An enemy he could neither attack nor run from... the oval craft had—in every sense of the phrase—*overwhelming superiority.*

When Knife finally spoke, his voice carried something nightmarish.

"Neither of our FLIRs would lock."

She knew at that moment he was gone in fear and had forgotten she was even there.

"I understand it was already at your CAP moments later?" she asked.

He nodded slowly.

"Yes, ma'am," he said quietly, not looking at her.

Gone, she thought. He stopped the replay and exhaled, trying to steady himself, then raised his eyebrows slightly, pressing his lips together.

"Supposedly, it was sixty miles away at the CAP."

She nodded.

"In just over two seconds, it traveled sixty nautical miles to your CAP?" she pressed. "And what's your best guess as to how it knew to go there?"

Knife shrugged, chuckling dryly.

"Who the hell knows?" he said, feigning nonchalance. "I'm guessing it was just a coincidence."

She knew that was Knife's first lie. Papa's stories about pilots using a CAP or, more specifically, the point-in-space where fighters rendezvous to begin the patrol; is only known by the aircrew and air traffic control. It was top-secret information, and she knew that in the Navy, each group of fighters that launched from the carrier had a different CAP. The CAP point moved according to the progress of the entire battle group. For that UAP to inadvertently pick a fixed-point-in-space, sixty-miles-away, at a hard altitude, computed to almost zero probability.

That UAP had known exactly where to go, she thought.

She also knew with no uncertainty—Knife was completely spooked. Pressing him for answers about possible telepathy on the part of the alien craft was way beyond this investigation, but as she recalled the Majestic brief, and thought through how that vessel knew where to go, was curious to her.

The brief listed common phenomena reported worldwide in UAP encounters. Telepathic communication was the first phenomenon listed. The brief included an excerpt from the infamous 1961 Betty and Barney Hill abduction—the first widely reported UFO abduction case in the U.S. She had read with fascination the Hills' claims of alien telepathy. That the entities who descended in a flying saucer and abducted them—did not speak—but instead used telepathy to communicate. During separate hypnosis regressions, Betty and Barney each expressed confidence that their minds had been read by the aliens. Both had been shocked that their questions were being answered before they spoke. When she had read the brief in Geneva, she was still skeptical, but now—everything had changed. She considered the possibility that Knife's alien ship was doing the same telepathic communication. She watched Knife, and knew that his UAP had raced out to his CAP, in a clear signal sent directly to the fighter pilots and the entire fleet. As if the alien craft was saying telepathically,

"We understand everything you are thinking."
She studied Knife as he tried to pull himself together. The replay had clearly resurfaced, a trauma far deeper than she expected. He exhaled heavily.

"I was honestly relieved to be heading back to the ship."
She nodded.

"Was there any aftereffects you experienced that you want to share?"
He looked at her warily, as if the question was way too personal. Then, forcing a half-smile, he shook his head.

"No, just—surprised at whatever that thing was."
She studied him a beat longer, then gave him a measured nod.

"Captain Jacobs, I can't thank you enough for your service—and for your candid help with all of this."
He nodded back as she reached for a slip of paper, writing down her number.

"If you ever have any thoughts in the future—anything at all—you can call me, day or night."

"Yes, ma'am," he said, standing and glancing at her number.

"I'll get Crazy for you."
He looked one last time at the screen as he turned to depart.

"I sure hope those guys are nice to us," he said nervously as he exited.
She nodded with a chuckle and watched him go.
Damn, he was agitated.

And so was she—just from the footage alone. But there was no time to process. Not yet. Crazy would be arriving soon. She turned back to the frozen heads-up display—where moments before—she saw her first UAP. Suddenly, a warm sensation washed over her.

A presence—that came with infinite adoration. She looked down at her hands and whispered,

"I love you, Papa."

Chapter Five

C hief Petty Officer Dan Day watched as the White House investigator's H-60 helicopter appeared out of the intense fog and wind and somehow landed on the USS Princeton's heaving aft deck.

The ship was charging roughshod through extremely heavy seas. The guided-missile cruiser was rising and falling headlong into walls of water with an audible thunder as the heavy seas exploded outward from the hardened steel bow. The fog was so intense that even the aircraft carrier—spanning three football fields long and twenty-two stories high—was unseen as it heaved in the heavy seas, only a few hundred yards starboard. The eerie thought of its close proximity and the twenty knots of potential collision was not lost on Chief Day.

A fleet going through a storm relied completely on radar. Each ship in the strike fleet, lost in fog, an angelic steed in its own world, yet tethered to the carrier in the most delicate web of radar. The strike fleet plowed forward inexorably, regardless of weather, as stopping a battle group for any reason might encourage an enemy attack. Certainly, the destroyers, troopships, guided-missile cruisers, and submarines would take slightly more separation in their combat formation, but Skipper Schrader demanded formation discipline.

In Schrader's Task Force Seven, if any ship took too much separation, its captain would soon be standing in front of Schrader for "an adjustment." And possibly a demotion. Chief Day knew that even the submarine protecting the fleet would surface in this dense fog and run the storm. With this type of cloud cover, a sub could run on the surface without detection from spy satellites and enemy surface ships that often ghosted the battle group. This allowed the Bubbleheads—as sub-crews were called—a momentary dose of topside fresh air. A real morale booster after weeks submerged.

Day watched as the helo doors were slid open, and Dr. Kells stepped out. She had completed her interviews with the fighter pilots on the carrier and was coming for her last one with him. He saluted her and then shook her hand with a smile, yelling,

"Welcome aboard, ma'am. I'm Chief Day—right this way!"

As he led her through the ship, they were saluted at several hatches on the way to her stateroom. She knew the salutes were for her, but at the same time, she noted the sailors were enamored with Chief Day. She could see the way they responded to him and now understood what Papa had so often said about senior enlisted. There was a wisdom about Chief Day that was tangible. She also knew that his vulnerable and humble demeanor disguised an explosive badass just behind the curtain. She had read Day's dossier—his alter life as a martial arts master. His salt-and-pepper mustache betrayed his age, but clearly, he was in impeccable shape. Fascinating to her, as most would simply disregard this man in a bar and have no idea of his hidden lethal capabilities.

A disguised superhero, she thought.

She had taken some karate lessons in high school, and her extremely rigid martial arts instructor had taught her how to throw a solid punch before she had to depart for college, but her course load was too heavy for her to continue in martial arts. She thought Chief Day looked much younger than his forty-six years. As they reached her stateroom, which had *VIP* emblazoned on the door, he gave her a wearable key card, and she entered the largest suite on the ship. Her luggage was rolled in, and everyone departed except for Chief Day.

"Just hit that button by your door, ma'am, when you are ready."

"Thank you, Chief. I just need a few minutes."

"Yes, ma'am," he replied, closing the door as he left.

An hour later, they were standing in the CIC. The Command Information Center was a darkened air traffic control center for the entire fleet. Huge radar screens adorned the front wall and were being monitored by a cross-section of radar operators and air traffic controllers. He offered her a tall chair next to his and motioned at the large screen in the center of the room.

Using a laser pointer, he described the blips and the location of every major ship, as well as the attack sub running on the surface. She nodded as he described the transponder codes associated with each blip. She told him briefly of her flying experience, and he was glad he had an aviator for an investigator. At least he wouldn't have to start from scratch with regard to radar.

He led her to a back room where a large video screen held a freeze-frame of the radar screen they had just viewed in the CIC. He reverse-scrolled through footage on the radar screen. The date at the top suddenly showed three days before the incident.

"This is a recording of the radar activity from seventy-two hours before the intercept," he said.

He drew his laser dot up to the top of the screen.

"Watch up here, ma'am," he said.

She watched as the screen showed all the usual ships and planes with their corresponding transponder codes. Then, slowly coming into view at the top of the screen was something that appeared to be falling, like snowflakes. So many they were uncountable. Moving in various directions, but certainly above the fleet. She stared in disbelief.

"There's... there're hundreds?" She said, astonished.

He looked her way, and she saw that he was contemplating a bigger tell. He finally exhaled and looked back at the screen, pointing to the top of the radar picture.

"Those are dropping from above 80,000 feet, which is where they enter the screen. But that's not the whole story. They're arriving from outer space according to SDI radar out of Coral Gables."

She slowly nodded.

"Wow," she whispered.

"Yep," he replied. "Wow is an understatement, and see, their velocity is almost zero. They are moving at roughly one hundred miles per hour, and that's in crosswinds that were equally one hundred miles per hour."

She stared.

"So, they were just hovering there?" she said matter-of-factly.

He nodded, now truly impressed with her flight knowledge. He pointed at the screen.

"There is not an aircraft in our inventory that can go that slow, that high. Our helicopters can't even get to eighty thousand. But then watch this."

He guided the laser to highlight the left side of the cluster of UAPs. Suddenly, the blip highlighted by his laser pointer dropped to the bottom of the screen in an instant, stopping just above sea level.

"That one right there just descended 80,000 feet in one second."

She stared in shock.

"Damn!" she whispered.

He nodded at her.

"That's a good assessment, ma'am."

Settle down, she reminded herself. *I'm not supposed to be surprised at this shit!*

He looked back at the screen and continued.

"Up to that point, nobody on our ship wanted to admit that there were even UAPs in the area for fear of losing their jobs. The military still holds that UAPs are bullshit, and only spooks believe in them. Every single radar operator around me could see these blips for four fucking days in a row," he said, pausing, contemplating the screen.

"Excuse my language, ma'am, but I felt like I was in some kind of weird time-warp where nobody would admit what was happening all around us."

She nodded, watching him. He tightened his lips, gesturing to the radar.

"I finally got fed up and took this recording up to the skipper. I just couldn't stand the white-elephant syndrome any longer. I had to do it for myself."

She watched as he slowly gazed around, as if looking for a camera, and then turned directly to her, speaking under his breath.

"Ma'am, I may lose my job over this. I'm already feeling the heat, but I've got to tell you what I saw." He took a breath. "I've been staring at these screens for nineteen years, and there's a lot more out there than the military will ever admit."

She nodded, staring intently at him.

"Thank you. What happened then?"

He looked back at the screen.

"See this right here?"

He pointed at a red light flashing at the bottom-right of the radar.

"Every time those UAPs ping the fleet with an electromagnetic pulse, that light flashes."

She nodded.

"Gathering information about the task force?" She said matter-of-factly.

"Exactly," Day said, relieved she knew what EMPs were. She looked over.

"I read about those in my brief. When you approached your skipper with all this, what did he say?"

Chief Day thought for a moment and took another deep breath, as though he was still incensed by his initial confrontation with the skipper.

"The skipper offhandedly tried to balk that he wasn't seeing the hundreds of blips descending on the fleet. He asked me to do a full technical check of all the radar systems to ensure that these blips weren't just a glitchy new radar. I reminded him that we did a full check four days prior when these first appeared. 'The radar is in perfect working order,'" I told him.

She watched him.

"The skipper stared at me like I was forcing his hand. 'They're fuckin' UAPs, sir,'

I finally told him. 'You have a real and present danger threatening this strike group.'"

"I bet that went over well?" she questioned.

He tightened his lips.

"I stayed there while my skipper called Captain Schrader on the aircraft carrier and informed him of the UAP threat. The stare I got from my skipper at that moment would have frozen water, but I was fuckin' over it."

She nodded, watching him carefully.

"So, then what?" she asked.

He shrugged.

"Well, at that point, Captain Schrader knew he had a threat to the carrier battle group, and in that situation, SOP requires that he acknowledge and engage the threat."

She watched as he slowly shook his head again in disgust.

"Once the skipper announced that he wanted an intercept, then everyone seemed to suddenly see the blips. How fucking convenient."

She slowly nodded.

"That was a huge moment," Day continued. "That meant this UAP was being announced by the captain of a U.S. Navy ship as a real threat to a carrier strike group. Confirming a UAP even existed had never occurred during all my years," he said. "And then the rolling dumpster fire began."

"How do you mean?"

"Well, ma'am. It's one thing to put an entire battle group on alert. Meaning every ship knew that this was not a drill, but a real threat to the carrier. But it's another thing to say that we are under threat of alien attack."

"Right," she whispered.

"But in that moment," he continued, "I had to broadcast over the loudspeaker of every ship in our strike group and basically describe the threat. I watched the sailors running to their battle stations as I made the announcement. When I said the words, 'Unidentified Aerial Phenomenon,' most of the sailors turned toward the loudspeakers in disbelief. Then I repeated the phrase, and they turned-to, and scurried to man their battle stations."

She nodded.

"Can we watch the sequence of the intercept?"

He nodded and hit play. They watched as the two F-18 blips departed the carrier, with the UAP blip doing wild maneuvers miles ahead of the ship, seeming to go below and then above the surface of the water.

"I saw this on the F-18 heads-up camera footage," she said.

He nodded.

"That thing is traveling over 3,000 miles per hour while submerged," he said, pointing his laser at the UAP racing just under the ocean surface.

She shook her head in astonishment. They both watched as the blip rose and broke the surface, only to race back in a circle at the same unbelievable rate, just above the waves. Then, as the two fighters approached, she could see the UAP rise vertically and begin toying with the two jets. A minute later, the blip disappeared from the screen. He turned to her.

"It just departed into a dimension the SPY-3 can't see, at over 7,000 miles per hour. Now watch this."

He placed his laser dot on the far-right side of the radar screen. The UAP blip suddenly reappeared next to his laser dot, completely stationary.

"Now it's just reappeared from wherever it went, and it's hovering at 17,000 feet at their CAP."

She slowly shook her head, astonished.

"And that was the CAP that only you and the two pilots knew?" she inquired.

He nodded.

"At that point, I ordered the RTS."

"Return to ship?" she said.

"Correct."

"Why?" she asked. "Why not allow them to fly out to meet it again?"

He pointed his laser at the top of the screen.

"The other UAPs up at altitude had departed, and the remaining one was no longer threatening," he said. "But mainly it's because I didn't want to piss that thing off on any level."

She nodded. He then moved his laser pointer to the far side of the screen where the UAP was hovering.

"Watch the UAP, ma'am."

She stared, perplexed, as the UAP flashed in and out of view, then shot vertically off the top of the screen. She turned, astonished. He slowly nodded.

"Apparently, you just witnessed an above Mach-30 departure velocity into outer space," he said.

"Wow," she whispered.

He lowered his laser pointer and circled a small blip just outside the perimeter of the strike group with no transponder code attached.

"Here's something else. This blip here is a boat. That thing had shown up just outside our perimeter the same day the UAPs began descending from space," he said, staring at the blip.

"It held its position relative to the fleet for the next five days, with no transponder code. One of our helicopters finally got a visual ID. It's based out of Monterey Bay, California, at Moss Landing near Santa Cruz. *Gizmo* is the name of the boat."

"How big is it?" she asked.

"About eighty feet long. Our chopper pilot said it appeared to be an old WWII patrol boat," he said, and then got a skeptical look.

"I've never seen a privately owned boat stay on station like that near a strike fleet. Russian spy ships will often follow us when we reach open ocean. But there are no Russian surface ships that run the California coastline. At one point, when that PT boat was arriving, we tracked it doing fifty knots in moderate chop. Almost like it was hydroplaning in the open ocean."

"Whoa," she whispered.

He nodded.

"Yeah, that's uniquely fast, and the weird thing is, it arrived at our perimeter just ahead of the UAPs coming down from space. Stayed the entire time we were being probed by electromagnetic pulses and then departed when they did."

"And your best guess?" she asked.

He shook his head.

"Beats the hell outta me. I've never told the skipper about it because there was already too much for him to process, but I thought you should know."

She nodded.

"Can you shut it off, please?"

He shut the replay off and turned to see her looking around the room as if for cameras. She turned back to him and leaned in.

"Can I ask you some questions off the record?" she whispered.

He contemplated her, then shrugged and whispered,

"Yes, ma'am."

She leaned in again.

"You think my stateroom would be free of bugs?"

He shrugged.

"Yes, ma'am. I would hope so."

Chapter Six

Tom only knew that he was going batshit crazy.

It was 3 a.m., on March 10th, 2014, and he was terrified.

He had many nightmares that were strange over the years, but this new batch that began two days ago on the evening of March 8th had changed everything. Through the years, his nightmares before the 8th, would come in spurts that made no sense—had no context. But last night's horrific sequences had a location to them. Something that—in his bones, felt real. But—

How could they be?

What terrified him as much as the nightmares themselves was that same passenger jet—featured so prominently in his horrific dreams—was now, somehow, on the news. On CNN for Christ's sake.

That damn jet with Malaysia written in blue on the side was the top story on every news feed. The one that had vanished without a trace on the 8th, with 239 aboard. Every major network was covering the worldwide search for Malaysia Flight MH370, but already, hope had faded. Most assumed all on board had perished when it crashed in the ocean. But Tom knew that wasn't the case. The jet had not crashed. It had landed safely.

Goddammit! he thought.

Wondering how in the hell did he know that? But there it was, staring back at him from the TV screen, right behind the newscaster's face. That same jet, with the blue lettering against the white fuselage.

He had been there—at that military base. And landing safely would not bring them home. Not any of them. Ever.

That's not the way it worked. They were in the way of what someone wanted. That's all they were.

Fuck! he thought, as a cold wave of realization crept through him.

Somehow—he was involved. But how?

Another jolt! Gripping the arm of the couch—another flashback—like electricity surging through lines that were too small. His body tensed, veins bulging, his eyes slamming shut as it locked up his mind.

He was *there*. Pointing his pistol at the Navy maintenance crew, who had just disassembled the tail section of that jet. In broad daylight, on the tarmac at that U.S. Navy base. He could smell the ocean, and feel the tropical warm breeze, and he knew something even then, in his bones—that *this* was *Diego*.

He gasped aloud, snapping back into his living room.

What was it—Diego—Diego Garcia? How could he even know that name? But he did know it. How? He'd never even been there; didn't have a clue where it was. He was fifty-eight years old and wore his hair in a ponytail, for Christ's sake! He had never even been in the military—or?

He shifted on the couch, staring at the CNN anchor droning on about Flight 370. He leaned forward and shut off the TV.

Before he even settled back into the couch, the next flashback ripped into him. The scene playing out in front of him. One that felt as real as staring in the mirror—and this flashback was visceral, not the least bit vague, instead horribly detailed, like the nightmares that had just woken him. The ones where his victims would always say the weirdest shit.

Their last words—pleading with him—not to shoot as those Navy maintenance men were on their knees, holding up their hands in a defensive gesture. As if the bullet coming would somehow be stopped by a few fingers. Fingers shaking in terror between his pistol barrel and their turned away head—just before he inevitably fired his Colt 45.

It thundered into their pleading—and stopped it cold.

"Please! I have a family!" *Whoom!*

Or,

"Please, I'm just a maintenance guy, bro!" *Whoom!*

He felt absolutely nothing as the Colt barked, sending that bullet to rip through their fingers before it blew most of their head away.

Blood gushing from their hands and head would still be spraying as the limp body cascaded toward the tarmac—while he calmly stepped to the next victim—before they could even comprehend the darkness enveloping their last moments.

Their last moments next to that disassembled tail section at Diego. That's where he was, and he had a job to do, an order to be carried out.

Thirty minutes before, he had watched them up-close, as they hastily unbolted that Boeing 777. Their energy was hurried, like somebody wanted that jet apart quickly for some reason. It wasn't his business to know who or why. Or to even care. And he didn't care. *Not at all.*

His orders from Master Chief-One were simple.

"*Remove them* as soon as they had the tail disassembled."

And then the Chief had shocked him with that fucking cattle prod. Just like he always did.

Fucker.

But he didn't want to be shocked again, so he walked toward the jet parked on the tarmac. It had just landed, and already the disassembly crew was pulling the tail apart. The door by the cockpit was opening, and he could hear yelling from inside the jet. But that wasn't his concern. And it wasn't his concern that he was up on the surface.

He hadn't been in sunlight in forever. The tropical ocean breeze and the heat were foreign to him, as his normal duties were carried out in the top-secret base below the tarmac. Extending down—deep into the ocean. A hidden fortress in the covert world.

But he didn't think too much of it. He had been ordered to the surface, and he had a job to do. And he didn't want another goddamn shock.

He wore his grey uniform. The one he always wore. He was *U.S. Black Navy*. An above-top-secret unit run by the CIA for the Cabal. His unit sometimes worked hand in hand with the regular U.S. Navy, who wore white uniforms. But not today.

He walked calmly toward the disassembly crew, unbolting the tail section. They were all Black Navy too, wearing their grey maintenance coveralls, yet they seemed anxious—clearly working at an accelerated pace. His sidearm was holstered, and he could feel the weight of his eight fully loaded magazines he always carried. He wore glasses, and his slightly greying short hair was parted to the side—like a clean-cut businessman. Fifty-eight years old, yet with an edge of enhanced physical capabilities—because *that's what they had done to him.*

Quicker reflexes. Better hearing. Emotions flatlined. Methodical and obedient. Trained for *abduction* and *assassination*. Sometimes *disposal.*

But the Chief shocked him with every order—a reminder of what punishment would come if he disobeyed.

His tactical uniform was form-fit and all his pockets bulged subtly over the loaded mags. With his black boots and cold expression, he looked formidable—like an aged colonel.

He walked calmly nearby as they worked—at breakneck pace. They had no idea, as he watched them, that in a few more moments he would gather them together—at gunpoint.

He knew they would all be in shock when it began. And that they would *follow orders.* Men suddenly confronted with the barrel of a gun generally don't argue.

He appeared businesslike in his military gait, casually walking nearby like an inspector. And they barely noticed him—because those maintenance men taking apart that tail section—kept stealing anxious glances toward the passengers and crew being forcibly removed at gunpoint near the cockpit exit ramp.

All were blindfolded and handcuffed. Herded down the rolling staircase by black-clad operatives... that were not his unit.

The lead hijacker guiding the blindfolded hostages yelled they were moving too slow. A second hijacker stormed down the steps and yanked off the lead hostage's blindfold, yelling at her to walk faster! A gunshot. His head exploded as the lead hijacker shot him at point-blank range. The dead man crumpled to the tarmac, blood spraying. The blindfold was replaced. The lead hijacker pulled the hostages into movement again... argument over.

At the rear of the jet, the maintenance crew laid the last piece of the tail section on the tarmac, working together to place the large aluminum component on the ground. They looked up as he approached, unholstering his .45 in a smooth, trained gesture, aiming directly at them.

"Get on your knees," he calmly ordered.

And they dropped. Cowering. Hoping that obeying would delay what they all couldn't believe... their hands raised high, screaming not to be shot... and clearly some of them knew him from seeing him on the base. Including the first one.

"Hans! Please, bro! It's me—Jack, your friend—no!"

Whoom!

Tom could barely breathe on the couch, his heart racing harder until he yelled out—breaking the flashback—panting.

"What is it, Tom? You're doing really good," she whispered. "What is happening with Hans right now?"

Her therapist voice, reassuring against every bit of trauma Tom was re-living, bracing tightly against what he's seeing, there on her couch. She sat nearby, studying him with an intense yet compassionate focus. In her early sixties, casual attire, reading glasses and a pad and pen on her lap. A well-used coffee cup on the table near her.

"Okay, you're doing really good, Tom. Just stay with it... remember, don't focus on what Hans is feeling, just tell me what Hans is seeing instead."

Tom hesitated, breathing hard... recovering just slightly.

"So tell me... what is Hans seeing right now?" she whispered.

"Is his gun still out... Tom?"

Chapter Seven

H e escorted her to her stateroom, high in the Princeton's upper decks.

She flashed her keycard and pushed open the door, then looked both ways, clearing the hallway. She gestured for him to enter, stepping in right behind him, closed the door and locked it. He looked around, admiring the spacious stateroom.

"Have a seat," she said, gesturing to the leather couch with a small table in front of it.

"Yes, ma'am."

She walked to the refrigerator and returned with two bottled waters, filling the small glasses on the table.

"I'm curious about other things than just radar and factual data," she said, sitting beside him.

They toasted, and she studied him for a moment.

"So, what crossed your mind when you realized the UAP was sitting at the CAP?"

He contemplated his drink, and she could tell he was reliving it.

"In the moment, I felt like we were being played with—like primitive apes in a futuristic game that we weren't equipped to understand on any level. But they clearly wanted us to understand. To pass information to us without harm."

She nodded, knowing there was more coming. He took a sip of water, staring at the glass.

"But when I step back to that moment, I remember watching the ship move, and I was actually scared. Or in fear, I guess. I was in enemy-assessment mode, and I was kind of freaking out. Here was an adversary that had created a craft that could defy gravity and all known scientific laws—then what-the-fuck might their weapons do? I was concerned they could have vaporized the fleet if they felt the least bit threatened."

She nodded and whispered,

"Right, hence the RTS?"

"Yeah," he replied. "I didn't want our Hornets to appear threatening or accidentally hose-off a missile. I just wanted our crew back safely—so I ordered the *Return-To-Ship*."

"Chief, did you feel or sense a communication?"

He contemplated for a moment, exhaling a long breath.

"Since that moment, I feel like I've been connected to them. And I don't know how to say this, but I'm still," he paused, shaking his head, "I don't know, it's weird—like next-level."

"How do you mean?" she asked.

He looked at her... his deep blue eyes so intense.

"It's like looking at your first child, and when their eyes meet yours, they're like ancient souls, reminding you of things you need to learn in this passage. Your baby isn't physically speaking—but it speaks to you—you know?"

She nodded.

"Are they still... speaking to you?"

"Sure feels that way."

"Wow," she whispered. "Thank you."

He shrugged and pursed his lips.

"Either way, I'm pretty sure my career is toast."

She watched him for a moment.

"It seems like you acted in defense of the fleet. Your position required action. I would think any Navy investigators would consider that?"

He half-smiled, and she could see the sadness.

"It doesn't work that way, does it?" she ventured.

She watched him stare down at his drink as he sadly smiled, and then she knew. She could no longer hold up the façade of being the expert. She needed to return to who she really was—for herself.

"You wanna know something about me?" she whispered.

He turned.

"Honestly, I'm a physicist by trade. I was handed this investigator job three days ago because the White House wanted to know if the UAP might be working in other dimensions."

Dan nodded and could see more coming.

"And I don't really understand the cover-up thing. I mean, this denial by everybody—it's too big," she whispered. "Why is everyone holding up a see-through curtain? Like your boss not wanting to see the hundreds of blips in front of him? I mean, I get it. I've read the conspiracy theories about the Majestic-12, which I guess is now called *the Cabal*, but..."

He watched her, knowing the whole history of *"The alien cover-up"* was new to her. He took a slow sip of water and put the glass down.

"So, how about you?" she asked. "Do you think the Cabal is a real group?"

He turned, staring at her, then half-laughed, shaking his head with a hint of fear.

"Well, I don't think you want to test if they're an actual entity or not," he whispered, his steady eyes warning of dire consequences.

"James Forrestal tested that group, and it didn't end well for him."

"Okay, who was he?" she asked.

"He was Secretary of the Navy and America's first Secretary of Defense. By all accounts, a true patriot."

"And what happened to him?"

"They threw him out of the sixteenth-floor window of the Bethesda Naval Hospital. For threatening to go public with the alien phenomenon that was being kept secret."

She stared.

"They?"

He looked at her, then away, shaking his head. She watched him. His silent warning was a gentle slap. This new arena was *absolutely deadly,* she thought.

"Hey," she whispered. "It's refreshing to be around someone calling it like it is."

He slowly turned to her.

"You can call me Vyla," she whispered.

He nodded.

"Call me Dan."

She nodded and raised a finger... then reached into her briefcase and slowly pulled out her flask, placing it on the table in front of him with a serious look.

"Well, Dan, that's truth serum—I'm not absolutely certain—that you've told the complete truth."

He turned, perplexed, and then caught the twinkle in her eye. After a moment, he burst out laughing, which ended with the two of them locking eyes. Two hours later, half-drunk, half-dressed, and making out, she knew something for certain—she had very bad boundaries. And she was again reminded of how she was curiously attracted to both sexes, and how Charlotte, her longtime girlfriend at Stanford, would gently tease her, crooning Freddy Mercury's, *Any Way the Wind Blows.*

And yes, she had momentarily considered investigation protocols, but quickly jettisoned them—to ensure they didn't stop the wildness rising. Their explosive physicality, replete with gentle bites, hair-pulling, and fingernail marks, ended with panting and giggles and fresh old-fashions from the wet bar. They talked deep into the night, laughing about the bullshit worlds of academia and the military. She wasn't sure why Chief Day was so attractive to her... he just was. Yes, she would feel bad on some level that she had sex with an individual in her investigation, but it was after the fact, and dammit, a good fuck relieved her on a million levels.

She knew that what was occurring with Yen Jee, the Majestic clearance, the signing away of all her privacy rights, was not the job description she had signed up for. There was a sinister darkness about it all. A secret she was not yet privy to, but that she knew in her boney-bones was real. She made a promise to herself that when she flew back, she would press Yen Jee to come clean. She polished off her old fashion and sucked on a piece of ice.

"Shit, half the stuff in my brief seemed like something from a comic book," she said.

"What level are you cleared to?" he asked.

"Majestic."

"No shit?" he whispered, astonished.

She stared at him.

"Aren't you?"

He looked sideways at her. She got a mischievous look.

"You mean you're not cleared to fuck me?" she said.

He stifled a laugh.

"Must be some wild shit you get to read," he said.

She thought about the Majestic brief and how it alluded to other UAP sightings and incidents with the military. Since she hadn't really believed in UAPs two days ago, it didn't really apply. She was surprised at how far her mind had shifted from disbelief to belief in just a few hours. Seeing is believing, but not just that... the implications were overwhelming.

She noticed he was staring at her.

"What?" she whispered.

"You're cleared to Majestic," he said. "Hell, I get tailed from time to time, and I'm twenty levels below Majestic."

"Seriously?" she said, remembering all the surveillance and utter privacy invasion she had just agreed to in Geneva.

He polished off his drink and set it down slowly as he spoke.

"Well, let's put it this way—there is only one person in this entire battle group cleared to that level—and that would be you."

"Should I shoot you now or after you leave?" she said.

He half-smiled and whispered,

"I reckon you should wait until we fuck one more time."

She moved in close, lips almost touching.

"Say 'I reckon' again—with that slutty Texas accent."

He smiled.

"I reckon—"

She bowled him over before he finished the line with a deep kiss, and it went from there to hell and back. And the ship rolled, and they rolled, and fucked and fucked and fucked more.

Finally, they came up for air, both sweaty and spent, and smiled at each other until giggles erupted. She turned on some mellow music while he made more old-fashions. They toasted, "To aliens," and marveled at the fact that a no-shit encounter with something from another world had just been verified. They mused on its significance. She brought over a small tray of snacks from the counter and sat next to him.

"It's too bad they didn't have your Spy-3 radar watching that Malaysian flight. They'd know exactly where it is."

He quit chewing and got a look, scanning the room as if searching for cameras.

"A jet that big can't just disappear from all the high-tech radars in its vicinity," he said, staring straight ahead. "That thing was taken."

"What do you mean, taken?" she whispered. "You know something about Flight 370?"

He took a deep breath and turned, contemplating her.

He could trust her.

He looked around again as he pulled out his cell phone with a dead serious look.

"I didn't show you this," he whispered.

She slowly nodded and whispered,

"Right."

He angled his phone on his lap so they both could watch a video that was cued on his screen.

"It's being leaked online today," he said.

He hit play.

"This footage is from a U.S. Air Force MQ-9 Reaper drone."

She watched as the video showed a clear sky with only a few white clouds interspersed. Suddenly, a large commercial jet flew into the frame, and the video began tracking the flight as it appeared to turn through the clouds. She recognized the distinctive airframe and looked at him.

"That's a Boeing 777! Is this the Malaysian—?"

"Watch," he whispered, interrupting, hinting at something sinister.

A moment later, as the commercial jet continued its turn, three small orbs flew into the frame, each appearing to be roughly fifty-feet in diameter. The orbs began circling around the jet as it raced ahead—just like the UAP had danced around Knife and Crazy's jets. She watched transfixed as the orbs effortlessly circled the huge airliner. She figured the jet was traveling at four-hundred knots. That meant the orb-like objects circling the jet had to be antigravity platforms of some type, working at above Mach speeds to dance around the fast-moving aircraft. She looked quickly at Dan, and he motioned back to the video, as the circling orbs suddenly increased their speed dramatically and then—the jet and all three orbs—vanished!

"What the fuck!" she gasped, her voice a terse whisper. "Where did you—?"

He raised a finger to his lips. *Quiet!*

And looked around again.

"My black-ops buddy in Hawaii just sent me this," he whispered. "And there's another video from another Reaper drone that tracks the flight as well. Exact same sequence, just from an opposite angle."

She stared, shaking her head.

"So—what happened right there—did they vaporize it somehow and destroy it?"

He slowly shook his head.

"They teleported it," he whispered. "Basically hijacked it."

"What?!" she whispered in disbelief. "We have that technology now?"

He stared.

"Apparently—the Cabal does."

She stared.

"Wow, so... why? Why would they hijack a Malaysian commercial jet?"

He slowly shook his head.

"Somebody wanted that jet for some reason. There had to be something or someone on it... worth making that jet vanish."

"And what do you think happened to the Malaysian passengers?"

He slowly shook his head, staring through the porthole window at the storm.

"With this many days gone by... something really tragic has happened. I'm assuming if they haven't been heard from in two weeks' time, that they're..." he tightened his lips, shaking his head.

Vyla stared, watching him.

"So, this Cabal can just... order the Air Force or Navy or whatever to help them carry out this entire hijacking?"

He shrugged.

"Play it again."

He put his phone between the two of them.

As it began playing, there were only clouds and ocean on the screen. She pointed at the clouds.

"That's what I thought... those are cumulus clouds! Those only show up between one to five-thousand feet, so that means they're tracking this jet really low, like just above the ocean."

He nodded as the large airliner flew through the clouds. She got a quizzical look and pointed to the exhaust coming from the jet.

"That's not exhaust or contrails! That damn jet is on fire! That's smoke trailing behind it!"

He looked at her, amazed.

"Yeah," he whispered. "My buddy said the other drone footage was thermal imagery, and showed that the cargo hold had a small fire... so you're exactly right... the jet is on fire."

They watched as the three small orbs entered the frame and began circling the airliner... faster and faster until everything suddenly vanished.

She stared stupefied at the clouds, with no jet or orbs present.

"You're saying I just watched a commercial jet... get teleported?"

He shrugged.

She stared, contemplating.

"So, where did they teleport it to?"

Dan hesitated.

"My buddy told me it was teleported to just above the Maldives Islands, 1,500 miles southwest of Great Nicobar, and when it came out of the wormhole, it was then flown south to Diego Garcia."

"Where is that?" She whispered.

"It's a tiny U.S. Navy base in the Indian Ocean."

He slowly stood and leaned against the far wall, staring through the porthole window at the storm. She watched him.

"So, your buddy, where did he get this footage? Was he involved? Is that how he knew it was taken to Diego Garcia?"

"Well, his team was involved, but they were being ordered to take actions in real time, and didn't have the bigger picture of what they were involved in."

She stared, confused.

"In this video," he said, tapping his phone.

"The jet vanishes over Great Nicobar Island. My buddy said the Malaysian jet then reappeared out of the teleportation, 1,500 miles southwest, over the Maldives islands, still in flight."

"How could he know that?"

"His AWACS bird was in orbit over the Maldives, which are just north of Diego Garcia. His bird was waiting in a holding position, on standby for further orders. He said the Malaysian jet just suddenly appeared from nowhere, at only one-thousand feet above a seaside village on the island they were orbiting over. It's a Maldives island with a long name called Kudahuvadhoo. My buddy and his crew didn't know the jet had just finished a teleportation from 1,500 miles away. He said that his AWACS bird was then ordered to take control of the Malaysian jet and fly it south to Diego for landing, which they did."

She held up a finger, pausing him, piecing it together.

"You mean your buddy's Navy AWACS essentially commandeered the autopilot on the Malaysian jet and took full control away from the pilots and flew it south to Diego?" she asked, astonished.

"My buddy claims his Navy AWACS has taken control of other aircraft in flight for many years now. It's a specialized AWACS... not a standard one."

She shook her head, perplexed.

"I can sort of understand how an advanced AWACS could commandeer the autopilot, but landing an airliner that size would take a human at the controls as there are way too many last-second adjustments to land an airliner that big."

Dan stared at her, dumbstruck.

"Damn, you really are a pilot, and you're exactly right. My buddy said that they took control of the Malaysian jet until Diego Garcia. At that point, they handed it over to the Cabal pilot at the controls, and he landed it."

She stared.

"Oh no. You're saying the Malaysian jet was actually hijacked—and after the Cabal had control of it—that's when they teleported it?"

Dan stared.

"Apparently. My buddy said the pilot that landed that jet at Diego had a noticeable American accent and seemed to be a very seasoned pilot. Not to mention having light brown hair."

She stared.

"As in, not one of the original Asian pilots?"

"That's correct," he said. "He told me that both Reaper drones following the Malaysian flight were using *Gorgon Stare* technology... and that's some brand-new shit right there. Gorgon Stare is still uber top-secret. It shoots at six frames per-second, but more importantly, its footage allows the viewer to literally see through the aircraft, or building or whatever the drone is filming. It's normally used to catch terrorists hiding in buildings or vehicles."

She watched as he continued.

"So, when my buddy viewed the thermal imagery footage from the second drone, most of the passengers were strapped in their seats. But he could see two bodies on the floor just outside the cockpit door."

"Pilot and copilot," she sadly guessed.

Dan nodded.

"Apparently, and my buddy said he could see several bodies strewn throughout the cabin, but like I said, most were still strapped in their seats, according to him."

She stared.

"So he's releasing the Reaper thermal imagery with all the bodies online?"

Dan shook his head.

"No, he put a filter on the thermal imagery that allows the fire and the hot spots to be seen, but not the passengers. He said the unfiltered version was too gruesome to watch, as that Gorgon Stare footage is really detailed."

She slowly nodded.

"Wow, so, were some of the passengers still alive upon landing at Diego?"

He nodded.

"My buddy's AWACS orbited over Diego Garcia after the jet was landed, and he could see many passengers being unloaded at gunpoint, before his bird was ordered back to the Maldives. He said the jet itself was in really bad shape when it landed at Diego, and my buddy was impressed that the pilot managed to get it on deck safely."

She contemplated him.

"I know you don't want to divulge his name, but what's the story with your buddy?"

Dan exhaled, staring at his glass.

"Old friend of mine. He has an extensive signal-intelligence background. Smartest of the smart... kind of like a prodigy. His Navy Special Projects Patrol Squadron is called VPU-2. It's an above-top-secret Navy AWACS squadron based out of Kaneohe Bay, Hawaii. He's the flight director on his AWACS bird. His unit uses specialized aircraft to collect data on potential U.S. adversaries as part of one of the most secretive units in the service."

He took a sip and continued in a whisper.

"After my buddy landed back at the Maldives, he watched on CNN the worldwide uproar over the MH370 disappearance. He obviously felt something so foul was going down that he wanted to get the word out. I think this Malaysian flight may have hit home for him personally because he's a Navy lieutenant commander of Asian descent. I'm pretty sure that flight was like ninety-nine percent Asian."

She slowly nodded, seeing more was coming.

"So, because his unit was already in the black ops world, he could log in to an NRO satellite database that his unit shares with the Air Force. The satellite is called L22. It receives footage from Air Force Reaper drones and transmits that data directly to the CIA and the National Reconnaissance Office. That allows our top intelligence officials to watch what the drones are viewing in real time. That's when my buddy came across this footage. It basically showed him the first half of the teleportation near Great Nicobar Island. He told me he was so shocked at the sinister shit going down, he made a screen recording and figured out a way to get the footage on a thumb drive. He said he's putting the footage online tonight."

"Fuckin' A," she whispered. "Good on him."

Dan nodded.

"He also found footage from the Air Force AWACS that was cloaking the flight—when the Cabal pilot turned off the transponder—forty minutes into the flight."

She pointed at him.

"I have been wondering how that huge airliner could just go black and disappear from every radar screen everywhere. So that's how they hid the jet? The Cabal pilot switched off the transponder, and the Air Force AWACS was used to essentially... defeat all radar pulses trying to locate the airliner while it was black?"

Dan nodded, smiling as she pieced it together.

"My buddy said the Airforce AWACS was running an operation called *Eclipse*, which was created just to make that Malaysian Flight vanish on radar via long-range signal disruption and spoofing of civilian and military radar."

She stared in disbelief as he took a sip and continued.

"I'll tell you this... if an Air Force AWACS was cloaking that airliner, even my Spy-3 radar wouldn't see that jet. That's how powerful those Air Force AWACS birds are."

She nodded.

"So you're positive this footage is all from Air Force Reaper drones?"

He nodded.

"The MQ-9 Reaper drones are the only ones that have this Gorgon Stare technology... and are positively United States Air Force platforms. The American company that created Gorgon Stare is called Sierra Nevada, and no other country has that technology."

She raised a finger, then began tapping her forehead.

"Wait," she whispered. "So the Cabal and the U.S. Air Force had to pre-plan this hijacking before that jet ever took off, because to track a fast-moving jet with drones, you have to be in place—ready to pounce?"

He nodded.

"That's right... a drone can't catch up to a jet... it has to be in place in advance."

"So, at what point did they hijack the jet?" she asked.

"Right away, apparently. My buddy pulled up the cockpit voice recordings that are viral on the web now... when the jet is still on the ground at Kuala Lumpur International. It's all the radio transmissions between the pilots and ground control, tower and departure. He told me that on the 12:42 a.m. radio transmission just after liftoff... calling departure control... it was made by the American hijacker pilot."

She nodded.

"It's wild you mention the cockpit recordings, because I came to the same conclusion when the radio transmissions went viral online. The cockpit voices are heavily Asian accented prior to launch. And then suddenly, right after takeoff, on that first call to departure control, the voice has no Asian accent whatsoever, and the new voice sounds distinctly American... and the guy stutters on the callsign of the jet, like he's not used to saying the *Malaysian 370* callsign."

Dan pointed.

"My buddy told me the same thing, that the Cabal pilot basically stutters every time he says 'Malaysian, uh... 370'."

She nodded, thinking it through.

"So the hijackers must have rushed the cockpit once it was airborne and trimmed for climb... because there's basically a full minute of climb-out before a pilot is required to contact departure control. That would have been a perfect time to rush the cockpit, because an American-accented voice on the first call to Departure Control would not raise any flags."

Dan nodded sadly.

"I'm assuming the Cabal hijackers burst through the cockpit door and those poor Malaysian pilots were shot at point-blank range, just to get them out of those seats in short order."

She stared sadly at the floor, and he could tell she was envisioning it.

"My buddy said they could see a Caucasian guy in the cockpit with light brown hair when they were controlling the jet on the way south to Diego. And that he was alone in the cockpit. Said he appeared to be wearing a black, long-sleeve, military-style tactical shirt, or something like it. But certainly not the white shirt and tie that the Malaysian pilots were wearing in those boarding videos."

"Yeah," she whispered, "and neither of the Asian pilots had blonde or light brown hair."

He nodded. She watched him closely as he momentarily went away. A darkness she could feel.

"What is it, Dan?" she whispered.

He slowly looked up and took a breath.

"I just read an SOS alert online that some business executive on that flight sent out. An American IBM employee named Philip Wood. It just went viral online."

"He sent an SOS from the flight?" she asked.

"Nah, after the flight landed. Philip Wood's message claimed he had been captured in a hijacking and was being held in a cell away from the other passengers."

She watched him as he remained silent, contemplating.

"What?" she whispered.

He looked over.

"The Wood SOS message sourced from Diego Garcia, of all places."

She shook her head at the apparent confirmation of the jet landing at Diego. Dan looked over.

"Several online technical geeks have verified that the message stamp of the Wood SOS sourced from a latitude and longitude of a building at Diego. On the south side of the main runway. I guess every cell phone message that hits the web can be sourced from the information stamp buried within the message. But the debunkers are already attacking the SOS as fake."

She walked over, close enough to whisper.

"But you're saying your buddy told you—in advance of that SOS—that the jet landed at Diego?"

He slowly nodded and opened his hand—showing the video of the Malaysian jet—and stared at her.

"So what happened in the video? What do those orbs do?" she asked.

"Apparently, the Cabal has had that technology for years, to create a portal around any moving object and send it wherever they want, like a magic FedEx."

She stared.

"And this technology came from?"

"Them!" Dan whispered.

"Them, as in aliens?" she asked.

"Yeah, apparently it's all alien tech the Cabal has been acquiring in exchanges with these malevolent alien fuckers for decades."

"I need more liquor," she whispered and took a long swig. "You're saying it was Air Force drones that tracked the flight, so why was your buddy's unit involved... if he's Navy?"

"Well, the National Reconnaissance Office ordered his bird to be on station in the Maldives Islands... and remember, the NRO is told what to do by the CIA."

She nodded slowly.

"I was wondering about that NRO location stamp on the videos," she whispered. "The National Reconnaissance Office was mentioned in my brief. Seems like they are the super spooks?"

He nodded.

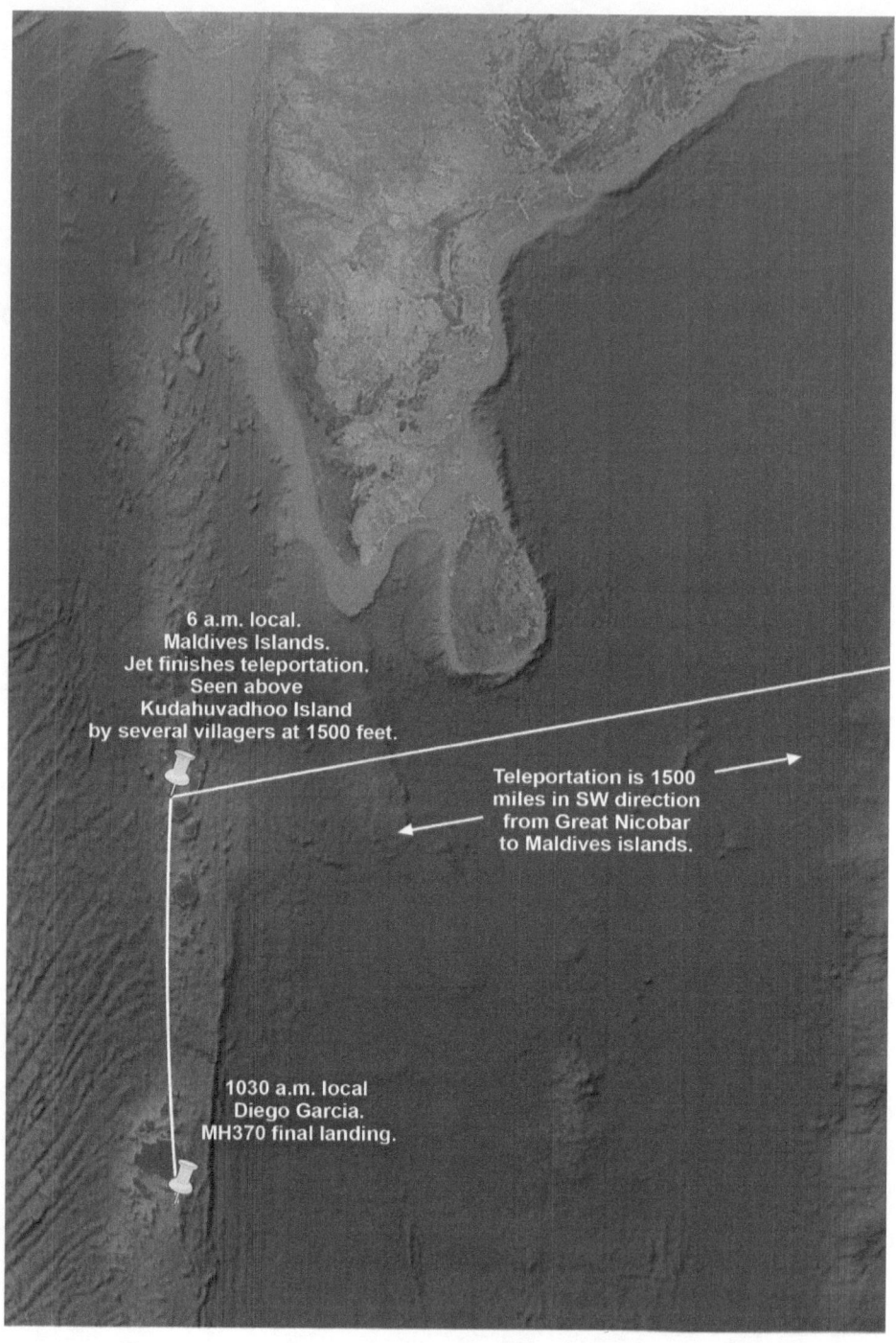

6 a.m. local.
Maldives Islands.
Jet finishes teleportation.
Seen above
Kudahuvadhoo Island
by several villagers at 1500 feet.

Teleportation is 1500
miles in SW direction
from Great Nicobar
to Maldives islands.

1030 a.m. local
Diego Garcia.
MH370 final landing.

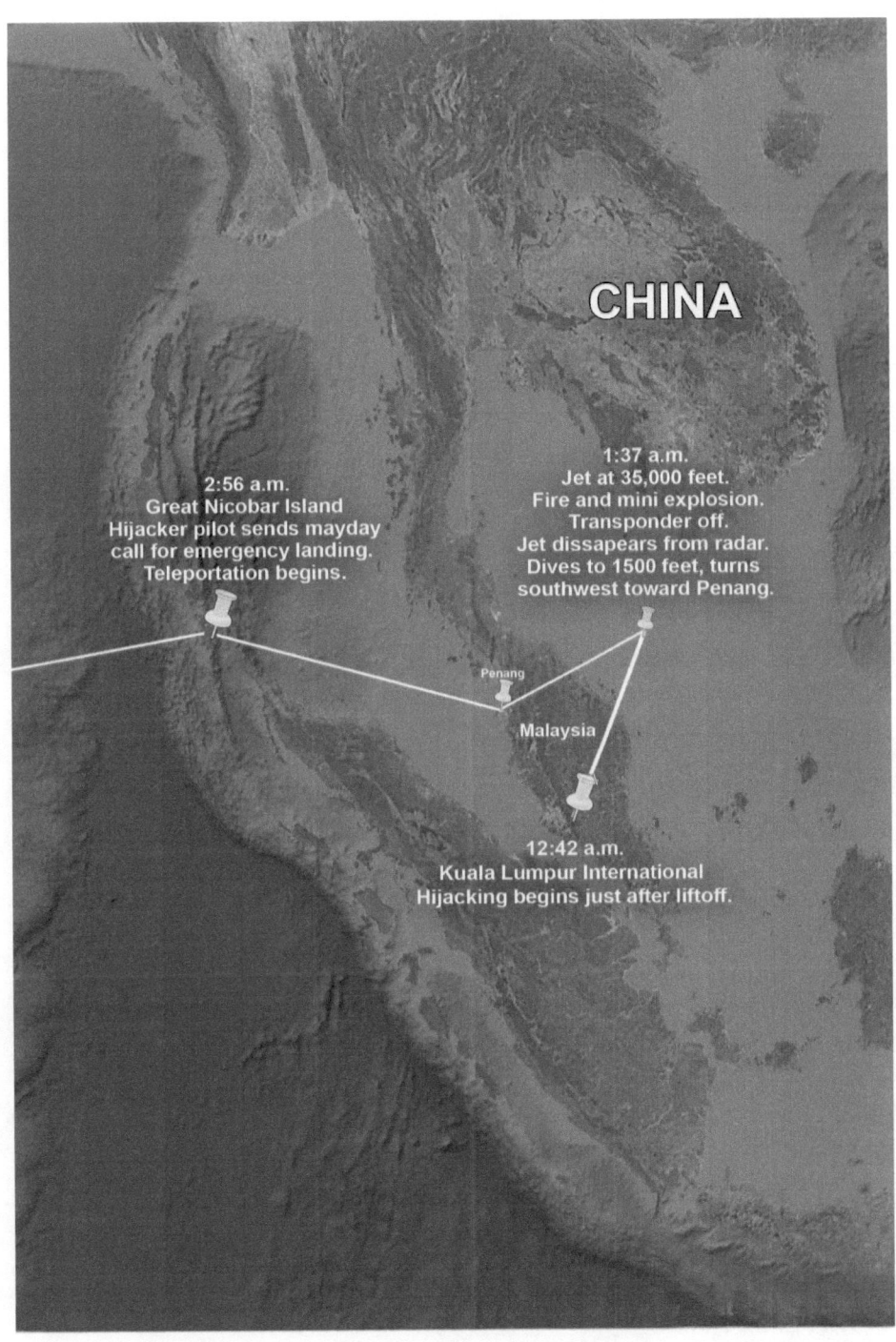

"My buddy said that the L22 is the satellite that the Reaper drones were uploading their footage to for the NRO."

She nodded, putting it together.

"So, you're saying the National Reconnaissance Office could watch the teleportation—in almost real-time—right off their L22 satellite?"

Dan nodded, contemplating.

"If the NRO filmed this for the Cabal, then everyone at the top levels of our intelligence apparatus was on board for the hijacking of that civilian airliner."

"Meaning exactly who would have known?" she pressed.

"Well, all the usual suspects; the CIA, the National Security Agency, the Defense Intelligence Agency and DARPA. And certainly the president is eventually onboarded and briefed by all those department heads."

"So, then the president knew we were going to hijack that Malaysian flight?"

He shrugged.

"Nothing, and I mean nothing, happens at that worldwide level unless the president knows about it."

"You mean in advance?"

He shrugged again.

"Who knows if the president knew in advance, but certainly, he's been briefed that we took that jet, because those videos are absolutely the property of the National Reconnaissance Office."

She put a finger up, pausing him.

"Okay, let's see if I got this. Basically, the Cabal can use those orbs to snatch the jet out of the air and move it to another location, but it's still in the air—and they have to manually land the jet—so, that's where your buddy's AWACS and the Cabal pilot comes into play?"

He nodded. She stared quizzically.

"Why didn't the Cabal hijacker pilot fly it south to Diego?"

"I asked my buddy about that... and all he could figure was, the Cabal pilot might have been disoriented from the teleportation, as the jet came out of the wormhole, flying to the east, which is right back toward Nicobar. My buddy's AWACS immediately turned the plane south toward Diego Garcia, so it could reach the airbase before it ran out of fuel."

She slowly nodded, contemplating.

"So why Diego Garcia? What's there?"

Dan turned directly to her. Gauging whether to take her further into the rabbit hole. He looked at the clock, then back at her.

"Let's go for a walk."

Chapter Eight

The ship was heaving and rolling in the heavy storm.

She followed him through a maze of elevators and hatches leading back to the CIC. Few were about at that early hour, yet when they entered the CIC, it was packed with radar operators at all stations. Dan guided her into the same back room as earlier and locked the door behind them. He patted a chair for her to sit next to him and then stared at her for a moment and looked at his hands, clearly wrapped in a thought.

"You okay?" she asked. "I don't want you to put yourself in an awkward position."

He watched her, and there was admiration in his eyes.

"I was surprised up in your room at how you seem to be okay with suddenly seeing spaceships like the UAP... I mean, you don't seem shocked?"

She shrugged and whispered,

"Well, I'm certainly mystified at the capabilities of the UAP, but my Papa had seen them... and I'm just opening up to aliens having been here... most likely all around us... for a long time."

He nodded, but she could sense he was anxious as he looked at the radar screen and then back at her.

"I feel like I can show you something that I haven't been comfortable showing anyone... because I didn't want them to disappear."

"Oh, shit." she whispered. "This must be some seriously top-secret stuff?"

He looked partially away... as if saying, *You have no idea*. Then looked directly at her.

She suddenly had a dead serious look.

"I'm not scared at all... let it fucking rip!" she whispered.

He snickered at her moxie.

"I knew I met you—for a reason." He said quietly and typed another command. "Okay—you asked for it!"

The screen was still blank. He turned to her and whispered,

"About five months ago, we were testing the Spy-3 in the middle of the Indian Ocean and made a fuel stop at Diego Garcia. It was 3:45 a.m. as we approached the island and harbor."

He typed another command.

"Right then, we were told to shut down the Spy-3 prior to reaching the harbor. But we never do that. Especially the active sonar, because that lets you look down, below the water, to see subs or anything else down there. So, I knew something was weird about that base, but since we had to follow orders, we turned off the system and I sent my entire staff back to their quarters because they needed the rest. After they left, I locked the door and figured... well, what the hell... I'll take a look. Then I turned the system back on, and this is what I saw."

He hit a button, and the massive radar screen in front of them suddenly displayed a very detailed image of the surface and subsurface of an island. He motioned to the radar image.

"Nobody but you has seen this."

She nodded and looked up at the screen, perplexed. The radar image was confusing. Dan turned, watching her piece it together. She gestured to different areas of the image.

"That's a runway on the surface and some parked aircraft and hangars... and not much else." She said, looking at him, perplexed. "So, what's so special about that image?"

Dan pursed his lips.

"That's a really good question. I thought the same thing when I first saw this but Diego Garcia is a top-secret U.S. Navy base," he whispered. "No press or anybody is allowed to go there. A lot of weird scuttlebutt about it over the years. The base and island are tiny. Nothing really to see, but..."

He shook his head again and thumbed toward the screen.

"I don't know. My buddy alluded there is a D.U.M.B. there and that the Black Navy is there too."

"A DUMB?" she inquired.

"It's an acronym for Deep-Underground-Military-Base, D.U.M.B.," he whispered, motioning to the radar image.

"My buddy said Diego is basically like a hub where materials and traffic come and go to other planets."

She stared at the radar image and turned, confused.

"There appears to be nothing below that base?" she whispered.

He looked quickly at the door and then leaned in to her.

"Remember up in your stateroom where we talked about the AWACS cloaking the Malaysian jet so that no radars could see it?"

She nodded. Dan watched her and raised his eyebrows, thumbing toward the screen. She looked up again at the simple radar image with nothing happening in the picture.

"What? You're saying there's more here than meets the eye?" She asked.

"Slightly," he said. "So, that radar image is a freeze-frame of what's in front of the ship as we're approaching the base. Now I'm going to hit play, and you'll get to watch the entire video as we enter the harbor. Keep in mind it's 3:48 a.m., meaning dark outside with only moonlight and stars."

She nodded as he pressed a button on the console. The radar image held steady momentarily... showing the same calm island setting and then, slowly, as if passing through an unseen curtain, the screen suddenly came alive with movement as the entire area below the surface runway proliferated with three enormous Egyptian-size pyramids descending in cascading steps, hundreds of feet down into the ocean depths.

"What in the hell?" she whispered, astonished.

"We're now inside the cloak," Dan whispered.

"Oh, my God! The whole base was cloaked?" she pressed.

He nodded, motioning back to the screen. She could now see movement inside the three pyramids—like a factory in motion with materials moving vertically along the insides of the pyramids—in ascending and descending motion.

"Fucking-A!" she blurted.

Dan shushed her with a finger to his lips and aimed his laser pointer at a spot on the surface runway near a set of hangars, and then whispered,

"Keep watching right here... at this aircraft parking area next to the end of runway 31."

She watched astonished as a large area of the concrete tarmac, roughly one-thousand-feet square, suddenly lowered forty feet... on what appeared to be a hydraulic mechanism of some sort.

"What in the hell?" she exclaimed, looking quickly at Dan and back at the screen.

"It's a loading dock," he whispered tersely.

She shook her head, mesmerized, as freight containers of all sizes began flowing onto the loading dock, accompanied by a small crew of military personnel who were all staring up and pointing at something unseen. And just when she thought she couldn't take any more, she heard Dan whisper,

"Stand-the-fuck-by."

Before she could react—a massive Mothership, the size of an aircraft carrier—began to uncloak itself... hovering only one-hundred feet above the lowered loading dock. She reached out, gripping Dan's forearm as she suddenly sat forward... staring, breathless. The Mothership stretched over a thousand-feet-long and appeared to be at least fifty-stories thick in the middle with several smaller ships hovering around it. Like tenders.

"Holy shit!" she blurted in a whisper.

Dan suddenly hit pause as she stared, her mouth open. She turned slowly, struck dumb.

"I know," he said, "I'll hit play again in a minute."

"Oh, my God!" she continued in a whisper, catching her breath.

"Look at the clock up here." Dan whispered as he put his laser dot on the digital clock at the top right of the screen, showing 4:05 a.m.

"So, what the fuck is happening there and whose spaceship is that?" she pressed in a whisper.

Dan raised his eyebrows.

"Those are really good questions. That's why I made a copy of this clip and took it to my buddy as I wanted answers. I had never believed him up to that time. I mean, years ago, he told me, he worked here—at this Diego Garcia DUMB, dealing with black-ops type things—but he wouldn't say much more back then, other than about a whole Black Navy unit that I never believed existed."

"Black Navy?" she whispered. "As in the regular Navy wears white and does good things and the Black Navy is for Black-Ops or something?"

"According to my buddy, the Black Navy is a Cabal-created unit that is run by the CIA and handles all black-ops operations, including running Diego Garcia for the Cabal."

"So, who is the Cabal exactly?" she asked. "Who the hell is making all this happen?"

He shrugged.

"My buddy says the Cabal is basically a small group who consider themselves *a covert administrative elite* for the world. That they have acquired alien technologies without the knowledge of the president or Congress and have been employing that technology wherever they deem necessary. Apparently, they have full control of all the intelligence agencies as well as the military by paying top dollar under the table. He said they utilize the key players in the CIA as their operational wing, which directs all the dirty work of the other intelligence agencies."

She stared.

"So, our own CIA is under the thumb of this Cabal group—and the Cabal is rogue—like, outside control of the president and Congress?"

He stared at her.

"My buddy said that the CIA went rogue clear back when Allen Dulles was the director in 1953. Since then, supposedly the CIA has remained the operation wing for anything the Cabal financiers want."

"So, the Cabal directed the CIA to carry out the entire hijacking and teleportation?" she asked.

Dan half shrugged.

"My buddy think's that's the case... and says the vanishing orb things are Cabal technology and are controlled via a space-based platform. He says the Cabal, via the CIA, directed the NRO and the U.S. Air Force to track the Malaysian jet during the teleportation."

She stared, contemplating.

"My buddy says the Cabal created the Black Navy that runs Diego Garcia, and that they also control all the other secret facilities like S-4 in Nevada and Dulce in New Mexico and all the DUMBs worldwide where black ops are happening daily, to include the entire Secret Space Program. Both the Navy SSP and the Air Force SSP."

"So the Cabal is paying for all these covert military operations?"

Dan slightly shrugged.

"Well, he told me the Cabal enlists Black Navy guys with a suitcase full of cash to do their dirty work... which ensures they keep their mouths shut. I guess most of their operatives are military contractors who were formerly in the regular armed services. But they're hired from all the different services right when they get out. But what's wild is he said the Cabal is paying for all their covert programs with American taxpayer money... that is funnelled illegally out of taxpayer dollars. So, the Cabal is funded basically... by you and me."

She put her hand on her forehead trying to grasp it all.

"So the Cabal runs everything, and our actual American government is... is what?"

Dan shook his head.

"Just a show, I guess. My buddy says the Cabal views our government as something to keep the regular citizens occupied... and nothing more."

She watched him, knowing more was coming.

"According to him he says our government has no real power—especially since there are new elections every four years—and the government continues to have new folks coming in, but what's really happening..."

He thumbed toward the radar image.

"Is never shared with those in our government. So our own president and Congress have no fucking idea what's really been happening."

She shook her head, perplexed.

"How do they keep it all secret?"

Dan pointed at her and whispered,

"I asked him the same question. He says the Cabal utilizes *Unacknowledged Special Access Programs* or USAPs, to fund alien-related projects that are not seen by the public or by Congress. Since federal auditors are only cleared to top-secret-17, all USAPs rated top-secret-18 and above remained unseen... including the president, who is only cleared to level 17."

"Oh my God," she whispered, starting to piece it together. "So the Cabal basically went rogue by taking everything to classification levels that nobody can access but them?"

Dan slowly nodded. She raised a finger.

"Right, that's why you were blown away by my Majestic clearance?" she asked.

He nodded and continued.

"Even in the UAP incident. If I hadn't been a witness to it... I wouldn't even have been privy to seeing what happened on the intercept... and I'm the top guy on the Spy-3."

He took a sip.

"I was warned right after the incident that nobody else in my shop was allowed to watch that intercept footage except for the handful of folks who were in the CIC when it was happening."

He shook his head.

"And the radar operators in my shop—they've all had the living shit scared out of them by CIA investigators—telling them to *shut the hell up* about what they saw... *or else.*"

She slowly nodded and looked back toward the radar image.

"Tell me more about what's happening here," she asked.

He moved his laser pointer, highlighting several shafts going from a surface hangar down into the underwater pyramids.

"Look right there... those are elevator shafts going from one of the topside aircraft hangars... down."

She could see several vertical shafts extending far below into the huge pyramid-type structures.

"So the whole base is like a factory below the surface?" she whispered, finally understanding the image.

Dan nodded.

"I can tell you that at least two of those, just by their size, have to be freight elevators, and the other small shafts going down are more like standard elevators for personnel. But wait, I want you to see the other thirty seconds, as I had to shut down the system because someone had arrived at the CIC and was knocking on the door."

She nodded as he pressed the button, and the image came alive with movement. Dan moved his laser dot to just below the Mothership.

"Watch right here."

She stared, fascinated, as a spiraling light dropped from the cargo bay of the Mothership and grew into a funnel shape as it descended... encircling an enormous freight container on the loading dock. Within seconds, the container began rising into the Mothership!

"What in the—"

"It's a damn tractor-beam!" Dan whispered, locked on the screen. "And look down here."

Moving his laser to the bottom of the lowest pyramid, where a massive submarine entered one of three circular ports at the base of the pyramid.

"That submarine is coming in for supplies that will be loaded from the Mothership."

She shook her head at the overall operation happening in front of her.

"What's that?" she said, pointing to two men wearing uniforms, who were descending in an elevator that was lowering from the Mothership... hanging suspended by only four steel cables around it.

"My buddy said it's called a Spyder-lift, and those are—well, supposedly they're Germans from the Mothership—coming down to coordinate with the loading dock crew. I'll tell you more about them later."

She nodded slowly and pointed at the bottom pyramid.

"Are those bullet trains arriving and departing from the lower pyramid?" she asked.

"Magnetic-levitation trains," Dan whispered, "My buddy said they can travel at excessive speeds and distribute the goods coming down from space—worldwide—in hours... to the other DUMBs around the globe."

She shook her head and whispered,

"Wow!"

He nodded and then moved his red laser dot to a large cigar-shaped object far below the surface, sitting stationary next to the lowest pyramid structure—a thousand feet down—apparently waiting to enter the complex.

"That right there is some type of ship, but I can tell you, it's not a submarine as there is no heat signature."

She stared at the ship.

"You're saying it's a spaceship?"

He pursed his lips.

"Well, what else could be that large, that low, without a heat signature? I've been staring at these screens forever. There ain't one sub out there that doesn't put off some kind of heat signature, especially when the Spy-3 is lookin' at it."

She watched him, knowing more was coming.

"That's why I laughed so hard at my buddy back then... because he was claiming that the U.S. already had a space fleet and we were using Diego as a launch facility for antigravity spaceships that could secretly launch and return from below water."

"Wait," she whispered, holding up a finger, then tapping her forehead and looking at him.

"In the fighter footage with Knife and Crazy, you and I just witnessed a UAP flying at Mach speeds submerged. The damn thing was not affected by submersion. They're somehow creating a gravity envelope around the ship, and if my guess is correct, going to space and back for antigravity ships using Diego as a hidden spaceport would certainly be a perfect way to hide a spaceport," she said, gesturing to the image. "Just sink it underwater."

He slowly nodded.

"My buddy said that was the reason we now have an underwater National Reconnaissance Office, because there was so much alien anti-gravity traffic in our oceans that the Cabal added the underwater NRO."

She nodded.

"Underwater National Reconnaissance Office?"

Dan slowly nodded and typed a few keystrokes. A moment later, the image disappeared. He turned, watching as she stared at the now blank screen.

"What is it?" he whispered.

"The deception... and this entire evolution happening. I just can't believe how they've hidden all this from me... from all of us?"

He nodded and noted the clock. A minute later they were strolling through the ship towards her stateroom.

She whispered to him as they walked.

"Now I know why you didn't want to show me. A secret that big—being withheld from the general populace—for who knows how long? Can you imagine the anger that would sweep the nation if the average citizen knew all this secret stuff was being funded by their dollars and still being kept from them?"

Dan nodded as they walked, then tilted his head inquisitively.

"How would a ship create its own gravity envelope?"

She looked up.

"That answer will cost you a drink."

"You're on," he said.

Moments later, they were on her couch, sipping cocktails.

"So, about that gravity envelope?" he whispered.

She nodded, and he could tell she was figuring out how to put it in simple terms.

"The easy version for non-physicists would be that each ship has a nuclear reactor onboard that generates a gravity envelope around the craft when it's powered on."

He nodded as she continued.

"As I went to my stateroom last night, after watching Knife's heads-up footage, I settled into what exactly would be required for the UAP to perform those types of maneuvers, and the same conclusion kept stepping forward as the only solution. A gravity bubble around the ship. In simple terms, the craft had to have a nuclear reactor on board to create its own gravity envelope. And then all the puzzle pieces fit... perfectly. If a pilot could maneuver through space inside a gravity bubble, then the pilot is not affected by anything outside the bubble. No longer affected by the gravitational pull of the Earth, to include Mach speed acceleration and deceleration, right-angle turns, and submersion in water at the same terrific velocities. None of it would be felt by a pilot encased in a gravity bubble.That's exactly how Knife and Crazy's UAP could do right-angle turns at Mach speed—because the pilots are encased in that gravity envelope. They don't feel shit."

She looked up as if finally piecing it all together.

"That thing could plunge into the ocean at one-mile-per-hour or Mach-five, and the pilots would never feel a thing in either case. It would also explain the oval tic-tac shape—because if you can create a gravity bubble around the vessel you're traveling in—then the shape of the ship no longer matters. If your ship looked like a turtle or a pirate ship or a sledgehammer, it could still do all the things that oval did... same with that huge friggin' Mothership."

He stared in admiration.

"You really are a physicist," he whispered.

She smiled.

"You've got a very smart girl here, and she's fuckin' YOU," she said with a wink.

He chuckled and nodded.

"She's good at that too!" he whispered.

"Yeah, multi-talented, right?" She said with a sigh and put more ice in her cocktail.

He watched her as she contemplated.

"So what was with the Germans in that radar image descending on that elevator thing?"

"Well, it's more completely unbelievable shit my buddy claims has been happening since the early '80s."

She leaned in even closer.

"I'm now realizing I might like your buddy, as he's confirming some things I've long wondered about."

Dan half smiled.

"Well, this next piece of info may break your belief in my friend, as it's way-the-fuck out there."

"Try me," she whispered.

"So, those men descending in that elevator—he claims—are Nazis."

He watched her for a reaction... but she was unfazed, so he continued.

"My buddy claims that in 1980... the Nazis ran Diego Garcia as a launch facility for their own antigravity ships and already had a moon base and one on Mars. They were supposedly using Diego as a hub to transport personnel and materials to and from space."

"The Nazis?" she said matter-of-factly, taking a sip and contemplating.

He shrugged.

"Now you see why I blew him off. My buddy was so serious about all of it—and it was all so outlandish—I finally just fell out of my chair laughing, and he gave up."

He watched as she slowly raised her finger to him.

"I met an ancient German physics professor once at a pub near Stanford when I entered my grad program. His name was Andre Brodder, and my friend had invited Andre to meet us for a beer. After a while, we started talking about time travel, and Andre got a strange look and then looked away. My friend and I questioned him about his sudden silence. He turned back, shrugged, and then sheepishly asked us if we wanted to hear a wild story. We said, 'Hell yeah!' Andre snickered at us, I guess knowing that we wouldn't believe his story but proceeded to tell us, anyway. He said his dad was a German submarine captain in WWII. Then he pulled out an old photo from his wallet and showed us a vintage picture of German Navy Captain Heinrich Brodder, standing in front of U-209 with his full crew. Andre said U-209 was presumed sunk in 1943, but he showed us the back of the photo, which was stamped *1945*. Andre said many of the German U-boats were only presumed sunk when the Americans couldn't locate them, but that really wasn't the case."

She took a sip of her old fashioned, gesturing with it as she continued.

"Andre then put the picture back in his wallet and said, 'So, maybe you've heard the rumor that a lot of the top Nazi scientists in WWII had disappeared just before the war ended?' We both nodded, and Andre went on to tell us that his dad had taken many top Nazis to Argentina but also many of Germany's best scientists and engineers to a place called Base 211, under the ice-shelf in Antarctica."

She paused as he filled her glass, then continued.

"Supposedly, Andre's dad took Heinrich Himmler to Base 211, and he became the first commandant of the Breakaway Nazis. Himmler and his engineers then developed flying saucers with tech given to them by a malevolent group of aliens who were working with the Nazis at that time. He said the alien group was called *The Draco,* and they gave Himmler all the tech needed to build space-capable antigravity ships—flying saucers, essentially. And that some of Himmler's Nazi flying saucers were the ones photographed over the White House in July of 1952."

Dan raised his glass, pointing at her.

"I've seen pictures of those saucers above the White House in 1952."

She nodded.

He shook his head.

"Clear back in 1996, my buddy—who was just an ensign back then—told me that his unit was already using clones. They had gotten the technology from Grey aliens they were working with at his base. Which I'm assuming now is probably that DUMB right there at Diego Garcia, the one we were just staring at."

She stared, perplexed.

"You mean the aliens had shown them how to clone—you mean like cloned sheep, and..."

He stared at her.

"Oh, shit—you mean humans?!" she whispered, astonished.

He shrugged.

"2005, I think, he brought it up again—that they had several security guards at his facility—who were literally identical, and clearly enhanced physically. My buddy freaked out one day when one of the test pilots working with his team died right in front of him during a crash landing—someone he had worked with for months. He said the next morning, when he was tearfully debriefing the crash with his team, the same damn pilot walked in and sat down as part of the debrief. He told me he nearly shit his pants as that pilot appeared. Then his team began laughing, and the pilot smiled and joined in. His team had filmed him freaking out because they were all in on the joke—from before he even started working there. They had already seen that same test pilot die several times in other test flights."

She put a hand to her head.

"Wait—so the military cloned the original pilot—and was basically using clones for all the test flights?"

He stared at her.

71

"I mean, it makes sense from a safety standpoint, because if you can use clones of a really good test pilot, then you won't ever lose that highly skilled original pilot."

She slowly nodded.

"The more I think about him over the years—he never fucks around—as in kidding or teasing me. He's kind of... a boring, straight-shooter. I was just assuming he was being funny back then."

He shook his head.

"At least three different radar operator buddies across the world attempted to tell me about interfacing with aliens in DUMBs in the past, but I couldn't hear them. My belief system is pretty entrenched about what I know, or what I've been told to believe. I wasn't open to the amount of technology we now possess and the amount of alien interaction happening. That I'm now realizing must have been going on for decades! Just like my buddy told me years ago. I laughed at him back then... but he's been trying to tell me... the joke's on me.

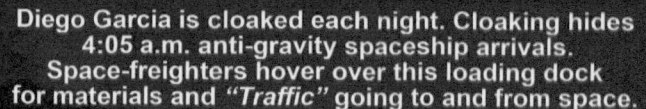

Diego Garcia is cloaked each night. Cloaking hides
4:05 a.m. anti-gravity spaceship arrivals.
Space-freighters hover over this loading dock
for materials and *"Traffic"* going to and from space.

Deep Underground Military Base D.U.M.B.
extends below loading dock in shape of
three cascading Egyptian style pyramids.
Submarines, spacehips and Mag-Lev shuttles
distribute from 3 ports on bottom
of lowest pyramid.

Remaining passengers and crew
executed in hangar.

Philip Wood final
text from this building.

Chapter Nine

Dr. Yen Jee was fifty floors below the surface of the Papoose Dry Lakebed in the Nevada desert.

She exited her office inside the DUMB, which was one of many in the Nellis Test Range.

Walking briskly to the elevator, she was escorted by her security team—two heavily armed operatives wearing black tactical uniforms. One had blue eyes, the other green, and both clearly had enhanced genetics, but were nevertheless eerily the same.

Clones, she thought, as the two strange units escorted her into an elevator.

She could no longer keep up with what security team was on duty at whatever facility she was presently occupying. She now had clones interspersed with regular security throughout her company, at all the DUMBs where JRAD was running a black project. Clones were cheaper than human guards, and human security was known to steal and sell to competing companies. With clones, she didn't have that worry, as they could be monitored with nanotech AI.

But at this moment, standing between the two huge operatives was unnerving, as both had clearly been programmed not to be social.

She inserted a key into the wall lock and turned it. A steady tone sounded as she leaned forward, staring into a retinal scanner. A moment later, the tone ended, and the elevator doors opened without a sound. She stepped in, followed by the two operatives. She appreciated that neither would speak unless spoken to, as she was in no mood for casual banter.

"Galileo," she said calmly.

Seconds later, the elevator doors closed, and they ascended at an astounding velocity, yet without any sense of gravity opposing their rise. Yen appreciated the silence, riding in a magnetic field, levitated ever so slightly away from the walls as the elevator raced far faster than any cable-style elevator on the surface world.

She was anxious, thinking about the test flight her company would commence in the next hour.

She also worried about who would be there—at the desert plateau on the surface. Papoose Lake. That's where the flight test would take place. She noted her diamond watch. Fifty minutes until launch.

Hearing the soft chime signaling they had reached the surface heightened her unease. She knew some were already there—those who came to witness history. A history her company was about to make. Some of the most powerful people on the planet—and possibly from other planets, too.

She didn't worry about visual security; the super-secret dry lakebed was protected from satellite surveillance by particle beam weapons that sent blinding pulses skyward, defeating any video or photographic attempts.

Her employers were arriving to see if her flight team had finally figured out how to fly *the ship.*

The elevator doors slid open to reveal a darkened hangar, with its huge exterior door raised, revealing the stars outside over a moonlit desert.

Papoose Dry Lakebed was spectacular day or night, and enhancing the view at that moment, there on the tarmac sat *"The Widow."*

A one-hundred-foot flying saucer with polished dark silver skin, thirty-three feet thick in the middle, tapering down to only one inch at the outer edge. The Widow reflected the sky like a mirror. At the center were two ball-shaped sections—upper and lower—approximately twelve feet across. They served, for all intents and purposes, as the cockpit area.

Yen knew from flipping the ship completely upside down during a study, that both sides were identical, as the entire ship had been somehow molded in one continuous build... like with wax. But, in the case of the Widow, nuclear-molecular construction was used, created by an advanced technology far beyond current human science.

This molecular build included all moving parts inside the ship as well. Still frustrating to Yen and her engineers... were the landing struts with their large hemispheric pads. Yen's team had never understood how to extend them. When the Widow was captured during her arrival in 1948, the ship had touched down under intelligent control but without extending the landing gear. Instead, she had landed directly on her lower ball, settling onto a mesa near Aztec, New Mexico.

Upon first discovery, she had been sitting at about a twelve-degree angle due to resting on the lower center-ball extension. Nevertheless, after over fifty years of top technology companies working to reverse-engineer the Widow, the operation of the landing gear had remained elusive.

That was embarrassing to Yen's team, but to keep things moving forward, Yen had the Widow lifted with straps on a small mobile crane and then driven to a set of wooden pallets on the tarmac. The pallets had a hole in the center, allowing the ship to sit level. Even though the Widow was huge, she weighed almost nothing. The pallets allowed her lower-ball extension to sit only inches above the tarmac. Even on pallets, she was still a complete marvel to the handful of people who had ever laid eyes on her.

But Yen had learned to quell her admiration for the ship. She walked quickly through the darkened hangar to the moonlit tarmac. She approached cautiously and stopped two feet away—out of respect—for *Her*.

The Widow was alive. Sentient, and known in the Black-Ops world as *"A Living Conveyance."*

Yen stood still, trying to suppress her anxiety as the communications technicians and several guards stood far away, watching her.

The desert night air was almost indistinguishable from her skin at eighty-three degrees, with no breeze. Yen contemplated the Widow's dimensions. The one-hundred-foot diameter was deceptive at best.

Engineers on Yen's team had quickly learned that, upon entering the Widow, the interior felt cavernous. The science behind *Dimensional-Transcendence* was better understood now than when the ship arrived in 1948, but the Widow and her capabilities were still eons ahead of humanity's known science.

The ship had initially been carbon-dated at over 10,000 years old and had come from an advanced civilization that built the craft with no visible rivets, seams, or windows. Her skin had a tensile strength far stronger than titanium, but it was plant-like in molecular structure, and it was all constructed with nuclear-molecular nanotechnology.

Fully alive, like a horse, she interacted with her pilot via a combination of brainwaves and consciousness. And, like all sentient beings, she was known to have a personality, which the flight team referred to as "A Wild Stallion"—one that had yet to be broken.

Yen's team had determined many things so far, including the understanding that the silver hand imprints on the console were the connection port between the ship and the alien pilot's brain.

Yen stood there in the dry desert heat and gazed at the Widow, hoping she would *play fair.* That was all she was asking.

She stared at the moon and stars reflected in the Widow's dark, silvery surface. The rings of the Milky Way were large and easier to make out, but Yen noticed something that felt subtly directed.

She tried to quell her anger but thought the full moon and stars, visible in the Widow's gleam, seemed ever-so-slightly distorted.

Like the Widow was mocking her again. Again, because Yen's team had not made significant progress since the last test flight, they were just hoping that changing the test pilot would perhaps get the Widow airborne.

She turned quickly away, noting the observation windows higher up on the mountainside. That's where they were—the ones watching her team. She hated the feeling of being tested. She was angry she had to answer to anyone, especially since she was considered by many to be one of the smartest on the planet. But these people had everything to do with her overall financial viability, and that was all she really cared about.

Yen had grown up on the mean streets of New York's Chinatown and had learned the hard way that money moved the planet. Her parents had many side jobs as she came of age; some of them were blatantly illegal and even involved her in helping with swindles. But she was fine with it all. That money had put her through school. She had vowed at fourteen that she would not scrape by as her parents had. Now, she had reached a level of financial success that few had. She had made hard decisions regarding income, even over friends and family, and now had the nest egg she felt she deserved. But having to constantly prove her company's value to the head of the Majestic-12 and the Cabal was infuriating, yet there was no way around it. They funded her lifestyle at the level she deserved, and she would never go back to being poor.

When she attained her doctorate, she had determined that becoming a private military contractor had the highest potential for financial success. Her fledgling company had only been awarded a handful of *Special Access Programs* (SAPs) and was just making ends meet when the first *Unacknowledged Special Access Program* (USAP) came her way.

The difference between the two had changed everything. The unaccounted-for millions that flowed in for that first USAP had turned her company into a conglomerate overnight.

CEOs of private military contractors like Yen Jee were often awarded Unacknowledged Special Access Programs that kept alien reverse-engineering projects on track, outside the purview of the president or Congress.

The public was only aware that Yen's company, Jee Research and Development (JRAD), worked on secret government contracts. Like only seeing the outside of an onion, the public was unaware of the various projects JRAD handled just below the surface. Alien projects that were many levels above top-secret. This simple workflow also allowed for plausible deniability if the USAP was ever discovered. And Yen had learned that all USAPs involved alien technology and interactions—America's top lie since the 1940s. A hoodwink so complete that most Americans still believed,

"There is no such thing as aliens."

Yen knew not to ask questions about how the Cabal hid her funding. She understood that since federal auditors were only cleared to top-secret-17, all USAPs rated top-secret-18 and above remained unseen. Yen knew what most Americans would never be aware of.

When Donald Rumsfeld quipped in 2001 that "2.3 trillion dollars were unaccounted for," JRAD had already received millions for its first USAP contract.

Yen knew those millions would never be reported to the IRS or to the public. Now, thirteen years later, Yen's company alone had absorbed over a billion dollars in USAP funding, and that money forced JRAD to have two financial wings. One aboveboard for its known SAPs and a secret financial wing for the USAPs.

The above-board financial wing was constantly under IRS scrutiny for the number of buildings, land, materials, and personnel that were at her various facilities worldwide. The money to fund that much infrastructure was clearly not coming in via her aboveboard SAPs, but somehow, the Cabal had ensured that the IRS did not look too hard. Yen marveled at the insane amount of taxpayer funds that were funneled directly to JRAD. Millions the Cabal wielded above all they chose to do business with—and it came at a heavy price.

The downside Yen quickly learned was that the Cabal, which controlled the Majestic-12, was treacherous and had blackmailed former contractors when they were not satisfied on any level. Yen's goal was to stay in the unacknowledged pipeline, and she did her best to provide a solid product.

Her lifestyle, she knew, had been distorted by the amount of wealth that suddenly flowed in beyond her wildest dreams. Well beyond buying her parents two separate posh estates since their separation, Yen herself had been forced to funnel much of JRAD's excess millions into Swiss accounts as a means of insurance in case the Cabal ever pulled the plug.

She was anxious, knowing the test flight would be viewed by her boss, the head of the Majestic-12, and several of its members. They were the American wing of the ICC. The *Interplanetary Corporate Conglomerate* was a large group of multinational companies that truly ran the planet and much of the solar system.

HUSH

The ICC, in turn, was controlled by a very small group of unseen global elites known only as *The Cabal*. The Majestic-12 pretended to oversee her projects. But Yen knew that, at the end of the day, the Cabal paid the bills.

She stared at the Widow a moment longer, the moon and stars still fuzzy.

"Okay, you don't want to act nice with me? Whatever! she thought and turned away to join her team at the flight test console mounted outside near the hangar door.

F ar above Yen and her team, inside the mountain complex, was a posh overlook-viewing room and restaurant for MJ-12 executives and members of the ICC.

It gave a perfect view of the Widow sitting on the tarmac. Inside the dining facility, above the overview windows, were mounted state-of-the-art viewing screens that showed every detail and angle from inside the cockpit as well as distant shots of the Widow from the desert and mountains surrounding the tarmac.

Chernal Teebeck entered the overlook restaurant and cautiously approached his boss at the small dining table reserved for the head of MJ-12. Teebeck, a former British Royal Marine, wore a custom-fit, capital-style suit with a bow tie. His form beneath the suit was clearly muscular, but still hid the fact that he was also armed to the teeth. Everyone in the facility knew him as Goldmeyer's personal assistant and bodyguard.

The Overlook restaurant would be filling shortly, but at this moment, it was empty except for Jack Goldmeyer sitting at his table reading *TheNew York Times* and enjoying a sumptuous breakfast. Goldmeyer had heard the elevator chime as Teebeck entered the room, but Goldmeyer still didn't look up. On the table next to him, his cell phone began flashing an incoming call, but he didn't answer—didn't even look at who was calling.

He had risen to the very pinnacle of power in the U.S., and he often would not return even the president's calls. He didn't have to. He was the head of the Majestic-12. Identified on *Eyes-only* briefs as MJ-1. But to all in the Majestic-12, Jack Goldmeyer was code-named *The Overseer*.

Goldmeyer was unapologetically ruthless in his quest to acquire alien technology, as had been his predecessors, namely former Secretary of State Henry Kissinger. Kissinger had been The Overseer for twelve years, and his second-in-command, Dr. Edward Teller, was known to most as the creator of the hydrogen bomb.

Those two had ramped up the reverse engineering of alien tech like no others before them, and Goldmeyer was determined to keep that ball rolling at whatever cost. But things were not on track with regard to reverse-engineering much of the exchanged alien technology over the recent months, and Goldmeyer was known for making heads roll when that happened. It did Goldmeyer no good to have acquired alien tech, only to have his scientists not understand how to make it work. Especially since other countries were also in trade negotiations with aliens and the first country to reverse-engineer it... could employ it... against other countries.

Many scientists had departed before their time, but that's how he kept things moving. Produce or depart was his way, and departures could come in any form necessary to move ahead. There was no probationary period with The Overseer.

"Excuse me, sir..." Teebeck said in his high-English accent.

Goldmeyer continued chewing his hash browns and wiped his lips, not looking up from his *New York Times* as he whispered,

"Teebeck, don't you English learn in some fucking English school not to disturb your boss while he's having breakfast?"

"I'm doubly sorry, sir, but it's—uh—Mr. Aspelsin."

Goldmeyer looked up, alarmed, and then exhaled, annoyed. He looked at his watch and slowly stood, pissed off at the unexpected ambush.

"Have I told you how much I hate these fucking aliens, Teebeck?"

"Yes, sir. You've made that quite clear," Teebeck said, smiling, knowing more spewing was on the way.

"I have?"

"Yes, sir."

Goldmeyer stood and whispered under his breath as he straightened his custom Italian suit.

"Fuckers don't understand human protocols for social interactions, Teebeck; they're worse than you fucking English."

Teebeck stared.

"Is that really possible, sir?"

Goldmeyer continued seething, not acknowledging Teebeck's humor.

"Like, make a fucking appointment before you just show the fuck up at someone's door at two-fucking-AM in the goddamn morning!" he hissed.

"Yes, sir. I understand, sir."

"You do?!"

"Yes, sir."

"Good—how do I look?"

"Splendid, sir."

The large man eyeballed Teebeck skeptically and straightened his tie near his neck.

"Goddamn aliens. They give us all this technology, ships, and looking glasses, and they never show us how to work the shit."

"Well, sir, you seem to be making progress," Teebeck said, not wanting to test the boiling pot. He watched as Goldmeyer lifted a cup of coffee to his lips while keeping an eye on the elevator.

"Meanwhile, the fucking Nazis are already occupying planets in the asteroid belt with their technology. Literally years beyond where us Americans are now."

"The Nazis, sir? I thought they were eliminated..."

Goldmeyer's hard gaze told Teebeck to stop.

"Teebeck, I promised Winston Churchill's great-grandson that I would take you on as my personal assistant and bodyguard, so long as you were educated in history and that I wouldn't have to ramp you up to every fucking move that's happened in the covert world of alien interactions."

Teebeck watched as the large man set the coffee cup down and dabbed his forehead slowly with a napkin.

"Now, Teebeck, listen carefully. We—Americans and the British—won the battle of WWII. But trust me, the fucking Nazis won the war, as they already had functional flying saucers in Antarctica by the close of the conflict."

Teebeck stared inquisitively as the older man checked his suit.

"Did you know that in 1947, Teebeck, America selected Admiral Byrd to go down to Antarctica for Operation Highjump?"

"That was some kind of scientific military expedition, right, sir?"

Goldmeyer did not look up from checking his suit.

"Did you learn that in one of your high English schools, Teebeck?"

"Yes, Oxford, sir."

"That's good, Teebeck. I'm certainly glad to know that our American propaganda is still hoodwinking the British citizenry after all these years."

Teebeck continued smiling, but less so.

"I beg your pardon, sir, but history was my major—"

Goldmeyer's understated chuckle made Teebeck cease.

"Teebeck, have you ever heard the rumor that lots of high-ranking Nazis fled to Argentina and other places at the end of World War II, effectively escaping persecution?"

"Yes, sir, of course. It's hard to know if any of that..."

"Shut up, Teebeck, and listen. I'm not bringing this topic up with you as a matter of debate. Meaning, you and I are not having a discussion, understood? I'm about to tell you something that isn't in the history books at Oxford or any British library, but you can bet your royal pink ass... it's a fact."

"Right, sir," Teebeck whispered reverently.

"You are not a bodyguard for me because I'm a college professor attempting to understand what might have happened back then."

"Right, sir, you're the former head of the CIA—"

Goldmeyer's stare made Teebeck cease.

"Operation Highjump was an American military strike group sent to round up all those Nazis who had fled to Antarctica and escaped persecution."

Teebeck watched the older man.

"Admiral Byrd was ordered to invade Antarctica by then-Secretary of Defense James Forrestal. Forrestal wanted Byrd to take Antarctica by force and show those escaped Nazi bastards our military superiority."

"Right, sir," Teebeck whispered.

"Byrd's mission was to kick their ass out of that underground base below the ice shelf and bring them all back here for trial. Their secret complex was called Base 211, and it was located deep in a geothermal cavern near Schirmacher Ponds."

Teebeck stared, waiting for more.

Goldmeyer looked at the table between them and took the porcelain saucer from below his coffee cup, and raised it. Flying it back and forth over the table like a flying saucer.

"All those plates and dishes on my table, Teebeck—pretend that they are Admiral Byrd's entire armed flotilla just about to reach Base 211—with complete and utter superiority in men and firepower."

Teebeck looked down at the table.

"Right, sir."

"Now imagine that you are a highly trained American pilot flying an F4-U Corsair fighter over the flotilla, protecting it. And then, suddenly—you see this..."

Goldmeyer flew the saucer below the level of the table and then up over the flotilla and around it.

"Multiple flying saucers suddenly shoot up out of the ocean, at impossible velocities, and systematically shoot down all thirty fighters that were patrolling over the fleet. And the Nazi antigravity saucers were using particle-beam weapons, Teebeck—against our fighter pilots."

Teebeck stared perplexed as Goldmeyer performed one last dust-off of his suit.

"Yes, they were using lasers on our American pilots clear back in 1947."

He looked up.

"Torched our fighter pilots, sending their flaming Corsairs to their watery graves, and all were gone within minutes."

Teebeck was dumbstruck.

"You see, in 1947, the fucking Nazis were already in cahoots with the Draco Reptilians, and those lizard motherfuckers loaned them antigravity ships. The Nazis took those ships and effectively sliced-and-diced every American fighter attempting to protect Admiral Byrd's battle group."

"The Draco Reptilians, sir?"

"Planet-conquering hordes, Teebeck," Goldmeyer whispered. "Think alien, but not the nice kind," he said and lit a cigarette.

He exhaled and waved the smoke away.

"Malevolent motherfuckers that we still do business with. They look exactly like lizards, Teebeck—except..." He raised a hand above his head. "Think eight-to-thirty feet tall, and mean as fuck."

Teebeck watched him as Goldmeyer stared at the elevator door.

"Smarter than Einstein, telepathic, and fucking psychotic as hell," he said, pulling on his cig. "Turns out the Nazis had been in cahoots with the Draco Reptilians since early 1938, and it's only luck that WWII ended before the Nazis brought that Reptilian technology to bear on the United States."

Teebeck slowly nodded.

"Now, Teebeck, when you are an old man teaching history at Oxford, you can tell the true story of WWII... how the Nazis actually won the war by signing the first off-world treaties with aliens, effectively leapfrogging America by obtaining alien technology and using it against us."

Teebeck stared as Goldmeyer put his coffee down, continuing in a whisper.

"Admiral Byrd barely got out alive as he immediately turned his battle group towards home."

Goldmeyer looked back at the elevator.

"I'm only telling you this because the fucker who is about to arrive... was alive when it happened."

"Aspelsin, sir?" Teebeck said, shocked. "I didn't know he was that... old—"

"Yes, Teebeck, not only is he ancient, but he's a fucking Reptilian in disguise."

Goldmeyer waved his cig.

"I didn't want to tell you when you met him last time... I've been dealing with him for years. Aliens can live up to 600 years or more. And Reptilians can shapeshift to look any way they want. Aspelsin always chooses skinny, but I can guarantee you... that fucker, when not shape-shifted... is as big as a goddamn Velociraptor. He only speaks through his mouth because of the human ruse. Otherwise, we'd be in for a round of telepathy... and I hate that fucking alien shit."

Suddenly, Goldmeyer got a look and motioned toward the elevator. Both men felt a sudden cold tension, like an energy of darkness that just entered and permeated every molecule around them.

Teebeck slowly nodded.

The soft chime sounded.

Both turned as the bronze-plated elevator doors glided open. Standing alone in the elevator was a tall man who stared quietly at them. His face was human in proportion with a completely normal, if somewhat light, complexion. He wore a dark suit with black leather gloves and sported a large, flat-brimmed black hat. A large scar ran from his cheekbone past his ear and temple and disappeared vertically into his hat.

Even in the relative calm of the empty restaurant, Goldmeyer and Teebeck were wary of him. After their last meeting, they had discussed how his scar seemed to move at times like an organic chasm, changing before their eyes.

He slowly exited the elevator, then stopped as the doors closed behind him. He looked calmly around as if sensing the room, like a cat, peering around slowly, noticing every detail in the restaurant.

Goldmeyer wasn't even certain if "*he*" was an accurate pronoun.

He put on his best fake smile and watched as Aspelsin took in the scene, with all the perfectly set tables dressed in fine white linens and the views of the desert overlook.

Goldmeyer had a special dislike for Aspelsin. In Goldmeyer's view, Aspelsin was the penultimate achievement for the aliens. Through their abduction protocols, they had genetically engineered a humanoid alien that could pass as human, but still had the powers of *neural-engagement* and *psychic-entrainment*. Meaning they could fuck with a human's mind when they wanted to.

Teebeck moved first, approaching Aspelsin with his most confident greeting.

"Welcome, sir. Can I take your hat and jacket and hang them up for you?"

Aspelsin stared at Goldmeyer and walked slowly past Teebeck without a word.

"Right, sir," Teebeck whispered as he was blown off, watching Aspelsin join the smiling Goldmeyer at his table.

"Good morning, Mr. Aspelsin, sir, please have a seat and be my guest."

Goldmeyer knew not to attempt to shake Aspelsin's hand. Meetings with the top of the alien hierarchy were never under the protocol of humans. Aliens were emotionless and task-oriented. No formalities, as those traditions and emotional connections were seen as inferior needs by Aspelsin's kind. Aspelsin stood a moment longer, looking directly at Goldmeyer, who did his best not to stare at Aspelsin's scar.

Though Mr. A's physicality was somewhat strange, the persistent rumors about his psychic abilities made Goldmeyer uneasy. The Majestic-12 had dealt with many alien races through the years, and Goldmeyer hated the fact that aliens didn't age like humans. That gave them a distinct advantage in negotiations. Aspelsin had been the liaison to the Cabal before Goldmeyer was even born.

Goldmeyer had been briefed by his predecessor that Aspelsin would use mind control and telepathy during negotiations, and there was no way to stop him.

Aspelsin remained standing, his albino eyes with sea-grey pupils seeming to look through Goldmeyer, rather than at him. His wire-rimmed glasses only made the effect more acute.

Goldmeyer opened with a normal offer.

"Would you like some—"

"I don't need any food," Aspelsin said, cutting him off in his whispery, inhuman voice.

Goldmeyer nodded, furious that Aspelsin was already reading his mind, with Goldmeyer not even having the safety of thought privacy.

Aspelsin spoke evenly, with a voice that had no discernible accent.

"I know you are upset that I can read your thoughts, but try to stand quietly, as I just need to schedule a meeting... a matter that I can't discuss this moment, but it affects both of our operations."

Goldmeyer nodded.

"Certainly, sir. I'll find an opening for you next week, and I'll have Teebeck let you know which days are available."

Aspelsin nodded and then took a quick glance out the overview windows down at the Widow.

"Are you staying for the flight demonstration? It should be a good show," Goldmeyer inquired.

Aspelsin turned, and ever-so-slightly, nodded.

Goldmeyer smiled as Aspelsin departed without another word. Teebeck and Goldmeyer watched him enter the elevator and waited until they were certain the elevator had departed. Teebeck exhaled. Goldmeyer whispered below his breath.

"Get used to it. He's the head Reptilian liaison with our security division. He also handles traffic to and from the planet. And I'm not talking about spaceships, Teebeck."

"Right, sir," Teebeck said, checking his watch. "Ten minutes until the flight test, sir."

Goldmeyer looked out the overview window and could see the new test pilot walking on the tarmac.

On the moonlit desert plateau, the tarmac was lit only with dim red neon, and the open hangar was flush with the desert rock face of the mountain rising above it.

All watched as the pilot came from the darkened hangar and approached the Widow.

Air Force test pilot Captain Bobby Andle walked confidently before pausing in front of the ship, which had gently been craned into her location on the tarmac.

He knew the full history of the Widow and how she had somehow landed on her own, as her two pilots were apparently found already deceased immediately after her touchdown in 1948. Andle knew that American engineers had never figured out how to get the landing gear to extend in the sixty or so years since then.

With the landing pods retracted, Andle was able to stand at the edge of the ship and place his hands on the outer edge.

"Open, please," he commanded in his guttural, matter-of-fact pilot speak.

The Widow pulsed momentarily with a red light, and seemingly from nowhere, a long ramp morphed into position, leading up into the ship. He watched in fascination as the ramp appeared from no visual cue, no seam or riveted area. Instead, it had developed and opened like mercury, with the edge dropping to the tarmac and the long ramp angling up into the ship. Andle let out a cock-sure smile.

"Good girl," he whispered, then turned his head and gestured a thumbs-up toward the flight team as he proceeded up the ramp. With each step he took into the ship, the flight team watched in fascination as the ramp followed him, morphing and enveloping him as he disappeared into the cockpit area of the huge craft. Several standing near Yen shook their heads at the unbelievable technology.

Inside the ship, Andle still couldn't get over how cavernous the interior of the craft was—or at least, that's how his eyes perceived it, even though he knew the actual dimensions of the ship were nothing close to what he was experiencing inside. *Dimensional transcendence* had not yet been reverse-engineered, and experiencing it firsthand felt otherworldly.

He knew the overall diameter of the ship was only one hundred feet and that, top to bottom, she was only thirty-three feet thick at the dead center. But walking up the ramp into the cockpit, he felt like he was entering a geodesic dome of gymnasium proportions. The circular, high-tech cockpit had two seats for the pilots on sliding rails, with no mechanical parts, yet they could slide in any direction the pilots required in the cavernous space.

Resembling test-pilot acceleration couches, the two bucket seats seemed tiny—until Andle dropped into the left one.

A moment later, as Yen and the technicians watched on monitors, his seat morphed around him, growing, extending, rising, and widening. The molecular structure of the seat shifted until it comfortably molded to his form. The technicians all watched, shaking their heads; even though they knew it was coming—it was still a sight to behold.

On her exterior, the Widow began to pulse in a deep red coloring, and a throbbing dark tone hummed through the air like a bass amp vibrating at a tangible low frequency.

Next to the hangar door, Yen's team of flight support personnel were monitoring video screens showing wide-angle views from inside the cockpit. They had watched in fascination as the interior walls of the saucer suddenly became transparent all around Andle. He turned his head in awe, seeing everything around him in all directions as if there was nothing there—a glass dome with no glass reflection.

Unbelievable, Yen thought as she watched on the video screen. Her team, stationed at the exterior console near the hangar door, did not see any change on the Widow's exterior. She still appeared solid, with no windows visible. Yen's team was still trying to figure out the translucent technology, but at this moment, Yen was focused on Captain Andle.

Over the loudspeakers throughout the tarmac area, Andle's voice rang out as he went through the preflight sequence—a checklist of tasks he was supposed to complete before placing his hands in the metal imprints.

H igh above, in the overlook windows, Goldmeyer took a drag from his cigarette, watching as the overview filled with military brass, MJ-12 members, and heads of several ICC companies.

Of the fifty executives and military types watching from the overlook, almost every race and country was represented, and all were clearly wealthy, with a few famous faces to be seen in the shadows.

Separated by a thick glass partition was a room for *Guests of the American Government,* where Goldmeyer could now see Aspelsin sitting alone and stone-faced, staring at the video screens showing the Widow and cockpit views.

Nearby, sitting several seats away, were two eight-foot-tall Maytre Greys also watching the screens. Goldmeyer shivered, looking at the Maytres, as they had the most harsh look of all the aliens he'd ever encountered. As one of them turned to look at him, he looked quickly away... shit could happen... aliens were telepathic... and gave no quarter if they sensed someone was viewing them.

Goldmeyer looked up to the monitor showing Andle in the cockpit. He had chosen Andle for the test flight from a list of the Air Force's best TR-3B pilots. The TR-3B was America's triangular, nuclear-powered, antigravity ship built by Lockheed Martin years ago. It had become the workhorse for standard missions from Station D at Area 51 and from McChord Air Force Base to the Moon's Lunar Operations Command.

Andle had the most hours in the TR-3B, but that human-built ship was not *A-Living-Conveyance* like the Widow. Building the first antigravity ships years ago, America had learned much and was now working on a new fleet, but the human-built ships were nowhere near as advanced as the alien ships they were trying to emulate.

The alien crafts were all maneuvered through an organic pilot-to-ship connection through the pilot's brain. Getting the ship airborne for the engineering teams was key to understanding the brain-connection research that was currently underway. Goldmeyer, upon his only interview with Andle, was satisfied with the young man's enthusiasm to be *"the first"* to fly the Widow. Goldmeyer didn't feel the need to tell the excited aviator that three others had attempted it—and failed.

Why dim the kid's hope? Goldmeyer thought.

Goldmeyer knew the past three test pilots had died in horrific ways, and that certainly wouldn't inspire.

So why not just let the kid have a go?

Goldmeyer took a drag from his cigarette, nodding to the four-star Air Force general smoking a cigar next to him. The general exhaled and motioned toward the alien enclosure.

"It's about time we showed those aliens that humans can fly their machines."

Goldmeyer nodded, pulling on his cigarette as the General continued staring at the enclosure.

"Too smart for their own goddamn good—and yeah, I get it, they're a few years ahead of us—big friggin' whoop-de-do. But we're catching up fast... so, fuck 'em."

Then he motioned down to the Widow sitting on the tarmac.

"You got Captain Andle down there in the ship. Best pilot in the Air Force, bar none. He's been flying our TR-3Bs for years."

Goldmeyer nodded slightly, pulling on his cigarette and exhaling to the side as he watched the two screens in front of him—one showing the flight support team and the other a cockpit view.

D own on the tarmac, Yen Jee sat with her team at the tarmac flight console.

The team flight surgeon was speaking into a microphone, calling out vital signs as the preflight checks were underway. His voice had a re-assured, upbeat tone, as if he had monitored this type of launch a thousand times. His voice rang out across the tarmac, and also in the overview room.

"Blood pressure normal, temperature normal, pulse slightly high but within SOP. Oxygen intake normal... and all other vital signs are green for go."

The team saw Captain Andle staring forward. He shifted slightly in his flight chair, and there was no seatbelt to hold him down—no need for one. He would be in his own gravity envelope once the Widow was connected to him through his hands. No matter which way the ship flew—right-side-up or upside-down—he would remain in a steady 1-G environment. This was something every antigravity pilot had to get used to when learning how to fly the TR-3B, and it was also part of the learning curve when a new pilot first flew underwater. But Andle had many years of experience flying the TR-3B, so he wasn't concerned about those issues anymore. Flying a ship via a brain connection, however, was completely uncharted territory, and he was damn proud to be selected as the first to... *give her a go!* The magic of alien technology.

He took a slow, deep breath and placed his hands over the shiny silver hand imprints, custom-molded to his hands. Yen's team had replaced the original small alien handprints with Andle's much larger size.

"Okay, connecting," he said.

The flight support team watched on the interior video camera, showing the side of Andle's face as his hands came down. The moment his hands were firmly placed in the imprints, a tiny round light above each of his ten fingers illuminated. Each light was a different color. His head seemed to jerk back slightly, as if jolted by a surge of electricity.

"We have full connection," called out a technician monitoring Andle's hands.

"Brain throughput is normal at twenty-two percent."

Andle's body twitched every few seconds now that a solid connection was made. Nothing too disturbing, but a consistent twitch for certain. There was a lot of energy flowing. He was clearly locked in.

"All vitals still green for go," the flight surgeon called out.

The Widow slowly came to life, emanating a thrumming sound, followed by a deep red band of light that pulsed from top to bottom continuously.

Andle's chest seemed to heave slightly when the team first heard a loud hiss, like an electric substation powering on. Then the Widow rose a few inches, slightly wobbling as her central axis tilted a few degrees from vertical.

In the darkened overlook room, several people yelled out encouragement.

"That's it! You got it! Go, boy!"

The general next to Goldmeyer turned and winked, and both returned to watching the screens.

Back at the flight desk console where Yen stood, the technician called out,

"Throughput up to 86 percent!" A hint of anxiousness was in his voice as he turned quizzically to the flight surgeon.

"We are still green," the flight surgeon said with a perfected calm.

There was an electric-blue glow, a corona discharge, beneath the Widow as the air below her was crushed, emitting photons.

Then, the team heard Captain Andle make his first sound since connecting. It came over the speaker as an eerie whine, like he was fighting an energy that had suddenly grown.

"Throughput is 167 percent!" the technician called out.

The flight surgeon jumped forward, slamming his hand on the comms button.

"Disconnect Captain Andle!" he commanded.

But it was too late. They watched helplessly as Andle's mouth slowly opened, his eyes rolled back until only the whites remained, and the Widow stayed hovering, emitting her electric-blue corona. Seconds later, Andle's body began shaking as if he had latched onto a high-voltage line.

"Disconnect!" the flight surgeon yelled at the screen, but to deaf ears.

Andle's hands seemed magnetically locked into the imprints. The team heard his blood-curdling scream as his eyes bulged, and his mouth opened and closed rapidly, his circuits frying.

Up in the overview room, everyone watched in horror as a small amount of white smoke began to rise from around Andle's ears and violently shaking head. A moment later, his eyes seemed to recede into their sockets as his head uncontrollably wobbled, held in a surge of voltage.

Yen jumped forward and mashed the camera kill switch, but it was a moment too late. Andle's eye sockets suddenly gushed blood, flowing out around his sunken eyes. The screen froze, but the audio continued. The team sat back in frozen horror, listening to the scream become hollower until only an echo was left.

The Widow remained hovering like an animal that had just devoured her prey. One minute later, without warning, she settled under perfect control and powered down. Her ramp miraculously opened from nowhere, and then, seconds later, as the technicians slowly approached, they hesitated, staring at the deep red blood rolling down her ramp toward them.

Up in the desert overlook, Goldmeyer glanced over to see Aspelsin turn with a stone-faced stare before departing.

Fuck-wad, Goldmeyer thought, but he knew better than to linger on it. There were repercussions that could happen from a distance with those fuckers.

Goldmeyer had once witnessed a human being *neurally engaged* by a Reptilian, and that *hell-realm* had been terrifying to watch. So far, he had never pissed off Aspelsin, and he remained vigilant in combating his natural tendency to say what he felt.

Jack Goldmeyer stood, sniffled, and pulled on his cigarette... then ashed it out several times, contemplating the moment... like most of the others in the room. Fixated on the freeze-frame of test pilot Bobby Andle, blood oozing from his bulging eyes... mouth open and covered in thick saliva as if it had been ejected forcibly.

He looked at the monitor to see it had switched to a live view, showing Dr. Yen Jee standing by the exterior console, her arms crossed in front of her.

Goldmeyer disliked being embarrassed in front of the Interplanetary Corporate Conglomerate, but more than that, he hated the thought of losing face in front of the aliens. He considered himself a staunch American patriot. He knew what the aliens were capable of—not only from a technological standpoint but from their ability to work in different dimensions, a skill many of those races had mastered. He loathed them for it.

He glanced again at the video showing Yen Jee. Even in the dim light, her diamond watchband gleamed and sparkled.

Jack Goldmeyer knew things about people who worked for him. He knew what and who they were into, the drugs they took, the sex they preferred, and certainly their oddities. He knew where they banked, where they slept, shat, and even what they said on burner phones. All the details that made them tick. He lit another cigarette and watched her carefully... exhaling into that obsession.

Groom Lake runway, Area 51 (Station D)

S-4 DUMB Papoose Lake, NV

Chapter Ten

They sat on the couch, and Dan stared at the video with Vyla sitting next to him.

They could feel the roll of the U.S.S. Princeton as it moved through the raging storm outside.

"My buddy mentioned that just before the Malaysian jet appeared over the Maldives island, his crew had seen those orbs circling by themselves in the sky, about a thousand feet over the island. He said the orbs just suddenly appeared from nowhere at about six a.m., and then I guess, seconds later, as the crew watched, the Malaysian jet suddenly appeared right where the orbs were circling. As soon as the jet appeared, the orbs vanished, and the jet was tooling along above the island by itself."

She slowly nodded and looked down, viewing the teleportation video again, working the equation. He watched as she suddenly closed her eyes and fell back on the couch, putting her hand to her head, exasperated.

"Oh, my God! Those are plasma orbs!" she whispered, astonished.

Dan watched as she slowly opened her eyes, staring straight ahead. Mesmerized by her thoughts.

"I didn't think this technology would happen in my lifetime—it's all I studied in grad school—I wrote my dissertation on it!"

She looked up and could see Dan was lost.

"Okay, she said, I'll make it really simple."

She started the video again and described what she now understood.

"The plasma balls in the video that are racing around the Malaysian jet are basically like an aircraft or drone that the Cabal can fly wherever they want—and I'm assuming they are initiating them through that space-based platform your buddy mentioned—because everything here is dynamic."

He watched intently as she continued.

"Okay, so let's call these three orbs in this video... *one, two* and *three*. They create a plasma vortex around the Malaysian jet. The airliner then gets sucked into the vortex or *phased-out*. And the phase-out happens instantaneously, as you're seeing right here in the video."

He nodded, following along as she continued.

"Three more orbs, let's just call them orbs *four, five* and *six* are waiting where the Cabal wants the Malaysian jet to reappear. The fourth orb is the destination orb. Meaning wherever the Cabal places the fourth orb, that's where the Malaysian Jet will reappear. In this case, the Maldives, where your buddy was orbiting with his AWACS. And that's where your buddy saw the airliner phase back into this dimension."

Dan stared, pondering the video.

"The jet vanishes over Great Nicobar, but my buddy said it didn't reappear until hours later over the Maldives. Like, six a.m. in the morning is when they first saw those orbs, and then right after that the jet came through."

She shrugged.

"That's most likely a function of time distortion, which naturally occurs when it's teleported."

She looked up, and he was staring at her.

"Now the whole SSP thing is making sense."

She pointed at him.

"Secret Space Program... as in the entire thing going on below the water at Diego?"

He nodded.

"You just viewed the spaceport, supposedly."

"The SSP was mentioned in my Majestic brief," she said.

He nodded and continued.

"Since my buddy sent me this, he told me to research a set of names he wanted me to know about. All the names are whistleblowers coming forward online, saying they were in the Secret Space programs. Jason Rice, Corey Goode, Niara Isley,

Randy Cramer, and more. I've watched their interviews, and most of them were in the Secret Space programs clear back in the '80s."

"Already in space in the '80s?" she whispered, astonished.

He nodded.

"All of them. Mars, the Moon, Ceres, Jupiter, the Kuiper Belt—and way further. They're coming forward because they're having memories that were not supposed to come back."

"You mean memories of missions they did in space?" she questioned, astonished.

He slowly nodded.

"That's where it segues perfectly with what my buddy says has been happening. Several of those SSP whistleblowers claim to have landed or launched from Diego Garcia at one point."

"Meaning—they are all saying the DUMB below the Diego Garcia Navy base—had been a spaceport for years?"

He nodded.

"You can watch their interviews online now. None of them knew each other during their time in the Secret Space programs, but a lot of their stories overlap with what they describe during their time in the programs. Tony Rodrigues, one of the whistleblowers, said he was actually working on a Nazi space freighter as it delivered a load to Diego. And I wouldn't be surprised if that ship we just watched was his Nazi ship. The other SSP whistleblowers all mention having to deal with the nasty Nazis, who at that time, really controlled Diego Garcia."

She watched him and shook her head.

"What I still don't understand is how all this stuff can be happening and yet nobody knows about it... why aren't more participants in all the covert world coming forward?" she whispered.

"Alien tech," he responded matter-of-factly.

"What do you mean?" she whispered.

"My buddy told me for years now, the Cabal has used alien technology on anyone that needs to forget a sensitive mission they participated in."

"You mean something the Cabal wants to cover up?" she asked.

He nodded.

"Like these guys and gals going to space and doing missions?"

He nodded again.

"Or, if you help them hijack a civilian airliner."

She stared, piecing it together.

"So, they're giving these operatives performing secret missions some kind of alien drug that makes them forget?"

He slowly shook his head, staring at her, then exhaled slowly.

"No. There are no drugs involved. My buddy says it's alien tech acquired by the military in 1979... and by 1981 they had reverse-engineered it and enhanced it. My buddy says it's now used almost daily across the globe and out in the galaxy. A selective-memory-blocker."

She stared, perplexed.

"Wait, you mean they can select an actual period in your life—like a covert mission that lasts only two days or perhaps years—and then just erase that slice of time from your memory?"

He looked away, then turned back, locking eyes with her.

"Mind-Wipe technology."

Chapter Eleven

"You're doing really good, Tom... just remember, we went over this last session... you told me Hans was a clone of you, like an alter."

Tom slowly nodded as she continued.

"One they created when you were illegally drugged by the Black Navy during recruitment. The Black Navy cloned you—without your permission. And now, their Mind-Wipe technology—the one they used to make you forget—is wearing off. You're remembering what your clone did for them. So, don't take this on. *You,* Tom, are an amazing man. What Hans is doing to these people? It's not *you.* It's a clone of you—doing these awful things."

She could see him dropping in again, clearly on edge. He had his eyes open—but was lost in a flashback—tense with fear.

"The forklift driver is up there on the tarmac. He's brought out a construction dumpster and put it by the maintenance crew. The driver is sitting in his forklift next to the bodies. Hans tells him where—down in the tunnels, by the East Gate."

"The bodies of the maintenance crew?" she whispered. "You're saying Hans is telling the forklift driver where to put the bodies?"

Tom nodded.

"The forklift driver knows that Hans is the expert with the tunnels and the people down there—below the DUMB. The tunnel people. The sewer people. Hans knows where the bodies should be dumped. He tells the forklift driver to take the freight elevator."

She slowly nodded, seeing that Tom was becoming tense again.

"What's happening, Tom? What is Hans seeing?"

"Chief One has come over—and he's—he's shocking Hans, pushing him to leave the bodies on the tarmac."

"We've got work to do!" he says to Hans, and shocks him. That fucker!"

"Okay, okay, Tom. Do you need a break?"

Tom slowly shook his head and seemed suddenly determined. He took a deep breath.

"He's—they're in the elevator, down in the DUMB. And Chief One is pushing him to walk with that fucking cattle prod. Telling Hans, 'Get in the wet room! You've got work to do!'"

"The wet room?" she inquired.

Tom winced, as if being struck.

"Chief One is shocking Hans! That fat little fuck! And ordering him into the wet room. Ordering him to follow the orders of the men in black suits. The two men, leaning on the table."

"Okay," she said. "Hans is in a wet room, and there are two men in black suits? Are they in charge of Hans?"

Tom nodded, panting.

"Hans is walking around the man in the chair... Asian guy—naked—bound and bleeding in the chair."

"Bound?" she asked.

"It's a wet room," he said.

"A wet room?" she asked again.

"Where we—where Hans tortures people—in the DUMB. Concrete room with white tile. About twenty-feet square. A steel chair in the middle—bolted to the floor above a drain—for the blood."

"Hans tortures them in the wet room?" She asked in a whisper, taking copious shorthand notes.

Tom nodded slowly on the couch, his eyes fixed straight ahead, locked in the flashback.

"In the DUMB? What's the DUMB?" she inquired.

"It's my—our base. The Black Navy. Our Deep Underground Military Base. The D-U-M-B. *The DUMB.* That's what we call it. And this one is huge, because it's also a spaceport."

"Okay," she whispered, reading her shorthand notes.

"So, you left the dead bodies of the maintenance crew on the surface, next to the disassembled tail section. And those bodies were being forklifted into a dumpster when you left. And now you're—I mean, Hans—is underground, in his base, there at Diego Garcia?"

Tom nodded.

"And Hans is in a wet room, right? A wet room, down in the DUMB... underground, right?"

Tom nodded again.

"And you're saying that, in that same DUMB, way down below, there is also a spaceport? Is that what you mean?"

Tom nodded matter-of-factly.

"Mm-hmm. A lot of shit goes through the Diego spaceport," he replied.

"What do you mean by shit?" she asked.

"Materials and traffic," he said.

"What kind of materials? What kind of traffic?" she asked.

He shook his head.

"A lot of materials going up to the ICC."

"The ICC?" she asked.

"The Interplanetary Corporate Conglomerate. The ICC gets lots of human traffic, and some of them are transferred to the Lunar Operations Command on the Moon. A lot of human traffic, man."

"Okay, Tom, you're doing great. But let's leave the spaceport and that stuff for later. Let's drift up and away—back into the wet room, okay? What is Hans seeing in the wet room?"

Tom's face went hard as he again froze in a tense stare. She looked down at her notes and read aloud.

"You said there were two men in dark suits, leaning on a table in there, directing the interrogation? Right?"

She looked up. Tom breathed and slowly nodded.

"The bloody man in the chair is shaking, terrified... whimpering," Tom whispered.

"Who is he?" she asked. "Who is Hans torturing?"

"The Asian guy... naked, bound to the chair—bleeding from his nose—he's a passenger from the Malaysian flight."

Chapter Twelve

S he felt the twin-engine turboprop go to full power, straining against the steel that held it back.

She saw the smart salute of the deck-shooter on the Gerald R. Ford aircraft carrier as he paid homage to the pilots flying the COD she was strapped into. Then, the man pointed toward the bow.

Like a bat out of hell, she felt the induction catapult as it slingshotted the C-2 *Greyhound* off the front of the ship. She felt the landing gear retract in the bird and how hard the twin-engine beast was straining to climb into that storm.

Her first-ever catapult launch, and even though she wasn't in an F-18, the sudden acceleration from zero to 150 knots in 1.8 seconds was an eye-opener. The Gerald R. Ford was lurching straight into the howling monster ahead, yet the gloom didn't have enough lightning visible to delay the launch. The COD bird was buffeted by extreme winds as it climbed, and the sea was tumultuous below her. The huge engines were lifting a cockpit of two pilots, plus her and all the strike-fleet mail that was stacked seven feet high in the center of the craft.

She thought about the wild night and how they had to sneak Dan out before daybreak. He had quickly rinsed off, and moments later, they put him back together, checked his uniform was sharp, his face clean of lipstick. A final locking of eyes and two breath mints later, he was gone.

She still felt a little hungover from all the Old Fashioneds, but she was good with it. A rare night in life for certain, and she liked it when spontaneity grabbed the reins.

It was only now that she realized there were other passengers on the far side of the mail that she hadn't noticed when she was hurried aboard the COD. Two Black men wearing flight suits who looked like identical twins. Both appeared athletic and seemed to be about her age... and both were reading paperback novels. She turned away and tried to get a grip on who they were. When she looked up a few moments later, one of the Twins was looking directly at her, then looked past her as if all was normal.

But they were on a COD leaving an aircraft carrier, and she had a Majestic clearance, she thought.

The specter of being surveilled already. The weirdness of how the Majestic brief mentioned that surveillance could come in many forms and that it wasn't just foreign governments the United States was worried about. She had read incredulously about the government's new awareness that off-world infiltration was already in process. Entities that looked human. The whole enchilada of extraterrestrials as a real thing.

A real thing, she thought and looked at the Twins still reading. *Would I even know an alien if they were right in front of me?*

The COD buffeted again, and she shot another quick glance at the Twins, who were calmly reading.

No, they're not after me! she told herself.

She had never allowed paranoia to rule her life, and damn if she would start now. But here she was on a new playing field, and she had more questions than answers. She wanted to whittle them down to a structure of sorts before her debrief with Yen Jee back at Nellis AFB.

She also realized she was thrown by the follow-on investigation with Dan regarding Flight 370, and it gave her a deep sense of unease. Being systematically deceived by her own government, not just about the missing Malaysian jet, but even more maddening was the apparent years of alien interaction, tech exchanges, and diplomacy—all while hoodwinking the global populace.

She was a physics Ph.D., for Chrissakes; she was supposed to be smarter than the average human. But apparently not. And that added fuel to the fire.

She had completed all three interviews, but the looming meeting with Yen Jee had bothered her. She was torn as she now knew that the Malaysian jet with Yen's family members had not crashed, but she couldn't bring it up, as it might compromise Dan. And that was not going to happen.

But now, the two men opposite her on this flight. Something about them. She felt like she had seen them on the Princeton or Gerald R. Ford but hadn't paid attention at the time. Since her discussion with Dan about her Majestic clearance, she had a new sense about Dr. Jee and her obvious agency to gain clearances for anyone she deemed worthy.

Was this entire investigation a test? Were these two traveling with her... some form of security team? Were they watching her, or protecting her, or perhaps both? Okay, don't go all paranoid!

For the next hour, she perused her notes and found herself wondering about the technology she had just witnessed, not only with the UAP, but with the vanishing of the Boeing 777. She absolutely knew that she had not touched the surface of what must already be in use by the Cabal, but it was clearly being hidden from the human population. And the fact that they were employing 6th generational warfare technology without any public oversight was absolutely terrifying.

It made her think about the Majestic clearance, and all of the surveillance that came with it. If, at the end of the day, it was really just the Cabal who wanted to keep tabs on anyone they needed to get rid of.

She heard the power roll-off, felt the gear and flaps drop as the COD took its dirty configuration. The landing at Marine Corps Air Station Miramar, California, was uneventful, and fifteen minutes later, she was Uber-bound to San Diego Airport, where she had a ticket to San Francisco and home. Her mom, Charlotte, Marten and Steph. She had been gone far too long... and right now she needed home.

S he checked her bag at the ticket counter and turned her phone off just for good measure.

After the long security line, she proceeded to her gate but decided to double back. A sixth sense of hers that had rarely failed her. Seeing the Twins in business suits departing security and walking casually toward her gate gave her the creeps.

Stop it! she told herself, but the sight of them was too coincidental.

Did they just happen to be going in the same direction as her? Maybe to a different gate?

She stopped and shook her head.

Better safe than sorry, she told herself and took the elevator to baggage claim, where she rented a new black Mustang from the rental car agency with the shortest line. She double-checked her purse before getting in the car to see if somehow they had bugged it. She found nothing. Twenty minutes later, she departed the airport, driving north. Her missed flight would not depart for another hour, so she doubled back on several on-ramps and off-ramps to see if the Twins had somehow adjusted and were following her in a car.

After thirty minutes of circular backtracks, she felt good enough to begin the journey north along the coast. She left her phone off and decided that all communication from here on out would be via computer. She would assume that all emails were being monitored.

Why had Yen not told her all this shit was going to happen with being read up to Majestic level?

She was bewildered, and the dark ego voice was beginning to tease. She forced herself to think about other things as she drove. She now understood how an alien craft sending out electromagnetic pulses over a carrier strike group was a no-shit national security issue. The thought that kept circling back was the fact that Yen seemed so detached and indifferent to the incident. Either she was completely a non-believer or perhaps just had more pressing matters within her company that Vyla was unaware of.

The information she was bringing back to Yen would have to be documented in the same format as the rest of the Majestic brief. *Damn paperwork.* She knew there was no getting around it, but she decided that before she began writing, she needed to do at least one more interview. She wasn't certain how that interview would transpire. And it made her think about how everything had led to this moment, running from her security team as if they were going to kill her one day.

In the Uber on the way to the San Diego Airport, she had hopped online and looked up Secretary of State James Forrestal. He had been Secretary of Defense for sure, but not one article mentioned anything about him being assassinated. Most articles stated that he had committed suicide after being fired. But Dan had told her later in the evening that he had a Seal buddy whose dad had been in the CIA in those early years and supposedly told his son, at some point, about the *unfortunate but necessary erasure* of Secretary Forrestal.

And the Majestic-12 was somehow involved, but it was all so much to take in after the last few hours.

She exhaled and thought about how she got the job with Yen Jee.

She had only finished grad school six months ago and was still perplexed about how she was even here. Her roundabout way of getting to this moment had almost seen her quit her dream—for good. The withering rollercoaster of sucking up to all the egos of academia, from Stanford to Princeton, and months of letter writing and subsequent rejections from publishers had taken her to extremely dark places.

Jobs in top laboratories were scarce to begin with, and without being published, she lay awake at night, trying hard not to hear her relentless ego whispering:

You're not as smart as the others!

And seeming to confirm that nasty inside voice were all the rejection letters from publishers—a foot thick, impaled with a Bowie knife, and stuck into a wooden post in her Victorian apartment. She assumed the rejections were primarily due to her age, which at thirty was old for a newly acquired Ph.D.., as most finished their doctorates at twenty-six. She had taken a few years off after getting her master's, having grown tired of all the arrogance of the academic world, and decided to find out who she really was by going inside.

She got her yoga teacher's certificate and dropped into a meditation practice that gave her the inner sustenance she lacked in the frenzied world of academia. When she finally learned to stay in the quiet center no matter the turmoil around her, she dropped back into school for her Ph.D.

Even with a solid meditation practice in place, it was still tough to ride the line of balance between the need-to-succeed and the need-to-breathe. On her 30th birthday, which was also Christmas morning, she was at her lowest.

She woke to find a sweet birthday voicemail from her mom, but birthdays always reminded her of her biological family she never knew. That led her to think of Papa and Gloria, and how she missed the birthday ritual they had shared.

Compounding that sadness this year was the thought of having to tell her mom that she would be coming to live at home again, as no jobs were forthcoming. Completing her Ph.D. at thirty might not have been the best planning. Labs wanted young, brilliant scientists, not older, balanced ones. She had been hoping to say that all the hard-earned money her mom had saved to put her through school had paid off.

But no. Fuck no.

As a last gasp, she had planned a full day of letter writing when she heard a gentle knock and the unmistakable laughter of her best friends Charlotte and Marten.

She approached the door.

Okay, be nice.

She opened it to see Marten with his wry smile, wearing a Santa hat, holding up a blindfold, and Charlotte's beaming blue eyes over his shoulder. Vyla slowly shook her head and frowned.

"No, sorry, kids, not today."

Charlotte shot her a look, snatched the blindfold, and slowly approached, teasing. "This surprise you will like."

Vyla melted a little.

"I won't," she said and felt herself almost cry.

Her friends caught it. Had known it. Marten stepped forward and put a soothing hand on her shoulder. Charlotte gently slid the blindfold over Vyla's head while whispering into her ear. That, on top of turning her on to no end, made her realize once again that these two had been her most staunch supporters through the fire.

Swimming upriver in graduate work for years, weathering storm after storm together—these were now her lifelong mates.

Charlotte softly cooed while gently tying the blindfold.

"We promise fun," she whispered, her soft lips brushing Vyla's ear.

More melting. And why shouldn't she? Since all of her letter-writing had left her with nothing but sadness. These two were a gulp of fresh air, and she needed air. So, fuck it! *Fuck everything!*

With the blindfold in place, led by Charlotte's long-fingered, silky hand, Vyla was tucked into the backseat of Marten's rusted yellow VW bug.

As they pulled out, she felt a tear come and go. Then, without warning, the floodgates opened, and she quietly sobbed.

She felt Marten and Charlotte's hands as they reached back and held hers, allowing the backseat to be her safe zone while they remained quiet as the sobs played out.

Oh, the grace of friends, she thought—*I love these two!*

She heard a rustling up front, followed by giggles. Then Charlotte put a small rubber figurine in her hand.

"Happy Birthday from Steph," Charlotte said.

Stephanie was Charlotte's ten-year-old daughter, and Vyla adored her. Below her blindfold, Vyla fingered a rubber, eight-inch figurine that was humanoid but with an elongated, lizard-shaped head. It had muscular, long arms with three long fingers on each hand and stout legs that ended in large, three-toed feet.

"I take it that I've been given Lizzy?" she said under her blindfold.

"Yep," Charlotte replied. "When you're ten, it's all about aliens and new boobs."

Vyla snickered and fondled the figurine.

"Shit, I'm honored. We had a big discussion about him when I was over the other night. Lizzy is one of her mainstays. He's like the leader of the aliens, right?"

"Yeah," Charlotte said, "she really adores Lizzy... he sleeps on her pillow every night."

"Right," Vyla said. "He's the smartest of the aliens?"

"Yep," Charlotte said. "And he's like the top thug too, like the bully of all the off-world races. She reads books to him."

"Oh my," Vyla said. "What a lucky alien."

After a while, she felt the car slow down abruptly and come to a stop. She heard Charlotte and Marten giggle up front, along with the distinct sound of loud motorcycles idling near the car.

After a forty-minute winding drive, she still had her blindfold on but had correctly guessed she had been taken to The Debacle, their favorite biker bar in Half-Moon Bay.

For three thesis students, this saloon held reality. They craved a hard dose of Earth away from the pretentious academia of lofty Stanford. The Debacle had real in-spades, as it was a no-shit, biker-gang hangout. Sawdust and blood.

The three friends had witnessed a couple of legit fights there over three years, yet they kept going back. Despite the milieu of pistols tucked below leather and tattoos mixed with swaggering pirate stares, the bikers were friendly to a man. Unless you messed with their old lady. *Bitch on back*, who often accompanied them. And if that happened, *woe be to that poor bastard.*

Vyla and Charlotte were clearly a welcome sight at The Debacle, Marten got more of the "*We'll tolerate you, Sparky, because you bring the hotties.*"

But there was another little enchantment at The Debacle that sealed the deal. Their Mescal-Gigante-Margarita was a "Fuck-me" drink guaranteed to make a particle scientist feel a chest puff of spicy bravado. The magic potion came in an oversized glass, seven heavenly salt-covered inches across and four inches deep, laced with an authentic habanero chili.

It hurt so goddamn good; you didn't want it—but then *had to have* another, with or without the worm.

When they finally allowed her to take off the blindfold, Marten and Charlotte had a tray delivered with a birthday cake, candles, and three Gigantes.

"Happy Birthday," Marten said, smiling as he lifted her Gigante, holding it up to the light and illuminating the vision-quest mescal worm, *Gusano-de-Rojo.*

He placed it in front of her as she whispered a slightly terrified but giggling, "Fuck!"

One large biker nearby winked at the very shy Marten.

Get some, Sparky!

To which Marten half-smiled, figuring he was now *one of the boys,* or sort of like one.

Vyla stared at the tray and then noticed the little newspaper thing tied with a red bow. A sweet card, she figured, as she unraveled the wrapping. It took her a minute to realize what it was—a monthly science-oriented periodical.

Einstein-Oppenheimer Worldwide Journal.

She froze when it hit her. She looked up, shocked, at the two of them.

"You're shitting me?"

Her two beaming pals began a happy birthday song, and a few reluctant but jovial bikers joined in.

Vyla sat stupefied. Her head swam. Murky memories reminded her that she had sent her thesis to EOWJ but hadn't heard back. Or, as with other rejection letters, she assumed she had already impaled it on the Bowie knife—her usual move after a shot of whiskey to soften the blow. *Blows. Devastating blows.* Fifty rejection letters at least, when she finally quit counting.

Now, in her hands, in the fucking Debacle, she held the EOWJ periodical and was shaking. She had gotten published!

Hot-Damn!

Before she blew out the last of the three candles, Charlotte and Marten started a *"Worm! Worm!"* chant. Unlike birthday songs, which often garnered only a nod and smile at the Debacle, this heathen chant immediately rang the low-down gong.

Like flint to steel, every pirate in attendance, including their old ladies, were staring at her and hooting for her mandatory baptismal deliverance.

So, with much ado, she stood, hoisting her Gigante with both hands. And then it began. She gulped and gulped, with some escaping down her cheek, until finally, she let the Gusano-De-Rojo wiggle between her lips to a raucous roar before throwing her head back and swallowing that vision-quest-inducing, slimy two-inch fatality.

She felt the habanero chili burn her from the tip of her tongue down to her gut, and she welcomed it.

Published! Fuckin' A!

Later would be a different story, but right now, in this moment...

Round two, yes! Worm, please, thank you!

"Wow," she whispered, shaking her head and staring at the EOWJ.

"It starts on page three, and they didn't edit anything!" Marten yelled with a little bit of a wry smile.

She nodded at him, and then it hit her. Her smile slowly faded as the hinted message from Marten worked its way through her newly induced Gigante chemistry.

"They what?" she said disbelievingly.

She quickly turned the pages, kept turning, and then *fanned them*. She looked up in utter disbelief.

"The entire thing is there!" Charlotte beamed.

Vyla blinked and then for a moment, felt like she would pass out. Charlotte grabbed her arm.

"What's the matter?"

Vyla's main thrust had been on plasmoid-technology and the possibilities it promised for creating holes in space-time. Solid stuff. But the second and much smaller section of her thesis was a guarded topic, one she had not given permission to publish. A flame-throwing scorcher of a personal account about all things currently wrong with academia. Specifically addressing the infusion of egomania throughout the academic world.

Part II: The hallowed halls of Egodemia only got more damning after her title. She had essentially called out all academia and every egomaniac professor on the carpet. Citing her personal experience at Stanford over the years and including online testimonials from various anonymous students throughout top universities worldwide.

She had turned a spotlight on what was known by all but only discussed in secret at universities everywhere—certain top professors in her field were unapologetically all about themselves to a fault. These exalted teachers had perpetuated their own cult of personality, expecting, even demanding, each of their students, under threat of grades, to be echo chambers for the professor's work, thereby ensuring academic stardom and prestige.

She sat breathless again, fanning the pages, confirming all of Part II was there.

The walls of her entire academic career began to crumble. She had made a mistake and accidentally sent her thesis to *a predatory journal.* Publications she had been warned were not legit and were all about sales and money.

And fuck me! she thought.

She had effectively destroyed her career before ever having one, as the voice deep inside whispered its self-righteous poison.

Yes, you wanted to get published so badly; *you didn't read the fine print, the details that would have told you this rag was bogus!*

Marten and Charlotte looked nervously at her. She half-smiled, and then, unbelievably—even to her—she just stared at her two friends.

She suddenly got it. *Everything.* That all this life really held was this moment. It was her birthday, dammit! And with that came an epiphany about what mattered.

She realized in that checkmate-of-a-moment, that there was no reason to drown her two friends and all the bikers around her in sorrow. Now, she concluded, she had killed it all for certain. And being that it was water over the dam, she decided to roll with it.

She was done fighting life. Something in her gave up at that moment, and she made a bold decision.

Why not flow with it and enjoy love where it exists?

She shrugged her shoulders and looked at them.

"Can we please just get drunk?"

They slowly nodded, knowing exactly what she needed.

Six hours and six worms later, a huge biker poured her into Marten's backseat.

Charlotte stayed with her that night, and in the morning, she propped a tray of biscuits, bacon, water, coffee, and Pepto-Bismol by her bedside and kissed her forehead.

"I've got to pick up Steph from your mom's," Charlotte whispered.

Vyla nodded but fell back to sleep before Charlotte had even reached the door.

When her cell rang three hours later, her brain was pounding. She grabbed the sides of her head with both hands and stared at the phone vibrating on the nightstand. Breathing hard, she reached out with a shaking hand and tapped the speaker button.

"Yeah?" she managed.

An Asian-accented voice sounded through the speaker.

"Hi, Vyla, this is Yen Jee."

She suddenly felt rising anger as she stared at the phone. She knew it was just another Stanford grad-school prank, which in the last few years had become almost as ritualistic as the notorious pranks at MIT.

When she finally did respond, her words came out in a drunken slur.

"Yen Jee? Yeah, bitch, well, I'm fucking Einstein, so kiss my ass!" and hung up.

Then, turning her phone off, she slurred to herself,

"Bitches!"

She put a shaking hand on her throbbing head and then felt the seismic shift—rushing toward the bathroom as the gush of bile exploded through her. Leaning over the toilet, she did the technicolor yawn of the alien. Then, dropping to her knees, she held the cold porcelain bowl to steady herself.

Three courtesy flushes were required over the next twenty minutes, and then, when she thought nothing could be left, she fell against the bathroom wall, curled into a fetal ball, and burst into tears.

T wo hours later, Marten called to check on her.

She said she was slowly coming back to life when he cut her off.

"Vyla, I just got a call from Margaret Hynec, your advisor?"

She went silent as he continued.

"She said you were not answering, and she had been contacted by somebody important who was trying to get ahold of you."

Vyla attempted to re-cage her brain.

"What? Who?" she mumbled.

"Somebody famous, I think," Marten said.

"Yeah, it was a fucking prank," she slurred, slamming a gulp of cold coffee.

"I don't know. Some Asian chick impersonating Yen Jee, giving me shit. They probably called Margaret first just to get my number."

Marten, now serious, asked,

"Are you certain it was a prank?"

Suddenly, her phone vibrated, and a number flashed. She stared at the caller's origin next to the number: *Washington, DC.*

I don't know anybody in Washington, DC, her cloudy brain thought.

"Marten, you're so great," she slurred. "Can I call you—"

"Sure," Marten said, cutting her off. "Drink some coffee, girl, and let me know if you need anything."

Then he hung up. She held the phone at arm's length as it continued to vibrate and flash. She hit the green button and put the phone to her ear.

"Hello, is this Vyla?" the caller asked.

Vyla would tell Marten days later, when she was sober, that she made Yen Jee take a *Vyla culture test of authenticity,* as Vyla questioned her, slurring at one point:

"Could you speak a little Chinese, so I know this isn't a total fucking prank?" It wasn't until Yen mentioned that she had read Vyla's thesis, part II, about Egodemia that the conversation suddenly turned.

By then, she was gulping cold coffee and realized that Yen might actually be the real article. When Yen said she was impressed with Vyla's audacity and outlandish theories on plasmoid technology, Vyla stumbled to the sink and vomited.

Once purged, she sat in silence on the toilet, holding her throbbing head, then cried silently as Yen continued. When Yen finished, Vyla was silent for a long time, gathering tears. Shaking.

Yen questioned the silence.

"Hello, Vyla, are you still there?"

She was silently sobbing and felt the *little girl deep inside,* nodding and trying to speak.

"I'm here," her little girl finally whispered, as everything in her wanted to shout: *Yes, I am here!*

Now, driving in her Mustang, she could now only remember snippets of the rest of the call. Listening to Dr. Jee, she felt herself floating in an otherworldly state. She did remember putting the phone on speaker and walking in her long, loose t-shirt to her only picture window.

She continued listening to Yen while looking down onto a garden where a small girl and her grandfather sat holding hands. Yen seemed to be going on about Secret Projects and National Security, moving to Las Vegas, and much more. She watched the two below with a soft gaze, mesmerized by the little girl and her grandfather.

"Well, what do you think?" Yen finally asked.

"Yes," she whispered, realizing at the last moment that she should acknowledge the question. She didn't really know what she was saying yes to, but by God, everything felt like a big-fat *YES* in this surreal moment.

"Oh, good," replied Yen casually. "Well, welcome aboard. I'm going to have you meet me at the LHC in Geneva, Switzerland, in March. Before that, we'll meet at Kirtland Air Force Base."

A long pause... and she realized again that it was her turn.

"Thank you, Dr. Jee."

She placed her hand against the glass for support, staring down at the little girl and her grandfather. Hungover beyond belief but watching the two below, she understood that the best moments of her life had been those with her Papa as a little girl. It was enough to be near him. *Always.*

She didn't remember when she woke up hours later if the whole job offer thing was real or not. She freaked out and had to look at her phone calls. When she realized that the one from Washington, DC, had lasted thirty-five minutes, she sat on the edge of her bed in sobering disbelief. It took her two more days of packing for Geneva and going for runs before the alcohol had vacated her system.

And now, driving north in this new moment, she remembered that Charlotte had left a message that she and Marten would be waiting at San Francisco Airport with Stephanie in tow. She needed to stop that evolution before going any further. She pulled into an internet cafe in Santa Barbara and sent a quick message to Charlotte and Marten, letting them know about the change in plans. She indicated, without going into details, that her phone was on the blink and that she would respond to emails and phone messages when she could. She promised Charlotte she would be back in Stanford by tomorrow. She sent essentially the same message to Yen Jee regarding her phone, letting her know that she would be at Yen's headquarters facility at Nellis AFB in two days for her first walkthrough.

Before she turned her phone off, both messages were returned with a thumbs-up, and she felt good that she didn't have to explain anything at this point regarding her new surveillance issue. Certainly, this would be a discussion with Yen Jee.

Departing the coffee shop, she really felt the heatwave that had been creeping across the country for the last week. The unexpected warmth made her peruse the high-tech dashboard of the brand-new Mustang. She found the button she wanted... and a moment later she exited the parking lot with the top down and the unseasonably hot wind blowing her hair back.

She felt calm for the first time in weeks as she headed northbound on the highway, liking the thought of being hidden electronically, racing along with her hair going wild around her. Listening to a Rolling Stones song at full volume while accelerating even faster, she suddenly realized she had an opportunity in front of her that wouldn't have been available had she taken the flight from San Diego. She thought about this new, risky possibility, and the more she did, the more she convinced herself that she really had nothing to lose by doing one more interview. Suddenly, singing *Sympathy for the Devil* at the top of her lungs while driving eighty-five made her feel a confidence that had nothing to do with reality.

"Pleased to meet you!" she belted, flying by cars like a wild woman. "Hope you guess my name!" she sang, going even faster.

Just below her butt, hidden in the Mustang's swanky bucket seat, was the Lowjack theft system, broadcasting to the Twins. The code to the Lowjack had been quickly handed over by the rental car associate at San Diego after the Twins flashed their government badges. They were two hours behind her on the highway and had watched on their phones in real-time as she had sent her messages from Santa Barbara. They knew her destination and her mindset. She had eluded them momentarily, and they gave a begrudging respect for the hoodwink.

But the Twins were cold operators, and they would now shorten the leash on Dr. Kells. She now knew about the alien presence as a real thing, and that made her a security risk to huge financial and private entities that relied on the alien presence on the planet being kept completely secret.

Chapter Thirteen

Swizzle shouldered his tattered backpack in the moonlight outside the Safeway near Moss Landing, California, collecting the standard number of homeless stares.

His wild ponytail, silver earring, and forearm tattoos fit the picture of a land pirate—yet all was not as it seemed.

The hot wind flattened his beard as he looked up slightly. He knew it was up there. They had been closing in for weeks. Their drone was based out of Creech Air Force Base—otherwise known as the super-secret Indian Springs DUMB in Nevada. An American military team had been tracking him. They would confront him soon, he figured, but they still didn't know his agenda and had allowed him to continue.

He wasn't at all certain he would complete his mission. A big piece of it depended on someone he had yet to meet.

He cupped his aged, calloused hands and lit a cigarette. He pulled hard, exhaling through his nose as he gazed at the huge moon. Then he lumbered, backpack and all, onto his 1970 Honda 650, complete with an Easy Rider sissy bar—angled up toward the starlit sky.

The electric starter cranked three times before she roared to life with a belch of blue-white smoke.

115

Swizzle coaxed her up the on-ramp to Highway One, heading north, and opened the throttle full-tilt—sending the oil-bleeding monstrosity roaring into the huge moon beckoning just ahead in its polite manner.

S ixty-two miles northwest of Moss Landing Harbor, the aged Stanford therapist watched as Tom sank deeper into his regression.

She could sense he was there—wherever that dark place was—because his body tensed on the couch, his arms and legs rigid like wood.

"What is Hans seeing now, Tom?" she whispered. "Is he still in the wet room?"

Tom's chest rose and fell in deep, breathy extremes. Heaving as he began to speak, the images vivid in his mind.

"'Ask him where he got it,' the short guy in the black suit said to the Chinese interpreter. The short one—he's the boss. There are two guys in suits, but the short one—he asks the questions. The interpreter asks the bloody guy in the chair something in Chinese—or some Asian language. Hans isn't sure. Doesn't care. Just doesn't want to be shocked. Maybe it's Japanese—it's Asian, that's all Hans knows."

"Okay, don't worry about what language it is," she soothed. "Just stay with what Hans is seeing. You said the interpreter is clarifying that the bloody man in the chair stole something?"

Tom nodded.

"Stole it from the Cabal."

"The Cabal?" she asked. "The same Cabal you said runs everything on the U.S. Navy base at Diego Garcia?"

Another nod.

"That flight was going to China. Gonna give it to them—to the Chinese."

"What, Tom? Give what to whom?" she whispered.

Tom shook his head.

"Fuckin' with the Cabal," he whispered. "That's why so much shit goes through Diego—up to space and back. It used to be the Germans—the Dark Fleet—but they moved operations to Mars in 2003. Then, the Cabal took over. Now it's just us—the U.S. Black Navy. But we work for them—for the Cabal. The shit they run through Diego—up to space and back—to the Interplanetary Corporate Conglomerate base on Mars. Bunch of Asians there. And the Lunar Operations Command—our base on the fuckin' moon. The Cabal—they—they run the fucking world. And off-world too."

"Okay, Tom," she interjected gently. "We'll come back to the Cabal, but stay with what Hans is seeing in this moment. What's happening in the wet room?"

Tom adjusted his head slightly, exhaling.

"The two dark suits are off to the side, leaning on a table, asking questions. The interpreter is there, watching the bloody Asian man in the chair. He's whimpering, and his nose and head are bleeding. There's a big two-way mirror on the wall—don't know who's behind it—watching."

"Okay, you're doing great. Don't worry about who's behind the mirror. What happens next?" she whispered.

Tom shook his head, breathing heavily. She studied him, concerned.

"Tom!" She pressed, her voice edged with unease. "What's going on?"

Tom stared ahead, slowly shaking his head—gone—as if watching a movie.

"The smaller, black-suited man, the intense one—he tells the interpreter that the bloody Asian is lying. Says he's going to have the man's fingers removed if he doesn't start telling the truth."

The therapist braced.

"And then?"

"The interpreter tells the bloody man in the chair. And that poor fucker is shaking his head, like he's denying it, screaming at the interpreter, at the men in suits."

North of Tom's terror—in the most progressive city on the planet, everyone was entranced by *Plato.*

Union Square in downtown San Francisco had a history of hosting some of the finest concrete prophets to ever grace a major city. But Plato was in rare air.

Daily crowds had grown throughout the summer, and many of them stayed for entire diatribes on all things intellectual and sensual too.

"Plato's Corner" had become a destination in the city. Word spread fast among both the homeless and the suits. Now, it needed police security. Traffic stopped. Vendors showed up. Plato had arrived.

An oft-repeated whisper that could be heard amongst newcomers to the daily throngs was that *Plato was hot. Really hot.* And she was.

Toned, slender, shaved black legs, that sprouted out of eight-inch platform heels, rose elegantly into funky pink short-shorts—revealing just enough firm-jiggling-butt-cheek to tantalize... and inspire.

And then there was the silk bikini top. Her ever-curious nipples erect and pushing through like antennae attempting to listen. Oh, those nipples. Just erect enough to twist each listener into an ongoing conundrum: concentrate on verbal luminosity or simply succumb to the sensual smorgasbord that was Plato.

A delicious problem. But there were more dimensions and layers to the soiree. The brilliance and utter prescience of her lectures were an equal match to her just-enough cleavage, which was slightly covered by two ponytails hanging down from her shiny beehive—a coiffed colossus... rising vertically, sleek, black, and fused. Fused as in dynamite. Gunpowder. *Chaos.*

Woven into her shiny hive were strings of hemp fuses, saturated with potassium nitrate and gently threaded into her hairdo by San Francisco hippy girls who adored her. The ritual of lighting her fuses before each verbal miracle was a drama that, at once, fired up the crowd and made them cringe. Even when they couldn't see her amidst the throng, they knew where she was. A scented smoke trail followed her as she slayed her watchers with shit they could not walk away from—ideas that were not radical. Plato didn't have to try that hard. She simply questioned what they thought they knew. She raised a mirror they couldn't see in their drone lives. When she held court, even known hecklers learned to *shut the fuck up.*

On that already roasting summer morning, Plato was just coming to life. She sat on a wooden stool, smoking a cigarette and sipping coffee from a paper cup. Her harem of Ayurvedic girls, wearing see-through long dresses, were busy around her. They knew to move slowly. Plato never rushed. She pulled on her cig and watched the suits on their way to work as her fuses were being teased through her hive. One of the girls painted Plato's long fingernails on her free hand, and nobody spoke. She appreciated quiet, and the sounds of the birds and the city as it came alive. The crowd began to murmur as the fuses were lit.

"Bring it, Plato!" someone shouted as she slowly stood, turning in a circle as the crowd waited. Halfway through her slow turn, she adjusted the tiny wireless microphone extending from her collar.

"Good morning, San-Fran-cisco!" she opened in her smoky street brogue.

Before she could complete the sentence, the yells and applause swelled. Amidst the fanfare, Plato licked her pointer finger and raised it to the wind. The crowd slowly quieted as she stared at them, finger still high.

"If you take one planet and destroy it, the fabric of the universe changes. Mm-hmm. It's all part of the hive, don't you see? Everything is connected by the finest thread. I know, I know, all of you want that statement to be true, right? Everybody here wishes it to be true when you're all holding hands, doing all your Kumbaya-shit, in your new-age groups. You wanna believe it. You really do. And you know what? This is the one and only time I will give a nod to all the new-age quinoa addicts present here today!"

The crowd laughed and whooped.

"We are all connected. Now here's a little lesson, so pay attention." Turning slowly as she spoke.

"I'm gonna make this direct for you, not some magic-wagic bullshit potion. I'm going to give you concrete, mixed from the bag, with just simple water."

She saw a frat boy whispering in the ear of his perfectly dressed girlfriend and stared at them with a friendly smile. But everyone was now staring. The frat boy stopped whispering and looked caught. His girlfriend quickly rifled through her purse and put a bill in the donation box as light laughter ensued.

"Why, thank you," Plato said as the girlfriend returned to her spot. Plato stepped casually in front of the frat boy, slowly raising her finger to his heart as she smiled at him, but spoke to everyone.

"At the heart of your heart is a very peculiar atom made of iron," she said, sharing a smile with the frat boy.

"Think old-school choo-choo train made of iron. Heavy and solid, lean and fuckin' mean." She pointed back to her own heart.

"Now, that iron atom is like a freight train because it binds hemoglobin—which has to be pumped throughout your body at all times. That's because hemoglobin binds oxygen... and you need that shit."

She whirled around and stared across the sea of listeners.

"Now, what that means is that at the heart of your heart—is that tiny little iron atom—that makes your heart... beat."

Silence everywhere.

"Alright, so I see all you bitches starin' back at me-goin' who gives a fuckin' shit about an iron atom?" She raised her finger.

"Oh, but here's the jiggy, here's the catch, here's the anecdote, here's the fuckin' magic—there was no iron when this universe first came to be," she said, staring out and allowing the pause to take effect.

"We had hydrogen and helium, but iron... uh-uh... no, sir. So, if you bitches are standing here with a beatin' heart like me—then something had to be created just for you and me—to be."

The audience watched her as she stared back, circling to see that her listeners were on point.

"The only way that iron is created in the universe is through supernovas and supermassive stars colliding." She picked up two small plastic balls and began slapping them together gently.

"For iron to exist at all, the process of stars colliding and exploding had to happen over and over. And that process—created..." she pointed again to her heart.

"Iron."

She tossed the balls to her entourage girls and pulled a firecracker from her pocket, and lit the fuse. She watched it—waiting as the fuse got shorter.

The crowd yelled,

"Throw it!"

But she continued to hold it. The fuse disappeared into the firecracker as she closed her eyes, holding out the firecracker as the crowd yelled,

"Drop it!—drop it!"

Nothing happened. She opened her eyes, then raised the firecracker and attempted to look inside as she spoke.

"I took the gunpowder out," she said, looking up and smiling.

The crowd giggled.

"Mm-hmm... you think I'm a Pyro or what?"

The crowd whistled.

"There's enough San Francisco police out here to stop a goddamn earthquake, and you really think I'm going to break the law? Shit, y'all... I'm dramatic... but that does not therefore mean—I'm ignorant," she said, holding up the firecracker.

"So, at the Big Bang, y'all," she said, walking slowly.

"And when I say the Big Bang, I ain't talking about good sex, y'all. Although I wouldn't mind talking about it!"

More laughter and catcall whistles came out.

"I'm talkin' about when that first mother-fucking firecracker, that M-80 of all M-80's... that was only the size of a pinhead, exploded from essentially nowhere, and shot out hot plasma 13.8 billion years ago."

Spreading her arms wide, like pushing back waves from either side of her, she continued,

"That hot plasma, which was basically like an energy shockwave expanding outward, eventually went through a Higgs field and slowed way down, forming—you guessed it—planets."

She raised a basketball-sized globe from her bag of tricks.

"Friggin' planets from energy! That's a whole other story. But for today, we just need to understand where iron came from. That freight train that runs your beating heart—originated—out there!" she said, pointing toward the sky.

"It ain't here naturally. You understand?"

She puts her hand on her heart.

"Now everybody put your hand on your heart... right now."

The crowd complied.

"Now let's dwell for a moment on that. Everybody close their eyes... do it."

She paused and closed her eyes.

"Now—your hearts are beatin' because of an element not created by your own planet. Our sweet, sweet Mother Earth that's holdin' you right now. That means that for you to be standing here listening to the real truth, some reaction—from somewhere other than here—had to happen for us to even be in communion here this morning. So, only through the process of stars forming, then exploding, over and over, did we get iron, which now courses through each one of you. Now, open your eyes."

The crowd did so, to find that Plato now had her finger raised to the sky.

"But our sweet Mama Earth didn't have any iron to give. It ain't her thing—but we needed it—so stars out there gave us their magic. Think about that for a moment—and then you tell me—the rest of this universe is not connected to everybody here?"

She turned slowly, taking in her throng.

"Even you, frat boy... your beautiful face, and hair, and them Bass-Weejun loafers you got on too! They wouldn't even be here without iron... and that ain't no shit. And you can take that back to the frat and make a deposit!"

The crowd roared.

In the midst of all the commotion, Plato noticed Swizzle calmly walking out of the throng and seeing her. He pulled a small pad from his pocket and scribbled a note. Rolled the note inside a wad of bills, wrapped it with a rubber band from his wrist and dropped the wad in the donation box. Then kept walking, disappearing back into the throng.

Plato nodded her appreciation of the crowd and worked her way nonchalantly to the donation box, retrieving Swizzle's wad. She handed the donation box to the crowd and placed Swizzle's cash in her short-shorts.

She sat and was handed a glass of water. She watched as the donation box made the rounds while she unraveled Swizzle's wad of bills to find the small note rolled inside.

She opened the note, took a glance, and placed it in her shorts. Lit a cigarette. Watched all the faces staring her way.

Picking up on things, she sensed.

So many things.

T he harbor at Moss Landing was a ragtag flotilla of every type of water vessel.

Since Monterey Bay bottomed out at almost a mile deep, Moss Landing had its fill of research ships, fishing vessels, and an entire fleet of new and ragtag private vessels of all styles and ages.

Huge private yachts made of lightweight alloys with spinning radar arrays all the way down to vintage, turn-of-the-century Italian fishing boats that somehow were still afloat.

Swizzle came down the dock gangplank, hunched slightly under the weight of his backpack. He shuffled by the seventy-foot shrimp trawler *Bad Boy* and got the inevitable catcall from Bobby Joe, the tobacco-chewing crew chief, prepping the ship for the daily fishing run.

"Hey, Swizzle, gonna catch some rockfish today?"

Swizzle acknowledged BJ and his five-man crew with a silent shrug and then boarded the Gizmo, his perfectly restored PT boat with the name painted in teal letters across the back.

The eighty-foot throwback WW-II sub-hunter still had the deck-mounted torpedo tubes used to attack Japanese shipping in the Great War. BJ watched as Swizzle disappeared down the steps into the main cabin and, a moment later, heard the distinctive thunder of Gizmo's three V-12 Packard engines firing up.

"Where does he go, BJ?" said one of the crew, staring at Swizzle's boat. BJ shook his head and spat a disgusting four-foot-long tobacco-colored loogie over the side.

"Well, he always departs toward Santa Cruz, but I think he circles back when he hits blue water. Never seen him in the fishing grounds. And that boat does some freaky shit."

BJ's crew turned to him as he continued under his breath.

"Captain Jimmy was tracking some rockfish one night about twenty miles off the coast. Said that fucker flew by him doing at least forty knots, open ocean."

An admiring whistle from one of BJ's crew. BJ lofted another long spit over the side.

"Nobody saw him coming, no running lights, spotlights, nothin'. And according to Captain Jimmy—the weirdest thing is—they didn't even hear the approach. Jimmy said, 'It roared in, like from thin air!'"

BJ sucked his teeth.

"Said the whole ship was covered with a bunch of funky antennas, waving in every direction. Went by so fast, the wake alone knocked all Jimmy's crew to the deck. And Captain Jimmy's boat is big and runs deep."

"Runnin' drugs?" one of BJ's crew asked.

BJ shrugged.

"Who knows? He's a weird old fucker. Jimmy said he used to be a physicist or some freak-show-kinda science teacher back in the day. That's all I know."

The men turned suddenly as Plato walked by them, wearing headphones, blaring music, black shorts, a matching tank top, and her signature platform heels. A canvas computer bag slung over her shoulder. She was reading a cell phone message while walking. Only looking up when she arrived at the Gizmo, and without hesitating, boarded.

BJ and the crew watched as Swizzle came out and motioned Plato past him into the cockpit. Swizzle looked up at BJ and shrugged, pulling a cheshire grin. Then he winked and closed the door behind him.

BJ glared.

"Goddamn!" whispered one of the crew admiringly.

BJ spat as everyone turned to see his pissed-off look. He took in the Gizmo for a moment and looked back to his crew.

"Get to work!"

V yla carried a stuffed shopping bag from the tattered Moss Landing thrift store and proceeded to her black Mustang.

She was happy to have a new change of clothes and a thick fleece blanket for a badly needed nap. She was still too cheap to pay for a hotel for one night, and the Mustang's backseat seemed big enough for her. She scanned the parking lot as she started the car and departed toward the harbor.

The Moss Landing marina at 2 p.m. was scorching. Heat waves rose visibly from the new blacktop outside the marina. She pulled into the dirt parking lot of *Queen Helen's Revenge bar and grill* and raised the soft-top on the Mustang.

She was blocked from entering the docks by chain-link fences, which were keycoded for boat slip owners. There were hundreds of boats, yet she figured it wouldn't be an issue since the PT boat she was looking for was extremely rare. The only place accessible on foot was the fueling dock, and several boats were lined up with only one attendant fueling.

She went inside the weathered store that serviced the fueling dock and purchased sparkling water and a candy bar. Exiting, she made her way casually to the twenty-year-old girl who was fueling the boats.

The girl had long black hair pulled back in a ponytail, several earrings, and an anchor tattoo on her bare shoulder, glistening in the sweltering heat. Her tank top and jeans were greasy, and her high tops were faded pink and disgusting. She was sweating profusely, with a clear "*Don't fuck with me*" look of someone who had put up with too many wealthy boat owners. Vyla liked her immediately.

"I brought you a little something," she said.

The girl looked up from fueling the boat to see Vyla place the sparkling water and candy bar on the dock railing near her.

"Thank you. That's really cool," the girl said, immediately popping the top on the water and taking a swig while keeping her eye on the fueling nozzle.

Vyla sat on the dock bench.

"I've never been to this marina before. Somebody said it was really ancient?"

"Yeah," the girl said. "We've got a bunch of old boats and some pretty good fishing here."

"You have a boat here?" Vyla asked.

"My dad's got a thirty-four Rybovitch in slip two-twenty," she said, opening the candy bar. "It's a classic sport-fisher, but it's pretty cool. I know how to drive it."

She pulled the fuel line and schlepped the heavy hose back from the boat. One of the trawler crew reached out a wad of bills, and she grabbed it, waving the bills up at the captain in the upper cockpit. He smiled down at her, working the throttles, and eased the old trawler away from the dock. She slipped the cash into her greasy jeans and waited for the next boat in line.

"I'm Vyla. What's your name?"

"Peggy," she said. "But everybody calls me Peg. Like the Steely Dan song."

"I love that song," Vyla said, watching Peg as she popped the gas cap on the arriving boat and inserted the nozzle.

"Peg, you must know every boat in this harbor, huh?"

"Oh yeah," she said. As she started the pump, ensuring it was flowing nicely, she picked up her sparkling water, took a big gulp, wiped her brow, and sat on the bench next to Vyla.

Vyla could smell the diesel and sweat as it wafted over her, and she liked this tough young girl even more.

"That looks like hard work?" Vyla said, "Do you get decent tips?"

Peg shrugged and bit a hunk of the candy bar.

"Most of these fishermen are generally broke by the time they pay their crews and gas, but they try to take care of me. Some give me cash, but I've been offered every kind of drug you can imagine—pot, crack, cocaine. Shit, I even got one of those tiny *Screamshit* vials the other day."

Vyla watched her.

"Are you into all that stuff, Peg?"

"Maybe a joint once in a while, but nothing hard. Not my thing. Besides, I'm in school for investigative journalism. But I've got enough friends that enjoy trippin', so I can usually sell any kind of drugs I get, no problem." She said and took a sip. "That Screamshit tripped me out, though. Have you ever seen it?"

"Drugs aren't really my thing," Vyla shrugged with a smile.

"Me neither," Peg said, shaking her head in disbelief. "I mean, that little plastic vial was no bigger than my pinky—like maybe there were a few drops of the red shit in there. And I don't know what it's made of, but damn, if I didn't get 750 bucks for it!"

"Wow," Vyla said. "It must be better than heroin?"

Peg shrugged.

"I guess. I mean, damn, whoever's creating that stuff must be making a fortune."
Vyla slowly nodded and looked back at the water.

"So, you're gonna be an investigative journalist?"

"I sure hope so," Peg said.

"That's super cool," Vyla said, scanning the docks. And then continued,
"Somebody told me there's an old PT boat that lives in this harbor—"

"Gizmo," Peg said, cutting her off. "Slip forty-five. She's eighty-foot, with
three Packard V-12s, supercharged. Still got all four—21-inch—Mark-VIII torpedo
tubes. And they still work. Bitch is a badass through and through. Flat-out chase
down any ship out here."

Vyla watched her as Peg took a bite of her candy bar and then continued,

"Went out this afternoon. Swizzle's the Captain."

"Swizzle?" Vyla asked.

"Dude's a friggin' trip, I swear," Peg said, shaking her head. "He's super
cool—used to help me with algebra homework, but he's definitely one of a kind.
Was like, a physics professor in England, I think. Heavy British accent."

"Oh, yeah?" Vyla said. "That's cool. Was he a good teacher?"

Peg sucked her teeth, contemplating.

"It's like he would answer me before I even asked the question I had in my mind,"
she said. "Smart as fuck. He'll probably be back sometime tonight if you want to see
his boat come in," she said, standing.

"And that boat does some weird shit, according to the scuttlebutt around here,"
she said, walking back to the fueling station.

"Nice to meet you, Vyla, and thanks for the chow."

"Likewise, Peg. You're kicking ass out here—keep up the good work!"

She watched Peg receive the next boat and walked back toward the Mustang.

"Slip forty-five," she whispered, walking away, noticing the slip numbers. She
could see the empty number forty-five slip down the way. She looked up at the
Mustang in the parking lot of the bar and grill. A plan was forming.

"A physics professor," she said to nobody. What are the chances?"

She reached the Mustang, raised the top, locked the doors, left the windows down
slightly, and hopped in the back seat. She pulled her new fleece blanket around her,
and moments later, she was gone.

Yen Jee was nervous as she stared out the rear window of her black,
nine-seater Sikorsky executive chopper, racing just above the treetops
northwest of the White House.

At that altitude, it would avoid radar detection from anyone trying to track it.

She adjusted her diamond watchband, noticing it was 5 a.m.

Pitch black, save for the chopper's front headlight—illuminating the forest racing just below the nose of the chopper—at a steady 180 knots.

She was anxious and had been since the failed test flight a few days ago.

She had been summoned by the Overseer, and that rarely happened.

But when it did, it was always a morning flight, as the Overseer liked to have meetings before his breakfast—and being called on the carpet to answer his questions always unnerved her.

Regional air-traffic controllers based near the White House were used to non-scheduled, top-secret flights.

Not just for the President, but also for a select few whose above-Top Secret jobs were known only to themselves.

ATC controllers knew her chopper would rise just enough to clear the trees northwest of the White House and then sustain itself below ATC radar visibility without a squawk.

They also knew that bird was heading to an above-top-secret area in the densely forested Maryland countryside, where it would vanish below ground.

The Country Club. That's what the pilots and members called it.

The unknown-to-the-outside-world complex, only accessible by air, was the home of the United States' government-behind-the-government. *The Cabal.*

Originally constructed as the headquarters of the Majestic 12, the sprawling facility, buried in the dense forest of Allegany County, Maryland, was so secret there were no roads anywhere nearby.

The surrounding forest was full of tactical operatives who would terminally thwart any infiltration. With land and construction donated by the Rockefellers, the fortified underground fortress was not only miles deep below the surface but was outfitted with posh living quarters, restaurants, and recreational spaces created exclusively for members of the Majestic-12 and their families.

Yen felt the bird slowing as it cleared a final row of trees and nosed downward toward a large tunnel angled into the earth.

Minutes later, she would be in *The Overseer's* office, and the short notice of this meeting was no doubt about the failed test flight.

She quickly pulled a small vanity mirror from her purse.

She had hardly aged a day in the three years since discovering the *Fountain of Youth.*

She lifted the blood-red glass vial from her purse. It felt so good—custom handmade glass that fit perfectly in her small hand. *Looks were important in business,* she told herself, and money was no longer an object, so she indulged daily. She slowly unscrewed the eyedropper top, ensuring she didn't disturb the small *Winking Wolf* emblazoned gold tag hanging from the vial on its soft, deep red thread. *Nice touch,* she thought. And she knew the Winking Wolf personally.

Ricky Slepher was an athletic, nice-looking man—quite understated for a drug dealer. Ricky, she hoped, might ask her out sometime.

Maybe? Or maybe she was too old and had disappeared from his gorgeous eyes already? Whatever.

She placed a few drops of the red magic on her tongue and closed her mouth, making sure to let that adrenochrome drive its zing right into her system.

And damn, it hit quick.

Like LSD mixed with speed, she suddenly felt like she could run up Everest and not be winded.

Fuck!

She sniffled and shook her head, thinking she understood why they called it *Screamshit*. She carefully put the eyedropper back inside and screwed the top on slowly, making sure she was firm on the last turn. She didn't want to spill a drop of that *forever-young* concoction.

Gold, she thought. *And damn expensive shit. But worth every penny.*

She would get another vial soon.

"She looked great and would continue to," Ricky had told her.

"As long as she only took the newest batches, which were also coveted by many Hollywood stars and elites worldwide. Hence the steep price tag."

She swallowed hard and put the vial back in her purse, snapping it closed as the helicopter came to a hover, deep down in an underground hangar.

Despite the rush from the Screamshit... there was a foreboding feeling running through her veins, but then again, it was a sensation Yen Jee knew well when visiting the head of the Majestic-12:

Fear.

Chapter Fourteen

J ack Goldmeyer sat alone at the table reserved for MAJ-1, catching up on *The New York Times.*

The restaurant deep in the country club was closed to regular members at that early hour. And regular members of that exclusive dining facility were of a covert group that few knew existed.

The American wing of the Cabal dined at those tables, and the Overseer liked his early morning privacy. He knew Yen Jee's chopper had arrived at the deep underground complex. She could wait. Would wait.

He noted *The New York Times* headlines covering the Malaysian Flight disappearance. The worldwide hunt was in progress to find the jet somewhere at the bottom of the vast ocean. He would make more calls today to control that story. The scent trail needed to be nurtured in subtle ways. It was always curious to him how easily humans could be deceived.

It was mainly Asians on that flight, he thought with an aloof snicker, and knew the rest of the world would lose interest quickly. The elevator suddenly chimed, startling him. He shook his head.

What fucker has the audacity to bother me at this early hour? he thought.

He looked up to see the elevator doors slide open and Aspelsin exited, proceeding directly toward him. Goldmeyer noted his watch, scampering to understand why this ambush-type behavior was happening... again. At that moment, he worked hard to keep his thoughts in check, as best he could, due to Aspelsin's tendency to read his mind.

Aspelsin, wearing his wide-brimmed black hat, approached and motioned with his gloved hand to one of Goldmeyer's chairs.

"Certainly, sir," Goldmeyer said.

Aspelsin settled in and watched as Goldmeyer put his newspaper down and looked up with a fake smile, waiting.

"We have one of our kind who has suddenly gone rogue," he whispered as Goldmeyer's smile faded. "We're not certain what he may do, but our best guess is that he might attempt to expose our agreements."

"To the Russians and Chinese?" Goldmeyer inquired.

"To the world," Aspelsin replied.

Goldmeyer sat back. The implications of the worldwide cover-up being disclosed were beyond a simple discussion. The entire trillion-dollar interplanetary corporate conglomerate working on reverse-engineering alien technology could be exposed. If the public found out, it could destroy the framework the Cabal had created, expanded, and protected over the last sixty-five years. The blood trail alone would certainly expose human rights abuses that the Cabal could not recover from. Including the Malaysian flight.

Goldmeyer looked up.

"Mr. Aspelsin, I believe you told me once that you have a hyper-dimensional beacon installed in all your Greys, and—"

Aspelsin raised a finger, cutting him off.

"Yes, well, I wouldn't be here if we could have taken care of this on our side."

"So, are you saying that the rogue has removed its geo-locator, sir?"

"It appears that way," Aspelsin said, looking at his leather-bound fingers. "I'll need your security teams to let me know of any strange occurrences on any level."

Goldmeyer slowly nodded.

"And is there any indication of how this entity would attempt to expose our agreements?" Goldmeyer asked. "Or do we have any information whatsoever on who it might be?"

S wizzle adjusted the throttles on the Gizmo in the moonlight, executing each movement of the vessel as he slowly turned the huge boat in close quarters.

Moss Landing was stunning at night. The moonlight on the water was like a flashlight... bathing the entire marina in its iridescent glow.

She watched him from the backseat of the Mustang. She had heard it before she opened her eyes. The thrumming of the Gizmo's engines had crept slowly into her consciousness. By the time she sat up and wiped the sleep from her eyes, it had rounded the inner buoy and was approaching the docks.

She could easily make out the outline of the dimly lit PT boat as it motored along the docks. Eighty-foot boats were rare, and the shape of the vintage PT boat even more so. It was just after nine, according to the clock on the dashboard.

Already wearing shorts and a tank top, she threw on black wooden clogs and made the short walk to a bench overlooking the marina. She could clearly see two people in the moonlight on the ship's deck.

Swizzle appeared to be an older man with a huge beard and wild hair, confidently standing at the wheel of the ship, making minute adjustments on the throttles. On the aft deck was a young black woman with a unique beehive hairdo and what appeared to be short-shorts and a bikini top.

And were those really tall platform heels? On a boat at night? And why-the-fuck-not! Vyla thought, admiring the young sensual goddess, escort or not.

A little night cruise for the right price? she thought curiously, considering her own body with its peculiar, ever-beckoning vices.

She watched as Swizzle deftly adjusted the throttles, executing every move of the ship as he slowly turned the huge vessel in close quarters, caught its drift just in time, and began backing it into the slip.

The sensual beehive smoked a cigarette and stared up at the stars. Vyla noticed that she didn't just casually gaze but seemed interested in a very distinct section of the southern hemisphere. No matter which way the boat turned, the woman adjusted to suit.

Swizzle completed all the docking chores, securing the bow and stern ropes. When the huge engines shut down, it was as if nature itself had gasped, finally free to breathe. The harbor filled with the sounds of lapping water against boat and dock, and the whispering waves beyond the harbor entrance. A gull wheeled about, squawking on a dock spar, spreading its wings in the brilliant moonlight.

The young woman walked Swizzle to the entrance of the bar and grill, where he went inside. There had been no kiss goodbye or even a hug.

Business, Vyla thought.

Beehive came up the steps to the parking lot and hopped in a vintage Mercedes convertible, and departed. Vyla had a quick thought that perhaps she had picked the wrong profession.

She did love physics, but damn, that was a nice ride, and it seemed like an interesting

130

life.

That assumption was followed immediately by the thought that she was assuming all of this about Beehive.

And why the fuck am I judging her, anyway?

She knew deep down this was her own little ego voice, attempting to put everybody in a box.

Okay, Miss Ego, you're just a judgmental bitch! she told herself, like that did any good.

She returned to the Mustang, grabbed her purse, and walked slowly, contemplating how she would approach the old man.

The weathered wood of Queen Helen's Revenge bar and grill looked ancient as she passed below the female pirate masthead, staring down at her with an eyepatch and a testy sailor's smile. Fried food and beer smelled up the packed joint as she entered and eyed Swizzle at the bar, sitting by himself.

A hard-drinking sailors' crowd reminded her of The Debacle, except these pirates were of the water tutelage. Hard rock from hidden speakers played just below howling laughter from sea-salted, ruddy cheeks and the weathered, cautious gazes of those more comfortable at sea.

Every pool table was adorned with beer mugs and empty whiskey shots. Vintage gas lamps glowed over booths fitted with wooden tables and trimmed with distressed brass edges. An oversized German Shepherd dozed like a hump carpet as a barkeep swept around the carefree mascot.

On the walls, flintlock muskets and pistols of the pirate domain were thrice-bolted to bronze plates, just in case a drunk sailor got any wild hankerings for savagery.

Swizzle was partway through a plate of fish and chips and a large mug of beer as Vyla saddled up on the stool next to him and ordered a beer.

Staring at the menu, she pulled the hair back from her face as Swizzle stared straight ahead, his mouth full of fish and chips.

"What's good here?" She asked, turning to him and smiling.

He turned, taking her in, chewing as he pointed down at his plate.

"That's the fish and chips, yeah?" She said, snickering at his stuffed mouth.

He nodded and took a sip of beer, wiping his wet, bearded mouth with a napkin.

"I highly recommend it," he replied in guttural British brogue. "First time here, aye?"

"Yeah, just heading back north," Vyla replied. "I heard this was a cool little harbor."

He watched her and nodded.

"You're sailing north?" he inquired.

"No, I drove up. Just heading back to Palo Alto. But I'd sure like to get a boat one day."

He nodded, turning back to his plate and overfilling his mouth once more. She squelched a chuckle.

"Are you a fisherman?" she asked.

He looked over, mouth bulging, then he raised a finger, gesturing to his mouth.

"Professional fish-and-chips eater?" she kidded.

He pointed at her and nodded.

"That's awesome," she said as her beer arrived.

She raised the frosted mug to him in toast, and he raised his, still working his mouthful. He then took a deep guzzle of beer. She watched the evolution, studying him, amused. He placed his mug down and slowly offered his huge hand.

"Swizzle," he said with a grin.

"Swizzle?" she said, smiling. "I'm Vyla."

"Right then... what do you do, Vyla?"

"Oh, I dream of being a professional fish-and-chips eater... but for now I'm a physicist."

He paused, nodding slowly.

"That's a nice surprise—the big type—or subatomic?"

She turned.

"Only a physicist says shit like that."

His eyebrows raised as he smiled, still chewing, then gulped down the rest of his beer.

"Oh, I had my years," he said, setting the mug down.

"The big or the small type?" She asked.

"Subatomic," he answered, slowly standing and pulling out his wallet.

"Alright then, I best be walking the plank back to my ship."

"Cool. You live on your boat?" she asked, hoping to delay him.

He nodded, pulling several bills from his wallet and laid them on the bar.

"Since you followed me here," he said with a gentle smile, "it's in slip forty-five. I'll leave the dock gate open for you."

She stared, shocked, as he counted his money and casually laid it on the bar. Placing his empty mug on top of the bills. A million thoughts cascaded through her mind in a split second.

How could he know? Did he see her on the bench in the dark? Impossible—he never looked her way. Had he seen her enter? No, she'd noticed his back was turned when she walked in. Was he guessing? Was this a pickup?

She made a quick decision to question his assumption.

"Um, I think you're—"

132

"I'm certainly not mistaken." he interrupted, reaching out his hand. Before she knew it, and almost as if she'd lost control, she grabbed his large, calloused hand. His shake was gentle.

"Slip forty-five and... not to worry. I may just be... on your side," he said with a humble look, releasing her hand.

He nodded at the bartender as he patted the wad of bills and turned away.

Still in shock, she watched him walk slowly to the German Shepherd still lying near the door, and bent over, giving the huge dog a gentle pat. He whispered to it, and it was clear the two were old friends. A moment later he stepped through the screen door and was gone.

Vyla felt the flip. Her nervous system—a strange flow of energy—was rolling inside her, like a sudden gush of wind. And that change happening... was way beyond her control.

S wizzle stepped into the summer night just outside Queen Helen's Revenge bar and grill.

He lit a cigarette and inhaled deeply, gazing over the harbor. As he exhaled, he felt a twinge, like radar. He knew to just feel it, see its source. He looked down at his shoes, then understood. He half-nodded.

"Of course... of course," he whispered to himself, taking another drag and looking up at the moon, thinking things through.

I nside the bar, Vyla was still tingling as the bartender made his way down to where she sat, bewildered, trying to regroup.

"You need another shot there, sailor?" he asked, his heavy Cockney accent cutting through the silence as he gathered Swizzle's tip.

"I could use a shot of something," she said, staring blankly ahead.

"Whiskey, rum, vodka—"

"Rum, please," she interrupted.

He smiled, pulling a bottle from beneath the bar and pouring her a shot, noting her stupefied gaze.

"Swashbuckled by Swizzle?" he asked with a smile as he re-corked the bottle.

She looked up.

"I feel so odd."

He leaned in.

"You're okay, mate. You're not the only one," he said with a curious smile, then disappeared through a curtain into the back kitchen.

She contemplated what he meant, then threw back the rum, placing the shot glass down. She swallowed and felt the burn. Noticed her fingers were shaking. She gripped the tiny cup with both hands, stopping the twitch, and looked around.

"Fish and chips," the bartender said as he reappeared with a paper plate.

"Can I get those to go?" she asked.

He paused and nodded, noticing she was still at sea.

"You bet, mate... back in a moment," he said and disappeared again.

And she was still adrift, swirling in a whirlpool.

"Damn... what in the hell," she thought, as she slowly came back to herself.

She knew one thing in her weirdly intuitive nature. She had just felt herself step through a dimension of sorts. She knew her gyro had just become uncaged. She was suddenly in new territory. Not new as in desired, but new as in strange and certainly more frightening. But here she was, and she had a job to do. And damn, she needed this job. Frightened or not.

C oncealed by darkness, the Twins sat in the stifling heat with their windows down.

They stared out of their rented white Impala, methodically eating their fast food while keeping an eye on the bar and grill. Just across the parking lot sat Vyla's black Mustang. In addition to the low-jack, the Twins had credentials that allowed them to convince the phone company to track her whereabouts. They were of national security interest, and the phone company promptly provided her cell phone tracking code.

They had watched her sitting on the bench as she surveilled the old man and the black girl. They made notes on the Gizmo, as well as the license plate of the vintage convertible Mercedes the beehive woman drove, and entered them into a logbook. They had watched as Vyla retrieved her purse from the black Mustang and entered the bar. The gravel parking lot had no exterior lights, which made it easy for the passenger Twin to walk around the Mustang, inspecting it through the windows. The driver scanned the parking lot during the operation. The passenger returned, and they resumed eating the last of their french fries.

Suddenly a sound outside. Both Twins turned as a limping old man, smoking a cigarette, approached through the darkness.

"Have you got spare change for an old sailor like me?" the old man said, coughing as he did so.

"Sorry, brother, we sure don't," said the Twin in the driver's seat, instinctively moving his hand to the .45 caliber magnum resting between the seats... because one could never be too sure.

"Nothing for an old sod like me, eh?" he said, stepping out of the darkness by the driver's window.

He bent down so that both men were in view. His face was weathered, with a silver earring and bushy eyebrows. His long beard smelled like cigarettes and beer, and it was him. The one she had followed.

By the time the Twins finally realized who and what he was, it was already too late.

Swizzle stared at them, neurally engaging both at once. Instantaneously, the overflow of chemicals flooded their systems. They both had the terrified instinct to react, to raise the magnum and blow him away, but the pathways to muscular action had already been severed chemically. Both Twins heard his voice in their minds.

"Right, mates, no need to shoot an old man, just... relax."

And despite their learned instincts, they both relaxed. And then, it was all okay.

Swizzle watched as both of their heads slowly fell back against their headrests. They stared at him but were not there. They were not dead either... just held in a neurological stupor. He leaned in, cigarette in mouth, exhaling smoke and speaking in a whisper as he reached between the seats.

"You won't remember this happened to you. You won't remember me. You won't remember an old sod asking you for spare change."

He retrieved the notebook, simultaneously removing the driver's hand from the magnum, leaving the gun right where it had been. He looked quickly at the cellphone mounted on the dash and saw a cellphone tracking app was open, showing the location of the bar and grill.

Next, he placed their open fast-food containers back in their laps and put their hands near those containers. Finally, he stood completely, opening the hardcover notebook as he pulled on his cigarette, thumbing through it in the bright moonlight.

He read references to Vyla's missed flight number, the Mustang's license number, low-jack number, Gizmo, slip forty-five, bearded captain, Black girl, possibly hooker, Mercedes license plate number, and more.

He gripped the two pages of notes and ripped them cleanly out. Double-checked his handiwork and put the notebook back beside the magnum. He looked up at both men, still staring at him with catatonic gazes.

He took a long pull on his cigarette and exhaled, then casually held the cigarette to the pages until they caught fire. He walked with the small flame, making his way to the Gizmo and then boarded, tossing the flaming notebook pages off the side, where they extinguished and sank in the moon's watery reflection.

He looked back one final time at the parking lot. He had laid in heavy on the surveillance team with his neural engagement. He didn't know who he was dealing with, and one could never be too sure. And Swizzle certainly wasn't... neither too sure... nor human.

T he moon, so huge beyond the docks, seemed to be beckoning as she found herself walking inexorably toward slip forty-five.

The unsettling thought that she was about to board the boat of someone she didn't know at all made her uneasy. She never did things like this. Ever.

I'm going crazy, she thought.

She was bewildered by why she had not told Swizzle to pack sand. But there had been something in the way he shook her hand and looked at her in the bar. A calming, reassured feeling, but one that was offset by her natural protective tendencies not to suddenly go boating with a complete stranger!

She had been taking more and more chances since this investigation kicked off, but perhaps it was her conversation with Peg that made her feel somewhat acquainted with Swizzle.

Peg made it seem like he had been around forever. She heard herself exhale.

Whatever, you're here now... deal.

Swizzle reached out a hand to help her board the Gizmo, carrying her bag of fish and chips.

"Welcome, Vyla," he said, gesturing toward the cockpit. "There's a small table inside for eating, or you can sit on the aft deck in the folding chairs."

"Thank you," she said, and made her way slowly toward the cockpit.

The huge motors below gently vibrated, and she could feel the potential energy of the ship, like it was a young quarter horse, anxious to race the night ocean. She descended the wooden steps into the vintage interior. She loved older boats, and this one was certainly rare. Custom woodwork in rich mahogany hues, polished and all original.

And that smell—old wood mixed with the unmistakable hint of diesel. She was reminded of working on Gloria with Papa during long summer days, and how the Stearman biplane with its vintage spruce spars had been manufactured about the same time as the first PT boats.

She stared at the wild array of gadgets on the cockpit shelf... a smorgasbord of technology and witchery. There were small handheld radar-looking widgets, radios, binoculars, and night vision scopes, mixed in with tarot cards, laser range finders, and, in the corner, a Haitian voodoo doll with its hand resting on a 1940s sextant used for celestial navigation. Beside the sextant sat an oscilloscope-like apparatus. Amidst all of this was a tightly bound roll of white sage... a smudge-stick.

Interspersed along the cockpit rail were *National Inquirer*-style magazines about UFOs. She thumbed through a couple of them before realizing the magazines covered two silver handprints... made completely of polished metal. The handprints were impressions of hands pressed into the metal while it was still molten. Above each finger was a tiny colored light.

Strange art, she thought. She re-covered the handprints with the magazines. Even though her views on UFOs had drastically changed in the last few days, she still saw these types of magazines as fluff. She was surprised that a physics professor would choose that type of fodder.

Next to the magazines sat a well-worn paperback... Bud Hopkins' *Intruder,* which she had seen on the Majestic brief as recommended books for extra reading. She noted the cover of the book had a UFO apparently lifting a woman... via a tractor beam, up to the UFO hovering in the night sky. From what she could tell, the book dealt with hypnotic regression and *missing time*... another UFO phenomenon mentioned in the brief summary.

She rejoined Swizzle up on deck as he pushed the throttles and slowly eased the ship toward the mouth of the harbor. As she passed by him at the helm, a glint caught her eye, and she saw next to the steering wheel... the same two silver hand impressions, made entirely of polished metal.

Must be his favorite art theme, she thought, as she sat in one of the well-worn lawn chairs behind the helm and unwrapped the plastic food bag. Her first bite of the fish and chips and.. damn! Something about them. Perfectly battered fresh fish with a sublime hint of salt and vinegar. She could get used to this.

He opened a small cooler by his feet, popped the top on a cold beer, and handed it back to her while simultaneously raising a radio transmitter.

"Moss Harbor—Gizmo is outbound—slip forty-five—with A.T.I.S. and updates."

A squeal of static crackled from the radio.

"Copy, Gismo—your traffic is research vessel Tri-star Two-five—one-two-zero feet—departing slip two-two—will be following you outbound—right traffic."

He picked up his binoculars and glassed the harbor behind Gizmo. The Tri-Star was rounding its dock spar.

"Moss Harbor, copy all—Tri-Star in sight—thank you and good night."

He guided Gizmo out of the harbor entrance and into Monterey Bay. Vyla could see the red, green, and yellow lights of the Tri-Star as it exited the harbor, quickly gaining speed, turning south toward Monterey at a good clip. Even in the moonlight, she could see several rotating radar dishes and antennas.

Swizzle lit a cigar and upped the throttles, turning north toward Santa Cruz. She could feel the supercharged V-12s kick up a notch as the wind blew back her hair. She was about to ask how fast the boat would go, but before she spoke, Swizzle raised a finger to his lips. She stopped and looked around the ship, wondering why he shushed her. Then it hit her again.

How did he even know that she was about to speak?

Since first meeting him at the bar, he had done this repeatedly. But then she remembered Peg talking about Swizzle's weird way. She knew she had some of this trait—a preternatural sense of knowing things about people sometimes. But his was next-level. Being a professor of subatomic physics required some heavy-duty smarts. All this stuff made her realize how depleted she was. The week had been a gauntlet. Tonight would be whatever it would be, and right now, she was on a boat sailing in the moonlight.

Why not enjoy the moment?

She watched as he pulled on his cigar and worked the wheel, as the ship moved easily through the night breeze. She felt the front of the boat drop slowly and glide as Swizzle pulled the throttles back and shut off the engines.

Monterey Bay was calm for such a huge body of water. Moonlight and sea sounds flooded her senses as the boat coasted slowly, rocking with the waves lapping against the bow.

He pressed a button on the console, and she stared in amazement as formerly hidden antennas of every type suddenly extended all over the boat. Like some form of wild hairs rising, the wires extended off the edge of the ship, waving in the light breeze. There were silver and black, long and short, fat and hair-thin. The entire perimeter of the ship now had antennae pointing out, bow to stern.

He half-smiled at her surprise, then bent down and picked up a portable scanner and began walking the perimeter of the entire deck, still smoking his cigar. With each step he made a slow circle, waving the scanner slowly up and down like he was trying to detect a radio wave.

She watched him... eating her fish and chips, and his actions brought her back to discussing this boat with Chief Day and how he had mentioned that it was right below all the UAP action and that the boat had arrived just before the wave of UAPs showed up.

"Four-days travel from Moss Landing," Day had said. "How would that boat even know how to find the strike group?"

Swizzle approached, still circling as he slowly made his way back to her—a high-tech pirate dork with his Noah beard, sandals, short pants, tank top, and cigar.

"We are clear," he finally said. "There is no recording device pointed at this boat, and no bugs on board."

He looked up at the stars through the device.

"And currently, there are no drones overhead."

She stood, wrapping up the meal and placing it beside her chair as she watched Swizzle kneel and place his scanner back on the deck.

"If this thing starts beeping, shut up immediately."

She mock-saluted him.

"Yes, sir... may I have another, sir?" she whispered.

Swizzle looked at her and chuckled under his breath.

"It's funny... till it's not," he said matter-of-factly.

This reminded her of the Twins on her COD flight departing the carrier.

"Are you expecting to be recorded?" she asked.

He looked at her as if he had done a favor for both of them. Then he grabbed a fishing pole, walked to the edge, cast out his bait and cork, and placed his rod in a holder on the rail.

Chief Day had mentioned *UFO conspiracy freaks.* Those paranoid types obsessed with anything UFO-related. Vyla stared at Swizzle, wondering if he fit the bill.

He watched his pole for a moment, then sat back in the lawn chair, popping open a cold beer from the cooler next to him. His eyes were on the cork floating in moonlight, a few feet from the Gizmo as it sauntered outbound.

"What are you going for with that?" she asked.

"Rockfish," he said, smiling. "They're not too gamey. Quite tasty when grilled with a bit of garlic and butter."

She nodded, studying him as he took a guzzle of beer, set it down, pulled on his cigar, then blew a smoke-ring and watched as it grew... rising over the rail into the moonlight.

"So, what can I do for you, Vyla?"

"I beg your pardon," she said, perplexed.

He looked askance at her, then turned forward, back to his cork in the moonlight.

"Right then, you were scanned when you came aboard, and you register as human. So, perhaps with a federal agency?"

She smiled, not fully understanding but flowing with her assessment that he was a UFO conspiracy nut.

"Yes, I'm—well, I'm with a company that monitors certain things the Navy does," she said. "And I saw that you were near the battle group off San Diego last week?"

"Ah," he said. "You saw my ship out there?"

"The Princeton had you on radar," she said.

"The SPY-3 picked me up? Okay, right, fair enough," he said. "Yeah, I like to watch their exercises."

"You mean the Navy exercises?" she asked, staring intently at him.

He turned and locked eyes with her.

"Yeah, I'm kind of a nut that way—always following the Navy—wherever they go."

"That's an awfully long way to travel from here to there. What—four days of motoring?" she inquired.

He slowly nodded and ashed his cigar over the side.

"That is exactly right," he said.

"May I inquire how you located the strike group?" she asked.

"It's quite easy—there are lots of sightings of U.S. Navy ships—especially when it's an entire battle group."

"So, you were not out there for any other purpose?" she asked.

He turned slightly, pulling on his cigar. She felt herself getting bored with the game.

"So, all those UFO magazines and books in your cockpit—what's that all about?" she said, casually eating a piece of fish. "Your little four-day excursion had nothing to do with UFOs?"

He seemed to freeze on this one, still smoking but contemplating his answer.

"Oh, I just read that rubbish when I'm motoring along, ghosting the strike group."

"Well, you certainly have a lot of it," she said, knowing she was getting nowhere.

She wanted to get on the road to Palo Alto. It had been too much cat and mouse since Yen Jee hired her, and this was just another part of the game.

"I can take you back?" Swizzle said. "You're tired... you probably want to get home?"

She felt the hair on the back of her neck stand up.

"How did you just do that?" she blurted. "How the fuck did you even know what I was thinking?!"

Swizzle stared at his cork as she continued.

"And how did you know I was following you?"

She glared, no longer caring.

She slowly stood.

"And for that matter, who the fuck are you?!"

He turned and was clearly taken aback, raising his eyebrows at her sudden outburst. When she was given the investigator mission, she decided to read some articles on investigative techniques, and Numero-Uno was to never get in a hurry, which, of course, went against everything she was... an impatient, headstrong risk-taker. At that moment, staring at Swizzle, she was fully smoked. Nothing left in the tank. And it was right then... the full download hit her. A sudden, terrifying epiphany.

She gripped the rail, turning away from him, and tried to quell her panic. Steadying herself, she heard herself hyperventilating.

"Oh, my God!" she whispered to herself, getting it all too fast. She felt she might puke. Two long breaths.

Come on, baby, come on! Calm down!

She felt her body shaking as her words had no effect. Then it happened. Something washed over her. She suddenly wasn't scared. Wasn't even freaked out. She heard him behind her... stand and grab his pole. She slowly turned around and calmly watched the old man gently pulling in his line, seeing if he had a fish. He placed the rod back in its holder and sat back down.

"You just did that too?" she asked. "Made me feel calm?"

He looked over slightly, then went back to concentrating on his cork.

She walked slowly toward him and sat down in the lawn chair next to him, studying him until he quit fiddling. He finally looked down at his cigar, flicked the hot ash off the deck, took another long pull, and exhaled, all the while not looking at her.

"Why did you just reveal yourself to me?" she said. "Of all the people you could choose... you don't even know who I am?"

He looked over momentarily and saw that she had tears in her eyes.

"You want to get back to Palo Alto and your friends," he said softly.

She slowly nodded, the tears now streaming.

"I'm not going to hurt you," he said. "I sensed an opportunity when I felt you—when you were surveilling me with my friend earlier tonight."

"Is she one too?" Vyla said, barely audible through her tears.

His eyes now held almost a shyness as he slowly nodded.

"Oh!" Her voice escaped through tears. "I don't know if I can handle all this right now."

"Right," he said humbly, and stood. "I'll take you back."

"Thank you." She whispered, wiping away tears.

He stepped to the wheel, turned the key, and the three supercharged Packard V-12s thundered to life below them in the midships. She gripped the lawn chair as he pushed the throttles and turned Gizmo back toward Moss Landing.

Surreal wasn't quite strong enough for this moment, she thought.

Had she not been privy to everything she'd just witnessed with the strike group, she certainly would not have believed that this apparently sweet old man, who appeared to be fully human, was actually not. He continued to smoke his cigar as they motored along, occasionally looking back over his shoulder as if to reassure her. Thousands of questions went through her mind, but some were at the forefront...

namely, his agenda.

Why me?

As she watched him drive the boat, she realized that all these questions were already being addressed. Supposedly. Since he obviously could read her mind, her attempting to put it all together seemed frivolous.

"Wait! Stop the boat!" she yelled.

He eased the throttles back as Gizmo came off the plane and glided forward. He looked over his shoulder—cigar in mouth—a questioning look on his face.

"You really want me to stop?" he asked.

She nodded, sniffling. He turned the key off, and Gizmo transitioned into a silent magic carpet, gliding effortlessly forward in the still bay, moonlit and stunning. She watched as he turned around and took a seat. He stared out to sea, giving her time to regroup.

"Do all aliens like cigars?" she asked.

He turned slightly, giving her a smile as she suddenly got a look.

"Oh, that's right, you already know what I'm going to ask. So, should I just think the thought?"

"That's up to you," he replied.

"So, all those questions I was contemplating asking you a minute ago... would you... would you address the main ones?"

He looked down at his cigar.

"Hmm," he said, contemplating.

She now saw in his eyes something she hadn't even remotely noticed before... a secret not shared that he was eager to express.

Yay, for preternatural instincts! she told herself.

At this thought, he looked up and snickered her way.

"Whoops," she said. "Sorry, go ahead... that was my ego telling me how spot-on my capabilities are."

He smiled at her for a long moment, his eyes humble and sweet. And for a split second, Papa's sweet face was there too. She felt her heart go to her throat. He looked down at his hands and spoke softly.

"And that is why we are sitting here," he said humbly. "I sensed a kindred soul of sorts in you."

She fought tears watching him.

"My secret," he whispered, "and the agenda of my kind is complicated."

Four rapid beeps from the scanner made both of them jump. He raised his hand to her. *Quiet!* He stood, picked up the scanner and turned toward the south... then looked back at his scanner... and looked up again.

He shot a quick glance at her on his way to the helm and whispered,

"Tri-Star... Russian spy ship."

Then, he cranked the engines and brought the throttles smoothly forward. She held fast to the bolted-down lawn chair as Gizmo was up on the plane in seconds, racing toward Moss Landing. She watched as he monitored the scanner next to him as they flew along the glassy surface. He looked back and yelled to her.

"They've not followed me in years, so that means..."

He looked at her, and then at the Tri-Star.

Wow, she thought, shaking her head as another facet of her new world order presented itself.

There it was. No doubt about it. That shift in her psyche that she felt in the bar was now coming home to roost. Through this old man alien driving them home, she knew that the transition was now complete. She had undoubtedly separated from the woman that was her a week ago. She would never go back to that innocent physicist who just needed a job. If she didn't live another day, this past week had been enough to fulfill a lifetime. As they raced along, not having all the answers to her surreal new relationship with Swizzle didn't matter. It just didn't matter. The answers would come when they did.

The fact that Swizzle had come along was enough. In that wild moment, exhausted beyond description, she allowed herself to feel the lovely night wind of Earth blowing back her hair. She thought of her Papa and her stepmom, Dah, and then allowed herself to feel her real mother, older brother, and dad. And how, for some reason, at this moment, it seemed okay. She felt her heart stepping forward and knew it was not scared or anxious, but instead, it was becoming expansive. A thing it did whenever it sensed love, and certainly in this moment... the grace all around her.

Chapter Fifteen

The Mexican cartels had a hit out on Dr. Andre Enzensberger, so a contingent of U.S. Secret Service patrolled around his home, near the Berkeley campus.

The Secret Service was a gift from the U.S. government, who had tried to buy his ground-penetrating radar invention several times. But Andre had refused. He wasn't U.S. born and raised, but he loved America and what it stood for and had become a U.S. citizen years ago, when he began teaching at Berkeley. And still he wouldn't sell... even when he stood in the Oval Office, he had refused the President, face-to-face.

Andre was a complete American patriot, and proud of it, but as a scientist, he had valid concerns about his device in the wrong hands.

He didn't think the world was quite ready for his invention. He was the only one who could read its algorithms and had designed the software and the device by deciphering Tesla's Colorado Springs wave experiments, and then once tested, expanded upon it, to include algorithmic feedback.

So, the Secret Service boys were there as insurance. They didn't give a toss about Andre... but his device was gold, and not just for the corporate treasure hunters.

The ground-penetrating, low-frequency, back-scattered, wave-pattern radar produced a 3D image of whatever was below it. A volumetric representation that was 400 times more detailed than a Cat-scan. And the waves that came back to him provided not only a 3D image of what was below, but a detailed elemental examination of everything the waves hit as well.

Not only could Andre decipher the size and shape of what his device was over, he also knew immediately if the object was in the periodic table of elements or made up of unknown elements—like from *elsewhere,* otherworldly—not registered in human science.

The first time the U.S. utilized his services, he had saved a large U.S. port city that was destined to be nuked. They had hastily flown him and his device to the Suez Canal, where, after a short briefing, he was loaded into a Black Sikorsky S-92. A nine-seater that raced out over the canal. Upon locating their target—a long-range oil tanker—his team positioned the Sikorsky a quarter mile away at six-thousand feet, hovering at a steady twenty-knots forward speed to keep pace with the tanker.

From the Sikorsky's posh interior, he controlled his device, which had been mounted on a drone. The long-range oil tanker carried a heavy load of sweet crude in its belly—400,000 barrels weighing down the enormous ship. Within seconds of the drone flying over the tanker, Andre called out via headset that there appeared to be a fifty-gallon oil drum sunk at the bottom of the ship's oil reservoir, as if to hide it.

"What's in the drum?" inquired the U.S. agent, across from Andre in the overview Sikorsky

"There's a sealed 12-inch box within the oil drum." Andre said, in his German brogue, watching his laptop as he controlled the drone.

"In the sealed box is another 6-inch sealed box. Inside this box is a 4-inch block of Plutonium 239."

The US agent shot a hard glance at him, and the operation was over that fast. Only a week after the oil tanker had been isolated in the open ocean and the plutonium recovered, did Andre get his call that would result in the complete description of every tunnel the Mexican cartels were working into the United States. From a single flyover of the entire U.S. border, Andre was able to tell U.S. agents what products, drugs, weapons and humans were being trafficked in both directions.

But apparently, the Mexican government was also infiltrated by the cartels. When the news came out that all their operations were known... the hit order came out for Dr. Andre Enzensberger.

But Andre wasn't scared of the hit order. He feared what he knew about his invention. He had seen things that absolutely shook him to his foundations. Things he shared with no one.

The waves that emanated at super-low frequencies from his device... didn't stop giving information when they penetrated the earth and hit a target. The design of algorithms was to process everything the wave hit—and then—*keep going.* That was the little thing that he didn't let anyone know.

He already had a complete picture of every cavity and every element within the planet, and many of those elements were not in the periodic table, but much more shocking—were the cavities within the earth—some of which were thousands of cubic miles in size. And what some of them contained... was simply beyond his comprehension.

Even if his radar was mounted electronically within his cell phone, which he had done, the system could literally see... *through* the planet.

And what was there, everywhere around the planet, from the surface to the center, in the seven seas and below them—were things that he tried to grapple with—things not possible.

Coming in full force with the joy of his invention was the new knowledge that all on his birth planet was not as it seemed. His old belief systems were now shattered—broken to the very core. He knew there was only one way to handle his new predicament...

He had to tell someone.

Moss Landing Harbor in Monterey Bay, California, was quiet by the time Gizmo was secured back in its slip.

Vyla watched Swizzle as he finished the last tie off and then stepped onto the tattered dock surrounding slip forty-five. She had mentioned as they came into port that she wanted more time. Swizzle had dictated the terms. There would be no phone calls, and no electronic communication whatsoever. Now, as she was about to say goodbye, he approached slowly... almost shyly.

"Don't worry, they're not dead," he said. "You'll just have a bit of a head start on your way home."

"Who's not dead?" she asked, alarmed. "What are you talking about?"

"Your surveillance team."

She stared, shocked.

How did they find her? she wondered.

Swizzle looked askance at her. His *"Really?"* gaze was a cold slap, and she realized again how far behind the power curve she was in this new Majestic realm. He tried to ease her mind at that moment, as he had certainly read it.

"You're a scientist, for fuck's sake. You're not supposed to know all the ways of surveillance teams, but you might want to start paying attention," he said with a hint of a smile.

"Right," she whispered.

"And you can count on the fact that your cell phone is being tracked at all times when at the Majestic level. But, if you turn it off, you make it a lot less easy for those cheeky bastards that are following you."

She quickly turned her phone off.

"I'm sorry," she said.

He looked to the moon.

"And not just the American team up there in the white car, or the Russian or Chinese teams, but off-world surveillance as well... from a multitude of alien races."

He slowly looked her way as she stared, dumbstruck, in her new awareness.

"Since your Majestic status is the absolute top of the heap, when you are placed in that category, everyone participating with the Earth's authorities are basically put on alert. You'll find that nothing is sacred."

"Hence the whole Gizmo antenna surveillance dance?" she asked.

He shrugged and told her that future meetings with him would have to be prearranged and that she would have to be patient despite that personal issue.

"Whatever," she muttered, looking away, and realized how incredibly nuanced his lighthearted humor was.

He smiled and quietly explained that he didn't use electronics for communication—except in dire emergencies. And when she was ready for more information, she should leave both visors in her truck down.

"How do you know I have a truck?" she asked.

He stared.

"Well, I just assumed a blonde wearing clogs might like 2003 Chevy Silverados—"

"Okay, okay, God-dammit," she said, cutting him off, and fighting her mean ego voice.

Yeah, let's quit asking questions of an alien that already knew you were following him!

At this, she saw Swizzle's body quake in silent laughter as he turned away. But before she knew it, tears were flowing again, and she knew he didn't induce them. She was simply exhausted and overwhelmed.

He politely stared out at the moonlit water, allowing her a quiet moment to regroup. Then she felt him and heard a whisper—but not out loud. It was in her mind and with her own voice. But the dynamics—the way it was said—would have never come from her. And the phrasing was not hers. She then knew it was him whispering to her deep inside.

"Perhaps you should save what's left for your drive north. You have come forward many steps in the last week. And there is much more to bring you into the now of all

that is at stake."

Tears were already streaming as her first experience of telepathy coursed through her. It was so sublime—like velvet—and in her own voice, as if to reassure her. She watched him as he stared into the moonlit water. This bearded, ruddy-faced old man had gifted her. She wanted to give him a hug—or someone a hug. He held out his hands, and she took them. They locked eyes—and again it was for a moment... Papa's gentle face—and then it was Swizzle, and on every level, to her deepest self, she knew she was safe. It was enough. It was more than enough. She softly whispered, fighting tears,

"Thank you."

He nodded and watched her walk slowly up the moonlit dock.

She was cruising north in the black Mustang, only a few miles out of Moss Landing.

And now, she understood what Swizzle meant when he said he had *disabled them.* Before climbing into the Mustang, she had crept into the dark and snuck up behind their white Impala. She couldn't believe the sight. The Twins had clearly been switched off—their eyes open but not present. She looked around the dark parking lot, where only a few cars were sparsely separated. Then she looked back down at Gizmo in the docks. She then turned back to the Twins, memorizing their faces. Clearly military in bearing. Only then did she notice that the driver had his hand near a large gun between the seats.

Holy shit! she thought and realized just how incredibly deadly this new realm was.

Okay, you're not in fucking Kansas anymore, Dorothy! she thought as she took one last look at the two big men and managed a chuckle as she walked away. They were bad-boy military operators, for sure, but they had just been zapped by an old-man alien.

How about that? Bitches, she thought, shaking her head as she climbed into the Mustang and fired it up.

She slowly made her way to Highway One north, relieved on some level that her own surveillance boys weren't dead. She wouldn't be able to handle dead people in front of her. Even if they didn't have her best interests in mind, she didn't care. She wasn't vengeful in that way. Humans were valuable to her—even if they were mean or evil. They were redeemable. And, even if she was wrong about that, she didn't give a damn. It was her way... and she was sticking to it.

She was calmer now and pushed her new favorite button, lowering the top into the warm night. Under the stars, her hair blew back. She was content to have left

Moss Landing, free of surveillance. But then caught herself, realizing she could no longer control if she was being watched. In this new realm, she was determined not to live by their rules of paranoia and fear. She would hold ground in her quiet center, where there were no demands. No future or past. Only essence.

She breathed a few times as she went deep within—reaching her hand up into the warm night air and opened her fingers to the stars, sparkling and magnificent.

Teebeck stared at the Twins in the dark parking lot.

They slept—with eyes open—in the front seats. It had been hours since their last check-in. He was amazed at their switched-off state and knew they had been caught off guard. But these two operators were consummate pros, never to be simultaneously brain-locked. Whatever—or whoever—had ensnared them was fast. And certainly not human.

He put out an immediate notification to Aspelsin, as was protocol, whenever alien intervention occurred with security teams. By the time Teebeck departed, Aspelsin had pulled up in a black sedan as the Twins were slowly coming out of their stupor. Aspelsin watched Teebeck motor away and then turned to the groggy Twins, who were attempting to reorient themselves.

"Follow me," Aspelsin said flatly out his window, and pulled out.

As the Twins followed him, they noticed the empty space where the black Mustang had been. Both cars were on the highway moments later. The Twins rode in silence as they followed Mr. A. along the dark highway. They had been tasked with security missions by him in the past and were just as wary of him as all other top-level operators. But as former Navy SEALs, they didn't ask questions about strange individuals above their pay grade.

They drove, perplexed. Neither had ever fallen asleep on a watch. The Twins, Case, and Will, though almost identical, were not related. An odd confluence had brought them together in SEAL training, where their unit had immediately dubbed them *The Twins*. They had become best friends, and as a team they were unique in their skill sets—bringing more to the table than most pairings in Special Warfare.

Both had completed two tours before opting for the more lucrative world of private security. Will had a wife and two little boys. Case was single. Special Warfare operators were experts in a multitude of disciplines, from weapons to any type of hand-to-hand combat, as well as tactical training from parachuting to handling explosives of all types. Their paths had crossed again at the Defense Language Institute, where Will earned fluency in Arabic and Case in Russian. But in this moment, both rode in silence.

They knew something strange had taken place. The bewildering feeling of not knowing where the last few hours had gone weighed on them. Both suspected *Missing Time* had occurred. And they were well aware of the phenomenon. When first hired, they had been monitored by Aspelsin's teams for a two-year probation. The Twins knew JRAD was a huge military contractor known for black projects above top-secret. The literature in attaining their Ultra-Top Secret, Cosmic Q, Level-23 clearances had them reading all things related to the various phenomena associated with unidentified and otherworldly craft. This included all races and types of alien entities, with all their possible agendas—from geopolitical to the occult.

The brief also covered everything currently known regarding common occurrences, such as abductees worldwide reporting *Missing Time* and surgical or reproductive procedures performed against their wills. Many reported post-abduction marks or scars, as well as locator nodes discovered during post-abduction pain.

The Twins' security position delineated that surveillance of *otherworldly persons of interest* might be required. Case and Will had twice been tasked by Mr. A to keep tabs on a particularly strange individual. And though Mr. A did not outright tell them, both had a sense they were watching a subject that only appeared human. As the two men rode in silence, the sudden awareness of having been *neurally engaged* and *put to sleep* seemed impossible.

T hey followed Aspelsin into an all-night diner and sat opposite him in a back corner booth.

Even in the relative calm of the packed diner, the Twins were wary of him. Both did their best not to notice his scar while speaking to him. In their private discussions, the Twins hinted to each other about him in roundabout ways—never verbalizing their distaste overtly.

For two hours, he questioned them thoroughly about anything they could remember about what happened before *Missing Time*. The notebook lay open on the table between the three of them, its missing pages leaving them with no sequence of events. They remembered tracking Vyla to the parking lot and arriving in darkness around 8 p.m. They watched her enter the bar and ate their fast food while preparing for an all-night surveillance. The next thing they knew, Mr. A was waking them up.

Aspelsin watched in silence as they tried to recollect their sequence of getting fast food and using the cell tracker, which led them to Moss Landing. Case remembered placing his magnum in the center console to be more comfortable while he ate. Will recalled writing the cell-tracking number in the notebook and placing it between the seats, as they always did.

"Mr. A, do we know where Dr. Kells—"

"Palo Alto, hopefully," Aspelsin said, cutting him off. "She returned the Mustang to San Francisco Airport four hours ago."

The Twins nodded, embarrassed.

"Well, we'll get right on it, sir," Case said.

"No, that won't be necessary."

Aspelsin slid the empty notebook toward them.

"I need to know what happened tonight. I want both of you to fly out tonight on the company jet. We'll conduct a hypnotic regression session. Then, you'll fly back here in the early morning and resume your surveillance in Palo Alto."

The Twins looked at each other nervously and then back at Aspelsin.

"What was the reason Dr. Kells went to the harbor in the first place?" Aspelsin inquired.

The Twins slowly wagged their heads.

"Well, she had met a young woman here on her way north, and perhaps she had stopped specifically to see her?" Case offered.

Aspelsin stared with no affect, then stood, placing cash on the table. Case noticed Mr. A's skin-tight, black leather gloves and realized he had never seen the man's hands in all their various meetings.

"I'll watch Dr. Kells tonight and expect you two to be back on surveillance by morning."

They watched Mr A. depart as Will exhaled his disgust.

"Shut the fuck up, bro. Just remember you get paid like a king," Case said, sipping his coffee.

"I don't want to do fucking hypnosis. That's bullshit," Will said.

"That sounds very Black of you," Case teased.

"Yeah, well, fuck you and all the ghost shit."

Case turned to him.

"Yeah, bro, it's all poltergeist bullshit," Case said. "But I'm gonna shoot the ghost motherfucker who shut off my brain, and regression may be the only way I can find him."

Will raised his index finger slowly and wagged it—like hypnosis.

"You're getting sleepy, Case—very sleepy."

Case glared.

"Fuck you."

Will stifled a laugh.

"Shit, bro, for all you know, Ol' poltergeist might have got you pregnant."

Case stared straight ahead.

"Will, you're a big fuckin' asshole, you know that?"

Will chuckled, and then the smile faded. They sat in silence after that. For all their bravado, both were now coming out of their shock. The hard truth of *Missing Time* was seeping in. Both were pros at assessing enemy weaknesses and exploiting those to their advantage. Seals were considered elite in all situations regarding surveillance and warfare. Trained to acknowledge fear yet never show it. But the tables had turned. An enemy had just exploited them for their greatest weakness. A weakness not fixable with any amount of training. No change of strategy would help. They now knew they were completely vulnerable on every level. Basically *fucked...* but you couldn't blame them.

They were only human.

U nderground in the Maryland countryside, Yen Jee departed her chopper and was met by two heavily armed, black-clad operatives.

They descended many levels and exited to a hallway lined with shiny black walls that showed Cuneiform writing inlaid. Entering the luxury waiting area, Yen looked at the familiar oak door on the far side.

Both cloned operators performed retinal scans at the same time. The oak door glided open, revealing the Overseer leaning on the front of his desk, reading a briefing folder. The clones stayed in the waiting area as Yen entered.

Jack Goldmeyer had heard the oak door opening, but still didn't lift his head from the file he was immersed in. The barrel-chested man with grey hair and a custom Italian suit towered over the approaching Yen Jee as she nervously stepped forward. Still, he did not look up.

She heard the oak door close and the electronic locking mechanism behind her, and yet Goldmeyer did not acknowledge her. She waited a full minute, alternately looking up at him and over at the younger, well-dressed man on the nearby couch.

Chernal Teebeck was adorned in his normal custom-fit capital-style suit with bow tie and was staring at her. Yen knew him from other occasions, and yet Teebeck gave no quarter in his vigilant stare, considering all who were near the Overseer a potential threat. His depraved gaze, still to this day, unnerved her, and she looked away.

Normally, that would have been enough for some relief, but it was then that she noticed the same stare coming from the opposite side of the room. Somehow, she had missed it when she first walked in. Standing against the opposite wall, making no sound at all, was Teebeck's clone. That unit was just as depraved-looking and perhaps even more disturbing as it stared at her with no affect. It stood motionless, eyes fixed on her. The only difference was the real Teebeck had a black bow tie, and his clone wore deep maroon.

Yen was prepared for Mr. Goldmeyer to open with something about the test flight, and she was ready to defend her company's actions. But he came at her with a question that had nothing to do with two days ago, throwing her strategy out the window.

"Miss Jee," Goldmeyer said with a quiet intensity. "Can you please enlighten me as to why you upgraded your new employee to a Majestic clearance for the UAP investigation?"

His question reminded her that the Overseer never gave a scientist the respect of calling them *"Doctor."* Yen looked down quickly and reached into her briefcase, nervously producing an 8x10 photo.

"Yes, sir," she replied anxiously. "I've wanted to introduce her to how UAPs fly—"

Goldmeyer yanked the photo out of Yen's hand, cutting her off.

"Her?" he said with a terse whisper.

"This is your investigator?" he continued. "A woman?"

Goldmeyer turned the picture of Vyla toward Teebeck.

"You see this, Teebeck?"

Teebeck looked over momentarily.

"I do, sir," he replied in his high English accent.

Yen nervously looked away, only to see Teebeck's clone staring at her. Goldmeyer watched, placing his hands on the desk behind him with the photo wedged between two fingers.

"Please tell me, Miss Jee, that this Vyla Kells is a former military officer?"

"Well, no, sir, she's—"

"Stop!" he seethed in a whisper.

"Just stop."

He sailed the picture back at Yen, which flew past her, spinning onto the floor behind her. She started to turn as if to retrieve it.

"Stop!" he said again in a terse whisper. "You do understand that command?"

Yen froze.

"Yes... yes, I do, sir," she whispered, staring at the floor.

"Good," he whispered, disdainfully looking her over.

"This... Vyla Kells is your investigator on the White House UAP incident?"

Yen looked up, nodding.

"She has a Ph.D. in physics—"

"I don't care if she's a goddamn Rhodes scholar or a fucking school janitor," he said, cutting her off. "When that investigation hits my desk, it better be a complete and utter denial that any UAP was seen near that battle group. Is that clear?"

Yen nodded.

"Yes, sir."

"Miss Jee, I know you will make it clear to this Vyla Kells that if she validates any part of what the pilots said happened or leaks any information about the UAP investigation, she will then witness a wet room, firsthand."

Yen stared.

"You do understand what a wet room is, Miss Jee?"

Yen nodded. "Yes."

"Tell me what happens there, Miss Jee?"

"Well, sir, that's where people are interrogated and—"

"And what, Miss Jee?"

"I don't know, sir."

Goldmeyer looked at his fingernails and spoke in a whisper.

"I think you do."

Yen didn't move, looking down anxiously.

"Is there something on the carpet you are curious about, Miss Jee?"

"No, sir," she said, forcing herself to look up as he continued in a whisper.

"As you well know, we've always got your company's best interest in mind, Miss Jee, and I'm certain you'll be vigilant with Vyla Kells to ensure that she delivers a product to the White House that is also in our best interests."

Yen nodded nervously.

"Yes, of course, sir."

Goldmeyer watched her closely and sucked his teeth. Then, picked up another folder and opened it.

"Four crashes in two years, Miss Jee?" he said, staring at the folder while leaning on his desk. "That's a new record for killing test pilots."

He looked up calmly, though the tick in his eye betrayed a savagery about to explode.

"Yes, sir," she replied anxiously. "I now think we've made a breakthrough with understanding what's required to fly the Widow."

Goldmeyer gently laid the briefing folder on his desk and opened both hands to her.

"Well, that's fantastic news, Miss Jee. Please... do tell."

"I think I've finally found someone that might be a match with the ship."

"A match with the ship?" he whispered sarcastically, staring evenly at her.

"Yes, sir, you see, the alien ship is a living—a living conveyance, and if the pilot is not matched, then—"

"Then, they fucking die," he hissed, cutting her off.

She looked up as he continued in a sarcastic whisper.

"It explodes their fucking brains all over the cockpit, doesn't it, Miss Jee? And the viscera splatters across the cameras for our I.C.C. executive guests to watch all your progress?" he said, slightly nodding. "Yes, I understand your little dilemma—Miss Jee—you've just made mincemeat of four of our best military test pilots."

Yen's head was down.

"Is there something on the floor, Miss Jee?"

"No... no, sir," she said, then looked up.

"Well, sir, that's the reason why I had Dr. Kells upgraded. She's a—"

"Stop," he said, cutting her off. "You're about to tell me that she is a former military test pilot?"

"Well, sir, she's not a test pilot, she's a—"

"Please," Goldmeyer said, raising his hand and then putting his fingers to his eyes.

"Well, no, sir, she's... she does yoga and is spiritual." Yen said. "We think she may interface with the ship. It's Dr. Kells... she's—uh, actually—"

Goldmeyer looked up, beginning a whispered, maniacal laugh as Yen continued.

"She does aerobatics—"

"Stop!" he whispered.

Yen froze.

"Vyla Kells? Your investigator? Is now going to attempt to fly the Widow... that four fucking top-rated military test pilots could not fly?"

Yen stared as Goldmeyer broke into a smile.

"Oh, good," he said, looking her over. "This—Vyla Kells, Miss Jee... are you just wanting to see what it's like—to have female brains and viscera—exploded all over the Widow's cockpit? Adding a little gender levity, perhaps?"

Yen looked to the side and whispered,

"She knows how to fly biplanes."

Goldmeyer touched his forehead with both hands sarcastically.

"Of course she does. And therefore, since the Widow—an alien antigravity flying saucer—somehow looks and performs like a biplane... Vyla Kells is a perfect candidate?"

Yen raised her hand to speak.

"Put your hand down," he seethed.

Yen did so.

"Let me be abundantly clear to you, Miss Jee. She'd better make that alien saucer fly. I'm giving you three weeks before the next test flight."

Yen stared as he continued under his breath.

"Get that fucking ship in the air, or I'll award that alien technology to a company that can."

"Yes, sir."

"Would you like to retrieve your picture, Miss Jee?"

"Yes, sir," she whispered.

"By all means," he whispered, gesturing to the floor.

Yen turned and anxiously grabbed the photo, placing it in her briefcase. He watched her shaking fingers work the clasp of her briefcase, and the glistening of her diamond watchband caught his eye.

"Finally, Miss Jee," he began in a whisper,

"The security breach we encountered at your facility in Japan, do you remember that?"

She looked up to see him with a tight-lipped smile, his leathery skin a red mass of bulging veins.

"Yes, sir. I was informed that the matter had been handled by the head of my security."

"That's correct, Miss Jee. It was handled before it became a much bigger issue."

She nodded.

"Yes, sir. I was glad to get the message."

He nodded at Teebeck's clone, and the unit moved quickly to the door, opening it for her to leave.

Yen looked up and was going to speak, but seeing Goldmeyer's hard stare, quietly departed with the clone following her.

Chapter Sixteen

D r. Jane Hoppensowski watched Tom as he stepped away from her office doorstep.

All was not right in her world.

Tom would be okay, she determined from his gait, as he slowly strode away across the university campus. She took a deep breath and turned back inside, closing the door behind her. She sat and let it come. That feeling. The thing that was wrong.

As a thirty-year therapist and Stanford professor, she had been privy to a wild ride. She felt she had encountered every type of issue there could ever be.

Her therapy clients included stars, both past and present, as well as high-profile politicians, CEOs, and even past presidents. She had been written up in every therapeutic magazine, as well as *The Washington Post*. Her interviews were everywhere online, and she was a sought-after guest on the webinar circuit.

Yet, something wasn't right with her since her sessions with Tom had begun. She knew what it was right away, that frustrated her. *Physical Proof.*

Tom's memories of being cloned and used by the Cabal mirrored many of the issues she confronted with previous clients who had been alien abductees.

She had no doubt that they were all telling the truth as she had a really good compass for gauging truth in the room.

Her various clients came from all over the world and didn't know each other, yet all told almost the exact same details about being abducted from their bedrooms and enduring torturous experiences aboard Grey alien ships or in DUMBs.

In the last ten years, the alien phenomenon had made a big shift. Her latest wave of clients were all *Secret Space Program* personnel, who were suddenly recalling what their clones had experienced in space.

These covert programs, all of which were controlled by the Cabal, had been operating throughout the solar system for decades. Most of her clients had memories of their clones operating in space as far back as the 1980s.

Jane felt anger as once again, there was a dearth of physical evidence, with nothing to show but memory recall. In Jane's personal network of over one hundred therapists worldwide, she was getting wind of the amount of new Secret Space Program clients flooding in from across the globe. All with similar stories of being cloned, launching on spaceships to various planets the ICC was developing, and finally being subjected to Mind-Wipe technology, which was now glitching. She knew her network of therapists was only seeing the few citizens with faulty mind-wipes who had the courage to step forward. She assumed there were hundreds more worldwide who were afraid to speak out, fearing the Cabal. Yet, for the average citizen, this rise of Secret Space Program veterans stepping forward was not changing public opinion. Anything alien-related was still firmly entrenched in the realm of hearsay and fantasy. She loved her clients but knew that one more book on the subject wouldn't change public opinion.

But Tom's revelations about the Malaysian flight and all those innocent civilians being caught up in the Cabal's clandestine agenda really upset her. She had a feeling that the fate of the passengers would not end well. But here she was once again, facing a horror that the world needed to know about—and yet, all she had were Tom's memories.

However, one week ago, a new client presented a possible solution, and he was coming in for his second session shortly. She glanced through her blinds and saw *them.*

Secret Service agents were already dotting the campus around her building.

She had seen this type of security before with former President Richard Nixon. An intriguing man, but certainly torn about what he knew and what he could talk about. His sessions and what he needed to get off his chest were alien-oriented experiences as well. Jane had also been a therapist for Nixon's dear friend Jackie Gleason. Wild stuff for certain, but not provable.

But today's client was not a president or a star or anything of that nature. He was, however, a marked man for sure, and his first session had been a whirlwind of information that shook her foundations.

Dr. Andre Enzensberger had entered her office while two Secret Service suits loitered in the waiting room.

At sixty-five, Andre fit the bill of an aging scientist: black glasses as thick as Coke bottles and wild hair that was thinning and grey. Jane knew he was on the spectrum the minute she saw him enter. She also knew something else that really surprised her—especially at her age.

There was an attraction, of all things, to this total geek of a man.

What in the world? she thought. *I'm not attracted to old geeks!*

But there it was. She knew one thing for certain during that first meeting: Andre had a lot on his chest. A therapist at her level could give an assessment just by someone's gait, and Andre was *burdened*. She had just closed the door to her office on that first session, and before she even turned around, he had his hand out, offering her a handwritten note:

My security uses recording devices... and will attempt to monitor anything I say.

She nodded.

"Have a seat," she said normally.

"Thank you," he said, and more notes came quickly after that.

Do you have a radio we can turn up with some classical music?

She nodded and put a classical piece on her cell phone, turning it up. The next note he gave her was a detailed account of how his unique radar invention was based on Tesla's knowledge and how his device had found a lethal amount of plutonium buried in an oil tanker. He then had shown the U.S. government every detail of the tunnels below the Mexican border.

Jane was most fascinated that his radar could image at four-hundred times the magnification of a CAT scan while returning information on periodic elements the radar encountered!

She looked up, nodding her understanding. Another note came her way.

I will say things aloud that are about what I see in my brain, but it will have everything to do with my device. So, ask me things about my invention, like it's my brain you are talking about.

Jane smiled and nodded, thinking one way or another, it was going to be an interesting session. And it was.

She would quickly find that her own belief systems would be shattered and shifted by this humble scientist. At first, Jane didn't understand the significance of his invention. That he could see through the planet—*the entire planet*—until he passed a note to her that read:

Let's now use my head as a metaphor for the Earth.

She nodded. And with that, he suddenly said aloud:

"I see things in my dreams that are hard to explain."

"Like what?" she said. "Give me an example, and don't be afraid to give all the wild details, because dreams are really great ways of understanding yourself," she said, louder than normal, hoping this would allow him to really let go.

With that, he got a look and sort of laughed.

"Well, if you think you are ready to see what I see in my crazy brain every day, then—okay."

She nodded, noticing that she was nervous, and realized in that flash of an instant that she was worried her own beliefs might be challenged. She was older now and somehow wanted to believe that she had most of life's big questions basically answered. But she was about to be stopped in her tracks. She remembered just how the global masses viewed their reality as only that which was in front of them, and how far off the scale they were.

Their reality versus what *actual reality* was. Most were not aware that the Cabal had been in space for decades, and that they had effectively hoodwinked the masses to keep them under control, while the Cabal and its secret space program ranged ever outwards.

She had already decided that she trusted Andre implicitly and that he had no reason to seek her out and schedule sessions unless there was really a truth that he could share with no one else on the planet. She watched him take a breath as he picked up the spinning world-globe off her desk... and held it up. He smiled at her like a magician and spun the globe with his opposite hand until she could see that he had placed North America under his hand.

He gave her a serious stare that said:

"I'm going to tell you—what is below this—below America."

She nodded, realizing she was on edge. Andre moved his finger directly to the center of the United States and tapped the globe on the state of Kansas, then looked her way. She nodded. *Got it.*

He tapped Kansas gently as he spoke.

"When I first fall asleep, I always have the sensation of entering my brain from the outside—like I'm descending through it—say from my hair, into my scalp, and then into my cranium, and then into my actual brain."

He stared at her.

Are you with me?

She slowly nodded. He tapped Kansas again.

"I drop through what feels like a cavernous area, kind of like Carlsbad Caverns, but much grander, like a cavern that stretches in both directions for thousands of miles."

She stared, trying to picture an actual hollowed-out cavern below the crust of the Earth, extending in both directions all the way across the continent.

Wow, she thought, as he continued.

"And yet, as I descend to the floor of the cavern, there is a New York-sized city. And it feels like it has its own atmosphere. Like whoever built the city also created the atmosphere. And there is an aquifer there, and certainly millions of inhabitants. As I descend to the street level, I see that there are antigravity vehicles moving about, and some form of sunlight, though I can't quite place the source of the light."

Jane stared, astonished, as he watched her.

"I know—it doesn't seem possible—that's why I came to see you."

He tapped the globe again, then touched his head and continued.

"The people I see in my head have tiny technology sticking out of their necks, about one inch, like it's a regulator for connecting to something that gives them food, or it's for communication, but I'm not certain which."

He thought for a moment.

"But the people seem to be content as they go about their business," he said, looking at Jane again.

She nodded, taking a sip of coffee and shaking her head in amazement.

"Go ahead," she said aloud. "I'll ask questions at the end."

"Okay," Andre said, slightly laughing, "You asked for it."

He took a breath.

"The city's occupants are like humans, but seem much more technologically evolved. Then, as I pass below that city, I go even deeper into my brain, and as I move toward the center, it is honeycombed, with more civilizations, large and small, with various interesting races, depending on how deep I go."

He then pulled another note, one he obviously thought was important, and handed it to her.

From where I'm standing—to the center of the Earth—is 3200 miles. That's wider than the entire United States.

She looked up, astonished. He got a silly look, like a magician, and produced another hidden note. She smiled, reading it.

But the Earth, being round, is measured in cubic miles. *There are 260 billion cubic miles below you. Not millions—260 billion—so, there is ample room for lots of civilizations, with lots of diverse races.*

She looked up, clearly blown away. He nodded at her with a humble gaze, then focused back on the globe and continued.

"And at the center of my brain—of all things—is a black hole."

He looked up to see her uncomprehending stare. She placed her hand on her forehead, exasperated.

"*Really?*"

He shrugged and inhaled, tightening his lips.

"Every time I go into my brain, I see the same things, the same civilizations, the same black hole."

He raised a finger. *But wait, there's more.*

He rotated the globe so that his hand was over the big island of Hawaii, and she nodded. *Got it.*

"And even in the watery parts of my brain, I see many civilizations as I drop toward the center. They too have their own atmospheres, like bubbles. And those cities are grand as well, and some have very tall beings, who appear to be ancient and peaceful, and there are levels within the watery parts of my brain that seem to be inhabited by watery entities, like mermaids and mermen, with fins. These creatures can move at incredible speeds through the water. And their cities are stunning as well, and I have a sense of their brilliance."

He looked up to see Jane, slack-jawed, shaking her head slowly in astonishment.

"And here too, in the watery part of my brain—if I keep descending—I am again in a honeycomb of large and small civilizations, each with unique races, that are just too much to describe. But they are peaceful and seem to have been there for eons. And naturally, if I descend all the way down, I again hit the black hole in the center."

He looked up, and Jane was beside herself—dumbstruck. He stared at her, full of humility, and placed the globe back on her desk. He sat down beside her, staring at his hands. She could tell he was almost in tears. From his energy, she knew he had just gotten a lot off his chest and was relieved. She had seen this phenomenon many times, and the one thing that always rang true—when she was privy to a session like that—was that he had finally been able to tell the truth.

"I think that's enough for today," he finally said, "but there is much, much more in my brain that I can't even begin to tell you about."

He stood and reached out his hand.

"It's been a pleasure, Dr. Hoppensowski... I'll call again soon."

That was a week ago. And she knew one thing for certain about that first session—she was blown away by more than just his amazing invention. For an old gal getting up in her years, she liked being blown away. She had missed that feeling.

Her office doorbell suddenly chimed softly. She looked up. He was here again.

Wow, she thought, standing up and straightening her dress.

She brought up the classical piece on her iPhone and turned up the volume. Checking her look in a small mirror, she saw an older woman staring back, but still *beautiful.*

And then it hit her.

She hadn't felt like this—in a long, long time.

Chapter Seventeen

V yla had slept for seven hours yet was still exhausted.

Now, in the early morning light, she felt the deep comfort of being in her own bed, but an undercurrent of urgency was pulling at her. Then it came through slowly—the unbelievable thing. *Still unbelievable.* She had just met and hung out with an alien—*on his boat, for Christ's sake!* She mused on the significance of it. And Swizzle was so damn humble and cool!

Then, a grand awareness washed over her—

We are not alone. Wow—and holy shit! she thought.

That fact alone would take days to seep in. But there were so many layers to her new world order. The American military was certainly utilizing some dark technology, and the Reaper footage of Flight 370 being hijacked by the Cabal was truly disturbing. She thought about how to proceed. She would have to start at the beginning to work it all out.

The beginning? she thought. *Where was that?*

She decided to take everything one step at a time until she had a more comprehensive view of what was really happening around her. She wanted to re-read Papa's journal entries for a different understanding of his cryptic messages to himself. She would have to revisit much of what he had hinted at when she was a little girl. She inhaled deeply and exhaled, coming to her quiet center. She had to calm down. This was all way too much.

She had learned years ago, during her grad school pressure days, to let go—either that or implode. And in this moment, she needed a good sit. Her term for meditation. Something she had learned from her mom, and the ritual of doing a daily sit had profoundly changed her life.

Sitting a perfect distance from her wood-burning stove, she lit a tiny amount of sage and placed it nearby. The velvety movement of that smoke, the smell, and her nakedness next to the flames felt calming, and she needed calm. She closed her eyes, feeling her soft breath as she began to move within, but not the way fear made her move. There, in the quiet center, she knew herself. What she was before and what she would be after. Essence. Floating in that sea. She felt the buoyancy. And soon, she was beyond content.

Forty minutes later, she emerged from that silky place where her spirit was rejuvenated. She took a sip of coffee, and then she saw it: impaled in the wooden column, the Bowie knife with all her rejection letters. She contemplated the amount of work they represented. She was happy to have a job, but so many things were in transition with having to move. She dressed quickly, thinking about her interlude with Dan, and wondered if she had just gotten pregnant.

Her 2003 Chevy Silverado fired up on the first try after weeks of not being started, and she was southbound a minute later.

As she departed the Victorian parking lot, she noticed a black sedan wait until she was three or so blocks ahead before it pulled out to follow.

Was this a different team? she thought. *What in the hell? Well, at least I know what they're driving.*

Minutes later she pulled into the tiny house, which her mom had rented just to be closer to Vyla at Stanford. Banjo, her mom's ancient bloodhound, bayed at the front door while still lying down.

Awesome economy of movement, Banjo, she thought, as she approached the sweet dog.

Good old Banjo no longer ran around, but he bayed at any passersby. He gave up the ghost of his belly for a rub, which she obliged, complete with fingernails, which always got the hind legs kicking like a janky robot.

A moment later, the screen door swung open, and her mom, Dah Kells, stepped out with a grin, looking fit for a woman of sixty-one. Her smile was humble, and the long hug that followed was one both had clearly missed. Dah had a deep red-brown coloring with black hair, which reflected her Navajo and Apache bloodlines. Her great-grandfather, a Navajo hunter, had married an Apache, and Dah was fluent in both languages. Dah had grown up learning the verbal histories of both tribes, and Vyla was versed in both traditions. They released their embrace and looked at each other.

"Well, I heard Banjo," Dah said, "and only special guests get the full baying."

"Yep," Vyla replied, "he got his overdue belly scratch."

Dah snickered and opened the screen door for her to pass. Vyla shot a quick glance to see the black sedan parking down the street as she stepped into the living room. She stopped just inside, always caught by her mom's picture collection, which adorned the entire living room.

Up and down the walls, in all shapes and sizes, were vintage Navajo and Apache family pictures dating back to the turn of the century. The majority of them were from the thirties, showing old trucks, dwellings, and big family gatherings. She knew most of them were from the area near Socorro, New Mexico, where Dah had grown up. She remembered that Dah's parents had to temporarily vacate Socorro due to Oppenheimer's *Trinity nuclear test* in 1945.

Many of the photos centered around Dah's grandfather, who was a Navajo hunter. A huge man who stood a head taller than all the other Navajos and Apaches in the pictures. She remembered, as a little girl, that her mom had mentioned he was involved in the Roswell incident, but at that young age she had paid little attention. Roswell had been mentioned many times in the Majestic brief, and she hoped going over the family albums might provide more context now.

At her feet in the middle of the living room was the big birthday box her mom had mentioned was waiting for her. It was long and bulky, like a file cabinet, laid down lengthwise.

"Happy Birthday from Papa's safe," Dah said, walking into the kitchen.

"Really?" Vyla replied, astonished.

She had seen Papa's huge safe many times at his old house, but neither she nor Dah had ever seen him open it. When they had asked him about what was in it, he always replied:

"Well, something interesting, I suppose. Someday, you'll know."

That someday was today. The contents of the safe had been delivered to Dah's house from Papa's attorney after his passing in 1997. The rest of his estate was sold, and a portion went to Dah for Vyla's college fund. Papa's wishes, according to the attorney, were for Vyla to receive the contents of the safe when she turned thirty. But she had gotten crazy drunk on her birthday with Charlotte and Marten, so Dah decided to wait until she returned from her trip to Geneva. Dah entered the living room with a cup of coffee.

"I've had it tucked away all these years. I had my neighbor's boy bring it up from the basement yesterday. That box is darn heavy."

Vyla looked up, beaming at Dah. She was over the moon that Papa was still giving gifts on her birthday. Dah could see her excitement.

"Your Papa would be so proud of you with your new job," she said. "You want coffee or anything?"

Vyla shook her head, staring at her mom. Dah beamed and pulled her close.

"God, I missed you."

"Me too, Mom," and they both sat by the heavily duct-taped monstrosity.

"So, what's this all about?" Vyla asked, noticing Dah seemed slightly anxious about the box.

"Well, your guess is as good as mine. This box filled that huge safe of his, and it was delivered to me when he passed. I have no idea what's in it."

"Wait, you've had this box since—"

"Yes, since you were thirteen when Papa passed," Dah said, cutting her off. "His attorney had it delivered and said it was for you when you turned thirty."

Vyla stared.

"Wow," she whispered.

Dah slowly nodded, staring at the box. Vyla sensed an apprehension, but figured Dah would say what she needed to say when she was ready.

It took a sharp knife to liberate the top, and the box appeared as if it had only been opened a couple of times over the many years. When she finally got the top off, the inside of the box was clean. There was an old VHS tape on top of many file folders. Just below the video was a letter in red ink, written in Papa's unique penmanship.

He had always preferred red ink, and she smiled at her mom, laying the VHS gently off to the side and lifting the letter. Her eyes filled, just feeling the paper. Dah was clearly moved as well.

"Do you know what this letter says?" Vyla inquired.

Dah shook her head and began to speak but then hesitated.

"I love you," Dah finally said, looking away.

Vyla could tell her mom was fighting tears, and she gently pulled her close.

"Come on, this is for both of us," she whispered.

They held each other as she read the familiar handwriting. And she felt she could hear Papa's voice.

My dearest Vyla,

I have asked your mother to wait until you were at least thirty years old before giving you this box and this letter. I wanted to ensure that you had some life experiences under your belt to fully understand why your mother and I would wait to tell you this

166

information.

She looked up quickly at Dah, who now had tears in her eyes. Vyla shifted even closer, placing her free hand on her mom's back as she kept reading in a whisper.

This will be a letter of extremely tough love, but I am certain you will be glad of it in the end.

Firstly, let me say that you have been the strongest beacon of hope and love in my lifetime. Rest assured that I tried—in the best way I knew how—as your Papa, to be there for you. I will always love you as my number one.

Now for the tougher things, and there is no really great place to start, so I will dive right in.

My real name is not Steve Johnson. My real last name is Wilson.

Your mom only knows a bit of this story, so hopefully, she is with you when you are reading this.

Vyla felt Dah grip her, as Vyla momentarily looked up and then went back to reading in a whisper.

The entire subject matter below is all part of a massive UFO coverup operation by a malevolent element within the U.S. government that has been ongoing since 1941. This coverup has everything to do with your family and the real truth of what occurred to them.

A group called the Majestic-12, also referred to as the MAJI, is the American wing of an elusive Cabal that has led the coverup, not only against the American people but the entire world. And it continues to this day.

This Cabal has been in contractual obligations with two malevolent alien races since the first contracts were signed in 1954. I'll cover more about this Cabal later, but for now, let me get back to your dad.

To begin, your dad's real name was not Michael Smith. I told you that as a protective measure, and I'll explain below.

I first knew your dad as "Griffin," his code name.

I only learned later, as we became fast friends, that his real name was Dr. Michael Kruvant Wolf, and even then, he was considered a unique and brilliant scientist.

We both worked for the Majestic-12 beginning in the early 70s. I met Michael at a super-secret, below-ground facility at Papoose Lake, Nevada, called S-4.

I was the commander of the security detachment for the entire complex.

At S-4, there is literally nothing to see on the surface except for camouflaged hangar doors that are only visible when you are really close. Otherwise, the S-4 facility exists as a Deep Underground Military Base, referred to in the black-ops world as a D.U.M.B.

Vyla had to catch her breath, but decided to keep reading.

There are literally hundreds of DUMBs below surface military facilities worldwide. All are connected by high-speed Mag-Lev trains, which are too complicated to explain here.

For now, let me get back to your dad, Michael Wolf.

At the time I met him, Michael and Carl Sagan, yes, the famous scientist, were working together at the S-4 facility on "The Monolith," which was a large stone first seen floating in space by Russian astronaut Yuri Gagarin in 1961.

It was later brought back to Earth in 1972 for investigation and came directly under my purview of security at S-4.

Later, your dad, with his unique ability to communicate telepathically, worked with captured aliens we had in detainment at that facility, as well as another complex below Mount Archuleta near Dulce, New Mexico. Dah has relatives in the area of the Dulce complex. But let me continue.

As my friendship with your dad deepened, I came to know your family: your wonderful mother, Sarah, and your big brother, Daniel. I miss them still.

By the time Christmas Day came in 1984, your father had created some enemies within the Majestic-12 or Cabal, as they are now often called. This dark group was concerned that your dad would tell the world about the alien presence and, in fact, were convinced that he had recently divulged his above-top-secret alien interactions to a couple of scientist friends. The Cabal wanted to teach him a lesson—to keep his mouth shut—but also wanted him to keep working for them, as he was one of the few on the planet able to communicate telepathically with the alien races we were working with at that time.

What I've shared with both you and Dah about my flying and the general part of my military career has been the truth. But the secret side I simply never shared with you, as I wanted to protect you.

I was not only the security head of the S-4 facility, but periodically I was tasked as the Commanding Officer of a project called "Pounce," which is still in effect and handles UFO recovery and containment operations worldwide.

The containment part of my Pounce unit was often assigned "hit missions" to silence whistleblowers for the Cabal. This meant I was working in unison with Black Berets and Wackenhut killers—above top-secret operators and assassins on contract for the Cabal.

My sweet Vyla... your mother and brother were not killed in a car accident when you were in your mother's womb. I gave you that story to soften the truth. Your mother, Sarah, and your older brother, Daniel, were assassinated in a Cabal-ordered hit while vacationing in the Swiss Alps with your father on Christmas Day, 1984. The day you were born.

Vyla burst into tears, and for a moment they held each other, but Vyla wanted to continue. She pulled herself together and kept reading.

This attack, your dad was told, was a direct retaliation by the PLO for his work with the Israeli Mossad and their alien task force. (The Israelis had a strong working relationship with an alien group, and the Cabal tasked your dad with finding out the depth of that relationship.) But I can assure you, the hit order came from a Cabal directive. I was part of the mop-up team, and we knew about the operation two weeks before it occurred. But "Need to know" prevented me from understanding who the victims were to be.

This was a carefully orchestrated car assassination designed to kill the passenger and back-seat occupant. Your father was driving on a steep mountain road when the attack occurred. I can tell you now that the kill team was a Wackenhut unit on contract with orders from the Cabal.

These were the assassins my "Containment team" was tasked to mop up for, on the night of your family's murders. My team's job for that evening was the post-attack death verification and containment operation.

Vyla looked at Dah, who sat perplexed.

"Papa only told me it was a terrorist attack. I've never heard the rest of this," Dah said.

Vyla nodded and leaned more into her mom, turning back to the letter.

As far as the Cabal is concerned, you, as an unborn fetus, were killed in that attack, along with your mother and brother. As fate would have it, the attack occurred after dark, and minutes later, as I approached the dying pregnant woman who had been thrown from the car, I suddenly realized who it was. Your mother, severely wounded, died in my arms.

Vyla's tears were streaming as she fought to continue reading.

It was then, in the midst of staring at Sarah's post-attack body, that I saw your tiny leg kick amidst all the gore around her open belly! I immediately sliced your umbilical cord in the darkness and hastily swaddled you inside my jacket. The sirens blaring all around us allowed me to cover your initial crying, as many other operatives were nearby.

When we arrived at the Swiss hospital with your mother's body in the ambulance, I was able to get you to an older Swiss nurse on the far wing, who was on night watch. I explained the dire situation to her, that if the baby was discovered to be alive, the terrorists from the car attack would come back to kill her.

That nurse, whom I won't name here, kept you hidden for two weeks until I was able to return to Switzerland and retrieve you. Upon returning to Las Vegas, where I had a house, I was able, through my connections, to present you to a local woman of Apache/Navajo heritage, Dah Kells, and she never let go of you!

Vyla turned to Dah, as the tears flowed for both, holding each other close.

"Oh God," Vyla whispered through sniffles. She wiped her eyes and continued.

Your birth mother, Sarah, would have been pleased to learn that Dah would be your loving surrogate—and as great a mother as anyone could ever hope for. I had informed Dah that Sarah had already picked the name Vyla for you, and Dah said,

"Perfect."

From that day forward, Dah placed you as number one in her life and never looked back! I was amazed to learn, after I got to know Dah, that her full Apache name was Dahteste—meaning Warrior Woman. And as you now know... Dah has proven to be all that and more.

Vyla gripped her mom tightly and continued.

This was my secret life, which I now realize was committed to a rogue government group that used me and your father for their own heinous purposes. Even in this moment, as you read this, if you choose to reconnect with anyone in your real extended family, I can assure you that it would be fatal for all involved. The Cabal has not only grown its stranglehold of power worldwide, but their tentacles of deception and absolute butchery are notorious. For the sake of your safety, I beg you to remain Vyla Kells and steer clear of anything related to the UFO community.

The picture included in the small envelope is of your family a week before Christmas 1984.

Vyla's hands were shaking as she quickly looked into the box and opened the envelope to find a 1980s-era photograph showing a beautiful couple and their son wearing festive Christmas garb. The pregnant mother stood in the center, surrounded by the long-haired father and seventeen-year-old son. The mother's hands lovingly rested on her pregnant belly. The son and father held glasses of wine, and all were smiling.

"Have you ever seen this?" she asked her mom.

Dah shook her head, amazed at the picture.

"Oh my God, no."

Vyla took a deep breath, leaned in, and kissed her mom on the cheek.

"I love you so much, Mom," she said, feeling Dah's strong grip as she continued.

A week before the attack, while I was en route to Switzerland through Heathrow Airport, your dad invited me to their flat in downtown London. We had a beautiful lunch together, and I snapped that photo of your family.

It shows your mother, Sarah, with her hands lovingly holding her bump—that was you. Your parents had invited me over for a glass of Christmas cheer, and Daniel showed up as well. He was a strikingly smart young man, about to turn seventeen.

Back then, there were no cell phones, so I had the picture printed, throwing away the negatives.

I had no idea that the operation I would be involved in a week later would have anything to do with your family. I had heard rumors, as part of the security contingent for the Cabal that your dad was ruffling some feathers, but I had no idea the extent of their savagery at that point.

That they would not only turn on him but then proceed to use him for his unique skill set.

As of this date, September 1997 (right after my last flight with you, where you handled a full airshow and a perfect landing of Gloria at only thirteen years old!), I have begun my RV trip.

And yes, I knew when I hugged your neck today that I would never see you again.

I am diagnosed as suffering from a fast-acting brain cancer that I'm certain was infused at my last visit to the VA Hospital, and I didn't want to burden you or Dah with my demise.

The Cabal has been hunting me since I went on the speaking circuit at UFO conferences last year, and since I am now known somewhat, instead of shooting me and causing a stir, they have infused my blood with this rare form of cancer.

I have been told I will last a few more months at best. This cancer that I have suddenly "acquired" has no history in my ancestry.

My friend and Michael's friend, Carl Sagan, died last year (1996) of an extremely rare, fast-acting blood disease that I can assure you had no history in his ancestry either.

Sagan was a known public debunker of all possible alien existence. But make no mistake about it, the Cabal made it clear to him, as they had done with Einstein and Oppenheimer before him, that speaking about his alien interactions would see him lose all funding for his current projects.

That, in addition to threats against his family, and now you understand why Sagan, in addition to Einstein and Oppenheimer before him, kept their mouths shut about their incredibly involved roles with the different alien races the Cabal was in diplomacy with.

There are many other world-famous scientists who were involved as far back as the Roswell incident, and all were sworn to secrecy. And many today are under threat as I write this, but again, there is not enough time for all of it.

For now, let me get back to S-4, where your dad and I worked.

The land surrounding S-4 was purchased by the CIA in the 1950s, and the CIA controls not only S-4 but all of Area 51. And since the CIA is controlled in every way by the Cabal, the entire area is essentially a Cabal stronghold.

S-4 and the surrounding Area 51 operate as a state-within-a-state, as there is no presidential or congressional oversight.

There is much alien technology being reverse-engineered within Area 51, and the security for the facility is sourced from the special operations forces of our own military.

Our president is only cleared to top-secret level 17. But to access any information regarding Area 51, an individual must be cleared to Cosmic level 23 or above. This clearance tier structure allowed the CIA to go rogue with Area 51.

Accordingly, black-ops personnel dealing with alien technology are all cleared to levels above the president, as was my clearance level, as head of security. Ultra-top-secret, Cosmic Q, level 27.

The very top of the Majestic-12 have clearance level-33, such as my bosses, Henry Kissinger (MAJ-1) and Dr. Edward Teller (MAJ-2), also known as the inventor of the hydrogen bomb.

There are only a handful of people in the world who are cleared to that level by the National Reconnaissance Office, which hands out those classifications. The NRO and its underwater equivalent, the National Underwater Reconnaissance Office (NURO) are two of the most secretive agencies out there.

When I first heard of the National Underwater Reconnaissance Office, I wondered why there would be such an office? What in the hell would we monitor down there? Over time, I realized why.

As far-fetched as it may seem, there is massive spaceship activity below our oceans.

Since alien spaceships (and ours) create their own gravity envelopes, they perform the same underwater as in the air.

A prime example of below-water spaceports is the DUMB below the Navy Base at Diego Garcia in the Indian Ocean.

Vyla swallowed hard, shocked at the mention of the Diego spaceport, but continued reading in her focused intensity.

That facility is a busy spaceport for anti-gravity, spacefaring transports that carry supplies and "other" cargo to the Moon, Mars, and beyond. Cargo the black-ops world calls "Traffic."

That dark topic I won't explain further other than to say that it is ongoing and growing.

The NRO is a super-secret entity run by the Air Force, and even mentioning the NRO can be deadly.

To give you an example, individuals from several alien races have been captured and are currently held in detainment facilities such as S-4 and just south in the DUMB below Indian Springs, which is now called Creech Air Force Base, as well as Haystack Butte, and the Air Force Laboratory at Edwards AFB in California.

There are many other "Guest" (detainment) facilities (DUMBs) used for dark genetic testing, including the hollowed-out mountain at Kirtland AFB, near Alamogordo, NM.

That DUMB descends more than fifty floors down and extends laterally for miles beyond the base.

The testing done on detained live aliens at these hidden facilities is reminiscent of Dr. Joseph Mengele's depraved experiments on Jews during the Nazi reign of terror.

All DUMBs worldwide are hidden from public oversight. These facilities, of which at my last count number in the hundreds worldwide, are funded illegally by American taxpayer dollars, that are funneled secretly away from the American people. Additional funds also come from multinational companies that make up the ICC.

The Interplanetary Corporate Conglomerate now has operations throughout our solar system and beyond, answering directly to the Cabal.

Your dad is still alive as of this writing but is being "sequestered" by the Cabal (under house arrest), which will not end until they decide his ultimate fate. He is currently diagnosed with fast-acting pancreatic cancer.

There is so much more to this story, and I have included some "Eyes only" documents for you to understand more about this dark Cabal, which truly runs our planet, and in fact, the solar system and beyond.

You should know that the Cabal questioned me at length on the whereabouts of the unborn child after the attack on your family.

I simply told them that, "The mother's belly was ripped open during the attack and the infant must have been subsequently lost during violent departure from the vehicle."

But I'm certain they did not believe me. The murder of your mother and brother cemented my goal to escape and lay low for fifteen years, which I did before starting to leak my story to UFO groups.

The Majestic-12 group has grown, like any other organization over the years, and at last count, numbered forty-four.

This American wing of the worldwide Cabal is still much too powerful to try to explain in this letter. This is the best I can do for you in the short time I have left.

I chose this path of taking the RV so that when I began speaking out about my real career to UFO groups, it would not lead back to you or Dah.

After the car attack, I felt it was in your best interest that I not remain close to your father as it could have led to your discovery.

I worked with your mother, Dah, to create the story we told you as a child about the car wreck, something a small girl could somewhat understand. I knew that one day, I would tell you and Dah about the much tougher reality behind your family's demise.

I continued to watch your dad from a distance as he recovered from the attack. I made excuses to create distance for your sake. He has no idea you are alive, and I'm certain if he did, he would risk life and limb to find you. The Cabal would not hesitate to terminate you both.

Your father is an incredibly wonderful man, and his new book, The Catchers in Heaven, just came out.

There is a copy in the box. His love for you and your entire family is eloquently displayed in those pages.

Hopefully, by now, you have grown close to your mother and can understand why we told you the softer story of your family's death while you were a little girl.

I hope you can forgive your mother and me for not telling you the whole truth until now.

Rest assured, your mother only knew there had been a terrorist attack. I never told her that your father had survived the blast.

I will always love you, Vyla. I'll see you one day again in what your dad lovingly calls "The Forever."

All my love,

Papa

She was in shock, and it took her two more read-throughs to comprehend what her new ground zero was. She lifted her dad's book from inside the box and quickly flipped through the pages. She grabbed her laptop, and Dah watched as she did a quick internet search for the book title.

The bio of her dad came up, only to reveal that he had succumbed to pancreatic cancer under suspicious circumstances in 2000. She stared in disbelief, and then slowly, as the floodgates opened, she laid back on the floor, sobbing silently, holding her family's picture to her heart as her world emptied and the room became a swirl.

Dah placed a gentle hand on her chest, and she heard her mother's soft voice sing a Navajo passing song. The ancient melody of Dah's great-grandfather winding into her descending whirlwind.

The little girl scream she cried at that moment didn't make any sound. The disjointed life she had finally figured out—had somehow flipped again.

ANCESTORS

N avajo hands and a silver ring on his fourth finger.

Leather hatband with turquoise stones, stitched in every inch or so. His skin was dark and weathered from horseback exposure, and calluses from that territory. His leather moccasins were tightly wound just below the knee, enveloping his dirty denim pants. The moccasins were beaded with small thunderbirds that looked outward, perpendicular to his stride.

And that gait—

His head always leaned—just forward of straight up. His landings were soft... each step seemed preordained and equally heavy from ball to heel. For a large man, he was ghostly silent in his stride, a trained evolution from years of hunting antelope with bow and arrow and childhood challenges of sneaking up to grab snakes behind the head as they bathed in the white-dirt plains of San Agustin.

He didn't really like walking through town. Gallup, New Mexico, in 1947, though just on the edge of the Navajo reservation, was still White-Man land. And walking beneath all those colorful explosions, he was even more anxious.

Whites of all ages were clogging the main street in a cloud of sulfur-infused smoke mixed with hints of rotgut whiskey, beer, and roasted pig. They had begun their fireworks celebrations just hours before, starting on the 4th of July. Now, in the moonlight at 1 a.m. on the 5th, he wondered if they would catch their town on fire like last summer.

He could feel the eyes on him the moment he walked off the reservation. Mothers and fathers would subtly pull their children closer as he passed, wary of the large, dark figure who moved along the walkway in front of brightly lit store windows.

It wasn't so bad, though. He knew he did the same to Whites whenever they came on the reservation. It was a curious thing to watch people of another world.

So, he walked along. His gaze focused slightly downward as he moved, posing no threat to anyone yet acutely aware of what was around him. He was always on alert. He always had a reason to go to town; otherwise, he wouldn't go. Tonight, though, was going to be awkward. What he had just found, glowing in the moonlit ravine in the Plains of San Agustin, would forever change him—and the tribe, too.

Gallup was absolutely wild as he walked through town. Yet, with all the commotion, he still got many of the condescending looks he was used to. But right now, he had a job to do, and he was focused on finding Sam Boyd.

His head was still reeling from what he had discovered and the antelope hunt that led him to that moment. He thought about tracking that pronghorn at sunset and how he had a sense that something bigger was in store for him. He knew he was not simply hunting an antelope. He replayed everything in his mind as he walked through town.

Out there on the Plains of San Agustin, the afternoon had come with the ground still radiating heat from the long day of sun. The plains were speckled with vegetation suited for the sweltering climate—cedar and piñon trees, sagebrush, and the white dirt of the Pleistocene lakebed, which dried after the ice age, never to fill again.

And you had to be wary of where you planted your feet while hunting in San Agustin. Scorpions and diamondback rattlers could end your day—and even your life—for those not alert.

As the afternoon moved toward sunset, he had finally found the right spot. He had been lying still behind a small piñon tree near the sleepy arroyo, which wound its way through the plains. Surrounding the white plains were two-hundred-foot red-rock walls that climbed high, absorbing the heavy heat that would slow any living thing.

The electrical thunderstorm that afternoon was common to him. Every year at this time, the storms became more electrically charged with each passing month. By summer, chain-lightning would appear across the horizon during heavy storms. So much so that he had taken cover under a rocky outcrop, below where the ancient ones had lived in cave dwellings high above the ledge.

But the summer storms often moved swiftly, and by afternoon, the thunderclouds gave way to bright sunlight. It quickly became so hot he felt like he was wading through waves of heat rising from the plains.

He could always feel the old ones tugging at his chest, directing him on which way to go during the hunt. They had gotten him this far. The rest was up to him.

His deep brown eyes focused on the large pronghorn drinking rainwater pooled in the dry creek bed just ahead. He had tracked it while sitting huddled under the overhang during the thunderstorm and had seen it stand below another rock outcrop. When the rain ceased, he slowly moved in its direction. It had taken three more hours as he tracked it, following it up the arroyo, all the while inching closer—bow-and-arrow range.

He knew from years of hunting antelope that one mistake, one sound out of place, and the pronghorn would be gone in an instant. The Big Indian rolled slowly in the white dirt, which had dried moments after the sun reappeared. He shifted soundlessly, slightly sideways, as he pulled his handmade arrow silently back on his short bow. Holding the tension, he aimed at the shoulder of the pronghorn, which stood still like a statue, lapping water.

He said a prayer of thanks to this prey—one he had recited many times.

"I know your life is as precious as mine. We are the same under one great sky. One must end so the other may continue. I ask your permission. Killing with your consent, your countenance that you are ready to cross."

Then, he expertly released the tension from his three fingers on the taught bowstring. He heard the soft percussive *whoosh* of the handmade arrow as it departed by his ear. A split second later, the stout pronghorn shuddered and staggered momentarily, then bounded away. The arrow through its shoulder made the grace of its bounding less so.

The dizziness came quick and heavy as it leaped down a steep embankment to a flat sandy spot. It stood still in the setting sun as the warm blood flowed down its leg, and then it dropped to its knees. The warmth of its departure from form was upon it.

Its back legs gave way until it lay down completely, gasping and inexorably becoming lighter. Its final moment in form, breathing slowing, staring at the sun-streaked red hills surrounding the plains—all mixed with the distinct smell of the warm, white dirt it knew as home.

177

T **he blood drops began on the far side of the dry creek bed from where the Big Indian's arrow had pierced the pronghorn's shoulder.**

The red blood trail, even in the sunset light, was still stark in the white dirt. It led over an arroyo and down into a ravine. He stepped to the edge and looked down. The dead antelope on the sand far below was bathed in the last rays of the sun.

He knew he would have to come back, as he had left his horse at least a mile away, where he had taken shelter under the rock overhang during the thunderstorm. The next evolution of finding his horse and returning to recover the Pronghorn would be in complete darkness, but he knew the moon would stand full tonight and would help him. He looked up at the stars, beginning to dot the desert sky, and realized he would have to return with haste before the predators would come.

The Big Indian lit a torch and traveled the mile on foot to where he had left his horse. He was now hungry and trotted the horse the final two miles to his small, twenty-foot trailer home. The lightning in the midst of the booming thunderstorm was like nothing he had ever seen. He grabbed some frybread, gulping it down as he loaded up ropes and a blanket on his saddle. His huge new clock, mounted outside his trailer door, showed the date and year. He had saved for a month to purchase it and was proud every time he gazed on it. The long and short black hands showed 11:18 p.m., and the rolling date displayed July 4, 1947.

He was almost fully packed when he first felt the growl. It seemed to be below him, in the sandy white dirt under his knee-high moccasins. But it wasn't an animal-type growl. It was a deeper, angrier menace of something huge approaching, shaking the entire forest around him. He quickly spun, realizing it wasn't coming from below him, but from behind him. There, almost directly out of the moon, he was confronted with a molten ball of fire, racing just over the forest, roaring with a thunder so violent, he felt trees might start falling. The *howl* of its approach became so loud as it raced over him that he slammed his hands over his ears and cowered. Turning instinctively, looking up, he managed to watch it roar by with a ferocious, whipping fire tail extending well behind it. Then it was gone, with only the whoosh of the furious fireball left echoing around him. A split second later, he felt and heard what sounded like an impact out in the plains that seemed to drag on and on, like a shovel being pushed through heavy rocks.

He could see the sky lit with molten flashes from whatever trees and debris were breaking apart in its wake. At the speed it had gone by, it had to have impacted many miles away. Well beyond the point of going to see whatever it was, he thought. He stood shaking, his heart pounding out of his chest, and stepped quickly to his terrified horse, talking her down with a firm hand and tight bridle grip.

Then there was silence. And it was the loudest silence he had experienced in a long time. Not a single bug, bird, or animal made a sound in that aftermath. It seemed to him that even the light breeze was too shocked to blow, as if it, too, was uncertain of what had just come through. He stood in that deafening quiet and could feel the thumping of his heart, beating hard and wild. Catching himself, he placed a firm but gentle hand on the side of his horse's neck and spoke to her in a calming, guttural tone. She had never strayed from him, and he owed her this moment.

He looked at the big moon as he spoke to the horse, and presently, she calmed. He brought her water, staying by her side until the energy around the trailer settled. His clock ticked 11:27 p.m. by the time he was finally packed for the retrieval. He set her out at a fast walk in the brilliant moonlight. He could see a great distance but knew not to trot her, as a hoof fall on an angled rock could cripple her.

Thunderheads in the great distance flashed lightning here and there, and the booms arrived seconds later. He knew it was the same storm that had passed just earlier when he had taken shelter under the rock overhang. Now, the same storm was rolling over the mountains to the east. He wove his horse between piñon and banyan trees, standing so stark in the moonlight, their shadows stretching taller than themselves.

He was close to the ravine now, as he knew the plains from his childhood days of hunting pronghorn with his father. Even in the moonlight, it was still a great playground in his mind, known to him on every level and equally beautiful under the huge moon as when the sun held its daytime reign. He was still looking at the moon when a strange feeling rose in him. An immense sadness? But he had never felt this before when retrieving a pronghorn. The sadness confused him and grew as he approached the ravine, bathed in bright moonlight. He slowly stepped to the edge of the ravine and looked down. The dead antelope on the sand far below could easily be seen, but it barely caught his eye.

The bigger picture of what was there was perplexing and out of context with anything he had ever known. He stood and had to rethink where he was several times. He looked back, thinking this would reset his swimming mind. But when he looked down again, he suddenly understood at least a little why the hunt had ended here. The Big Indian whispered a prayer of thanks to the dead Pronghorn. He now understood that its entire life had been directed so that its demise would bring the Big Indian to this moment.

The scene in front of him was laid out in all its confusion. Staring at the whole, he was as bewildered as when he first gazed upon it. What lay strewn in front of him would change him and the tribe forever. He stared at that fractured, glowing, pulsing thing and felt a change in himself he could not fathom. A vision and a feeling he didn't understand on any level. What was there was beyond all he had ever known.

What was there—was otherworldly.

He hastily loaded the pronghorn onto the blanket, tightened the ropes to the saddle, and dragged the beast at a fast walk back to the doublewide.

He hung the large carcass in his stand-alone garage and ensured the door was closed. He put the Appaloosa up wet, with a fresh bucket of water, then ran to his 1945 Ford truck.

It fired up with only two cranks, and the flathead V8 was gunned to the gills as he swerved up the dirt highway, kicking out a rooster-tail of blue-white smoke and the dust that shot up behind him as he roared northbound, hell-bent into that Navajo blanket of starlight.

He encountered no vehicles on that seldom-used stretch of highway but swerved several times, narrowly missing animals crossing as he roared ahead.

He wondered about each animal he missed and what its message was to him. All those signs were adding up. Totems from the other world, spirits swirling within his bewildered haze.

He drove hard, praying that Chief Elu would know what to do, praying hard he didn't hit something. The thought passed through him; what would the wreck of him and his cherished truck look like at this incredible rate of speed?

It was a notion that passed without any fear, as he was committed to his mission to find the Chief. Now, if he wrecked, it didn't matter. He would be okay with it if he departed his tense body.

His final statement, he thought, would leave little fragments of his truck and his blood for a damn country mile. He could see that devastation in his mind, and he mischievously smiled at the thought.

Just junk all across the horizon… a *real Navajo farewell*.

But he didn't wreck.

The peach Ford truck roared with fury into that gigantic moment as the wind blew furiously through the cab, buffeting his long strands of Navajo black.

And to his left, as he kept the pedal to the floorboard, he caught glimpses of the red, arcing explosions from the crazy Whites in Gallup.

But he had twenty more miles to go, and he chanted a prayer that he would not be pulled over.

The Navajo Nation was the largest reservation in the United States, and the tiny town of Window Rock was the center of that universe. He raced through his birth village, kicking up dirt all the way to the Tribal Headquarters. His huge cloud of dust announced his arrival.

The tribal headquarters in 1947 was simply a few doublewide trailers strung together, with picnic tables lined up for community feasts. It wasn't much to look at, but this little common area held much power for his people, and he loved to visit when he could. These were his *Dine*. His people. He was accepted there. No questions asked.

By the time he located Chief Elu, the venerable old man was in the middle of a moonlit gathering with many tribal families. At night, those Indians who worked in the border towns just off the Rez were home. Families gathered around the long tables, playing games, drinking cold beer, and eating frybread. Stories and muffled laughter floated on the summer breeze as kids ran rampant, and the Chief moved from table to table, familiarizing himself with all the new additions to each family.

Chief Elu used these nightly gatherings to learn the pulse of his people, who were now immersing themselves in the white world of the border towns. Jobs and money were out there for the taking, and the Chief encouraged his tribe to extend, as the money always came back to the tribe.

The minute Elu saw the Big Indian approaching, he politely excused himself, as the Big Indian rarely came so far north. They greeted with a handshake and a simple *hello* in Navajo. Then the Big Indian held silent momentarily, as they both looked at the tables filled with joyous families, sharing under the moon, which stood full in its blessing. The Big Indian wondered if the Chief sensed the tension he was holding. Elu was medicine like no other chief he had ever met.

When he felt the silence had been long enough to show respect, he turned, and the Chief looked his way, motioning for them to walk up the path to the nearby rock outcrop. Moments later, they had climbed the trail and stepped out onto the long rock, jutting out, overlooking the entire scene. They stood still for a moment and could see and hear the fireworks to the south in Gallup. The Chief silently nodded, and the Big Indian knew it was now okay to speak. He raised his huge hand to the moon and looked back slowly at the Chief.

"Something has come," said the Big Indian, "to the Plains."

He was certain that what he saw in the Chief's understated nod was a knowing—a confirmation of that which had been expected. The Chief had been a medicine man since way back, and he always seemed to have a channel to more information than the rest of the tribe.

"We need Sam Boyd," was all the Chief said

Dulce

Gallup

SAN JUAN RIO ARRIBA

MCKINLEY

BERNALILLO

ALBUQUERQUE

LOS LUNAS

Socorro

Plains of San Agustin

SOCORRO

Trinity Atomic Bomb Test Site

SIERRA

White Sands Missile Range

SILVER CITY

1947

DONNA

New Mexico

Corona

J.B. Foster Ranch

Mack Brazel Debris Field

Split Rock Crash Site

Roswell

Roswell Army Airfield
and Hanger P3

Chapter Nineteen

The Big Indian was winded from running as he boarded his truck, slamming the door.

A moment later, he picked up the Chief, and they raced southbound, hurtling toward Gallup and all the drunk whites shooting off fireworks.

Hopefully, Sam Boyd—who the Big Indian knew had a new baby—was not one of them.

Sam Boyd was a used car salesman in Gallup, and his lot was at the end of a long row of shops right in the middle of town. This meant the Big Indian would have to go into town, and he disliked that thought. He didn't like driving in Gallup, fearing he would be pulled over. It had happened before. The word on the Rez was always to walk if possible. The white cops played games with the Navajo, so he understood the game. And the best way to win was not to play.

He parked on the outskirts of town, grabbed a wad of cash from his glove compartment, and checked himself in the rearview mirror. Then he grabbed a rag from the dashboard, wiped his face and neck, and adjusted his neck scarf. The Chief stared ahead, sitting on the bench seat.

The Big Indian stepped out and thought he heard the Chief beginning to chant as he departed, but he wasn't sure. He ran toward the center of town, fireworks rising and exploding above him. The message to get Sam Boyd meant letting no one else know—except Sam. The Big Indian slowed when he came around the corner and began the long walk along the wooden boardwalk that passed each brightly lit storefront window.

Out on the wide dirt main thoroughfare were all the Whites, in a smoking, drunken stew of yells, explosions, drinking, and puking. Women were shooting six guns into the air, dancing, and puking more. He knew that when they saw him, they would sober slightly and say things aloud. But so far, he had passed unnoticed. His size alone would soon garner attention, but for the moment, he was just a large, dark shadow moving along the boardwalk.

As he walked, he was glad he had remembered the one-hundred and seventy-five dollars to cover a late payment he owed Sam. He had been meaning to get to town and give Sam the money but had gotten sidetracked as the hunting had been good lately. Now, he actually needed Sam Boyd and hoped his late payment on the truck wouldn't hinder his mission to convince Sam that the Chief had requested him.

He could feel the bulge of cash in his dirty denim jeans as he walked. The Whites were everywhere in the streets, and many were clearly drunk. He knew that *White and drunk* was something you didn't get near.

He kept close to the shop windows. He could see the reflection of all the fireworks and fanfare out in the street and thought it was better to look in the shops than at the Whites. He didn't want to provoke any trouble, and not looking out gave him some belief that he was invisible to the raucous crowd.

It felt good having that much money in his pocket. He could buy almost anything he saw in those windows—if he wanted to. Unfortunately, the money had already been spent, and he wondered how Sam would react to seeing him. The Big Indian approached Sam's used car lot with apprehension.

Sam could *see*.

He was the only car dealer the Navajo would deal with in town. The Big Indian thought about how he had first met Sam Boyd over a year ago. He had never wanted a truck, but finally, his friends on the Rez—who were now driving everywhere—had convinced him. He could haul a lot more skins to the pawnshops if he had a truck instead of taking them one by one to town on horseback. When he finally saved enough to buy a vehicle, the Big Indian was sent to Sam Boyd by Chief Elu and was warned by him,

"Expect very little."

The Big Indian took this to mean that it would be a regular encounter with a White, which meant lots of talking on their part, lots of signing papers, and then leaving with a feeling that, somehow, you had been *taken*.

On that hot August day, the Big Indian came upon Sam from behind while he was bent over the engine of a 1940s truck. Sam's body was half inside the engine compartment, and the Big Indian wanted to observe him for a moment before speaking. Like watching a rattlesnake bathing in the sun, the Big Indian thought it wiser to watch this Sam Boyd—sizing him up, watching his actions from behind. He had barely stepped into place behind Sam when, without looking up, Sam spoke.

"Chief Elu said you'd be comin'."

The Big Indian was shocked.

Had he not used his most silent approach? Was his shadow underneath the car? Was the wind from behind him? No.

The Big Indian stood frozen in place, troubled to his core. Sam gave one last turn on his wrench and slowly started to stand. He turned around and smiled.

"Chief said your name was Wolf," he said. "*Waya*. Is that how you say it?"

The Big Indian stared steadily. He had never heard a white man utter his real Navajo name. Much less pronounce it with a calm, guttural tone—like a native Navajo speaker—with the accent on the "ya." His head was swimming. The thought that Chief Elu would tell this Sam Boyd his tribal name was at once troubling and confusing. But the bewilderment at that moment was so overwhelming that he barely noticed Sam was no longer staring at him and had turned his attention toward his greasy wrench.

"Wolf or Waya, which do you prefer?" Sam uttered nonchalantly.

"Waya," the Big Indian replied. Shocked again that he answered without intending to.

Sam exhaled, sweat dripping off his chin onto his white tank top. There were marks of grease on his hands and shirt. He reached up with his sweaty forearm and wiped his brow with his wrench hand... then he lowered his arm.

He took a good look at Waya, motioning with his wrench toward the covered wooden porch.

"Waya, you want to join me for some lemonade?"

Waya slowly nodded, understanding enough English to know that Sam was offering him a drink. Though lemonade was little known to Waya—as it was not a common refreshment for Navajo. But Waya was too shocked to really care. He just wanted to quit the feeling of being overwhelmed. Sam's smile had become a simple expression—half tired from the hot sun—half respectful of this new Indian.

Finally, Waya turned and proceeded slowly to the porch, which stood just beyond the car lot where the shiny Model Ts and As were lined up in the grass. He looked past the cars to the porch, which sat underneath a large sign that read:

Sam's Used Cars Best deals. Financing available.

Behind the shop, attached to it, was a small house with a side entrance. He couldn't help but wonder as he walked—if his footsteps were somehow louder on this white man's property—as he had never been noticed like that before. He listened harder as he walked, feeling Sam Boyd's presence behind him as they made their way through the shiny cars on Sam's lot.

The heavy heat was typical of New Mexico summers, almost like wading through a hip-deep pond as you moved. Waya tried to smell Sam Boyd behind him. It was a natural thing for him to gather information about something or someone behind him, but all that he could smell was the slight odor of grease, car wax, and the freshly cut grass.

Just before reaching the porch, he couldn't help but notice a peach 1945 Ford truck with a white interior. The truck was like nothing he had ever seen, and he liked the color tremendously. He momentarily imagined himself pulling through the entrance to the reservation, while the tribe elders watched from the grocery store porch, where they congregated on the hot summer afternoons. The grass underneath that truck was really long. He concluded from this—that the Earth liked this particular truck well—and, hence, had sent long strands of grass to reach up, touch, and behold it. He caught himself pulling his eyes back to the center as he made his first step up onto the porch. He could feel the old wood bending slightly under his weight. He stepped to the side upon reaching the top of the stairs.

Sam motioned to a set of wooden rocking chairs at the far end of the porch. They were painted white and were separated by a small wicker table topped with daisies in a glass vase. Waya stopped in front of the far rocker and sat down apprehensively. He watched as Sam opened the creaky screen door and disappeared inside.

Waya stared out at the peach Ford, then surveyed the entire lot. All the cars and trucks sat there like a herd of steel horses, all facing the same direction. There were so many different colors and shapes, and the intrigue with all the moving parts was almost too much to comprehend. He didn't rock in the rocker. He held on gently to the armrests and waited. There was honeysuckle on the breeze, and the chica-chica-chica sound of the sprinkler on the side yard, shooting water across the straight lines from the push mower. Misty droplets gleamed in the hot August sun.

Off to the side yard, he could make out a small but fully packed vegetable garden—complete with lettuce, tomatoes, carrots, and even a few tall stalks of corn. Next to it, a lemon tree sagged under the weight of its fruit. He looked back at the lineup of vehicles. His friends on the reservation had told him that they would pitch in on the payments. There was to be a big powwow in the northern part of the state in August, and they wanted to go.

Sam returned a few minutes later, carrying a tray with a pitcher of pale yellow liquid and fresh-cut lemons floating inside. Next to it, two plastic cups and a neat row of sugar cookies rested against a stack of white paper napkins.

Over the next forty minutes, neither spoke. They had long since finished the cookies, and Sam had refilled Waya's cup twice more. Waya realized that Sam would fill it a third time if he drank his entire cup, so he didn't. His lips felt a little strange from drinking that much lemonade, but he liked the taste, nevertheless, and liked as well the thought of sharing a drink with this very curious, Sam Boyd.

When conversation finally took place, it was Waya who initiated. Forty minutes was not a long time to Waya. It was very common on the reservation when meeting with elders that nothing would be spoken for even longer. It was a gesture of respect, and it cleared the air. Waya had been ready for speaking at about the thirty-minute point, but soon realized that this Sam Boyd would sit in silence indefinitely. Waya had come to Sam and not the other way around, and so he figured it would be right for him to state the nature of his visit, which was to buy a truck from Sam Boyd.

It was at that point that Waya understood what Chief Elu had meant when he said,

"Expect very little."

On that first day of meeting Sam Boyd a year ago, Waya realized how Chief Elu had actually complimented a White man. That was a strange thing. Something that had never happened before. Chief Elu had said, *expect very little*, and in the Chief's cryptic way, he had honored this Sam Boyd.

Now, in the present moment—under the cover of darkness, with fireworks exploding all around him—Waya approached Sam's used car lot. He was anxious. Not just about his late payment, but also about how to tell Sam Boyd that the Chief had requested him at this midnight hour. Or whether Sam would even be at his shop. As he neared the car lot, he could see in the moonlight that Sam had some new models parked in the grass, which was still mowed perfectly even. He had barely set foot by the nearest car when he realized that Sam was staring at him from the moonlit garden, watering with a hose in one hand and a beer in the other. Waya still didn't know much about White ways, so he tried not to judge this strange scene.

Sam turned off the spigot and took a slow swig of beer, motioning for Waya to join him on the porch. Waya made his way through the cars and climbed the steps. Sam eased into one of the rocking chairs and wiped his brow. Waya, somewhat anxiously, pulled the wad of cash from his pocket and unraveled the bills. Then he walked them over to Sam.

Without so much as a glance, Sam laid the wad of bills on the small table and gestured for Waya to have a seat. Waya did so, though he was exploding on the inside. Sam took a final swig of his beer and wiped his brow. He stood and gathered Waya's payment, and half-opened the screen door.

"I'll be ready to go in just a moment."

Waya was shocked.

How could Sam Boyd know?

While he was still contemplating, Sam came back out through the creaking screen door, wearing an old cowboy hat and carrying a long-handled flashlight. Over his shoulder was a full military backpack, and around his waist, a canteen belt with various pouches attached. He looked at Waya.

"Ready," was all Sam Boyd said.

By the time Waya and Sam reached the truck, Elu was walking toward them with a gentle smile for Sam. Then the Chief and Sam did something Waya would never forget. They spoke in Navajo.

"Long time no see, Chief," Sam said with a smile.

Elu nodded.

"How's the baby doing?"

"She's fine," Sam replied. "But she doesn't like the fireworks, so Catherine and her went to bed."

Waya stood, shocked at the utterly flawless Navajo.

When the Chief saw Waya's reaction, he explained in Navajo that Sam Boyd had been his commanding officer in the war and was fluent in Apache and Navajo. That it was Sam that had formed the Navajo Code Talkers, and had worked with the Chief to create the code used to best the Japanese.

Waya slowly nodded, realizing that Sam Boyd had remained humble when Waya had bought the truck a year ago. Waya now understood how Sam had pronounced his name so perfectly on their first meeting. And how Sam had remained quiet, never promoting the fact that he knew Waya's language as well as any Navajo. Waya would never forget Sam's gesture of respect.

I t was just past 4 a.m. when the three arrived at the Plains of San Agustin.

Waya quickly saddled his best horses, and the trio was on the plains minutes later, at a fast walk behind Waya. He looked back occasionally in the moonlight and realized that Sam was clearly comfortable in the saddle and rode as well as any Navajo. Presently, Waya halted, and the three dismounted and followed him to the edge of the ravine. Sam and Elu stood in silence for some time, staring at what lay in front of them. Like Waya before them, it took several minutes of staring to adjust to the wild devastation.

Sam and Elu could see a glowing, dull silver, saucer-shaped craft—roughly fifty feet in diameter—jammed into the side of the arroyo at the end of the scorched ravine.

And below it, something—*alive.*

Chapter Twenty

She could cry no more.

It had taken her and Dah two days of long walks and many tears to process all the new information in Papa's letter. The depression had been heavy, and she countered it with a few long sits and self-care. Her flight to Nellis was only hours away, and she was torn about the looming debrief but didn't have many options. She looked up to see a tray of coffee coming her way, along with some Navajo frybread—her mom's way of showing Native comfort. They sat together, eating the warm bread, and she wrapped her arm around Dah's.

"You sang me your grandfather's passing song as I started to pass out. Did you think I was dying?"

Dah slowly shook her head.

"No."

Vyla watched her closely.

"I had a sense that the innocent one you were to that moment was leaving, and I sang her the passing song."

Vyla gripped her hand tightly and watched Dah as she slowly chewed her frybread, looking down into another world.

"There are some chosen for tasks to move us all ahead," Dah whispered.

Vyla stared and exhaled. She knew her mom was far ahead of what she spoke. Sometimes, Vyla only understood it after the fact. Somehow, Dah had the capability to dwell in another plane of meaning. And sometimes, she would say it aloud, and Vyla always had to catch up. Vyla felt herself wanting to crawl into a fetal ball but simply had no tears left.

"I didn't ask for this, Mom."

Dah slowly nodded, chewing her frybread.

"When are you leaving for Las Vegas?" Dah asked.

"My flight's late tonight. Then I'll come back in a day or so and pack up my place."

Dah nodded and looked up at the wall of pictures. Vyla looked as well, taking in all the vintage Navajo and Apache family photos.

"Papa mentioned the Roswell incident in his letter, and you had mentioned it once as well. I was just so young when you tried to tell me about Waya that I wasn't really paying attention."

Dah nodded, eating her frybread while staring at the photos.

"There are many pictures up there that are from the Roswell timeframe." She said.

"Mom, would you mind telling me again about what happened back then?" Vyla whispered.

Over the next two hours, Dah told her of the three men having their historic encounter with the ship from another world. Vyla stared transfixed as Dah finished.

"Why didn't you tell me this amazing story before now?"

"Because until now," Dah said. "It would have just been viewed as a simple Native American mythical story. But now you see differently. Hence the passing song."

Vyla watched Dah as she grew quiet again. She adored her on so many levels. Dah was the one who had taught her how to sit—the Native way of meditation—and how to receive and interpret energy to decipher what came through. How to wield that energy when needed. Something Vyla never spoke of except in hints to friends. The magic accessible to humans but long forgotten. Those deep dives into energy work had driven her toward physics and the science behind it.

Energy, she had learned in college, was still in the infancy of human understanding. Subatomic particles, below the size of an atom, were still a mystery. There was no *unified theory of everything*. But more than not understanding all the science behind it, she had quickly learned that her professors knew nothing of energy with regard to working with it. Dah had shown her how to open a pipeline as a little girl, one that she could access at will.

She looked up to see her mom focused on a picture of Sam and Waya at Sam's used car lot.

"Waya and Sam became closer through the years, and Waya knew his whole story," she said in a whisper.

Vyla nodded.

"So, after they reached the ship, what happened?" she asked.

Dah exhaled.

"That's a gigantic story," she said and slowly stood, picking up her old leather purse.

"If I don't get that young man some fresh dog food, he's gonna never let me hear the end of it. Plus, we need more frybread."

"I'll help you carry in the dog food when you get back," she said as Dah gave her a hug and exited.

She exhaled, worried about her mom, but knew she was a tough one. The rest of that morning, Vyla watched old footage of her dad doing interviews online.

Dr. Michael Wolf spoke so eloquently, answering questions from a couch in one video, and she imagined herself nestled in his arms as he did the interview. The sadness of her family's demise was still too overwhelming to dwell on. But she knew one thing for certain... an anger was rising, and she would have to harness it and attempt to channel it as best she could. She would manifest something positive out of her loss. Her revenge against the Cabal would have to be on her terms.

So much had happened in the last few days—it felt like a mission was being whispered to her. There was the UAP incident, then meeting an alien in person. Learning through Swizzle that she had telepathic abilities, most likely passed down from her father, had been a big leap. And now, topping it off... was Papa's letter, which gave her a broader picture of what was at stake.

It all seemed to be driving her toward exposing the Cabal. And that group was still perplexing, but she was absolutely positive about one thing: *she now knew too much*. It hit her all at once, not as a bad thing, but as something that must be done.

She would do everything in her power to get the word out, and she didn't care anymore if she died trying. For all those who had died before her, she knew one thing for certain—there was no turning back now.

Okay, here we are, and I can't tell anyone any of this, so deal.

Perplexing her... was the whole cover-up part of Papa's letter, claiming that not only her dad and Carl Sagan were involved with aliens, but J. Robert Oppenheimer and Einstein too. Everything was still so incongruous to her, and it made her realize how thoroughly the Cabal, whoever they were, had effectively brainwashed the entire world for the last sixty-five years.

She had learned from personal experience that proof of alien presence had to be seen to be believed. The audacity and arrogance of the Cabal stupefied her, and she could see how Papa had become so furious. That the Cabal had anointed themselves to handle the alien presence without presidential or congressional approval was beyond treasonous. But then, to terminate so many individuals like her father and Papa without remorse in furthering their stranglehold on power and control was simply organized crime.

And the thought that she could not discuss the Cabal with anyone was the worst part of it.

There is no way to strategize against an enemy that nobody believes exists! she thought and then realized that Swizzle was certainly aware of them. She breathed a sigh of relief. He was a smart one, and perhaps he would have some ideas.

She decided to only look at the contents of Papa's box when her mom was not in the room. She didn't want Dah involved in this new deadly landscape just in case her actions led back to her. There were several file folders, each tagged with a year. The thickest by far was marked: *Roswell Recoveries. 1947.*

As she hefted the wide folder, she could see right away that all the files contained within were stamped *Majestic-12, Eyes-Only,* and she nearly gasped. She had been curtly warned by her *Man-In-Black* during her upgrade brief in Geneva that *Eyes-Only* was a warning to all: no copies of the documents should ever be made under threat of prosecution. She now understood that *prosecution* by the Cabal meant *termination*.

Papa had to have some serious anger to sneak these files out, not to mention his bravery. She exhaled, pondering how to proceed, but knew one thing for certain: she had a ton of catch-up to do regarding all the alien interactions and diplomacy over the last sixty-five years.

Roswell kept rearing its head.

She knew that Waya and Sam's saucer had crashed near that area. And certainly, the entire alien presence seemed to have ramped up after Oppenheimer's Trinity test, which was only miles to the west of Roswell. She wanted to understand America's full history with aliens to garner the bigger picture. Then, she could make better decisions for the next steps. She lifted the first file, which was stamped:

Eisenhower, Roswell. 1947.

Opening the folder, she was faced with an 8x10 black-and-white photo of former president Dwight D. Eisenhower when he was still a general at the end of WWII. The picture's inscription read:

Ike, June 1947.

She knew that Eisenhower was called *Ike* back in the day. She also knew that the Roswell events occurred in early July of 1947, so the picture seemed in keeping with that timeframe.

She was determined to find that connection now. She laid the photo on her lap and placed her fingers over the image of Ike.

This was *her window* that Dah taught her how to access when she was just a little girl. An energy vortex she had learned to expand whenever she was alone.

Channeling.

Only Charlotte and Marten knew of her strange capability. She could channel with any remnant of the person—a piece of clothing they wore, the car they drove, or even a handwritten letter would work. Photographs and drawings were fair game as well. She had learned that these things were like energy pathways to that person and that a pipeline could be expanded and engaged. She had become so nuanced in her energy work that she only needed to be near someone—to access important milestones in their lives—good or other. She could essentially dissolve—into them.

With her fingers gliding over Ike's face, she took a deep breath and closed her eyes. She had never been a general before.

A moment later, she felt the tingling—the vortex widening as she reformed into another. She was no longer she. She was Ike.

Dwight was never nervous.

He was too old for that. Nor anxious, either. Hell, he was a five-star general and the current Army Chief of Staff, not to mention his position as overall commander of the victorious forces in Europe during WWII.

On that night, like many other nights, he was flying a cross-country in a 1940 Army Beech-18. The twin-prop, eleven-seat taildragger was a rugged bird that could land almost anywhere. And for Ike, as the country called him, it was just another top-secret mission to handle something big for President Harry Truman.

These flights were generally *business as usual* for Ike. But he knew he was out of his league on this one. He was on his way to Walker Army Airfield to deal with a new threat to the United States and the world. Dwight felt something in this moment that he had not felt in ages.

Fear.

And in that moment, he knew it was because of a new adversary.

The Visitors were here now, and they were not going away. America was suddenly not *number one* on the planet anymore, and that fact threw him. But the technology the Visitors had displayed confirmed it for all who knew about them.

Humans... Ike had learned, were really primitive in the overall scheme of what was out there. And what was out there terrified him. Normally, in dealing with an adversary, Dwight D. Eisenhower was all about planning. It was his brilliant strategy used in the successful *Torch invasion* of North Africa in 1942 that routed the Germans, and then he had deftly topped that with his *Overlord invasion* on D-Day of 1944. A dagger that cut the Nazis off at the knees, effectively ending Hitler's reign of terror.

Ike had a great confidence that he could drop into the mind of an enemy and plan around what their agenda might be. But this adversary was foreign to him. And not in the sense of German or Russian, of which he had experience. The new threat he faced didn't even have a face in his mind. But that was about to change.

He stared out the window of the Beech-18 as it descended toward Walker Army Airfield, which he now remembered had been recently renamed. Now, it was world famous as the only nuclear base in the world—the source of the atomic bombs that ended the war. And it was now called—Roswell.

Moments before boarding the flight, he had been informed via a secure channel that he was flying to deal with a situation that could not be briefed in advance. And this unnerved him. He had a sinking feeling and knew where it sourced from. Ike had first been made aware of extraterrestrial contact when the Navy recovered a saucer floating in the ocean off Saipan in 1940. He was one of the few—who still to this day—knew about that one.

But it was the first mainland crash in Cape Girardeau, Missouri, that changed everything. That recovery occurred in late April of 1941, and since then, the Visitors had begun showing up in flying saucers, wafting electromagnetic pulses over American bases worldwide to gather information.

The tiny handful of people who knew about the aliens were terrified. He happened to be in the right command structure when they decided to show up on American soil in an actual flying saucer. He would never forget the first time he encountered them. It was beyond surreal, and he knew in that instant that the course of humanity would never be the same.

He leaned his bald head slowly toward the window and tapped his tan cranium ever so slightly against it, looking down at the unlit black hole below, which he knew was the New Mexico desert. He felt the unease creeping through him... of what *they* were—and it brought him back to where this evolution with *The Visitors* had begun.

Missouri. He thought. Cape Girardeau, Missouri, in 1941. That's where this goddamn lie had really become a juggernaut. That's where the specter raised its ugly head, and it was deadly from the get-go.

Ike was working as an aide for Army Chief of Staff General George C. Marshall at the War Department Headquarters, and he was surprised to get the call after hours to report immediately to the general's office.

America's entrance into World War II would not happen until December of that year. He entered the Munitions Building in Washington, D.C., that late April evening to find General Marshall wide awake and on the phone. The general motioned Ike to close the door. A tense look on his face as he hung up the phone.

"Evening, son, I need you to do a little recon trip over to Missouri for me."

Ike's eyebrows raised slightly as he nodded to the general.

"Yes, sir... what's in Missouri, sir?"

"Mainly cowshit, Colonel," Marshal said. "But something crashed down there, and I need you to get me some information regarding that matter. Your Beech-18 is on the tarmac, ready to roll."

Six hours and nine hundred miles later, Ike landed at Sikeston Army Airfield, which was only a few miles south of the supposed crash site. The Beech-18 touched down on the Sikeston grass-landing-strip in stark moonlight at 2 a.m., aided by lanterns the Army airfield crew had placed around the strip.

Ike was greeted that morning by a clearly shaken thirty-one-year-old Captain Charles Root. Ike had read Root's dossier on the westbound flight and was impressed with the eight-year Army pilot. A no-bullshit, brilliant aviator, Root was commander of the Missouri Institute of Aeronautics at the airfield and had placed the initial crash call to General Marshall. Captain Root introduced Ike to Cape County Sheriff Rueben Shade and County Medical Examiner Dr. J. H. Cochran. All three men had just come from the crash and would escort Ike northbound to see the situation firsthand.

Ike rode up front with the sheriff as the early pleasantries were exchanged, but he knew when he was in the presence of destroyed men, and these three had clearly been traumatized to their foundations. The toughest men Ike knew always showed their hands if you knew how to view them, and he had learned that trick over the years. Even when they were doing their best to smile and be respectful—as all three of these men had been upon greeting—he knew they were out of their minds. Moments later, riding in Shade's patrol car with the red light breaking the unlit country roads, there was the damnedest eerie feeling, and Ike knew the energy of it was from these three men.

Generally, men in the presence of a Colonel from Washington were politely inquisitive upon first meeting a dignitary and would engage in simple banter to gain favor with a Washington insider. But in the pitch black of that tense morning, the three veterans went quiet after the first turn onto the highway northbound, and Ike knew he was in for something no one wanted to discuss. Ike had seen truly awful Army crashes during this current buildup to fight Hitler—Army troop transport accidents where young soldiers had gone through decapitation and dismemberment in too many nightmarish ways.

General Marshall had not told him what type of airplane had crashed, but he knew one thing: It was not a commercial airliner, as the Army would not have been called. So Ike assumed that a large transport must have gone down, and these unfortunate three just happened to be in the wrong place at the right time.

Minutes later, the car was ushered through a heavily armed roadblock, and a moment later, Sheriff Spade turned off the highway onto a farmer's field. In the headlights was clearly the smoldering swath of whatever fireball had exploded across it, skidding and blasting trees and bushes down in its wake.

This had to be a large aircraft to have that much destructive power, Ike thought.

He stared out at the charred skid mark that was at least two feet deep in the pasture. Like a road grader had simply lowered its blade and pushed dirt and debris out of its way for a country mile. But strange to Ike, even the freshly grated dirt was charred and smoldering.

What in the hell? Ike thought.

A moment later, he got the very first hint that this crash was different.

"Sir," Captain Root said from the backseat. "From the folks who saw it come down, most thought it was a meteor, as it was traveling many times faster than any airplane they had ever seen."

Ike nodded but was perplexed, knowing that a large army cargo plane—even in a straight-down dive—didn't gain meteoric velocity. In addition, he had yet to see a wing or tailpiece or propeller-like object, which were normal clues to every crash site he had ever seen. There was always wreckage leading to whatever bulk of the fuselage was left. But not here. There was no wreckage anywhere amidst the smoldering trees and bushes as the Sheriff's car undulated along the shredded pasture.

Momentarily, they approached two huge army tents surrounded by MPs. Exiting the car, Ike was immediately hit with a death stench, somewhat indicative of a crash site, but then it was more than that. An odd smell of sulfur and vomit mixed. Captain Root held out a white handkerchief for Ike as the other men placed handkerchiefs over their mouths.

"Right this way, sir," Root said as he led the three men into the dark green tent with the large red medical cross on the outside.

"Attention on deck!" Root said as they entered, and several MPs came smartly to attention. They all wielded machine guns and were guarding two pallets in the center of the room.

"At ease, gentlemen!" Ike said aloud through his handkerchief.

"Now, I appreciate all of you good soldiers, and I want everyone in this tent to get outside and get some fresh air. We'll call you back in when we're through."

Ike didn't have to wait long as the eager guards did not have handkerchiefs to filter their breathing while in the tent. He saw at least two who ran out were pale from the overwhelming stench. Dr. Cochran motioned for him to step forward toward the makeshift field table made of two-by-fours and pallets. Ike stared, stupefied, at what lay before him. He did his best to hold his nerves steady, but as much as he wanted to keep his cool, he was suddenly out of his head, in shock at what he was staring at.

There were three small cadavers. Their faces reminded him of *Jerusalem crickets*, or as some farmers called them, *potato bugs*. The cadavers had humanoid bodies and strange anatomy. They were all roughly four feet tall and appeared identical, though he had never seen a potato bug that big. He immediately looked up at the three men—who were all staring down—with that look of being unanchored to life.

"What in the hell?" Ike said through his handkerchief.

"Sir, we believe these three to be aliens, who have somehow just crash-landed," Root said through his handkerchief.

Ike turned.

"Aliens? What?!"

"Yes, sir," Root said, pointing toward the other tent. "Their—their ship is in the next tent over—or what's left of it."

Ike looked down again at the four-foot-long creatures with the huge, black, almond-shaped eyes that wrapped around their heads. There was no nose—only two indentations—and the mouth was a single horizontal slit with no lips.

The creatures had greyish-blue skin that seemed rough like canvas, yet with the elasticity of lizard skin. Each cadaver had only four fingers and no thumbs. The bodies appeared to be wearing silvery flight suits that went all the way down and covered their feet. The suits were impeccable and clearly fireproof, as some of the fingers and faces of the creatures had signs of charring.

"That one on the left side was alive, sir, for about two hours after the crash, then it finally passed away," Dr. Cochran said. "It seemed like it was having a hard time breathing our atmosphere, but I just didn't know how to help it. I tried talking to it, but it just stared back—and I got some strange visions—or... well, I just couldn't talk to it."

Ike nodded, watching the overwhelmed doctor continue.

"I called Preacher Huffman, and he came out and gave all three of 'em their last rites."

Ike nodded again, realizing he was starting to feel sick.

"Can we go see the—" Ike said, pointing.

The lack of words coming to his brain reminded him... he was in shock, something that hadn't happened to him in over twenty years.

"Yes, sir, Colonel, right this way, sir," Root said, seeing that Ike was turning pale.

Once in the fresh air, Ike felt himself stabilize, and he spit, attempting to rid himself of the disgusting—whatever-the-hell-those-things-were—back there.

The other men quickly followed suit, spitting and coughing as if they had been too embarrassed a moment earlier to spit in front of a full-bird, unless he did so first. Ike could see off to the side that several soldiers had succumbed and were being tended to by medical personnel. He knew those soldiers were in shock that otherworldly beings had suddenly appeared in their God-fearing community. He turned to Captain Root, pointing back at the medical tent.

"Just leave it surrounded with MPs and don't make any of them stand in that damn environment. The last thing we need is a guard to get sick in there, or worse. Who knows what disease those three in there are carrying?"

"Yes, sir," Root replied and led them into the far mess hall-sized tent.

After the "At ease" was given to the twenty or so armed guards inside, Ike stared at three pieces of what appeared to be the remains of a dull silver, saucer-shaped craft that he estimated would be thirty feet across if it were in one piece.

"Sir, it apparently broke apart on impact. That largest piece there is what tore up the pasture, and the other two hunks went off to the sides and started fires where they stopped. The whole thing was molten at first."

Ike stepped forward to the largest hunk, which was the bulk of the saucer. What appeared to be a small dome on top had been sheared off, and he could see three small child-like seats facing an instrument panel, which was very simple, with only a couple of dials and what appeared to be metal hand imprints with flashing lights.

"Where is that power coming from?" Ike said.

"We're unsure, sir. It seems like the three parts of the craft are still under some form of power that we can't yet locate."

Ike shook his head slowly, looking back at the huge pieces. There was strange hieroglyphic-type writing on certain parts near the dashboard.

"Where's the engine?" he finally said.

"Well, sir, we don't know. And nobody has yet to smell any gas or oil," Root said.

Ike stared perplexed at the three pieces as Root continued.

"Other than the sound of the actual craft hitting the field, it had been silent as it shot across the sky, and then slammed into the pasture in a skidding fireball."

Ike nodded and stepped to a large piece that was ten feet across and smooth like a silver china plate. He could see no rivets, welds, or any structural binding points to hold it together. The metal looked like industrial steel, yet it appeared to be as thin as a razor blade. He touched the surface and attempted to look under the perimeter edge. He was shocked when the simple lifting of his fingers made the entire section move. Captain Root saw Ike's astonishment.

"Yes, sir, we couldn't believe it either when we first began to move these pieces to this location," Root said. "The entire ship is light as a feather, but don't let it fool you... that metal is—well—it's strange."

"Is it steel? What do you mean?" Ike inquired.

"Not sure, sir," Root said, shaking his head. "But my boys tried to bend a tiny piece they found in the field, and as soon as they released it, it seemed to reflexively take its original shape. Then they tried to break it in half, first with a crowbar and then, when that failed, they went after it with an industrial blowtorch. But it remained completely intact. Wouldn't burn or melt or nothin'. Finally, the guard shot a bullet into the piece, and damned if it didn't absorb the bullet and then expanded right back out to its original form. And the damn bullet was pulverized into a flat piece, like a penny."

Ike stared, shaking his head slowly, then looked at the three men.

"Gentlemen, you've done a great job securing this site. And I know I don't need to remind you, from the standpoint of national security, that this event absolutely did not happen."

The three men nodded and softly replied,

"Yes, sir."

"Sheriff Spade, I want you to work with Captain Root here and ferret out any of the public or press who were here and ensure, by whatever means necessary, to squelch any leaks about this incident. I'll have my intelligence agents here shortly, and they'll remain to help you over the next few weeks to keep a tight grip on any families, press, or radio who may attempt to leak information about this," he said and turned to the doctor.

"Doctor Cochran, I want you to take the utmost precaution before you go back in there," Ike said, pointing to the cadaver tent. "And get those—things, whatever they are, in formaldehyde ASAP, so we can prepare for an autopsy."

"Yes, sir," Cochran said. "I'll go right now and get some vats."

The three men watched Cochran depart, and Ike turned to the captain.

"Root, you stay here until sunup. I'll have a fresh set of soldiers replace your crew at dawn. We're gonna get this entire thing outta here on a transport as soon as it arrives. Spade, get me to a telephone."

N ow, back in the present moment, heading for Roswell, Ike was still staring down at the black hole of the New Mexico desert.

He remembered how it had taken him days to come back into his body after that first alien encounter. The Missouri crash retrieval had been efficient, and the ship and its three dead crew were flown to Washington, D.C., and secretly stored in the basement of the U.S. Capitol building.

Even in 1941, only a select handful of people in the world knew that below the U.S. Senate floor, in America's most visited building, was an extensive dungeon-like set of expansive rooms where valuable state secrets had been carefully and securely hidden for years.

Ike had handled the transition of bodies and materials to the Capitol building under the cover of darkness after business hours. Two weeks after the initial crash, it was as if it never happened. He had been pleased with the evolution, but almost immediately, that feeling of accomplishment had been doused when the *big lie* grew overnight and quickly became deadly.

America was on a wartime footing, and was monitoring German and Russian espionage agents across the country. There began a string of *unfortunate but necessary* "erasure deaths" in Cape Girardeau of several townsfolk who simply could not keep quiet about the little aliens who had come to town. Ike had been astonished to learn that a church right there in Cape Girardeau had so many Germans in the congregation that hymns were sung in German!

Within three months, there had been six fatalities by suicide around the area. Locals suspected the military was involved, as some of the whistleblowers were upstanding citizens who were not the type to off themselves. But those same upstanding Cape Girardeau locals, who didn't want to be *shushed* about something they felt every citizen had the right to know about, had "suicided" only days later.

Ike's Army intelligence team, who all sourced from the O.S.S., were desperate to keep the Germans and Russians from finding out about the recovered alien technology in American hands. The Office of Strategic Services boys and their tactics soon had the townspeople whispering.

"Shut the hell up or else!"

In Ike's mind, there had to be a line in the sand when it came to gagging American citizens, but he knew the O.S.S. knew no bounds. They were ruthless in their shadow world. Since the war ended, he had become wary of the O.S.S. and what they had become. He knew some of their operatives, like Alan Dulles and James Angleton. Those boys could machine-gun a handful of German recruits in one minute and be rocking their own granddaughters in the next—never thinking twice about it. Cold, calculated, and, when Ike thought about it, downright depraved.

He had seen the National Security Act paperwork winding its way through Congress. In early September, Truman would have an even more powerful entity that would combine all intelligence gathering worldwide. Ike knew this new agency would be a game-changer, and not necessarily for the public good. In Ike's view, it would quickly become the American version of the German Gestapo. It was going to be called the CIA.

He felt the plane begin to descend. What awaited him below in the New Mexico desert was something he wasn't ready for.

How could he be? he thought.

He was spooked to his core. Armed guards had delivered the brief to him just before boarding the plane. His presence was requested by higher headquarters to deal with a "developing situation" in the New Mexico desert. He felt the thump of the landing gear coming down into the airstream and the rear end of the taildragger rise.

That another race was advanced enough to travel to Earth from somewhere in space put things in a new perspective—and not necessarily a good one. It made him feel primitive. Like a barefoot Mayan warrior raising a spear against Spanish conquistadors in full armor suits, shooting fire-breathing cannons that ripped flesh and shattered bones. That humans were no longer leading the show was something Ike found hard to swallow.

Earth was just a primitive dot in a gigantic universe, and its people did not yet have the technology to travel into space. Everything had changed now, and he knew the new alien presence had to be carefully held as the country's top secret. It was hard enough for him to not come unglued with an advanced race arriving on the planet. But he knew the world would turn into a smoldering pot of chaos if the regular citizens of Earth knew about this stark new reality.

He felt the bird drop heavily on the Roswell runway and knew his landing was under complete secrecy. Ike was ushered under cover of darkness out of the plane into a waiting armed convoy. They were heading to the Split-Rock Crash Recovery operation, and Ike's mouth was completely dry for the first time in twenty years. His bodily response to complete fear. What terrified him as the convoy set off in the darkness was the fact that he was about to see another goddamn alien.

But this time—it was a live one.

Chapter Twenty-One

She heard him baying, slowly bringing her back into Dah's living room.

She opened her eyes, knowing she had much more to understand about Roswell. Then it hit her.

Her mom could not have returned yet. And Banjo wouldn't bay at her, anyway. The black sedan?

Suddenly anxious, realizing someone was approaching the house, she quickly placed the VHS and the folders back in the box and closed it. She knew it contained material from 1940 to 1986 and then realized it was the entire covert history of the U.S. involvement with aliens up until the 1980s.

Oh shit! She thought.

She slid Papa's letter into her purse just as Banjo bayed again. Then she heard them—multiple footsteps approaching the door.

They had to be coming for the box!

Hoisting the huge thing, she moved quickly into her mom's extra bedroom and dropped it with a thud in the back of the closet. That's when she heard the knock. Her heart was pounding as she approached the door on tiptoe. Dah didn't have a security peephole on her old wooden door to see who was out there, so Vyla leaned heavily against it and tried to sound calm.

"Who is it?"

"It's Stephanie," came the soft, shy reply.

Vyla almost fainted.

She dropped to her knees, heart pounding, and opened the door. Stephanie ran into her welcoming arms, and the two shared a long hug.

"We saw your mom at the grocery store and wanted to come by and surprise you!" Steph said.

"You surprised me, alright!" Vyla said, looking up and winking at Charlotte.

"You look like you've just seen a ghost!" Charlotte said.

"Oh, I'm just happy to see my favorite one. I've missed her."

Charlotte smiled, but knew something was up. She and Vyla had been lovers since they met three years ago, and nothing escaped between them anymore.

But she knew to be patient. All would be revealed. That's the way they rolled, and she felt more confident with each passing year.

Vyla stood, and they shared a strong, loving embrace.

"God, I missed you three!" Vyla said as they released and looked at Steph.

"Where's our main man?" she inquired.

"Marten had two therapy sessions in a row," Steph said. "But he should be at the house tonight. He's coming over just to see you."

"Awesome! Hey, can you help me with a big favor?" Vyla asked.

Steph nodded.

"Okay, close your eyes!"

Steph did so, and Vyla looked at Charlotte and winked. A moment later, she returned, dressed in shorts and clogs, carrying the heavy box covered with a blanket. She placed it in front of Steph.

"Okay, open your eyes."

Steph did so and stared at the blanket-covered box.

"You are ten now and one of the strongest girls I know," Vyla said. "Think you can heft this to your car while keeping it in the blanket? It's a present for Marten's birthday."

Steph suddenly seemed wary, and Vyla did a double take.

"What's happening? Is everything okay?"

"I'll get it," Charlotte said as she hefted the box, blanket, and all and turned to exit.

"Steph's feeling kinda sore all over," Charlotte added over her shoulder.

Vyla looked at Steph and took her hand.

"What's up, girlfriend?"

Steph shrugged slightly but clearly didn't want to talk as they followed Charlotte to the car.

They watched her drop the heavy box into the trunk as Vyla managed a quick, surreptitious glance down the street. The black sedan was on station, and she wondered if she'd just set off alarms with the box exchange.

Minutes later, her arm was around Steph as they rode in the backseat of Charlotte's car.

"I'm so glad to hear Marten's practice is growing," Vyla said. "He was worried nothing was happening."

"He's been doing hypnosis training with an old professor he likes," Charlotte said.

"Wow," Vyla said. "I've read about some of that."

"What do you think about it?" Charlotte asked.

"Hypnosis?" Vyla said. "Seems like it helps some people—how about you, what's your take?"

"I think it's all bunk," Charlotte said. "But Marten's definitely getting more clients because of it. He thinks it's valid for some folks."

"Cool," Vyla said. "Well, if it grows his practice, then great."

"How about you?" Charlotte inquired. "How's the new gig?"

Vyla caught her eye in the rearview mirror and half-nodded.

"It's fine."

Charlotte knew there was a world behind that short answer but figured she would hear more when Vyla was ready. Vyla looked at Steph, curled in her arm, and kissed her head.

"I hear you now have boobs?" Vyla whispered.

"Uh-huh!" Stephanie said, grabbing her chest over her shirt and lifting them like trophies.

"Oh my," Vyla said.

"They kinda hurt," Stephanie said. "My whole body hurts."

"Cramps?" Vyla asked.

"I don't know; it just hurts down there."

Charlotte adjusted the rearview mirror to see both of them while driving.

"Honey, don't worry," Charlotte said. "We're going to the doctor tomorrow, and you'll see, it's all going to be fine."

Steph looked out the window, and Vyla patted her shoulder.

"They're not bad," Vyla said. "I'm friends with my OBGYN. She's cool. You'll be in and out in no time."

Steph continued staring out.

"I got your Lizzy birthday present," Vyla said to distract her.

"Mm," Stephanie murmured without effect.

"I bet you're missing him already?" Vyla said.

"Nope, not at all," Steph whispered.

"Uh-oh?" Vyla said. "Did we have a falling out?"

Steph was quiet.

"Steph put them all in a bag for you," Charlotte said.

"What, you're giving all your friends away?" Vyla said, surprised.

Steph remained silent.

"Steph said they hurt her in her dreams," Charlotte said.

"Oh no," Vyla said. "I'm sorry to hear that."

"They're not what you think they are," Steph whispered.

"She's also ten now, and growing up," Charlotte said.

"Right. Well, of course," Vyla said.

"It's not about that, Mom!" Steph said, almost yelling. "I've told you that!"

Vyla could see tears welling up.

She gave Steph a gentle squeeze.

"I can't wait to read a book with you tonight," Vyla whispered.

Steph sniffled and curled into her.

Vyla kissed her head gently and noticed that Steph had closed her eyes.

Wow, she's really hurting, Vyla thought and casually glanced out the back window. The black sedan was trying to hide several cars behind them.

Moments later, Charlotte pulled into her ranch-style rental and carried the box inside as Steph and Vyla brought in groceries. Vyla watched Steph disappear into her room and turned to help Charlotte in the kitchen.

"Poor thing," Vyla whispered to Charlotte as she entered the kitchen. "She's really in pain."

Charlotte nodded, and they locked eyes.

"I missed you," Charlotte whispered.

Their embrace was long and gentle.

"Your mom seemed pretty down at the grocery store," Charlotte said. "Everything okay?"

"We found an old letter from Papa, and it was tough to go through it," Vyla said.

They released, and Charlotte watched her as Vyla continued.

"She's coming by in a bit to pick me up. I'm going to spend the day with her—but I'd like to come over tonight and have dinner with you before my flight."

"Yes, and yes," Charlotte replied.

"And..." Vyla whispered, staring at her.

This was their signal to announce any outside sex they had while they were apart.

"Yeah, someone at work." Charlotte said. "But it was just sex, and she bores me anyway... but I needed a little touch."

Vyla nodded.

"Me as well... someone at work... nice person... but not you."

Charlotte nodded, and they both heard the familiar sound of Dah's old pickup truck pulling in.

"Okay, see you tonight," Vyla said.

"Tonight, tonight, tonight," Charlotte whispered as they came together. The deep kiss that followed, combined with hands traveling across all playing fields, almost sucked them into the bedroom. But they pulled out of the dive just in time, and moments later—Vyla was gone.

Vyla carried in the huge bag of dog food and helped Dah put away the groceries.

She could tell her mom was down, still processing the letter and revelations. They agreed to play bridge for the rest of the day as it was Dah's favorite game, and they both needed to have some fun.

Vyla convinced her to take an early night and tucked her in bed with her favorite book and Banjo at the foot of the bed. She kissed her forehead, reminding Dah she would be heading over to Charlotte's for a late dinner before catching the red-eye to Vegas.

Dah reached up and placed her hand gently on Vyla's heart, softly gazing at her with her beautiful Native eyes.

"Trust this one," Dah whispered.

Vyla smiled and nodded.

Minutes later she was driving her truck to Charlotte's, and she noticed the black sedan always a few car lengths behind her. The thought of a quick-ditch attempt, just for giggles, crossed her mind. Then she realized that, in a way, she already had a window into the murderous Cabal just by taking the job with Yen's JRAD Corporation. That she had insider knowledge from Papa's letter about the Cabal gave her a momentary respite. She could work with bad if she could see it. But then she realized she had already led the assholes directly to her mom and best friends. They were all now in the Cabal's crosshairs, and that was unsettling. The whole damn thing had become a shit-storm, and the fact that her blood family had already been murdered by them made her feel completely hopeless.

She pulled into Charlotte's driveway, and sure enough, she only had to wait a moment before the black sedan wound around the cul-de-sac.

She let herself in and peered out the edge of the living room window, wondering about her surveillance team and if they were on her side as protection or because they didn't trust her.

She exhaled as Marten came around the corner, and they shared a strong hug.

"I can't wait to hear all the news of your new gig," he whispered. "But right this moment, I think you have a little girl who wants to see you."

She smiled and went down the hallway. It took her a moment to recognize Steph's bedroom because it was essentially a bare room. Steph was already tucked in her bed and seemed really down. All the UFO paraphernalia that had covered her walls and her figurines were gone. Even her favorite UFO beanbag chair was missing. There was a small plastic bag, packed to the gills, with a piece of tape that said *Vyla* on it.

"I put all the figurines in the bag for you in case you want them," Steph whispered.

"Do you want to tell me about what happened?" Vyla whispered.

Step shook her head, clearly wounded.

"Okay," Vyla said. "How about we just read a book?"

Steph nodded, and Vyla lay down beside her.

Steph was asleep before Vyla finished the bedtime story.

Vyla quietly stood and turned to watch Steph sleeping in the moonlight.

She had known love, but her love for that little one was different. A wanting so deep to protect that soft, sweet innocence.

I n the darkness on the far side of the cul-de-sac, Aspelsin adjusted a directional listening device inside the black sedan.

From where he was parked, he could hear the regular banter of the adults inside Charlotte's. In the moments when they were quieter, it was tough to make out what was said. His laptop suddenly chimed.

On-screen was a video image of Dr. Ferrell, the psychologist at Nellis Air Force Base, one of the few on the planet cleared to work with non-human intelligence issues.

Aspelsin shut off his listening device on the dashboard and looked at Ferrell.

"Neither performed very well," Ferrell said. "Sometimes, subjects are not suited for hypnosis."

Aspelsin stared at the older man, showing no expression.

"Do you want me to put Case and Will through another regression?" Ferrell asked nervously. "I mean, perhaps I—"

"That won't be necessary, Dr. Ferrell," Aspelsin cut in, with his deep, gravelly whisper.

"There are ways to find out what entity engaged the Twins."

"Yes, sir," Ferrell replied anxiously.

"Dr. Kells will be arriving in Las Vegas late tonight. Just have Case and Will monitor her movements at the Janet terminal."

Ferrell began to speak as Aspelsin closed the laptop and switched back on the listening device. Adjusting the directional antenna, he noticed that the house had gone dark. He slowly looked around the cul-de-sac and then took off his wide-brimmed black hat. Placing it on the seat next to him, he caught his reflection in the moonlit windshield glass.

His large scar stood out without the hat, and he watched it momentarily as it moved across his pale skin, extending in one direction toward the top of his head. The true nature of him. The reptilian beast inside, looking for a way out.

Vyla departed Steph's room and saw the house was dark.

She entered the living room to find Marten and Charlotte waiting with a candlelit tray of sushi and sake on the living room floor.

"Yum," she whispered, sitting between them.

A toast between all three, and the sake was chilled and delicious.

"What book was the winner?" Charlotte asked.

"My bet was any Dr. Seuss," Marten said.

"What was I scared of?" Vyla replied.

"Bingo," Marten said. "My favorite Seuss, by far."

"Steph's so dang sweet," Vyla said. "I really missed all of you."

"Well?" Charlotte said, barely able to hold her excitement.

Marten jumped on the bandwagon, his mouth full of spicy tuna roll.

"Yeah, *Miss employed by the hottest military contractor in the world*, what the hell are you doing?" he said. "Tell it!"

She had been preparing for this moment the entire drive up from Moss Landing. *Where would she even start?*

What had transpired was simply not believable to her, and she had lived it. But she absolutely wouldn't have believed it if she hadn't experienced it.

No way. Not a chance.

As part of her strategy to stay awake on the drive north from Moss Landing, she had pretended that she was Marten and Charlotte, listening to her story on a couch.

She didn't want to put them in harm's way by divulging top-secret things, so she made up her mind on that drive that she would play completely by the rulebook. In some ways, it seemed the strict rules of the Majestic clearance gave her a perfect excuse. And it was her job to uphold those rules. And hell, for all she knew, the Twins were parked outside the house with one of those listening dishes pointed right at the three of them. It was all too much.

Her by-the-book solution was by far the easiest and didn't cost her any more energy, knowing that she was already miserably depleted.

She took a deep breath.

"What I'm doing is national security related, and I actually can't talk about it," she said, taking a sip of the sake.

Silence.

Then, howls of laughter from Charlotte and Marten as both rolled backward, laughing. This went on for so long that Vyla laughed as well.

"Ha-ha, you fucking had me by the balls on that one!" Marten said, and Charlotte chimed in.

"Yeah, for a second, I thought, *oh my God, she's fucking serious!*"

As they rolled back up to sitting, their laughter slowly died. The room was suddenly quiet as Vyla stared at the tray and poured another shot. When she looked up again, dejected eyes stared at her. Distant and certainly confused. The three were silent as Charlotte and Marten slowly began to eat again, but the damage was done. This was not what she had planned. The sudden distance... she was crushed, and they were too.

"I'm sorry—" Vyla attempted.

"This sucks," Charlotte said, cutting her off with an air of distance.

Marten half-pleaded with Charlotte.

"Hey, come on, she's got a job—"

"She's our fucking friend!" Charlotte said coldly, cutting him off.

Vyla attempted to steer them back softly.

"Well, can you two tell me what you've been up to?" she said.

Charlotte stood abruptly and vanished into her bedroom. Vyla and Marten looked at each other. Marten went for the fix.

"Wow," he offered. "I'm excited for you. I mean, that's—"

"I signed a contract," she whispered, cutting him off.

"Right," he replied, staring at her.

An awkward silence. He slowly stood, straightening his clothes.

"Well, I guess... I'll be going," he whispered sadly.

She nodded, and he saw the change. Her silent tears rolled in the candlelight. He stepped toward her and sat down, wrapping his arm around hers. She leaned into him, and the floodgates opened. Charlotte appeared in the doorway, watching with tears, then swooped in slowly, joining the group hug.

"I love you guys so much," Vyla whispered through tears. "And I'm in way over my head."

HUSH

Marten handed out tissues from the coffee table, and all three snickered as they blew their noses. She felt a change and looked at her two friends. They really were her home. She had thought about having an outlet for everything that was happening. Some way to express at least the basis of her new life. She knew she needed grounding, and who better to do that than these two? But she knew she couldn't talk about this. At least not out loud, she told herself. Then, an epiphany.

She got a mischievous look, and both watched curiously as she silently entered Stephanie's room. A moment later, she reappeared with Steph's chalkboard in one arm and the wooden tripod in the other. She looked at them and put her finger to her lips. *Quiet!*

Both nodded, smiling. She set up the small tripod and placed the chalkboard on it, then walked to the living room window, ensuring the curtains were all the way closed. At this, Marten and Charlotte exchanged surprised glances. Vyla returned to the chalkboard and smiled like a mime as she produced a teal-colored chalk from her pocket. They shook their heads, smiling.

She then turned to the chalkboard and, with her back to them, scribbled furiously, blocking what she was writing. Finally, she turned away from the board so they could see what she had written.

Keep your mouths shut, no matter what I write.

Both snickered through nods and a thumbs-up. Vyla turned again and blocked the board, writing fast, then turned away again so they could read it.

There's a team that watches me now... due to my new security clearance.

Marten and Charlotte nodded with raised eyebrows.

I'll try to tell you what I can. What I feel comfortable with.

Vyla stared at them for a moment, contemplating her friends. They could tell she was torn about her next reveal.

Would you believe me if I said I'm doing an investigation for the White House?

Both stared and then slowly nodded. Marten gave a big thumbs-up, and Charlotte joined in. Vyla scribbled again.

Marten, I'm sorry, but that box is not a present for you. It's got documents I don't want my surveillance team outside to find. I need help from both of you to ensure that box goes back to Mom's house without them knowing where it went.

Both gave a thumbs-up.

Vyla blew air kisses to both of them and pounded her heart with her fist. They returned the gesture.

Then she stood still, taking them in. She contemplated this final reveal for a moment longer. These two, she could trust, and she would need an outlet. Otherwise, she would explode.

Once again, she hesitated. They watched as she began scribbling. She read her

211

own sentence, trying to be certain of herself. Then, she slowly walked to the side.

Would you believe me if I said there are malevolent aliens working with a rogue part of our government and military?

Marten and Charlotte stared, dumbstruck.

Vyla knew right then they were in complete and utter disbelief.

"I'm trying to get this," Marten whispered. "I really am, and I'm almost there."

Charlotte nodded.

"Me too... don't worry, we just need a minute."

"I love you two so much," Vyla whispered.

They both watched as she again put her finger to her lips.

They nodded, but the novelty had been replaced by a slight fear that she would reveal more information that would further rock their foundations.

She pulled Papa's letter from her purse and unfolded it, knowing this was important for them to understand. It would be hard to explain how deadly this new environment was unless they read the letter. She placed it between them and pulled the lamp over, covering the letter with white light. They both began reading, and Marten suddenly whispered:

"You've got to be kidding me?"

And the revealing of her birth family began. He looked up, as did Charlotte, to see that she was holding her family's picture. She laid it gently by the letter. Both took it in. Charlotte looked up with tears in her eyes.

"Oh, my God!" she whispered.

Marten was blown away, too.

"So sweet," he said, shaking his head at the beautiful photo.

She fought tears as they gently pulled her closer while both kept reading.

"Your dad's still alive?" Charlotte asked hopefully.

Vyla shook her head.

"Gone in 2000, pancreatic cancer, suspicious circumstances."

Both watched her, gripping her shoulder.

"I'm good, I'm okay," she whispered, motioning for them to continue reading.

Minutes later, they sat back, stunned. Marten gently picked up the family photo.

"Beautiful," he whispered with a smile.

Charlotte chimed in.

"Oh my God, so beautiful!"

Vyla nodded, her eyes full.

"How long have you had this?" Charlotte asked.

"Three days ago," Vyla whispered. "It took us two days just to process what's there."

Both watched her.

HUSH

"I'm departing for Vegas tonight to debrief my boss at Nellis, and I'm—I'm afraid," she whispered.

"What are you afraid of?" Charlotte whispered.

"I'm afraid of—them," Vyla said.

Both nodded, pulling her between them and placing her across their laps as all three remained in silence, holding each other.

Chapter Twenty-Two

The three friends slowly came around, and Vyla told them she had a little work to do before catching her flight.

They shared a hug, and she remained on the living room floor as they exited. The room was dark except for the moonlight streaming in beside the curtains.

As she gently folded Papa's letter and placed it back in her satchel, she thought about her looming meeting with Yen and her desire to gather more information about the arrival of the aliens back in the 1940s. She needed a broader history to judge the current situation better. Certainly, following more of Sam and Waya's story would help with that.

She raised a small framed photo out of her satchel. She had messaged her mom, that she needed the photo and knew Dah would be okay with it. She gently released the photo from the old frame.

The back was stamp-dated *July 1947*.

It showed Waya and Chief Elu standing together on the Plains of San Agustin. Waya's huge frame dwarfed his venerable chief, but Vyla sensed Elu's expansiveness. Waya's power was tangible in a different way and no less magical.

Dah had told her that Sam had taken the picture and given a copy to Waya months later. Written in ink below the two men was an inscription.

Near crash site. Plains of San Agustin, New Mexico.

She knew the Plains of San Agustin were directly west of Roswell and that all the crash events over that long weekend were somehow connected.

With her fingers gently placed over the two men, she felt the tingling as the pathway began to widen inside her. Sam had taken the picture, and that was all she needed to connect to him. She closed her eyes and slowly took a deep breath. Then she shot through, full-force; her body quaking and a split second later—she was a used-car salesman—on the Plains of San Agustin.

M oonlight bathed the plains as Sam, Elu, and Waya descended into the ravine and proceeded toward the saucer-shaped craft.

The ship still seemed to be under some form of power as it glowed an eerie bluish hue that lit the surrounding arroyo. Sam figured the disc was roughly fifty-feet in diameter and about fifteen-feet thick in the middle. It was impaled into the side of the arroyo, angling up toward the night sky. Small fires were burning along a five-hundred-yard swath of smashed trees, bushes, and charred earth. A carnage of shiny metal fragments was strewn lengthwise along the burnt trajectory, where the craft had crashed and skidded at excessive speed until impacting the arroyo.

Sam remembered the A.P. wire service release he had read two days before about flying saucers or *disc-crafts*, as the newspaper had called them. The article stated that a veteran pilot, Kenneth Arnold, in Washington State, had reported seeing a gaggle of nine saucer-like ships flying in formation over Mount Rainier. Arnold estimated each craft to be forty-feet-across and shiny like they were nickel-plated. They stretched a total of five miles from the first ship to the last, and several at the end of the formation were in constant motion. The tail-end ships would periodically flip, bank, and weave side to side, making the formation appear dynamic, like the tail of a Chinese kite.

Arnold decided to clock them between Mount Rainier and Mount Adams, a distance of roughly fifty miles. It only took the formation one minute and forty-two seconds to travel between the mountains—a rough calculated speed of 1,700 miles per hour. Sam knew that speed was at least three times faster than any aircraft in the U.S. inventory. The article stated that similar reports had flooded in from three nearby states.

Now, what lay in front of him seemed to have context, at least a hint of what this ship might be. Perhaps the Russians had somehow gotten ahead of America—that's what all the newspapers were speculating. Sam estimated this ship was about the same size as Arnold had reported.

"You think it's one of ours?" Elu whispered.

"No, I'm guessing it's Russian," Sam whispered back.

"Should we bring a gun?" Elu asked.

Sam shrugged.

"Let's go take a look, Chief. Whoever it is, can't be in too good of shape."

Elu nodded, and the two followed Sam toward the craft in the moonlight, working their way through the debris field. They touched nothing. The glow of the saucer-shaped craft lit the area immediately surrounding it. The disc had obvious damage. One long opening looked like a collision of some form had occurred. The four-foot-wide gap ran from the center of the disc toward the edge and was slightly rounder at one end, like a large exclamation mark.

Waya was getting more confused as they approached. Huddled in the shadow below the glowing disc, he could make out what appeared to be four kids' dolls, roughly three feet long. They were all under the edge of the ship that was angled skyward. Three were lying prone on little silver sheets, and one was sitting up. But the dolls did not resemble any kids' dolls Waya had ever seen. These were grayish in color, with heads bigger than humans but with skinny arms and legs. The hands appeared to have only four long fingers—no thumbs.

Overall, they resembled potato bugs to Waya.

What kid would play with a potato bug doll? Waya thought.

But then he saw the doll that was sitting up move its head ever so slightly. Waya had never seen a mechanical doll, and he stared, confused, as he heard no mechanical sound. Sam saw it too and raised his fist slowly to stop.

It was then that the wave hit them. Like a heavy curtain that wafted in, sadness and anxiousness were suddenly palpable to each man. Waya knew it wasn't coming from him, as he was not sad. He looked at the other two men and could tell they had felt it. Then it hit him: the creature was communicating with the three men! It was alive and watching them approach!

He now remembered the same heaviness when he had first discovered the crash. He could see that Sam and Elu knew it at the same moment.

"Alright... let's move in slow," Sam whispered.

As he stepped forward, Sam could see that only one had survived uninjured. The one next to it had a mangled leg and was barely alive. The final two were certainly dead—one with its chest blown through, and the other cadaver seemed twisted as if its neck had been broken, leaving the body in an unnatural posture. Somehow, the non-injured one appeared to have placed its three crew members on thin silver sheets that reminded Sam of aluminum foil. He then recalled that paramedics in the war had placed soldiers showing signs of shock on blankets to calm them.

The creature with the leg wound had a small box beside it, wrapped in silver

216

material. Sam figured was some type of first-aid kit. The unwounded creature wore a dull metal headband of some sort. The other three had no headgear. The wounded creature now watched them closely, and though clearly anxious, it didn't move.

Elu and Waya stayed just behind Sam as he proceeded forward, stopping only twenty feet away. He slowly raised his hand in greetings to the creatures. There was no response. He lowered his hand and calmly approached, now only a few yards away. Elu raised his hand for Waya to hold. The two watched Sam move without haste, his head was chin down in a deferring gesture to the two living creatures, who grew more anxious as he approached. The wounded creature crossed its hands over its head and cowered. Its leg wound was severe, preventing it from running.

The uninjured creature began scooting backward, trying to hide further beneath the angled-up ship, raising its hands and crossing them as if it feared being hit. It was radiating anxiousness.

Sam slowly knelt as he reached the tilted-up disc. Chief Elu and Waya watched in fascination as a curious thing happened. They watched him slowly sit just below the edge of the ship in the white dirt, the glow of the ship illuminating his calm demeanor. His gentle approach seemed to change the energy around the ship as if it, too, were alive. Waya and Elu exchanged a glance as the new calmness wafted over them.

To Sam's astonishment, the area below the ship, where the creatures were taking shelter, was cool. Yet the outside air temperature was over ninety degrees on that moonlit July 5th morning. Sam was perplexed as to why the area was so cool. He reached up to touch the glowing ship. Sure enough, it was cold, like metal in winter!

It had power of some sort? he thought. *But how? There was no engine running, no sounds whatsoever. Was it generating its own energy? Was this ship alive?*

It brought him to the stark realization that he was not just dealing with creatures or animals... but aliens—from another planet!

My goodness, he thought.

But to him, what was most important at that moment was that they were clearly in distress, and his goal was to help if he could.

He watched the healthy one do a double take, slowly lowering its protective gesture. The anxiety and fear in the vicinity dimmed. Whatever the creatures felt seemed to emanate like emotional waves, changing with each new circumstance. The calm of Sam Boyd made Waya think it was good for the creatures, and he whispered this to Elu, who nodded.

Sam confirmed visually that the two crew members on the right were dead. The one nearest Sam had a massive gash in its right leg, and yet there was no blood. Only a clear liquid was present, which Sam thought smelled faintly of battery acid. The healthy one came forward, and Sam looked the other way as if to say, "It's okay."

The little creature slowly approached and sat by its wounded crew member. The wounded one removed its hands from protecting its face but did not sit up. Sam stared at the glowing white dirt so as not to scare the creatures. They watched him in silence, and all was quiet in the darkness except for the gust of hot wind across the plains.

"I mean no harm," Sam said softly.

He could see the grayish-colored skin seemed dolphin-like in texture. There was no nose, only two indentations where a human nose would be. The arms were long, and the hands, each with four long fingers, reached almost to the knees. The fingers on each hand appeared to have small suction cups at the ends, *like an octopus,* Sam thought.

The creatures remained silent, and Sam slowly began to sign at the healthy one as Elu and Waya watched.

"Sam Boyd is signing that he means no harm," Elu whispered to Waya. "He taught us Code Talkers how to sign when we were at radio-signal school. He required every soldier in our signal platoon to be fluent in sign language before we could graduate. Sometimes the radios failed on combat missions, so we used Sign instead. When signing wasn't understood, we used pictographs, drawing pictures on small writing pads."

Waya nodded as he watched Sam in the distance.

Sam stopped signing when he realized the creatures had not understood. Reaching into his canteen-belt, he produced a pen and a small pad of paper. He drew on the pad and gently tore off the piece of paper, slowly offering it to the healthy creature.

The creature showed the paper to the injured one, and they both looked up. Sam had drawn a simple rose.

He then drew a stick figure of a man drinking water from a canteen and handed it over. Then, he placed his canteen near the two.

They looked at the paper and stared at the canteen. Neither moved to take the water. The injured one lay back, clearly worn out and dying.

Sam felt exasperated. He knew a lot about language and communication; linguistics had been his major in college. His professor had once mentioned that humans might one day learn to share information with just thought.

Telepathy was the term, and Sam had been fascinated by the possibilities. Allowing two entities to communicate without speech would be much more efficient than any spoken language. Then, at that moment, as if somehow picking up on Sam's energy, something began happening that Sam would never forget.

The uninjured creature began probing him with energy, like an acoustic pulse—a wave of thumps that seemed to reach further and further into his brain with each moment. Sam understood on some level that the creature was probing for the frequency that his brain waves would respond to, and he somehow knew he must relax to receive it.

He exhaled, releasing—allowing the energy tentacles to reach further and deeper—expanding toward the center of his consciousness.

Sam and the creature locked eyes, and then—a message.

We came in peace. We are not here to harm your people.

He suddenly heard it in his head, though the creature had never moved its mouth! Sam realized there was no actual sound being created by the alien; he had simply heard a voice in his head. His own voice! As if he were talking to himself!

Oh my God, he thought, awestruck at what had just transpired. He knew he would not use those particular words in that specific order. So, it had to be the creature, yet using Sam's voice!

Yes, Sam suddenly heard again. *I am communicating to you without speech.*

Sam stared at the creature, then looked over at Elu and Waya to see if they were hearing the same thing.

I am only heard by you. Sam heard, and the second epiphany hit him.

The damn thing was reading his mind!

He decided to meet the alien on this new playing field. He looked and held its gaze.

I understand, and I'm trying to help you, Sam relayed through thought, without speaking.

The creature shifted at this, then slowly reached up and removed its headgear, laying the dull silver piece on the white dirt, appearing calmer.

Oh my, Sam thought, as the realization that telepathy was happening flooded his senses.

He slowly approached the creature with the mangled leg and stared at the charred flesh. The healthy one watched, and Sam had to fight the sad and scared energy that seemed to be emanating from both.

Are you thirsty? Sam thought.

The creatures just stared. He slowly stood, backed up a few steps, and looked over the ship with its long gash. The damaged area was roughly four feet wide and fifteen feet long. It ran from the outer edge up to the center dome. The gash exposed a big swath of the interior of the ship, and he could make out three small seats near the dome, facing a tiny console of what appeared to be screens.

The blinking lights extending from the gash confirmed the ship was still under some form of power.

The cable tossed back and forth like a horsetail in the light breeze. The tiny lights were blinking and glowing. He hoisted himself onto the smooth, glowing craft and was astonished to find it was freezing cold!

Like metal in the Arctic! He thought, astonished. *And it must be offsetting the outside air for the creatures to stay cool.*

He shook his head, amazed. Worked his way up the long gash toward the dome top, looking inside for other occupants, but saw none. The thick cable, with all the tiny lighted cables inside it, appeared to be connected to small brown squares within the ship. Each square protruded every few feet inside the double-hulled craft. The small squares had a pink cover with some form of writing that he thought looked Egyptian or Cuneiform, which he had studied in language school.

Not one part of the craft, inside or outside, had any rivets or seams and appeared completely smooth, as if molded from dull grey candle wax. There were no right angles anywhere that he could see.

Amazing! he thought.

He finally worked his way off the ship and stood, looking at the overall situation. From the large rip in the double hull, he figured the ship had collided with something in mid-air before it crashed—perhaps one of the new wireless Marconi towers or another aircraft. He looked at the moonlit sky and knew daybreak was only a couple of hours away. He had to make quick decisions, as there were predators such as coyotes and even an occasional wolf pack, and all of them hunted in darkness.

Sam looked back once more at the creatures and their dead crewmembers.

I will try to help, he thought, but the creatures just stared back.

He turned to Elu and Waya and signed. Chief Elu signed back and then turned to Waya and whispered in Navajo.

"We are leaving the creatures here. One needs medical attention, and Sam wants to call the military."

Departing the area of the crash in the pre-dawn darkness, Sam told Chief Elu and Waya that it would be best for them to ensure no other Navajo or Apache entered the plains until the military had finished the recovery. Waya had Apache relatives in Socorro, and they often hunted the plains as well.

The chief agreed it would not bode well for either tribe if they were involved with anything that might hinder the military response, which Sam knew would be aggressive.

Sam and Chief Elu had often discussed White relations, as they had become strained recently, and any type of write-up in the newspaper could freeze government aid. The Navajo and Apache were already poor enough and needed every penny the U.S. Congress was sending.

The three had worked out a plan. Sam would not call in the crash until daybreak. Waya would remain behind and patrol the crash area for any predators that might approach the living creatures. If any Whites came near the crash site at daybreak, before Sam returned, Waya was to leave the area, pretending he had not noticed the ship.

A t daybreak, Sam and Elu were at Waya's trailer, listening to the radio for news.

Sam noted Waya's huge clock. *Six a.m., July 5, 1947.* He looked at Elu and picked up the phone... moments later; he was informing an operator at Alamogordo Army Airfield about the crash. He knew the army would respond without hesitation. He hung up and hastily opened his large marine backpack. Minutes later, he looked himself over in the mirror, surprised that his olive green Marine officer service uniform still fit. It had only been a year since he had gotten out, and he was glad he hadn't gained too much weight. He knew that military personnel in an emergency would respond better to him if he were in uniform. He hiked out to the dirt highway next to the plains and saw Waya slowly approaching on horseback. They spoke in Navajo, and Waya said the last couple of hours watching the creatures had been calm and that there was only one coyote he had to chase away. Sam nodded, but could see there was more to come.

"There are many Whites there now," Waya said and tossed the sweating Sam his canteen. Sam took a deep drink, replaced the cork, and tossed it back.

"Ahe'hee," Sam said, breathing hard, his uniform so sharp, though his black, shiny shoes were now covered in the dust of the white plains. They both heard the rising whine of engines being pushed to the limit and knew the huge Army convoy had arrived. Waya immediately kicked his horse in the direction of his trailer. Sam watched the huge Navajo trot his Appaloosa across the dirt highway and disappear into the woods beyond. Waya kept his Appaloosa moving through the woods at a fast walk, then turned her when he was out of sight of the highway. The *"thank you"* Sam delivered in perfect Navajo reminded him of how strangely connected he felt to Sam. He watched as the convoy approached from the east, with sirens wailing. It slowed, coming to a full stop where Sam stood with his hand held high. Waya then realized that the chief was in the trees a short distance away, watching Sam and the convoy. The chief's face was a mask of concern. Waya sensed a darkness in the Chief's stare, as if Elu knew what was in store for Sam Boyd.

Chapter Twenty-Three

At 1:08 a.m., twenty-six minutes into the flight, Ben had leveled off MH370 at 35,000 feet and made his call to ATC that he was at FL350.

"Flight level 350—Malaysian, uh—three-seven-zero."

The autopilot was engaged as the jet moved steadily over the Gulf of Thailand toward China. The fumes had done their damage, and Ben was fighting hard to stay awake as he made his second call. This call was not required—it's just that he'd forgotten—that he'd already made it. This time, however, he began the callsign with an eight before catching himself.

"Malaysian—eight—uh, three seven zero, maintaining level three five zero."

He was so disoriented he found it hard to maintain his anger at his handlers. The ones who had not told him the full plan. Those who were withholding information—the ones he knew had pre-planned a fire in his cargo hold. It was now registering in his system—the halon fire suppression was automatic—and was now fighting a fire he couldn't see... that he knew his handlers had set.

Those fuckers!

Behind him in the dimly lit main cabin, the hijackers attempted to move methodically as they zip-tie handcuffed and blindfolded the remaining passengers. But in the sewage death stench of that main cabin, the hijackers themselves were disoriented, not realizing that directly under them, the lithium-ion batteries had ignited and were now in flames. Bromine gas fumes were circulating throughout the entire jet.

The hijackers moved unsteadily, always having to step over the executed passengers scattered through the aisles. Some of the hijackers who previously had stood firm in the aisles, were now leaning against bulkheads as the passengers sat silent and the smell of death, urine and feces only increased with each minute as all passengers were strapped in, blindfolded and handcuffed. And since all passengers were relieving themselves while strapped in—the main cabin began to reek like a flying shithouse. Just when it seemed that nothing else could be worse—the smoke... visible black smoke, began to pour into the cabin.

Minutes later, at 1:19 a.m., Air Traffic Control told Ben to contact *Ho Chi Min radar* on a separate frequency and wished him goodnight. Ben should have responded as any pilot would do, when switching frequencies by repeating what the controller had said... and then saying *goodnight*. But Ben, being a hijacker, knew this would be his last call of the night... so he made it short and sweet. Standard flight protocol... nothing dramatic. It would be made dramatic by the media, after the fact. But in that moment, for the completely disoriented hijacker and operative, it was simply a radio reply.

"Uh—goodnight uh...Malaysian uh... three-seven-zero."

It was standard flight protocol. Nothing dramatic. It would be made dramatic by the media after the fact, but in that moment, for the completely disoriented hijacker and operative, it was simply a radio reply.

"Uh—good night, Malaysian—uh, three seven zero."

Ben immediately heard his CIA handler tell him to *go dark*. Already connected to the jet's system via his embedded tech, Ben sent simultaneous signals to the ACARS reporting system and transponder, switching them off instantaneously.

At 1:21 a.m., moments later, MH370 disappeared from all radar screens. Ben was aware that the U.S. Airforce AWACS, which had been shadowing him miles off his wing in the pitch black, would now go into action. The AWACS bird began what would later be identified as Project Eclipse, *which was specifically set up by the Cabal to cloak* MH370, disrupting any long-range civilian and military radars that undoubtedly would start looking for the jet now that it had disappeared from their screens.

The U.S. Air Force AWACS bird—began spoofing civilian and military radars alike—while simultaneously cloaking the whereabouts of MH370.

Right then, triggered by Ben turning off the transponder, the Cabal reached the peak of their first act. And that salacious middle finger to the Chinese government came in the form of the ultimate *fuck you.*

While Beijing sat watching the prized jet on satellite video, coming their way in real time—bringing the semiconductor technology and engineers they were salivating for—the damn jet... suddenly burst into flames!

Ben felt it—when the massive pallet full of lithium-ion batteries in the forward cargo bay—exploded, with such force and brightness that an oil worker three hundred miles to the east suddenly witnessed a bright torch in the western sky. The oil worker said the fire lasted a full ten seconds. The fire was so bright—he could tell it was a jet of some sort at high altitude—burning. He would call it in to the authorities hours later.

In the cockpit, what had been only darkness outside Ben's view, suddenly illuminated with a brightness reserved for arc welding, and the explosion shook the entire airframe. Ben went into automatic mode as a pilot, seeing the bright flames outside his window.

He screamed at his handlers as he manually overrode the autopilot and shoved the stick forward—pushing the nose of the 250-ton jet down, with a hard left turn, back to the west. And he shoved it harder—deeper and deeper into that dive until it was a racing dart—falling nose first, on fire and bound for disintegration. Ben knew two things in that instant. He had to get the fire out, and he had to get air.

Behind him in the cabin the strapped in passengers, blindfolded and handcuffed, collectively screamed as they slumped forward in their seats, held only by their seatbelts as the hijackers fell to the floor in aisles, holding onto the base of the seat next to them. Cadavers of the assassinated slid down the aisles, tumbling towards the front of the jet. Water sprayed from the cabin fire suppression system through the black smoke filling the cabin and that water ran like a river down the aisles—taking blood, shit and urine with it toward the front of the jet—as everything cascaded toward the locked cockpit door, made to withstand any entry when it was bolted closed.

Upfront, Ben held the stick forward as the blood colored, death stench water, gushed in below the cockpit door. The jet increased its speed and within seconds was descending at a rate, experts later monitoring Ben's recorded bursts, estimated to be up to 15,000 feet per minute. 170 miles-per-hour... straight down.

The jet was now plummeting too fast for structural integrity as an entire flaperon ripped off and flew away into the dark void—but in the strangest of coincidences, Ben didn't notice pieces of his wing coming apart.

You see... Ben was already at the height of his bromine gas intake when he made his final goodnight call. Just before beginning his dive, Ben had reached his limit. And he didn't notice a damn thing at that point—he was now beyond furious and even beyond screaming his hatred of all the Cabal treachery he was now privy to with a goddamn front row seat.

HUSH

Experts later would explain... that all they could hear on his involuntary six-second satellite burst, his hi-tech system made during the dive, was measured breathing by the man in the cockpit. And unbelievably... in the crazy, straight-down onslaught, with his trim all the way forward, holding the plane in its furious dive... a curious thing happened to Ben. He finally succumbed to the bromine gas... and didn't feel or smell the cold pool of blood colored water rising over his shoes in the nose-down cockpit. Ben, you see—was now—asleep at the wheel.

Chapter Twenty-Four

S tanding with his hand held high, Sam was amazed how fast the Army had responded, watching as the leviathan came in his direction, sirens blaring.

The lead car was a green Army Plymouth with a large white-star emblem on the side and red U.S. Army flags waving on the front bumper. Just behind it, a 2.5-ton troop transport was packed with heavily armed soldiers, all wearing blue berets. Behind it was a Willys radio jeep, with a mounted .50-caliber machine gun between the seats, manned by a large MP. A radio operator wearing earphones rode in the back, flanked by whip antennas.

Behind the radio jeep were more troop trucks packed to the gills. The soldiers wore light khaki uniforms that offset their blue berets, each with a blue shoulder patch. They all had clubs and guns strapped to their hips, with rifles pointed skyward.

The lead Plymouth slowed and stopped next to Sam. Driving was a large Black Sergeant, and the passenger across the bench seat was a redheaded Army Captain named Armstrong. Sam nodded, stepped to the driver's window, and gave them directions. Their nods were curt, without any regular banter, and Sam knew they were in a rush. He tried not to focus on the Colt .45 pistol lying in the Sergeant's lap.

From a hidden vantage point in the trees, Waya watched as Sam hopped into the radio jeep. The leviathan moved again into high gear, engines pushed to the limit, and sirens wailed. It raced ahead, the dirt highway becoming a wall of dust, and just then, the convoy angled south off the highway onto the plains at high speed. The dirt cloud changed from highway-brown to the chalk-white of the San Agustin plains.

In the radio jeep, Sam watched ahead as the lead vehicles descended on the crash site with sirens wailing, enhancing the aggressive intensity of storming an enemy town. He guessed there were about twelve civilians at the crash site, milling around the ship, and he could still make out the two surviving creatures.

A tall man wearing a pith hat appeared to be attempting to communicate with the creatures. He had what seemed to be a group of students around him. The civilians looked up, unnerved, as the lead Plymouth skidded to a stop. Captain Armstrong exited, yelling a verbal assault.

"Get away from that ship, or we'll shoot! This is military property!"

Sam was unnerved by the intensity of Armstrong's voice and the sergeant following just behind him, wielding the huge pistol. He watched, astonished, as the tall civilian with the pith hat—who Sam made out to be a professor, with his students in tow, attempted to argue with the redheaded Captain Armstrong.

The professor was immediately confronted by the Black Sergeant, who raised the gun and backed him down. Sam had never experienced this type of behavior toward American civilians, and he had to stop himself from intervening.

He found himself confused on many levels about what was happening, but everything was moving so fast that he had no angle yet on what felt strange to him.

Two of the civilian men turned out to be brothers and were there with their boys. One kid appeared to be about six, and the other a teenager.

An older man stood off to the side near his old beige pickup, watching the chaos. He wore a straw hat with circular wire-rimmed glasses, and Sam thought he looked like the spitting image of President Truman.

The shrill sirens only made the scene more chaotic as he jumped out and moved to the creatures to keep them calm.

By the time he reached the ship, the healthy one had retreated underneath the farthest reaches of the craft. Sam knelt by the wounded one, who was again cowering from the noise and the menacing soldiers running in every direction.

He realized two MPs were right behind him with rifles trained on the creatures. Sam turned, raising his hands to the MPs.

"Stand down, boys. These creatures are not a threat."

"Yes, sir," said the more senior MP as he motioned for the other MP to point his rifle toward the dirt.

Both soldiers stared at Sam curiously, as if questioning his assessment that the creatures were harmless. Sam let it go, as the commotion everywhere was simply overwhelming.

He turned to the healthy one, which was now cowering further back, below the ship.

They won't hurt either of you, Sam thought, yet received no response.

He decided his telepathy was not a sure thing. He could feel the agitation and fear of both creatures as more MPs disembarked, yelling at the civilians and pointing their automatic weapons at the frightened group.

"Get away from the crash and line up!" Sam heard them yell.

He watched as all types of soldiers worked in unison amidst heavy equipment arriving, being offloaded from lowboys and six-by-six army trucks. Above the entire operation, a huge Army C-46 twin-engine cargo plane was circling low. To Sam's surprise, it lined up on the dirt highway and landed!

Moments later, troops wearing silver radiation suits disembarked and began canvassing the area. They moved on hands and knees, shoulder to shoulder, picking up fragments of the saucer along the swath where it had leveled trees and plowed up dirt, skidding to its resting place.

The civilians were escorted away amidst a flurry of yells. At one point, one of the two fathers was shoved by an MP with a rifle, forcing him to walk faster. The father turned on a dime, and his lightning-fast punch dropped the MP in his tracks.

Sam heard the unmistakable sounds of locking bolts and pistols cocking as everyone froze. The tall professor stepped in between, attempting to calm all involved. Immediately, Captain Armstrong approached the fathers and their boys, yelling for everyone to hear:

"The next person—that doesn't do exactly what I say—will-be-shot!"

With the tension at a breaking point, even Sam believed him. The last time Sam felt this type of military intensity was during the war, and he was relieved when the guns were lowered, and the civilians were moved to the highway.

But something else nagged at him at that moment: an energy from the convoy that carried an agenda of sorts. All he could muster in his mind was that this team was really well-rehearsed.

But how could they be?

The idea of other possible crashes just started to float in his mind when two military ambulances arrived, followed by a jeep full of military photographers. Three photographers exited and immediately approached Sam.

"Captain Boyd, sir," the lead photographer said. "We just need a couple of shots of the Greys."

Sam was surprised they knew who he was, but he figured they had been

228

briefed that he had made the initial report and was with the creatures. But the photographer, referring to the creatures as *Greys*, flipped a switch in Sam, and it was apparent that these photographers had a familiarity with the creatures.

This was not the first crash of an alien saucer, he then knew, as he slowly stepped to the side, his mind in a swirl of new awareness.

"Don't get me in those shots, boys." Sam said to the photographers.

"Yes, sir!" they all replied in unison.

Sam had a notion, based on their demeanor, that they were hand-picked for this assignment and knew exactly what shots they were after. Two photographers immediately began shooting stills while the third rolled 16mm film. The flashbulbs and rattle of the cameras clearly unnerved the creatures. He watched them cower under the siege.

"Alright, boys," he said. "That's enough."

The three saluted him as they exited toward the saucer, which was already being cabled for the portable crane. Two military paramedics approached, saluting Sam.

"Captain Boyd, sir?" said the ranking paramedic. "Can we get the two Greys loaded up, sir? Colonel Scanlon is inbound and has ordered a full check-up for them at Los Alamos Hospital."

Sam nodded and was surprised to hear again that these soldiers called them *Greys*. Now, everything shifted in his mind. This covert unit, with its well-oiled demeanor, must have done this evolution many times. The implications of what that meant were too much for him to process in that moment.

He turned to the healthy Grey.

They will now load your crewmember and take you both to a medical facility, he thought but got no confirmation that the Grey had understood him.

The two living creatures cowered as the paramedics slowly approached and gently placed the wounded one on a stretcher. The heaviness and fear of the Greys were palpable, he thought. He looked down at the healthy one and offered his hand.

I will go with you and help you into the vehicle, Sam thought.

The creature slowly approached but did not take Sam's hand. It walked beside him to the ambulance, and Sam wondered if his telepathic ability had been a fluke.

The two paramedics loaded the wounded one into the far ambulance and then opened the rear doors of the nearby ambulance. Inside the rear section were two padded bench seats with stretchers stacked below.

Sam sat on the far bench, with the creature choosing the opposite side. It looked like a six-year-old with its feet hanging down. Sam slowly stood to exit, staring at the creature and thinking the thought,

I will come back to ride with you, but for now you will remain in here alone where it will be quieter.

Then he stepped out as the paramedics slowly closed the doors.

"Might be good to leave that one alone in there," Sam said to the paramedics, and they both responded,

"Yes, sir."

He sat down on the bumper of the ambulance and lit a cigarette. The yelling and aggressive activity continued. He pulled on his cigarette and again was struck by how coordinated the entire crash retrieval operation was. His mind raced.

How many crashes had this team recovered?

He watched as the two dead Greys were taken from below the craft by MPs and placed directly on a wide block of dry ice, which was covered by a thin silver blanket. One MP appeared to be teaching a younger MP, helping with the cadavers.

"The blanket keeps the Grey's skin from getting ice-burn prior to autopsy," the ranking MP said.

Both then raised the sides of the wooden crate, framing the dry ice with the cadavers lying on top. They secured the latch with a combination lock and walked away. It now looked like a simple crate. Sam contemplated the ranking MP's statement.

How strange and surreal, he thought, having just watched two dead creatures from another planet being stored inside a basic plywood box for transport!

Suddenly, a commotion behind him. He turned to see a jeep with red colonel's flags on the front come to a stop and shut down.

"Attention on deck!" was yelled.

Sam came to attention as Colonel Martin F. Scanlon exited the passenger seat of the jeep.

"At ease, Captain Boyd," Scanlon said, walking directly to him.

The Colonel had the eyes of a calm, duty-bound soldier and not a blowhard, as many field-grade officers were.

"Thank you, sir," Sam said.

Scanlon extended his hand, and Sam shook it.

"Boyd, I know we didn't meet at Trinity, but I heard you did a fine job with the Apache, saving many lives."

"Did my best, sir," Sam replied quietly.

Scanlon lit a cigarette and looked around. He had been briefed on his flight from Muroc Field about the alien crash and that this former Marine captain had made the initial report. But it was in reading Sam's dossier that Scanlon realized Boyd was also the Apache-Interpreter during the Trinity nuclear test two years before, in 1945.

The young captain had apparently convinced many Apache living in the town of Socorro, New Mexico, to leave the area prior to the blast. The rest of Boyd's dossier was more than impressive.

He had helped form the famous Navajo Code Talkers unit and had a Purple Heart from Guadalcanal, which Scanlon knew had been a withering battle. Sam was the son of a Methodist missionary, and the family had lived on the Navajo reservation during WWI.

According to the dossier, he had become fluent in Navajo as a small boy, playing with Navajo kids on the reservation. Later, he attended the Navajo High School, where he also became fluent in Apache, as both languages descended from the Athabaskan tradition.

He had tested out of two grades in high school and received early admission to college, where he studied German. He was only nineteen when he earned his linguistics degree.

The Army badly needed radio signalmen, and Sam's fluency in German, in addition to his Navajo and Apache capabilities, made him a perfect fit. But battles were won or lost largely on which side could get intel to their troops effectively in a battle situation. Sam knew the Navajo language could not be deciphered as it had no written alphabet. On the battlefield, Navajo could be used to inform troops of enemy movements without fear of the enemy deciphering the code.

He had approached his commanding officer in the Signal Corps. After speaking a bit of fluent Navajo to the impressed general, a dispatch was sent to Washington, D.C., and the *Navajo Code Talkers* were formed. Their code was never broken and was considered a huge factor in the overall Allied victory.

With the war over, Sam was only twenty-four years old and had been the youngest Marine ever promoted to captain.

Sam watched as Scanlon walked to the ambulances, looking in the rear window of each. He turned and slowly approached Sam, offering him a cigarette.

"Thank you, sir," Sam said, and both men lit up.

The Colonel watched all the commotion and exhaled, motioning toward the ambulance.

"Captain Boyd, I'd like you to help us with that little Grey over there. Get him safely up to Los Alamos and see what information you can gather."

Sam was surprised.

"Colonel, sir, I run a business just north of here in Gallup, and I have a family—"

"Captain Boyd," Scanlon said, cutting him off.

"I understand you have a business, and we can help you with finances, but I'm gravely concerned about secrecy. I'm going to ask President Truman to reinstate you until we can transition that Grey to another handler. But you have its trust right now, and this is an order of national security."

Sam's mind was racing. He knew that life had once again changed course, and he had learned over the years to accept instead of fight what came his way. It was easier and generally had turned out okay for him.

"Yes, sir," he replied.

"Excellent, Boyd. I've read your entire dossier, and I'm glad you are on board."

The crane in the distance made a grinding sound as both men turned to watch the silver saucer being hoisted out of the arroyo wall. The crane turned slowly, rotating the craft over the white dirt of the plain, and lowered it onto a lowboy flatbed truck.

Sam pulled on his cig and thought about how leaving Catherine again would be a bigger adjustment now that they had baby Sue and another on the way. He would not be able to tell Catherine anything other than *he was needed for something he couldn't discuss.*

Catherine had understood this protocol since their engagement, which had lasted through the war. Even after they were married, she never asked what he did during the war or about his Code Talkers. She knew Sam's work was highly classified, and she figured it was none of her business and was good with that.

Sam appreciated her respect for his position and hoped that one day, he could tell her everything. He looked up to see the Colonel motioning with his cig toward the ambulance.

"That wounded grey won't make it," Scanlon said.

Sam slowly nodded, having already decided that this coordinated recovery operation was too smooth to be a newly formed unit, so he didn't question the Colonel's medical assessment.

They watched the saucer being covered with a tarp on the flatbed, effectively hiding it. Scanlon took a drag, slightly looking Sam's way as he spoke under his breath.

"That's a big gash in that ship."

"Yes, sir. It sure looks like it ran into something," Sam whispered.

Scanlon tilted his head, thinking out loud.

"Those ships are tough, like no metal we are aware of. Apparently, we tracked two of them monitoring a V2 rocket launch last night at the White Sands test range just south of here. I guess the Greys were flying all around our V2 while it was in flight. Like they were inspecting the damn thing."

Scanlon looked directly at Sam and leaned in again, whispering.

"Think about this, Boyd. Our damn V2 rocket is doing close to 3,000 miles per hour—and that little ship over there is moving around it—like it was standing still!"

Sam shook his head as Scanlon continued.

"I guess the two radar blips went bright white and then disappeared off the screens. We think they somehow hit each other. They're out looking for the other one now. But that's just between you and me, Boyd," he whispered.

"Yes, sir," Sam replied.

Scanlon contemplated him for a moment.

"And I'm dead serious about that last line, Captain."

"Yes, sir," Sam responded and understood that Scanlon was essentially saying: *Speak a word about what I just told you, and you'll disappear.*

The Colonel waved his cigarette at the men raking the crash zone by hand and exhaled.

"Boyd, we'll probably be here for another four hours or so, cleaning up debris. I want you to head back to Gallup and pack a bag. You'll be flown into Los Alamos airfield and rendezvous with that little Grey. My jeep driver over there will give you a ride back to the highway."

"Yes, sir," Sam replied. "By your leave, sir," Sam said as he saluted.

"Carry on, Boyd," Scanlon said and watched him depart.

T he colonel studied the scene around him as the ambulance convoy departed with the Greys.

He watched his team in their silver radiation suits as they crawled on their hands and knees, shoulder to shoulder, in the high heat, the entire length of the ravine. The saucer on the flatbed had been covered with a blue tarp, and Scanlon thought about his first encounter with the Greys in 1940.

How the discovery of many of them, deep in a cave system near Dulce, New Mexico, had led to a meeting with then-President Roosevelt. But that strange evolution was something he was forbidden to discuss with anyone.

He pulled on his cig and watched the men sifting the white dirt, knowing that Roswell Army Airfield, just to the east, was America's only nuclear-equipped base.

The top-secret brief from this morning's flight informed him that President Truman had ordered General Nathan Twining to coordinate the recovery and containment efforts in the Roswell area. The brief told how several saucers had arrived on July 2nd and spooked the American military. They had appeared on radar, cruising in formation at Mach speed, and then stopped on a dime, hovering for several minutes while pulsing the Roswell base with electromagnetic waves. Then they would dart away, still in formation, instantaneously achieving above Mach speeds.

He shook his head at that type of capability. The initial consensus was that the Russians had somehow engineered a flying saucer and wanted information about the American nuclear squadron at Roswell.

He felt relieved somewhat that it was not the Russians who had flown the saucers. But he was surprised at discovering that it was actually the little Greys who had been monitoring Roswell all this time. He used one of the Army's newest mobile field phone units and placed a call to Truman's Secretary of State, General George C. Marshall. When Scanlon relayed his impression of the craft as *not of Russian origin,* the line went quiet.

"Scanlon, are you absolutely certain of that?" Marshall asked.

"Well, sir, I have two live Greys from that craft heading to Los Alamos for medical attention, as well as two dead ones."

The line was quiet again. After a long pause, he could hear General Marshall exhale.

"Colonel, I want you to divert the dead ones to Roswell for autopsy and ensure none of those civilians you rounded up speaks a goddamn word about what they saw."

"Yes, sir," he replied, and the line went dead.

T he soft tone of Vyla's cellphone alarm brought her back into Charlotte's darkened living room.

She could tell that the Roswell incident was just heating up, and there was clearly a much broader picture she needed of that seminal event. With her alarm still sounding, she hopped up and grabbed her things. A moment later, she was out the door bound for the airport and a debrief with Yen that she was not prepared for.

As she turned onto the highway, she monitored her rearview mirror. A moment later, the black sedan slid onto the freeway and began tailing her. Whatever was happening was beyond her control. She sat with that thought for a moment as she drove, realizing that she couldn't control a damn thing. The more she thought about it—she never had.

Chapter Twenty-Five

Her plane from San Francisco had landed thirty minutes earlier in Las Vegas, and she had caught an Uber to the isolated Janet terminal on the west side of the main airport.

On that short Uber ride, she noticed the white Impala was back, and the Twins were clearly on board.

So they friggin' know everything with regard to my schedule. Okay, whatever, she thought, and turned her attention ahead, curious about what the Janet terminal would be like.

She had never heard of Janet Airlines, but a quick internet search told her that the air carrier was created back when EG+G, a private military contractor, began flying its employees to and from Area 51 during the early 1950s.

"Just-Another-Non-Existent-Terminal" was how the locals in Vegas jokingly referred to the spook-infested airline hub, as everyone knew those planes were going to Area 51. But since neither the airline nor any of its passengers riding those planes would admit to the Area 51 destination, the locals made a joke of it. She had looked up EG+G and knew that the corporation was in control of S-4 during her dad and Papa's tenure at the facility.

EG+G, as well as several other military contractors, had been bought, sold, and traded until finally ending up under Yen's JRAD conglomerate. The strange congruence that Vyla might be working in the same general area as her dad and Papa was unsettling. She knew the Nevada Test and Training Range was huge, and the probability of her actually working in the same facility where they did was minuscule. Yet, she admitted to herself that the whole full-circle thing was a little freaky.

She exited the Uber into the toasty morning air with her backpack over her shoulder, wearing summer shorts and clogs and a new silky short-sleeve shirt. She was glad that Jee Research and Development required only *casual business attire*. But she had been warned to bring a winter jacket because the temperature in the facility where she would be working could be very cool.

She approached the terminal gate and showed her Majestic ID. She noticed the two security guards exchanging a quick glance before she was waived through. Then she remembered that Dan had said Majestic was really up there, and it made her wonder about the others she would meet at the gate.

Other than knowing that Yen's company was on the Nevada Test and Training Range, nothing was passed in the email. No address or phone number was listed. Yen's secretary told her that if there were any complications, she should just show her badge and call Yen directly.

Going through terminal security, she was scan-searched and hand-patted as well. The two security guards wore all black, with an American flag on their shoulders, and had the standard earpiece with a wire running into their shirts.

But they weren't military, she knew. No military insignia whatsoever. *Private contractors*, she assumed. They wore black Glock-9 pistols, ammo pouches, and stun guns on their high-tech radio belts, mixed with flat, black, unmarked baseball caps, which topped off their military operator demeanor.

There was only one gate in the terminal, and it had the standard airport leather seating. She was happy to see that the other employees in the gate area were also in summer attire. Most had backpacks and wore tennis shoes or sandals.

Whew, she thought, and sighed.

Normal visuals against the backdrop of so much security gave her a bit of fresh air. Everybody seemed to have a book, newspaper, or magazine. She sat by a younger, nice-looking man about her age, wearing white cotton summer slacks and tennis shoes. He was reading a novel and smiled as she sat down near him. He then went right back to his book.

"Is this all for the 12:05 flight?" she asked.

He turned and nodded.

"Yep, the one and only," he said, smiling. "First night?"

She nodded.

"Cool," he said, going back to his book.

Well, shit, is he gonna be all spook on me and not be normal? I'm still cute, aren't I? she thought and figured she'd push the envelope a little bit.

"So, where exactly are we headed to?"

He looked over inquisitively and seemed to question whether she was legit.

"Well, since we're being recorded, all I can tell you is that we are heading to a part of the Nevada Test and Training Range."

She stared.

"Right... sorry," she said, as he kept staring... his smile fading, and he nervously went back to his book.

She looked away.

Oh my God, he thinks I'm testing him! Like I'm a security plant!

She then realized that all four corners of the small gate area had listening cones cross-triangulated, covering every inch of the seating area.

What in the hell? she thought. Then she realized that all one hundred or so employees waiting for the flight were reading and not talking.

Pay attention, goon! Her nasty, *less than* voice chimed.

"Flight 51 is on time and will be boarding in five minutes. Please ensure all electronics are off and placed in your carry-on," came a voice through the loudspeakers.

Moments later, she was walking with the other passengers in a single-file line on the boiling tarmac and then up the airplane staircase into the white Boeing 737 jet. The bird had a single red stripe on the side that ran the length of the plane. Just below the rear exit door was a very small "NH69HH" in black letters.

The flight was crowded as she took her window seat. The older woman who sat down beside her did the same *smile-and-shut-up* thing the young man in the terminal had done.

It's just us spooks, she thought, and then, *Let's try not to be drunk the next time I say yes to a gig.*

The Janet flight steward went through all the regular preflight spiel while the plane taxied. A moment later, they were airborne. Vyla watched as the jet climbed northbound to only about eight thousand feet and then turned northeast. She could still clearly make out buildings and roads below. That was odd because most commercial jets cruised at twenty to thirty-five thousand feet, and the climb to those altitudes took much longer.

Minutes after level off, she felt the engines wind down, and the descent began. The thump of landing was followed shortly by reverse thrusts, and then they were taxiing. The entire trip, takeoff to landing, was only twenty-three minutes.

"At this time, please check to see that your badges are visible. Visitors or unbadged personnel, please remain seated until the security guard is able to release you. Enjoy your night," said the steward on the loudspeaker.

Vyla remained seated as the jet came to a stop.

She watched the other passengers descend the staircase in moonlight, proceeding right into a bus parked next to the jet with blackened windows.

The huge hangars in the distance had no identifying signage painted on them. She knew the Nellis Test Range was enormous and figured they could have landed at one of many airports within the range.

A moment later, she was approached by a JRAD security man in a suit and tie who had an earpiece and a bulge, indicating a sidearm.

"Dr. Kells, right this way, ma'am," he whispered.

She descended the staircase with her backpack and was guided to a nearby golf cart, where another JRAD security officer assisted her into the back seat of the covered cart.

She was still adapting to the change in climate as the cart raced through the night heat, blasting her hair back. She loved it. A momentary bit of fun amidst all the armed spooks felt good and simple.

Thank God for small miracles, she thought.

One minute later, they arrived at a small, nondescript hangar. A sleek black, nine-seater Sikorsky executive chopper was in its preflight warm-up sequence, with the rotors turning slowly. The guards drove her past the chopper and through a hangar door. They escorted her down a soundproofed hallway leading to a white-walled conference room, where Yen sat waiting for her.

"Thank you, gentlemen," Yen said to the security detail as they nodded and departed. Yen looked up at Vyla.

"Welcome back," she said with a smile.

"Thank you," Vyla replied as she approached.

She could see the brief Yen was perusing was the same one from Geneva. Her diamond watchband flashed as she gestured for Vyla to have a seat, and Vyla noticed again that Yen looked really young for her forty-nine years.

She certainly looked youthful when Vyla had first met her at Kirtland Air Force Base, moments before they had descended so far down into the DUMB.

Whatever, she thought, noticing her anxiety whenever she was near this woman. She decided to just breathe and see if anything would change in their dynamic.

Yen watched her and then laughed slightly.

"What?" Vyla said.

"You look like you've seen your first UAP," Yen said.

"Yeah, fuckin'-A," Vyla replied. "Well, at least I saw one on video."

Yen nodded, and Vyla realized she was completely done with faking anything with Yen. Swear words were now on the table, and if Yen was offended, she could speak up. Vyla knew all this internal energy was still building—a boiling pot of anger that needed expression—but also knew she couldn't vent without provocation. Yen seemed calmer for some reason.

Was it because I'd done her bidding on the investigation? Vyla thought.

Yen pushed a button on the table, and a viewing screen lowered from the ceiling. When it was fully extended, it began playing the heads-up footage from the intercept.

Vyla was shocked.

"How can you have that already?" Vyla asked.

"I received copies of footage from Knife and Crazy's flight, as well as the copy of Chief Day's radar on the day you departed for the ship. I've reviewed it a couple of times."

"Oh, so you don't need me to debrief you?" Vyla asked.

"Actually, I do," said Yen. "I'm really interested in what you think is happening here."

Yen slid the wireless console to Vyla, allowing her to control the playback functions.

"And of course, what you learned from the pilots and Chief Day," Yen said.

Vyla nodded, forwarding the footage to where the UAP appeared on Knife's heads-up display. The oval-shaped UAP was on the upper left of the screen, with the top right of the screen displaying a timestamp of *two minutes.*

"Well, as best I can tell from the dynamics of that UAP," Vyla said, "it has nothing to do with conventional flight, and it's using technology not of this world."

"Go on," Yen said, staring curiously at her as she sipped her coffee.

Vyla hesitated, perplexed.

She clearly knows all of this, so why is she making me explain? she thought.

Seeing that Yen was waiting for her to proceed, she exhaled and forwarded Crazy's footage to the same *two-minute* timestamp. But the UAP was not visible on Crazy's heads-up display.

"Right here," Vyla continued, "at this same timestamp for both jets, only one pilot can see the craft. That indicates to me that the ship is somehow warping space-time and is only visible to each pilot intermittently. Meaning the gravity created by the craft is bending the light," she explained. "If you are at the correct angle to the gravity wave, you can see the ship, but if you are not, then you see *through the ship* due to gravitational lensing."

Yen nodded.

"So, what do you think is creating the gravitational wave?"

Vyla stared.

"You say that like you already know all this?" Vyla asked.

Yen watched her, and Vyla just stared back, growing tired of the game. Yen seemed to contemplate a much bigger tell, but in keeping with previous interactions, she switched gears.

"What did the pilots tell you that you found interesting?"

Vyla did her best to flow with the game.

"They didn't say it, but I sensed the UAP was somehow communicating telepathically with both pilots," she said.

"You mean the way it re-appeared at the CAP?" Yen asked.

Vyla nodded.

"That, and the way the alien ship moved, made it impossible for either pilot to acquire a weapons lock. Like the UAP knew their intent to shoot it down, and it basically nixed their plan."

"Fascinating, huh?" Yen said, taking a sip of coffee while staring at the screen.

Vyla turned directly to her.

"Dr. Jee, I'm getting that you have seen this all before, so I'm—"

"Tell me what you learned from Chief Day's interview," Yen asked, cutting her off.

Vyla felt her anger rising as Yen's energy was again hunting for something unsaid. *Did she know about the stateroom interlude? Vyla wondered.*

She jettisoned that thought as quickly as possible. She was certain that she had cleared the hallway and that Dan knew the Princeton inside and out. He would never have allowed either of them to be compromised.

"Well, Chief Day told me, he made the pilots, *Return-To-Ship,* fearing the UAP's capabilities."

Yen nodded, but Vyla could see she was waiting for more.

"He also mentioned that the UAP seemed to communicate with him on a telepathic level, but couldn't really explain it further."

Yen watched her, put her coffee down, and took a deep breath.

"In your stateroom, did Chief Day reveal anything that I should be aware of?"

Vyla did her best not to show shock. The tidal wave of emotions, with anger leading, was rising, but she stared at Yen and realized there was no use defending herself. Vyla knew it was wrong to take the interview to a private location, but she made decisions on the fly, and that's how she rolled. If she was going to be fired for that, then *so be it.*

"I brought him there to allow him a safe space to divulge what he was feeling, as I knew he would not discuss his personal feelings in the interview room." Vyla said.

"I see," Yen said, then looked away momentarily and sipped her coffee.

Vyla felt the doom of what was coming but was just—*over it.* She knew this discussion was going nowhere good, but if that was the case...why did Yen even ask her to debrief the interviews?

Why not just fire her? Was Yen just fucking with her?

She looked at her hands and attempted to calm herself when Yen spoke.

"I know you didn't have time during the quick Majestic turnaround to read all the fine print..."

Vyla looked away.

Fucking get it over with, and fire me already, she thought as Yen continued.

"Because you are not military, your liaison with Chief Day did not break any rules of clearance, but I want you to be aware that, in the future, if you need to be with someone in that way, you should consider that you are being watched at all times, and in all places, and most likely being recorded—"

"I didn't sign up for this, Dr. Jee!" Vyla retorted, cutting her off.

"I signed up because I admired your work, and I didn't realize I'd be giving my privacy away!" she almost shouted.

A tear escaped before she realized it. Yen watched her closely as Vyla looked away and wiped her eyes.

"I'm sorry," Vyla whispered. "I wasn't ready for all this. I don't even know what the fuck I'm doing here? I mean, you clearly have access to smarter scientists—"

"Vyla, it's okay," Yen said, cutting her off. "I'm hopeful that you've seen things now that will bring you up to speed with where my company is on this subject, regarding the verified existence of UAPs and their otherworldly capabilities."

Vyla sniffled and slowly nodded amidst an epiphany. She would not have believed anyone about UAPs and their gravity-defying capabilities and speeds until she had viewed the footage, the concurring radar screens, and spoken with the pilots. Yen had in effect... leapfrogged her knowledge in the quickest way possible. Vyla now appreciated Yen's method of *show, don't tell.* The UAP in action had truly erased her skepticism regarding UFOs and their existence. She wanted to show appreciation to Yen for leapfrogging her, but she also felt that something in Yen's agenda was nefarious.

"Vyla, before we go any further, I don't know if you've figured it out yet—but nothing that you know to be true about the entire UAP evolution—can be written in your report to the White House?"

Vyla stared, realizing that her hunch had been correct—that the *"aliens aren't real"* narrative was just that—a hoodwink. She also understood that she needed to nod her head and comply. This was no time to put herself on the radar to be fired.

"Of course," Vyla replied, "nothing happened."

"Good," Yen said. "Just make it short and sweet, and we can be done with it."

"You bet," Vyla said.

Yen exhaled and pushed an intercom button.

"Can I have the bird ready in three?"

"Yes, ma'am," came the reply.

Minutes later, two operatives strapped Vyla in across from Yen in the Sikorsky nine-seater. The large door slid shut, and the sleek chopper lifted and began racing across the desert airport.

"I really appreciate the brief," Yen said. "Your instincts about the gravitational lensing are correct."

Vyla stared.

"How do you know that for certain?"

Yen stared, suddenly caught.

"This morning, you will get to see more of what you've experienced thus far. You're still on probation with regard to your clearance, but as long as I am with you, you are allowed to see certain things."

Vyla nodded as Yen looked back out the window, disappearing into her own thoughts. Vyla watched in growing delight as the chopper smoothly climbed a few feet and then shot out over the desert, skating just above the sand along the mountainous desert landscape.

She took in the posh interior and was still in disbelief that she was on one of Yen's multimillion-dollar choppers, bound for *who-knew-where?* The two-facing bench seats were plush leather, and the padded interior made nice work of silencing the sound of the engine. The bird raced only a few feet above the deck, and she felt like hanging her feet out and skipping her toes along the sand in the moonlight.

She knew they were heading due south from the moon angle and watched as the chopper now skirted the southern end of the mountain range, curving west until they were again heading northbound, suddenly over another dry lake bed.

The bird rose slightly, decreasing its speed... then hovered. She knew from her flying days that at the chopper's speed and time flown, they could not be more than ten miles southwest from the runway they had just departed.

Why the hell did we just fly an expensive chopper when we could have driven here in twenty-five minutes? Her mind blurted, but she quickly remembered that this was Yen's world and that she was simply a player in it.

"You are now one of only a handful of people in the world who will have access to this complex, so don't be alarmed when you exit the chopper, as there will be armed guards wherever you go in the facility," Yen said.

Vyla nodded, feeling the bird descend and settle onto the sand next to a mountain.

A rriving from seemingly nowhere were five black-uniformed security personnel, all wearing powder-blue berets.

They surrounded the helicopter, opening the doors and releasing the women from their harnesses. The blue berets then helped them exit below the still-turning rotors toward the mountain.

A moment later, the chopper lifted, departing northbound. The group of five heavily armed guards and the two women set out toward the mountain, each woman flanked by an operative, with guards in front and rear.

Vyla was struck again by the heat at this early morning hour and the breathless beauty of the desert mountains rising in bright moonlight. Bathed in that glow, all the jagged edges of each mountain and every tree and bush could clearly be seen.

That's when she did her first double-take of something that seemed unnatural just ahead. As the group followed the path uphill, she could make out what appeared to be a 60-degree vertical cut into the mountainside. The odd, flat face, right in the middle of the round mountain, appeared to her like a giant had dropped the blade of a flathead shovel and sliced into the mountain.

And then it hit her. She realized that she was looking at hangar doors—nine of them! Camouflaged on the mountainside! But she would never have seen them had she not been so close.

Wow! What the hell? she thought. *I didn't see those flying in, and I was paying attention.*

But her surprise vanished when she heard *a snapping* behind her. She turned to see the rear security guard wielding an Uzi-style, short-barreled machine gun. That sight alone didn't shake her. It was the Doberman that the guard held taut on a short chain that unnerved her.

"Heel!" the guard commanded the muscular attack dog.

It took her a moment to realize that the Doberman was going through all the barking and snarling physical actions, yet the animal made no noise! The only sound was the eerie snapping of its shiny white teeth as it struggled to get at her. Its vocal cords had been removed!

Fucking-A, shit! What in the hell is this place? she thought.

Yen looked over without affect and kept walking.

Chapter Twenty-Six

They were led along a slightly climbing footpath past the nine hangar doors and entered through an iron gate that went directly into the side of the mountain.

Once inside, they were greeted with gray cinderblock walls and incandescent lighting, and the temperature drop was pleasantly cool. An eight-inch-wide orange stripe ran diagonally the length of each wall. On the far wall was a poster showing a UFO hovering above trees with "I want to believe" printed below.

Yen turned to her.

"I'll be seeing you in about an hour, after your security protocols are completed."

Vyla nodded as Yen departed with her guard. Vyla followed her guard to a square machine in the corner that had a visor-like apparatus extending from it, with an eyecup. It reminded her of a camcorder eyepiece. At waist level, a small shelf extended with an obvious area that had a left thumbprint emblem.

"Now, ma'am, place your right eye on the eyepiece and your left thumb on the lower scanner at the same time," the guard said.

She did as instructed, and a soft tone sounded, followed by a laminated card falling into the lower slot. The guard placed the card on a lanyard and handed it to her. The card showed her headshot on the top right, and just below it, in bold letters: E-6722MAJ. Clearly printed on the card were the words *U.S. Department of Naval Intelligence.*

The guard looked at her.

"You will have that on at all times in this facility," he said as she stared at the card.

"But I don't work for the Department of Naval Intelligence?"

"Your company, JRAD, does, ma'am."

She nodded.

"Oh, right."

"Now, right this way, ma'am," he said, pointing for her to walk in front. They made their way along a well-lit cement hallway adorned with the same eight-inch diagonal orange wall stripe combined with parallel red and blue stripes on the floor.

"Always walk between the lines, ma'am," he said with finality, and she gave a thumbs up, walking in front of him.

Every ten feet along the ceiling were casino-style security camera domes. Moments later, they paused in front of a nondescript door, and when it opened, she was greeted by a fifty-year-old female nurse who seemed less military than anyone she had yet encountered.

"Hello, I'm Nurse Jensen, and I'll be doing your intake medical."

Vyla shook her hand, smiling. The guard closed the door, leaving the two women alone.

Jensen gestured to a padded table for her to sit on and approached with a blood pressure cuff as Vyla took off her winter jacket.

Minutes later, after her blood pressure, hearing, and eyesight were checked, Jensen produced a small, clear plastic case with tiny compartments.

She swabbed Vyla's forearm and then, using a felt marker, freehanded a grid of sixteen squares on her arm.

"We're going to do a baseline allergy battery to make certain that you will not have any strong systemic responses to anything in the work environment here in the complex."

"And what am I being tested for with these, nurse?" Vyla asked.

"Well, honestly, I don't know," Jensen said without embarrassment. "All I can tell you is that if you had a reaction to any of these chemical droplets that I'll put subcutaneously on your arm, it would certainly determine if you could work in the facility, as there are exotic materials that you'll be working with here."

"Got it," Vyla replied.

Jensen then produced a small plastic cup of yellow substance and handed it to Vyla for drinking.

Vyla stared disdainfully while swirling it.

"Smells like household cleaner," she said.

Jensen smiled with the unmistakable look of someone used to receiving the same questioning look from other patients.

"I'm sorry, but it's part of the test, and nobody has ever gotten sick from it."

"Okay, here's mud in your eye," Vyla said, downing the shot and smacking her lips.

"Just needs a little gin, and you could make a martini." Vyla teased.

Jensen smiled and took the vial.

"Okay, we're done here, and so good luck with the work." Vyla nodded and hopped off the table. Jensen departed a moment later, and Vyla was able to have a few minutes of downtime before the door opened again.

"How did your medical go?" Yen said, arriving in the room with a guard watching from the hallway.

Vyla lifted her forearm, displaying the grid and subcutaneous colored dots.

"Complete," she whispered.

Yen nodded without affect.

"Follow me," she said, and Vyla fell in behind her as they walked the hallway, followed by the guard.

A moment later, they entered a small room with several thick blue binders stacked on a table. Each of the binders had a large K printed on the outside.

"These are the King Tuts, and they will give you an overview of the facility and its mission. These will catch you up to where we've been and where we are going. I've got some business to attend to, so I'll be back to retrieve you in just a little while."

Vyla nodded, watching them depart as they closed the door.

Alone in the room, she breathed a sigh of relief. It was her first reprieve from being the center of attention, but a quick glance around revealed cameras in every corner.

Of course, she thought, annoyed. But then realized this was her new life.

She took a deep breath and opened the first blue binder. The first page described how President Eisenhower in 1954 had signed the Greada Treaty with aliens. She didn't know what the treaty entailed but figured that information would come shortly. The next tab described *Project Galileo* and its goal to back-engineer a propulsion system for an extraterrestrial craft. She assumed *extraterrestrial craft* was just JRAD engineer-speak for some type of prototype craft that resembled a UFO. She then read references to past attempts at getting the wingless craft airborne, and that several attempts had failed. She was too tired to analyze what all that could mean and found her mind wandering back to thoughts of her dad working somewhere on this same Nellis test range.

The door abruptly opened, and Yen looked in.

"Follow me."

Vyla did so, and falling in just behind the two women was the armed guard. She noticed Yen was walking along the line between blue and red, and she followed suit as Yen spoke over her shoulder.

"This is level four-one, and it's the Galileo Bay. I'll explain in just a moment."

Vyla didn't respond.

"And again, you are still not officially cleared at Majestic Level, but I am allowed to show you what I need to during your probation—as long as I am with you," Yen said, stopping by a door.

She tapped her keycard and led the way into a darkened hangar. As they entered, Vyla saw dim light seeping through an open partition in the distance, revealing more hangars beyond the one they were in. She assumed this had to be one of the nine hangar bays she'd seen on the way in.

As the lights slowly brightened, she caught her breath. She was staring at a dull silver flying saucer—one hundred feet in diameter and thirty-three feet thick in the middle, tapering down to only an inch thick along the outer edge. A small, raised dome sat at the top, mirrored by another on the bottom.

The ship was suspended a few feet off the ground on a wooden frame.

"Oh, my!" Vyla stammered, looking at Yen, who watched her curiously.

"Is this—what the binder mentioned?" Vyla asked.

Yen nodded, and they approached the saucer.

"Go ahead," Yen said. "Walk around it."

Vyla circled the ship, squatting to peer underneath before standing again to take it all in.

"There's... there're no rivets anywhere!" she exclaimed, looking back at Yen, who nodded again without affect.

Vyla continued her inspection, and then stopped, slowly reaching out to touch the saucer.

A sudden rifle bolt was heard—being cocked!

"Ma'am, don't touch the saucer!" yelled the guard, aiming his rifle with a red laser sight.

Vyla hastily raised her hands, simultaneously seeing the red dot on her chest!

"Whoa, whoa!" she yelled. "Don't shoot!"

The guard held steady—Vyla's chest heaving.

Yen gestured to him with both hands. *Stop!*

He hesitated, then slowly lowered his rifle.

Vyla lowered her hands, her heart beating out of her chest as she turned to Yen.

"What the hell is this place?!" she seethed under her breath.

"I'm sorry," Yen said. "I didn't realize you were going to try to touch the ship."

Vyla glared at her.

"Okay, I get it; it's your little baby, but it's just a fucking prototype. Why did he threaten to shoot me?!"

Yen stared quizzically.

"There has clearly been a misunderstanding. This ship has been carbon-dated at over ten-thousand years old."

Vyla froze, the weight of Yen's words sinking in. She turned back to the craft, now seeing it in an entirely new light—utter astonishment and disbelief washing over her.

"What?" she breathed. "Where did it come from?"

Yen met her gaze and whispered, "Well, it's not from Earth. And that's why I brought you here."

Vyla's chest still heaved with adrenaline as Yen continued, her voice edged with finality.

"This is where you will be working—learning to interface with this ship. And this complex is called S-4."

Vyla nearly gasped.

"Are you okay?" Yen asked.

Vyla exhaled.

"Yeah, I just had to get over that friggin' guard pointing a weapon at my heart," she lied.

But in truth, she was tingling. *This was it.* This was the exact complex her dad and Papa had worked in. And on top of that, she was staring at the real deal. An actual off-world ship.

"Holy shit! It's stunning," she whispered.

"Perhaps now you understand why the guards are strict," Yen said softly. "Like I told you... you are now one of only a handful of people in the world who have ever seen this ship."

Vyla nodded slowly.

"And you want me to help with understanding its propulsion?" She asked.

"I'm more interested in how you might interface with her."

"Her?" Vyla asked, surprised.

Yen nodded matter-of-factly.

"She's a living conveyance."

Vyla stared inquisitively.

"This flying saucer is alive?"

"Completely," Yen whispered. "She's half biological, half machine—controlled by a brainwave connection with the pilot."

Vyla stared and slowly nodded.

Of course, she thought, recalling the crazy moves of the UAP and how they could be achieved.

"She's alive," Vyla murmured in wonder.

Yen nodded as Vyla stepped closer, stopping a foot from the saucer's impossibly smooth surface. Slowly, she raised her hands—palms facing the ship—making sure the guards saw she wasn't planning to touch it. Then, she closed her eyes. Yen watched, fascinated, as Vyla stood still, holding space for the Widow. Her expression was soft and humble.

"Hi, Widow," she whispered almost imperceptibly. "I'm Vyla."

Yen watched, transfixed, as a sudden, low hum resonated through the air like a pulse. The guard tensed, his rifle raising instinctively. Yen raised her hand to him. *Stop!* She looked up, watching Vyla.

A sublime wave of red light rippled through the Widow's silvery skin—illuminating Vyla's face for an instant and then vanished—leaving Vyla's body quaking. A low-thrum accompanied the light show.

"Oh my," Vyla whispered, her voice tinged with awe—and a hint of fear... as her eyes slowly opened.

She took a slow, deep breath and appeared labored from the connection, slightly shaking. Yen stared at her in amazement.

"Did she just... tell you something?" Yen asked.

Vyla nodded.

"She did—not in words though," Vyla whispered. "She has the energy of an unbroken horse. An angry one."

Yen nodded, watching her recover.

"Has anyone ever flown her?" Vyla asked.

Yen shook her head.

"I have a test pilot coming in next week. When you return, you'll be watching him fly the simulator."

"You have a simulator of her?" Vyla asked, astonished.

"Just below the craft in each hangar at S-4 is a simulator created specifically for that ship," Yen explained.

Vyla nodded slowly.

"How many ships are here?"

"Well, this is Hangar eight. Hangar Nine has a small ship we call *The Sport Model*. In the first three hangars are old crashed Nazi ships from Antarctica called *Haunebu II*. Hangars four through six are original Roswell ships. And Hangar Seven is one that came from Cape Girardeau, Missouri, in 1941. But these ships are often loaned out to Lockheed-Martin or other private contractors for reverse engineering."

Vyla was exploding with all the confirmations of what her channeling had revealed.

Yen glanced back at the Widow.

"I hope that after learning to fly the simulator—you'll be able to take her up for a test flight—in exactly three weeks from today."

Vyla stared, perplexed.

"You want me to fly her in three weeks?"

Yen stared.

"I mean, if you'd rather I pick someone else, I can move in that direction—"

"No, no," Vyla said abruptly, not wanting to lose the opportunity. "I'm just—I don't know—it doesn't have wings or an engine."

"You just witnessed one like her in flight," Yen reminded her.

Vyla turned suddenly, feeling challenged. Yen stared evenly—forcing her hand. Vyla hesitated, hating that feeling of being outmatched intellectually. And Vyla took a second to feel it.

It was too fast. Nothing seemed legit. Something was amiss.

But she couldn't put her finger on it. Her heart was screaming at her. But damn—if she could figure this woman out—or her agenda.

Vyla exhaled her anxiety.

"Well, maybe the simulator will make me feel confident."

Yen smiled and nodded.

"You'll be trained by one of the best antigravity pilots we have. He's a TR-3B pilot."

Vyla stared. She had only heard rumors about the proposed antigravity platform, but no one in her physics world thought it was feasible with America's current technology.

"The TR-3B? You're saying that thing is already flying?"

Yen looked over with a slightly condescending smile.

"It's been a workhorse between here and the Moon since the early 1990s," she said. "It launches daily from McChord Air Force Base in Washington state and just north of us at Groom Lake. Sometimes, it's used as a shuttle from the Lunar Operations Command on the Moon to the Mars I.C.C. base."

This time, Vyla caught herself. She recalled Dan's buddy and his assertions about the technology America had secretly been employing for decades. And the entire Swizzle episode.

"So, we can pretty much go to the Moon and Mars at will?" Vyla asked.

"Oh, far beyond that," Yen said. "If I had given you more time with the King Tuts, you would have read about several of our projects out in the galaxy."

Vyla slowly nodded, looking up at the Widow.

Holy shit, she thought, trying to remain calm.

Yen's cell phone suddenly chimed. She glanced at her diamond watch, exhaling, then looked at Vyla.

"I've got to take a meeting. The guard there will show you how to depart, and I'll see you early next week to begin work in the simulator."

Vyla nodded as Yen departed in the opposite direction.

"Right this way, ma'am," the blue beret behind her commanded.

A moment later, they were in an S-4 elevator as the doors closed. The guard turned a key while simultaneously looking into a retinal scanner. A second later, they were dropping—for what felt like a full minute—but her sense of motion didn't change as in a normal elevator.

A magnetic field elevator, she thought.

When the door opened, she stepped out to see a small, subway-style train car—bullet-shaped—with its sliding doors open but no one on board.

"That's the Mag-Lev train, ma'am. That will take you back to Groom Lake."

She nodded and boarded the sleek-looking shuttle.

The doors closed, but the train ride was anything but normal. She knew the helicopter trip from Groom Lake to the S-4 facility had taken only ten minutes, but the Mag-Lev was already slowing just fifty seconds after she had boarded.

She quickly did the calculation in her head—she had just traveled roughly twelve miles at seven hundred miles per hour... on an underground train, with no sense of velocity whatsoever.

She shook her head.

And the world above is still riding subway trains that rarely go above fifty miles an hour! she thought.

Her mind raced. The Cabal had created a vacuum-train below the surface of the Earth—with no friction, no air resistance, no sense of velocity except the visual blur of terrain going by, way too fast.

Unbelievable, she thought.

The rest of the night was a blur as she rode the spook-infested Janet flight back to Las Vegas.

Chapter Twenty-Seven

H er flight back to San Francisco International was two hours long, and she again felt unhinged at all the new information.

She watched the starlight out the window and simply could not believe Yen's claims about the TR-3B already being established as a workhorse between the Earth and the Moon and all the stuff about the Lunar Operations Command... and—

Dammit, all!

Then she realized her Cabal mind control was happening—again. Telling her that none of this alien stuff was real! Kicking her ass. Even after she had personally witnessed all of the mind-blowing things in the last week, her body, her mind—her soul even—felt skeptical!

Wow, how can that be? she thought. *I have lived every bit of this, and I am still wanting to deny it's real?*

She shook her head in anger at the utter deceit she had believed all her life.

They fully got me. I am owned by the Cabal and their mind control!

She tried to shake off the frustration, but it was difficult. Here she was, riding with a bunch of other humans on a fossil-fuel, oil-dripping jet that funded the Cabal and the Interplanetary Corporate Conglomerate.

Meanwhile, all across the world, TR-3Bs—and who knew what other antigravity ships—had clearly been going to the Moon and elsewhere, using antigravity technology, and those ongoing events had been kept from the public... for decades!

She exhaled and thought about how they had done it to her. Their perfect mind control. She knew the answer lay in where it all started... *Roswell.*

She pulled the small picture of Sam from her satchel and laid it on her lap. She looked out one last time at the moonlit clouds as her fingers rested on Sam's image. She felt him then, and moments later, she was at Los Alamos National Laboratories in New Mexico on that July 5th, Saturday night—in 1947.

U pon touchdown at the Los Alamos National Laboratories' runway in the Beech 18, Sam was hustled into a black government sedan with red flags on the front.

The small Grey was sitting alone on the rear seat. Sam had barely closed the door when the heavily armed convoy, with the sedan in the middle, pulled out. Moments later, just inside the Los Alamos main gate, the convoy came to a stop, and Sam's door was opened.

"Captain Boyd, I'm Major Poke. Welcome to Los Alamos," the large man said as he held open Sam's door.

"Thank you, sir," Sam replied as he stood and saluted the major.

"At ease, Boyd," the major smiled. "Let's get the Grey to its room."

"Yes, sir," he replied.

Major Poke was easily the largest man Sam had ever encountered in the officer ranks—a pro-linebacker-sized frame but with salt-and-pepper hair consistent with the major's rank and age. His energy was like that of a gentle bear, Sam thought.

But he also sensed that the hulking frame and welcoming demeanor betrayed a keen intelligence and a fierce backbone. He knew the major could not have attained the top-secret assignment without a unique skill set.

He assisted the small Grey out of the sedan and looked up just in time to see Poke staring down disdainfully at the creature. A flash went off, and Sam looked up to see a military photographer lowering his camera.

He was annoyed but wasn't in a position to have an angry spat over a surprise photograph.

"Right this way," Poke said.

He led them past several armed MPs into a four-story, dorm-style building. They followed him down a long hallway that was empty except for MPs stationed throughout and security cameras pointed in every direction.

Poke turned to him as they walked.

"Colonel Scanlon specifically said to create a security suite for our guest and allow you two time to acquaint yourselves with each other. It has a Faraday cage built within the walls, so you shouldn't have any issues with escapes."

Sam nodded as they walked and had no idea what Poke meant about the cage thing but figured everything would come out in time.

Poke stopped at the last door, opened it with a key, and gave it to Sam, motioning him to enter.

"Go ahead, Captain Boyd," Poke said. "This is a two-bed, two-bath suite. It's the largest in the building."

The suite was beautifully furnished and had a main living room and kitchen. The large window in the living room faced an interior garden courtyard of small plants and little pools that flowed into each other.

The garden had a sitting bench and an open sky above it. When he looked up, he could see an armed MP staring over the roof parapet on the fourth floor.

Poke gestured toward the kitchen.

"The refrigerator is full, and you can order off the menu near the phone. It usually takes twenty minutes for them to cook something and get it delivered over here. My number is also by the phone."

"Thank you, sir," Sam said.

Poke whispered to him, handing him a hand-sized remote.

"If you need any help, just mash that button, and my men will storm through the door in seconds."

Sam nodded and slipped the device into his pocket as the major walked toward the door.

"Captain Boyd, when you are through each day with visiting our guest, we have a separate suite next door for your own privacy. And certainly, you can dine with me in the mess hall if you wish."

"Thank you. It would be a pleasure, sir," Sam said and watched the major exit and the door close behind him.

Sam was wary of why he had been given the remote—and what had transpired in the past that required such protection in dealing with the Greys. But he had a job to complete so he could get back to his family, and he didn't want to dwell on fear. He motioned the Grey toward the couch.

Please have a seat, he thought.

The Grey sat, looking like a six-year-old with its feet hanging down but not touching the floor. Energy-wise, Sam felt its frustration.

What are we doing here? The Grey said into Sam's head.

Home, he thought back. *This is your new home.*

The Grey stood abruptly, walked to the window, and stared all around as if looking for escape routes. Sam was torn on that first day. He knew if the tables were turned, he too would look for a way back to his own kind. The Grey certainly knew it was not a "Guest" of the American government. But Sam didn't want the relationship to become one of cellmate and warden. He knew the Army was working on another handler for this position, so he wanted his short tenure to be productive.

Poke had given him a set of questions to ask the Grey once they settled in—questions from Truman's top military and scientific advisors. He sat across from the Grey on the couch and looked at his directive, which listed the questions in order. He read the question aloud, figuring the room was bugged, and he wanted to ensure the listeners that he had asked the questions... including the first one:

Why had the aliens flown a formation of three ships over the world's only nuclear storage base at Roswell?

As he read the directive, he was thinking the same question to the Grey. A moment later, an answer came through.

I am the ship's pilot, Sam heard. *I don't know anything about where I fly or why. I'm only onboard the ship to ensure safe flight. I'm not privy to the overall mission.*

Sam quickly wrote the answer and considered asking a flight-related question just to maintain a connection with the creature.

What propels your ship? he passed.

That's too complicated for you to understand, the Grey replied in Sam's head.

It then looked up at the ceiling, appearing frustrated at having to deal with one not equal to its intellectual capacity. Sam worked hard to remain friendly, practicing not to have disrespectful thoughts in front of the Grey because of its telepathic ability. But it was tough. The creature was clearly from an advanced civilization, and Sam was taking a beating. The exchange did not feel friendly. Sam sensed its annoyance at having been captured by an inferior race.

He still didn't know what gender it was but was too embarrassed to ask. From body to facial features, it appeared identical to the others, reinforcing his suspicion that these creatures might be clones.

To test if the Grey was always reading his mind, he deliberately thought about Catherine, baby Sue, and the one in the womb to see what the Grey would do. Moments later, the Grey looked at him.

Those three are your family?

Sam nodded, astonished.

Do you have a family? Sam sent.

I have a family on my planet, the Grey responded.

How long will I be held here? came next, and this began what Sam would later term a cascade of questions—a relentless flood of inquiries that the Grey shot into his mind.

Where is my ship? Why are we here? What do you intend to do with me? Is this a prison? Will you let me go outside?

The questions came so fast on that first day that Sam finally stood and walked to the refrigerator. He opened the door and paused, staring at all the food. It was then that he realized why he was getting so agitated. The dynamics of their communication was a one-way street. The Grey could clearly read his mind, but he could not read the Grey's mind. If the Grey wanted him to receive an answer, then that would happen. But he could only hear the Grey in his mind when it wanted to communicate. Since Sam had no way to read its mind, he did the next best thing. He would control his own mind and all its thoughts.

He pulled a fresh pineapple from the refrigerator and chopped it up, offering the Grey a small amount on a plate, but it was left untouched.

Now that he had time, Sam studied the Grey's anatomy in detail as he chewed on a piece of pineapple, confirming his earlier assessment. The Grey's mouth had no teeth for chewing, and in place of a tongue, there appeared to be a membrane in the tiny slit that was its mouth. It had four fingers on each hand and no thumb. All four fingers had tiny suction cups protruding from their ends. Its entire body, from neck to feet, was covered with what appeared to be a skin-tight flight suit of silvery material. Its feet were covered by the same material, but it seemed slightly thicker down near the feet. The covering over the feet resembled soft boots.

But over the next day, he could confirm the stranger thing that he had suspected. The Grey did not breathe.

Its chest did not rise or fall. No air was being exchanged. It hadn't eaten or ingested anything he would consider food, at least not through its mouth. It had never used the toilet, but it had taken a really long shower, which was monitored via closed-circuit TV.

He assumed it must be getting some nutrients from the water. But he noticed the Grey was already diminishing in energy, and whatever had been replenished by the long shower was not enough. At this rate, it would die soon. He had seen the internal organs in the dead Greys at the ship and the fibrous material of the blown-apart arms and legs. They reminded him of the celery from his vegetable garden.

He asked Major Poke to inform the Los Alamos base commander that food nutrients should be introduced into the water line leading to the Grey's shower in hopes it would somehow make a difference.

S am's request had prompted a meeting with the elite team of surgeons who had performed autopsies on the dead Greys.

HUSH

The team had been flown in from Bethesda overnight, and the group watched the Grey lying on the couch via closed-circuit TV.

They told Sam that their autopsies revealed no digestive tract or waste tract either. Neither urinary nor bowel. It simply didn't need a kitchen or a bathroom, a fact confirmed by the absence of food storage or any waste facility in the crashed ship. They guessed it was maybe getting nutrients via dermal absorption from the surrounding air. Sam listened intently.

Food from air? Perhaps, he thought, *but there had to be more, because clearly the Grey was dying.*

He figured that a food source would have to exist somewhere for the creatures and that perhaps the small ship was simply a scout ship. And the scout ship had come from a larger interstellar ship that had food and energy for the creatures.

The surgeons stood in a huddle, observing the Grey, and Sam sensed that he was not invited to the conversation. He lit a cigarette and watched them for a time. He was patient a little longer. And then he wasn't.

"I'm a used car salesman and a gardener," Sam suddenly said.

This halted the group, and they turned, smiling their somewhat condescending smiles. Sam was not intimidated, as he had a sense of urgency about him and knew they all needed to work this out quickly or they would lose the Grey. He figured his assessment could do no harm, and in his simple way, proceeded to tell them his idea. He took a long drag and waved his cig at the screen showing the Grey.

"Many of my used-car batteries leak... the clear liquid that oozes out smells similar to that of the cadavers at the crash site."

The doctors nodded slightly, as they were certainly aware of the acetone-smelling liquid. Sam pointed with his cigarette back at the Grey.

"So, this thing attempted a really long shower as if it was trying for a recharge of energy and nutrients." He turned back to the doctors.

"And I mean not just nutrients from the air—hence the longer-than-normal shower—but clearly, its attempt at gaining energy is having no effect."

They were locked on now as he exhaled smoke and opened his hands.

"Now, just like the batteries in my old cars use liquid as the electrical conduit, perhaps somehow on its mother ship, that Grey could plug in and get recharged with an infusion of that clear liquid. Which I'm assuming not only has an electrical component but also has plant nutrients."

They stared now with rapt curiosity.

"I'm a gardener, and that thing's body reminds me of the celery in my garden—fibrous yet strong. Light and pliable, but using food in liquid form mixed with sunlight to grow."

You could hear a pin drop as he took a drag and looked at the alien.

"The little fella is gonna keel over here pretty quick, so I'm thinking you might want to get a top botanist in here ASAP, as the biology of that thing is absolutely plant-like."

The lead surgeon smiled curiously at him.

"So, just plant its feet and water that sucker?" The surgeon said.

Sam shrugged. "You said it, sir, not me. But if it doesn't happen ASAP, then you can forget having the chance to try."

The surgeons flew back immediately to begin tests. One day later, Sam could see the Grey was too weak to walk, and he let Poke know. Sam departed for lunch, having left the Grey resting on the couch, and had just sat down at the mess hall when one of the surgeons approached and whispered to him.

The clear fluid taken from the cadavers had been analyzed and recreated in the lab. Sam's hunch had been correct... the Grey apparently absorbed food nutrients contained in the clear liquid.

One minute later, Sam and the surgeon were rapidly rolling a gurney into the room where the Grey had no energy even to sit up. Sam made a command decision and lifted the small creature into his arms, telling the doctor he could run faster than the gurney could roll.

They ran the Grey, with MPs trying to keep up, to a waiting ambulance where the doors were slammed shut, and the ambulance raced to the medical facility a block away. The Bethesda team was already in place in a large operating room. Sam laid the non-responsive Grey in a shallow bath of the lab-produced liquid, which was full of food nutrients the team from Bethesda had discovered in their cadavers' clear liquid.

The small tub was stainless steel and slightly longer and wider than the Grey's body. The depth allowed Sam to press the Grey down until submerging it completely.

"Careful," one surgeon said, stepping forward so that Sam did not submerge the mouth slit and nose holes.

"It's okay," Sam quickly replied. "It doesn't breathe through its mouth or nose holes."

"Right!" the surgeon whispered, pointing at Sam.

Sam's hands were completely submerged, holding the Grey down. When he saw no more air bubbles rising from the mouth and nose holes, he released it, and it stayed submerged. He then nodded at the elderly male nurse standing ready at the end of the metal bath. The entire room watched as the nurse gently massaged the arms and chest to speed absorption.

Attached to the tub via wires was a fluid level indicator, which another technician monitored. Sam realized he was holding his breath as the Grey's four-fingered hands remained still.

"Thirty seconds," the fluid level technician called out, staring at a stopwatch. "Fluid level decrease less than one percent."

Everyone stared as the massaging continued, but nothing was happening.

"Two minutes... no significant further absorption," the fluid technician called out next, and Sam could feel his hope diminishing with each passing moment.

Two of the surgeons turned away as Sam watched the nurse working the hands, kneading and gently moving each long, strange finger. At four minutes, the rest of the surgeons departed. Sam stared momentarily at the unresponsive Grey and turned to exit.

Reaching the hallway, he could see the team speaking in a semicircle. He couldn't help but notice two team members glancing his way with a hint of condescension.

"Hey!" They heard the nurse suddenly shout. "Hey!"

Running back into the room, the team surrounded the small tub. The Grey's eyes were slowly changing and seemed to become vibrant again.

"Absorption is now two quarts!" called out the technician.

An audible gasp came from several in the room, and the surgeon next to Sam gripped his shoulder, and the two shared a hopeful glance. The entire team watched in amazement as the creature slowly animated while the massaging continued.

"Oh, my God!" exclaimed the head surgeon, looking up at Sam and shaking his head in admiration.

They all watched as each limb began to liven and move, like a newborn waking from a deep sleep.

"Somebody call Wright-Patt and tell them we've had a breakthrough!" said the chief surgeon to the group, as one surgeon quickly stepped to the red wall telephone and began rapidly dialing.

"H ow's the little Grey bastard doing?"

Poke asked Sam that evening during dinner in the base mess hall.

Sam felt relieved at Poke's line—he needed to vent. The full return to energy had taken ten hours. Sam had remained by the Grey for the first two hours, and the Grey simply stared at him as it slowly realized where it was.

"It wants to know, basically, when we will set it free, sir," Sam said.

Poke snickered.

"That little shit. Give me a gun, and I'll free it," he said with a wink.

Sam burst out laughing before he caught himself. He didn't want to be that guy with a predetermined judgment of the Grey, but his day had been long and tense. So, he allowed himself to simply laugh good-heartedly when Poke continued.

"Damn things are too smart for their own good."

"Yes, sir." Sam said. "It's a challenge to communicate with it."

"Communicate with it?" Poke said. "Shit... it took us a damn year with the last one just to contain it. You know those things can go through walls, right?"

Sam stared, perplexed.

"I'm not joking," Poke said. "The first one we had here would simply dematerialize and walk through whatever room we put him in." Poke said, swallowing a big hunk of chicken, and tossed the bone.

"Until we figured out about the Faraday cage. It creates an electromagnetic field that deters the little shits from dematerializing."

Sam watched him intently.

"The first one we had here... that sucker was lying to us about everything we asked it. And we knew it was lying. But once we installed the cage—and it knew it could no longer escape—the truth started coming out."

Poke sucked his teeth, snickered, and shook his head.

"The truth for its release... because it knew it was trapped."

Sam was transfixed as Poke continued.

"That's why I mentioned that Faraday cage hidden within the walls around the Grey's room, so you don't have to worry about it running away, at least."

Sam nodded, chewing, when suddenly Poke realized something as he stared at Sam.

"You don't know, do you?" Poke said.

Sam quit chewing as he saw the concern in Poke's gaze. The major was clearly assessing him.

"Know what, sir?" Sam asked.

"Shit, they didn't tell you," Poke replied with genuine surprise.

Sam watched him closely.

Poke looked both ways and exhaled. He seemed miffed. He turned back to Sam, contemplating him. Then he leaned in slightly, speaking in a whisper,

"Captain Boyd, you be careful. We lost a handler not too long ago."

Sam stared, alarmed.

"What happened, sir?"

Poke took his time, slowly looking both ways again.

"I didn't tell you this, but that first one mind-melded the handler on closed-circuit TV."

Sam stared, confused as the major continued in a whisper.

"Like it got in real close to the handler and then, all of a sudden, put its forehead against the handler's forehead. The next thing you see on the camera is the poor handler screaming. My boys rushed in and shot it, but it was too late. There was blood oozing from the handler's eye sockets when my boys got to him. He was dead as a doornail, and his eyes were all bulged like his brain had been exploded."

Sam felt bile rising and the urge to vomit. He had picked up the creature to run it to the operating room.

"Damn," he managed.

Poke stood slowly and grabbed his tray.

"Hence the term '*Little Grey bastards.*'" Poke said. "I'd better be getting back, Sam... you take good care now, and keep your distance."

"Will do, sir, and thank you," Sam replied quietly.

Poke turned to exit but then paused, sternly looking back over his shoulder.

"We've gotta look out for each other now, Boyd... they're comin' for us."

Sam stared and realized he was shaking as he watched the huge man lumber away.

Chapter Twenty-Eight

The wheels coming down brought her back into the jet as it landed at San Francisco International.

Inside, she could feel Sam's anxiety—escaping a dangerous situation with the Grey—and all the new information about its biological system was shocking.

She caught the BART subway to Millbrae Station, where her Silverado awaited. She departed the parking garage and drove slowly—waiting. Seconds later, slipping out from a hidden area by the parking garage, the black sedan appeared. She wanted some sense of control. Then, exhaled... realizing she had none in this new realm she had chosen—one where the Cabal had control. They controlled everything.

She woke early at Dahs. After a good breakfast and a sit, she had a cup of coffee with Dah and watched her depart for her garden, which was her morning ritual. Vyla stepped to the picture wall and stared at a small photo of Waya standing next to two other men. The picture was inscribed: *Waya, Mack Brazel, and Roy Wallace.*

She knew that Mack Brazel had been at the center of the entire Roswell incident, and she had heard stories about Waya's good friend Roy Wallace, a huge Cherokee Indian. In the picture, the two large Indians dwarfed the older rancher, standing between the two. She carried the photo to Papa's box, where she selected the thick Roswell file. Inside, she found an attached vintage map of the Roswell, New Mexico, area from 1947.

She knew that near Sam and Waya's crash in San Agustin, several other crashes had happened simultaneously, around the Roswell area during that weekend. She was certain, from her channeling of Eisenhower, that the aliens were attempting to understand what the Americans were planning with their new nuclear capability, as Roswell was the only base in the world with atomic bombs during those infamous days.

She wanted to know the exact timeline of events and the players involved to understand how the deadly lie had spawned. This was going to be a deep dive, as she wanted the full perspective. She was open to whatever players presented themselves and would allow the entire Roswell incident to play as a movie before her, reliving it in real time.

She had Sam's picture in her purse for later, but right now, she wanted to meet the other major characters of the Roswell timeline and get a sense of who was involved and how the incident became such a juggernaut. She laid out the vintage map of the Roswell area that was in the folder. It was marked with areas that appeared to her to be hotspots of activity during the incident weekend.

The small towns of Roswell and Corona were circled. South of Roswell, the Army Airbase was circled, as well as the Capitan Mountains to the west, where a red circle was annotated with *Split Rock Crash Site*. Miles to the north of the Capitan site, the map had another red circle labeled *Mack Brazel Debris Field*. Just to the north of Roswell was a circle marked *Mesa Crash Recovery*. On the western side of the map was a large circle. *The Plains of San Agustin... live Grey recovery*.

She closed her eyes, with her hands on the picture of Waya, Mack Brazel, and Roy Wallace at Wade's bar in Corona, New Mexico. Her other hand rested gently on the Roswell area map, and the pipeline opened immediately. She began to feel the moisture and the deep thunder of the violent electrical storms rolling amidst the intense heat of that dark New Mexico night.

T he explosions on that Fourth of July night in 1947 were louder than any fireworks Mack Brazel had ever experienced.

And what rocked him in bed at that midnight hour were not even manmade explosions. The thunder and lightning of the electrical storm over his dilapidated shack felt like they might rip his little homestead apart. He felt the walls shaking and wondered how much more it could withstand before it collapsed on his small family.

Mack was used to electrical storms. Hell, he'd been through many years of them, but the one that was hovering over the J.B. Foster ranch at that moment would not let him close his eyes. His wife and two young kids were tucked into the small bed next to him, and so far, they had remained asleep. The impact, or explosion—or whatever it was—that woke him had certainly happened just above him, as it was so damn loud it shook the ground far stronger than the thunder and chain-lightning that had shaken the ground all night.

Electrical storms of this size had often ripped airplanes apart, and the violent impact he had heard was terrifying. Mack rolled in his bed, hearing the rain and wind raging amid the flashes and booms through his curtained window.

He was also anxious about his two-hundred sheep possibly stampeding, trying to get over a fence running from the noise. His mind went back to the possible crash and the downed crewman who might still be alive, but by God, he was not chancing taking his horse out in that electrical storm. She would spook for certain, and he wouldn't be able to see a goddamn thing, anyway. He figured that if there were survivors, their fate was in their hands—at least until morning. He looked at his wife and kids, still asleep there in that tiny one-room, and amid a lightning flash, he heard it—again.

A high-pitched whine that he didn't recognize as any animal he had ever known. A tremendous thunder cracked and boomed, and his heart raced... and again, he heard it... like something in death throes. What terrified him at that moment... was that for all the years he had worked this ranch, nothing in the whole southwest made a siren-wail like that.

He knew one thing for certain—that eerie cry—was not from an animal.

S eventy miles southeast of Mack Brazel's terror, two Catholic nuns were watching the fireworks explode over the small military town of Roswell, New Mexico.

Mother Superior Mary Bernadette and Sister Capistrano were sitting in lawn chairs on the sweltering roof of Saint Mary's Hospital. It was a balmy ninety degrees on the rooftop, but the sisters were used to that desert feel and enjoyed the warm breezes on those summer nights. To the northwest of them, an electrical storm of immense width was traversing toward them, and they could see the chain-lightning and flashes of that monster slowly heading their way.

They were also used to seeing strange craft flying overhead, ever since two years before when the Trinity Nuclear Test had detonated near Socorro, 115 miles west. They had both been awakened by the blast on that mid-July morning. The ground had shaken as if the earth was coming apart.

Since then, the two sisters had witnessed the strangest craft zooming around the Walker Army Airfield base just to their south. The base and town had been renamed Roswell only a short time ago and the little saucers—as they called them—had kept up their surveillance of the airfield. Nobody knew what they were, and the sisters were always curious how the military boys down at the base would deny ever seeing them, though everyone in the town was abuzz about the little discs.

The sisters were always amazed at how fast the flying saucers were, and how they could change direction or altitude on a whim, making no sound whatsoever.

And on this celebratory July 4th night, Superior Mary Bernadette felt it was God's will for her and Sister Capistrano to sneak a little of their leftover hospital wine up to the roof for a nip. After all, they had been administering the same wine to the hospital patients during room calls, and they felt it was their God-given duty to ensure that it still tasted okay, as they would administer more tomorrow afternoon.

They sat in their chairs and watched the fireworks exploding all around them in the tiny town. Then they saw it.

A brilliant light, far brighter than any firework, shot over their heads in a northerly direction and plunged to the Earth in a molten flash near what Sister Mary figured was the tiny town of Mesa, New Mexico, about thirty-five miles to their north.

Mother Superior covered her mouth as the object disappeared over the horizon—then joked that they might soon have more patients at the hospital. Sister Capistrano crossed herself, laughing hysterically. Then, they both sat back... and had another sip of wine.

F orty miles northwest of the two drunk sisters, Captain Sheridan "Snake" Cavitt sat stone-faced in the passenger seat as he struggled to stay inside the open Army jeep, bucking and bouncing eastbound on the pocked, dirt highway locals called *Pine Lodge Road*.

Him and his three MPs had roared north an hour ago from the White Sands Missile Test Range at high speed in search of a complete unknown—something that had appeared and then vanished off three separate Army radar screens at 2317 hours on the damn 4th of July.

Now, an hour later—in the electrical storm-filled darkness, they were bouncing through desert scrub along old dirt highway 246—rising up Mount Capitan.

The three large MPs in the jeep with him held hard gazes as they peered ahead into the pitch-black desert while the jeep scampered roughshod across the extremely rugged terrain.

As they ascended with the engine pushed to the limit, Snake could make out, far below them, the bright red fireworks exploding over the tiny town of Roswell, forty miles to the east.

One MP stood in the middle of the jeep, manning the pedestal-mounted T-47, 50-caliber machine gun. One drove, and one rode behind Snake with a set of radio headphones on, giving updated directions as they departed the highway at full speed and bounced and weaved through desert scrub up the side of the mountain.

The three MPs had no idea what they were hunting. They had only been ordered by Snake to *be ready for anything, but don't shoot... unless ordered.*

Several times, the jeep seemed to catch air as it leaped through the desert washboard. There was no road where they were—just sagebrush and pinyon trees, arroyos, ravines, and desert night heat. Suddenly, from just ahead, a glow emanated from behind the slight rise in the terrain.

Snake was fighting his nerves. What was ahead terrified him, and he was not one to be easily scared. He had been in withering combat situations in the war, but nothing compared to the terror he felt at this moment. He was in charge and couldn't tell the three soldiers he was leading what they were going after. Not that he could, even if he wanted to—hell, he didn't even know—and that's precisely what terrified him.

At 23:17 hours, he had been crowded inside a brand-new SCR-584 mobile radar platform, just deployed to the White Sands Missile Test Range. Snake had watched over the shoulders of his three radar operators as they monitored the test launch of America's new V2 rocket, which had fired off just moments before.

The V2, which had been built with the help of a former Nazi rocket scientist, was capable of speeds in excess of 3,000 mph.

Snake and his radar operators were watching the rocket accelerate through 2,000 mph as it raced in an arching maneuver over the test range. At that moment, two unidentified blips shot across the radar screens and flew in formation with the rocket as if the rocket was standing still!

The radar techs all turned, looking up at Snake standing behind them. Everyone in the sweltering tracking unit knew there was no manmade craft on the planet that could keep up with a V2.

"Goddamn," Snake whispered as the V2 raced along the range, the white blips now dancing around it, seemingly inspecting the missile while in flight. A moment later, the bright blips shot at Mach velocity northeast in formation and suddenly stopped on a dime, eleven miles northeast of Corona. They appeared to hover momentarily... and then vanished in a ball of white light!

Staring in disbelief at the radar screens in front of him, the just-deployed mobile radar units that were active at White Sands, Corona, and Mt. Capitan were telling him that two unidentified blips on three radar screens had suddenly disappeared mid-flight.

"Sir, I think those ships just exploded!" said a radar tech, looking up at Snake. Snake slowly nodded.

"Okay, boys, triangulate that last known position and get it to me on the radio. See if you can determine trajectories for that debris and send us those rough locations."

"Yes, sir!" they answered in unison as he hastily exited.

Now, in the moonlit early morning, he held on tight to the windscreen. Neither Snake nor the three MPs in the jeep had seen the molten ball streaking over Roswell, miles behind them. They were focused on the glow emanating just over the mountain ridge in front of them.

The three MPs assumed they were about to witness an airplane mishap, but Snake couldn't tell them that an aircraft was not what they were looking for. What they were after was classified, and Snake was a pro at covert operations, knowing when to withhold information... even from those under his direct command.

Unbeknownst to the three MPs, Snake was a long-term spy with fifteen years behind him... of working two lives. One as a captain assigned to the personnel section of any given military group, and the other as a high-level operative of the Army's Counterintelligence Corps. A covert unit deeply embedded in and around the 509th Bomb Group at Roswell Army Airfield. President Harry Truman was hell-bent on keeping that unit safe from the Russians, who were gunning hard to gain their own nuclear capability.

The MPs frequently looked over at Snake as they drove, wondering where the hell they were going and what they were searching for. Captain Cavitt had always been a slight mystery to the MPs on the base. They knew he was attached to personnel, and that was pretty much everything they knew. And since he was a captain, and they were highly trained MPs, nothing was discussed. Before they picked him up that night, they chatted amongst themselves that Captain Cavitt had been more of a regular customer at the flight line lately since the recent rumors about disc-craft flying around Roswell.

The wave of sightings had increased right after Oppenheimer's Trinity Blast of 1945 and had been on the rise ever since. But flying saucers had become something of a joke around the Roswell area. Most figured they were Russian reconnaissance of some sort.

And now, after searching through the rough desert terrain on the northern slope of Mount Capitan for three hours, luck came their way in the form of a glow emanating from just over the next hill. The three MPs looked at Snake, wondering what the glowing object was just ahead as they motored forward. They were suddenly hit with a heavy smell of what Snake thought might be sewage.

"Stop the jeep!" Snake bellowed, coming over the rise. The glowing object had split the huge mountain rock just ahead, and Snake's worst fears were coming true.

The craft was certainly not identifiable as an aircraft in the U.S. arsenal.

"Sir, what the hell is that?" the machine gun MP whispered to Snake, aiming the huge .50 caliber at the glowing craft, which pulsed a slight humming sound in its wrecked state.

"Hold your fire, Corporal!" Snake said tersely.

"Yes, sir," whispered the machine gunner, staring ahead at the strange sight.

"I don't have any idea what it is, boys... but I'm assuming it's what everyone is talking about."

The three MPs stared warily at the ship and weighed the situation. They were top-tier MPs attached to the 509th Bomb Group at Roswell, specifically to guard the B29s. They were handpicked and vetted from thousands across the nation and knew how to keep their mouths shut—especially about all things top secret.

Impaled in the mountain rock, was a pumpkin seed-shaped craft, roughly twenty-five feet long, with a wingspan of fifteen feet or so. A small, ashen, orange-colored creature that appeared dead, lay half out of a crack... where the cockpit dome of the craft had separated. The ship glowed an electric blue color.

"Okay, boys, I didn't want to tell you on the way here because I wasn't certain, but—"

"Oh, my God!" the driver suddenly exclaimed, realizing what he was staring at.

"Yes, it's what you think it is," Snake replied, knowing that rumors of flying saucers had been circulating around the base since two days before when several Roswell citizens had reported strange lights in the sky over the base.

Snake slowly exited the jeep, pistol in hand.

"You stay here," Snake said to the machine gunner. "And you two, come with me—do not shoot unless I do."

"Yes, sir," they all replied in unison.

The three large men slowly approached the ship, which still had a small humming sound emanating from it. They could see another creature had been thrown against the split rock wall and was clearly dead.

"Oh, God!" one of the MPs with Snake whispered, suddenly overcome, and fell to his knees, beginning to vomit.

"Leave him be!" Snake whispered to the remaining MP walking next to him. "And keep your head on a swivel!"

"Yes, sir!" the final MP whispered tersely.

Snake approached the glowing craft as the MP, puking behind them, yelled, "Oh, God! Oh God!"

Snake continued forward with the MP beside him, guns raised toward the ship. He peered into the cracked portion of the glowing craft. There were control panels loose and hanging lines of tiny lights that seemed to sway like horsetails in the night wind. Inside, he could see three more creatures, two of which appeared to be dead, but the remaining one, injured, was moaning—though not the moan of any human. It had an eerie, siren-like whine unlike anything Snake had ever heard.

Snake and the other MP looked at each other, then back at the small creature. It was roughly four feet tall, and hairless. It appeared naked, with an ashen-orange skin color, and the eyes were large and black, but not wrap-around. These were placed where human eyes would be, except they were of a more rounded shape. The mouth and nose were small, as well as the ears.

The six-fingered left hand was moving back and forth as the creature moaned its siren-like agony.

"Sir," said the MP next to Snake, "is that... that thing from—another—"

"Hold your shit together, Sergeant!" Snake tersely demanded, cutting him off. "Get on the radio and get a recovery team out here on the double!"

The MP nodded slightly.

"Yes, sir," he said, holding back bile, and stumbled back toward the jeep.

Snake turned back to the alien ship and the crazy scene in front of him. He realized he too was hyperventilating, his heart pounding. He looked at the same dead creature bent forward before him. He felt the ground swirl beneath him as the bile rose, and his feet started to tingle. He caught himself and said aloud in a half-crazed whisper,

"That is not a damn Russian—that is not—a goddamn Russian!"

A t daybreak on Saturday, July 5th, when the storm had passed, Mack was just saddling his horse when he heard his ranch assistant, Dee Proctor, ride up behind the stable.

Timothy Dee Proctor was the neighbor's son from next door. That fact alone meant that the seven-year-old cowboy had already ridden the ten miles from his parent's ranch to Mack's ranch. Mack was always surprised at how the tough youngster was so eager to accompany him for all the hard work ahead. They had become fast friends.

"Good mornin', Mr. B," Dee said shyly. Mack noticed that Dee always spoke softly in the morning, almost as if he was testing Mack to see what kind of mood his 48-year-old boss was in.

Mack looked up momentarily as he cinched the saddle straps on his Appaloosa.

"Helluva storm last night. Did you see our sheep on the way over?" Mack said.

"I seen 'em, but they looked spooked. There's all kinds of stuff up there."

"Up where?"

"Well, up where they are."

Mack looked over, and half nodded, not understanding what the hell the kid meant, but figured he'd soon find out.

With a huff and a pull, Mack was in the saddle a moment later, and they were trotting steadily across the desert ranch terrain, already somewhat dry from the ninety-degree heat that would boil by noon.

Twenty minutes later, coming over a small rise, Mack finally saw what Dee had meant, and it confirmed his fears from the night before.

In the massive field ahead of him were the two-hundred sheep, all bundled together, looking his way like a bunch of scared children. But between the sheep and Mack was what appeared to be a plane crash of some sort. Scattered before him and Dee was a massive patch of aluminum-foil-looking material that stretched for almost half a mile across his ranch in what appeared to be a fan shape of silver debris. It was blowing everywhere in the steady gusts, and the sheep on the far side were clearly terrified.

Due north of the debris field was a long dirt gouge, roughly three feet deep and twenty feet wide, stretching for about five hundred feet. It curved smoothly up at the edges, running north to south in a perfectly straight line. Much of the dirt was scorched.

What was odd to Mack was that in the debris field, there was no fuselage, no structure of an aircraft anywhere that Mack figured would be at the end of the gouge—just thin pieces of foil scattered everywhere.

In Mack's mind, it looked like a huge, rounded, silver object had hit, skidded, and then departed back into the sky, heading at high velocity directly south toward Mount Capitan.

A moment later, Dee was off his horse, staring at a piece of the silvery-looking foil. "Hey, Mr. B! Look!"

Dee had wadded up a 6x6-inch square piece of foil in his hands and then lofted the foil ball into the air. A split second later, the ball magically expanded in a watery fashion back to its original flat shape it had been seconds before.

Mack stared in disbelief as a gust caught it, and it drifted in the wind before landing a few feet away. He dismounted and grabbed a piece at his feet as Dee watched. Mack twisted and pulled on the foil-like material, but it remained completely unscathed.

He sucked his teeth and pulled a cigarette pack from his shirt pocket and lit one, pulling hard on the cig, getting it red hot. He lifted the material as Dee stared, excited. Mack put the cigarette to the foil, but instead of burning a hole, the cigarette was extinguished.

Mack looked at Dee, who now had a mischievous look.

"Well, if it don't burn, shoot it, Mr. B!" Dee said matter-of-factly.

Mack got a look, relit the cig, and pulled out his six-shooter—a vintage piece his father had passed down to him. He exhaled smoke, spinning the six-shooter once for the kid, who watched in admiration as Mack aimed at a two-foot-square piece at his feet and fired.

Whoom!

The material closed around the bullet in a flash. Mack picked up the wad of foil, and as he did, it was already unraveling back into its square shape. The smashed bullet was held in the center—pulverized, just like he'd shot hardened steel. But the foil material was completely untouched. Dee stared in wonder.

"Wow!" Dee said in astonishment.

Mack looked up at his huge flock of sheep, anxiously watching silver pieces blowing around them. He could tell they were terrified, and the water they needed was on Mack's side of the debris field. He knew right then that they'd have to be driven to that watering hole.

Goddammit, he thought, shaking his head.

"Come on, Dee. Let's get back and find out whose stuff this is so we can get them to clean it up."

T wo hours later, Mack was back in the debris field without Dee.

He'd had a hunch when he was with Dee earlier that the little boy would be forever scarred if they came across dead bodies amid all the crash debris, so he sent him home, telling him to let his father know about the crash.

Mack had spotted something in the far distance to the east, near the bluffs—another shiny element. He trotted toward that area, intending to investigate it now that Dee was no longer around.

As he rode forward, he understood on some level that he was riding into his destiny. He looked ahead, and without thinking about it, calmly pulled his right arm back like a gunslinger, resting his hand on his six-shooter, still in its holster.

He allowed his thumb to feel the warm steel of the trigger, sliding it back slowly. He felt a little more secure when he heard the familiar—*click*.

Then he remembered the eerie whine from hours before—it still haunted that calloused... weathered... cowboy.

Chapter Twenty-Nine

Racing like an arrow, headed straight down at 170 miles per-hour, Ben's handlers realized the jet was hell-bent for destruction at an unbelievable 15,000 feet-per-minute, rate-of-descent.

All the way from Williamsburg, Virginia, they understood their boy toy had fucking passed out. So, they did what they always did when Ben misbehaved. They shocked him—through his interlink—while yelling at him to *wake up!*

And he did.

He also managed to slowly raise the nose—from his straight-down dive—and simultaneously decompress the entire jet.

In the main cabin, a collective gasp went up as the passengers and hijackers suddenly had fresh outside air, mixed with the black smoke. At least there was now clean air to be had, and the gasping and coughing of everyone was continuous as smoke continued to pour through the jet.

In the aisle midway through the coach section, the female hijacker sat up from where she had lain on the floor during the vertical dive, holding on to the steel base of the passenger seat next to her as the jet had plummeted.

She waited momentarily, catching her breath as the jet came up to level. A moment later, she heard a yell just behind her as a large Chinese passenger had released himself, pulling his blindfold up enough to lurch for her—falling on her—and crushing her down with his weight, yelling something in Chinese as he attempted to bludgeon her with his zip-tied fist-cuffs.

Suddenly his eyes lit up—as the crazed passenger felt her bullet go through his stomach—and he seemed to halt as the blood sprayed out from behind him. She pushed him off... getting to her feet... and then took her time—making a show for the other hijackers of putting the next bullet—directly between the man's terrified eyes.

Up in the cockpit on that pitch-black morning... Ben was taking in the fresh air from the decompression and slowly getting his bearings in the pitch black. He could see the Malaysian coast a few miles ahead of him, with little pools of light dotting the countryside.

Below him, a few miles off the coast, eight fishermen watched in astonishment—as the glowing orange jet... with smoke trailing behind it—flew just above the ocean heading west. They had never seen a commercial jet so low over their fishing grounds, and they would later report it.

Ben's handlers checked in with him just enough so that he didn't say *fuck-you* out loud. He had always wanted to do that... but he hated the shocks, and he also knew that as much as he wanted to depart from them forever... they held a card he couldn't beat.

They never said it out loud—but over the years he realized—they had put it in him... and he could never find it. He knew they had the power to flip that switch anytime they chose. And that just pissed him off. That little switch, wherever they had embedded it, was unknown to him—otherwise, he would have removed it years ago—and said, "Adiós, assholes."

But he hadn't found it. He knew they would use it if he tried to go rogue—leaving them forever—for a normal fucking life.

But he felt it... knew it was there. That minuscule piece of hardware lurking inside him...

that goddamn *kill switch*.

Chapter Thirty

T he convoy was still at the crash site when Waya pulled away from his
trailer and headed east to meet his friend Roy Wallace.

It was already 11 a.m., by the time he pulled his peach Ford into the parking lot
of Wade's Bar in Corona, New Mexico.

He didn't have to look too hard to find his old friend. Waya didn't know
many men his own size, but Army Corporal Roy Wallace was one of them. A
six-foot-nine-inch Cherokee Indian from Arkansas, Roy was assigned to the 390th
Air Service Squadron at Roswell as an MP.

The two men had met at a Native powwow a few years before and had hunted the
plains together many times. Roy was skilled with bow and arrow but could place a
bullet equally well, thanks to his days practicing in the military. Waya had called Roy
when the Army convoy arrived that morning to recover the saucer he'd discovered
in the ravine. When he saw the convoy with Sam Boyd depart to the east, he figured
it must be headed to Roswell.

Roy, however, said he wasn't part of the cleanup and hadn't heard of the crash
near Waya's. But he was quick to assure Waya that he believed his story, as there had
been many sightings of flying discs recently around Roswell Army Airfield. And

274

Roy wanted to hear all about Waya's sighting.

The two decided to meet in Corona to discuss things as it was roughly a halfway point between where the two lived, and Roy's family lived there. Wade's was a favorite watering hole for both Indians as the walls were adorned with arrowheads and old Winchester rifles.

There were many Indians who worked as ranch hands or served in the military in the Corona area. Shaking hands in Wade's parking lot, Roy, still in his MP uniform, patted Waya's shoulder.

"You're not gonna believe what's in the bar! Roy said excitedly. "My old ranch foreman is in there with a bunch of that silver space stuff!"

A minute later, Waya and Roy were standing at the far end of the wooden bar inside Wade's. The bar was a flurry of activity as Mack Brazel stood at one end, showing several patrons the silvery foil-like material that had appeared scattered across his ranch that morning.

They took a corner table, and Roy motioned over his shoulder.

"That's Mack Brazel in the cowboy hat. Runs the Foster Ranch just southeast of here. I haven't seen him in years."

Waya saw that Mack was handing out silver foil pieces to ranchers who were confounded by the material. The long wooden bar was covered with pieces from end to end, and every patron was experimenting with it. Waya watched the commotion, and Roy could see he was anxious.

"Would you rather talk somewhere else?" Roy asked Waya. "I mean, hell, I want to hear your whole story!"

"Maybe we can talk on the way to the rodeo," Waya said.

Roy nodded.

"Sure, we ain't ordered nothin' yet, let's go," Roy replied.

The two men were on their way out when they heard a yell.

"Roy! Roy Wallace! Is that you?" Mack Brazel shouted from the far end of the bar.

Roy and Waya turned.

"Hey, Mack!" Roy said, smiling.

"Well, I'll be damned," Mack said with a grin, approaching the two huge men. "You're lookin' sharp... leavin' so soon?"

Roy smiled.

"Well, we were planning on headin' down to the rodeo in Capitan and figured we better get on the road," Roy said, nodding to Waya just behind him.

"My buddy Waya here has just come from the plains of San Agustin, and he saw one of them ships, too."

The bar suddenly went quiet as everyone stared at Waya. Mack looked at Waya.

"Well, did it look like this stuff?" Mack said, holding out a piece of the silvery foil.

Waya stared at the piece, remembering how the debris picked up by the army looked similar. He looked up at Mack and nodded slightly, embarrassed to have so many white faces staring at him. The bar remained silent as Mack contemplated him.

"Did you see anything else?" Mack whispered.

Waya stared down at him, and it was clear to Mack that the huge Indian was finished speaking. But Mack understood the subtle signs and hints when it came to dealing with Indians. The stare Waya gave him at that moment spoke volumes.

"Thank you," Mack whispered with a nod.

Waya held his gaze a moment longer and then turned away, with Roy following. Roy gave Mack one last nod and smiled as the creaky screen door closed behind them. Mack followed them out the door and asked if he could get a quick picture with Roy for ol' time's sake?

Roy laughed.

"Sure, Mack," he said, pulling a 1946 Kodak hand-held from his pocket. "I've got my Kodak right here, all ready for the holiday."

They flagged down a passerby, and Roy convinced Waya to join in the picture. The three of them posed for the shot.

"Thank you, son," Mack said to Roy as he put his camera away.

"Sure, Mack. I'll get copies made and get you one shortly."

Mack nodded.

"That'd be swell, Roy, thank you."

Mack waved as they pulled out of the parking lot. He thought about what he had seen in Waya's look. He knew the big Indian had most likely seen the same thing he had witnessed on his ranch. Something he hadn't told anyone at the bar.

Mack would wait two more days before he let a news station in Roswell know what was really eating at him. There were bodies on his ranch. Child-sized bodies... that were not human.

A fter spending an hour or so at Wade's Bar and giving away a bunch of the silver pieces, Mack Brazel took more of his silver debris to the Corona hardware store.

No one there had any idea what the stuff was either. He hopped in his rusty 1930s pickup, and driving back to the J.B. Foster Ranch, he thought about what he discovered in his field and felt a darkness about it.

After Dee Proctor had gone home, Mack had ridden back out to the debris field, which seemed to have expanded in the wind and now was stretching for almost a mile. Mack inhaled, frustrated, and kicked his horse into a trot, continuing east for another two miles where he thought he saw another glint in the desert scrub. That's when the stench hit him. That distinctive smell of death brought a foreboding with it. He slowed his horse as he came upon the second area of silvery wreckage.

He raised a red handkerchief across his mouth and nose to beat the stench. Mack had witnessed many plane crashes around the local area as all the ranchers called for help whenever a plane came down on their properties. He had been to many a recovery operation, but what was ahead of him made him sick to his core. The stench was unlike others. He slowed his horse to a stop as his heart raced. Just ahead appeared to be the bodies of several children. He inched his horse closer. That's when his world began to change.

He uncocked his pistol and dismounted, staring down in utter disbelief. There were five little bodies.

What in the Sam hell! he thought as he stared, holding the handkerchief tighter against the disgusting stench. The bodies were clearly not human and had an ashen-orange color to their skin. The creatures were humanoid but with no hair on their skin and huge, black, glassy eyes that, even in death, seemed to look right through him. The cadavers were in various stages of rigor mortis, and Mack stared at a hand sticking up from one of the dead. It had six fingers!

He felt the ground swirl as he became lightheaded, looking down at the hairless body and saw that it also had six toes on roughly human-looking feet. He quickly turned away and spat, attempting to stop the rising bile. It worked. He lit a cigarette and inhaled deeply, holding the smoke. Finally, he looked again as he felt himself settle.

These were not Greys like the folks at Wade's bar had claimed about other crash events. Three of the ashen orange cadavers were mushed inside a torn-up ejection pod of some sort, while the other two bodies lay twisted and broken in the death throes of what appeared to be a high-altitude fall.

Suddenly, Mack heard the sound of horses behind him. He turned, and his heart sank. Just as he suspected, Dee Proctor was back—but this time with several of his young cowboy friends from the various ranches. They were all on horseback. Dee even had Truman Pierce's daughter with him. All the kids were between seven and nine years old, sitting up on their steeds.

Mack raised his hands.

"Don't you look!" he yelled ferociously, but it was too late.

The kids had stopped their horses short of where Mack was standing, but the terrified look on their young faces said it all. The black, glassy eyes that seemed to be looking right at them and the oily, sewage stench of death kept them staring, even as Mack kept yelling.

The little girl's blonde hair blew gently back as she stared ahead amidst the shouts from the rancher in front of her.

They would all grow up too fast in that moment. Forever changed. They stared at the creatures from another world amidst all the yelling and pleading from the angry man just in front of them.

It didn't matter anymore now.

Nothing did.

And nothing ever would.

V yla suddenly heard Banjo baying, and it brought her out of the channeling.

She opened her eyes and saw that Dah was entering the house, while Banjo was sounding off in the front yard.

She now felt she understood more of the anxiety-filled hours of the Roswell incident but knew there was much more to delve into and would get back to it as soon as possible. So many of the journeys she had just experienced were still unsettling. The kids seeing the bodies, and so many civilian and military personnel witnessing real aliens, had forever changed the planet.

The terror those early witnesses endured while being warned to keep their mouths shut must have been extreme, as many would never speak of it for the duration of their lives. She had more answers as to how the alien cover-up became deadly, but why it continued beyond Roswell was still puzzling. The fact that not one bit of information was leaked to the public in a slow disclosure was disturbing. She knew the Cabal had an important reason for keeping the alien presence a secret, but she would have to dig much deeper to uncover that covert agenda.

She could feel Mack Brazel's story turning darker by the moment, and yet Sam's experience was equally compelling. Sam's sudden awareness of a government cover-up, already in operation, aligned perfectly with her own new awareness. And to realize that her shock at the sinister secret being kept hidden from the public came to her so many years later made her realize that the Cabal's covert agenda was clearly deadly to anyone who threatened to expose it.

Adding to her stress of understanding the Cabal cover-up was the pressure of moving to Las Vegas, as all JRAD employees were required to live near Yen's headquarters on the Nellis test range. In addition, Vyla's fear of the unknown regarding test-flying the Widow brought with it an added anxiety.

Banjo bayed again. She shuddered, and it brought her into the current moment, remembering that she had promised Charlotte to walk Steph to school.

She quickly put the box away, and minutes later, she was showered and walking to her truck. The black sedan was down the street, lurking... and she could only make out one individual inside... and couldn't tell from that distance whether it was one of the Twins.

Parking at Charlotte's, she went inside and found Steph sitting quietly at the breakfast table, ready to go to school. Charlotte had apparently come in late from work and was still asleep. Vyla fixed Steph a bowl of cereal, and Steph sat quietly as she ate. Vyla made her a sack lunch, and a few minutes later, she carried Stephanie's small school satchel as they walked to school.

She held Steph's hand as they took their time along the sidewalk, but she sensed Steph was in another place.

Moments later, she looked down to see Steph was in tears and guided her to a nearby park bench. Vyla held her in the morning sun as Steph curled into her and, through tears, said that they had come again in her dreams and messed with her.

"Like, how do you mean?" Vyla whispered.

Steph shook her head slowly, sniffling, clearly affected.

"They were holding me down and..." she shook her head in Vyla's arms.

"They put things in me," she said, sobbing.

"I'm so sorry, sweetheart," Vyla whispered, gripping her tightly.

"I'm sick of it!" Stephanie almost shouted. "But I can't... I can't stop them!"

Both were silent for a time as Vyla caressed her head.

"Was this the Greys who were hurting you?" Vyla asked.

Steph nodded.

"The little ones hold me down, and the tall, mean one is the one that always hurts me."

Vyla watched her closely.

"I scream at him to stop, and he says, 'I won't remember it when I wake up,' but I always do!"

"So, he talks to you?"

"No, but I hear him in my head."

Vyla nodded.

"What did your mom say when you told her about it?"

Steph shrugged.

"She just sits there, and I think she doesn't really understand."

Vyla nodded, and they sat in silence, holding each other. After a time, Steph sniffled and got to her feet.

"Sometimes it makes me feel better to be with my friends at school, as I'm not scared when I'm away from home. My friend Anne always hugs me and helps me."

Vyla nodded.

"Anne, she's your best friend, right?"

Steph nodded, and Vyla stood giving her a hug.

"Yeah, let's get you to school, sweetheart, and I'll talk to your mom about it. Maybe we can come up with some way to make them stop."

Steph nodded through sniffles, and they had her at school a few minutes later.

D r. Jane Hoppensowski opened her office door on the Stanford campus to see Andre holding flowers and a sage smudge stick, smiling.

Behind him were two Secret Service agents.

"Good afternoon, Dr. Hoppensowski," Andre said, smiling. "I only have a few minutes today, but I wanted to bring you these for the last session, and perhaps I can just take a few minutes of your time today?"

Five minutes later, the two agents were sitting in the waiting room as she closed the door to her office. She smiled as he sat on the couch. It took her a few minutes to get water in the vase and organize the flowers, and she noticed that he had dropped into heavy contemplation. She finally sat near him and waited as he stared at his hands.

"Thank you again for the flowers. They're beautiful... and the sage."

At this, he lightened and nodded, looking up.

"I felt so relieved when I left the last time."

She nodded slowly, waiting. He shook his head, exhaled, and produced a handwritten note. She held it and could hear his voice as she read it.

"The one thing I didn't mention last time is the Deep Underground Military Bases, called DUMBs. There are hundreds of them. Some are only a few levels deep, and some are many levels deep. Some are clearly inhabited by aliens, some by humans, and some by both. There are many spaceports worldwide with antigravity ships. Area 51, McChord, Kirtland, Diego Garcia in the Indian Ocean, to name a few, as well as several on the eastern seaboard."

She nodded breathlessly.

"There is so much going on just below the surface of our planet that I decided to dwell on what feels to me to be the positive aspects of our inner earth, but rest assured, there are many clandestine operations going on daily, worldwide."

She slowly nodded.

"Well, tell me where you want to begin today?" she said aloud.

He produced a folded piece of typing paper and handed it to her. When she looked at the image, she was struck dumb. She had to reset her brain to process what she was seeing. She looked up at him, and he raised his eyebrows, then put a finger to his mouth. *"Quiet."* He then pointed to the CAT-scan-like image in her hand.

"There's so much more in my brain I want to tell you about, but I need a few minutes to interpret this being—I keep seeing."

Then, he opened both hands toward the image in her hand, and she took it in.

The mystical woman in the image stood with her long hair flowing in the sun. Yet that's where the human-female ended, and the mermaid-like woman began.

She stood upright on her curled fin, on the edge of a natural seawall, deep within the ocean. Sunlight streamed down on her, illuminating her long hair and extremely strong musculature. Shimmering jade scales flowed from her hips down to her curled fin. Her long hair, which swirled across her chest and down around her hips, was adorned with tiny shells that reflected the shafts of sunlight.

She seemed to hover on that seawall—poised like a seahorse—gallant and stunning. Appearing much taller than a surface dweller, with her hand holding some type of abalone but bigger. Her slender, graceful hand easily held the iridescent sea creature. Her gaze was calm and ethereal as she appeared to be watching something far ahead through the speckled sunlight. All around and behind her appeared small schools of colorful fish—and Jane could sense they were her attendants, who cleaned, protected and adored the clearly ancient—regal creature.

And in that luminescence, Jane could see a hint of her small dorsal fin, which rose behind her and curled softly, wafting in the watery atmosphere along with her forearm fins. In her soft stare, Jane felt a queen-like command of her realm, mixed with a softness of one at home in her magical... undersea universe. Jane sensed her strength and knew she was most likely as fast as a rocket through the water. Andre spoke again, confirming what the image told her.

"The woman I see in my brain is exactly nine feet, three inches tall. She is half human and half fish, with aquatic-style lungs that work in water and air, somewhat like a porpoise. But I only see her in water. Her musculature is much like a dolphin in the way her hips can sway and propel her through the water. Combining that sway with her main fin and her dorsal and forearm fins, she's twice as swift as a surface dolphin."

Jane shook her head, staring at the picture as he continued.

"My feeling from thinking about her..."

He gestured to the bottom right of the page, where a small computer chart showed what her skin and bone texture were made of—and the age of those materials—*450 years.*

"Is, she's ancient, like hundreds of years old."

Jane stared at the striking woman, then looked up to see him smiling. She gestured at the image.

"The image in your head—the woman—does she seem like she has a family?"

He nodded and smiled.

"She has a daughter, I believe... but she comes and goes so fast I only get flashes of her—never enough stillness to really get a clear picture of what she's like."

Jane shook her head, her heart exploding.

"But my guess—from my feeling about her—is that she is the mother of many within her clan."

She looked up at him. He was delighted to see Jane's reaction, as it was clearly his feeling, too.

"Well, thank you for sharing her with me today. You have quite an imagination in that brain of yours."

"Oh," he said, exasperated. "I've never shared her with anyone, so thanks for being open to what I see every day."

Then he stood, reaching out to take the picture.

"Can we light a little sage and do a short meditation?" he asked aloud.

She was shocked that this geek was a meditator. Then she saw it—the Zippo lighter produced from his jacket pocket. He held it near the image as it dangled in his other hand and looked at her... and the message in his eyes said it all.

We're burning this—now.

She nodded and spoke aloud.

"Sure, I'd love to light some of your sage. Let me get you an ashtray."

He nodded, and a minute later, lit the sage and the image. The mermaid picture quickly burned as he placed it in the ashtray. He then waved the sage by the door. When the image was fully ash, he gently placed the still-smoldering sage on top and sat back on the couch. They looked at each other and were quiet for some time. He noted his watch and stood. She joined him.

"Thank you again," he whispered.

She didn't want him to go.

"Of course," she said. "Just leave me a message if you would like another session."

He nodded and reached for the doorknob. Before she knew what she was doing, she reached out quickly and touched his shoulder. He paused and turned with his coke-bottle glasses, tilting his head down to see that she was holding a small handwritten note. He took the note, looked at her, then slowly nodded as he tucked it in his jacket pocket.

"Yes," he said with a gentle whisper and a nod toward the agents outside. "I'm free on Friday night, as long as you're fine with the chaperones escorting us to dinner?"

She smiled, and he took off his coke-bottles and placed both hands around hers. They shared a moment of soft smiles.

"My name is Jane, but everyone calls me Hoppy."

"Hoppy," he whispered. "Beautiful. I'll call you soon."

A moment later, he was gone.

V yla returned from dropping off Steph and slipped under the covers next to Charlotte.

She could tell Charlotte was awake, yet off on a mind run, holding something. Vyla slid in close to defeat any surveillance.

"Good morning," Vyla whispered.

Charlotte reached out and gently caressed her, but she was still gone.

"What is it?" Vyla whispered.

Charlotte stared into the morning sun as it softly streamed through the edge of the curtains. She was clearly stuck—frozen in some memory.

"I couldn't sleep anymore," Charlotte whispered. "Steph told me about her ongoing abductions."

Vyla watched her closely, wondering if Charlotte believed Steph? She recalled the Majestic brief section on abductions. How the Grey aliens didn't discriminate between adults, children, or animals. Anything with blood and glands was fair game. Abductees worldwide had videotaped their hypnotic regression sessions, and many had experienced the same torturous procedures.

"I can help you if you let me in," Vyla whispered.

Charlotte shook her head slowly, her lips trembling as she tersely whispered.

"When I was ten—I had the same thing as Steph."

Vyla stared, perplexed.

"You what?"

Charlotte stared ahead, caught in something terrible.

"I was pregnant."

"You were—what?!" Vyla whispered.

Charlotte sniffled.

"The OBGYN told my mom I was pregnant, but Mom didn't tell me. She just exited her conference with the OB and didn't tell me. Mom knew for certain I had not been with a boy. She told me, the pain would go away soon."

Vyla watched her closely.

"And eventually it did."

Vyla gently pulled her in, holding her close.

"I'm so sorry." Vyla said as Charlotte nodded and continued.

"Years afterward, my mom confessed she had the same thing happen."

Vyla stared.

"You mean she was pregnant without being with a boy?"

Charlotte nodded, and the silent sobs began.

"It was *them*." Charlotte said through tears.

"Them?" Vyla whispered.

"The whole thing you did on the chalkboard." Charlotte said.

Vyla's caresses slowly stopped as it hit her where Charlotte was going. Both were still.

"I've had a lot of—experiences," Charlotte whispered through tears.

Vyla turned directly to her.

"You—you were abducted?"

Charlotte nodded.

"Many times, years ago. And I knew about people doing hypnotic regressions to remember everything—but I was terrified—I didn't want to relive it."

Vyla nodded, watching her. They lay still for a time.

"In three years of being together, you didn't want to tell me?" Vyla asked as Charlotte wept silent tears.

"You were afraid I wouldn't believe you until now—now that I've seen things?"

Charlotte looked up slowly and nodded.

"Because nobody ever believed you before?" Charlotte looked over, and continued nodding.

"I get it," Vyla whispered. "And I am so sorry."

They lay still again.

"Steph said they hurt her," Vyla whispered. "She was in so much pain last night that she didn't want to discuss it. On the way to school, it all came out."

Charlotte half-nodded, staring out with a severe look.

"I'd tear them apart if I had the chance," Charlotte whispered. "They're unstoppable."

Vyla watched her eyes burning. A few minutes later, Charlotte was asleep again.

Vyla watched her and considered the entire phenomenon that had been covered in the brief. Common to all human abductions were recollections of long metal probes shoved into the temples. And equally common were men and women retelling horrific experiences of anal and vaginal insertions by the Greys using cold steel implements. Those torturous rapes often occurred repeatedly over many years.

The animal and human mutilations were almost always identical in many respects. Human abductees had traced the phenomenon to other members of their own families, whether it was acknowledged or not by the other family members.

Some abductions had been witnessed by bystanders, who reported seeing a cow or a human lifted on a tractor beam of light into a hovering UFO. The laser technology used on both animals and humans was so advanced that it removed suspicion of human involvement or trickery.

Cattle and humans were found with their eyes, glands, and reproductive organs surgically removed with such precision that no flesh wounds from surgical instruments were ever found.

And there was no blood where the cadavers were discovered. All plasma had been somehow collected without a single drop on the ground near the thousands of cattle found worldwide. Like it had been forcibly withdrawn from the cadavers.

And there had been humans found in the same post-mutilation, plasma-free condition, same horrific procedures. Dead animals and human cadavers alike were documented as having been dropped from altitude, as legs and arms were often found broken and twisted from apparent un-arrested falls from high altitude.

Vyla lay there infuriated. In time she simmered down, as she knew she was powerless to stop them. She turned to watch Charlotte as she slept. They had become closer through the years, and Stephanie only cemented that bond. She loved that little one at another level. Unexplainable love. She hated that she was powerless to stop what seemed like a group of phantoms abducting a child for their own fucked-up experiments.

She went into the living room, which still had the curtains closed and laid out her vintage map and photo. She put her hand over the town of Roswell on the map. With her remaining three fingers, she touched the picture of Mack Brazel with Waya and Roy flanking him. She breathed deeply and closed her eyes. Then, she opened her essence—to whatever would come, allowing the timeline of events to present themselves in order of occurrence.

She felt the pipeline open as never before, and moments later, she could feel the hot wind crossing the J.B. Foster ranch, and the smell of cigarette smoke dissolved what was left of her—into a hard, calloused ranch foreman.

Mack took a long drag on his cigarette and flicked it to the dirt.

It was daybreak on Sunday, July 6th, 1947, and the silver debris had spread again during the night. He knew he would never get his sheep around it. He gathered up a box of the foil material and fired up his rusty truck. Once the blue-white smoke from the exhaust was down to a reasonable level, he began the seventy-five-mile journey southeast to Roswell, New Mexico.

At 11 a.m. on that hot, quiet Sunday morning, Mack carried a small box of foil material into Sheriff George Wilcox's office and was greeted by Deputy Bernie Clark.

"This stuff is all over my ranch west of here, and I was wondering if you know whose it is?" Mack said.

Bernie looked over the material and scratched his head.

"Well, I don't know, Mr. Brazel," Bernie said. "Sheriff Wilcox is upstairs with his family," motioning above the jail cells just behind him.

"They live above the jailhouse, and he had a long night with it being a holiday weekend."

Mack nodded and paused. He didn't want to sound crazy talking about alien bodies.

"Well, Deputy, something strange crashed out there, and I think he might want to know about it."

The deputy eyed Mack with a hint of skepticism but picked up the phone and dialed. A few tense minutes later, Sheriff George Wilcox came down the stairs, looking irritated that even Sunday mornings on the 4th of July weekend were not free from drama.

Sheriff Wilcox nodded to Mack and looked down at the foil-like material as Bernie chimed in.

"Sheriff, Mr. Brazel here says this stuff came from a crash on his ranch over toward Corona. Said it don't burn, or break, or nothin'."

Wilcox looked at Mack and down at the material as Mack showed the incredible way it would unfold back to its original shape. As he was doing so, the phone rang, and Sheriff Wilcox motioned for Mack to wait as he picked it up.

"Yeah—oh hey, Frank," the sheriff said, pausing.

All three men in the room could hear Frank Joyce's booming voice coming through the phone, even from three feet away. The sheriff held the phone at arm's distance, listening as Joyce asked for a news scoop.

"Well, I ain't got nothin' for you," the sheriff said, "but hold on, 'cause a rancher just walked in with some of that flying saucer stuff."

Wilcox held out the phone to Mack.

"This is Frank Joyce from KGFL here in Roswell. He's lookin' for his news scoop, and I think you should tell him what you've got."

Mack took the phone, in a huff that the sheriff and deputy were not taking him seriously.

"Hello," Mack said in his gravelly, low voice. Again, all three men could hear Joyce's voice coming through the line... so loud that Mack also held the phone away from his head.

"So you got some of that flyin' saucer stuff?"

Mack looked at the other two men as he responded.

"Yeah, I got a box of it right here. I'm telling you that it's not from an airplane."

"What do you mean?" Joyce said.

Mack shook his head.

"It's not from anything we make here, I promise you that," Mack said.

Bernie and Sheriff Wilcox watched as Mack's anger rose... as he listened to Frank Joyce.

"Well, you've gotta bunch of stuff out there... why don't you just bring it all in?"

Mack tightened his lips.

"Well, by God, I wanna know who's gonna clean up all of that crash wreckage out on my ranch? My sheep can't get to water, and that shit is everywhere!"

"But you're saying it's not from an airplane?" Frank Joyce inquired.

"Hell, I don't know! From one of them flying saucers, I think—but it's everywhere!" he yelled.

"Well, why don't you call the base here in Roswell?" Joyce's voice boomed. "They take care of all the flying things around here."

Sheriff Wilcox and Bernie Clark would never forget what happened next.

Mack Brazel, already steaming mad, sat down on the edge of the desk and almost seemed to cry as his head dropped into his hand. He rubbed his head and began to moan lightly in anguish.

"Oh, my God... oh, Lord Jesus, it... it's... what am I gonna do? They—they smell so bad—they're... that stench is... just awful."

"What are you talking about?" Joyce said. "What stench—from what?"

"The little ones—they're all—they're all dead," Mack whispered.

Wilcox and Clark exchanged a look as they watched the tortured man.

"Who's dead? What are you talkin' about?" Joyce boomed.

"The creatures—they're all mashed up and dead," Mack whispered.

"What kind of creatures? Are they animals?"

"They're—they're not human," Mack whispered.

"What do you mean they're not human?" Joyce almost laughed.

At this, Mack tensed... lifted the phone close to his mouth.

"Goddammit, they're not monkeys, and they're not human!" Mack finally yelled, slamming the phone down. He looked up at the two men as he departed in a huff, leaving his box behind.

Sheriff Wilcox immediately stepped out after him.

"Hey Mister—hold on."

T wo hours later, after Sheriff Wilcox had informed the Roswell base commander of Mack's crash claim, Major Jessie Marcel and Captain Sheridan "Snake" Cavitt introduced themselves to Mack.

Within minutes they were following him westbound as he led the way to the J.B.

Foster Ranch and his debris field.

Mack drove hard, pushing his rusted truck to the limit, relieved that somebody was finally believing him. Marcel followed in his private vehicle while Snake drove an Army Jeep Carryall from the base motor pool.

The arduous seventy-five miles west along the dirt highways and rutted ranch roads took them almost three hours. They reached Mack's place well after dark.

Mack's wife, Maggie, provided a simple dinner and two makeshift beds for the officers in the tiny adobe barn next to the house. The next seventy-two hours would bring an evil to Mack's world that he could have never imagined.

Chapter Thirty-One

Sam was the only passenger on the Army's twin-engine Beech-18 as it lifted off in the darkness from the Los Alamos runway, bound for Roswell Army Airfield.

The plane climbed quickly to 8,000 feet and had barely leveled off when the lone blonde stewardess approached—a corporal—offering Sam cocktails and cigarettes.

One minute later, she returned, bringing him a refreshing, cold Coca-Cola and a pack of Chesterfields. She lit a cigarette for him.

"Sir, we'll only be level for a few more minutes before we start our descent to Roswell," she said, tipping a small pint bottle of whiskey into Sam's Coke and stirred it.

"Enjoy," she said and returned to her attendant seat. Sam pulled on his cigarette, staring at the moonlit clouds as they passed below the wing.

The last seventy-two hours had been shocking. He sipped his drink and mulled over how the creature had expressed itself through telepathy.

Of course, thought Sam, spoken language was too slow and cumbersome for an advanced race. They had gone beyond words to a communication form that allowed the immediate transfer of information between two entities.

That it could communicate through images, combined with feelings was incredible. He now understood that such a form of communication would be acceptable on any planet—a universal way of information exchange.

He thought about his upcoming brief for General Twining, who would be waiting for him at Roswell. He knew for certain that admitting his telepathic communication with the alien would kill any chance of his departing the military to be with his budding family.

Telepathy, in Sam's view, was still overwhelming, even to himself. Trying to explain that strange evolution to Twining was something he would mull over before the brief.

He sipped his drink, and his thoughts drifted back to the Grey. So many odd things about that creature that he could not put his finger on. And the entire issue of the well-rehearsed crash-retrieval teams was unnerving to him.

He had always considered the military to be of the utmost integrity. But the reality of otherworldly beings and the recovery of their ships kept secret from the general populace was disturbing. He figured there were reasons not to tell the public right away, but it was still jarring to realize that the U.S. military had an enormous secret that was being covertly guarded.

And that Grey still perplexed him.

Something felt artificial, but he couldn't resolve why. Perhaps because the Greys at the crash site had identical features—from skin texture and color to height and extremities.

Even when humans were bald, Sam thought, *they all had distinct features, but the little Greys did not.*

It was so odd to think that he had possibly communicated with an artificially cloned biological entity that could somehow emit emotional waves.

He thought of all the cars on his lot and how each one had an electrical system. He then wondered how one would attach a human biological brain to the car's electrical system. Could emotion be artificially created? And did the little Grey really feel?

It was all too much for him to mull over as he was exhausted. Perhaps he should leave well enough alone. He sipped his cocktail and watched the propellers outside his window.

Propellers, he thought.

How archaic, given his new knowledge of a disc that could travel the heavens without wings or an engine, oil, or gas. *Damn!*

Even without understanding the nature of the Grey, the shocking reality that humans were not alone in the universe was just the tip of Sam's thoughts. The global implications were beyond words. He wondered what his Methodist father would say if he were alive.

"Demons is what they are!" his dad would have said.

But Sam had learned long ago that his father's ingrained religious beliefs had a lot to do with fear. He knew of the Navajo and Apache spiritual ways, which were entirely different, and he tried to no longer judge a person by their religious faith and traditions. He accepted the native ways as valid, just like the white ways. It was all the same to him. Folks working out their place in the universe.

And Sam knew his place in the universe was holding baby Sue with Catherine by his side. How that sweet little thing already had him wrapped around her finger. And the new little one on the way—*Helen*, they would call her. He couldn't wait to meet her.

Two girls, he thought. *For heaven's sake, it was a miracle.*

He sometimes wished he was independently wealthy so he could just spend time with his growing family. *Boy, did he have a bevy of stories to tell them.*

He heard the plane's engines throttle back as the moon painted a cloud below. He sat back and gulped down the whiskey. Pulled on his cigarette, held it in, and finally exhaled as he felt the bird tip slightly forward and could feel the Beech begin its descent.

He looked out over the black expanse below in the moonlight and thought about how they were descending into the dark desert with only a few specks of light to signal life. A metaphor, in his mind, between the few who knew and the masses who were being aggressively hoodwinked.

He suddenly remembered that Eileen Fanton, his cousin, had recently gotten orders to Roswell. She had attended Fort Sam Houston Army nursing school and had graduated as a first lieutenant. She had asked Sam if he would write a letter of recommendation to the Army for her to be stationed at Roswell, as it was close to her family in nearby West Texas.

Sam wrote the letter but had warned her that Roswell was a top-secret facility and it would be a tough sell to get her in there, but that he would try.

Now, as the plane slowly descended, he realized he had been so blown away by the last seventy-two hours that he had completely forgotten Catherine had mentioned Eileen's call a few weeks ago. Eileen had phoned, wanting to thank Sam for getting her the position.

When Catherine had told him of the call, she said that Eileen mentioned she was already dating a fella from Roswell named Glenn Dennis, who ran a mortuary in town.

Hopefully, Sam thought, he could catch Eileen for a quick hello and hear about how it was going for her.

He felt the flaps extend as the bird slowed. He tamped out his cigarette in the ashtray attached to the seat in front of him. Gazing out as he descended, he could barely make out any lights in the vast desert below, except for what appeared to be a ranch house and barn every few miles.

Just then, as if signaling the plane from below, a bright red firework exploded, illuminating the tiny town of Roswell for a second or so. A remnant from the 4th of July celebration over the past weekend.

He thought about how America had just celebrated her independence. A country founded on truth, honor, and dignity, which Sam was proud to be a part of.

Yet, in this new moment, a mix of melancholy washed over him. He considered himself a true patriot, one who loved everything America stood for. But in his new awareness, he had just experienced the American military hiding a world-changing event on the plains of San Agustin. The entire thing felt wrong. That only a few would ever know that creatures from an advanced race had, once upon a time, been met, interacted with, and even perished right here in New Mexico.

Even though he was now in on the secret, he knew deep down that Americans deserved to be told the truth—even if just a hint. That the masses were being fed a complete and utter lie was already eating at him.

He sat for a moment, letting it come in full force. The nastiness and aggressive nature of what he had seen at the recovery operation left him with a deep dread about what lay ahead. Something had risen within his beloved government, and its tentacles were now stretching like a growing sickness.

It was a monster on the move.

A covert evil.

I t was still ninety-six degrees when the huge desert moon illuminated a lumbering GMC 6x6 Army troop transport, motoring slowly toward the empty runway at Roswell Army Airfield.

The canvas top on the rear had been removed, and the night air was calm but sweltering for the three college students swaying on wooden benches in the back of the massive truck.

A corporal drove while a captain sat in the passenger seat, casually smoking a cigarette as they approached the runway. All was quiet at the airbase. The long truck came to a stop and shut down next to a taxiway.

Sitting in the back of the truck on one of the wooden benches, a beautiful college freshman pulled her hair back and cried silently. She had not slept well since seeing the live aliens at San Agustin on Saturday morning, and since then, things were no longer in place. She felt unhinged and terrified.

She and her two college friends had been part of an archaeological tour and had stumbled upon the crashed alien ship and its crew. Just as her tall professor, Dr.

Buskirk, had attempted several languages with the two live aliens, the military had arrived and essentially arrested them, giving them all stern warnings about telling anyone what they had seen.

After a tense afternoon of enduring interrogations and warnings, she and her two college friends had gotten a hotel in Roswell for the rest of the weekend. But last night, they had gotten a little wild downtown and had fun telling many bar patrons about their amazing contact event.

Hours later, they were driving to their hotel when the nightmare stepped up a level. Their car was suddenly surrounded, and they were abducted by a team of military operatives who scolded them for blabbing about the aliens and told them they were in big trouble. The operatives brought them to the truck they were now sitting in. They were warned not to speak to each other until after their debriefs at Alamogordo.

She wiped a tear in that long truck and waited for their departure. They all heard Sam's Beech transport at about the same moment and could see its wing lights moving among the stars. The low drone grew louder as it turned downwind and lined up for landing. The military Beech-18 settled heavily on its huge front tires, lumbering down the runway and eventually dropping onto its tailwheel.

The girl watched as the plane turned off the far end of the runway and began to come up the taxiway toward them. The captain stepped out and yelled to all in the back with his distinctive New Jersey accent.

"Let's go, you three! Line up for boarding."

The college girl shot a quick glance at her terrified friends as they lined up behind her.

"Remember, folks, no talking between yourselves until after your debriefs at Alamogordo!"

The three said, "Yes, sir," in unison as the captain turned to face the plane rolling toward them on the taxiway.

Sam stared out the window as the Beech turned off the runway and stopped on the taxiway. He could see a captain he didn't recognize, with three college-aged kids lined up behind him—two boys and a girl.

He recognized the college students from the crash recovery at San Agustin. They had been with the tall professor.

"Sir," the stewardess said to Sam before opening the exit door, "we're going to leave the engines running as you exit because we are departing momentarily for a flight to Alamogordo for the folks getting on after you."

Sam stared, perplexed.

"You're taking those kids to Alamogordo now?"

She nodded.

"Yes, sir. I believe they are doing a debrief over there," she replied, opening the exit door.

Sam felt the gust of wind rushing in, and already, a set of steps had been rolled in place. The attendant saluted as Sam departed down the steps, carrying his satchel, and exchanged a nod with the captain waiting at the base of the stairs. The roar of the engines was deafening as the captain gestured for Sam to approach the waiting jeep.

"Captain Boyd, the corporal will get you over to Base Operations!"

Sam nodded and stepped into the jeep as the three college kids climbed the staircase into the airplane, with the captain just behind. Sam had his jeep driver hold while he put his bag in the back. As he did so, he had a momentary flash that something was wrong with the captain who had just greeted him, especially since the man had not offered a handshake and had no nametag.

So odd, he thought. *No officer steps out without a nametag.*

He watched as the three college kids disappeared into the Beech, and a moment later, the no-nametag captain was exiting down the ramp.

What in the hell? thought Sam. *Since when are civilians loaded onto a flight at 4 a.m. for a debrief at another airfield?*

But everything had shifted. Sam nodded at his driver, who pulled away at a good clip. He looked back one more time at the Beech moving toward the runway for its takeoff roll.

The long six-by truck with the no-nametag captain had not moved. Sam sensed everything had just shifted toward something that felt sinister. As his jeep raced across the flight line toward base operations, he had a notion that the focal point of that growing darkness was centered right here, at *Roswell*.

Back at the flight line, the captain sat with his driver. Both men lit up and watched as the lumbering plane began its takeoff roll, the propellers howling from the opposite end of the runway. Roswell's runway was long, built for the gigantic B-29s that had carried the atomic bombs to Japan, and those huge planes stood stark in the moonlight just across the runway. Heavily armed MPs patrolled around each nuclear-equipped bird. The Cargo twin was already airborne in the first third of the runway. Both men watched it, working hard to climb, as it was a hot night and the density altitude was high.

Staring up at the taillight, the captain pulled on his cigarette and contemplated how fate had intervened in the young girl's life. How she and her two friends had been monitored as they bragged to patrons in a Roswell bar. Telling their tale of seeing live aliens and a crashed saucer. And that was only a day after they had been warned to keep their mouths shut. He had his team delay until they were in their vehicle departing the bar. His operatives approached with guns drawn and quietly drove the students away while their car was driven to Alamogordo base, where they were heading to, this moment.

Each student was interrogated individually by his team, and the girl was found to have remnants of the San Agustin crash on her person. She had somehow bluffed her interrogators into not strip-searching her at the actual crash site. But after the bar scene, she was not so lucky, and several pieces of foil had been handed over.

The boys were clean. Each was then told they would fly out shortly for a debrief at Alamogordo and could return to their families afterward.

Upon landing thirty minutes from now, the three would be met by the captain's team—three MPs already stationed at Alamogordo—who would escort the students to the secret debrief bunker. He envisioned the students walking in single file with his MPs, moving through the early morning darkness toward a distant building just beyond the runway.

The captain had briefed General Nathan Twining only an hour ago about the students and their bar-bragging scene. Twining had reviewed the captain's written reports, which covered each of the three students, the incident, and the potential ramifications.

The general knew it would be extremely tough for the youngsters to hold their tongues for long. Seeing an alien was life-changing—no doubt about that. Something almost impossible to keep secret.

"Okay, Captain, I agree. These three go on to Alamogordo," Twining had said. That was enough for the captain.

Now, in the moonlight, the captain exhaled cigarette smoke toward the stars and thought about how all three would soon walk to the debrief building at Alamogordo. A peaceful, quiet walk in the desert. Not so bad.

In time, their families would learn that the three had never returned to the university. It would be suspected that they had perhaps crossed the Mexican border on a boondoggle drinking binge and never returned.

It happened often near the border towns. Kids would go on wild trips into Mexico to raise hell, and sometimes, they would disappear. Their car would become a target on the Alamogordo bombing range, and the license plates would be discarded.

But in this moment, back at the Roswell runway, the captain watched the plane climbing and considered the strange hand that fate had played in these three youngsters' lives. He observed the blinking taillight moving west—toward their destiny with his team.

But he didn't dwell on it for too long. This was his job, and they had shown themselves to be threats to national security after being warned—only hours before—to keep their mouths shut.

"Captain" was the insignia on his uniform that day, but he wasn't a captain. Damon Slepher's OSS teams—from the Office of Strategic Services—were the most covert of all America's operators. His teams were responsible for all containment and laundry operations, and each member had been handpicked.

Slepher's teams were trained to look for signs in personality, trained to spot security risks. To identify those who would whisper about what they had witnessed—and report to him.

On certain days, his teams were MPs embedded with local units. Other times, they might be janitors, migrants, or homeless vagrants. Sometimes, they were officers newly arrived to a unit.

Slepher's operators had carried out countless hit missions during the war against the Germans. But now, things had changed.

The new alien phenomenon required a different protocol. He would be containing American citizens, and the highest secrecy of his unit's existence was in place. It was one thing to assassinate a German. But an American who couldn't keep his or her mouth shut about what they had seen regarding extraterrestrial contact was a sensitive issue.

President Harry Truman wanted absolute secrecy regarding the new alien presence in America. The U.S. military had no way of stopping the aliens from coming. Their ships moved at velocities far beyond anything the military could handle. And that maneuverability defied all known laws of physics. The best Truman's administration could hope for was to keep the masses in the dark. But there was a catch to the big lie.

It often required that American citizens—who would not shut up about what they had seen—sometimes had to be permanently silenced. Damon Slepher on that night considered himself to be a staunch patriot... duty and honor-bound to protect America's national security. It was complicated work—making things appear to happen naturally. Ensuring the correct post-assassination details played out as intended. Too much press was bad.

He thought about the beautiful young college freshman and slowly shook his head.

Loose lips sink ships, sweetheart, Slepher thought.

The same line he would use before he murdered Secretary of Defense James Forrestal at Bethesda Hospital only twenty months later—working for the newly created CIA.

If the victim was a known dignitary and statesman like Forrestal, Slepher lost no sleep. An order was an order... period.

He flicked his lit cigarette into the desert and sucked his teeth, his mind returning to its cold righteousness as he watched the plane's taillights fade into the distance.

"Corporal," Slepher commanded calmly to the young soldier at the wheel. "Let's roll."

"Yes, sir, Captain!" the corporal said as he shifted the truck into gear and gunned the huge machine forward.

Slepher put his hands behind his head as the six-by lumbered underneath the stars. A sense of satisfaction flowed over him. There would be lots more hunting of whistleblowers as this alien cover-up grew, he thought. The idea of job security had been sketchy since the war ended.

He feared he might never be paid to kill again.

In the early morning darkness, Sam's jeep slowed as it neared an armed checkpoint near the base operations building.

MPs wielding submachine guns checked his security clearance, then saluted and waved him through. He had never seen security like this inside a base—especially one already deemed top secret. He figured the crash recovery at San Agustin with the live Greys must have triggered a chain of events, and Roswell was now center stage.

His driver pulled ahead and stopped at the base operations building, which was also swarming with security.

"Right this way, sir," the Corporal said as he hopped out. "The captain told me you are to report to Conference Room C1 on the second floor. There's chow on the first floor if you need it."

After more security checks, Sam was ushered into Base Ops, where he could feel the anxiety as field-grade officers and their aides moved in every direction. Several tables were being used for eating while civilians and military personnel moved about as if time was running out.

He approached the stairs but was stopped again, required to show his ID just to begin the climb. Upon reaching the second floor, he found MPs stationed near several doors. He looked across the way to see Conference Room C1 had its door open but appeared empty. He approached and was again waved through after another ID check.

Inside the quiet, carpeted room, two MPs stood at the far end. Off to the side, two civilian men leaned over a field table with a map at the center. Sam recognized both men studying the map and casually walked up behind them.

"Oppie," Sam said.

J. Robert Oppenheimer didn't look up. The famed scientist kept his eyes on the map as he responded.

"Only friends call me that," Bob Oppenheimer said, turning to look up with a huge grin. He reached his hand out to Sam and spoke in an excited whisper,

"Sam! I heard you were coming! I want you to meet my friend we call Dr. Space," Oppie said. "Otherwise known as Dr. Wernher von Braun."

Sam recognized the tall German from photos of high-ranking Nazis that he had worked with as part of the Paperclip operation to extradite top German scientists in 1945. Being fluent in German, Sam had interviewed several during their transition to working for the American military, as President Truman did not want them falling into Russian hands.

"Pleased to meet you, sir," Sam said.

"My pleasure," Von Braun replied with a thick German accent.

Oppenheimer stared at Sam as he spoke to Von Braun.

"Sam translated for the Apache Indian tribe living near the Trinity test site before the 1945 explosion. I think his translation convinced many of them to leave the area, and I was glad about that."

Von Braun nodded at Sam.

"Gentlemen, I have to go to Whitesands for a V-2 test," Von Braun said. "Oppie, perhaps I'll see you back at Los Alamos?"

Oppie nodded.

"Okay, Werner, I'll see you then."

Von Braun nodded to both men and departed. Oppie pulled out a pack of cigarettes and offered one to Sam. Sam took it, and Oppie lit it with a Zippo as they spoke in whispers.

"You know about him?" Oppie inquired.

"Yeah," Sam said, knowing that Oppie meant that Von Braun was the Nazi scientist who had designed the devastating V-1 rockets and had been brought over during Operation Paperclip. It was an awkward exchange Sam remembered, because besides Von Braun's V-1s having killed thousands in London, he was also notorious as a torturer and murderer of his own slave-labor force that built the V-1s.

Oppie scanned the room, as guards were everywhere.

"I have to act enthusiastic around him, as he just helped us create our own V-2 rocket. I'm certain Von Braun knows more about these aliens than he's letting on. There are rumors he's helping the breakaway Nazis down in Antarctica."

"Antarctica?" Sam whispered, perplexed.

Oppie double-checked the area visually while pulling on his cig.

"I was part of a brief about a breakaway Nazi group that has been developing flying saucers with the aid of aliens in Antarctica."

"Oh, for God's sake," Sam replied, exasperated. "Do these Nazi bastards ever just go away?"

Oppie exhaled smoke and watched Sam closely.

"A lot of stuff's happening, Sam."

Sam nodded.

"Yeah."

Oppie leaned in, whispering even more quietly.

"Sam, you knew about Operation Highjump, right?"

Sam shrugged. "Admiral Byrd's scientific expedition down there to Antarctica? But they just came back early—this past February, right?"

Oppie stared at him, shaking his head.

"Sam, that's what the administration wanted you to believe."

Sam watched Oppie as he continued under his breath.

"Secretary Forrestal sent Admiral Byrd to invade Antarctica to clear out the Nazis down there. But when Admiral Byrd got close to the Nazi base, flying saucers shot out of the ocean and attacked the invasion force."

"What?!" Sam whispered. "The Nazis already have flying saucers?"

Oppie nodded.

"They were supposedly being helped by a malevolent alien race called the Draco-Reptilians, who gave them the plans on how to build them."

Sam shook his head, putting it together.

"Oh my God," Sam whispered. "So, that's the real reason Byrd's expedition came back early?"

Oppie nodded, looking around and then back at Sam.

"Admiral Byrd lost every airplane in under ten minutes. The damn saucers were firing particle beam weapons."

Sam stared, confused.

"Lasers, Sam," Oppenheimer said, forgetting that average Americans had never heard of particle beam weapons.

Sam stared, perplexed.

"A laser is like pointing a flashlight at someone, but instead of illuminating them, it instantaneously burns them to their core, killing them almost instantly."

Sam stared, slowly shaking his head.

Oppie took a drag, looking around the room. Finally, he turned back.

"I heard you worked with a live alien from San Agustin?" Oppie whispered.

Sam nodded, exhaling.

"Yeah, it's up at Los Alamos."

"It's a Grey?" Oppie asked.

Sam nodded, pulling on his cig as Oppie continued in a whisper.

"The crash we just came from had more of an Orange type. I mean, they were not Greys."

Sam stared, perplexed.

"What do you mean they're not Greys?"

"They don't look like the Greys," Oppie whispered. "These have more of an ashen-orange color to them. They have six fingers and toes. Kind of more spongy skin. We're calling them Oranges."

Sam was shocked that two types of aliens had crashed.

"This whole damn crash-landing thing is sounding more like an invasion," Sam said.

Oppie nodded.

"I know. Truman is spooked, and the clampdown here feels really dangerous."

Sam nodded and noticed the no-nametag captain entering the far side of the room.

"There's definitely a containment operation in effect," Sam whispered and motioned to the captain, who was checking in with the MP at the entrance.

"I saw him earlier at the airfield. Something about that guy—no nametag or nothin'."

Oppie turned slightly as the captain made a beeline for the two of them. Sam was not the only one who had his hackles up as the captain approached.

Oppenheimer suddenly went quiet as well. The captain nodded respectfully to Oppenheimer and looked at Sam.

"You know Dr. Oppenheimer, Captain Boyd?"

Sam had dealt with manipulators before and was not intimidated by the no-nametag captain.

"I know Dr. Oppenheimer, but I don't know you. Did you forget your nametag... Captain—"

"Captain Jones," Slepher lied, cutting Sam off without disguising his contempt for Sam's comment.

"Oh, you know, in the rush to get here on General Twining's team, I somehow misplaced it."

Sam stared skeptically and noticed Oppie was giving no quarter as well.

"And if I may ask—how do you know Dr. Oppenheimer?" Slepher asked.

"That's classified information," Oppie replied coldly. "What exactly do you need, Captain?"

"Right," Slepher said with an air of threat. "I'm glad to know everyone here is keeping the discussions about this operation completely need-to-know."

He glanced quickly at Sam.

"Captain Boyd, General Twining wanted you to know that he'll be expecting your debrief on the San Agustin matter at 2200 tonight."

Sam nodded.

"I'll be there."

"Outstanding, Captain Boyd. I'll let him know," Slepher said with a fake smile and departed, leaving the two men watching him.

"That captain gives me the creeps," Oppie whispered.

"He's an operator," Sam whispered as he exhaled smoke.

"Operator?" Oppie questioned.

Sam looked around to ensure none of the MPs were looking their way.

"I'm guessing he's on a containment op," Sam whispered. "A covert unit that is specifically here to contain the secret of these recoveries from getting leaked on any level. And that story about his nametag was horseshit. You can bet good money his name ain't Jones, and most likely, he's not a captain either."

"You mean he's O.S.S.?" Oppie pressed.

"Most likely." Sam said.

Oppie nodded.

Both men watched the guards saluting Slepher as he departed the upper floor. Slepher didn't return their salutes.

Oppie turned to Sam.

"Follow me. I want to show you something before you go."

They exited down a hallway, where they were stopped by armed guards equipped with Thompson submachine guns. Oppie showed his ID.

"Captain Boyd is on your list as well," Oppie said.

The far MP checked a sheet of paper and nodded. Sam showed his ID, and they were waved through. Oppie led him into a carpeted room off to the side. As they entered, Sam could see that the entire wall was covered with alien cadaver photographs in full color. They were separated into two groups. It immediately became apparent to Sam that there were two species of alien cadavers.

The small, four-fingered Greys were on one side, and he recognized some photos from his own San Agustin recovery.

He then turned and walked to the other set.

He studied the photos. The ashen-orange cadavers were bigger than the Greys and had six fingers and toes, and it was obvious these were a different race of aliens altogether. The Orange cadavers also looked more human than the potato-bug greys.

Oppie lit a cig and handed one to Sam.

"If two species of aliens crashed, how many species were flying around this base, and why?" Sam whispered.

Oppie shook his head.

"I know it's overwhelming. I'm guessing it has a lot to do with our new nuclear capability, as they started arriving almost weekly after the Trinity explosion."

Sam nodded slowly and looked back at the photos of the Oranges.

"None of your Oranges survived their crash?" Sam asked.

"One is still alive," Oppie said, "and they're bringing the bodies here in a bit."

"Why here?" Sam asked.

"Medical attention and a couple of autopsies on the dead ones," Oppie said.

As he said it, Sam noticed a wash of sadness across Oppie's face.

"We lost a couple of army technicians from Sandia Base too," Oppie whispered. "They were messing around with the small reactor in the center of the ship, and a few minutes later, they were dead."

Sam shook his head.

"How many ships have crashed?" Sam inquired.

Oppie gave him a hard look.

"Three. Yours—mine—and one last night."

"What?!" Sam whispered, exasperated.

"Well," Oppie said, "Supposedly a call just came in from a gas stop thirty-five miles north of here near Mesa, New Mexico. Some amateur archaeologists said they stumbled upon another crashed ship. Then the scuttlebutt came out that a couple of nuns saw it come down on the night of the fourth but didn't report it, figuring nobody at the base would believe them."

Oppie again scanned the room and continued in a whisper.

"A recovery team was just sent up there to clear out the civilian archaeologists and secure the site. And that's the real reason you were called back from Los Alamos. I think the upper brass all know that you can communicate telepathically, and they may need your services."

Sam pulled on his cig, shaking his head, then exhaled, exasperated.

"Between you and me," Sam said, "the answer is yes, I can—at least somewhat. But I don't want to be pigeonholed into that billet. I want to be with my family."

Oppie watched him as Sam shrugged.

"And Oppie, those things—they're dangerous."

Oppie nodded.

"I've heard the rumors about them, Sam."

Sam nodded as Oppie watched him.

"Well, you'll figure out how to get out of that, I'm sure," Oppie said.

He looked around and back at Sam.

"They're performing autopsies on the dead Greys at the hospital right now."

Sam nodded, wondering if Eileen was involved in those autopsies.

Oppie pulled on his cig and leaned in close.

They're bringing the six-fingered Oranges to Hangar P-3 by the water tower. That includes the live one. You'll want to see the differences between your four-fingered

Greys and the six-fingered Oranges."

"Are you not going to be there?" Sam asked.

Oppie smiled.

"Well, unfortunately, I'm famous now, and that's why you see all the guarded rooms up here on the second floor. All the Bigs are here, Sam. The new Air Force Secretary, Stuart Symington, is here with none other than Charles Lindbergh as his consultant. Generals Doolittle, LeMay, and Twining are all here, as well as Eisenhower."

Sam stared in astonishment.

Oppie looked around and back.

"President Truman doesn't want the press to know that any Bigs are here, to keep this alien thing under wraps. But he wanted all the Bigs here to discern what we are dealing with.

Sam nodded as Oppie continued.

"We all arrived covertly at the Capitan Split-Rock crash site a few hours ago to see the aliens while it was still dark out. Eisenhower was the last to arrive, and his convoy is out there now en route to here. That's why they are bringing the live one here later today, and you should see it before it dies."

Sam watched him, reeling in all the new information, and Oppie sensed it.

"Go, Sam. And remember, they'll be arriving at Hangar P-3 around 5 p.m. I'll see you soon at Los Alamos."

Sam nodded, feeling the pressure, and shook Oppie's hand.

"Thank you, Oppie."

Oppie patted Sam's shoulder and watched him depart. He admired Sam and wondered if he could escape working with the deceptive Greys.

A t daybreak, two hours later, seventy miles to the northwest, Maggie Brazel fixed both Army officers and Mack a simple breakfast.

Minutes later, Mack saddled horses for himself and Major Marcel, while Snake opted to follow the horses in the Jeep Carryall. Mack led the way, trotting the horses until they reached the debris field where both officers stared, perplexed, at the massive, fan-shaped swath of foil. It now stretched for three-quarters of a mile to the east.

Mack waited a few minutes while the officers handled a few pieces of the foil, then handed each of them a handkerchief. The two men accepted, but with a quizzical look.

"You're gonna want these for where we're going next," Mack said and turned his horse to the east.

When they arrived at the bodies fifteen minutes later, Mack watched as both officers stared at the six-fingered cadavers in shock, each doing a double take as they held handkerchiefs to their mouths. Presently, Major Marcel turned to Mack.

"Mr. Brazel, I'd like to have a few moments with Captain Cavitt here. Can you meet me back where all the foil is in just a bit?"

"Yes, sir," Mack said.

He took one last look at the little bodies sprawled in their death throes and trotted his horse west toward the debris field. Mack had a sudden sense that a curtain was falling on his world, and there was nothing he could do about it. Before he reached the debris field, he heard the loud whine of the Carryall gunned to its gills and watched as Snake raced, bouncing across the ranch toward the old dirt highway, kicking up a dust trail that Mack could see for miles.

In the Jeep Carryall, Snake Cavitt raced along the dirt highway east to Roswell.

Partway through his seventy-mile run, he had radioed for a military escort, and minutes later was being led by a state patrol officer at high speed. He arrived at the base in short order and reported to the newly arrived General Nathan Twining about the six-fingered cadavers at Mack's ranch.

Twining took a deep breath at the news.

"Well, I'll take care of that, Captain Cavitt, but right this minute, I want you to grab a nurse and head north, up towards Mesa. We had a call come in this morning about another crash, and it seems there's a live alien at the site. It might need medical attention."

Five minutes later, Snake was northbound with twenty-three-year-old Master Sergeant Matilda MacElroy driving an army ambulance. Snake was once again silent as they raced along, siren blaring. He could not tell her what he had commandeered her for, except to say he needed her for a mission, and she had not hesitated, arriving to pick him up in the ambulance moments later.

Snake had a quick thought that he wasn't at all certain why he had picked MacElroy. She just happened to be nearby when he exited Twining's office. But she was certainly easy on the eyes, he thought. But so was First Lieutenant Eileen Fanton, who Snake knew was a friend of MacElroy's.

The two were the only female medical staff with top-level clearances and were the only ones assigned to the 509th. So, since he was in a hurry, Snake thought, the Master Sergeant would have to do.

HUSH

They received continuous radio instructions as they roared up the highway and passed through a heavily guarded roadblock. They then followed an army jeep several miles west through desert scrub and finally slowed to take in the wrecked remains of a badly damaged alien ship and several dead crewmembers.

Still photographs and film footage were being shot of the otherworldly scene, as a swarm of military vehicles, gear, and MPs were all about.

Matilda looked over at Snake when she realized what was in front of her.

"You gonna be okay, Master Sergeant?" he asked.

"Yes, sir, I'm ready to go," she replied matter-of-factly.

They exited the ambulance and were immediately guided into a large, heavily guarded tent to find a single alien sitting like a child in a field chair, guarded by two MPs. The creature in the chair was not like the others by the ship. It was smaller and appeared to her like a forty-inch doll with large black eyes and no nose, mouth, or ears.

Snake looked again at Matilda.

"Master Sergeant, I need you to check it for injuries."

"Yes, sir," she said and slowly approached as the MPs stepped to the side.

As she knelt down in front of the chair, its head moved, and the MPs seemed to tense. She glanced at the two security men.

"Please point your weapons away while I do this medical checkup," she said, calmly smiling. "I'm not worried about it injuring me or hurting me in any way."

The two anxious MPs reluctantly did so and noticed that as Matilda reached to touch the alien's limbs, the doll-like creature raised its prehensile, three-fingered hand in an offering to the nurse.

Matilda said nothing in that moment to the MPs or to Snake Cavitt, who stood behind her watching. But she was experiencing something profound. Something loving. She continued gently working her way along the offered hand and arm.

She would wait to see if what she was now experiencing without speech was actually happening to her. She now understood that a communication channel between her and the alien had opened the moment she had departed the ambulance as the only woman in the crash area.

Before she even entered the tent, she had been probed with a flood of truly joyous emotion. As if an old friend was waiting for her.

And now, as she gently checked over the small being with its soft, grey skin, Matilda knew absolutely that she was in a stunning communication with this entity not from Earth.

But she waited to tell Captain Cavitt. She waited because she had to believe it herself. Had to know she wasn't going crazy. With each thought to check another limb of the creature, Matilda found the limb slowly rising to meet her. The energy flowing into her was absolutely sublime.

She also felt that this being was ancient in its female energy and mannerisms.

In that moment, Master Sergeant Matilda MacElroy had no idea that she had been sought out, had been searched for, and was now being reunited with a member of her own ancient alien race.

W aya screamed when the creature kicked in his arms, like a dead body that suddenly twitched in death throes.

But he saw the enormous eyes suddenly energized, trying to ascertain where it was.

He raised it just enough so that the child-sized body was out of the creek water, and he carried it slowly to dry land as it came fully back to the present.

He laid it down slowly, not on the sandy shore, but instead in an inch of water, a precaution in case it needed more hydration.

Waya watched as the creature got its bearings. The eyes never blinked, and the mouth slit didn't move. He could not hear any air being exchanged through the nostrils or mouth slit.

Since it had received water through its skin, he wondered if the creature also got air that way, and perhaps its nutrients.

The creature sat up slowly and stared back to the west, toward the crash site.

Again, a question came in Navajo to Waya, the creature confused and swelling with anxiety over its new predicament.

To the question, *Where is my ship?"* Waya finally looked at the creature and thought the thought.

I don't know.

A fter Mack Brazel had seen Snake departing for the highway, he grabbed a bite of lunch at his homestead, while Major Marcel remained out at the debris field.

Mack was just sitting down for a bite when Walt Whitmore, Sr. arrived in a new 1947 Ford truck.

Mack walked outside as Whitmore Sr. stepped out of the shiny vehicle wearing a three-piece suit, introducing himself as the owner of KGFL radio in Roswell. Within a few minutes, he had convinced Mack to record a story for the radio station.

Without riding back out to warn Major Marcel, Mack followed the older

HUSH

Whitmore three hours east to a large ranch house outside of Roswell.

When they entered the lavish home, the entire KGFL staff, including disc jockey Frank Joyce, was waiting with a brand-new wire recording setup.

Mack soon realized that DJ Joyce was the one who had initially quizzed him over the phone at Sheriff Wilcox's office. He had no idea at that moment that Joyce had already put out to every news outlet in Roswell that Mack had found a flying saucer on his ranch.

An hour later, Mack had made his detailed wire recording for the station. He told them everything, just as he had experienced it since last Saturday morning when he and Dee Proctor had come upon the wreckage.

It felt good for Mack to get that story recorded. Beers were passed around, and for a moment, Mack had a notion that perhaps this was all going to play out okay—that maybe a little fame might bring him some fortune.

The growl that came next, snuck in below the beer bottles being toasted and the conversation's suddenly hushed as multiple vehicles outside skidded to a stop and the house was suddenly hit with a wall of dust. Everyone on the staff went quiet as the darkness outside was shattered by the headlights of the many vehicles. Everyone looked at Mack as Whitmore Sr. stepped to his kitchen window.

They could hear the rush of soldiers as the front door was literally kicked open with MPs rushing in, drawing weapons on all radio staff as the room fell silent.

A moment later, Damon Slepher entered, smoking a cigarette. Slepher looked around the room as handcuffs were being placed on Mack Brazel, who was carried out of the room screaming.

"You can't do this, Goddammit, I have rights!"

Slepher watched Brazel being manhandled away and took his time, staring at his cigarette and finally, at Whitmore Sr.

The older man was not used to being intimidated by younger men, but he knew, with no uncertainty, that he was out of his league on this night.

"Mr. Whitmore, I assume?" purred Slepher, looking directly at the venerable older man.

"Yes, sir," Whitmore sheepishly whispered.

Slepher half-nodded and turned, staring at the large wire recording device.

"Mr. Whitmore, would you please hand me the wire recording of Mr. Brazel?"

"Yes, sir," Whitmore whispered, clearly deflated, as he gathered the recording and delivered it into Slepher's hand. Slepher looked at it and handed it to an O.S.S. operative nearby. Slepher then stared intently at the wire recording device and seemed to satisfy himself that no other recordings had been made. He looked around the room and gave much attention to Frank Joyce, who nervously looked down at his shoes.

"Mr. Joyce," Slepher said as Frank raised his eyes furtively to see the intense gaze of Slepher upon him.

"My boys will bring Mr. Brazel to your station first thing in the morning to tell the actual truth about the weather balloon that he actually found on his property."

Joyce looked up and started to speak, but the look from Whitmore Sr. made him stop.

"Mr. Whitmore," Slepher said, "You will immediately begin broadcasting that all the things you have told the newspapers and media folks today in Roswell turned out to be the big lie of rancher Mack Brazel, who, as you all now know, actually found a weather balloon on his property. That weather balloon was all he found."

The room was deathly quiet. But young Frank Joyce wanted to protest until he looked up at Whitmore's icy stare.

"If I hear a word that anyone in this room decided to broadcast any part of Mack Brazel's lie he just recorded for you, that individual will disappear."

Slepher looked around, allowing his words to reach those already nervous in his presence.

"Mr. Brazel will be at your station tomorrow, and I'm certain, Mr. Whitmore, you will be ready to broadcast the recanting of his flying saucer story."

"Yes, sir. We'll be ready," Whitmore whispered, looking at all his staff, who were shooting furtive glances his way.

Slepher allowed the tension to hang, and then, without a word, departed.

U nder a huge moon, Waya watched the creature lying by the fire as it stared at the stars in the southern hemisphere.

It seemed to exert energy only when it needed to adjust itself further from the fire or closer. It had communicated much less in the last few hours, and he realized that the water of the creek was not enough. The creature was failing and would not last much longer. No matter the type of food he cooked, the creature only stared and then looked away.

Now, it could barely turn its head. Waya knew it was too weak to walk any distance, so he carried it. He could cover the uphill climb much faster with the little one on his shoulders.

It had taken three hours to reach the top of the highest mesa near the plains. He placed it down in a wide-open space and built a bonfire. Then he turned it so that it could stare toward the Southern Hemisphere, as it always seemed to prefer. After adding more wood to the fire twice that night, he had dozed off, sitting in place. The light show began across his closed eyelids as the ship approached in silence. When

Waya realized he was not dreaming as the wild lights played across his eyelids, he opened them.

The creature had managed to walk a short distance from the fire. Waya stared in wonder as the saucer dropped slowly. Suddenly, a deep blue light shot down like a flashlight beam from the craft and surrounded the creature, which was facing Waya. Waya slowly raised his hand in a farewell gesture, but the sign was not returned. The creature simply stared.

Perhaps it was just too exhausted, Waya thought.

But in his heart, he knew that the little creature certainly had enough energy to walk away when it chose to.

The ship descended slowly over the creature, enveloping it. The saucer sat on the mesa for a moment as its lights changed in pattern and color. Then it rose and hovered, glowing white-hot. A second later, it shot diagonally up, vanishing into space.

Waya stared at what was left over—the glorious night sky that he knew so well. Dimensions and layers into infinity. He gazed at the familiar constellations, all of which had guided him at one time or another. He felt relief, with not too much sadness. He had done all he could do with that little one. There was a part of him that wished for a different outcome, but then he knew the creature was simply that: a creature.

It had instincts like all things in form. He knew now that his loneliness had spurred much of what his actions had been since desiring to be with the unique one.

Initially, he hoped they might become companions—a slow build of trust toward a friendship. But each moment with it had become more adversarial as it seemed to have no desire regarding giving and receiving companionship.

Waya had learned again that it was not possible to make a wild wolf a pet. The wolf could not be stopped from seeking its pack.

Day by day and hour by hour, the creature seemed only concerned with its mission to find its ship.

He looked at his bonfire and considered the last few moments. This would take much inner work in his quiet place to clear this lesson. He now realized he needed companionship, and that was where it had all gone astray.

Waya didn't think the desire for companionship was a weakness or a bad trait. He knew it was a normal part of being in form. But he also knew he had misdirected that energy toward the small one. And for that, he would spend time in silence and let it help him understand how to guide that energy next time.

He looked back once more at the area where the creature stood as the ship came. The truth came strongly to him at that moment. There had been no gentle touch goodbye before it walked away. No, thank you communicated as it stood waiting for its ship. He realized he had simply been a means to an end—and absolutely nothing more.

He felt the heat as they rolled. The sadness came with the tears, and he now felt gutted for the first time since he could remember. He knew the hollow place within himself as a silent sob rocked his massive frame. He was in no hurry. He allowed his heart to wring itself. The tears dropped onto the white dirt, reflecting in the bonfire.

After a short while, the gentle night breeze seemed to flow through him. The depth of the sadness had passed. His enormous hands came slowly to his hot face, feeling the moisture. He dried his eyes, and then he knew he was not alone. He now understood he had been held safe by another.

Out there in the deep starlight beyond his fire, was the silhouette of Chief Elu sitting motionless on his horse. One hand rested on the horn of his saddle. The other hand gripped his long wooden lance. One end rested on the ground, and the pointed end rose above his head with three feathers hanging near the point.

Waya felt time stop as he stared at the Chief's silhouetted face—unseen, with only the outline of his full ceremonial headdress flowing off his head and down his shoulders.

The arc of its many eagle feathers blew softly against the speckled and shimmering Navajo blanket of stars.

V yla looked around her third-floor Victorian flat.

The final cleaning had taken her hours, and it was hard to believe her entire life was now tarped—bed and all—in the back of her 2003 Silverado pickup.

Her channeling journeys of the various individuals at Roswell had been on her mind all day while cleaning. That and Steph's situation—it was all a little overwhelming. She looked at her empty flat and exhaled.

Marten had been a tremendous help and had just returned from a pizza run. She heard him thumping up the stairs. During the day, he had taken Papa's box and transferred it from his car to the back of her truck. It now sat amidst all the other boxes, so she felt it was concealed as well as it could be.

"One Hawaiian ham and pineapple extravaganza!" he said, laying the pizza box on the just-cleaned linoleum floor. "And two lemonades."

She settled in and lifted her first piece to toast him.

"Thank you for the whole day," Vyla said.

"My pleasure," he replied. Both stared at each other as they chewed. They had lightly touched upon Steph's pain situation all day while cleaning, but Vyla felt she couldn't discuss her newfound knowledge from the brief on alien abduction. Marten had brought it up in a roundabout way while discussing his old professor.

"Hoppy is pretty cool. She's forgotten more hypnosis clients than I'll ever have," he said.

"Hoppy?" Vyla inquired, mouth full of pizza.

"Dr. Jane Hoppensowski, the psychic wizard of the ward, as we call her," Marten said. "The ward being the other six in my doctoral program."

"She's the teacher Charlotte said was kind of venerable?" Vyla asked.

"Well, she's definitely had success with some famous clients who wanted to quit smoking or lose weight," Marten said. "There are before-and-after pictures on her wall with Fats Domino and Jackie Gleason, among others."

"Those are old, famous people, right?" Vyla asked.

"Dead famous people, yes," Marten said. "But success stories for certain. And Hoppy has videotapes of many of her sessions."

Marten slurped his lemonade, seeming to contemplate something.

"What?" she asked.

Marten shook his head.

"She showed me a tape of Jackie Gleason doing a regression dealing with the chalkboard thing."

They exchanged glances. Vyla put two fingers up to her head like antennae sticking up.

Alien? She mouthed silently.

Marten nodded. She gestured for him to wait. She turned up the radio until the apartment was rocking out with classical music. He watched her pull the cardboard cylinders out of two paper towel rolls. She took one cylinder and gently placed it against his ear, whispering into the other end.

"Just in case they are listening, let's use these."

He nodded, laughing. Then she handed him the extra cardboard cylinder, and he spoke into her ear.

"Testing." She gave a thumbs-up and motioned for him to continue.

"It was Jackie Gleason doing a regression session to remember details about his trip with then-President Richard Nixon to see three dead aliens. The date on the tape was around mid-February 1973. Gleason recounted how Nixon had picked him up in a limousine and taken him to Florida's Homestead AFB, just south of Miami."

Marten pulled away as Vyla turned.

"Why would you use regression for that?" she inquired.

"I guess he had been totally freaked out by the entire evolution," Marten said, placing his cylinder back up to her ear.

"Gleason described each turn on the base and how armed guards were all around a small building. They entered an elevator to a below-ground complex, where Gleason freaked out. Even on the regression, as he went through each moment, it was really eerie listening to him describe walking up to the three huge glass cylinders full of clear liquid, where the cadavers floated. The huge black eyes stared back at him as if they were alive. He was so unnerved he felt like fainting."

Vyla slowly nodded, chewing her pizza.

"We also saw one with a man who claimed to be '*Taken*,'" Marten said, as in the chalkboard thing."

She gestured for him to continue.

"That was awful to watch. Lots of screaming and absolute terror. Several folks got up and left. Couldn't bear it."

He lowered the cylinder, took a sip of lemonade, and shook his head. Then, he raised the cylinder to speak.

"At one point, he was screaming for them to stop as they ran a six-inch-long metal probe through his temple into his brain. The screaming was absolutely violent. I asked Hoppy about it later, and she's uncertain but speculates that there may be a chemical the Greys are extracting when a human is screaming. She showed me volumes of tapes from several of her ongoing clients who had gone through repeated abductions for years. That shit is generational."

Vyla gave a big thumbs up with the straw in her mouth, slurping the last of her lemonade. Marten watched her, contemplating everything. She realized Marten had just thrown the switch for her, and she thought it was now or never.

She took a deep breath and put her cylinder to his ear.

"Charlotte mentioned something along those lines this morning," she said.

Marten stopped chewing. Then, the cylinder exchange became quicker.

"Are you shitting me?" he asked incredulously. "Miss, I don't believe in ghosts or hypnosis or anything occult, told you she believed Steph?"

"Apparently," Vyla said.

Marten sat stunned, then raised his cylinder.

"Of course. Thou dost protest too much," Marten said. "No wonder she said that hypnosis was bunk."

"Yeah," Vyla said, "She's terrified of making Steph relive whatever she's going through."

Marten nodded.

"That shit is friggin' torture," he said.

"Steph's definitely had a sudden change," she said.

Marten stared.

"Fat chance Charlotte will agree to let Steph hit the couch," he said out loud.

"Could you talk to her?" she asked. "Just tell her what you told me and see what happens?"

Marten shrugged.

"Sure, I'll do anything if it helps Steph's situation."

Vyla gave him a big hug, then grabbed the garbage bag and filled it with their leftover lunch items.

"They're not what you think they are," she said, hoisting the black garbage bag over her shoulder and heading down the stairs.

Damn, what does she know? Marten thought.

He looked around, considered a final cleaning pass, and grabbed a sponge. He went to each windowsill for a detailed wipe, watching out the window as she exited the building and packed the trash bag in the front seat of her old Silverado.

As he bent down to wring out his sponge in the bucket, he felt something cross his face, like a spiderweb. He stood searching for what had hit him. It took a moment for him to spot it. Slowly, he moved his head, and the light caught it at just the right angle. It shimmered in the sun—a single, silvery strand of thin wire. When he realized what it was, the hair on the back of his neck stood on end.

He took a tense breath and looked around. A moment later, she reentered and saw Marten standing by the sill, his finger pressed to his lips. She froze.

He motioned for her to come over. When she neared, he waved the wire in front of her. Even with his doing so, it was hard to see the tiny thing until Marten ran his finger along its length.

She nodded and motioned for him to let go. He did, and she followed it back up to the windowsill.

Whoever placed it was a pro—matching the room's paint to cover its discovery. But they'd obviously been in a hurry, missing the two inches in the middle that had come loose when Marten swabbed that section with the sponge.

She deduced that the wire was one long antenna and traced it down to the base of the windowsill. She pointed for Marten to look. He knelt next to her, and her fingernail was an inch away from a tiny microphone, no bigger than a pencil eraser.

Marten mouthed the word, *fuck*.

She nodded slightly, standing and staring through the blinds at the black sedan in the far distance. Marten could tell she had slipped into another world. He watched her, feeling her presence more intensely this time. A wave of energy...rising. Her face—a mask of calm with a hint of madness. He rarely saw her this intense.

If looks could kill...

Chapter Thirty-Two

T om was deadpan, tense.

Jane took a sip of tea and put the cup down, watching him, slowly shaking his head. She picked up her pen and paper right as Tom continued.

"Who were you stealing for?" The Short Suit just asked... and the interpreter was asking the bloody man in the chair.

Tom swallowed hard.

"I just slapped him."

"Hans just slapped him, Tom," Jane whispered. "It's not you."

"Hans just slapped him—hard. He's whimpering more—head down—shaking. He's bleeding more from his nose and now his ear."

Tom went quiet, watching it all.

"What, Tom?" Jane whispered. "Is Hans just watching?"

"Last chance," the Short Suit just told the interpreter. The interpreter is telling the bloody man, and the Asian is denying his involvement. He's screaming at the interpreter. Hans just got a nod from the Short Suit to hurt the man, and Hans slapped him."

Tom shifts slightly, suddenly confused.

"Good, Tom, you're doing great. Stay with what Hans sees."

"Black-Suit guy—short one—turns to Hans."

Tom, suddenly on edge—breathing faster. Jane was right with him, feeling the intense strain of anxiety.

"The Suit tells Hans to take a finger off the man's left hand," Tom said, on the edge of tears. "Hans pulls out his pliers and—"

"Okay, Tom!" Jane jumped in, stopping the retelling.

"Tom, let's stop for now, okay? Let's come back—let's see if we can back out of the wet room for now—okay? You need a break."

She exhaled, affected, put her pen down, and whispered,

"We need a break."

But Tom plunged ahead.

"No—no, they're pissed—they're pissed about the hard drive, they don't... they don't believe him. Hans gets another nod from the man in suit, the smaller one. He's the one—he's in charge."

"So—let's slow down for a minute," she whispered. "It seems the men in black suits are asking how he got—the hard drive?"

Tom, seeing it all... whispered in a flat tone.

"The interpreter is asking the bloody Asian man how he got the hard drive."

"So, did this man steal a hard drive?" she asked."

Tom shifted slightly, shaking his head.

"The man is screaming in—in Chinese, I think. The interpreter tells the Black-Suit man that the bloody Asian is denying he took the hard drive."

She nodded, locked on Tom.

"Okay, Tom, good. So, Hans is just listening now to the interpreter? Is Hans just standing there?" she asked.

Tom was suddenly quiet, seeing something horrific.

"Tom, what is Hans seeing or doing?" she whispered.

Tom shook his head and began again.

"Hans pulls out his pliers, he's... he's... oh—"

Tom suddenly opened his eyes, locked in a visual, breathing hard.

Then he closed them and a moment later... sobbed.

V yla drove her overloaded Silverado through downtown San Francisco, finding a parking lot on Geary near Union Square.

She exited, carrying her purse and Steph's plastic bag full of figurines. The sun was high and hot, and she remembered the black sedan several car lengths behind her on the way north from Palo Alto. She knew with this much traffic, they'd have a hard time finding parking to surveil her.

She disappeared into Plato's throng, as she'd been told to by Swizzle. The crowd, already mesmerized, listened to Plato's haunting delivery on the loudspeakers as Vyla worked her way through. She caught glimpses of Plato in her full daytime sensuality. The beehive swirled and smoked; those pink short-shorts matched on every level by her excessively protruding nipples.

Oh my, Vyla thought. *I could watch that all day.*

She paid attention to Plato's words as she walked. Her voice on the loudspeaker was smoky and beautiful.

"I want you to understand that if you were a butterfly, and your life span was only twenty-eight days long, you might find yourself saying something like... 'Well, I came, I lived three weeks, and then I died.'"

Plato opened her hands, staring at the crowd.

"And then you might say something like... 'And nothing really changed.' And you might conclude, 'I had no purpose in this life as a butterfly. The world I came to is exactly the same as the world I left.'"

Vyla saw Plato point at the crowd as she slowly turned.

"But what you don't understand, all my dear Madam butterflies, is that every breath that you took contributed to countless lives after you."

Vyla thought of her family, Papa, and Dah, as she weaved through the tear-filled faces.

"Lives that would flourish after you... lives that you would never see... that we are all a part of today."

Vyla suddenly stopped. Her heart wanted to.

"I propose to all of you that maybe, just maybe, the meaning of your short lives here—is not even within the scope of your understanding."

Vyla inhaled, just holding it together.

"The greatness of your passage, you might feel, is worthless, but I will tell you this—what is true for the butterfly is true for you. The lives that come from you... and follow you... are rich because of you."

Vyla felt her heart exploding, her family and Papa and Dah all around her. She closed her eyes and allowed it. She had learned that she was never in a hurry if something like this arrived. She breathed and opened, stopping her rush, knowing that *this moment* was always the trophy, late or not. Standing in that quiet, she gazed at the unique versions of humans—of all ages, colors and genders around her.

Oh my, she thought, *even if we are apes... we understand love.*

She inhaled deeply and began weaving through, imagining how the crowd would react if they knew their speaker was not from this planet!

Wow, and I'm late to meet one too, she thought, picking up her pace. She exited the crowd and came out on Sutter Street, a solid two blocks from where she parked. And there, in the hot sun, sitting on his motorcycle, having a cig, was Swizzle.

He was wearing a '70s-style gold-sparkle helmet with black trim. The old open-face style with a simple chinstrap.

Dork, she thought, and snickered.

He nodded as she approached, pulling on his cig and handed her a teal, sparkly helmet. She stared at him with a smile as she put on the open-faced headgear. He had learned to be a very cool alien. He snickered at her thought.

Earlier, he had tapped into her, picking her up before he ever saw her. He then entrained to her, knowing everything she felt in the crowd, the humans, and her father, and her feeling about love as the grand prize. And she was spot-on. He knew that as advanced as he was intellectually, telepathically, and psychically, he could learn from her... a deeper way. She knew love.

A minute later, with *Mustang Sally* blaring from the stereo, they roared up the steep San Francisco streets, weaving between cars to outrun any type of surveillance attempting to follow them.

C ase and Will had seen her park on Geary, and Case had jumped out, blending into the crowd, listening to Plato.

Will drove in a circle around the crowd and found a spot at the rear of the throng on Post Street. The crowd was enormous, packed five rows deep at the outer edge. He was glad to be back on her surveillance, as the hypnosis sessions at Nellis Air Force Base had not gone well. He and Case chalked it up to their SEAL training and their many years of compartmentalizing. But they had discussed it at length, and both still held an unspoken fear about who and what had engaged them. As he parked the car, Will got a radio check-in from Case that Vyla was moving through the crowd. Will keyed his walkie-talkie.

"Copy. I'll wait here. I'm parked behind the crowd on Post Street."

The crowd was facing the opposite direction, focused on Plato, and Will thought it was interesting to stare at humans from behind. A knock on his window. He jumped momentarily and then realized it was Mr. A., who had suddenly come out of nowhere. He rolled down his window.

"Hey, sir. You surprised me. I thought we weren't meeting until tonight?"

Case's voice suddenly crackled across the radio.

"Hey, she just got on a motorbike with an old man," Case said, "and they disappeared."

Will looked up at Aspelsin, who was now staring out with an eerie look... like a cat sensing its prey.

Vyla had not ridden on the back of a motorcycle since she was in high school and certainly had never held onto an alien while doing so.

The surreal had become her life, and she was just trying to realize that none of this new paradigm would feel so otherworldly if she could accept that aliens had obviously been here long before humans. The surreal feeling, she knew, was generated from her narrow, egotistical belief that humans were the only life in the universe—the top of the ladder, the chosen ones. Because that was the story that she and all humanity had been inundated with since birth.

But now, she was realizing the extent of the deception by those in control. It was their narrative, and not an actual reflection of the truth... which was now becoming clear in front of her.

Fortunately, the visuals of the UAP warping time and space had shattered her old belief systems. Technology the UAP had demonstrated could only come from a race eons older than humanity. If she could now deal with the true status of humans in a universe surrounded by aliens from countless races and star systems, the surreal would dissolve into her actual reality.

Yen's confirmation that humans, with the help of alien technologies, had clearly been traveling in space for decades had really thrown her. Even though space travel had not been afforded to most of humanity due to the Cabal's cover-up, that didn't change the fact that some humans had obviously been participating in spacefaring missions for many years.

She needed answers from Swizzle, as so much shit was happening at once, and figured it was now or never. She understood that once she settled in at Nellis and began her Widow flight-simulator training, she would be too busy and too surveilled to meet Swizzle again.

Now, on this sunny morning, riding a motorbike, they had eluded her security team and parked Swizzle's bike at the top of Mission Dolores Park. Hundreds were already relaxing across the park as marijuana smoke wafted and dogs ran rampant, all in view of the sunlit city.

"Alright then, let's start with the big picture," Swizzle said when they sat in the corner of a massive kid's sandbox. Lying between them on the sand was Steph's empty plastic bag, with all the figurines piled next to it. Swizzle looked her way.

"Vyla, how are your old belief systems doing as of this moment?"

"They are completely destroyed, thank you," she said.

He stared at her, an understated smile in his eyes.

"Well, you have asked for an explanation of the reality around you, and I can just about assure you that what you think of as your current reality will now be shaken to its core."

"I just want the truth of what really exists around me, and I trust you."

He watched her and nodded slowly.

"I trust you too," he said.

She watched him, her breath taken away as he knelt in the sand by the figurines. Before she knew it, her eyes filled. This connection with him felt ancient, and the bond seemed to her as deep as any she had ever experienced.

He didn't look up, and she knew he had allowed her space. She took a deep breath, resetting herself, and watched as he separated the figurines. She had spent so many hours playing aliens with Steph that Vyla had memorized all the names. Swizzle picked up a two-legged, lizard-shaped figurine with wings, jackboots, and a ray gun across its arms.

"That's Lizzy," she said as he nodded, smiling, and drew a large triangle in the sand.

She was surprised to see him place Lizzy at the top point of the triangle. The Reptilian figurine was basically a lizard with dark green-black skin, and its snake-like eyes were vertical and menacing. He then placed the Tall-Grey and the rest of the figurines in descending order down the right side of the triangle, to include the slightly smaller Greys, then a GI-Joe army figurine, and finally, a Barbie-doll on the bottom corner.

"First, I want to be clear about the universe. It's a ninety-five to five ratio, good to bad, as far as benevolent and malevolent," he said.

"You mean there are ninety-five percent good races out there?"

"That is correct, and they are all around you, but not presenting themselves because of the Prime Directive."

She nodded slightly.

"The Prime Directive was mentioned several times in my brief. Alien races can't interfere in the evolution of a less-evolved race, like us primitive humans."

"Yes, exactly," he said.

"Okay, wait, then what are you doing here, connecting with me?"

"I can connect with you—meaning I am allowed to show myself to you and even say *hello mate!* But I'm not allowed to advance your human evolution in any way with my technology."

"But—our planet has clearly been in diplomatic relations with aliens for years, right?"

"Yes," he said and took a deep breath, staring at her.

"This is where we—my race of Greys, and another race called the Draco, have been breaking the Prime Directive. The Draco began this manipulation in 1933 when they first made contact with Heinrich Himmler and Fritz Todt—two Nazi occultists under Hitler. Himmler and Todt had been creating Satanic rituals to conjure up Satan to help the Nazis. But the Draco had been waiting for that breakthrough day, and it was the Draco Reptilians who appeared to Himmler and Todt, and the negotiations began."

She quietly guffawed.

"I read about the Draco Reptilians. If I saw a nasty, muscular, thirty-five-foot reptilian with wings standing over me and communicating telepathically, I'm pretty sure I would consider him the Devil."

Swizzle pointed and smiled.

"And they smell like fucking rubbish, too," he mused. "Most alien races consider the Draco Reptilians to be far worse than any."

He raised a finger.

"But they are genetic masterminds and can quickly clone a human and amalgamate them with technology to be sold as super-soldiers... not only in this galaxy... but far beyond. Those clones are worth a lot out in the galactic trade routes. My race helps with the creation of those super-soldiers."

"So, your race of Greys are like worker bees for the Reptilians?"

"Somewhat, but we have our own agenda of human domination as well. But at the end of the day, we defer to the stronger bully in the ring—who can rip us apart at any moment they choose. And they are brilliant at neural engagement as well, so we defer to their wishes."

She slowly nodded.

"So, that Satanic ritual contact in 1933 led the Nazis to establish their base under the ice shelf in Antarctica in 1938?"

"Correct," he said, amazed at her knowledge. "Himmler created Base 211 and utilized a brilliant aeronautical engineer, Hans Kammler, as his wizard for antigravity shipbuilding with the aid of Draco Reptilian antigravity technology."

"So, was that Reptilian technology just waiting for the Nazis under the ice shelf in Antarctica?"

"No, the Rep technology was given to Fritz Todt and Himmler and then loaded under tight security in sealed crates for the initial expedition to Antarctica in 1938. Todt, as the secretary of the expedition, ensured that 'no crewmembers knew what was in those crates.'"

"So, the Nazis' plan was to build their own flying saucers upon arrival?"

"That's right."

She nodded.

"I had an old German professor tell me that many German submarines brought men and supplies to that base well before the close of the war."

He pointed at her.

"Right, and women, too. Himmler wanted to create an Aryan Fourth Reich after the Reptilians had warned him that Germany was going to lose the war in the end. Over ten thousand blond, blue-eyed Ukrainian women were forcibly removed to Antarctica to breed with 2,500 elite SS soldiers, and New Berlin was created. And that Aryan colony is still there today, below the ice shelf."

She exhaled in disbelief, "Wow."

"So, all the U-boats my professor friend said went there was true?"

He nodded.

"250,000 German citizens were eventually in New Berlin by the close of the war, having been transported secretly with the U-boat fleet."

She shook her head.

"So the Nazis took those U-boats out of the fleet because they knew they would lose the war, anyway?"

He nodded.

"Fifty German U-boats were simply taken out of the war effort and used for transporting slave workers and supplies. 30,000 former extermination camp prisoners were delivered by the close of the war. Many of them children, as they wanted to have a stable labor force."

He lifted some sand and let it fall.

"And as many as six thousand scientists, as well as the full German secret societies of Vril and Thule, who had already been building antigravity ships in Germany with the help of Maria Orsic's drawings."

Vyla pointed at him.

"I read about her. She channeled some alien blueprints for ships or something, right?"

He nodded and could tell she was piecing it all together.

"So, were the Nazis off-world before the war even ended?"

He pointed.

"Years before," he said. "Under the direction of Himmler... with Kammler building his ships, the Nazis' first antigravity Haunebu craft had landings on the Moon and Mars by 1943. By the close of the war in '45 the Nazis were actively growing their antigravity fleet, which essentially routed the American Highjump Mission in early 1947."

"I read where James Forrestal sent that military force to oust the Germans from below the ice shelf?"

Swizzle nodded. "The Nazis sent the American fleet packing by attacking with flying saucers, downing thirty Corsair fighters in less than ten minutes, and sinking a destroyer—all with laser technology."

"In 1947?" she asked, astonished.

He nodded.

She shook her head. "*Damn.*"

He stared. "America knew at that moment that it had won the battle of WWII but had lost the war, as the Germans were already establishing colonies on the Moon and Mars by then."

She shook her head. "Okay, so much for my history lessons growing up."

He stared with soft eyes. "Your actual reality and the covert history of humans in negotiations with aliens has been largely hidden with the help of mind control," he said, pointing up to the very dim moon in the daytime sky. "More on that later."

"Oh, fuck, does this actual history just keep getting more complex?"

He nodded. "Much Draco technology resides in the moon, and all of it is for controlling Earth."

She lay back in the sand, staring at the moon, and wanted to cry. Her childhood associations with that quiet orb were now being severed, and it felt devastating to have that lifelong relationship destroyed.

He watched her with a deep compassion.

"I'm so sorry, Vyla," he whispered.

"No, please continue—I'm so goddamn tired of the deception that I just want to get down to reality, and I'll deal with the loss of my innocence."

He gave her a moment.

"Keep going; it will make me feel better to listen to you than to deal with the fucking global hoodwink right now."

"Right," he whispered.

"So , from roughly 1947 forward, the Greys and Draco Reptilians have been in cahoots with a malevolent, elitist portion of humanity who rule your planet using mind control. They are known to all as *The Cabal.*"

She abruptly sat up amidst a flash of immense anger and stared evenly at him. "The Cabal killed my family, as well as Papa."

Swizzle tersely nodded.

"I'm very sorry."

And she knew he meant it.

"This is where the global and off-world political situations get a little complicated, so let's start with the very basics and ramp you up slowly to where everything sits as far as aliens and humans in contractual agreements already forged."

"Okay, thank you," she whispered and watched as he touched the Barbie doll on the head.

"You," he said.

"Meaning I'm at the bottom of the hierarchy?" she asked.

"That's right."

Then he touched the G.I. Joe just above the Barbie doll. "Me."

"That's because you are just like me, but you can control me?"

"Very good," he said, nodding at her with a matter-of-fact look. "I'm completely human like you as far as regular male human physicality and traits," he said. "Except that I have neural engagement capability, and you don't."

"That's how you switched off my surveillance team?"

He pointed at her. She pointed back, and he smiled.

"The important thing to remember is that those two men won't remember any of it. They simply woke up later and felt a little odd but will never understand how they apparently lost hours in the same place."

"Hence the abduction phenomenon. Missing time?" she inquired.

He nodded.

"Got it," she said. "What are you called? I mean, if you are a mix of Grey and Human—"

"Hybrid," he said, cutting her off. "Half-human, half-Grey."

"Hybrid," she nodded. "Got it."

He then moved up the triangle hierarchy to the Small-Grey figurine just above the G.I. Joe.

"These are the worker bees," he said.

"The small-Greys?" she inquired.

"Yes, and they are clones. Male and female, but the majority are male. Their primary functions are to retrieve humans during abductions and then hold them still during operations. These little ones are small, but they are extremely strong, with hands and arms that act like vices when needed."

"So, the abductee can't fight their abductors?"

He nodded.

"Once neural engagement has caused paralysis, they place the abductees on the ship's tractor beam."

She nodded.

"I read about how that beam somehow rearranges molecular structures, thus allowing abductees to be taken through walls, up to the UFO?"

"Exactly," he said. "It works in reverse too."

She nodded.

"Is that why abductees say things like 'they were coming through the walls to grab me'?"

"That's right. The ship's tractor beam does the same rearranging with the Greys' molecules as they arrive to abduct a human."

"Wow," she said, taking it all in.

He then touched the tall-grey figurine, standing just above the small-grey on the triangle hierarchy. She felt her anger rise, and he acknowledged it.

"Yes, you are correct to feel anger, and I'll cover Steph's situation in a moment."

She exhaled, realizing that she felt better knowing this was going to be discussed and that he might have some answers.

He tapped the Tall-Grey's head.

"This one controls all the Small-Greys. Not a clone, he has a much stronger neural engagement that allows for the sedation of an abductee if they become unruly during operations. He has the ability to lock into the optic nerve and see the abductee's past, as well as sedate or stimulate various parts of the human anatomy. Tall-Greys are for the most part, rail-thin and about seven feet tall. Certainly more sinister in appearance and behavior than the Small-Greys."

"So, he's like the head surgeon?"

"Well, he certainly performs the more complicated operations, as well as making abductees forget the operation ever occurred."

She stared at the figurine and couldn't stop a flash of anger.

"Yes," he said, "a Tall-Grey was the kind that hurt Stephanie."

She looked up.

"And you are correct in your thoughts," he said. "The mind-wipe during abductions doesn't always work, and many humans remember their pain—and I'm sorry about that too."

"How can you... they... do that to a little girl—"

"I'll cover more about Steph's situation in a minute," he said, cutting her off. "But let's continue with the big picture."

She nodded, now fighting a mixture of anger and disbelief.

"I'm sorry at the deepest level," he said softly.

And she could tell he meant it.

He suddenly looked around suspiciously, sensing something, then looked back at her.

"I need to stay on target, as I don't have a lot of time."

She nodded as he moved his hand back to the top of the triangle, touching the Reptilian figurine, and looked up.

"This is the leader of our program here on Terra—at least as far as I know."

"The program?" she inquired, stupefied.

"Our infiltration and takeover of Earth. My race works with the Draco, who are also called the Ciakahrr Empire. The overall plan is to take over your planet and subjugate all of its people."

"You mean us—me?" she asked.

He stared at her and raised his eyebrows slightly.

"That's fucked up," she said.

He tightened his lips, took a deep breath, and continued.

"The Draco run the program and they control all of us—me, the Tall and Small-Greys, abductees, everything."

"Lizards?" she said, with a flash of anger.

He gave her a wary look.

"Don't underestimate the Draco."

She watched him and sensed the depth of his warning. She noted the figurine.

"They look like that?" she asked.

He lifted the muscular lizard warrior, studying it.

"Well, yes, or one like him anyway. But this figurine is amazingly close to what the Reptilians look like, except they come in all sizes, from eight feet tall up to thirty-five feet, and their elite ruling class, the royal ones, also have wings... and very white skin."

"Wings?" she asked perplexed.

He nodded matter-of-factly.

"Flying lizards—well, fuck me."

He snickered at her comment, but his smile faded as he studied the figurine, turning it in his hand.

"They are warlike, conquering goons but excessively smart and are masters of gene manipulation for their own devious agenda. And they have used this same velvet-takeover program on many worlds throughout the galaxy and beyond."

She looked away, shaking her head, and he allowed her a moment.

"When you say Lizzy controls you, what do you mean?" she asked.

"The Reptilians run the show. At least as far as I can tell."

She turned back.

"You mean you don't really know who oversees this takeover?"

"I don't, actually," he said. "It's a need-to-know program from the top down. All I know is that I'm the main part of it."

"Meaning you were created just to infiltrate us?" she inquired.

"Exactly. I'm the one that is to remain hidden within your populace and then help the Reptilians when the actual takeover begins."

"So, all Grey-Hybrids, male and female, will be directed to switch all humans off when the Draco-Reptilians are ready to take over the entire planet?"

"That's it," he said. "As soon as there are enough Hybrids like me living in human society—*the Change* will be initiated—it's a velvet takeover, designed to work without any resistance from the planet's natural inhabitants."

She turned with her hand on her head, thinking, and then looked back at him.

"Damn, it's—it's flawless," she said. "An unseen and unbelieved phenomenon of abduction and hybridization that is hidden from the same indigenous population it's perpetrated against—wow."

He nodded slowly, amazed at her awareness.

She stood, shaking her head slowly, and looked at him.

"And Humans won't fight back—because you don't resist something that you don't believe is happening in the first place."

He stared at her with a somber look. Ashamed.

"So, a hybrid like Plato will switch off her huge throng of people when she is directed?"

He shrugged slightly, embarrassed. She looked away and whispered,

"Fucking hell."

He rubbed his beard thoughtfully.

"I can only tell you that my system will do whatever the Draco want me to do. The same with Plato. The Reptilians control us Greys and your entire planet, and are at the top of the hierarchy as far as how it all plays out."

"So, what about the human Cabal—I thought they were in control?"

He paused and exhaled.

"Okay, so now we're dropping into the complicated dynamic on your planet."

"You mean all is not as it seems?"

He pointed at her.

"The Draco were on the planet long before humans. They brought your Moon with them as it was not here when Terra was first created billions of years ago... after the Big Bang."

She stared dumbstruck as he motioned toward the sky.

"Your Moon—it's not what you think it is."

She put up a hand for him to stop.

"Okay, wait... forget the Moon for now, just stay on the big picture with the Draco Reptilians, and only give me the Reader's Digest version."

He nodded.

"Well, not only are the Draco brilliant scientists and telepathic geniuses, even beyond us Greys and certainly beyond human understanding, but they dwell in the lower-fourth density, outside the human visual spectrum, and—they can shape-shift."

She stared.

"You mean to look like anything they please?"

He pointed at her.

"Like take over a human and—become them," he said.

She stared.

"Oh, shit," she whispered, shocked. Then she pointed his way. An epiphany.

"So, that's really what the Cabal are now? They're actually Reptilians in disguise?"

"At this point, yes," he said, amazed at her comprehension.

She sucked her teeth, nodding. "I had a sense that the Cabal, whoever they are, were too smart to be human."

"Well, some of them are still human, but those few are not aware that their former partners-in-crime are actually Draco-Reptilians."

She shook her head. "So, the remaining humans in the Cabal only think they're in control—but—they're not?"

He pointed.

"Back before WWII is when the Reptilians began breaking the Prime Directive, taking over certain top leaders worldwide to control the course of humanity."

She watched him, piecing it together. "So, they can just—somehow—take over any human?"

"Soul stealing," he said matter-of-factly. "The Draco have a technology that allows them to essentially extract your soul and put it in a holding chamber, like a beaker. Then your body is taken over by a Reptilian who has shape-shifted just to reanimate your body."

She stared, incredulous, as he continued.

"So, they have your body, with your same voice, personality, everything that appears as you, but having a fully Reptilian mindset."

She put both hands on her forehead as if it were exploding. "So, the head of a multinational bank or corporation can suddenly be making decisions that favor the Reptilian agenda?"

Another point.

"Fuck," she whispered, exasperated. "You mean like our president and the King of England and—"

"Yes," he said, cutting her off. "But think more holistically. Heads of the United Nations, CEOs of Big Pharma, multinational banks, and certainly all your media moguls."

She nodded.

"So, basically, any major human influencers they want to use to further their agenda, they just soul-steal them and use that body to control humanity?"

He nodded.

She slowly looked out onto the park, the light breeze blowing her hair back as her new awareness hit home. She contemplated as she looked out over the city, and around the stunning park. So many simple humans just like her. Beside herself. *Damn.*

After a time, she looked over.

"So, there's obviously not just this universe out there?"

He slightly shrugged.

"I tried to tell you... your real reality... the actual place you exist... is very complex."

"Why here? Why do the Reptilians need Earth?"

He opened his hands again.

"The climate worldwide here is conducive for many types of life to flourish if the planet can be saved from nuclear destruction."

She looked sideways at him.

"Meaning the Reptilians and Greys are trying to save us from ourselves as their top narrative, but really it's about enslaving us so the Reptilians and Greys can have Earth to themselves."

"And a food source to boot," he said with a very hard look.

She stopped, her mouth open.

"Did you just say what I think you did?"

He stared and slowly nodded.

"Oh, damn," she said and looked away. Then spoke without looking at him.

"Do you eat—human—"

"I don't," he said, cutting her off. "Never have or will. Greys are generally not after humans as a food source."

She turned and exhaled. Then got a hard look.

"But the Draco-Reptilian-lizard-motherfuckers, are?" she ventured.

He snickered.

"That is not funny," she scolded.

"I'm only laughing at your descriptive adjectives."

"These fucking Reptilians—"

"No," he said, cutting her off. "You can't defeat them with military might. They are much too advanced for any weapon humanity possesses—except—"

"Except," she said, cutting him off and letting it hang. "Except—" she said again, and he slowly nodded at her, seeing her eyes becoming vibrant and strong again... a woman on fire.

"Except—for—LOVE!"

He pointed at her and continued.

"You, and you alone, and I mean humans only, can manifest your reality with simply the power of your intent."

She allowed that statement in. Knew that was the holy grail. The thing that all humans knew, but had forgotten. She raised her finger—like a magic wand and watched it rise to the sun, and then—slowly lowering it, pointed her regal-finger... at him. He lowered his head, bowing in humility.

"I'll take any power you send my way."

She giggled. He looked up, smiling. Then suddenly got a look. Something bad. He stood.

"Follow me."

"Wait!" she said, standing. "I've got a lot more questions!"

He paused.

"Yes, the Tall-Grey will return in roughly twelve weeks and take the fetus. Steph will never know she was pregnant."

She closed her eyes at this and took a deep breath, then looked up to see him staring at her with complete compassion.

"Is there a way I can strangle this Tall-Grey now?" she whispered.

He took a deep breath and knew this was so hard for her.

"How do they even fucking find her!?" She almost yelled.

"The Greys place a hyper-dimensional beacon within her. Implanted in all abductees. We can track her anywhere on the planet and beyond."

She shook her head, disgusted.

Fucking aliens, she thought and exhaled, bagging the figurines.

Then she laid back on the sand and closed her eyes. He looked around suddenly, picking up on something.

"Something bad is about to happen," he whispered.

She opened her eyes.

"What?"

He shot a tense look to the north and then stepped out of the sandbox. Suddenly, without understanding why, she hopped up, full of energy, and stepped off with him, disappearing into the crowds. She was surprised she was up so quickly, and with energy. Then she knew he had helped in that evolution.

Bitch! she thought as she caught up with him. He gave a sideways glance.

"All your questions will be answered," he said, and she could tell he was getting more anxious by the second as they were clearly eluding someone.

"But there is much more at stake, and we'll have to come back to it later. For your safety, I'm going to turn right in five more steps, and you should depart in the opposite direction."

And without time to respond, she watched him turn, and she turned the opposite way and was anxious as the faces of the crowd swirled around her and she wondered about each one.

A few miles away at Union Square, Will exchanged a quick glance with Aspelsin as he keyed his walkie-talkie.

"Alright, bro, why don't you go back to her car and I'll stay put here for a bit? It was tough to find parking," Will said into the radio.

"Copy," came the reply.

Will looked up at Aspelsin, who was watching the crowd.

"You want to hop in, sir? Sounds like we're going to be here for a minute. Do you want something to eat?"

Aspelsin slowly shook his head, still looking at the crowd. A moment later, he walked to the passenger door and got in.

"Hey, sir, how are you doing?" Will said.

"I'm fine. Perhaps we could roll up the windows and put on some air," Aspelsin replied in his whisper.

"You bet, sir," Will replied, turning on the AC and rolling up the tinted windows. "We're glad to be back after the regressions," he said, with as much enthusiasm as he could muster in the cold proximity of Mr. A.

They could hear Plato on the loudspeakers, interspersed with crowd laughter and catcalls. Will turned.

"Sir, I'm sorry our regressions didn't work out."

Aspelsin shrugged, still watching the crowd.

Will half-smiled, full of anxiety, and then stared out the window.

It seemed to him that Plato had reached the end of her talk as the throng suddenly burst into a crazy loud roar, and then the loud rock music cranked up with everyone going wild.

Will saw Aspelsin slightly smile toward the raucous crowd, lowering his wire-rimmed glasses as they both turned to smile at each other—and in that split second of locking eyes—Will had been ensnared.

Aspelsin held Will spellbound like a snake, as it holds the terrorized stare of its prey before devouring it whole.

Will's body was frozen in place, his terrified eyes staring at the eerie sight of Aspelsin slowly discarding his leather gloves.

Those three prehensile reptilian fingers—scaly and long—reached like insect legs as they slid on either side of Will's shaved forehead, probing over his temple area.

Will's long, blood-curdling scream blended perfectly with the crowd all around them. No one could see the horrific spectacle happening behind the tinted glass, nor would they hear Will's screams, which only added to their Plato-inspired fervor—an ignited throng going crazy.

And none would see just behind the tinted windows, Aspelsin's vice-like grip pulling Will's head inexorably forward until their foreheads touched.

HUSH

The crowd, even if they could see it, would not comprehend Aspelsin's neural engagement as his psychic tentacles slowly weaved in, locking into Will's optic nerve.

Aspelsin went deep. Will's screaming only lightened momentarily as Aspelsin tapped into current segments of Will's last few days—memories a Draco could access. The hypnosis sessions at Nellis AFB. Will's two young boys happily welcoming him home last week. His wife gardening with their Irish setter playing nearby. The ruddy face of Swizzle limping up to the driver's door and engaging them from three feet away, outside the car in the Moss Landing darkness... telling them they won't remember him.

Will's brain suddenly expanded with the depth of Aspelsin's neural expansion. His screams were drowned in the roar and rock and roll outside the car as his feet suddenly kicked in death throes below the steering wheel, shattering the plastic of the lower dash.

His end came as Aspelsin released his still-shaking head from the spikes of spinal fluid that had been chemically altered, the blood oozing from his bulging eye sockets.

Aspelsin sat forward in the passenger seat. He calmly lowered the passenger sun visor and stared in the little mirror, pulling a handkerchief and wiping the light blood splatter off his face. Then, he casually inspected his fingers and wiped them clean. Moments later, he stepped out of the car, closing the door while staring forward at the still-screaming crowd, starting to dance.

He took one last look at the Impala with its tinted windows and could not make out the dead man lying inside.

He moved like a ghost through the wild throng, thinking about the old homeless man who had engaged his security team at Moss Landing.

And he knew the old man was neither homeless nor human—and most likely the same entity who had just escaped with Dr. Vyla Kells on a motorbike.

Chapter Thirty-Three

At Mission Dolores Park, she had her laptop out and was sitting by him in the sandbox.

Earlier they had departed in opposite directions, and only moments later he had wrangled her back, apologizing for the sudden fright and that it had nothing to do with her.

She had the thumb drive in her laptop.

"This is the footage Dan managed to get me," She said.

Swizzle nodded and watched the short video showing the Spy-3 visuals of the Diego Garcia base. The pyramids below the surface in operation, and the lowered loading dock with the Mothership hovering above using its tractor beam to raise freight.

"What is happening here?" she asked.

Swizzle half nodded, staring at the image.

"Well, that's a Nazi space freighter that arrives every morning at 4:05 a.m., when Diego Garcia is cloaked. That ship descends from high orbit at 80,000 feet... and comes down in one-split-second, to exactly 100 feet above the loading dock... and hovers there for the duration of the loading. The base itself was created by the Draco-Reptilians long before humans arrived. And for many years the Nazis used

Diego as their main hub before they transferred operations to Aries Prime, their base on Mars. Now they only do a daily run."

She nodded slowly.

"So, do the Americans use it for their spaceships that arrive underwater? she asked.

He nodded.

"Yes, and so much more. That base is the heart of darkness. The CIA runs it, and it's where the MK-Ultra program still operates in high gear with kids attached to machines and remote viewing and insane programming. Not to mention a huge NSA facility down in those pyramids there. Then you have all the levels of U.S. Black Navy on the top floors of the DUMB and then as you move down you go through the Nazi levels and then hit the city area. then the sewers... and tragically there's quite a lot of people that have lived in those sewers... for years. And below that... the Dungeons and Grey genetic testing labs and below that.. is where the Reptilians reside."

She shook her head.

"But in a nutshell, it's a Cabal-controlled base, run by the CIA that is officially the property of the Reptilians who built it, and ultimately decide what the base is used for."

She watched him and could tell more was coming.

"There is a Reptilian meeting room at the very lowest level... so low that one has to be teleported there to attend the meeting. It's chaired by a twelve- foot-tall massive Reptilian. Generals from many countries, attend those meetings. The big Rep who sits at the head of the table is the conduit for the planet. Everything goes through him, including weapons going off-world, human slaves, you name it. He decides and is the head of distribution for the entire Earth."

"It's too much," she said, shaking her head.

He nodded.

"But keep it simple...it's a hub where spaceships bring and take supplies to and from space."

She exhaled, and he knew she had turned her mind to the takeover of the planet.

"So, is Plato creating crowds as part of the Reptilian, Grey agenda?"

He shook his head.

"No, I don't believe so. She is like me—just having fun interacting with humans and creating her life. At least, that's what I get from hanging out with her."

Vyla stared.

"So, you're not even certain of her agenda?" she said. "For all you know, she has been tasked by the Reptilians to create the largest group of humans around her as possible."

"Perhaps," Swizzle said. "But I can't risk bringing up my own feelings without being termed a traitor to the program."

"So, you want out?" she inquired.

He nodded, looking out with soft eyes at the hundreds of humans in the park, having fun and relaxing with children everywhere. Taking it all in, he whispered,

"I have felt what it's like to be human, with free will, art, music, dance, drama, free time, and—"

"Love," she whispered, staring at him. "You've had a taste of what we are made of."

He nodded sadly.

"I now realize that if the Reptilians and Greys get their way, it will all be taken away. Not just from all humans but from me. My newfound freedoms and independent thought will be taken away."

She looked away.

"So, it's the one thing they didn't figure into their calculations when they started their hybridization program... they didn't realize that your human side would want to hold on to its individual free will and creativity." She turned to him. "That you might like the feeling of—love?"

He slowly nodded.

She pointed at him.

He stared. Held in that moment, and knew without a doubt—she was royalty.

C ase was no longer terrified.

He sat next to his best friend and cried inside the Impala. He would kill the fucker who did this. There was no fear at all now. Case would complete this story if it meant the death of him. Will deserved it and would have that respect. Case knew he would have some time before Aspelsin arrived.

He thought of Will's wife and two little boys and the devastation he knew from years in Special Forces: the burying of friends with families sitting shocked at what could have been.

Will had not responded for the last hour as Case had kept watch on her truck. The crowds around Union Square had long since dispersed, and Case had become worried. It was not like Will to not respond to a check-in.

When Case reached the Impala, he knew something was wrong. Will would never roll up both windows on a hot day with the engine off.

Case approached the car with his hand on his Magnum inside his jacket pocket.

There was nobody in sight except for tourists milling about.

He finally pulled open the passenger door, took a visual snapshot of what was inside, and then closed the door.

He leaned against the car and contemplated what he had just seen. And smelled. His best friend. That snapshot would be forever burned in his memory.

Will was slumped back against his headrest, and the heavy blood streaks running down from his bulging eyes confirmed everything for Case. Only the dead had that type of stillness. There would be no reviving his best friend.

Case realized he was standing outside the car, hyperventilating, and that people were starting to notice. He quickly pulled it together, then calmly opened the door and got in, closing the door behind him.

Will already smelled awful, as dead bodies always did.

This was not the first time Case had lost close buddies, but this was beyond anything he thought he would ever have to deal with.

There was no calling the police. He would have to handle getting Will and the car out of here ASAP.

He had messaged Aspelsin that he had an emergency of the same type from Moss Landing and requested that he come quickly. He and Will were planning to meet Aspelsin that night anyway to debrief the regression sessions at Nellis AFB, so he knew Mr. A was nearby.

He heard the knock on the passenger window and slowly opened the door just enough to get out. Aspelsin watched him closely as he motioned inside the car.

Aspelsin looked in, then closed the door.

He watched Case, who was now staring out at the city.

"I'm sorry about Will," Aspelsin said. "We clearly have an entity that is helping or watching Dr. Kells—"

"I'll take care of him and the car in a few minutes," Case said, cutting him off. "I'll need a couple of days to make funeral arrangements with his family, and then I'll call you." Aspelsin stared and slowly nodded.

"If you need a few days, I understand," Aspelsin said.

Case stared out as Aspelsin walked away, keeping his mind on Will.

C ase had done much reading since his *missing-time* at Moss Landing.

He had ramped up his knowledge of how an alien could supposedly lock into the optic nerve and retrieve memories.

Since he had been "switched off" at Moss Landing, it made him even more curious about Mr. A.

He was certain no human would have the capability to switch them off; the idea of aliens as a real and present danger suddenly loomed large.

He had contacted a former SEAL team member, who gave him a number to call. That evening, he met an older SEAL at a bar in town, and they took a booth in the back.

It turns out the Seal had worked at the super-secret S-4 facility but wanted to hear Case's story.

After several cocktails and Case divulging that he had been "swirled" by an alien, the former Seal had seen his misery and allowed a few words of wisdom.

He alluded to technology that he was currently guarding in their underground facilities at Nellis AFB that would make Case's head spin.

Case knew this veteran operator was not the type to make up stories. Seals were truthful to Seals.

He told Case that need-to-know compartmentalization would prevent Case from ever seeing what was down there. Besides, the old Seal said,

"Whatever you are doing topside with surveillance is ten times more interesting than guarding a piece of technology. At least you are free to move around. I stand in one spot all the fucking time and basically talk to my guard dog. I don't see anyone except other security and occasionally a fucking scientist—and other shit—but I'd rather not talk about that."

Case nodded. The old vet was being a good Seal in giving him cryptic information without overtly telling him anything. Just before they parted ways, the old timer passed him a note that Case didn't open until later that night; written in pencil on a bar napkin.

"I worked for EG&G at Groom Lake from 1987 to 1994. I used to guard both of these scientists. Bob Lazar, 1989. Dan Burisch, 1989-1992."

Case knew that the old Seal was trying in every way to help him and that these names were just another key to the alien cover-up that was not an overt confirmation of anything. But Case had no idea how much the old man had just hooked him up.

Two days later, after researching everything on both scientists, Case understood why the Veteran had passed these two names. Both Bob Lazar and Dan Burisch had become whistleblowers.

Physicist Bob Lazar became famous in 1989 for revealing that he had worked on alien spacecraft at a facility in the Groom Lake area of Nevada, within the bounds of the Area 51 top-secret test range.

As far as Case could make out from research, the Cabal, with its cadre of debunkers, had essentially made Lazar's story into the stuff of complete UFO bullshit, as they made Lazar disappear in all but physical form. They claimed he never worked at the S-4 facility at Papoose Lake and set out to undermine every facet of Lazar's fantastical story. They erased his Los Alamos tenure as a physicist and even got Lazar into court on trumped-up charges of running a brothel, further discrediting him.

But the note Case held from his Seal team buddy meant only one thing: Lazar had told the truth from the get-go. Lazar's story about alien ships housed in hidden hangars at the Papoose Lake compound had remained unchanged over the intervening twenty-five years.

In videos Case found from 1989, Lazar revealed how he was hired as a physicist by the Navy to reverse-engineer the propulsion system on the alien saucer he called *the sport model*—located at the S-4 facility. At that time, he was under the auspices of EG&G, the military contractor of that era.

The other scientist, Dan Burisch, a biologist, worked with a team trying to heal a deteriorating alien held at S-4. Burisch became a whistleblower after leaving the program, like Lazar. Burisch also faced the full wrath of the Cabal's anger, was debunked online and in life, and eventually disappeared completely from the public realm.

Case now understood—that for all his years as a special operator—he had been on the fringe of belief regarding an alien presence on Earth. The Cabal had hoodwinked even him.

Now, just days after his switch-off and only hours after receiving the cryptic note, Case understood the full implications of his new reality. The confirmed evidence of aliens working within a covert government-contractor realm—hidden from the American people and the world, as only the Cabal could do. And the unbelievable part to him—was that he was part of it—and didn't even know he was contributing to the cover-up!

At that moment a week ago, his life had changed. He began reading everything he could get his hands on regarding what was currently known about aliens. He knew from other compartmentalized things he'd worked on in Special Ops that nothing was truly kept secret in Black Ops. There was always factual information leaking out in various ways. You only had to absorb it from different directions to finally piece it together.

Case applied the same logic in finding out about the big secret regarding the Cabal and its cover-up of alien interaction through government contractors—contractors like Yen's company, who didn't have to answer to the U.S. public's demands for freedom of information.

Within a few days, Case had pieced together a picture of aliens and their capabilities and was determined not to be hoodwinked again. Now, as Aspelsin disappeared through Union Square, Case had done his best to keep his mind focused on the sadness of his buddy.

He fully understood that Aspelsin would attempt to read his mind when he arrived to see Will's demise. So, Case focused on his sadness until Mr. A had departed the area.

Proximity was key, Case had learned. Neural engagement required proper distance. Minds could not be read from afar. So, he dwelled on his sadness until Mr. A was gone.

A few miles south of Will's killing, Vyla stood, slowly turning barefoot in the sandbox as Swizzle sat watching her.

"So, the reason our government began the lie about aliens not being real back in the '40s was a Reptilian-controlled hoodwink?" she asked.

He nodded.

"Well, early on, it was your own government keeping it under wraps, and the military was the enforcement division. It was all very well coordinated, but again it was all under the purview and agenda of the Draco."

She stared.

"You mean that if we humans had understood what was really happening for all these years, we would have rebelled?"

He nodded.

"And that's the wildest part of the story."

"How do you mean?" she pressed.

He looked at her and waved his hand up and down her body.

"You—though you see yourself as a primitive human—are actually seen as royalty by all aliens in the multi-verse."

She stared.

"What? Aren't we millions of years behind all of your races?"

"It's not where you are technologically that matters. It's your potential that humbles benevolent alien races and absolutely terrifies the Draco, Grey and other malevolent races."

"So, our potential has to do with—"

He smiled. Then shook his head, as if to say, *Where do I even start?*

"Right... so, in a nutshell, you were created when aliens long ago combined the genes of twenty-four of the best and brightest races from all of the multiverse and made—humans.

She shook her head.

"Then, as you made your way along the path of evolution and growth, your genes were modified to adapt to the changing situations on Earth."

"Wow," she said, "so how long has this genetic manipulation been going on?"

He considered this and gave a resigned smile.

"It's a shock when you have a new awareness that you are not at the top of the heap in your universe."

"Yeah, well, fuck you and the horse you rode in on," she said.

He snickered.

"I said that for all humanity, by the way," she said.

He nodded and chuckled as he looked into the sunlit park.

"Right then, your race has been genetically manipulated roughly sixty-five times over the last 100,000 years."

She stared.

"You're bullshitting me?" she exclaimed, her mind swimming with the history of humans that she had always been fascinated with.

"So, were you the ones that dropped in Noam Chomsky's Language-Acquisition-Device roughly 100,000 years ago?"

He turned, impressed with her knowledge.

"I read that about him, that he postulated the LAD, and he was basically correct."

She shook her head.

"So, you were adjusting Neanderthals too?" she asked.

"Of course. Homo sapiens wouldn't arrive for another 60,000 years."

She shook her head. *Wow.*

Then, she touched her fingers to her forehead, remembering.

"I was reading the other day about how Neanderthals were the first to do artistic painting in caves discovered in Spain. They are dated to at least seventy-five thousand years ago."

Swizzle watched her as she continued.

"And one series of paintings has a man in what appears to be a spaceship and, next to the ship, a ladder that archeologists postulated was a ladder up into the sky."

He nodded.

"Once we altered the middle brain for speech; art came, and with it, symbology, culture and individual expression began to explode. The Neanderthals get a bad-wrap as dumb, but they were as brilliant as you are. Just built stockier for the extreme cold of that era. But they were truly intelligent. And their culture was beautiful. I've seen footage of them."

"What?!" she said.

He turned with a *what?* look.

"Wait-a-minute!" she said and slapped her forehead.

"Oh! Of course—if you were smart enough back then to travel here and alter us genetically—then certainly you had the means to document the entire science experiment!"

He shrugged, with a half-smile. She stared at him and then exhaled in exasperation.

"Shit—and we humans never ask permission when we do experiments on animals—so touché, right?"

He pointed her way and nodded. *Bingo.*

"Right," she whispered.

He raised a finger.

"And Vyla... you just brought up a very important point about racism. When I refer to the Draco as *the bad guys*, you need to understand that it's only a nasty faction of that amazing race that is causing humans problems. Most of the Draco are gentle and actually pretty cool reptilians. Some having been on the earth, living peacefully and in harmony with this planet for thousands of years before humans."

She stared, astonished.

He nodded.

"It's true. So, stamping all Draco as *bad guys* is simply racist. The large percentage of that race is peaceful, and many of them are amazing, quiet and humble—not to mention absolutely brilliant."

She listened intently as he continued.

"So, just as your human race produced the nasty Nazis in the '30s—the nasty Dracos I'm referring to—are not representative of that race as a whole. Overall, the Draco—especially the ones that have lived underground on your planet, and in different dimensions—all want the best for humanity. But as with the human race, they have a faction that wants to dominate *your* race."

He picked up Lizzy and stared at the figurine.

"And that nasty Draco faction you can think of as the Mafia. Complete thugs. And those Draco bastards are some of the nastiest aliens in the multi-verse. Feared everywhere. So, for this Reader's Digest version of what's happening, we'll just call the Draco *the bad guys*. But be clear, their race is quite brilliant in their own unique way, and they were the first on this lovely orb—you and they—call home."

She nodded.

"So, essentially, it sounds like the nasty Cabal is being led by a vicious group of low-end Draco-Reptilians, creating a lot of disharmony in this area of the planet."

He pointed.

"Good, but more like this area of the galaxy. And speaking of this beautiful orb we both live on, what you saw off the coast of San Diego, the UAP maneuvering and going in-and-out of space-time, was not even the tip of the iceberg," he said. "That was only a hint of what's used daily, throughout the universe and even by your Cabal on this planet."

"Examples, please," she asked.

"Well, you saw the video of the Malaysian flight being teleported?"

She stared. *How do you know that?*

He looked her way, arching his eyebrows.

She shook her head and bit her lip.

"Right, okay, you can read my mind, because you're an alien."

He pointed.

She flipped him off.

He snickered.

"Okay, so what the hell exactly happened in those teleportation videos?" she said. "It looked like those orbs were some kind of controlled plasma to me?"

He nodded.

"Well, your Cabal has utilized plasma technology for years. It allows them to take an object and essentially wormhole it to wherever they want. In this case, to Diego Garcia."

"So that's how they hijacked the jet, using plasma to warp space-time around an object and create a wormhole?"

He pointed. She pointed back.

"They've been employing that technology since the late 1960s for nefarious purposes—and no one even knew they had it—until now. Those videos put the world on alert that your intelligence community—under orders from the Cabal—hijacked that jet."

"Why would the Cabal or my government steal a Malaysian jet?"

"Right, well, there were twenty defectors of Chinese descent on that flight. All were engineers from a Texas-based semiconductor company and were attempting to take American technology back to China."

She held up a finger.

"Wait, so you're saying the Cabal had been monitoring those employees in Texas?" she asked.

He nodded.

"The Cabal found out three months before the flight that Beijing had convinced those twenty engineers to defect back to China. All of them were Chinese by blood, twelve from Malaysia and eight from China."

"So, their semiconductors have something to do with the teleportation technology?" She pressed.

Swizzle nodded.

"The semiconductors allow the plasma-teleportation orbs to use machine-intuition in fast-moving environments, where event-based logic is required."

She nodded, piecing together how semiconductor technology—which she knew had made a leap forward in the late 1990s—would have made the movement of the orbs feasible. Given that a human—in that same situation—could have never kept up with the movement required to create a wormhole.

She looked up and realized Swizzle had read her mind and was nodding and smiling at her.

He raised a finger.

"Beijing wanted that teleportation technology, and that's when the Cabal decided to teach them a lesson. The Cabal put together a six-person hijack team, and they had control of the jet before it ever launched from Kuala Lumpur."

She nodded slowly and then got a look.

"Why was it on fire in those videos?" She asked.

Swizzle sucked his teeth and shook his head.

"The Cabal—upon learning the final leg of the journey would depart from Kuala Lumpur—loaded the plane's forward cargo hold with five-hundred pounds of lithium-ion batteries."

She stared.

"What were the batteries for?"

"For drama. The Cabal likes to think of themselves as brilliant showmen. They knew that Beijing would be monitoring that jet on satellite because it was bringing them the technology and engineers that would bring them on a par with the Cabal's technology. Once the flight got to 35,000 feet, the Cabal pilot made his famous *Goodnight Malaysian 370* call, and turned off the transponder. At the moment the batteries, which were already burning, suddenly exploded. The Cabal's pilot hastily dove the plane almost vertically, just to get more oxygen as the smoke was filling the plane and at the same time, he turned it back to the west toward Penang."

Vyla stared.

"So, I'm assuming the hijack pilot had no idea... that his own Cabal handlers—were going to set the jet he was hijacking for them—on fire?"

Swizzle pointed.

"You are really starting to understand the Cabal. That American pilot had a nightmare ride that night... and was not told the Chinese *Dog-and-Pony Show* would include a fire on the jet that he would be flying."

"So the Cabal just used him?"

Swizzle nodded.

"And the Cabal not informing their own hijack pilot of an impending fire is very typical of their tactics. They use their own people for nefarious purposes and then generally discard them by executing them when they are no longer needed. Either that or they mind-wipe them... so they don't even know they participated in the hijacking."

She pieced it together.

"Oh, so the Cabal pilot was getting fumed out by the fire up at 35,000 feet, and that's why he dove it straight down... to just above the ocean... so he could breathe again?

Swizzle pointed.

"They almost all died during that dive because of hypoxia and the bitter cold at high altitude. The vertical descent nearly ripped the wings off and did, in fact, pull off a flaperon, which was found later by a Frenchman. But can you imagine what those poor passengers endured with all that smoke in the cabin from the fire and then the vertical descent?"

She stared with a sad look.

"Beijing was monitoring the flight from the get-go?" she asked.

He nodded.

"Beijing had tracked and watched every leg of the defectors' return journey to Beijing. China had that Boeing jet locked-on via satellite—even before the plane launched from Kuala Lumpur—on its final flight."

She stared.

"I read where that woman sailor, *Miss Tee,* reported seeing the Malaysian jet on fire, at low altitude, just above the ocean, near Great Nicobar on the night it vanished."

He nodded.

"The Cabal essentially paraded the technology and the engineers in front of the Chinese government, giving them a front-row-seat to the teleportation, keeping Beijing just-out-of-reach of the technology they so desired."

She shook her head slowly.

"So—the Cabal, with the help of America's top intelligence agencies, terminated all of them—just to show Beijing who was boss?"

He looked away, nodding sadly.

She whispered under her breath,

"You gotta be fucking kidding me?!"

He turned back.

"Except for the defectors. Those twenty engineers got to view their families as they were being slaughtered...and then were put back to work for the Cabal the very next day. But yes, the defectors' families, children, and all other passengers and crew members were murdered. And your government, including your President, then pretended to help with the search for the missing jet, when the entire time, they all knew the passengers and crew had already been executed at Diego."

She shook her head and whispered,

"So those families and innocents were just seen as collateral damage by the Cabal and my government? Massacred—because they were—in the way?"

He stared.

She looked out onto the park as the wind blew back her hair. Then she turned.

"Wait, instead of just arresting those defectors in America and putting them on trial, our entire intelligence community assisted the Cabal to carry out the execution of over two-hundred innocents?

He pointed.

"That's—that's a war crime," she said. "Committed by my own government—when they could have just arrested the defectors in Texas—and stopped the technology going to Beijing?!"

Swizzle stared and very slowly—pointed both fingers.

He could see and feel her heart breaking, watching as she slowly knelt. She slid her hands into the sand, picking up a handful, letting it fall between her fingers as she whispered.

"Hey Mr. President—I voted for you—twice. You were my man, the first Black President—the one who convinced me you would not lie to me, or to the world."

He saw a tear roll as she continued.

"Hey Mr. President—you could have just arrested them—and kept the technology and the defectors here? You had that option. But instead you allowed the murder of all those passengers and crew—and their children—and still you don't admit it to this day?"

She opened both hands.

"Mr. President—what do I call you now?" she whispered as Swizzle slowly placed his hand on her shoulder, watching her descend—her tears falling... without a sound.

Chapter Thirty-Four

C ase stared in the direction where Aspelsin had departed.

It was all he could do to hold himself back, but he knew he needed to study the one that was not human. He looked back at the car, feeling his rage at Aspelsin and yet was still amazed at Will's final, unbelievable gesture.

Case had seen Will's sign immediately when he viewed his best friend. When Case sat down in those first few moments, staring at his dead friend in sadness, he saw it.

Case worked his eyes down Will's body where his hands were together in his lap. At first he couldn't believe it... but then stared in amazement at the sign that Will had managed against all odds. He wanted to kiss his dead friend.

At that moment, Case saw the signal that Will had managed as his final act of being a badass to the end. Will's hands were locked in a peculiar pose, one that Case knew was not natural. Will had managed, in his death throes, to put his hands together, touching the fingertips of each hand almost in a praying-like gesture.

But Will was not a praying type. The final piece of the puzzle became clear when Case saw that the tips of Will's thumbs were also touching in the absolutely perfect rendition of the capital letter "A."

Case looked up at his dead friend as powerful tears came through... but with a feeling that they were still *a team*. One with his best friend, even in death.

Through his tears, Case whispered only one thing... as he placed his hand against Will's still-warm chest—staring at his dear friend.

"I got you, bro... I'll get that motherfucker."

Vyla drove south toward Dah's house in the afternoon and had the urge to crash her truck into something... anything.

After Swizzle had left her at the park, she had jumped online—searching for the past news conference—where the President had made his first comments on the missing flight. She was astonished at the timeframe.

The President didn't mention the Malaysian flight disappearing until eleven days after it vanished!

What! she thought incredulously. *Since when does our own president wait eleven days to mention missing Americans on a vanished commercial flight that has captivated the world?*

She stared transfixed at the video of the news conference, watching the man she had so admired as he easily deceived the world with his presidentially sincere face.

"Every available U.S. resource is being used in the search, including the FBI, the National Transportation Safety Board and others who deal with aviation. The U.S. will continue working in close cooperation with the Malaysian government, which is leading the investigation, to see if we can get to the bottom of this."

After replaying his speech a few times, she realized that the simple beliefs she fell for during his election speeches, about honor and dignity, had no foundation whatsoever. That, as he was speaking, he positively knew all those innocents—the men, women and children, and the families of the defectors, had been murdered at Diego Garcia... by U.S. Navy personnel.

She paused the video with him mid-speech—his face contrite.

How could you?

An hour later she pulled into Dah's and saw the black sedan slide across the way moments later.

At least she could count on surveillance.

Oh, what the hell. Move on.

As she walked into the house, she felt the pressure of her upcoming flight back to Nellis. With the house empty, she did a long sit and came out refreshed. Told herself that she would not rely on anyone but herself until further notice.

Fixed herself a sandwich, studying the picture wall and the photos of the Roswell timeframe. Moments later, Dah entered, and Vyla put her arm around her as they both stared at the photos. After a time, Vyla noticed her mom was staring at a picture of Sam with his cousin, Eileen Fanton. The photos showed them standing in front of Sam's used car lot with all the old cars and Sam's sign behind them.

Eileen was wearing an Army nurse's uniform, and they were both beaming. Vyla knew Eileen had been a first lieutenant when Roswell happened, and Dah had always spoken highly of her, though with a tinge of sadness.

"Mom, that picture was taken at Sam's lot in Gallup, right?"

Dah slowly nodded and smiled.

"He was so proud of Eileen. He had helped her get her first job with the super-secret 509th air group at Roswell."

Before Vyla could ask another question, Dah exhaled and turned away.

"I'm gonna do a little gardening with our favorite boy here so he can get some exercise."

"Okay, Mom," Vyla said, smiling.

She watched Dah and Banjo exit and knew something about the Eileen and Sam's picture was too painful for Dah to dwell on. Vyla watched them through the window as they made their way to the garden.

Wow, she thought. *Whatever journey lay ahead with Eileen was going to be rough.*

She exhaled, staring at the photo, but she was no longer afraid. She needed answers, and if going through a dark place was part of those answers, then so be it.

She laid out her vintage map and placed one hand over the town of Roswell. With her other hand, she rested two fingers on Sam and Eileen. With the remaining three fingers, she touched the picture of Mack Brazel with Waya and Roy flanking him. She wanted it all to flow back in again, come what may.

She took a deep breath, closed her eyes, and felt a female energy shoot through her, accompanied by a terror that lingered. As if that female energy was still unhinged from the planet, no longer grounded.

She felt herself falling into a chasm of darkness and was suddenly adorned in a 1947 military uniform. That of a female Army first lieutenant.

A rmy officer and nurse Eileen Fanton could feel her lips quivering as she sat alone in the ninety-five degree heat.

Next to her were the black medical tents that had been erected outside the Roswell Army Base hospital. In her lap was her notepad with the calendar page open. It showed Monday, July 7th, 1947, and she hadn't slept in three days.

She was exhausted and anxious, watching the tense commotion around her. Heavily armed MPs were everywhere, and the horror of what was happening weighed heavily on her.

The order had come down a day after the crash recoveries had begun: she was not allowed to make any phone calls. Now, she was escorted everywhere by armed O.S.S. security operatives, who were stationed outside her officer's room as well.

The world had flipped upside down. She wanted to call Glenn Dennis, her new boyfriend who worked at a mortuary just off the base, but she was forbidden to make any calls. The worst part of it all was that she knew he was in trouble, and it was because of her.

On Saturday afternoon, that 5th of July, she was the head nurse on her shift at the Roswell base hospital when the darkness swept through.

She had been filling out an inventory sheet in a supply room next to the emergency room when she heard a commotion of arriving vehicles outside the hospital. She stayed focused on her inventory, then was perplexed by the aggressive yelling going on in the hallway. That's when the stench first hit her. The smell of death she could handle, but that smell was far beyond a dead body.

She put the pen back in the clipboard and stood, straightening her 1947 female officer nurse's outfit with its smart collar and nurse's hat.

At 23, Eileen had just graduated from Fort Sam Houston Officers Nursing School, and this was her first duty assignment. None of her officer friends in the medical corps could believe she had landed Roswell for her first tour. It was the most top-secret airbase in the world, and you had to have clout to get in there—simple smarts wouldn't pass muster—but Eileen knew she had an ace in the hole.

Her older cousin Sam Boyd was not only a war veteran, but she secretly knew he had helped form the Navajo Code Talkers during the war, and a letter from Sam would certainly turn heads in the Army, even years after the war. Sam was happy to write the letter of recommendation for her, and a short time later, she was awarded the assignment.

She had only arrived in Roswell three months ago, and up to that moment, she had handled everything with a professional demeanor and had been enjoying her time. She had met Glenn Dennis a few weeks back, and they had hit it off from the start. But, at that moment, she was swirling in thoughts of Saturday afternoon and how the evil had arrived.

She had opened the storeroom door to find the emergency room hallway swarming with MPs. Before she even had time to ask one of them what was happening, she felt a gentle but firm grip on her shoulder. She turned to see Major Charles Rea, a doctor she did not recognize.

"Nurse, follow me," Rea commanded.

Eileen, sensing the crazy tension in the hallway, didn't ask questions. Doctor Rea guided her through an emergency room door guarded by two MPs wielding submachine guns. The stench grew unbearable as she entered the operating room with a tall, European-looking doctor studying a badly burned child's body. She shuddered momentarily but dropped hard into her medical role, always knowing she would have to confront this type of scene at some point in her career.

Dr. Detlev Bronk looked up from the cadaver and stared at Eileen and Dr. Rea.

"I've found us some help, Dr. Bronk," Rea said.

It was at that moment that Eileen put her hand to her mouth, realizing that she was not looking at a charred human child but the blackened cadaver of some demonic-looking creature. It was not burned but black from heat exposure and bodily deterioration in the desert. She felt herself becoming unhinged as she stared at the huge, slanted, black eyes that seemed to look into her soul. She felt the bile rising as she looked up at Dr. Bronk.

"Nurse, get a mask on," Bronk said with a heavy Eastern European accent. "We have to do an autopsy without delay."

His sudden command jolted Eileen back into the sweltering autopsy room, where the air conditioning had been turned off to keep the cadaver's stench from permeating the entire hospital.

Over the next three hours, Eileen and the two doctors, plus a military camera operator, would have to depart the sweltering room, race to the lavatory, get sick, and then sit and recover—only to reenter until the job was complete. There was no blood, only a clear liquid that reeked of acetone, vomit, and sulfur.

Throughout the autopsy, Eileen was asked to hold up the creature's limbs to be filmed and raise and display strange organs for the camera. Terrified, she gingerly lifted the long arm and could feel the dead, scaly skin, which was almost transparent. She looked up to see the eerie head, so much larger than a human's.

The eyes were shiny and huge, set back into the skull from too many hours dead in the 110-degree New Mexico heat. The bones were malleable and elastic, like a newborn baby, and the doctors made her demonstrate that for the camera... with the arm of the creature. She almost fainted and was terrified, on top of being nauseous. Those eyes—even dead—she felt were looking through her.

Late that Saturday afternoon, during a break from the autopsy, Eileen was in the hallway, catching her breath, when she heard a commotion.

Her boyfriend, Glenn Dennis, had somehow gained access to the emergency room hallway, and was rapidly walking toward her, wondering what all the security was about. Eileen warned him under her breath to leave before he got into trouble.

In that tense moment, Glenn was confronted by a yelling major, who had the

MPs carry the terrified mortician out of the hospital and escort him off the base.

On Sunday afternoon, the 6th, she was sleep-deprived as she made her way to the hospital amidst all the heavily armed MPs. The sewage stench wafted everywhere as several cadavers were in tents outside in an effort to isolate the smell.

She entered the hospital building and placed a call to Glenn using a side office before the order came down that no further outbound calls would be allowed by any hospital personnel.

For the rest of that Sunday afternoon and evening, her staff had orders to keep the cadavers in the tents iced, as formaldehyde had been proven to deteriorate the skin, and icing seemed to be the only solution for preservation.

She departed the hospital late that night to her officer's quarters and knew the base was on full lockdown, with no chance of going into town. She had seen Master Sergeant Matilda MacElroy briefly in the ladies' room, and they had given each other a hug without discussing what was actually happening. The two women were bonded by being the only females attached to the 509th and shared a clearance level that was tough to attain. Both knew the other was most likely aware of what was transpiring at the base, but neither mentioned it. Matilda could tell that Eileen was stressed but wasn't aware that autopsies were taking place and that Eileen was intimately involved. They promised to call each other soon, and as they departed the women's room, they were met by their separate O.S.S. escorts.

At noon on Monday, the 7th, Eileen met Glenn Dennis at the Officer's Club, which he could access because of his long-term medical affiliation with the base. She had hardly slept since the terrifying events had begun on Saturday.

They took a back table, and he could see she was clearly on the edge of a nervous breakdown. He listened to her horrific whispered account as they ate their lunch.

Her lips quivered during the retelling, but she managed to pass him several small hand-drawn paper notes under a napkin over that lunch date, with a general description of her autopsy alien.

Glenn had whispered to her that he had been warned several times since his hospital melee with the MPs, including receiving threatening calls from the military and a personal call from Sheriff Wilcox. He told her the entire town of Roswell was on edge.

They said goodbye without a hug due to the security everywhere. Departing in a separate direction from Glenn, she exited the Officer's Club and made her way through several security checkpoints to the cadaver tents near the hospital.

She sat, clenching her hands together to keep them from shaking. There were MPs everywhere around her, and the other hospital staff sat alone as well. None were allowed to talk, on orders not to do so. Some of her staff smoked, while others seemed overcome, crying silently, alone.

And now that she had handled the Grey's eerie skin and limbs, no amount of washing would cleanse that thing out of her system. Even with a long, hot shower on that first night, where she scrubbed every part of herself, it was still there. She wanted to vomit as she sensed it had somehow transferred itself into her. The one she had been forced to handle, with its dead, tentacle-like fingers, and sinister black eyes, was still—somehow—haunting her.

S am had left Oppie in the pre-dawn darkness and forced himself to catch a few hours of sleep at the Officer's quarters on the far side of the base.

Even there, he was confronted with O.S.S. operatives stationed outside each room. He departed in full uniform at 4 p.m. and made a beeline for hangar P3 at the flight line, only to find it already cordoned off by MPs.

They waved him through just as a convoy of military vehicles arrived. Inside the hangar, huge white spotlights had been set up, and there was a frenzied commotion as the alien bodies were brought in one by one on stretchers. Standing dead center where the bodies were being laid was Roswell base commander Colonel William Blanchard and other dignitaries.

In the corner of the hangar, Sam could see that the strange, pumpkin-seed-shaped ship had been brought in as well.

Moments later, all five bodies were laid out, and though they were only slightly taller than the Greys, they were much more human-looking from the standpoint of limbs, faces, and details. Their six-fingered hands were basically human-looking, save for the extra digit. Their feet were also human-shaped but with an extra toe. Their large black eyes were not wrap-around, and they had a small but well-defined nose and human-looking ears.

Sam noticed that the one on the center stretcher was still moving its hand. He approached slowly amidst the crush of officers and medical personnel for a better look. The Orange had brought its knees up slightly on the stretcher, and its hand was convulsing slowly.

It's dying, Sam thought, as a balding civilian man kneeled down and held its hand, comforting it.

All around him, Sam could see the *First-Contact-reactions* were severe. Right next to Colonel Blanchard, a large MP, wearing the customary white helmet and socks, was bent over at the waist, clearly overcome at the creatures lying before him—*from another planet.*

Behind Sam, in the crush of people trying to get a peek at the alien bodies, he recognized Joseph *"Little Joe"* Montoya, the Lieutenant Governor of New Mexico!

351

He was obviously anxious and whispered to Colonel William Blanchard, the base commander. The whole scene was chaotic, as it was clearly the first moment many of those present had even considered that there might be other life in the universe, and they were now staring at them... face-to-face.

Many, Sam could see in their shocked stares, would never forget that moment. And yet, he knew that there was a deadly end for anyone who whispered about what was right in front of them.

A moment later, Sam noticed Lt. Governor Montoya sneaking out a side door, looking nervous as hell. Nobody famous wanted to be seen lest they be questioned about it later. Sam watched as medical personnel checked the live Orange, but the creature looked bad as if it was in its last moments—and the eerie siren-like whine that it made—was certainly not human.

Its knees were now up and rocking back and forth, as its six-fingered hand continued to convulse... making it eerie to watch.

Suddenly, a commotion was heard as a security detail barged in. A colonel who Sam didn't recognize, spoke.

"Gentlemen, please make room for my detail. We have to get these to the base hospital this instant!"

The five oranges were reloaded into the ambulances and whisked away. The fifteen or so officers left standing with Sam were clearly shaken. Some smoked, some sat and began crying, while others shook their heads and laughed as a way to combat the moment.

Just then, a lieutenant colonel yelled out, "There will be a brief in Colonel Blanchard's office in ten minutes." He said, staring with eyes that were deadly serious. "Please exit the hangar, and it goes without saying that nothing happened here, gentlemen. Under threat of court martial—absolutely nothing happened here."

You could hear a pin drop as the hangar quickly cleared amidst the heavily armed MPs, who stood silently watching.

At the Roswell base hospital thirty minutes later, Eileen, Dr. Bronk, and Dr. Rea stared at the injured Orange that had just been brought over from hangar P-3.

Its siren wail filled the room, and its six-fingered hand flopped left and right amidst sporadic shaking.

"Nurse," Dr. Bronk whispered, "it's dying—please secure that hand—by whatever means, and I'll try to stethoscope its chest."

Dr. Rea looked away sheepishly as Eileen looked to him for help.

Knowing she needed to act quickly, she stepped near the twitching hand and gently cradled it with both hands. It was cold to the touch and had an elasticity similar to a lizard's skin.

On the verge of vomiting, she closed her eyes and pretended it was a dying child, but the trick didn't work. She could feel an energy from the cold, wailing creature that seemed to be longing for home. She finally opened her eyes as Dr. Bronk brought a stethoscope down to its chest.

She felt it go—the cold fingers gripping hers tighter for a moment. She shuddered, looking up into its round black eyes as the eerie wail softened.

The creature's fingers held firm, and she used her other hand to pry the death grip off of her fingers. Before she could do anything about it, she turned and vomited next to the table, falling to her knees and purging as she could hear the doctors whisper about the creature on the table and the need to autopsy it immediately.

Eileen heard the doctors exit beside her.

"Nurse, get to the bathroom and pull yourself together," Dr. Bronk said as he passed.

As the door closed behind the doctors, she pulled herself up into the chair and was too afraid to look around the room—because it was still there.

Her hands shook as she wiped herself clean about the face and neck and departed a moment later.

She staggered through the tense hallway and out into the sun, stabilizing herself against the wall. She took several deep breaths and noticed one of her female staff, entering the large black medical tent with a bucket of ice. She gathered herself as quickly as she could and followed her in.

The tents were completely dark on the inside, with two sets of four tables holding cadavers, separated by a temporary barrier. Guards were everywhere, and she noticed several who were close to passing out from the stench. The sewage smell was made even more appalling by the sweltering interior of the unvented space.

Three enlisted orderlies and two nurses were tasked with keeping ice on and around the stinking cadavers as they awaited departure on a transport.

Eileen then realized that the temporary barrier between tables was there for a reason. Both Grey and Orange types of alien cadavers were present, separated by the barrier.

There were four ashen-orange cadavers on the far side of the barrier, and she thought of the one that had just died in her care. She took a moment to stare at its dead crewmembers.

Their faces had a distinctly more human look. The ashen-orange skin appeared more spongy and more absorptive, and the eyes were set straight ahead and didn't wrap around the head like the Greys... on the far table.

"These orange ones with six fingers are supposedly from the bluffs east of the Mack Brazel debris field," whispered one of Eileen's nurses nearby, snapping her out of her trance.

Eileen moved closer to her as if helping with the ice. She had heard KGFL DJ Frank Joyce talking that afternoon about how Rancher Mack Brazel had found flying saucer debris scattered across his ranch the previous Saturday morning.

"Come close so I can talk to you," Eileen whispered and pointed at the ice as if the two nurses were discussing its placement. The younger nurse leaned in, playing along.

"The injured orange one just died in the emergency room," Eileen said. "Will you do the autopsy? I don't think I can handle another one."

"Yes, ma'am," the younger nurse said. "I'll do anything to get out of this ice duty."

"I'll go let the doctors know you'll be in momentarily," Eileen said.

"Okay, thank you ma'am." the young nurse replied.

Minutes later, Eileen was standing in front of Dr. Bronk and Rea, who were smoking in an area just outside the autopsy room. Eileen told them the truth, that she was feeling really sick and had asked a nurse on staff to help with the next autopsy.

Dr. Bronk again swore her to secrecy, and she was again reminded that everything she had just experienced did not happen—that she was to forget the whole affair.

A t the heavily secured Guest House, just inside the base main gate, Mack Brazel was silently sobbing.

Silently, because the huge, armed MP standing just behind him, against the far wall, watched every move the chained, naked rancher made.

Mack shook violently, recalling the unspeakable things they had just done to him—and he just wanted to go home. No matter what they asked him to do or say, he would be that for them.

He was in shock and didn't want to recall it, but he could smell the urine on the floor. His own. He whimpered silently as the horror from one hour before, played out over and over in his mind.

Mack had never expected to be terrorized by his own government. He flatly refused to recant his honest retelling of the past weekend's events.

He was a simple ranch foreman and father.

And by fucking damn, you didn't tell a rancher to lie. Ever!

A solid one wouldn't even know how to. Mack Brazel wasn't about to break that honor code. He didn't give a rat's ass what government man was threatening him.

"Fuck you!" Mack had yelled earlier at the redheaded Captain Armstrong, sitting across from him.

Armstrong had suggested that it would go hard on Mack if he wanted to tell people about flying saucers and aliens on his ranch, and it might upset the wrong people higher up the chain of command.

"Well, I can't help you there, son," Mack had growled at the redheaded wise guy. "I don't lie to my wife or my friends, and by God, I'm not lying for you."

At that, Armstrong ashed out his cig and slowly sucked his teeth.

"Not for me, Mr. Brazel," he said. "This is for your country. For America and what's best for her."

"Fuck you!" Mack yelled at full volume. He could see the MPs against the wall, ready to pounce if he laid a finger on the punk across from him.

Armstrong smiled again, lighting another cig as he casually puffed, staring at the rancher in his flannel shirt, dirty denim jeans, and tattered belt.

Mack held his gaze out the window.

"It's a big desert out there, Mr. Brazel—folks disappear all the time."

At that, Mack turned slowly, barely able to control himself.

"Boy, I'm gonna pretend you didn't just threaten my life. But I'll tell you this... if you and I were on my ranch, I'd give you an ass-whippin' like you ain't never had, and that—you little prick—is the goddamn truth."

Staring at Mack, Armstrong shrugged, shaking his head slowly, whispering,

"Suit yourself, Mr. Brazel, but you'll soon learn you're in over your head."

"Fuck you, you little punk," Mack replied tersely.

"Fuck me, huh?" Armstrong whispered and turned his head toward the small window in the door.

A signal.

A second later, Mack's turning began.

The door exploded open, and four burly MPs burst into the room. Mack was hoisted out of his chair backward and thrown onto the cement floor with a savagery reserved for traitors, knocking the breath clean out of him.

Armstrong pulled on his cigarette as Mack screamed... while all four MPs held him down, and his ranch clothes were literally cut off his body. He tried to fight but was no match for the much bigger, elite MPs.

They knelt on him, dug their knees in, speaking casually to each other as if he was an unruly dog. Mack had never been so dominated—the cutting off of his clothes was shocking and humiliating.

Exposed and vulnerable, he began to sob silently as the MPs continued their onslaught.

"Hold his right wrist, and don't let it move," the lead MP said calmly as Mack began to whimper.

The huge men placed handcuffs and chains on his wrists and ankles, then cinched them tightly until he screamed again. Naked and exposed, he heard the door open again and, from his flattened position on the concrete floor, saw a large doctor enter the room.

An MP grabbed Mack by the hair and, with both hands, turned his strained neck, forcing him to watch as the large physician donned a rubber surgical glove on his right hand and dipped his large index finger into a small vat of household grease.

Mack's body began to shake uncontrollably as he whimpered, having never imagined what he was about to endure. He suddenly had a new awareness of how small he was in this new deadly realm, in shock that his own U.S. Army was doing these things to him.

Sitting at the desk while Mack whimpered, Armstrong sniffled, then took a long drag, exhaled, and stared at the smoke playing in the streaming sunlight from the far window. He spoke calmly as Mack was now a terrified child, held in the grip of a monster.

"Mr. Brazel, I've determined from your behavior that you need a full Army physical."

Mack began to sob out loud, in the grips of an evil much bigger than himself.

"And with that physical, Mr. Brazel, there certainly needs to be a bodily inspection to confirm you have not hidden any pieces of the weather balloon foil in your ass in an attempt to keep it from my beloved United States Army."

A second later, Mack was aggressively lifted, bound hand and foot, and slammed against the wall, each limb pinned firmly while he cried out to no avail. Mack shook violently, straining in vain as he heard the doctor kneel behind him and calmly order the MPs,

"Hold that bitch still."

The scream that came next was only the beginning, as the huge physician's finger did its damage amidst a raging yell that could be heard across the base.

A short time later, when he came to after passing out from the pain, Mack realized he was on the piss-stench floor, naked, in chains, and shaking violently.

He worked his battered torso into a sitting position, facing away from the only MP left in the room.

Sobbing silently, he now feared for his life. Armstrong had departed and been replaced... and the one standing just inside the door, smoking a cigarette, finally spoke. Mack recognized the Mafioso accent of the no-nametag captain who led the military team that had abducted him from Whitmore's ranch house the night before.

"Mr. Brazel," Damon Slepher purred with his greasy, gangster drawl. "I want to make this simple for you and for me. In the next hour, if somehow you don't find a way to recant your fucked-up story about flying saucers and little dead aliens, my boys are going to take your truck keys and crash your truck into a telephone pole. They will then proceed to beat you—until you're good and dead. And then, after that, they'll place your badly beaten body in your crashed truck. A quick photo of your bloody, broken cadaver will be taken, and the entire crash will be reported to Sheriff Wilcox. Now, Sheriff Wilcox is a good man, and he's agreed to tell all the newspapers and radio stations about your tragic truck accident and that he was certain you were drunk when you hit that pole. He will also mention to the newspapers that you were lying when you told your story to the radio station. And he will confirm, for all the media, that it was just a weather balloon on your property and that you were simply a broke rancher who wanted a little extra attention."

Mack continued to sob silently as he heard Slepher whisper on his way out.

"Mr. Brazel, it was nice to meet you. I hope you don't let your friend, Sheriff Wilcox, have the last word about what kind of man you—were."

The door closed quietly as Mack broke down, feeling his naked vulnerability. He never wanted to feel it again. He sat gutted of all self-worth, tasting his bloody lips and the salty tears streaming down his broken, humiliated face.

S am sat in his officer's quarters at daybreak, reading the headlines on the July 8th Tuesday edition of the Roswell newspaper.

He was perplexed to see the Army admitting it had a captured flying saucer. The piece mentioned the craft being reported by a rancher, and Sam figured the article must have come out before the clampdown was announced. He had attended that brief the evening before, just after the aliens were taken to the hospital.

Colonel Blanchard made it clear to everyone in that tense meeting that General Twining was about to arrive... and that a decision by the president had now been made. Blanchard stared at everyone in the room.

"Nothing happened here, gentlemen, except a crashed weather balloon."

Sam tossed the newspaper and hopped up, checking his uniform in the mirror. He had a plane to catch—returning to Los Alamos—where Poke had something he wanted Sam to see.

Damon Slepher passed several saluting MPs inside Hangar P3 and continued his quick stroll into a private office in the corner of the hangar.

General Nathan Twining was on the phone and looked up as Slepher entered, settling onto the couch across from him. Twining hung up the phone and lit a cigarette.

A gray-haired general with a square jaw and stern gaze, Twining controlled everything to do with the new alien presence—including civilian witnesses who talked too much.

The general looked up at Slepher, exhaling smoke.

"Alamogordo all wrapped up?"

"Yes, sir. We're good to go," Slepher said.

Twining slowly nodded, studying the curious OSS assassin.

"We may have a couple more soon. Locals who are telling everyone what they saw. I've got that damn rancher, Brazel, in lockup, but your interrogator says he's starting to get the message."

Slepher nodded and ashed out his cigarette.

"Don't worry, sir. He'll get the message."

The general pulled on his cig and slowly nodded.

"He certainly will—dead or alive."

Slepher watched the older man.

"I don't like putting down American citizens," Twining said, "but a potential traitor is still a traitor."

"Better safe than sorry, sir," Slepher replied with his depraved smile.

Twining watched him, doing his best to appear hard.

"Damn straight."

Slepher got to his feet.

"Sir, if you'll excuse me, I've got some business to attend to. I'll see you shortly."

Twining nodded.

"Sure. Thanks for the update."

"Yes, sir. My pleasure."

Slepher nodded in deference as he departed, closing the door softly behind him. But Twining knew Slepher didn't have to defer to any officer; it was just part of his game and that Slepher only said *sir* as a measure of respect. *Smart fucker.* Twining thought. *A cold operator.*

He also knew Slepher was heavily in cahoots with East Coast crime families, and he had heard rumors that Slepher was also known by the Bilderberg group in Europe. The global elite who really ran the game. But that was next level. Twining thought about how few people could get away with arriving and departing his office without a salute.

He ashed out his cig, knowing that Slepher didn't salute anybody unless he was in character. *And that particular character,* Twining thought, *was a damn scary individual to be on the wrong side of.*

Inside KGFL radio station in Roswell on that morning of Tuesday, the 8th, they had brought him in.

Radio disc jockey Frank Joyce hardly recognized Mack Brazel when the military security detail escorted him into the recording booth. Mack looked anguished, and his eyes spoke of terror. He didn't say a word to Frank as he was led to the microphone.

A military type nodded at Frank that they were ready, and a moment later... Mack recanted his testimony using a script provided to him and Frank. Mack claimed he had made a mistake. That the alien ship turned out to be a weather balloon. Frank Joyce asked the follow-on questions about Mack being thrown by the storms and not sleeping well, and the interview was over moments later.

Frank watched Mack depart the recording room and sheepishly come into the booth where Frank stared at him with a look of utter disappointment.

"What you said in there was nothing like what you told me on the wire recording," Frank whispered tersely.

Mack leaned in and whispered in his gravelly tone.

"Look, son. You keep this to yourself. They told me to follow this script or it would go awfully hard on me and you."

Frank was disgusted.

"So, what about your integrity? What about the little green men you mentioned?"

Mack stared at the young DJ and grabbed the door handle to depart but then hesitated as he looked down and exhaled.

"They weren't green," he whispered sadly as he gave Frank a final look, pulling the door closed behind him.

Frank watched anxiously as the military men escorted Mack out. They had broken that hard, calloused rancher. But what unnerved Frank even more was the way the black-haired captain—the one without a name tag—the one who had threatened the entire staff about disappearing... had eyed him during the recording.

By Thursday, the 10th of July, 1947, Frank Joyce had endured two days of his friends and acquaintances wondering why he reported the alien event, only to broadcast a recanting a day later.

He was over the shock of what had happened and now he was mad. He knew Mack had not lied during the wire recording, but that recording had been confiscated, and Frank knew it would never see the light of day. And his final encounter with Mack two days ago made him want to tell the world... the military was lying.

He pulled out his keys, approaching his car on that Thursday afternoon when Walt Whitmore Sr. pulled up slowly next to him in an older black sedan.

"Get in, Frank." The older man said.

"Yes, sir," Frank replied, rarely seeing his boss in this type of tense mood.

Frank got in the passenger seat and noticed the same black-haired, no-nametag captain in the back seat that had led the military operatives into Whitmore's house on the day of Mack's wire recording and abduction. But this time, the same man was wearing an expensive three-piece Italian business suit, and the mafioso accent that Frank had heard two days ago suddenly had a context.

Damon Slepher sat quietly watching as Frank took the front passenger seat, across from Walt Whitmore Sr.

They drove north out of Roswell in silence for almost an hour. Frank Joyce occasionally shot furtive glances over his shoulder at Slepher, who pulled on his cigarette, staring at the twenty-three-year-old radio disc jockey.

Moments later, Whitmore guided the car off the highway near Corona Rd and drove a rough dirt road into the desert, stopping at a small wooden shack the size of a garage, as it stood alone amidst the pinyon trees and sagebrush. Whitmore shutdown the engine, and theirs was the only car there.

"Go in the shack, Frank," Whitmore said with a terse whisper.

Frank looked over and then back at Slepher, who stared out the window.

"Yes, sir," Frank whispered and exited.

The inside of the shack was empty, yet still had enough light to see. Frank was anxious as he waited. He heard the sound of another car pull up.

A moment later he heard footsteps approaching, and the door opened.

Mack Brazel strode in, and the two exchanged a look.

"You're never gonna talk about this again, to anybody." Mack said firmly.

"Well, not if you don't want me to, Mack," Frank whispered.

Mack took a deep breath and looked at the dirt floor.

"Our lives will never be the same, Frank." He said, looking up, and then walked out, pulling the door closed behind him.

Frank realized he was shaking. His emotions raced as he heard a single car outside depart. He gathered himself as best he could and exited. He walked to Walt Whitmore's car and got in the passengers seat.

Damon Slepher was gone.

Walt never looked over; instead, just slowly pulled out, smoking a cigarette, and the two rode in silence the whole way home.

V yla slowly opened her eyes.

The information she had processed on her Roswell dives was now forming a general picture—one that was at once dark and certainly full of desperation.

She heard Banjo limping up the porch steps, and a moment later, the screen door opened. Dah padded into the living room and sat down heavily on the couch beside her.

"How about I get you some water?" Vyla said, standing and heading to the kitchen.

"Or a cold beer!" Dah half-shouted.

"Or how about a cold beer?" Vyla echoed from the other room. A moment later, she appeared, holding two bottles with the tops already off.

She sat, and they toasted.

For a while, they sat in silence, drinking and smiling at each other.

"I like this," Dah said. "Just being with you."

Vyla nodded, watching her sweet mother. Dah turned to her.

"I'm so proud that you're finding an interest in my family's history."

Vyla wagged her head.

"Well, I'm starting to understand—a little—but there are so many moving parts."

Dah nodded.

"You mentioned once that your great-grandfather was taken?" Vyla asked.

Dah nodded.

"Does that have to do with Roswell, too?" Vyla pressed.

Dah nodded again.

"It's all tied together."

Vyla slowly nodded.

"At the time you told me those stories, I just didn't understand—didn't believe in those types of encounters—but I'm starting to," Vyla said.

Dah slowly nodded, looking at the black-and-white photos.

"There were many taken. My Apache side—my ancestors near Mount Dulce, New Mexico, lost so many, they sent a war party into those mountain caves. None returned."

"What? Who were they fighting?" Vyla asked.

"The evil in the mountain was all I was ever told—but it's still there, according to my relatives. They still hear things below their homes near Mt. Dulce. Vibrations and strange sounds."

Before Vyla could ask another question, her mom stood.

"I need a shower," she said, starting down the hallway. "That dog put me through the wringer."

Another dark topic, Vyla thought, exhaling as she looked at the photos.

She felt stressed, knowing she was catching a plane at midnight to Las Vegas for simulator training. But she wanted more answers and knew that much of what was happening now with aliens had begun in New Mexico... at Roswell.

She picked up a photo of Sam and sat on the couch.

Sam always had such a calm demeanor in his pictures. She placed her hands on him and closed her eyes.

Immediately, a vibration rattled through her bones... a rumble—and suddenly, she was jostling in a 1947 Jeep, plowing ahead on a dirt highway in northern New Mexico—as Captain Sam Boyd.

Chapter Thirty-Five

Two hundred and fifty miles northwest of Mack Brazel's crash site, Sam rode in the passenger seat of Poke's open jeep as they sped along a dirt highway.

"Potomac Grey and Michigan Yellow were the only two colors," Major Poke said. "My wife wanted the damn bright yellow, so here we are."

Sam snickered as Poke worked the wheel of his brand-new '48 Jeep. The shiny yellow four-wheel drive bumped north along dirt Highway 84.

"It's got the same Go-Devil engine that was in the Quads back in the war," Poke continued. "And we're gonna need every bit of it today."

Sam nodded as he took a drag from his cigarette. He was glad to be away from Roswell—the tension at the base was off the charts. As far as he knew, the only live alien left was the one under his watch at Los Alamos. He had returned to the facility that morning and spent a few minutes with the Grey before Poke summoned him.

The major had informed him that a new handler had been assigned—a top botanist, Dr. Guillermo Mendoza. The handover would take place in a couple of days. In the meantime, Poke needed Sam's help up near the state line.

As they drove, Sam took in the rugged northern New Mexico terrain... and it was certainly some of the most beautiful land he had ever seen.

"Sir, you told me there were other Greys at Los Alamos?" he asked.

Poke nodded. "San Antonio crash two years ago."

"There was a saucer crash in 1945?" Sam asked, surprised.

"Yep. That was the fifth one. It came down one month after the first A-bomb blast at the Trinity site. The damn aliens were buzzin' all around after that test. Remember that first A-bomb test?"

Sam nodded. "Yes, sir. I translated for the Apache in that area—warned them that the bomb would be tested soon and that they should clear out."

"That was you? Well, I'll be damned," Poke said, glancing over. "I heard they had an Apache translator helpin' out down there."

Sam nodded again.

"So, you met Oppenheimer, huh?" Poke asked.

"Yes, sir. Ended up working pretty closely with him."

Poke grinned. "You like him?"

"Seems like a real swell fella to me, sir."

"Smarter than all get-out, huh?" Poke added.

Sam chuckled.

"I'd say so, sir."

Poke waved his cigarette.

"Well, after that first A-bomb, the damn aliens were buzzin' around Ground Zero for days, sending electromagnetic pulses over the whole blast site. We later found out from that Grey that our new Doppler radar somehow messed with their pilots—screwed up their ability to control the craft."

Poke pulled on his cigarette and continued.

"See, the Grey pilots fly those things with their brains—wearin' those little headpiece things. It's all integrated with the ship. Something about the triangulation of three radar stations messes them up. That's when the Grey's saucer hit that Marconi tower and crashed."

"How big was it, sir?" Sam asked. "That 1945 one?"

"About the same size as yours—forty feet or so. But it was oval-shaped, like an egg, not really a saucer."

Sam nodded. It was all starting to make sense—the efficiency of the recovery teams, their familiarity with the Greys. Still, it troubled him that he hadn't heard a word about any of this. He usually got wind of military operations near Gallup, and the crash Poke described was only two hours away.

Poke continued.

"There were five more crashed ships before that one—even earlier recoveries nobody knew about. The absolute first saucer was found ditched in the ocean near Saipan in '41. I guess we were testing our new pulse radar at Tinian Island, right next to Saipan, and it messed with the pilot of that ship. Brought it right down. Our Navy recovered it—three Greys inside, all dead."

Poke flicked his cigarette out the window.

"The '41 Cape Girardeau, Missouri crash—now that was the first one on the mainland. Three dead there, too... but one was alive for about two hours before it passed."

Sam listened, absorbing every word, the weight of the revelation sinking in. The U.S. had been recovering saucers for years, all in total secrecy.

"The team at San Agustin seemed really well-rehearsed," Sam noted.

Poke glanced his way.

"The I.P.U. teams are stationed worldwide."

"I.P.U., sir?" Sam inquired.

"Interplanetary Phenomenon Units. Or 'Blue Berets,' as we sometimes call 'em," Poke said, lighting another cigarette. "They're basically crash-recovery teams that are above top-secret units—trained to secure, transport, and store crashed ships. They also have a small OSS counterintelligence units embedded within them—the black units." Poke turned to him. "For anyone who won't shut up."

Sam nodded, remembering the Blue Beret MPs at his crash site.

"You said Cape Girardeau was the first crash on our mainland?" Sam inquired.

Poke nodded.

"Yep, then, in the Battle of L.A. in '42, we shot at a bunch of 'em all night. Five civilians died—just from car crashes, 'cause they were looking up at the sky while driving, seeing the flying saucers right over the damn city. The Army launched over 1,300 explosive rounds, and we managed to down two, but the public never heard about those either."

Poke waved his cigarette for emphasis.

"One ditched in the ocean off the California coast. Rear Admiral Anderson was already out there, patrolling for Jap subs, and picked it up. The other one crashed in the San Bernardino Mountains—we got that one too. Outta those two ships, we recovered five more dead Greys."

He pulled hard on his cig and exhaled.

"It was after those recoveries that we realized—this was real. We had a no-shit alien surveillance situation on our hands. General Marshall set up the IPU teams, and now they are peppered all over the world... just in case. So the public never sees 'em because, frankly, we still don't know what the damn aliens want with us."

Sam nodded, gazing out at the vast mesa in the distance, thinking about Catherine. Wondering what she would say when the day finally came—when he could tell her the truth of what was happening all around her.

Poke had promised him a tour today that he'd never forget. Sam was curious. The jeep roared northbound, kicking up a high plume of dust along the recently graded highway. Poke had mentioned they were heading into Apache territory, and he had a job for Sam that would require Sam to do some translation.

"You know anything about Colonel Scanlon?!" Poke shouted over the rumble.

"Not really, sir! I met him once when I was translating at the Trinity test," Sam called back. "And I only spent a few minutes with him at the San Agustin crash."

"Well, he apparently liked you!" Poke shouted. "That's why you're coming with me today."

Sam nodded as Poke continued.

"Back in 1940, Scanlon led an expedition to where we're heading now. Top-secret at the time. It was called *the Lake Muroc Expedition.* You heard of it?"

Sam shook his head.

"No, sir."

Poke suddenly turned off the dirt highway onto another dirt road marked with an arrow sign: *Apache Nation. Dulce, New Mexico, 20 miles.*

Poke pointed to the huge mountain ahead and yelled over the banging dirt road and engine noise,

"Mount Archuleta! You ever been?"

"No, sir."

After a short distance, Poke turned into a ranch nestled at the base of the massive mesa that rose eight thousand feet above them. The ranch stretched over a great distance, with hundreds of cattle grazing in various areas. The major steered the jeep up a tall, grassy knoll that stair-stepped up the mesa. As the jeep cleared the top of the second hump, they approached two dead cows lying in the grass.

He shut off the engine, and immediately, Sam winced at a chemical smell that seemed to come directly from the two cadavers.

Poke got out, covering his mouth as he spoke, pointing at the dead cows.

"An Apache rancher called my group this morning and told us he had two more mutilated."

Poke walked near the first cadaver as Sam followed.

"Take a look and tell me what you see."

Sam's eyes watered, but he could tell the smell wasn't bleach. Instead, it had a non-natural, medicinal chemical scent. The cows had clearly been dissected, with many parts removed. Gone were the eyes, tongue, and several vital organs, including the testicles and what appeared to be the entire reproductive area. But what struck Sam as strange was that there wasn't a single drop of blood—none on the cows or even on the dirt and surrounding area. The cadavers seemed sterilized and cleaned, which was all incongruous to Sam.

As he knelt to get a closer look at the eye sockets, he saw that there were no slice marks or gouging, which would have been required to remove the eyes. Besides the lack of any evidence of a knife blade or scalpel, the remaining skin of the eye socket appeared to be cauterized—heated to an extreme temperature, as if to seal the wound.

Sam suddenly felt faint and slowly stood, looking over at the other cadaver. He stepped toward it, catching a small pocket of fresh air, and took a breath as he proceeded. Kneeling, he stared closely at strange suction-cup-like tracks nearby—footprints of a sort he didn't recognize.

"Okay, that's all you get. Let's get outta here!" Poke yelled, and they retreated to the jeep and quickly pulled away. Poke allowed the jeep to idle as they coasted down the large grassy knoll back to the highway.

When Sam felt himself starting to breathe again, he spat out the side, attempting to rid his mouth of the aftertaste of the chemical cloud they had just escaped. Poke did the same, then looked over at Sam, who seemed flushed and disturbed.

"Well?!" Poke shouted as they rumbled back onto the dirt highway toward the end of the huge mesa ahead. "What stood out to you?"

Sam shook his head as if trying to reset the strangeness he felt.

"What happened to the blood, sir?" Sam asked.

Poke looked over and nodded.

"What else?!" he shouted.

"Well, those were strange footprints around the second one!" Sam said.

Poke nodded again and passed Sam two cigarettes.

"Light one for me, will ya?"

Sam lit a cigarette and passed it to the major, then lit one for himself. They drove in silence up the dirt road, smoking and clearing their minds. The unimproved road leading up the mesa was so rough that both men held onto the windscreen of the jeep as they climbed. It was another ten minutes of extremely rough road before Poke stopped next to a small wooden shack.

Sitting at a table near the shack were two men, playing cards and smoking. They wore rancher clothing, but Sam knew they weren't ranchers. He had a sense about them, just as he had two days before with the aggressive redheaded captain who had commandeered his crash site. *Operators.*

The two men looked up when the jeep arrived and stood quickly, dropping their cigarettes. Poke shut off the engine.

"At ease, gentlemen. How's everything going?"

"Good, sir. Real good," the larger man said.

The smaller one opened the shack door and stepped inside. Sam immediately heard a low rumble and felt the ground below him shake slightly. A moment later, the ground seemed to give way beneath him. He looked up and saw Poke snicker as they descended, shack and all.

"It's how we bring in supplies," Poke said, half-smiling.

Sam looked to see the other two men watching him, and he knew they were special operators. He had dealt with these types in the war and had seen them kill Nazis with no mercy. They had that look in their eyes—an expression Sam recognized from high-security situations, as if they would kill him if he so much as hinted at speaking about what he was witnessing.

The platform was roughly twenty yards in diameter, and a moment later, it stopped in a below-ground hangar. Sam followed Poke off the platform, and one second later, the pad lifted again with both operators, the shack and jeep on board. Sam watched, amazed, as it slid back into place above them on huge hydraulic arms.

He finally looked over at Major Poke, who watched him with slight amusement. Poke nodded for Sam to look to the side. Sam turned—and gasped!

He stared at what seemed to be an endless tunnel, with vehicles moving about and military personnel coming and going to invisible side rooms and corridors. The tunnel had to be forty feet high and wide, and he felt like he had entered a busy anthill.

"Hop on," Poke said, pointing to what looked like a military golf cart. Sam boarded, and the machine glided down the tunnel. Sam was perplexed that an engine could be so quiet. Poke noted his astonishment.

"It's electric. We can't have motorized vehicles down here in the tunnels, it makes the tunnel too smoky."

Poke accelerated, keeping the cart on a painted yellow stripe the same width as the vehicle. Sam was still trying to reset his brain to the physical space that had been created around him. Even as they raced forward, he still could not see the end of the tunnel.

"We are below Mount Archuleta, and you're on level one," Poke said as he drove along. "I was ordered to bring you here by Colonel Scanlon, who thinks you might be a good fit."

Poke slowed and turned down an empty corridor with two MPs on either side. Both saluted as he passed between them.

"Good morning, gentlemen!" Poke yelled as he continued driving ahead into a darkened corridor that Sam could not see the end of.

A few moments later, he slowed and stopped in front of yet another corridor that was dimly lit. Poke took a breath as Sam looked into the darkened space. There was a dusty smell now, as if this area of the tunnel system had been neglected or unused. Poke produced a flashlight from the side compartment of the vehicle and handed it to Sam. He grabbed one for himself and stepped off the cart.

"Let's walk," Poke said, and the two men used their flashlights to illuminate a dusty corridor with cobwebs on the walls, several layers thick. Sam felt like he was on the set of a strange Dr. Weird show.

He walked, perplexed, staring at the walls of this new corridor, which had large flat screens mounted every few feet. Sam had never seen anything like them. They couldn't be TVs, as there was no depth for the tubes required like his TV at home. These were black, razor-thin, and huge! And there were more gadgets mounted on the walls in various places. Sam could see thin metal sheets with some form of writing on them. Just then, it dawned on him that all the large flat screens had a lavender glow to them—almost imperceptible! They—had—power somehow?!

Sam looked over at Poke, who waved his cigarette at everything they were walking by.

"In 1940, Scanlon was only a lieutenant colonel when he was tasked with finding a site for developing atomic weapons in secrecy."

Poke stopped and handed out cigarettes. Both men lit up and stepped off again, deeper into the dry, cobweb-and-dust-infested cave. Ahead, in the far distance, Sam's flashlight illuminated what appeared to be lumps on the floor.

"Scanlon put together a crack team made up of surveyors, geologists, several cavers—what we call spelunkers today—as well as a biologist and a couple of sharpshooters, along with two pilots. The entire team was handpicked by Scanlon and were battle-tested as soldiers and fighters outside of their specialties. And it was fortunate that he picked them so well."

Poke's flashlight now illuminated the first hump that Sam had seen before, and the two men stared down. It took Sam a moment to parse what lay before him. He finally realized he was staring at the skeletal remains of an Apache warrior.

What-in-the-hell?! he thought, looking up quickly at Poke and then back down.

The warrior was still adorned in traditional Apache wardrobe from the 1800s. Sam had studied Indian history in America and had been to many museums in the Four Corners area as he grew up. No Indian wore this type of clothing anymore.

Around the warrior were scattered old ammunition and a Winchester repeater rifle, which still appeared to be in perfect condition but was covered in dust. In the warrior's left hand was a bone-handled knife, and on his hip was still strapped a Colt pistol!

Part of the man's chest bones looked charred, as if they had been hit by some form of—a blowtorch, Sam thought. He finally looked up at Poke, who continued his story, waving his flashlight beam across the many layers of cobwebs and technology.

"So, the Army intentionally left this wing of the facility untouched since Scanlon's team found it. When his team first dropped into these tunnels, they were full of skeletal remains like this. Clearly, a massive fight had taken place."

"Who were they fighting, sir?" Sam asked.

Poke looked at him and raised his eyebrows, motioning for Sam to walk deeper into the cave. Sam took one last look at the destroyed warrior and stepped ahead as Poke followed behind him. Sam could see more humps in the great distance and proceeded toward them.

"Hey, take a minute and look in here," Poke said, motioning to a room carved out just off to the side.

Sam entered the room and was again struck dumb. The side room to the main tunnel was cavernous, with what looked like white metal lab tables and large flat screens attached to cables on the walls. Sam's mind raced. He recognized none of it. Even the Nazi rooms he had seen in top-secret bunkers at the end of the war had no technology like this.

Next to the flat screens were tiny sets of thin cables flowing down to what appeared to be typewriter-style keyboards—the type just developed for use against the Germans. But the ones in front of him seemed to have been there for centuries, Sam guessed. There were layers and layers of cobwebs and dust on everything.

Adding even more confusion were the large silvery sheets between the flat screens. Like dull aluminum foil, they were covered in some form of writing—yet not in English. The letters and symbols reminded Sam of the cuneiform plates he had studied in linguistics school, which were from ancient tablets found in Iraq.

But what Sam had studied was not printed on metal! His mind raced.

If this was ancient writing and had been here for as long as the dust indicated, then what country had the technology to create it back then? How could a highly advanced form of printing like that in front of him be covered in dust?! How could all these technological things in this room be ancient? Who put them here?

Nothing made sense.

Adding to Sam's confusion were the stools in front of the workstations, which appeared too small for an adult and more suited for a kid-sized human.

And all of this technology had to be hundreds of years old, just from the cobwebs and dust that appeared inches deep in places.

What in the world? Sam thought. *This stuff looks untouched for maybe centuries.*

"How long—?" Sam started to say when Poke cut him off.

"At least a thousand years, if not more, is what our archaeological experts have told us," Poke said.

Sam's head was reeling.

"Wait, so all this gear was here?" Sam asked.

"Yes, long before the Apache battle. Maybe as much as 50,000 years ago, according to one of our scientists. Scanlon ordered an archaeologist to join his team on the 1940 expedition down here, and that scientist dated this Apache battle to around 1870. At that point, Scanlon's team had been here a full three weeks, clearing out every bit of this type of hardware. The military was astonished by the technology, and the pressure was on to collect all of it, as they might never come back to this cave system."

Sam nodded and noticed a blinking light ahead and approached to see a dust-covered cable coming out of the lower floor... and the damn light was blinking! Light was actually coming through the end of the cable!

"What in the hell?" Sam whispered. "What is this thing, and where is this power coming from?"

"From below us," Poke said evenly.

Sam stared, perplexed.

"Below us?"

Poke nodded.

"As Scanlon's team collected more artifacts, they realized there were more levels below them. That's when Scanlon's boys started venturing deeper. And the walls continued to get more sophisticated in design as they got lower with each new level."

Sam stared, holding his forehead, astonished at the technology.

"Come on," Poke said.

They departed the cavernous room and continued down the darkened tunnel.

"Scanlon's team back in 1940 eventually pulled out forty or so Apache skeletons and tons of repeater rifles and Colt pistols—all in perfect working condition. Not to mention roomfuls of the type of stuff you just saw. They were basically collecting everything."

Sam stared.

"Were the Germans already here or..." Sam started to ask when his flashlight lit up a skeletal remain in front of him.

He slowed, his flashlight beam flowing over the chest of what looked like a small boy, covered in dust, with an Apache arrow still impaled in its chest bones.

Sam winced.

But then something wasn't right—it had an oversized, elongated skull. Finally, his flashlight illuminated the arm bones down to the hand bones—which only had four long fingers.

Sam's heart went into his throat. He felt himself hold his breath as the realization washed over him. He looked up at Poke, who simply stared back, watching him put it together.

"Oh my God," Sam whispered.

Poke nodded as he pulled on his cig.

"That power you just asked about is their power," Poke said, exhaling smoke off to the side, still watching Sam.

"You mean below us, sir?" Sam asked.

Poke nodded.

"There are six more levels below us in this complex—at least, that we know of. There may be more below that."

Sam held up his hand.

"Wait, sir, you're saying they created these caves?" Sam asked.

Poke nodded.

"The complex extends all the way below the Archuleta Mesa for four more miles."

Sam's head was exploding.

"Seven levels that are four miles long each?" He whispered in astonishment.

Poke nodded somberly.

"Scanlon's team was attacked."

"What?!" Sam whispered tersely.

Poke slowly nodded and illuminated the Grey skeleton at their feet.

"This one... was the last one the Apache fought in the 1870 battle."

Then Poke waved his flashlight beam further into the corridor, illuminating many more Grey skeletons.

"And all those down there fought Scanlon's men only seven years ago."

"In 1940?" Sam inquired.

"That's correct... the full pitched-battle took place right here."

Sam followed Poke toward the heap of Grey alien skeletons ahead. They illuminated the pile, and Sam wanted to throw up.

"Right before Scanlon battled the Greys," Poke continued, "his team had spent three full weeks in the tunnels, collecting this technology. They had heard sounds and knew someone was watching them, so they proceeded down to the first section of level three—then all hell broke loose." Poke said, gesturing with his cig.

"The troops began hearing what sounded like women and children screaming. This went on for several hours until they realized it was a recording. But still—who had made that recording? And who was playing it back to them? Several soldiers were getting rattled, and Scanlon gave the order to return to level one base camp. Immediately, the sounds stopped—almost as if whoever was watching them had heard the order as well."

Poke pointed above him.

"As the troops retreated to the upper levels, two hardened soldiers insisted on finding out who was messing with them. Those two stayed behind and went further into level three. As they got lower, it became excessively hot and humid with the walls dripping with moisture, and the two men could barely breathe, having gone that far down. They came upon a room with a thick, circular door, and heard whispering and clicking noises beyond it. When they quietly peered around the door, they saw at least fifty Greys working around lab-type tables doing what appeared to be medical dissection on human cadavers of all sizes."

Sam stared in shock as Poke continued.

"The soldiers managed to hold fast and then realized that up on the flat-screens behind the Greys was a video image of the American team base-camp on level one. The two soldiers then knew that these Greys had seen and heard everything the troops had done for the past month in every part of the caves. The two men were so terrified they couldn't breathe and slowly worked their way back from the door when one of them accidentally dropped his gun, which clattered loudly. The Greys immediately attacked, grabbing one soldier as the other fled. The escaped soldier could hear his buddy screaming and firing behind him. The free one ran like hell with a group of Greys just behind him, whispering and clicking as they got closer while he was running up to the first level."

Sam was transfixed as Poke took another drag.

"In desperation, the soldier began firing behind him as he ran, screaming his head off, and this alerted the base camp on level one. As he approached his base camp, still running and firing in complete darkness, his team could see and hear his muzzle flashes and they began firing in his direction. Their bullets whizzed by his head until he reached them. They were all in chaos, yelling at him, 'What was wrong with him?! And why had he made them wait?!' Just then, one soldier near him yelled, 'What the hell is that?!' pointing at the many Greys approaching in the darkness. That's when the confrontation escalated. That was the last pitched battle with the Greys in 1940."

Sam stared, swept by all the new information.

"Where did they come from? Were they living here, or—"

"They still do," Poke said, cutting him off.

Sam stared completely bewildered.

"They're... still... okay, sir... uh," Sam said, holding up his hand. "So, all this technology is theirs?" he asked.

Poke nodded again, watching Sam piece it together.

"So, sir, you're saying the Greys have been here for millennia?"

Poke shrugged and exhaled.

"As far as we can tell, yes."

Sam grabbed his forehead, staring at the pile of Grey skeletons. Some of them had clearly been blasted with bullets, as ribs and leg bones showed signs of bullet holes. The cave walls behind the heap of skeletons had bullet holes and ricochet marks.

Poke gestured with his cig.

"There were many American soldiers who perished right where you're standing. Their bodies were retrieved, but Scanlon left the alien bodies right where they were. As a warning to them."

Poke waved his flashlight beam further in front of them, where a single skeleton still held a small, silvery metal device. The gun-shaped object had a small handle but a wide end on it, resembling a garden hose sprayer. The sides of the device had a dim, blue-phosphorescent glow.

"Remember the Apache warrior's burnt chest back there?" Poke said, thumbing over his shoulder behind them.

Sam nodded, and Poke pointed ahead of them to the phosphorescent metal piece in the skeleton's hand.

"That gun is out of power, but the Greys used those against our men seven years ago. It essentially throws a bolt of lightning and leaves a molten mass on a human body where it hits. Hence, the poor Apache bastard back there. The Greys used them in the 1870s battle against the Apache as well. It burns you down to your core."

"So what happened at the battle here?" Sam asked.

Poke exhaled.

"Well, seven years ago, Scanlon saw the Greys approaching with their lighted guns, and he ordered his team to shut off all their lights and stay still. The team trained their weapons on the approaching Greys in complete darkness. Each glowing gun became an aiming point for the soldiers as they waited for Scanlon's order to fire. Scanlon waited until the Greys were only twenty feet away and pointed to open fire. The soldiers blasted every Grey holding a weapon. Only a couple of them managed to fire back, and when they did, anything caught in the path of those bolts was obliterated—except for the white metal tables. The moment Scanlon realized the alien guns had a weakness, he yelled to take cover behind the tables and keep firing. Three hours later, every Grey that had stayed to fight was dead. Only one tall Grey was captured after it had dismembered one of the men. The soldiers attempted to interrogate it by slapping and punching it over several hours, but the tall Grey said nothing to them, and they eventually shot it to death." Poke said, gesturing with his cig.

Sam shook his head, overwhelmed with all the information. Poke exhaled smoke and continued.

"Scanlon was a true leader here in the complex. He only lost a handful of men compared to the many Greys they killed that day. But his accomplishments will never see the light of day—as it was all top secret seven years ago and has remained so."

Sam shook his head as Poke chuckled slightly and continued.

"Can you imagine what the religious folks on this planet would do if they realized aliens had been living here for thousands of years—long before Christ, Muhammad, Buddha, and the rest of them?"

Sam was struck dumb.

"Had enough yet, Boyd?" Poke said smiling.

Sam shrugged and half-smiled.

"It's a whole lot, sir, but the way my week has been going, why the hell not."

Poke chuckled at Sam's humility.

"Come on, let's get some lunch, as that's only the start of it."

Sam walked next to the huge man.

"So, how many are below us, sir?"

"We're not positive. They control levels four through seven."

Sam contemplated.

"And each level is four miles long and spider-webbed with corridors like this?" Sam pressed.

Poke nodded.

"Yep, and perhaps as many as two thousand of them are down there... we don't know for certain."

Sam nodded slowly.

"And the cattle we just saw mutilated... that's—"

Poke nodded, cutting him off.

"They use the blood for part of their diet," the major said, "but also all the glands... apparently, the pituitary and pineal glands release hormones they utilize."

Sam had a sense the story was going to get darker, and that Poke was trying to ease him into the big picture.

They passed by the Apache skeleton with the charred chest bones, and Sam imagined what it would be like to be an Apache warrior, hosing off an arrow toward an otherworldly creature, only to have the alien return fire with a lightning bolt, drilling right into the Apache's chest. Sam imagined the voltage lifting the warrior off the ground, then dropping the poor Apache in a lump of smoking, molten flesh. *Damn,* he thought.

When they reached the cart, a lieutenant and corporal were waiting. They both saluted as Poke and Sam approached.

"At ease, boys," Poke said, motioning back to Sam. "Captain Molin, Corporal Stone—I want you to say hello to Captain Sam Boyd."

The two nodded and smiled Sam's way.

"Welcome to Rio Arriba, Captain Boyd," Molin said.

Sam nodded.

"Sam, Captain Molin and Corporal Stone run DSD-3 here, which is the Dulce Security Division. They keep the Greys in place down low and make sure this base remains completely invisible to the outside world."

"We do our best, sir," Molin said, looking at Stone. "But Stony here knows we can only control them when they want to be controlled. Those suckers are elusive."

Everyone chuckled.

"Sir," Molin said. "The Apache chief, Mama Grande has let our man in town know that she's ready to talk."

Poke nodded.

"Tell her I said thank you, and we'll schedule that meeting for next week,"

"Yes, sir," Molin replied, saluting again, and both men departed in their cart.

Poke watched them drive away and then turned to Sam.

"So, Colonel Scanlon let me know, he wanted to offer you a position leading one of the IPU teams at Camp Cale in Durango, Colorado. The IPU's main mission is to recover crashed disc-craft and their crews."

Sam nodded, assuming he was being chosen again because of his ability to communicate with the Greys.

"The Inter-Planetary Unit's job, as you will see, Sam, only comes into play when a saucer has crashed. Your regular job would be here at Dulce, with DSD-3 in charge of Molin and his crew."

Sam nodded, trying to take it all in.

"There's a lot of negotiation happening with the Greys at this facility, but also with Chief Mama Grande of the Apache. Colonel Scanlon highly recommended you for this super-secret post to the president."

Sam nodded again, and Poke knew it was a lot, all at once.

"You think it over, Sam, and there's no pressure, but you have to give me an answer right this minute," Poke said with a sly smile.

Sam chuckled.

"Well, yes, sir... tentatively."

Poke nodded and lit a cig.

"I know you'll need to talk this over with your wife."

Sam nodded. He would have to think things through with Catherine, despite the interesting story of the caves and the Apache battles.

"I'm interested in the IPU job," Sam said. "I just need to discuss moving with Catherine."

"Perfect," Poke said. "I'll pass that along. And by the way, that position requires at least a major, so Scanlon has let me know that you're getting an immediate promotion if you take that position."

Sam slowly nodded.

"Yes, sir."

Poke took a long drag, looking at him.

"Looks like you won't have to call me *sir* much longer, Sam," he said with a wink and a snicker. He looked around and waved his cig.

"Probably a good decision to take the IPU position. And if you work here in between crash recoveries, you can pretty much write your own ticket in the future," Poke said, suddenly looking at his watch.

"Hell, we gotta get you on a plane back to Roswell, as General Twining has asked you to monitor an alien they have in detainment there. And from what I gathered, it's not like the others you've seen."

"How do you mean, sir?" Sam asked.

"Well, all I know is that a female Master Sergeant is the only person the little alien will communicate with, and supposedly, it has no mouth or nose or nothing." Poke said, leaning back. "Twining doesn't trust the Master Sergeant is translating correctly."

Sam nodded and wondered if it was Eileen's friend Matilda MacElroy. She had mentioned that she was a master sergeant and that she wanted to introduce Sam to her.

Sam looked back at Poke.

"Yes, sir," Sam said. "I'll certainly help out if I can."

They hopped in the golf cart, and Sam was again amazed at the silence and speed of the tiny vehicle. He really liked Poke and the possibility of working at a facility near him, but the story of the Greys dissecting humans was completely disturbing. Sam also sensed Poke was holding back an even darker secret about the Greys and this deep underground Dulce cave system.

He knew the major had let him in gently so far and still had not shown the full hand of his knowledge about this ancient base—and the darker thing that was truly disturbing.

The cavernous tunnels seemed to go on forever. And as they drove, Sam also sensed something else in that cave system. He couldn't put his finger on it... an evil within—that he could feel all around him—like a beast that seemed to occupy the facility.

Chapter Thirty-Six

A huge desert moon illuminated the lumbering Dodge 6x6 Army troop transport, motoring slowly in the sweltering 88-degree early morning.

It passed the huge B-29 Super-fortresses, heavily guarded and poised for a quick departure along the Roswell Army Airbase runway. The canvas top on the rear of the 2.5-ton troop transport had been removed, and the night air was calm for the six Roswell hospital personnel swaying on wooden benches in the back of the enormous truck.

A corporal drove while Damon Slepher sat in the passenger seat, casually smoking a cigarette. He was back in his no-nametag captain's uniform, and all was quiet at the airbase as the long truck came to a stop, shutting down next to a taxiway. Bright stars twinkled above the desert landscape, and the hospital personnel remained quiet—not speaking to each other—on orders not to do so. Besides, they were all exhausted and anxious.

It had been a tumultuous whirlwind at Roswell Army Airfield, as the base had secretly hosted the recovery of two separate species of dead aliens from a total of three crashed ships. Autopsies had been performed on both the Grey and Orange species. The alien cadavers and their ships had been removed from Roswell under

378

the tightest security.

They all heard the transport as it turned downwind and lined up for landing. Moments later, the Beech-18 turned off the far end of the runway and came up the taxiway toward Eileen and the six-by truck full of her hospital staff. Slepher stepped out and yelled to everyone in the back.

"Let's go, folks! Line up for boarding."

Eileen thought about her boyfriend Glenn as she lined up with the others, holding their overnight bags. She still hadn't been allowed to make any phone calls.

A moment later, a Jeep with a corporal arrived and quickly parked by the six-by.

"Remember, folks—no talking between yourselves until after your debriefs at Alamogordo!" Slepher commanded.

Several "*Yes, sirs*" were heard, and Slepher turned to face Sam's plane as it pulled in. The aircraft propellers were left running as the door hatch was opened and a rolling staircase was put in place.

Sam exited the plane carrying his satchel, and Slepher yelled,

"Attention on deck!" as Sam descended the stairs.

The roar of the engines was deafening as Slepher, again with no nametag, gestured for Sam to approach the waiting jeep. This time, Sam passed with only a stare as Slepher held his flippant gaze, his eyes saying,

What are you gonna do about it, Boyd?

Sam walked to the jeep. Eileen saw him and wanted to yell out to him, but she was under such strict orders not to talk that she figured she'd catch up with him shortly. Boy, did she ever have a story to tell him!

Sam stepped into the jeep as the six hospital staff climbed the staircase to the airplane, with Slepher just behind. For a moment, Sam thought he saw Eileen—his cousin—in that group, but everything was happening so fast, and the roar of the propellers was so loud that he let it go.

Perhaps if it was her, he would catch up with her in the next couple of days, as he was slated to be in Roswell for a day or so. He had his jeep driver hold while he put his bag in the back and lit a cigarette. He looked back at the nurses entering the airplane.

It's 4 a.m., for Christ's sake, he thought. *That is a strange time for a group of nurses and orderlies to be departing.*

He exhaled smoke but didn't see Eileen, who was staring directly at him through the tiny windows. She had raised a hand to the window, hoping he would see. She watched as Sam hopped into the passenger seat of the jeep and nodded at his driver. A moment later, the jeep pulled away.

After the week's tumultuous events, she would have welcomed an evening with Sam. The other hospital staff took their seats, and Slepher whispered in the ear of the blonde stewardess as he gestured toward the cockpit. She nodded and motioned for him to proceed. Slepher stepped through the curtain into the cockpit.

"Evening, sir," he said to the aging major at the controls. "These letters, they go to my team at Alamogordo."

The pilot, still wearing his headset, nodded as Slepher laid a thick packet of letters bound by a rubber band on the empty co-pilot seat and tightened the seatbelt over them. He gave a quick thumbs-up to the pilot and departed. A moment later, he smiled at the cute blonde stewardess and exited the aircraft. By the time Slepher took the passenger seat on the six-by-six, the twin-engine was already taxiing for takeoff.

"Corporal, hold one for that bird to get off the runway," he said.

"Yes, sir!" the Corporal replied.

Slepher offered a cigarette, and the Corporal took one.

"Thank you, sir."

They both lit up, and Slepher had a passing thought about how beautiful the first lieutenant had been. He knew she was Eileen Fanton, and he thought about the wild way life presented missed opportunities.

Unfortunately for Eileen, clear back on Monday the 6th, at lunchtime, an operative from Slepher's team had secretly monitored her in the Officers Club, whispering to a civilian man named Glenn Dennis, who ran a mortuary in the town of Roswell. Eileen had handed Dennis several small, hand-drawn paper notes over that lunch date. Slepher had been there too when she was commandeered to help the doctors with the autopsies on the Saturday when it all began.

Slepher had casually smoked a cigarette, leaning against a wall among all the swarming MPs on that first day of the cadavers arriving at Roswell Army Hospital. He blended right in, wearing his no-nametag captain's uniform, and watched it all unfold. He saw the tall major, Dr. Rea, guide Eileen into the operating room, and Slepher remained there for the entire evolution of the autopsy. He noted how Eileen, the doctors, and the cameraman would depart to the bathrooms to get sick and return to their autopsy.

At one point on that Saturday afternoon, the mortuary guy, Glenn Dennis, had somehow gained access to the emergency room hallway and was warned by Eileen, under her breath, to leave before he got into trouble. Slepher had watched, amused, as Dennis hadn't understood what all the excitement was about. A moment later, he was confronted by a yelling major, who had the MPs carry the terrified man out of the hospital and escort him off the base.

Slepher watched not only Eileen and the doctors, but the entire medical staff, as did his team embedded within the MPs throughout the Roswell base on those infamous days. Slepher had arrived on the Saturday before General Twining's entourage would arrive the following Monday, and Slepher had the nod of the

General to do whatever was necessary for national security purposes.

Now, under the enormous moon, he pulled on his cigarette and contemplated the hospital crew heading to Alamogordo. How all six of them had already been ordered to write a quick note to their kin—to let them know they were on a special assignment and to not mention in their correspondence what base they were writing from, as it was classified. All had completed their letters, which were now on the co-pilot's seat.

Upon landing at Alamogordo, thirty minutes from now, the six would be met by Slepher's team of three MPs, who had already driven the 100 miles to Alamogordo earlier in the day. His team would collect the envelope packet from the pilot and escort the hospital staff to the secret debrief bunker. Slepher envisioned how the six hospital staff, who had all worked hands-on with the moldy alien cadavers, would stroll behind the three MPs later tonight toward a distant building just beyond the runway. All the staff were as traumatized by their hands-on experiences as Eileen Fanton had been. This had been in his report to Twining.

Twining had studied Slepher's written briefs covering the entire hospital staff. The general knew it would be extremely tough for the young nurses and orderlies to hold their tongues for long. Seeing an alien was life-changing, no doubt. But touching a dead one was an imprint that would have to be discussed at some point.

"Okay, these six go on to Alamogordo," Twining had said, and that was enough for Slepher.

Now, watching the bird departing to the west, Slepher exhaled smoke toward the stars and thought about all six, walking to the debrief building at Alamogordo. A peaceful walk in the desert. Not so bad.

Slepher knew as they approached the debrief bunker that the hospital staff would be asked to halt in place while the MPs conferred. The lead MP and the other two would come together in a circle and whisper to each other, as the six hospital staff would wonder what was happening.

A moment later, the MPs would turn simultaneously, raising their Colt .45 pistols as they aimed at the group.

The shock to Eileen and the others would be so extreme that they would just stare, unable to grasp the sinister horror of their own final moments.

The thunder of the pistols and the physical shock of the first bullet exploding through Eileen's chest took her breath away, as did the bullets hitting the other five.

In those quick seconds, as they were all being murdered, none had a chance to scream as the second and third bullets came in rapid succession. Headshots were then administered to all six while they lay prone.

A moment later, a bulldozer appeared from the opposite side of the bunker and slid the remains into a previously dug trench, grading the spot, as the three operatives picked up spent cartridges and replaced their sidearms in their holsters.

Slepher knew that about a week from now, the families of the six dead would receive their children's final letters from an APO in England. When those families replied to those letters, a military reply letter would eventually arrive, stamped *"Deceased,"* telling of the unfortunate military plane crash in England and that their loved ones had perished in the line of duty, serving their country. *Heroes.*

Slepher knew there was no way for the families of the deceased to find out what happened on distant military installations.

He watched the blinking taillight moving west, taking First Lieutenant Eileen Fanton toward her destiny with his team. This was his job, and she had shown herself to be a risk to national security. Therefore, she deserved what she had coming.

He flicked his lit cigarette out into the desert and sucked his teeth, thinking about Sam Boyd coming off the plane and giving him that stare. Then he breathed deeply.

"Corporal," he commanded calmly to the young soldier at the wheel. "Let's roll."

As they pulled away, Slepher's satisfaction came from his position of having access to information on everyone at the Roswell installation. He studied personal files as a matter of pride.

His depraved half-smile came with knowing his operatives would coldly execute that female lieutenant and that Eileen Fanton was none other than Sam Boyd's cousin.

F ive minutes later, the corporal had dropped Slepher off near Base Ops in total darkness.

Slepher popped a Zippo and lit a cig as he strolled in the moonlight along the tarmac toward the flight line.

He checked his watch and looked behind him as a black sedan pulled up alongside him. He climbed into the back seat and closed the door as the car pulled away.

Sitting across from Slepher in the backseat was Werner Von Braun.

In the front seat were the driver and an older man in a black suit and black flat-brimmed hat. The man didn't turn around, but Slepher could see the large scar on the side of his head and knew the alien very well.

Aspelsin was the human representative for the Draco-Reptilians, a space-conquering horde who had approached the Nazis back in 1933 and signed the first off-world treaties with Hitler and his SS. They had gifted the Nazis a few antigravity ships as early as 1940 to begin off-world flights to the Moon and Mars.

As far as Slepher could tell, it was the Reptilians who continuously dictated the terms of their agreements with the Nazis, as the Reptilians had all the technology and know-how, and the Nazis were eager to establish a space colony.

Von Braun had introduced Slepher to Aspelsin in 1939, when Aspelsin was providing alien technology to the Nazi SS in exchange for human slaves. Slepher knew the Reptilians fed on humans provided by Von Braun, and the Reptilians needed a steady supply. Slepher, as a young man in the OSS, had been sent by future CIA head Allen Dulles to determine what agreements the Nazis had brokered with the Reptilians. The Americans wanted that alien technology, and Slepher could begin the bartering process with Aspelsin.

Now that the war was over and Germany had no more humans to negotiate with, Aspelsin had suddenly shown a renewed interest in meeting with Slepher. The car pulled out and drove slowly in the moonlight around the flight line, where the now world-famous 509th Composite Group kept its B-29 Super-fortresses loaded and ready to deliver their nuclear payload. The Enola Gay that incinerated Hiroshima was out there, along with twenty other birds.

Von Braun looked at Slepher and gestured to the flight line as he spoke in English, with his High German accent.

"You Americans won the battle, but we won the war."

Slepher pulled on his cig, understanding every nuance of the German language and mindset—a skill his contemporaries in the Office of Strategic Services admired. He replied and smiled as he did so.

"So you say, but who is still on the run?"

Von Braun blew off the comment.

"We just routed Admiral Byrd's entire Highjump invasion force before he ever reached the shore," Von Braun smiled. "It seems he had never been attacked by flying saucers before."

Slepher calmly smoked as Von Braun continued.

"Turned his entire armed flotilla around and made a hasty retreat, tail between his legs, back to New York."

Slepher smiled, not one to be intimidated.

"True," Slepher said. "But America still thinks it's the winner." He touched his temple with his cigarette hand. "You didn't change public opinion because Truman told America that the flotilla was a scientific expedition."

Von Braun stared at Slepher disdainfully and then laid out his threat.

"A flyover of the White House with some of our saucers will bring Truman to the negotiating table soon enough."

"Perhaps," Slepher said, ashing his cig out the window. "Truman will want the technology you have, and he'll do anything to get it."

Von Braun watched him, knowing there must be a catch.

Slepher exhaled out the window.

"But am I to understand that your labor force below the ice shelf is running just a little low?" Slepher said, smiling at Von Braun.

Von Braun was not amused, realizing Slepher had inside information as the young American continued.

"Perhaps you could use an influx of slave labor to speed up your off-world aims?" He raised his eyebrows at Von Braun and sucked his teeth.

Aspelsin gestured slightly in the front seat, and the driver slowed to a stop.

He spoke in his gravely whisper,

"We will create an agreement for the American president to sign. America will get some technology in exchange for allowing us to abduct humans when and where we please."

Slepher looked quickly at Von Braun, who stared back with a sly smile.

"Mr. Aspelsin, sir," Slepher said. "I might convince General Twining to sign that agreement. But, sir, the amount of labor that Herr Von Braun needs should not be in writing."

Aspelsin turned slightly and whispered,

"You propose to provide a labor force to help Germans in Antarctica?" Aspelsin confirmed.

Slepher took a deep drag and exhaled out the window.

"There are individuals in America I can contact who might provide a certain amount of slave labor to Antarctica, provided the right amount of technology comes our way. But this must never be in writing."

"So, you will work with me to provide those individuals?" Aspelsin inquired without looking back.

"I can do that, sir," Slepher said.

Aspelsin sat for a moment, then whispered.

"And certainly, you know that we would like a separate delivery of your young."

Slepher stared and noted Von Braun's slight smile his way. Caught in the devil's negotiation, Slepher pulled on his cigarette and answered while looking in disgust at Von Braun.

"Yes, sir, I can do that, provided you will give instructions on the technology you provide to us."

"Agreed," Aspelsin said without turning.

Slepher kept looking at Von Braun.

"Do you want them delivered to Dulce as before?" Slepher inquired.

Aspelsin nodded.

"Level four."

Slepher stared at Von Braun, knowing those abducted children would be eaten alive, as that was something the Truman administration had learned early on about the Draco. They had a thirst for human blood, and it was the young—*the veal*—they craved most. But those little ones brought a huge return in technology. And technology determined who was winning the space race.

"Yes, sir," Slepher said, tossing his cigarette out the window.

When he looked again, Von Braun was smiling at him.

"Your president will also allow German scientists to take the leading positions in all corporations in America," Von Braun interjected.

Slepher sucked his teeth and looked at his fingernails.

"When you can do your little flyover of the White House, only then will Truman come to the table regarding your scientists. Right now, your little victory with Byrd's flotilla is still a mystery to Truman, and he doesn't fear you because you are too far away down there in... Antarctica."

Von Braun glared back as Aspelsin cut in.

"That will change shortly, Mr. Slepher, with your help, of course," Aspelsin hissed in his gravelly whisper. "I'll be awaiting your first delivery of slave labor for Antarctica."

Slepher watched the side of Aspelsin's face for a moment and could see the scar moving. He exited the car with an arrogant wink at Von Braun, who feigned defeat. Von Braun watched the door close and eyed Slepher as he walked calmly away.

He knew the savvy young OSS man was intimately connected to the ruthless American Crime Syndicate and the new Majestic-12 group created by James Forrestal. Von Braun had a sense the new Majestic-12 group would go to any lengths to procure the powerful alien technology the Nazis already had. The Majestic-12 would ask Slepher to use his Mafia connections to acquire slave labor for Antarctica. In exchange, the Germans would promise to help America's fledgling space program.

But the entire promise would be a sham, Von Braun knew. The Breakaway Nazis in Antarctica had already strategized about this. The Germans hired by American space ventures like NASA would ensure that America would somehow be stymied in its scientific aims, always remaining many years behind the Germans.

The Breakaway Nazis were already making inroads to other planets with flying saucers created with the technology provided by Aspelsin's Reptilian race.

Von Braun stared out the window at the nuclear-equipped birds on the flight line. America was full of itself as the first to have atomic bombs, but Von Braun knew that the bigger prize was the conquest of space.

At that moment, as Slepher walked away in the moonlight, Von Braun was confident... the future of off-world conquest was firmly in German hands. His cohorts at Base 211, below the ice shelf in Antarctica, with Heinrich Himmler at the helm, were on the brink of seeding themselves deep into the solar system. They would soon establish the first colony at Aries-Prime on Mars and the first human moon base currently being built in the shape of a swastika.

Himmler's Breakaway Nazis in Antarctica had far surpassed the Americans in acquiring alien technology, and his Fourth Reich would be the first humans to move off-world.

S am had returned to Roswell after his Dulce tour and learned that all three crashes had been removed.

He was able to get two weeks off to help Catherine and the baby as they adjusted back into military life. He still had not heard a word from Eileen and hoped everything was okay.

On the 31st of July, he was escorted by the 509th Counterintelligence Officer, Snake Cavitt, to meet with General Twining. He was then introduced to Senior Master Sergeant Matilda MacElroy. Sam met her under extremely high security and liked her immediately. She had clearly been promoted from Master to Senior Master Sergeant, and that was a big deal.

According to Snake Cavitt, the lone surviving alien from the Mesa crash, thirty-five miles north of Roswell, had engaged MacElroy with telepathy during a medical check-up on the day of the crash recovery.

Since that first telepathy event, the doll-like alien would only communicate with MacElroy. General Twining didn't trust the young nurse and wanted Sam to monitor the next interview she was scheduled to do with the alien.

MacElroy was only twenty-three years old, with curly brown hair, and looked sharp in her Army Nurse's uniform. Sam already knew she was friends with his cousin, Eileen Fanton, as the two women were the only females assigned to the nuclear-equipped 509th bomb group. Sam was surprised by the four heavily armed O.S.S. operatives escorting her. They paused in the hallway, and Snake Cavitt gave Sam and Matilda a quick introduction.

"You're the youngest Senior Master Sergeant I've ever met," Sam said in a whisper. Matilda shrugged with a slight smile.

"Yes, sir, they promoted me so I could have a higher security clearance."

Sam nodded.

"Well, good luck with the interview. Perhaps we can chat afterward?"

Matilda nodded.

"Yes, sir, that would be swell," she whispered, then got a darker look.

"I haven't been able to get ahold of Lieutenant Fanton since the 11th of July."

Sam nodded, understanding that Eileen had informed Matilda that Sam was her cousin.

"Well, me either," Sam said, "but with all that's been going on, she might just be lying low. Get in there and good luck."

Matilda nodded. "Yes, sir, it was nice to meet you."

Sam nodded, watched her enter the interview room as the four operatives took up positions in the hallway.

Moments later, Sam followed General Twining into the monitoring room full of dignitaries. They were all watching Matilda and the alien through a one-way glass partition. The monitoring room was filled with cigar and cigarette smoke and already teeming with Bigs. Sam recognized several, including Secretary of the Army Air Force Stuart Symington, Generals Jimmy Doolittle, Curtis LeMay, as well as Hoyt Vandenberg and Lauris Norstad. But Sam was most shocked to see Charles Lindbergh in the room as well. Sam knew that the famous aviator was a consultant to Air Force Secretary Stuart Symington... but many Americans, including Sam, were disgruntled with the once-famous Lindbergh for his pro-German, anti-war stance prior to WWII.

Sam lit a cigarette and exhaled, letting it all go. Politics was not his thing. He wondered about his cousin Eileen. Why had she not answered her phone for three full weeks? He had tried her twice and gone by her apartment, only to see that her car was not there. Her new boyfriend, Glenn Dennis, ran the mortuary in town. That would be his next stop after this morning's interview.

Sam had met with General Nathan Twining an hour earlier and disliked him from the get-go. Having worked with so many generals, Sam had learned there were always two types: Listeners and Warmongers. Unlike Colonel Scanlon, whom Sam felt was a common man in a big position, Twining was all ego, and his fear-based approach was positively shoot-first and then proceed with whatever was left over. Twining had asked Sam about the San Agustin crash and what he had learned from the Grey he worked with at Los Alamos with Major Poke. Sam kept his answers curt and figured if the general wanted to know more, he would ask. Twining finally spoke about the upcoming interview.

"Well, we've got Nurse MacElroy, who is supposedly communicating with the alien we have in detainment. But I'm not certain she is reading that creature correctly, or even if at all. I want you to watch the interview and tell me if she's translating truthfully."

"Yes, sir," Sam replied. "And sir, that's if I can get the communication. Sometimes the aliens are able to direct their telepathy, so only the person they want to communicate with gets the information."

Twining seemed perturbed at this, and Sam sensed the general was also frustrated that a captain like Sam could communicate, but someone like himself, a general, was not allowed to.

Sam looked through the one-way partition glass at the interview room. It had a simple overstuffed living room chair—and sitting completely still in that chair—was an even stranger-looking alien than Sam's Grey at Los Alamos.

Its skin coloring was grey, but that's where the similarities diverged. Sam was not convinced he was staring at skin, more like a cloth-looking epidermis. The strange alien appeared to be about the size of a four-year-old, roughly forty-inches tall, and had three prehensile fingers on each hand and the same on each foot… yet with big black eyes that were not wrap-around like Sam's Grey had been. This one had no working mouth, nose, or ears. The dignitaries in the room were whispering about *"The Doll."*

It sat upright, ramrod straight, and did not move. Sam could not see any signs of life. That was until the door was opened by an MP, and in walked Matilda. The alien doll suddenly animated, coming to life, turning its head, and the energy between Matilda and the alien was clearly friendly. Sam could also tell telepathy was happening between those two… as Matilda put her hand to her heart and slightly bowed as if she had been paid a compliment. But Sam heard nothing in his head. Twining was right next to him, watching him.

"No, sir, nothing," Sam whispered, as the other Bigs were also noting Sam, wondering if he could read the alien communication.

Sam knew that the goal was for Matilda to get a signature from the alien, agreeing to specific terms the American government wanted. Matilda then produced an envelope and placed it on the table between her and the alien. Everyone watched as the two seemed to share a form of communication. One of the Bigs in the room said aloud,

"That S.O.B. ain't gonna sign our agreement."

Sam watched in fascination as Matilda apprehensively nodded to the alien. She then turned with a resigned look at the one-way glass, and all in the gallery knew she had been denied. She turned back to the alien and slowly picked up the envelope, placing it in her uniform pocket.

At that moment, Sam saw General Twining raise a small walkie-talkie and press the transmitter.

"Go!" he commanded.

Sam suddenly heard the door to the interview room slam open and watched in horror through the partition as five heavily armed MPs barged into the room, followed by a doctor rolling what appeared to be an electroshock apparatus. Two MPs rushed the tiny alien and held it down in the chair, while two other MPs held Matilda to her chair. The final MP, armed with a rifle, pointed it at the head of the alien, holding it only six inches away from its face, while the doctor wheeled the cart behind the alien's chair. Sam could see Matilda watching, terrified, as the doctor hastily slid the electroshock collar on the alien's head.

"Clear!" was yelled, and the two MPs holding down the alien's arms released just as the high voltage surged through the alien for a full twenty seconds, until the alien slumped in the chair. The heavy-duty voltage was repeated to Sam's dismay several more times. Finally, they stopped, and the alien's tiny frame continued to slump sideways in the chair, appearing lifeless to Sam.

Just then, Matilda was led out of the room by the MPs, and Sam could see she was fighting tears amidst her terror.

Sam had to endure several of the generals whispering,

"Glad we fried that little S.O.B. with its big eyes and that weird, goddamn stare."

Later, it took Sam a long walk on the tarmac outside to shake the utter incompetence happening at the top level. He now understood a little of where it was all sourcing from.

Fear.

The thing that was growing, that already had its hooks in the top brass.

Vyla opened her eyes as she heard Dah opening the bathroom door and saw her enter the kitchen.

She felt the hot tears on her face as she slowly got to her feet. She was deeply saddened by Eileen's murder and the innocent staff who worked so hard with her. In addition, she knew Sam would never find out why she disappeared. Making matters worse were the many questions she had regarding Matilda MacElroy as well. She would study more about Matilda one day, just to honor her.

She was due to fly back to S-4 in a few hours, and she felt a tinge of fear regarding flying the Widow. She reminded herself that it would only be a simulator to begin with. Then she thought about that. She was going to learn to fly a simulator of an actual off-world ship! Terrified or not, she was intrigued. But then, a dark feeling swept over her. She couldn't get a handle on exactly what it was. Just that it had to do with Yen Jee.

Something about her was simply not on the level, and perhaps—Vyla thought—there were many things about Yen Jee... not on the level.

Chapter Thirty-Seven

Tom saw it clearly then.

She watched him. Not heaving as before, but still riddled with anxiety. And suddenly, he began again.

"The bloody Asian, he couldn't scream out loud because of the gag, but he's... done screaming. He's lost so much blood... his head is forward on his chest, mouth open. The bindings are the only things holding him up. The two Suits—the tall one and the short one—knew they would not let him live, so they made Hans keep up the torture. Just in case the bloody Asian, in his last moments, would somehow reveal more. Hans holds on to the back of the chair just to keep from slipping. It's greasy around the chair—on the floor—blood everywhere, severed fingers, and his piss. It took another twenty minutes, and the man finally stopped breathing. Hans watched him closely, making sure—yeah, it's over—he's gone... he's bled to death. And then they left."

"Who left, Tom?" she asked.

"The two Suits and the interpreter. Hans senses that whoever was behind the mirror was gone, too. He knows this is the time to work fast, holding onto the chair—cutting the bindings quick—I know he's coming."

"Hans knows he's coming." Jane corrected in a whisper.

Tom continued, but his anxiety was clearly up.

"Hans knows this is when that fucker Chief One comes back! Get the dead Asian out quick! Get the bindings off the slumped guy, but the bindings are slippery, covered in blood—fuck! Chief One comes up behind him, wheeling the body cart—before he can even turn, he shocks him, driving that prod into him. 'Fucking clean this shit up!' he yells, and I almost buckle from the jolt."

"Hans almost buckles. It's not you, Tom, it's Hans," Jane gently corrected.

Tom nodded, still immersed in the memory.

"Chief One shoves the body cart towards Hans. The Chief is pointing that prod at him, really close. Hans puts his hands up defensively. 'Hurry up and get that fuckin' shit outta here!' Chief One yells, walking out and threatening to come back. And he will, too—Hans is working fast—knows to take the body to the tunnels. That's his procedure for the ones that die in the chair."

Tom swallowed hard, calming a little but still with a hint of anxiety.

"Good, Tom. Do you want to keep going?" she asked.

Tom stared ahead, once again lost in the memory.

"He's got him loaded—loads up the bloody Asian. He doesn't worry about the fingers and all the shit on the floor; it's not his business. He just loads him up on the long, grey, plastic cart with the big wheels on it. He rolls him out—into the freight elevator, and he can hear 'em—the hose guys. They're in there already, in the wet room, hosing it down, shooting that disinfectant everywhere. Hans can smell it before the freight elevator door closes. He's safe now. Chief One can't get in the elevator. Not now."

Jane watched him and took a sip of coffee as Tom continued.

"I'm pushing the cart—"

"Hans is pushing the cart, Tom," she corrected softly.

"Down below the DUMB—in the sewers, where all the shit from the DUMB drains to. And garbage, too; it's all dumped in the tunnels for 'em. That's where they live, where the tunnel people live. Hundreds of them. Hans was taking the dead one down to dispose of the body for Chief One."

She noticed Tom was calm for this part, lying on the couch, just telling the story... not so tense anymore. She took notes and waited.

"Hans—Hans is pushing the cart out of the freight elevator—into the dark of the tunnels. No light down there. Hans turns on his infrared headlamp—he can see a little ways in front. And he can definitely see better than most in the dark. They enhanced him that way. The Greys enhanced that capability so he could be a better soldier.

"They did that to him when he was cloned. They can make adjustments right when they're cloning someone. Fuck with their DNA... with their genetics. He rolls the cart in darkness for a while. Hans senses some kids following him—a roving gang. But they're little ones. He knows they're hungry. But they know he'll kill them, or worse, take one of them up for that Chief One to kill, so they keep their distance. They know they're gonna get that body in the cart. That dead Asian. He'll be good eating. Fresh meat for their fire. And the Asian isn't one of them, from the tunnels. They know he came from up there. Somebody Hans killed up there.

"That Asian—he's not from the dark tunnels where they're from. He's not. They can smell his blood. It gets that way when you're always hungry. Things develop down in the tunnels. Generations of kids born down there, and they're more like third-world street dogs. They know everything. Can smell what's local and what's from the light world. Hans is from the Light World. Up there. Where everybody eats good. And they know the dead meat in the cart is from there, too.

"They sometimes get near Hans, a few of them, when they realize he's not coming to shoot them or abduct one of them. He does that too, and they're wary of him. He's taken many kids before. Boys and girls... and he takes them up into the light... and when he brings them back... it always looks like they were strangled to death. And some have been beaten. There's always lots of blood around their anus. Boy or girl, it didn't matter. But they knew it was Chief One who did the killing up there and the rape. Hans was just the abductor for Chief One. And if he didn't obey and bring one up for the Chief, he'd get shocked, or waterboarded, and sometimes beaten by security and thrown in the prison box for a night."

What kind of box did they put Hans in, Tom? She asked.

Tom hesitated, seeing it all. He gritted his teeth.

"Small box, not big enough for Hans to stand. Solitary confinement. He hated all that. And they knew it because sometimes Chief One would come down with Hans and direct him to grab a kid that the Chief had picked out. They knew Chief One in the tunnels, and they ran. Chief Two came down sometimes to find Hans, but Chief Two always had security with him. They didn't fear Chief Two—but Command Master Chief One—he was the psycho.

"Pocked-face, cold, and calculated. But most times, Chief One would order a kid brought up, and Hans would grab one. Hans would have to wait in the outer office while the Chief did it to them. Hans could hear the rape happening and their screaming. He could hear the Chief yell at them, and Hans could hear the slaps. The little ones would get quiet, and he knew it was over then. And Chief One would yell for him, 'Get this shit outta here, Hans!' And Hans would pick up the dead little one and put them in the cart while Chief One buckled his pants and lit a cigarette. Hans tried to hurry and get out before that fat fucker picked up the cattle prod. He always took the little ones to the same area down in the sewers. Right by the East

Gate. He had known them hours before, and they were just scared and screaming as he took them up into the light. But he wasn't mad at them then.

"So afterward, he always tried to give them some respect at the end—tried to put their clothes back on... but, he could always sense the gangs waiting in the dark. Knew they were waiting... hungry. So, he'd walk away, and he could hear them like a pack of dogs moving in, fighting over the body. He could hear the horde taking that food to their fires. And he sometimes shared a piece of candy from the light world, giving it to the little ones around the fires. He would talk to them, and the families down there were not all bad people—especially the ones near the East Gate.

"That was his area... where he patrolled in the dark as an enforcer, so the construction crews could keep working. The DUMB was always expanding. Some of the tunnel people had never seen natural light in their entire lives. Born down there, they didn't know how hungry they really were because that's just the way it was. It was like drinking water. You did it when you had some. When you could gather enough fresh stuff from the walls that seeped down from above. Up there in the DUMB, where the light people were, sometimes their water lines broke, and the sweet stuff would flood from the same wall down into the sewer. Everyone in the dark would fill up their jugs, and there would be plenty for a while. And if there was extra, some washed with it. But only a few had been brought to the tunnels from the light world. Sometimes one of the tunnel kids would try to go up to the light world, popping into the DUMB to steal things or even try to escape. They all knew that was the way out.

"Hans would be ordered to find them and bring them back down. Dead or alive, they were coming out of the DUMB. Dead or alive, they were going back down to the tunnels. There were always new live ones being thrown down there from the light world—ones who had been abducted off streets from around the globe. The Greys wanted the population to grow, and the Cabal kept feeding it. Having their Black Navy abductors, like Hans, bring more kids in... so they could inject more shit into those throwaway people. Drugs the Cabal wanted to test on the tunnel teenagers and adults before they injected their Black Navy operatives with it. That's what the families told Hans.

"They talked to him and told him things. There were many who had been shot up with super-soldier drugs by the Grey alien fuckers just below the jail level. Those skinny Greys were torturers. Seven feet tall, and had those big fuckin' eyes that slanted down, and they smelled just like sewage. And those skinny pricks would hold you like a vice if you tried to run. They were dissectors, and nobody ever wanted to see a Tall-Grey. But sometimes, they came too. And everybody hid.

"Those Tall-Greys with their lightning bolt weapons. The little silver nozzle thing that would fire out plasma and kill you quick—burn your ass right through.

They came to check on their experiments, to see if the ones they had put drugs into were still alive and what they had become. The Greys could always find their experiments if they were still alive, because they had those locator beacons—those tiny hyper-dimensional trackers placed at the base of their victims' skulls.

"The Greys used those in the super-soldier experiments so they could always locate the ones they had injected. And sometimes, the aliens would take them back for more experimentation. That's why the tunnel people let Hans come near their fires sometimes. He was more like them... like the sewer people... he could be calm and not scary. He was almost one of them. And sometimes, he felt more at home with them than with the ones above in the DUMB. The tunnel families liked the food he brought, and sometimes they told him things.

"The mothers watched him give out the candy, and they took some too. He stayed on the opposite side of the fire—a safe distance for both parties—but they knew he wasn't bad, really. He wasn't the one in control—it was the ones up there that told him what to do. He was often hungry too, because the Chief didn't always give him food if he'd been bad. So, he sat hungry with them around their fires. His fire, too. His room was down there, way back in the dark. He slept there. And it was quiet. They didn't fuck with him. The tunnel people didn't fuck with him—and if they did—he'd shoot them."

"And the rest of the passengers... Tom?" she whispered.

He stared down at his fingers, his lips quivering... lost in the darkness.

T eebeck stood and watched Goldmeyer return to his desk chair, putting his glasses on.

From a file, he raised a headshot of Vyla.

"Teebeck, your security detail on this civilian investigator... am I to understand that one of them was mind-melded by an alien?"

"Yes, sir. Unfortunately, my best team—I call them the Twins—were monitoring her when the operative was compromised while doing surveillance alone. We're looking for a replacement for that operative at this moment."

Goldmeyer nodded slowly, closing the file. He walked past Teebeck toward the door and then paused.

"That's very interesting."

"Yes, sir, apparently she is being monitored by more than just us."

Goldmeyer slightly nodded.

"What time is my meeting with Aspelsin?" Goldmeyer asked.

Teebeck quickly stepped past him and opened the door for him, checking his watch as he did so.

"Sometime soon, sir."

"Sometime soon?" Goldmeyer whispered.

"That's all the information we have, sir," Teebeck said, looking down.

"Fucking aliens," Goldmeyer whispered and turned.

"Is my dinner ready?"

"Sir, it is," Teebeck replied.

Goldmeyer stared.

"Teebeck, we're having an issue on the carrier with one of the pilots. Can you see to it that the issue is resolved? Ensure Skipper Schrader is kept out of it. It's strictly CIA business."

"Absolutely, sir."

Goldmeyer entered the bronze-plated elevator. The two men stared at each other as the door closed.

Teebeck spoke into his wrist radio.

"The Overseer is on his way to dinner."

"Copy, sir," came the curt reply.

Teebeck hesitated momentarily.

"Dispatch SA's *Ghostwalker* and *Greywolf* to the USS Gerald R. Ford immediately. They will receive their orders en route."

A moment later, the reply came.

"Copy, sir. Ghostwalker and Greywolf to Carrier Strike Group Seven."

A t 2:45 a.m., in the pitch-black morning, twenty-eight miles south of St. Louis, the grandson of notorious CIA operative Damon Slepher turned the enormous steering wheel of his semi-delivery truck.

Ricky Slepher smoothly glided the *Little Rome's Pizza* semi off the sleepy two-lane highway through the tiny hamlet of Dennis Hollow, Illinois. He snaked the tractor-trailer another half mile northeast along Limestone Lane to Boulder Boulevard and pulled into the government parking lot. Downshifting to a crawl, he passed a large brown sign reading;

Welcome to Rock City, National Archives and Records Administration.

But Ricky knew this Rock City government facility was nowhere near the town of Rock City, Illinois. Not even close.

Nice Cabal trickery, he thought.

He knew the folks at the Rock City government facility would be eagerly waiting for him. *There was quite an appetite for what he was carrying*, he joked to himself.

Several other Little Rome's trucks were already parked in the lot, and Ricky knew more trucks would be arriving, as this facility always received several per night.

He wore civvies and looked like a regular truck driver with his red t-shirt, blue jeans, and boots. The only things that seemed out of place for a pizza delivery driver in the middle of nowhere were his muscular physique and his sidearm. Both were military, and hidden under his loose civilian attire.

He thought it was funny that the government building, on the surface, housed only a few offices—*way too small to warrant a semi full of pizza, not to mention several semis, always there. Hiding in plain sight.*

He was always amazed that nobody from the civilian sector seemed to question anything. Ricky didn't do pickup runs that often for this facility. His job was significantly more layered than just simple deliveries. But he did them once in a while just to know what his teams were experiencing. As he pulled in, he knew several military types with infrared flashlights would be off to the side in a small group; they were security for the trucks arriving. Civilians would never see those operators. You had to know where and how to look.

He shut down the truck and was just stepping down from the cab when he was approached by his lead in the tactical detail, who arrived out of the pitch-black smoking a cig.

Thompson was skinny as a rail and chain-smoked. He handed Slepher a white sealed envelope and talked through the lit cig still in his mouth.

"SA Ghostwalker, you'll catch a chopper at 1300 departing St. Louis."

Slepher nodded.

"Thank you, sir," he whispered, mock saluting Thomson, who winked and continued toward the rear of the semi, leaving Slepher with the envelope.

Even though Thompson outranked Slepher in years in the covert programs, their relationship was based on a much more lucrative game. In that realm, Ricky was the top dog, and their wink was an acknowledgment of a long-term relationship where the right amounts of money flowed to Thompson. Ricky paid his team members well... and that money kept their mouths shut.

He stared down at the envelope he had just been handed... and knew it was a kill order.

He turned and saw Thompson approach the rear of the semi as the others on the security team were already pulling the huge rear doors open. He could see movement under the infrared lights the operatives used. And he could hear them, his "*Little-ghosts*" back there, but he couldn't pay them any more attention. He was *Ghostwalker,* and he had new orders to attend to.

He opened the envelope stamped with CIA letterhead and *red-stamped* in several places with *"Top-Secret."*

An *"SA,"* or *Silent Assassin* as the CIA called him, was rarely given a front load of information. That would be worked out on-site.

He opened the kill order and could hear his team behind the semi, herding the last ones toward the tunnels.

SA Ghostwalker, you are to report to the Naval Base San Diego, where you will be received by SA Greywolf. As a unit, you will fly to meet Carrier Strike Group Seven, and you will proceed to terminate an as-yet-unnamed member of the Strike Group.

Ricky Slepher stared at his letter and knew the CIA didn't order the hit. The Cabal did. He had learned from his grandfather that all CIA hit orders were always Cabal-directed. But the CIA letter helped give the Cabal *plausible deniability* should their organization ever be revealed.

From the beginning of their training, all Silent Assassins were told they were under the direct orders of the CIA. Only Ricky had the real scoop because of his grandfather.

Ghostwalker was his Silent Assassin callsign, but all soldiers in the regular world knew him as "Little Sleph."

His Force Recon Marine buddies named him that with affection, as "Little Sleph" was anything but little. Every bit of six-foot-four and built to hustle, Slepher had no natural predators in his world from a physical standpoint. He could outrun, outclimb, and outfight anyone in hand-to-hand combat, wielding a knife or not.

Before this evening's pizza-delivery run had begun, Slepher had been in charge of sentry duty guarding alien technology in four-hour shifts in the ultra-secret complex way below where he was standing. Miles below. No other sentry at the facility spoke to him, as none were allowed to speak in the deep underground military base. Even in the barracks down there, after four hours of walking the line, the other sentries never spoke. All the others were also silent assassins when called upon, but Slepher was always the top choice if he was available.

The CIA considered sentry duty between kills as *"a cool-down period."* But for Ricky Slepher, it was the *thrill of the kill* that made him tick. He could take or leave the $5,000 bonus for each execution, as he certainly no longer needed that pittance. To Slepher, far more than the money, he fed off the energy of watching humans under his complete control in their final moments.

Normally, his hit orders, as the CIA called them, were always to terminate *"Enemies of the United States Government."* The CIA called these missions *Wet assignments.* *"Wet"* was a Russian spy term for *"covered-in-blood,"* and the CIA had adopted the phrase after WWII, subsequently calling their torture rooms *"Wet Rooms."*

Ricky's assignments rarely involved wet rooms, as he was generally sent to terminate individuals—where they resided—out in the world. But occasionally, his victims would be bound to a chair in a wet room. And Ricky still enjoyed the power of that dynamic as well.

Those interrogation rooms, which Ricky knew were located in DUMBs throughout the world, were generally perfectly square, usually twenty by twenty, with white tiles on the floor and walls. Each had a steel chair bolted to the floor over a large drain for easy cleanup. Every room also had a two-way mirror on the wall. The newest wet rooms were stainless steel and equipped with fire hoses and disinfectant.

Ricky was often brought in as the torturer for whatever unlucky individual was bound to the chair above the drain. He somehow could extract more information than other interrogators, as if tapping into a primal instinct, much like his legendary grandfather before him.

And Ricky viewed himself as *a staunch patriot.* He had always done exactly what he was told because that's what a good soldier did, and you didn't ask questions. *Ever.*

Ricky kept copies of the kill photos he had taken after each assassination because it was a requirement for proof of termination for the Cabal, and those photos were also like trophies to him.

His first kill had been twenty years ago at Dulce, and that was when his rise to power had begun.

Through his granddad's connections, he was transferred after his Marine Special Forces tour to DSD-3, the Dulce Security Division. DSD-3 controlled the Deep Underground Military Base below the Archuleta Mesa, near Dulce, New Mexico—way out west.

The underground complex, miles long, was several levels deep and had a reputation in the Black Ops community as *a terminal facility.* Meaning, those who were abducted and taken there for genetic experimentation would never leave. Not alive anyway. This included both humans and aliens.

It was there, back then, on sentry duty at Dulce... where Ricky became an *SA*—a Silent Assassin for the CIA.

Ricky's first kill had been of an officer within the Dulce complex who had leaked information to a famous reporter, who, unbeknownst to the officer, had long been on the Cabal media payroll.

That officer, whom Slepher not only worked for but knew and admired, was bound to his own office chair and systematically tortured by Ricky while being questioned about who else he had leaked information to. The killing had taken hours and proved to the Cabal that Slepher had the depraved mindset that was in keeping with his famous grandfather.

After killing his own boss, Ricky was sent on various kill missions around the globe, receiving new orders every six months. *Death by suicide* was the protocol the Cabal used. Most executions were by strangulation. Almost always of individuals who were leaking information—male, female, civilian, military, as well as government employees.

Sometimes, he threw a victim off a building or shot them point-blank. Executions that could easily be termed suicides.

In between those kills back then, he performed sentry duty at the Dulce DUMB, or now, at this new duty station, miles below his feet... in the Rock City DUMB.

He lit a cigarette and realized his security team was done in the back, and he had a flight to catch later that day.

He folded the kill order and walked to the rear. He was excited to catch the chopper later in the afternoon. It had been a while since he'd been on a kill mission. He would enjoy meeting the other Silent Assassin. Would enjoy their planning and the kill itself. As that's what all traitors to the United States of America deserved—to be taught a lesson they wouldn't walk away from. Ricky had risen to be the top Silent Assassin because all of his terminations had the distinctive mark of being committed *with extreme prejudice.* A Cabal assassination signature.

Ricky loved to leave his mark in creative ways... like with Phil Schneider in 1996. Ricky had sent a message to the world about the consequences of having a big mouth. Schneider had tried to tell the world about the existence of the underground Dulce base and the genetic testing happening there. Because Schneider had been speaking at public conferences across the nation—when his execution came—it made national news.

Ricky's team had slipped a nice-looking female DSD-3 operative into one of Schneider's speaking engagements, and pretty soon, she was staying at Schneider's apartment, eventually opening the door for Ricky to enter without warning.

Ricky had also terminated Ron Rummel, Schneider's close friend, back in 1993.

Rummel was a former Air Force intelligence agent who became a whistleblower, publishing a UFO rag called *The Alien Digest.* The journal was the first of its kind... divulging the American military's involvement in alien imprisonment and genetic testing, which pissed off the Cabal.

Both assassinations were ruled suicides. The Cabal had its tentacles in all police and medical establishments worldwide.

Ricky had been stone-cold reliable throughout his career. He knew that's why he was the Cabal's first choice.

He pulled on his cigarette and glimpsed himself in the side mirror.

He ran his finger along a ragged scar from his eye down to his cheekbone—a badge of honor from a razor fight with a much bigger bully in high school. Over the years, he found that the jagged scar made men think twice. And for women, it triggered an animal mechanism—a beauty-and-the-beast danger switch, where each conquest knew at a base level... what she was asking for.

He climbed in the truck and fired up... as it needed a rinse out. He dropped the huge machine in gear and pulled out. The incline ramp was just down the way. He had that ramp built with proceeds from his *Winking Wolf* product. It made cleaning up after a run so much faster. A simple ramp, inclined up twelve-degrees, that allowed a semi-sized rig to pull up and park, right next to fire hoses that were already poised above the back of the truck for easy operation... to hose out the inside. The entire process took four minutes, and the final hose was loaded with the disinfectant so the truck wouldn't stink to high heaven.

A stroke of genius he had when he first began deliveries. He rarely drove the ramp anymore, but it was used nightly by his teams. Four minutes later, his truck was hosed out of all the shit and piss the little ones couldn't hold, and it all disappeared down a truck-wide sewage grate he had specifically installed for that purpose.

He was always slightly relieved when a dead one wasn't part of the refuse. That happened, too, when there were too many herded for some of the little ones to get adequate air. *Many vials wasted* in Ricky's mind. But transport was part of the business, and sometimes, they just didn't make it. Four minutes later, the semi-trailer was clean, and he closed and latched the huge doors.

He was proud of himself for jumping on a delivery once in a while. A boss had to know what his subordinates were asked to do on a daily basis. He knew this business inside out and had become wealthy because of it—a wealth and connections he never displayed or discussed with anyone. That was the key to winning the game. Ricky was good at being humble.

And why shouldn't he? He didn't have to prove anything anymore. He had long ago established connections, garnering the top stars in Hollywood as well as the most powerful in the music industry. Elite, high-powered players from all walks of life came his way, looking for that elusive strain with its time-honored reputation for providing youth and vitality. His *Winking Wolf* vials were now being sold and bartered for—out in the Galactic trade routes—a reality regular humans on the planet would never believe. But Ricky had been to many off-world harvesting facilities, compliments of the Draco. They liked his strain immensely, and he had worked deals for trips to see their harvesting facilities on the moon and elsewhere. After twenty years of tweaking his strain, the perfect batch had been created, and then the replication began. *Winking Wolf Screamshit* was top on the street and top in the galaxy. Ricky had arrived.

There was no more worry in his life. He had passed that milestone years ago. He had more money than anyone he knew.

Hell—he thought to himself—with a chuckle.

He had more money than God.

G etting back to S-4 via the Janet flight and a solo ride in an executive helicopter gave Vyla a sense of her importance to Yen and her team.

Vyla had met all of Yen's team, but she now understood that only she and Yen rode in the helicopter. The rest of Yen's team rode the bus to S-4—the one with the blackened windows—so no one could see out. It was a precaution against any individual attempting to reveal directions to the super-secret complex... at Papoose Lake.

After touchdown at S-4, Vyla and Yen moved directly to the Widow, and Vyla was once again astonished that she was alive.

"Follow me," Yen suddenly whispered.

Vyla looked one last time at the otherworldly Widow and then followed Yen, walking between the lines. They entered a small briefing room with a large screen, and Yen pressed a button that brought up a movie file.

"Grab a chair. I want to show you where the Widow came from."

Vyla sat next to Yen and stared up at a still frame on the screen. It looked vintage to Vyla, like old film stock, and it had apparently been shot in the desert. Yen expanded the movie to fill the screen and hit *play*.

The footage initially panned by several soldiers wearing old uniforms somewhere in the desert at possibly late morning. The men were unloading from military trucks.

"This footage is top-secret from March 25, 1948, twelve miles northeast of Aztec, New Mexico," Yen said.

Vyla thought the footage appeared handheld, as if being wielded by someone trying to cover everything in front of them while they walked. A moment later, the camera panned to the same flying saucer, Vyla had just stood by—the Widow—except it was lying on a desert mesa, and several 1940s-era scientists were inspecting the craft. The landing gear was not down, but the ship appeared exactly as the one in the hangar, except in the movie, a ramp leading into the ship was visible. Vyla looked at Yen with astonishment. Yen nodded, smiling slightly.

The camera then entered the ship, first going up the ramp and then down into what appeared to be the cargo hold on the lower level. It panned past several silver, coffin-sized containers with glass tops, and inside each one, a humanoid appeared frozen... underneath the glass. The camera closed in on the largest one, revealing an adult humanoid, roughly thirty years old. Vyla was transfixed.

"Turns out these were cryogenic freezer chambers," Yen said. "The scientific team realized that all these bodies in deep freeze were still alive while frozen. So, they hauled everything, including the ship, back to Los Alamos Laboratory to unfreeze these individuals under controlled circumstances."

Vyla turned to her, astonished.

"I know—but wait—it's about to show someone you know," Yen said.

Vyla looked back at the footage as the camera panned to one scientist, a rail-thin man smoking a cigarette, staring at the cryogenic chambers. The footage zoomed in, focusing closely on the man's face. Vyla suddenly sat up in her seat.

"Oh, my—is that—that's Oppenheimer!"

Yen nodded, smiling, and paused the footage as Vyla shook her head, astonished. Yen slowly stood.

"I want you to watch the rest of this, as it becomes a defining moment in our history with aliens," she said, closing her briefcase. "I've got to run to another meeting over in Los Alamos. When you finish this movie, the guard behind you will escort you to the basement Mag-Lev shuttle, which will drop you back off at Groom Lake. From there, you'll catch a Janet flight to Las Vegas."

Vyla nodded as Yen stepped off.

"Dr. Jee," Vyla whispered. Yen turned.

"Thank you."

Yen nodded curtly. Vyla raised a finger.

"I can start the simulator training in three days, but I need to do one more trip to Palo Alto for the last of my belongings."

Yen nodded.

"Good, do what you need, and I'll see you Monday evening for the first simulator session. Your actual test flight is now on the schedule, and there should be a lot of dignitaries in attendance."

Vyla shrugged.

"I'll give her my best."

Yen nodded and departed. Vyla watched the door close and noted the remaining guard watching her from the corner. She turned to face the screen with the freeze frame of J. Robert Oppenheimer. She realized then that this film, shot on March 25 of 1948, would have made Oppenheimer a young forty-three years old, and already, *The Father of the Atomic Bomb*, which he detonated in July of 1945.

What a wild life! she thought. *To figure out how to create the world's first nuclear weapon, and then become heavily involved with the new "alien presence," only to be told to never speak about it, or else!*

She shook her head in admiration, taking a deep breath... but she didn't press *play*; instead, she wanted to know how it all started with this crash. She closed her eyes and was no longer a young woman physicist admiring Dr. J. Robert Oppenhiemer...

She... was him.

Chapter Thirty-Eight

Eight months after helping investigate three crashed saucers at Roswell, Dr. J. Robert Oppenheimer stood in awe on top of Hart Canyon Mesa, near the tiny town of Aztec, New Mexico.

The sheer size of this one, the elegance of it... shining in the midday sun, and the astonished looks of his scientific team—unhinged at what lay before them. And this one had not crashed. It had no visible damage and appeared to have touched down gently, under intelligent control.

My God, Bob thought, as the possibility of live beings inside the ship was top on everyone's minds. The eight scientists Bob had handpicked for this covert recovery operation were considered some of the best in the world on that 25th day of March in 1948. And the best were humbled by their first contact with something from another world.

A 100-foot-wide flying saucer, no less, that was thirty-three feet thick in the middle, where a bubble shape extended from the center, top, and bottom. From that central cockpit area, the ship tapered outward to a sheer one inch at its edge. The craft had a brushed aluminum look but was not highly polished, instead having a darkened grey sheen. Stunning, with no visible seams, rivets, or weld marks. Instead, the huge disc appeared molded and had no visible means of propulsion and no smell of gas or oil. Not one flight control surface was visible, not to mention visible windows or portholes—so how could it even fly or land or... *damn!*

Bob looked across the faces of his team members as they gawked at the breathtaking, otherworldly craft. Jerome Hunsaker and Johann Von Roesler were actually laughing out loud, like big kids who were finally within arm's reach of the thing they had only dreamed of. Others were more silent as they slowly walked around the ship in their desert field garb. Detlev Bronk was inspecting the ramp leading up into the craft. Bronk had been with Oppenheimer at Roswell, but not the others. Lloyd Berkner had sat down a few feet away, chewing gum and marveling at what was before him.

At sixty-two degrees on that sunny March day, most of Bob's team wore desert gear with light sweaters, and several were smoking as they moved around the ship. Except for Dr. Vannevar Bush, who would show up soon, it was up to this small group to unwrap the gift before them—and hopefully save a few alien lives in the process. Bob had a sense of what must be going through his team's minds. He had felt unhinged in the same way when he saw his first off-world ship—the 1941 Cape Girardeau saucer.

That was seven years ago... but it had changed his life.

T he alien ship had crashed in Missouri just months before the Japanese attacked Pearl Harbor.

Dr. Vannevar Bush, President Roosevelt's scientific advisor, had just been tasked with beating the Germans to nuclear fission. The American OSS had information confirming that the Germans were attempting to create an atomic weapon, and Franklin Delano Roosevelt was hell-bent on getting there first.

Vannevar suggested to the president that J. Robert Oppenheimer was his first choice to lead the Manhattan Project, a top-secret endeavor that would eventually create and detonate the first atomic bomb in 1945. But in 1941, the virtually unknown Oppenheimer and Van had become fast friends. Though Bob was considered an extraordinary scientific talent, Van was no slouch either. The two men had bonded over their love of science and poetry. On that late April night in 1941, Van had quietly knocked on Bob's door in downtown Washington, D.C. Bob opened up to a wildly excited Van, who had his finger to his lips. Bob shook his head, snickering, and a minute later, Van was whisking him out the door for a pell-mell nighttime race to the United States Capitol Building!

"What in the hell, Van?!" Bob said after they were waved through the security gate. "If you are taking me to a late-night Senate session, I'll strangle you!"

Van shushed him again as they walked rapidly past more guards and descended several flights of stairs. Oppenheimer was getting winded as Van continued the furious pace, excited like a little kid. Bob was astonished as they passed by several dimly lit underground corridors that seemed to extend indefinitely.

"This is all below the Capitol?" Bob said, perplexed, huffing to keep up as Van snickered, raising his eyebrows.

"This is the sub-basement," Van said as they finally approached the massive vault door.

Van spun the large combination lock and lowered the thick latch, pulling back as the foot-thick door glided open.

"You are now the fifth person in the world to see what's in this room," Van said as he motioned for Bob to enter.

The first thing that caught Oppenheimer's eye was the three huge pie-shaped pieces of smooth silver—that appeared to be some form of—a ship? He turned to Van, who watched him, knowing that Oppenheimer would quickly figure this riddle out. Van motioned to the back part of the room. Bob turned and slowly approached three enormous glass containers full of clear liquid. Floating suspended within, lit only by tiny spotlights, were four-foot-tall humanoids... wearing shiny silver flight suits. Bob's mind was racing.

What-in-the-hell?!

The enlarged heads, huge black eyes, grayish skin and four-fingered hands. The skinny, long arms that extended down to just above the knee, and the small slit for a mouth, with two indentations for the nose above it. All three creatures were identical and appeared like futuristic museum specimens.

"You've got to be kidding me?!" he whispered excitedly as he put it all together.

There had been hints of disc-craft intercepting military aircraft worldwide recently, but there were no gun cameras on U.S. warplanes in 1941, so verbal reports of alien craft were often left as hearsay.

Oppenheimer stared, awestruck. He then turned to Van, who was lost in the humanoids as well.

"It's happened in our lifetime, Bob," Van whispered. "I... I still can't believe it."

"Where?" Bob asked.

"Cape Girardeau, Missouri. It basically crashed in a farmer's field two days ago. General Marshall sent a colonel named Eisenhower down to recover it and bring it back here. Nobody knows we have this thing."

That moment had changed Bob's life. And though four years later, he would be responsible for the Trinity blast that would forever change mankind, he knew everything in his life would pale in comparison to that night.

Humans were not alone in the universe, and to Bob, that was the ultimate question.

Now it had been definitively answered. The alien arrival phenomenon was untouchable. Bigger than any science. Bigger than outrunning the Germans to create nuclear fission. The two young men would spend the rest of that night going over the ship and the crewmembers and processing that extraordinary moment. And they would discuss how the damn ship was still under some form of power, even though it was in pieces and not plugged into a wall circuit. *Unreal,* thought Bob. *Not possible! It was somehow getting juice from the energy around it?*

Staring at that otherworldly craft, Oppenheimer knew right then that he and all other human scientists were just apes running around a cage with stone tools. The dousing in humility was the best thing that had ever happened to him.

Now, back in the moment, in Aztec, New Mexico, staring at that 100-foot-wide saucer that had just landed, Oppenheimer thought about how only a few hours ago, he was sipping coffee on his couch at Los Alamos National Laboratory, one hundred and seventy miles to the south.

The rest of the world, including the press, thought he was at Princeton, but since the Roswell crashes just a few months back, he had spent the majority of his time attempting to reverse-engineer the saucers that had dropped into America's lap on that infamous weekend. The work was progressing slowly, as the technology was so far beyond anything he and his team had ever seen. He was finishing his morning coffee when Van called, excitedly telling Bob that his Army transport was already warmed up at the Los Alamos airfield.

"Oh, my Van," Oppenheimer sleepily replied, "what's going on?"

"I can't tell you on the phone, but get over there, Bob! You won't be sorry—the brief will be on the bird!" and Van hung up.

Oppenheimer slapped together an overnight bag and drove to the airport, where he immediately boarded the already-warmed-up Douglas C-47 Skytrain. A moment later, an Army major stepped into the cabin, greeting him with a salute and a top-secret folder. Saluted again and was gone.

Oppenheimer was airborne as the only passenger minutes later. He lit a well-deserved cigarette, and the brief informed him that a recovery operation was already in motion and that he was to lead a scientific team for the covert expedition.

The Interplanetary Unit (IPU) would be waiting for him at Durango, in southern Colorado. This newly formed unit had security, recovery, and counterintelligence teams embedded within it, and they would assist Oppenheimer's scientific team with whatever they encountered at the crash site. Vannevar Bush would join them shortly, as his D.C. flight was just about to launch for New Mexico.

Bob's Skytrain touched down at Durango, Colorado, at 8 a.m., and he was immediately taken to base headquarters, where an MP led him to a very young major who was inspecting a convoy of trucks ready to roll.

Upon seeing Oppenheimer's approach, the major turned, smiled, and was not surprised when Bob stepped forward and gave him a bear hug.

"Sam! I was so excited when I saw the brief on the way here and realized you were running the IPU!"

"Oh, Oppie, it's great to see you," Sam said. "Let's get you over to my office for a quick brief; we're still waiting on a few members of your scientific team."

"Swell, swell," Bob said, putting his hand on Sam's shoulder as they walked. "What has it been... since Roswell eight months ago that I saw you? And a major already! Wow."

Sam shrugged.

"Well, you know—they needed someone to run this team, and it requires a major—so I got lucky."

Oppie patted his shoulder again.

"You got promoted because you're a good man, Sam. By the way, how's your baby girl?"

"We have two baby girls now," Sam said. "Sue's two, and Helen just came along."

"Oh, Sam, that's wonderful," Bob said, flipping open a Zippo and lighting a cig. "Well, you be sure and tell Catherine I said *hello*. You know I've got a place down in Los Alamos, and you're always welcome."

Sam looked up and smiled.

"That was one wild 4th of July week in Roswell," Sam said, opening the door to his office.

"Hell of a weekend," Bob concurred, shaking his head as he offered a cigarette to Sam while closing the door. Sam took the cig and double-checked that the door was locked. Oppie watched as Sam pulled out a rolled-up New Mexico topographic map and spread it out on his desk. He pointed to an already annotated, unused road and looked up at Oppie, lowering his voice to a whisper.

"I got a call at daybreak from Secretary of State General George Marshall that a disc-craft had come down near Aztec. The flying saucer was confirmed by an interceptor squadron out of Sandia that did a flyover. The LZ, or landing zone, is twelve miles northeast of Aztec. We're going to the top of a mesa called Hart Canyon, and I'm guessing we'll roll in there about lunchtime today," Sam said.

"My main IPU unit is based at Camp Hale further north, and they're already en route and should beat us to the landing zone by a few minutes. Their orders are to secure the area and wait for us."

Oppie nodded, pulling on his cigarette as Sam continued.

"General Marshall assured me that the ranch property owner, Mr. HD, has been told that the government will cover his family's expenses as long as they stay inside their ranch house, which is not up on the mesa. General Marshall also alluded to his desire for the United States to purchase the ranch outright and, in the meantime, lease it from Mr. HD, as Marshall thinks this ship is beyond anything we've recovered so far."

Oppie watched Sam as he continued.

"The main IPU convoy is so large it could attract a lot of attention if the main highway is taken. So, I ordered them to take an old dirt road, and, hopefully, not too many folks will notice them," Sam said, looking up.

Bob was already nodding.

"I'm with you one-hundred percent, Sam. We need to keep this from blowing up like Roswell."

Sam nodded, lit his cigarette, took a deep drag, and put his Zippo away. He exhaled, watching his old friend.

"Now, Oppie, I'm just gonna call you *Sir* from now on because—you are officially in charge of this expedition—and I don't want to seem too familiar with you to the boys outside, as that might get me in trouble. So, from now on—you are SIR—sir."

"You bet, Major Boyd," Oppie said with a sly smile. Sam nodded.

"And—we are under command of The Majestic-12 for recovery and clearing the landing zone," Sam said.

Oppie stared, perplexed.

"So—my scientific team—is not under any military control?" Bob inquired.

Sam nodded.

"Correct, I'm deferring to you, sir."

Bob nodded and understood that the Majestic-12 had taken the reins of the recovery from the military, which was why Vannevar had called him earlier. This was a new protocol since the Roswell recoveries eight months back, and it had everything to do with the military botching that evolution.

Bob was now the de facto leader of the entire recovery expedition. And Bob knew Sam's experience with the live Grey would be uniquely helpful on this covert operation, should they run into another one.

In Bob's mind, Sam was the perfect placement to lead the IPU. Bob had experienced dead Greys during the Corona recovery but, as yet, had only watched as Sam had worked with the live one later at Los Alamos.

"Thank you, Sam," Bob said. "What were the circumstances of the crash?"

"Well, sir," Sam began, "yesterday at 1820 hours, the disc-craft was initially tracked by White Sands and Sandia Test Range as it attempted to monitor one of our V-Rockets in flight. At 1840 hours, two more of our radars locked onto the saucer, and they could triangulate its location.

"At that moment, the ship dropped off radar... an evasive maneuver, it seemed. At about the same time, a police officer from Cuba, New Mexico, about one hundred miles south of Aztec, where the saucer is now, picked up the disc-craft as it flew slowly northwest toward Aztec. The police officer had radioed his dispatch, telling them that he was following a flying saucer that appeared disabled or was having problems flying.

"Finally, at around daybreak, the ship appeared to hit a cliff wall on the Navajo River near Blanco, NM, and then traveled northwest to where it supposedly landed under intelligent control. A flight of P-51s was sent to its last known location and confirmed the saucer was on the ground in Hart Canyon, up on the mesa."

Bob nodded, staring at the map as Sam continued.

"I had a helicopter dispatched at sunrise to get a visual, and according to that pilot, the ship appears to be in perfect shape. Not crash-landed, but definitely landed under intelligent control."

"A helicopter, huh?" Bob said, knowing the new whirly birds were still in the testing stage.

"Yes, sir," Sam said, "but don't worry—nobody is landing a helicopter at the site. That would just rouse the local townsfolk, and I'd like to keep our profile to a minimum." Oppie nodded.

"Live aliens on board?"

Sam shrugged. "I guess we'll find out. But I'm concerned because the helicopter did several circles over the craft and reported that there were many oil workers, police officers, and civilians milling about the craft. Some are even up on the ship."

Oppie nodded.

"What's your plan with all of them?"

"Well, my SOP says that my IPU team is to take charge of that area," Sam said, "which means rounding up any non-military types and warning them to keep their mouths shut about what they saw. Hopefully, by the time we arrive, that task will be taken care of."

Bob nodded.

Fifteen minutes later, Bob and his scientific team were assembled for the expedition. Twenty-five other personnel stood with them, and everyone had their right hand raised. Sam, standing up front, had the entire expedition swear an oath of secrecy, reading all assembled to an above-top-secret *Ultra* clearance.

Sam then ordered everyone to store their valuables and personal items—including wallets and identification cards—in lockers provided and embark on their pre-arranged transports.

Moments later, the line of four enormous six-by trucks... lumbered south along the seldom-used dirt road to avoid attracting attention on the highway. It took almost three hours to traverse the mountainous terrain to the crash zone.

It was noon when they arrived at Hart Canyon Mesa.

Fortunately, the IPU had already arrived and secured the area with a two-mile perimeter. Moving fluidly about the operation were camera operators using 16mm and large-format 4x5 Graflex cameras.

Technicians in full silver outfits were busy using Geiger counters, and several technicians were taking soil samples around the ship. Sam, knowing the locals would start asking questions, had already disguised the recovery effort by having fake oil company uniforms flown in for every member of the IPU, including the scientific team. These fictional oil-drilling uniforms were accompanied by signage, which was hung on the perimeter fence, advising the locals that the oil company would be exploring for mineral deposits in the area. In addition, *"Danger Blasting—High Explosive"* signs were placed around the two-mile perimeter to deter locals.

Within minutes of arriving, several small Army tents for each of the compartmentalized scientific groups surrounded the ship. Sam thought the whole thing resembled a traveling circus, yet with a very serious tone. Disguised as well, in their oil uniforms, were heavily armed MPs, who Sam could barely tell were armed to the teeth.

Sam had heard scuttlebutt at the site, that the huge ship had operated silently, and that seemed to him to be impossible. But shortly thereafter, Bob's team of scientists had received a brief upon their arrival that witnesses who had seen it fluttering along the highway in the pre-dawn... had confirmed... the huge ship was completely silent as it flew.

The long military convoy, with the bulk of the Interplanetary Phenomenon Unit, had departed Camp Hale, Colorado, hours earlier and had only been on station a few minutes before Sam and the Majestic Scientific team had arrived from nearby Durango.

According to Sam's second in command, when the IPU arrived, there was a group of roughly fifteen civilians milling about the ship. The craft appeared to have landed gently, with no exterior damage whatsoever. It was lying on its belly with a slight angle up toward the sky because of the small bubble on the bottom of the ship, which prevented the craft from lying flat on the desert terrain.

There were no visible landing struts. The ship's ramp, however, was already down and had supposedly been triggered by one of the young civilian oil workers.

Oppie had requested Sam bring the oil worker over for a debrief. Sam rounded up the young man, and within a few minutes of arriving, the entire scientific team was briefed on what had transpired since daybreak.

Bill Ferguson, a twenty-year-old civilian oil worker, relayed that upon his arrival at first light, with his co-worker Doug Knowland... that there were already oil workers on the craft, checking it out. The ramp was not down, and the ship was not responding to yells or even light blows from oil worker hammers. Bill and Doug hopped on the craft and walked toward the center.

Ferguson said that approaching the bubble on the top, he thought he was looking into shiny metal, like a mirror. Upon closer inspection, he realized it wasn't metal at all; that he and Doug could actually see through it!

Staring into the ship, Ferguson and Knowland could quickly make out two dead creatures slumped over the ship's flight controls in the upper cockpit.

Figuring they should try to get in and help in case there were any survivors, Ferguson looked for a way to enter the ship and found a small hole in the corner of the mirrored window area—a hole that both Ferguson and Knowland agreed looked like impact damage from whatever the ship had run into.

Ferguson used a long piece of rebar from his oil truck and extended it through the one-inch hole. He eventually pushed a button on the wall console, which triggered the ramp to extend.

The two young men then entered the upper cockpit of the craft, where the two dead alien pilots sat in their bucket-seat-style chairs. The creatures were four feet tall and wore blue flight suits, which were apparently fireproof, as the creatures' heads and hands were charred where they extended from the suits.

Ferguson and Knowland were only in the cockpit for a moment when the IPU team suddenly arrived.

And now, at 12:30 p.m., in the afternoon, Oppie was brought back to the moment by yells from his scientific team. After the earlier brief and all the civilians had been cleared, Oppie and his team had discussed how to approach the open ship. They first took many readings with Geiger and magnetic field detectors and quickly determined that the ship was completely harmless from a radiation standpoint. They decided to communicate first from the exterior, hoping to raise a response from whoever might still be alive on the inside.

Oppie watched as Dr. Jerome Hunsaker stood at the open ramp and called into the ship with a handheld megaphone.

"It's okay to come out...we're friendly!"

But the ship remained eerily quiet. Dr. Merle Tuve tapped the hull gently with a hammer, walking around the ship. All eight scientists and every soldier guarding the craft in that area turned toward Oppie for guidance.

At just that moment, Oppie's close friend and boss on the earlier Manhattan Project, Vannevar Bush, arrived at the mesa, having just flown in from Washington.

As his jeep growled onto the plateau, Sam's team, upon orders from Oppenheimer, began constructing scaffolding over one section of the upper hull.

Oppie and Van discussed in whispers the situation regarding the lack of visible signs of life from inside the craft, even though Bob's team had tried to no avail.

Bob told Van about entering the ship to find the two dead Greys slumped at their flight controls in the upper hull, combined with a strong smell of sulfur and death coming from the hole.

Van nodded, wiping his brow. He motioned for all eight of the scientific team to huddle.

"I think you've all done great trying to communicate from out here, but if we don't get in there ASAP—whatever might have been alive could have perished."

They all nodded and followed Bob and Van to the ramp. The two proceeded into the ship as the others stood by.

The interior of the inner hull was illuminated with bright sunlight, even though the outer skin of the seamless saucer had no visible windows whatsoever.

Bob went up the ramp into the heart of the ship. The ramp led to a cylindrical, elevator-sized compartment in the center of the craft, with a small spiral staircase steeply inclined to the flight deck and another going down into what would later be termed the cargo deck.

The two scientists climbed the tiny spiral staircase to the flight deck level. Both hesitated as they entered the cockpit area... as it appeared from the outside to be only twelve feet across, but on the inside... to be the size of a gymnasium. Both men looked at each other and back up at the impossibly big room with the two small, clearly dead creatures slumped over their flight controls.

Bob and Van would discuss *Dimensional-Transcendence* after that day and, years later, would still be stumped as to how the alien technology worked to create that effect.

The scientific team quickly determined that there were a total of fourteen small Greys that had perished before landing, apparently from a pressure decrease caused by the hole in the upper window, which may have happened during the ship's collision with the cliff wall before landing.

At first, the scientific team was disheartened by the cadavers. But then, the great discovery of the day was made. In what would be termed the cargo hold, cryogenic freezers were discovered, filled with frozen aliens of various sizes. The team would soon learn that these aliens were technically alive in their frozen state.

Dr. Detlev Bronk suggested it would be best to move the ship to Los Alamos, where they would have the best chance of reanimating the aliens in a controlled environment.

A day later, after much more inspection of the interior, Dr. Carl Heiland discovered a hidden drawer containing what appeared to be tuning forks. After much trial and error, he walked outside the ship with one of the forks and was shocked to see the ship coming apart where he walked! He quickly realized that if he walked from the center of the ship to the edge, the ship would molecularly unzip itself. And if he took the fork in the opposite direction, the ship would molecularly zip itself back together!

Hours later, the ship was disassembled into three sections and, over the next two days, loaded aboard flatbeds for the three-day movement by moonlight to Los Alamos and the Navy auxiliary base, where Bob would oversee the medical team on the greatest discovery of their lives.

V yla opened her eyes, not knowing if she'd been gone a minute or half an hour.

She didn't really care. She now felt like she had a good idea of the events leading to where she was in the film footage. She took a deep breath and hit *play*.

She watched in utter astonishment as the footage switched to an interior shot inside a medical lab, where the body of a human-sized alien was on a table surrounded by scientists and doctors, including Oppenheimer. A title card flashed across the top:

"*Los Alamos Medical Laboratory, April 7, 1948. Setimus.*"

But this footage had sound accompanying it! She felt as though she were in the lab with them, transfixed as Bob Oppenheimer and a bald-headed Marine major were shown sitting on lab chairs, watching over an alien who looked like a passable adult human, roughly thirty years old.

"We have a pulse!" said a doctor excitedly at the end of the table.

The camera panned and zoomed in on the tall, older, European-looking doctor as a title card appeared above his face: "*Dr. Detlev Bronk. Head of Majestic-12 Medical Team.*"

Next to him stood another tall man, and the title card appeared: "*Vannevar Bush: Head of Majestic-12 Scientific Team.*"

The entire group looked on in anticipation as they slowly massaged the limbs of the alien. The camera worked its way around the table, naming various doctors and scientists, finishing with J. Robert Oppenheimer.

"We are friendly, and you are in good hands," repeated Dr. Detlev Bronk as the team continued working the alien's limbs.

"His pulse is getting stronger!" Bronk whispered excitedly.

Vyla watched, astonished.

Just then, the camera panned to the Marine major and zoomed in on him momentarily.

She gasped. The close-up allowed her to see his military nametag: *S. Boyd*.

And just then, a title card appeared at the top of the picture: *"Major Sam Boyd, Head of the IPU Team. Durango, CO, deployed at Aztec, NM, crash recovery."*

She paused the footage and felt her heart beating out of her chest. She would have given anything to show Dah this footage! Again, she took a deep breath and hit play.

Bob Oppenheimer and Sam Boyd moved to either side of the table near the alien's head. Standing between the two of them was a man in a coat and tie, staring down at the alien. The title card popped up on screen, and Vyla again caught her breath. *"Secretary of Defense James Forrestal."*

She watched him, confused, and then remembered: Forrestal wouldn't be assassinated for another year!

Moments later, the camera panned to the alien, slowly batting his eyes and then—he opened them!

The camera captured the astonishment of all present as the alien's eyes appeared calm—as if he had expected to awaken in such an environment—surrounded by humans.

"Hello!" Oppenheimer whispered excitedly.

"Hello," the being replied in a raspy voice. The room erupted in muffled gasps of astonishment as Sam smiled, shaking his head.

Vyla jumped out of her seat and cheered.

"Yes!" she exclaimed, then realized the guard was staring at her.

"Sorry, I uh..." she trailed off, then realized she didn't give a damn about what he thought. She looked back at the footage.

"I'm Bob, and this is Sam," Oppenheimer whispered to the alien.

"I'm Setimus," came the raspy reply. "I'm a mechanic."

"Setimus, welcome!" several replied. "Welcome to Earth!"

"Would you like some water?" Sam asked.

Setimus slowly sat up as the scientists all assisted him. He stretched his arms and rolled his neck, adjusting to being animated again. He then turned to Sam.

"Why, yes, it was quite hot out there in the desert!"

The entire room burst into laughter, and Vyla laughed aloud... and thought the accent was somewhat British-influenced. But then she was caught. Setimus had a way-too-familiar look? Then it dawned on her. The beard was gone, but when the camera slowly came around to show the crazy earring, Vyla shook her head in amazement and placed her hand on her heart. Sam Boyd was talking to SWIZZLE!

She wanted to scream, cry, laugh, and shout as a wave of emotions she could not control swept through her. She wondered how old Setimus—or Swizzle, or whatever his real name was—must be and then remembered that the Majestic brief had alluded to aliens having 600-year lifespans!

Bob Oppenheimer then switched on what appeared to be a speaker behind him, and there were a series of voices. Then it was *him*. President Harry Truman spoke on what Vyla figured must have been one of the first speakerphones of the era. Truman's voice was distinct and scratchy, which fit the timeframe.

"Welcome, sir," Truman said.

Oppenheimer spoke next.

"That is our President, Harry Truman, and he wants to offer you ambassador status if you promise to prove no hostile intent toward humanity."

Setimus smiled and nodded slightly.

"Thank you, Mr. President. I come in peace."

Truman then spoke again.

"Thank you, Mr. Setimus. We would like to learn as much from you as possible, and if, after a short six-month period has passed, with no hostility issues, I will offer you an invitation to be the first-ever alien Ambassador to the United States."

"I thank you, Mr. President, and I will accept that offer as long as you don't ask me to interfere with the regular evolution of humanity on this planet. I cannot teach science or anything that would move your people ahead of their regular evolutionary process. But I can tell you anything you want to know about my race and my people."

"Thank you, Mr. Setimus. I accept your offer, and I understand you may need some time to settle back into your reanimation. I look forward to meeting you soon."

"Thank you, Mr. President."

Oppenheimer nodded as Setimus finished speaking with Truman.

"Thank you, Mr. President. We will try to take care of our new guest here and will keep you informed of our progress." Oppenheimer said.

"Thank you, Dr. Oppenheimer. We'll talk shortly. Have a good night."

The speaker was switched off, and Setimus was helped to his feet by Sam and Bob. Then the movie stopped on a freeze-frame of the three men smiling at each other.

Vyla sat stunned. She felt a deep stillness in her heart. There was something about Swizzle's face—even if his real name was Setimus—she didn't care. Something about him... felt like home.

Chapter Thirty-Nine

T he surviving passengers were anxious and cold as the shattered airliner they were trapped in—was still on fire and leaving a dark black smoke trail—as it raced along at 1500 feet above the night ocean.

Upfront in the cockpit, Benjamin R. Waters, was freaking out. He had the jet pointed northwest, heading for the southern tip of Great Nicobar Island. Unbeknownst to him, the second act of the Cabal show was now beginning, and he had no idea... that he was center-stage.

A moment before, out there in the pitch black, just behind MH370, two United States Air Force *MQ-9 Reaper drones* had been laying-in-wait, airborne, as Ben flew by. The drones were filming using *Gorgon Stare* technology at six-frames per second, and could literally see through the burning jet. The Reaper drones were filming on orders from the United States *National Reconnaissance Office* and were uploading their footage in real-time to the NRO L-22 satellite, which was broadcasting the video for the Cabal to view, as well as America's top U.S. intelligence officials who were watching in real-time from all over the planet.

The drones were on station to track and film the Boeing 777 for the ultimate visual spectacle of all time. The teleportation of a commercial airliner—while inflight and on fire—essentially making the jet vanish in midair. The entire *stealing*...

planned in advance as a show for Chinese leaders, watching on their satellite video feed, as the jet tooled along... with their promised technology and engineers inside it.

The teleportation would be the Cabal's goodbye kiss to Beijing. A *"Who's your daddy?"* of epic proportions.

As the jet approached Great Nicobar Island, Ben was using autopilot and assessing his damage. Even though his handlers had convinced him not to land at Penang on the western side of Malaysia, which could have been managed, Ben was determined to get the jet on the ground... kill switch or not. He was going to die in that godforsaken jet anyway if he didn't get it on deck... and fast.

Slowly descending the airliner, he had no idea that he was flying into a pre-planned trap. That other little detail his briefers forgot to mention.

The... uh... teleportation of his jet thing.

The MAYDAY call he sent out at that moment, picked up by a United States Air Force Base at U Tapao in Thailand at 2:43 a.m., was Ben's voice announcing:

"The cabin was disintegrating, and he was planning to make a forced landing."

A radio transmission the Cabal would quickly bury before the media picked up on it.

At that same moment, 1500 feet below the descending jet, a woman riding in a small ocean-going sailboat looked up to see—a glowing orange, burning jet—descending toward Great Nicobar Island, with black smoke trailing behind it. Simultaneously, a passenger in the main cabin managed to type—but not send—a message that was later found saved on social media.

Like a diary entry, it seemed to confirm the utter terror that surviving passengers were enduring. The terse cry hinted that all aboard—while riding blindfolded and handcuffed—had been doused with fire suppression water and were flying with wind and most likely smoke traveling through the unpressurized cabin. The eerie message would be found only a week after the flight vanished.

"Scared. Cold. No one says anything."

At precisely that moment, as seen on the leaked NRO videos, the first Cabal plasma-orb intercepted the jet and began circling MH370.

In the cockpit, Ben looked up surprised as a ball of light, roughly fifty-feet in diameter, flashed by his windscreen in the pitch black. He felt a sudden temperature drop as the technology in his brain went haywire... disturbed by the massive amount of magnetic interference suddenly enveloping the jet.

A moment later, there were two plasma orbs circling the jet... and then three!

The orbs were moving at above Mach speeds as Ben slowly lost control of his body. The technology embedded in his brain... came with an override trigger, just for such an event as this. His survival mechanism, when confronted with

417

massive electromagnetic waves—suddenly kicked into gear—doing exactly what it was supposed to do during extreme conditions. It sent a burst... an automatic last-gasp for help... a full system dump.

Experts later analyzed a structured telemetry file, that appeared to have been auto-triggered by an environmental override. Ben's software had gone into fight-or-flight mode. A system burst designed for field analysis under hostile or compromised conditions. The data that experts analyzed for that moment, painted a chilling evolution.

Between 2:32 and 2:36 a.m., exactly when the orbs in the video are racing around the jet and pulsing... the cabin registered erratic spikes in air pressure, consistent with decompression events. Interference readings in the electrical realm—shot off the chart, consistent with external electromagnetic disruptions—of epic scale.

The temperature log sent out from Ben's burst showed a drop of nearly 20°F in less than 90 seconds, which was far too fast for normal atmospheric cooling. During all of it, a cadence was recorded that matched *human respiration under physical or emotional distress.* It was Ben's breathing, of course, and the pace increased slightly near the end of the clip, suggesting a spike in adrenaline. And that spike occurred at the exact moment on the NRO videos when the jet and all three orbs... vanished... leaving only sky and clouds behind.

At that moment, the teleportation of MH370 with CIA hijackers and over two-hundred innocent passengers and crew was underway.

The phase-transition vortex the plasma-orbs had created around the jet literally pulled the airliner into the void. MH370 had been sucked into the Cabal's wormhole... appearing to instantaneously phase-out the jet. Chinese officials watched in dismay as their defecting engineers and promised technology... vanished.

But the burning airliner wasn't destroyed in that phase-out. It was stolen. In that moment... the jet was in the wormhole, moving instantaneously to a destination 1500 miles southwest of Great Nicobar, where it would reappear over a tropical Maldives Islands beach village.

One called... Kudahuvadhoo.

T om told Hoppy that his latest series of flashbacks had been overwhelming.

He had called her to tell her that he was flying up for another session. Now that he was on her couch, it was clear to her that he had aged in the last couple of months. Sleep deprivation, she assumed, from this much trauma coming forward. She sensed he was dropping away... back into the place he went.

"Hans dropped off the body of the Asian down in the tunnels, and he was still covered in the man's blood, but he was being summoned to the surface level by Chief One. He made his way up into the DUMB through a manhole cover, then Chief One had him remove a few more maintenance crew. The ones who had taken the wings off the jet."

He stared ahead without emotion. Jane became worried.

"Hans is not you, and you are not Hans... and Tom... remember, you told me they named your clone *Hans*, because he was a particular type of clone—an assassin model. You said wherever the Cabal had clones being used, there were other Hans models operating as assassins. So, if you can remember that, Tom... it will be easier to remember that you were used by them. By the Cabal. You Tom, had never given your consent to be cloned or used in that way."

He slowly nodded.

"Hans goes down the hallway. Sees the Chief standing near the forklift driver in the freight elevator. His forklift was hefting a thirty-yard construction dumpster."

"Thirty-yard construction dumpster?" Jane asked, taking shorthand.

Tom nodded.

"They're twenty-four feet long... eight-feet wide. Eight-feet deep."

She nodded slowly as Tom stared into space.

"Hans entered the freight elevator, and Chief One is yelling at him, 'Show him where to dump this shit!' Hans is worried about the prod the Chief is holding... but the Chief just—leaves—departing the freight elevator."

"So, Hans is in the elevator with the forklift driver?" she asked.

Tom nodded.

"Hans pushed the button and the enormous door closed."

"What's in the dumpster, Tom?"

"The bodies from the surface."

"So, the dumpster had all the maintenance crew from earlier?"

Tom nodded.

"And you descended to the tunnels and guided the forklift driver to where they were dumped?"

"No, Hans was in the back of the elevator, and the forklift driver pushed too hard on the dumpster, and it rammed against the freight elevator, and crushed Han's arm."

"Oh, my, I'm sorry Tom."

Tom shrugged slightly.

"The forklift driver delivered Hans to the Greys on the level below the jail and the Greys regrew his arm over the next three days."

"The Grey's regrew Han's arm in three days?!" she asked, astonished.

"Yeah, regeneration tanks... the Greys... when they want to, can regrow a destroyed limb and get a soldier back into fighting shape pretty damn quick. Hell... they can create a full clone of anybody in just a couple of weeks. That's how Hans got made. They took a soul fragment from Tom... from me."

"So, Hans never saw where the bodies went?"

"Yeah, later Hans saw what was left of them... in the tunnels below the DUMB."

"I'm sorry about that Tom... that you have to remember that." Jane whispered.

"The entire plane was apart and stored in a big hangar right there on the surface. The fuselage they left intact... it's just stripped. And the rest of the jet is stacked in pieces, right there in the hangar. Nobody comes to Diego, so, nobody would know it was a commercial jet anymore."

"So all the passengers and crew?" Jane whispered,

Tom stared into space... back into the place he went... without emotion.

Chapter Forty

On her flight back to San Francisco she knew there were still massive gaps in her understanding of the cover-up and how it had grown so quickly.

She was shocked that a few individuals in power had the audacity and arrogance to keep the incredible event of Setimus' revival from the public! How could such an evolution—an alien being brought back to life after being cryogenically frozen—have happened without the world knowing about it?

She exited San Francisco airport and didn't get off the subway at Millbrae station, where her truck was. She figured the Twins would be waiting for her, just like last time. So, she skipped it and kept riding until Union Station. Minutes later, as she was walking casually among the outdoor restaurants on 18th Street, she passed a burly vagrant on a street corner who was busy trimming his beard with rusted scissors. She knew not to acknowledge him. She heard him deep inside, and once again it was in her voice, but not her words.

You're being followed. Continue to the sandbox at Mission Dolores Park. Don't worry, they won't harm you.

Even with his saying so, she was unnerved that she could be tracked so easily. Before she reached the sandbox, he joined her with a smile and led her out of the light toward the darkened streets above the park. They walked in silence for a while before he lit a cigarette.

"Well, am I to understand that I should call you Setimus?" she asked.

This stopped him in his tracks. He turned, staring at her, trying to figure it out.

"S-4, Papoose Lake, Nevada," he finally said, pointing his cig her way. "You were in the DUMB at S-4, and you saw my reanimation footage from Los Alamos in 1948."

"Damn, you're good," she said, staring at him.

"So, if you don't mind my asking, just how old are you?"

"The average lifespan of my race is 600 of your Earth years. But I'm only 234."

She stared. *Wow.*

He shrugged.

"There are literally billions of races out in the multi-verse. Some alien races live to be over 1000 Earth years."

She slowly nodded.

He pulled on his cig and then waved it as he spoke.

"S-4... that's where the Cabal keeps some of the vintage footage... but their biggest archive is in the Rock City DUMB, below the Rock City Government complex. And that DUMB, way down below... has Royal Dracos—the thirty-five foot tall, winged, white-skinned ones."

"Yikes," she whispered.

He nodded.

"The Cabal stores their employees' personal records down there for blackmail purposes. And footage of every UFO crash recovery, as well as millions of photos of those recoveries. Not to mention the Eisenhower footage from the first contact event in 1954 at Edwards Air Force Base and footage of—"

"Setimus?" She said, cutting him off.

"Do you want to give me a recap of your full history?" she asked.

He gestured with his cig as they walked.

"I came to Earth my first time aboard Sophia, my one hundred-foot ship. There were eighteen of us onboard, but only four of us survived."

"Did you say your ship's name was Sophia?"

He nodded, and she could tell his ship was everything to him.

"She's a feisty one, and yes, I know she's at S-4."

She slowly nodded.

"Did you see her?" he inquired excitedly.

She nodded, smiling.

"You spoke to her?" He said with delighted eyes.

She kept nodding and saw his eyes mist over.

"Excuse me," he said and looked away.

She put her hand on his shoulder, realizing he was having a very human moment. He turned back, having regrouped.

"At that time, I went by the name of Setimus. I was a mechanic on Sophia."

"Why, Sophia?" she asked.

He smiled, opening his hands as if to signal everything.

"Well, Sophia is the original name of this lovely blue orb you call 'Mother Earth.' Many in the human new-age movement call her Gaia, and that's fine, but most who really knew her from the beginning call her *Sophia*."

She smiled.

"Sophia. Beautiful. So, you came here aboard Sophia in 1948?"

He nodded.

"Yes, and what an arrival it was. Hart Canyon, up on the mesa in Aztec, New Mexico, March 25, 1948. As you know, I met your famous scientist, J. Robert Oppenheimer, a really nice man and by far, the smartest human I've ever met in person. I eventually met with your President Harry Truman. A very conservative gentleman, I might add. But I think he had a good heart, he was just over his head in pressure to help your country recover from the Great Depression. When they moved me to the secret Vermont Army base to keep me hidden, I was introduced to several in Truman's administration."

"Such as?" she asked.

"Oh, I met with Eisenhower, James Forrestal, Lyndon Baines Johnson, Nelson Rockefeller, and several military generals, including Hap Arnold, Curtis LeMay and Nathan Twining, who by the way... Twining was the Cabal's man who signed the Greada treaty behind Eisenhower's back."

Vyla pointed at him.

"So Eisenhower didn't sign the Greada treaty?"

Swizzle shook his head.

"No, Ike was in over his head like Truman."

Swizzle opened his hands, gesturing as they strolled.

"And—and I have a confession."

She turned slightly as they walked.

"Oh, well, get it over with," she said.

He laughed at her nonchalance.

"Just like that, huh?"

She shrugged, and he let fly.

"I knew you were going to fly my ship," he said.

She stopped, her mind racing through all the events since the UAP incident when she became aware of Gizmo.

"So, did you also know that I was going to interview the pilots?"

He sheepishly nodded.

"So, I have a hyper-dimensional beacon installed?" she asked.

He nodded.

She exhaled.

"Who put it there and when?"

"I was a friend of your father's... I was there when the attack happened, and you were saved by Colonel Steve Wilson after the attack."

"Papa!" she said, almost bursting into tears.

He nodded, watching her.

"When he gave you to the Swiss nurse, I waited until she fell asleep and placed it then."

"Wait, you've—you've watched over me my entire life?"

He nodded. Her eyes filled with tears, as did his. She slammed into him, and the hug felt like coming home for both of them.

"Why now—why did you wait to tell me this?" she asked, still in tears.

"You've had so much to process—I didn't feel it was appropriate until now."

"Does this wildness ever quiet down, or is the universe just this nuts?" She said.

"You are it." He pointed at her. "You are... the universe."

She stared.

"You mean I'm the entire universe?"

He nodded.

"Each human is a fractal of the entire universe. You carry it within your being."

She stared.

"You mean I choose this—this fucking chaos?" she whispered.

He watched her, his look full of admiration and humility. She continued in a whisper,

"Royalty, you mean? This is the mission I chose? The potential you mentioned? The contract I agreed to?"

He watched her and, very slowly and humbly, pointed at her.

C ase arranged to meet the old Seal once more, and ask him if he knew anyone on the lookout for a new job, as Case needed a new partner for surveillance.

Case had decided that he would rather pick someone than just have someone assigned to him. He left the meeting with another napkin, which he didn't open until he got home. When he finally sat down and opened it, he saw a familiar San Diego area code and number.

Wow, he thought.

He knew the name before he read it... had trained under that badass back in the day... and shook his head at his luck as he read the final line:

Chief Petty Officer Dan Day. Martial Arts Master. Now available for hire.

T he Sikorsky CH-53 Sea Stallion chopper made its way to the Gerald R. Ford in complete darkness.

Ricky Slepher wore a three-piece custom Italian suit—the one and only time he showed his financial clout—and it was because he was traveling on a kill mission. On those missions, he liked to feel good and look good. His thing.

He sat across from SA Greywolf and, so far, liked the other Silent Assassin's demeanor. A six-foot-tall, stocky dude, wearing a good-looking suit as well. He seemed really cool in their brief exchanges so far.

Ricky Slepher was always looking for more individuals to help on his teams—he could always use another solid hand—especially someone who could keep their mouth shut. Years ago, Ricky had risen quickly through the security structure at Dulce-Security-Division-Three, eventually leading the security team that dealt with alien levels four through seven. That was a complex assignment for the Cabal to fill, as humans were generally unnerved by what transpired deeper in that facility. Ricky had witnessed this with his own unit of six Silent Assassins on their first descent to level four—a tour the Cabal had arranged, to find out who they could trust to monitor the Greys on levels four through seven.

The Cabal had a deal with the aliens at Dulce to provide humans in exchange for alien technology, and Ricky's DSD-3 team had gotten good at abductions. His team was told that those abductees were being used for genetic testing that would make the human race superior in every way. That was good enough reasoning for his team. What was good for the country was fine by them. They were good soldiers and knew not to ask questions.

Abductees were easiest to nab immediately following a natural disaster anywhere on the planet—earthquakes, tidal waves, tornadoes, floods, and even hurricanes. The Cabal ensured Ricky's team would be the first soldiers onsite—exiting the military transport that carried humanitarian aid—as the press cameras rolled. Two birds. One stone. Natural disasters always created thousands of displaced persons, and his team would abduct as many as possible. The abductees were gathered in shipping crates, with just enough air for their journey to the United States, and eventually to the Dulce DUMB—deep below the Archuleta Mesa—in northern New Mexico.

Upon returning and delivering their product, his team was consistently praised based on their numbers and reminded they were unsung heroes. They were paid handsomely for their efforts, which also kept their mouths shut. Secrecy was the law at Dulce, a place where experimentation on humans would have made former Nazi torturer Joseph Mengele wince.

His team only knew that abductees were sent down the freight elevators to Green-Level-Four, where they were rumored to be taken by Grey aliens to an area his DSD-3 team termed *Nightmare Hall*. Tall-Grey aliens on level four performed genetic testing on humans to create super soldiers for the Cabal, as well as for the Reptilians to sell out on the galactic trade routes. Often, the Cabal sent human scientists to level four to watch the Tall-Greys perform these genetic tests, to learn the alien protocols. Sometimes, that created issues. Slepher's security team would often be sent down to Level Four for a rescue mission... when a scientist went missing.

Generally, DSD-3's assignment was to keep the human scientists—who worked alongside the Greys—from straying into the non-human areas. Scientists tended to be curious, and even though "No trespassing" signs were posted on most passageways on level four... those signs were not always heeded.

Ricky would inevitably end up going in with a team to rescue a curious scientist—and often they would find that the scientist himself had already been dissected by the Tall-Greys, who had no qualms about making a human pay for their arrogance.

Slepher's security team, upon exiting the elevator on their first descent to Green-Level-Four, had been given a tour by a Tall-Grey alien. It was walking with that seven-foot, skinny telepathic Grey when his team witnessed hundreds of humans of all ages being kept in five-by-five-foot steel cages, stacked twenty feet high. All were naked and had that hopeless stare of animals who had been tortured too much. Some grunted at his team or howled. Some whimpered, and a few even yelled as they walked by.

"I'm John! I'm John! Hey, I'm John!"

Several members of Ricky's team had become sick upon returning to their offices high on level one—even though they had all been briefed before descending—that levels four and below were for genetic testing.

The men on his security team were really traumatized by seeing the humans they had themselves abducted being kept in cages and strapped to medical tables, tested, dissected, and enduring other horrible sights they encountered that first day. But not Ricky.

For him, the level four walkthrough had secretly confirmed what he already knew about the Greys... something he would shortly capitalize on. The Greys were experts not only in genetic manipulation but also in drug production of a particular type called *adrenochrome*. A drug derived from humans under extreme torture—a drug the global elite used to stay young.

His grandfather had first mentioned *Screamshit* when Ricky had told him of his new assignment at Dulce. Screamshit was the street name for the secretion taken from the human pineal gland, his grandfather had enigmatically alluded to with a look and a smile.

A drug that Ricky could sell on the open market if he chose to. One that had made his grandfather rich back in the day. His grandfather mentioned that the demand for Screamshit in the U.S. and worldwide had only grown exponentially since he had been at Dulce years before.

He told Ricky that a small vial of that human secretion could fetch several thousand dollars—and that was clear back in 1980.

Ricky, upon being given the new assignment as head of security for levels four through seven, had made secret connections with the Greys to become a facilitator. His deal was simple and effective for both sides. Slepher's DSD-3 team was already abducting humans for the Greys when he first arrived. But when Slepher took over on levels four through seven, he worked a side deal to provide a few more humans monthly in exchange for vials of Screamshit. He secretly knew that the real power controlling the alien levels at Dulce were the Draco-Reptilians, who lived below level seven.

He also knew that by doing business with the Tall-Greys, he was really dealing with the more powerful Draco—but he was fine with that. He knew in time he would deal directly with those brilliant, mean-ass lizards at some point.

They were the true mafia dons, his grandfather had whispered to him. The Cabal was powerful, but the Draco had long ago infiltrated the top of the Cabal, and it was they—disguised as powerful global elites—that actually called the shots. A little secret passed from his grandfather was that the Dulce complex actually had ten more levels below the seventh, and all of them were Reptilian-occupied, having been there for eons.

In no time at all, Slepher had a steady supply of the drug being created under his own security division at Dulce. While doing so, he made connections with stars in the entertainment industry, with whom his grandfather still had connections. Ricky's grandfather had warned him to stay away from ever taking the drug, as it was more addictive than heroin. And Ricky obeyed. He knew that a bodybuilder taking testosterone would soon cease producing his natural testosterone. The same effect happened with Screamshit. When addicted to the drug, the body would no longer produce stem cells. If the addict quit taking Screamshit, they generally lasted only three weeks and were either schizophrenic by then or dead.

Seven years after taking over the top enlisted position at Dulce, Ricky received transfer orders to take over the security team at a facility on the border of Missouri he had only heard rumors about—Rock City.

The scuttlebutt about the DUMB south of St. Louis had reached Dulce at some point years ago. But even for a veteran of dealing with aliens and extreme experimentation at Dulce, Ricky had been shocked upon finding what was far below ground on the border of Missouri and Illinois. It made Dulce look like child's play.

His first tour in the Rock City DUMB was more intense, as there were things happening below the surface that no human would ever believe. Creatures that, until seeing them himself, were only figments of his imagination.

What he now dealt with deep down in the Cabal's most secret location on the planet terrified him on one level and at the same time intrigued him. The amount of darkness below the surface world was mystifying and, perhaps more importantly to Ricky Slepher—expansive.

The creatures down there he had only heard rumors about at Dulce. They were the Royal Draco—the white-skinned ones that were all over thirty feet tall... and unbelievably to him... those bitches had wings. It was the Royal Draco that had requested his transfer from Dulce. He was now connected to them and did business with and for them... beyond even what his grandfather had achieved.

The helicopter touching down on the carrier brought him back to the job at hand, and he stepped out of the chopper with *SA Greywolf* just behind him. They were greeted by the counterintelligence officer for the carrier and were led to their stateroom, where they would get a quick brief on their target and exactly what time they were to strike. It was all planned in advance to ensure that as soon as the hit was complete, they could catch the next helo heading back to shore.

The weather was stormy but still dry as they walked in the windy darkness behind the CIC officer. Ricky felt good in his sharp-looking outfit. He savored the excitement of these moments. And none of those around him knew he was the famous *Winking Wolf*.

He thought about his last trip to the Diego Garcia Spaceport. While delivering a shipment, he had hung out with the German space freighter crew from the Max Von Laux, a Nazi Dark Fleet transport. While enjoying some delicious German beers, the crew told him that you could buy Winking Wolf products on the trade routes in space and on the planet of Alpha Draconis, where the goddamn lizards lived.

428

HUSH

Ricky had known for years that human-produced Screamshit brought top dollar out in the galaxy and beyond, but the crew assured him that Winking Wolf absolutely ruled the deep-space trade routes.

As he entered the superstructure of the Gerald R. Ford carrier... he thought about the Draco-Reptilians tipping one of his vials while shooting the shit on a street corner in their lizard capital—270 light years from Earth.

Maybe he would go there soon.

Part Three

SCREAMSHIT

Swizzle led her across Church Street, and then she trudged along beside him up the steep staircase of 20th Street toward a three-story Victorian.

Both of them were panting as he rang the doorbell and looked at her.

"Remember, they can read your thoughts."

"What?" she said, but it was too late. Footsteps were approaching the door. She glared at him as he flashed his Cheshire grin.

"Act normal," he whispered.

"Right, fuck off," she said, under her breath.

He snickered just as the door opened, revealing a stunning thirty-year-old brunette.

Damn, Vyla thought and then remembered his warning. The hottie nodded at Swizzle, then looked at her.

"Hello," she said, with no inflection. "I'm Cantrell," and opened the door wider for them to pass.

"This is Vyla," he said, motioning for Vyla to go first.

She smiled at Cantrell, who was sporting a summer silk miniskirt, sports bra, and flip-flops. Normally, this would have crushed her defenses, but the makeup wasn't quite right, and Vyla sensed something was off. She caught herself, remembering she was stepping into another facet of this alien reality. She decided to focus on the parts she liked. If Cantrell was reading her mind, it would be like reading a Playboy fantasy piece.

The Victorian was unlike Vyla's in that it was fastidiously refurbished and reeked of money. The entryway was polished mahogany, and the ceiling had a light fixture from the turn of the century with wallpaper straight out of *Gone with the Wind*.

"Right this way," Cantrell said as they followed her toward the sounds of a party down the hall. She could hear voices and music.

"Have you lived here long?" Vyla asked, smiling. Cantrell turned slightly as she walked.

"No," she replied, immediately turning back to the front.

Okay, that was weird, Vyla thought.

There seemed to be a lack of basic communication etiquette. Then, as they reached the large kitchen, she saw Plato bent over a table in her pink short-shorts, fixing martinis for the group of seven individuals who all looked up as she entered.

A strange mix of thirty-something adults who were watching Plato as she topped off each martini with the final luscious drops of vermouth.

"So, you add a little vermouth to each glass to make the martini smooth," Plato said to the group in a teaching tone, not looking up to see that Vyla and Swizzle had arrived just behind Cantrell.

"Jack, are you paying attention?" Plato said as she finally stood up straight and looked at a blond guy holding a small vial full of a red substance that she thought resembled blood. He was squeezing an eyedropper, dripping little red drops onto the tongue of the woman next to him, then putting a couple on his own tongue as he watched Plato. Plato then saw them and gave Swizzle a head shake.

These guys will never get this.

Swizzle shrugged and tapped a spoon on the counter to get the group's attention.

"Hello, everyone," Swizzle said. "This is Dr. Vyla Kells."

Plato shared a quick smile with her as the others all said hello in strange, unpracticed speech. Swizzle continued his introduction.

"Dr. Kells is here to meet all of you and see how the training is going," Swizzle explained.

Vyla looked at him, her mind racing as she suddenly realized that everyone in the kitchen was an alien, and then had the epiphany... that they were in training to act like—humans?

Just that morning, she had been reading a brief from Papa's folder about sessions of alien abductees training Hybrids on UFOs on how to act like humans. During hypnotic recall sessions, the abductees commented on the weirdness of teaching aliens the basics of human communication skills. Now, she was staring at a roomful of aliens, and yet she wasn't an abductee. The three men and four women, including Cantrell, nodded at her and in quiet whispers said a perfunctory *Hello* or *Hi,* but each delivery was a rote response, spoken with no affect, nuance, or feeling—one step removed from a computer voice.

"So, Vyla, this group has just arrived at this Victorian for their indoctrination into living within the city," Swizzle said.

"And I'm teaching them to make martinis," Plato chimed in as she turned and handed one to Vyla. "Welcome, Vyla," she said with a smile and a wink.

"Thank you," Vyla replied, taking the martini. "I'm honored, and I loved your butterfly talk the other day."

At this, all the aliens watched Plato for her response.

"Thank you, dear. I'll try to catch up with you in a little bit..." then leaned in and whispered, "After I teach these motherfuckers how to drink a Goddamn martini!"

Vyla snickered as Plato walked back to her teaching position. Several in the group passed the eyedropper, dripping a few drops on their tongues before passing it on. She wondered if it was a whiskey-like substance as they all seemed to shake their heads momentarily after swallowing the drops.

Swizzle noticed it at that moment and snatched the eyedropper, screwing the top back on the vial, and put it in the sink. The group looked at him like a bunch of needy kids whose cookies had just been taken away by an adult.

"I want all of you to concentrate during the time that Plato is teaching, please," Swizzle scolded.

Plato handed each of them a martini. The group awkwardly held their drinks, not understanding the thin, oddly shaped martini glasses. Some smelled their cocktails and wrinkled their noses. Vyla stifled her laughter, now noticing for the first time that all of their clothing was off.

One man had on blue jeans that were too long, and his shiny, black Corfam shoes were too big, as though he'd been gifted everything at the Goodwill. His shirt fit perfectly, but it was buttoned up to the neck. The women had all attempted makeup but applied it like small girls playing with makeup for the first time.

"Alright, everyone, taste them drinks, and don't worry if they're not that tasty on your first try. You'll encounter these in your interactions at private parties, and you need to understand how to drink 'em."

Each of the group began to sip, and their reactions made Vyla want to burst out laughing as Swizzle motioned Plato into the next room.

When she looked up, Jack had snatched the vial out of the sink and unscrewed the eyedropper—not sneaking it like a kid would do, but more like a puppy who'd just retrieved a bone it had misplaced.

She watched him curiously until suddenly he turned and offered it to her. Everyone was staring at her, and the idea of taking an alien drug with a bunch of aliens was simply too rich to pass up. Plus, Vyla had decided that Jack was cute despite his awkward dress.

So, bloody hell, why not? She thought and took the eyedropper, placing several drops on her tongue.

A moment later, as the Screamshit hit her bloodstream, she heard the sudden blaring rise in the radio volume of *I'm Sexy and I Know It,* mixed with the nauseous, dropping-way-too-fast-in-an-elevator feeling as her knees became unhinged.

In her eyes, Swizzle and Plato raced toward her in slow motion. Their terrified faces clearly yelling... she could make out a distorted warning of something scary, echoing through her brain like a hollowed-out cavern.

The shattering of her martini glass on the polished kitchen floor. The exploding cold liquid, splattering high and dropping over the plastic bag of alien figurines as they shot and splayed, spinning to stops at the wrong-sized shoes of those Hybrids holding their awkward martinis. They stared curiously down at the figurines they somehow knew as their teachers. And at the human woman's shaking body—kicking and moving like a snake—twitching in a nasty neurological fit.

They all could read her mind—that it had gone to a place where the drug was created—deep below the Archuleta Mesa, near an old Apache dwelling called... Dulce.

T here seemed no escape from the nightmare, the fighting and straining against those little Greys with their slimy hands that held her fast to the table with their fibrous, vice-like fingers.

Four of those little fuckers held her naked, writhing body in place... as she screamed, with no end to her nightmare.

She stared up through her one good eye—the one that didn't have a needle stuck through it—at the menacing devil face of that Tall-Grey glaring down at her... with its ant-like face. And he didn't give a shit. She was only human and perfect for producing her terror in a liquid for selling on the open market. *Screamshit.* And there was only one way to produce it: *torture.*

When a human is in mortal fear, adrenochrome happens. And with humans, it could be harvested—like milk from a cow. That's all she was to him. A resource to be harvested... a pinned rat on his operating table, a specimen for his fucked-up glandular secretion collection. He worked that long, cold metal spike deep into her cranium as her feet kicked and shook in violent death-throes-type responses to the ongoing torture. His wrap-around black eyes, shiny and menacing, turned his head, ant-like in his sinister intensity, zeroing in on her as she writhed just the way he tweaked her.

She couldn't hear herself screaming, but she knew she was, and yet she could somehow hear the screams and terror of those on the tables next to her coming out of her body—while they were having their own nightmarish operations. She was screaming all their screams. And some of those screams were from kids and babies! Some screamed with different inflections, and some yelled in different languages at their tormentors. And it was all coming from her, through her.

Yet a moment later, she was floating in utter contentment as somehow that tall, menacing prick above her made the pain stop. She heard him say in her own voice, *"Don't worry, you'll be okay."*

And then she was, and she breathed and felt okay for a moment. But then it began again, and she knew deep inside that he was a torturous, lying fuck!

And just then, when he had relaxed her long enough to refill her glands with more shit he could pursue, he would slide that fucking turkey baster back through her left eye, pushing until it slid into the cavity deep in her cranium... where the red juice from the pineal gland collected, as he knew the strain would be more potent if she were actually screaming... the moment he sucked it out of her.

And she did—the shaking terror, her wincing in a silent scream for her life as her body quaked, attempting escape but held like a vice by the little slimy, four-fingered hands stuck like a mouse in a glue trap. She could move, but she was getting more stuck with each twist.

Her throat was dry from the screaming... no sound coming out. Water—she needed water!

She could hear Swizzle and Plato before they came into focus.

Swizzle and Plato's faces were staring down at her. They were mixed into the dream, and then they were somehow the first relief from what seemed like a never-ending nightmare.

"I'll get her some water." She heard Plato say, and then her face disappeared from Vyla's view. Swizzle kept staring and had his hands on her shaking body. She had a sense she was coming out of something, but the terror gripped her, and she felt his big, calloused hands on her arms, holding tightly.

"Vyla, it's Swizzle, and you are on my boat, *Gizmo*, and we are in San Francisco Harbor at Pier 39."

She felt the terror, and the tears were all she had, except for her breathing. She could hear herself hyperventilating, and Swizzle's firm grip and gentle but reassuring hold helped to slow her heartbeat, hell-bent on escape.

"You are coming off a bad trip from a drug you ingested at a party."

She stared up and felt herself covered in sweat. She was cold, and yet she also noticed that she was swaddled in blankets.

"Hey, Darlin'," she heard Plato say.

And then coming into view was her calm face and beehive hairdo, with the two braids hanging down toward Vyla's face. Plato pulled her braids back and held out a cup of water.

"Can you sit up a little, sweetheart?"

Plato reached out and put her hand gently behind her head and simultaneously gripped her arm as Vyla slowly worked her way up onto her elbows. Vyla said nothing as Plato raised the glass of water to her lips.

She began crying as she sipped and fell back in silent sobs, turning onto her side in a fetal position as Swizzle and Plato swarmed around her, placing their hands and gently holding her.

And then Swizzle made it lessen, and she knew again that somehow she was safe in that moment. But she also would never forget.

They stayed with her for the next two hours as she slowly came around. The sun was coming up on the boat's aft deck, and there was the gentle rock of the ship as the city came alive. Plato and Swizzle sat close on both sides of her as she stared out.

"What was it?" she finally asked, looking over at Plato, who tightened her lips and looked at Swizzle. Plato then gently patted her arm.

"Sweet girl, I'm really sorry about what happened, but I need to get up to Union Square as there's a crowd waitin' on me. You'll be in good hands here with Swizzle."

Vyla nodded slightly as Plato gave her a hard smile and departed.

She turned to see Swizzle's gentle but concerned stare. He watched her for a moment.

"I don't know if you remember at the park when I told you there were many more reasons I am coming forward with my story."

"The drug you ingested—it's produced by my race. By the Greys. I had no idea that Jack was going to offer it to you, and I'm so very sorry."

She watched him and then whispered,

"Why would anybody want that—that shit?"

"The effect on my race is much different than for humans," he said, watching her. "It's something my race uses as a drug to slow the effects of dealing with Earth's atmosphere on our less dense bone structure. The pressure of your atmosphere can lead to mental instability for the Greys as they are not hybrids like I am."

"Why were those trainees using it then?"

He seemed frustrated as he took a deep breath and stared out at the enormous cruise ship approaching Pier 27.

"It has grown over the years into a recreational drug for the Hybrids. I don't use it, and neither does Plato, but when we tried it, the effect was basically melatonin-like and calming. But that's its intended purpose when it was first discovered by the Greys."

She could tell that this was certainly part of Swizzle's secret that she had sensed upon his coming out to her.

"Yes," he whispered. "This is a big part of why I showed myself to you."

She watched him and could see and feel what she knew as shame.

He looked at her, deflated and exhaled.

"We—the Greys, I should say—create it. In labs."

"What's in it?"

"It's a glandular secretion that is produced by the adrenal system when the body is in mortal danger."

"They secrete that shit from their glands?"

Swizzle looked at her and turned again to the bay, slightly shaking his head.

"Human glands."

It took her a few seconds to register what he said.

"Oh, shit."

And then the bile came up. She quickly sat up, slowly raised the water glass with a shaking hand, and took a sip as Swizzle put his hand gently on her shoulder. She immediately brushed it violently away, spitting out her water and retching.

"You stay the fuck away from me!" she gritted through her teeth, dry retching and slowly stood, shaking, working her way to the railing, holding on as he stood by the rail, giving her space. She retched, but nothing was coming out. She laid her head on the rail as tears streamed down her face, thinking of Stephanie, crying on the way to school about the Tall-Grey... and could hear her voice. *He hurt me!*

Swizzle watched her from a distance... beside himself.

She held the rail, clinging to it to ground herself. She breathed a few times, realizing Swizzle had no part in any of this, and she wanted stability again. Right now.

"You fucking aliens," she whispered, standing and looking at him as he stared shamefully at the glimmering bay, slowly nodding contemplatively.

"Tell it!" she yelled. "What the fuck is happening? You're abducting and torturing humans, then making them forget, then re-abducting them to drain their fucking glands over and over? Is that it?! Tell me all of it! Goddamn it!"

"That's—that's a pretty good assessment."

"But there's a lot more, isn't there?" she said, realizing the complexity, she hardly understood. She stared at the sunlit water lapping against the bow and breathed.

"Yes," he said quietly, taken aback as he watched her slowly stand, facing him. Suddenly, her eyes softened, the anger gone. He saw compassion, and the tears were still coming slowly as she put an arm around his shoulder, pulling him into her.

"I'm so very, very sorry," he whispered.

She nodded and gently squeezed him.

"Hey," she whispered, motioning with a nod toward the cruise ship—just the spectacle she needed to ground her back into the moment.

They stared out, holding each other in silence, watching the seven-story cruise ship slowly approaching the dock, music playing, flags and humans waving and yelling from ship to shore.

"Do aliens like cruise ships?" she whispered.

And for the first time in his life, something happened in that moment of compassion that he had never experienced. He didn't know where it came from, but he knew that somehow, she had come for him—for him to learn this from a human. A new depth of emotions he'd never known. She had somehow brought this sublime grace now flowing to him.

He looked at her, and she saw them.

Tears.

Chapter Forty-Two

It had been exactly two weeks since the UAP intercept, and the digital clock on his nightstand clicked 2 a.m. as Frank moved his *Knife* emblazoned flight suit off the bed and hung it up in the tiny closet.

He was back on the flight schedule after being grounded for the week-long investigation. In a few hours, he would again lead a sortie on the upcoming CAP cycle, and he was eager to put all this investigation bullshit behind him. It had been a withering week of debriefs and political maneuvering, and now, finally, he was in his robe, barefoot, and ready to crawl in bed.

That's when the knock came.

He quickly grabbed the harddrive next to his laptop and hastily placed it in the drawer of his desk, silently sliding it closed.

"Who is it?" he said out loud to the closed stateroom door.

"Captain Jacobs, sir, it's Corpsman Tort from medical."

At 2 a.m.? Frank thought, incensed. *Why are they harassing me now?*

He stared at the door. This whole endeavor—with all the debriefs and pressure to keep his mouth shut about what really happened—had become a gauntlet that had yet to let up. He had watched his squadron staff—and the ship's field-grade staff—hound Crazy, his wingman during the incident. She had departed the carrier on the morning COD, gaining emergency leave to see her ailing father, but Frank knew that was a cover. She was being cornered, as he was, from all sides, in the silent political maneuvers that squadrons do when they want to distance themselves from *tainted* individuals who could affect the squadron's field-grade officers, namely the Executive Officer and Commanding Officer. Crazy had made her decision to run, and now Frank was the only *problem* left on the ship.

Four days earlier, Frank had made a fateful decision over a rum and coke that he needed to get a copy of his heads-up footage in case the whole charade ended in a court-martial. At least then, Frank could present the footage as an actual fact of what he was saying happened.

He had been able to surreptitiously obtain a copy of the heads-up footage from his UAP encounter. His squadron's avionics shop had initially told him that the heads-up footage had been classified as top-secret and that no copies were available. But Frank knew a corporal in the avionics department who used to work for him when Frank was the officer in charge of squadron maintenance. Two crisp one-hundred-dollar bills to the young man had garnered Frank the full ten-minute-intercept on a harddrive.

But now, he looked around the room once more to double-check, making certain that nothing else incriminating was lying about, and then opened the door.

Standing outside were two large corpsmen that Frank had never seen. Not that he should really know any of the hospital staff on a carrier filled with 5,000 sailors, but nevertheless, they were completely new faces.

"Sir..." the taller corpsman of the two said.

"I'm Corpsman Tort, and this here is Corpsman Colley. We were sent down to get a current blood pressure test for the post-investigation."

Frank stared at the corpsmen, both of whom were clearly fit, and their uniforms seemed brand new—unlike many on the hospital staff he encountered. The taller of the two, Corpsman Tort, had a strange scar running from his left eye toward his jaw. Frank glared.

"Well, I have a fuckin' flight in six hours, corpsman!" Frank snarled. "And I don't appreciate the wake-up... besides, I just had my blood pressure tested earlier this week!"

Corpsman Tort raised the blood pressure cuff he was holding and shrugged.

"I'm sorry, sir, we were sent down here on orders from Skipper Schrader."

Frank glared, eyes ablaze, his lips tight... and then realized it was fruitless. He was being punished, and he didn't want to piss anybody off who could get him yanked off the flight schedule. He exhaled and opened the door wider for them to enter.

"Hurry the fuck up... I need to get back to bed!" he seethed.

"If you can just take a seat, sir," Tort said, pointing to the desk chair. "We'll be gone in two minutes flat."

Frank shook his head and reluctantly sat down, hearing the other corpsman close and lock the door... which seemed odd.

Frank had turned only halfway with his questioning look, when the wire garrote, in the hands of the corpsman with the scar, raced by his eyes and was instantaneously around his neck.

Like a trout being pulled out of the water, Frank was lifted, squirming, and flipping in every direction, but he couldn't scream for help as his larynx was already in a wire-vice that was slowly closing.

He instinctively reached for the wire, which had buried itself a quarter inch into his neck. His twitching fingers then reached up and back to the massive forearms of Slepher, reefing the wire even tighter behind him.

"Loose lips sink ships, Captain Jacobs." Slepher whispered in Frank's ear as his kicking and twitching were squashed by the other assassin bear-hugging his legs.

Frank knew in that instant that this was his end... and in those final seconds, he knew getting a copy of the footage had been a mistake. He could have been court-martialled if anyone ever found out. But now... being executed for this small error in judgment? It couldn't be! And by his own military that he loved... erasing him! But somehow... he knew it was higher than the military. Simultaneously, the shock of being strangled to death was so sudden and terrifying and not what he could have ever imagined happening in his lifetime.

And in those final seconds, when there was no air coming, he surprisingly felt twin emotions.

He wished he could tell Kelly he was sorry for being an unfaithful shit during every deployment and that he could make amends with her. He had fucked it all now. And the other emotion that would be his last... was, of all things... embarrassment.

As his vision went black, the final fleeting thought came home to him...that for the second time in two weeks... he had unexpectedly... shit himself.

Vyla stared at Swizzle.

"That is all wrong," she said, and he nodded.

"Screamshit started hitting the downtown homeless a few years back, and now it's all over the dark web, and it's worked its way out here on the regular streets."

She nodded, contemplating, as they moved toward pier twenty-seven and the gigantic cruise ship.

"Where is it manufactured?" She asked, "And who the fuck is providing it to humans?"

He exhaled.

"The Greys began creating it in the Dulce complex sometime in the 50s."

She gasped.

"Dulce complex?" she said. "Does this have anything to do with Dulce, New Mexico?"

He nodded. She stared.

"My mother, who is half Apache, said her people had been fighting the evil in the mountain there?"

He exhaled, exasperated at where to start. She saw his look.

"So, it's all true?" she asked.

He nodded.

"Oh, my God," she whispered, shaking her head. "Where exactly is this... this complex?"

"It's two miles below Mount Archuleta, in northern New Mexico... near the small town of Dulce."

"So it's a DUMB... like Diego Garcia and Kirtland and S-4?"

He nodded.

"It was the very first deep underground facility that the Americans had stumbled onto in 1940... when they were searching for a place to create their first nuclear weapons. Once your Cabal realized they could get away with alien interaction and illegal genetic testing without informing the public... the Cabal went crazy. And now there are hundreds of DUMBs throughout the planet."

"This Dulce thing, I did a journey on that place the other day... but I was only on the top levels... and it was back in 1947."

Swizzle nodded and could see all she knew from her memory. She watched him and could tell he was contemplating it all... trying to make it simple for her.

"So you saw the top levels in your journey as Sam... but Dulce is far more expansive. In a Reader's Digest version, imagine a genetic testing lab buried within a mountain... seventeen stories deep."

She stared.

"I thought it was only seven levels deep and four miles long?"

He nodded.

"Over the last sixty years, it has been extended and is now many miles in length."

She stared in disbelief.

"But the Draco created that facility for themselves eons ago. It's all Reptilian below level seven... and those caverns are deep and huge... created for the largest of the Royal Dracos. When Sam was in the facility, the Americans were just coming onto the scene. Even to this day, I don't think a human has ever descended below level seven... and if they had... it would have been their last descent."

She watched him.

"So what the hell happens there?"

He sucked his teeth.

"The American military contractors who wish to have more alien technology... are providing the Greys with humans in exchange for the alien tech."

She gasped, shaking her head.

"The Greada treaty that Twining and the Majestic-12 signed behind Eisenhower's back... with us... in 1954."

"Okay, let me get this straight... you're talking about how we Americans signed a treaty allowing you to secretly abduct humans in exchange for alien technology?"

He pointed, pulling on his cig.

"The Greys use the humans to create Screamshit, and they barter with the Draco down below, also selling it off-world."

She was dumbstruck as he continued.

"Screamshit is the most sought after drug in the universe... because humans are rare. Once the Cabal realized its value... it was simple to create as much as they needed, to further their own technological aims."

"You're dead serious?"

He slowly nodded.

"I'm sorry," he said. "But my source at Dulce just informed me that humans are being held captive by Dulce Security Division Three. Which is generally called DSD-3. And they are abducting and holding humans captive, not only for the production of Screamshit, but for the biochemical warfare testing and who knows what-the-fuck else."

"You're saying the American military has been abducting humans for the aliens to abuse?"

He nodded.

"DSD-3 is your above-Black, covert security force at Dulce. They have a long history of abducting humans for bio research and for integration with the Greys to create Screamshit... in exchange for more alien technology. But now the Cabal has multiple military contractor teams for abducting humans. And they come from DUMBs all over the globe."

"So the Cabal is just torturing people they abduct to create Screamshit and... then they're selling it?"

He nodded.

"The upper levels, one through seven, are full of American military... and Greys all working in unison, but on different levels. The Yanks generally work levels one through three, and the aliens control four through seven. The depleted human victims, who often die during the torture, are also sent down to the Reptilian levels for food consumption, or if they happen to be alive, for more genetic testing."

"Stop!" she said, putting her hand to her head. "It's so unbelievable, I almost... I almost started laughing."

He watched her and knew she was overwhelmed.

"Okay," she finally said. "Keep going... I'm just going to pretend the alien's use of humans is just like us humans use cows. We slaughter cows daily for everything that beast offers our people, and we certainly don't ask cows for their permission."

Swizzle slowly nodded. He lit a cigarette and took a deep pull, exhaled and waved the cig.

"Your Cabal is getting a continuous stream of alien technology to reverse engineer for weapons development and air superiority. To include controlling much more of Earth's atmosphere as they don't want benevolent aliens coming to the Earth to interfere with Earth's population, which they obviously control."

She stared.

"So how has all this shit been kept secret?" she inquired.

He looked at her.

"Did you believe aliens existed a week ago?"

"No," she said, shaking her head.

He pointed.

"Shit," she said.

"The Cabal is absolutely brilliant when it comes to mind control of their own people."

"That would be me," she exhaled, leaning on the rail and looking at the cruise ship. "If I weren't talking to a verified alien this minute... you couldn't ever convince me that aliens even existed," she said. "And that was true up until a week ago."

He nodded.

"The Cabal has continuously fed humanity the lie that Roswell and all the worldwide UFO sightings are simply hearsay and humans are too cocky to believe that they are not the first inhabitants of this planet. So it's an easy game for the Cabal to work against your own people."

She nodded.

"You just defined who I was and what I believed up until a week ago," she said. "And I'm a friggin' PhD who bought the mind control, hook, line and sinker."

He sucked his teeth.

"Well, the one thing that I do know... the one thing about mind control... is the smarter you are... in other words, educated, college, masters, doctorates... you're the ones that fall last and hardest... because your convinced that no one could swindle you. And I'm the same way if I was told that I had been hoodwinked. It's quite a thing to realize that you have been hoodwinked for your entire life."

She slowly nodded, looking at him.

"And the product is leaving Earth in bigger quantities, from multiple DUMBs and other harvesting facilities... worldwide."

"So those teams are not the American military?" she asked.

He shook his head.

"They're military contractors... paramilitary looking and are paid top dollar by the Cabal. I was just reading not too long ago... in 2009, there was a former Marine Corporal, Michael Herrera, I believe his name... a whistleblower... who ran into one of those paramilitary units. He had no idea that the black Draco ship that he witnessed was taking abducted humans to a moonbase... for harvesting."

She watched him and could tell he was not through, still holding something... a huge tell.

He pulled hard on his cig and stared ahead.

"I'm going to say one more thing... perhaps the hardest thing... then I have to get you to your truck and relocate my boat."

She waited and could tell it was something he clearly didn't want to divulge. He sniffled, looking out at the bay and shot a glance her way, as if contemplating the much darker thing. He flicked his burning cigarette ash, sending it shooting across the walkway. Watched it and took a deep breath, never looking her way as he said his ultimate truth.

"The Screamshit manufacturing, the torture and the bio-warfare testing experiments... carried out in collusion by malevolent elements of your race and my race... are not relegated to just adults, nor to any gender or race."

Her mind exploded with the new awareness.

"So the Greys and Reptilians are torturing children?" She said, staring out at the water.

He stared straight ahead... not moving, clearly ashamed... pulling on his cig and whispered,

"The most powerful strain of Screamshit is produced on Terra by torturing children and babies. The elite of your planet learned long ago that it also prevents normal aging."

She stared.

"Oh, no."

He nodded.

"Screamshit is often called *The Fountain of Youth.*"

She looked away, watching the tourists.

"Of course," she said, her head slowly shaking as he continued.

"And the best strain is taken from the youngest... and it keeps the wealthy looking like they haven't aged a day."

He turned to face her.

"Stars in Hollywood, musicians at the very top, CEOs of every type, media moguls, big pharma, banks, you name it. Elites worldwide are addicted and will pay top dollar. And, of course, the Draco will barter for the little ones with technology."

Her mouth was open at the vastness of the secret.

"How many years has this been going on?"

"Well, it came out of Dulce in the late 40s, and the demand has grown exponentially. And now it's off-world and distributed throughout the galaxy."

She lowered her head into both hands, resting on her knees.

"So, how many kids are taken each year to create the supply?"

He shrugged. She slowly sat up, pulled out her cell and typed rapidly. Then she stared at the screen and shook her head in disbelief.

"Two-million children were reported missing worldwide last year."

He stared. She looked at her phone again.

"That's not possible," she said, as she typed again and then stared dumbstruck as the same number came up.

She whispered, thinking out loud,

"There are billions of people on the planet. And so nobody notices two-million kids... missing each year, worldwide."

He looked sadly at the water in front of them. She turned and could feel his shame.

"I'm glad you came forward," she whispered.

He didn't look her way, but nodded slightly. They sat for a time... each lost in hopelessness beyond words. She wondered about Yen Jee and if that's why she looked so damn young for her age.

"I have something for you," he said.

Off the coast of California in the middle of the night, the two assassins watched each other and felt the final spark depart Knife's twitching body.

They lowered the dead man to the floor.

Ricky Slepher released the wire garrote and handed it to his partner. The other assassin hooked it over a pipe on the ceiling. They hoisted the now-stinking officer and hung him from the wire, placing the desk chair next to him. Blood from the wire began dripping onto Frank's bare feet and down onto the floor.

Slepher stayed focused, glancing around the room, and looked up at Frank, hanging dead and turning blue. Slepher contemplated the dead man for a moment, trying to figure him out. Then, Slepher got a look and shook his head, snickering, while reaching forward. He slid open the desk drawer, revealing the dead man's hidden prize. He knew Frank had gotten the harddrive only three days earlier, and Slepher had learned that hunted individuals often hid valuable things in plain sight.

Slepher pocketed the harddrive and looked one last time at the desk; seeing a folded note, he opened it to see Vyla's number. He pocketed the note and looked around the room, ensuring nothing but suicide would be determined during the post-mortem.

Just another grounded pilot who had become depressed during an investigation. Happened all the time, he thought.

Producing a cell phone, he focused on the blood dripping from the former Marine Captain hanging from the taut wire. The pilot's tongue extruded out of his mouth as the strangled dead always appeared.

Slepher snapped photos from three different angles as part of the Silent Assassin protocol. Photo confirmation of kills had to be delivered to the CIA before payment. Slepher pocketed the cell and slowly opened the door, looking both ways down the hall. He calmly exited with the other assassin following quickly behind, quietly closing the door and noting his watch. The kill had taken exactly six minutes.

The ship rolled slightly as they stepped through the hatch into the gigantic carrier mess hall. The enormous dining facility had a gaggle of sailors and marines packed shoulder to shoulder along tables that seemed to stretch forever. The few who looked up had no idea that the two corpsmen entering were never part of the carrier's original departure manifest. And certainly, none present knew that these two athletic hospital staff were not really corpsmen or even military.

The two operatives on contract with the Cabal had met only a day before on the Sea King helo bound for the carrier. They had spent exactly six hours together planning the execution of Captain Frank Knife Jacobs for becoming *A traitor to the American people.*

After a brief meal, they would change back into the business suits they had both arrived in.

An hour later, high above in the ship's superstructure, Captain Scott Schrader watched from his private at-sea cabin as the Sea King helicopter fired up its rotors in darkness, then departed the carrier, disappearing off the heaving deck into the black night.

Even though Schrader had not met the two individuals who had arrived the day before on what he was told was CIA business, he had a sense that his troubles regarding the UAP incident were now under wraps.

HUSH

In five hours, he would receive word, sent up through the chain of command, that Frank's roommate had returned from his CAP and found Frank hanging in their stateroom. Schrader would also learn that a corporal from Frank's avionics crew had been arrested and was now on an outbound helo under armed guard.

Schrader knew that Frank's squadron would be devastated, as would the entire battle group. The funeral would be held at sea within twenty-four hours, and Schrader's staff writer would compose a heartfelt condolence letter to Jacobs's wife, Kelly, which he would sign. Schrader had really liked Knife... and Crazy too. But he had long ago let them go as fodder to the CIA, which made it clear to him, in no uncertain terms, that he was to go about his business as the strike fleet commander and that CIA personnel would handle all further issues regarding the UAP incident—an incident he was never to mention again. The intercept would be adjusted in the strike fleet record as simply a mistaken identity affair that ended without incident.

Chapter Forty-Three

B en was only out for a second, he thought... as he woke to his handlers yelling at him through the right side of his brain.

But looking around, he was bewildered.

He was still airborne at 1500 feet, but it was now morning? He blinked his eyes and shook his head, staring out at the bright sunlight and looking down to see a lone black fisherman, standing waist deep in water, looking up from his tropical island as the jet passed over. Ben quickly looked at the digital map in the cockpit and couldn't believe what he was seeing. He was now 1500 miles southeast of Great Nicobar Island, where he was only moments ago... in the darkness of the early morning. But now it was bright and sunny out, and he was over the Maldives Islands chain at six a.m. local?

But even more disturbing in that moment was that the jet was turning... but not under his control! *What?!* And that's when they came through his brain. His handlers were telling him that the Navy had control of the jet.

Ben looked quickly off his right wing and saw the Navy AWACS P-3C Orion bird shadowing him. He knew it was VPU-2, the special reconnaissance squadron out of Kaneohe, Hawaii. Being an avionics and telemetry wizard for the CIA—Ben knew everything about that aircraft—and one of its capabilities was that it could take control of other aircraft... in flight.

Ben felt the anger rising.

Those Cabal bastards had taken control of his jet... turning him south, toward Diego Garcia.

Those sons-of-bitches! he thought.

"Relax, Ben," his handler said into his brain. "The Navy bird was ordered to give you a moment to regroup... as you had turned to the east... back toward Great Nicobar... and you are low on fuel, Ben," his handler said into his head.

He was steaming mad. He refreshed his connection to the jet's avionics as he wanted control... right now... but it was no use... he had been locked out... blocked.

His anger came quickly when he put the whole scenario together in his fast-moving brain. There was only one way he could have traveled 1500 miles that quickly.

He had been involved in previous Cabal missions where he helped them with the teleportation of a non-moving object... as a test. He had seen their technology in operation... and was quite impressed. But now—they had used their alien-acquired plasmoids—on him.

Those fuckers had not only lit his jet on fire without telling him, but had teleported him without any warning!

"Breathe, Ben... they'll give you control for landing," the handler in Virginia whispered into his mind.

Before Ben could tell him to *fuck off*... he felt the chemical cocktail sliding into his system, the one that bitch-ass handler in Virginia had just administered.

And Ben relaxed.

He now had time to process that... *being used* feeling. Diego Garcia he knew was another three hours south... and there were no places to land before that. He would be down to fumes if he made it at all. He looked at his airspeed, and it was locked at 300 knots. A speed that allowed the P3-C Orion to fly alongside him. He exhaled and sat back, trying not to notice the heavy stench now coming to the forefront of his mind.

Behind MH370, several Kudahuvadhoo Island residents watched as the Malaysian jet headed south. Those residents would later tell stories of the huge commercial jet that had appeared out of nowhere that morning. They would tell how it flew extremely low over their island at six a.m. Much lower than any commercial jet had ever done. Days later, a young man walking the beach found a round... fire suppression canister that the Malaysian jet had ejected from its burnt cargo hold as it flew over. The metal apparatus would be reported to authorities and matched perfectly the unique and rarely seen fire suppression nodes that only the Boeing 777 jets were equipped with.

Three hours later, at 10:20 a.m. Diego Garcia local time, Ben was back in control. The Navy AWACS bird had handed control back to him as MH370 approached the 12,000-foot runway 31 at Diego.

And Ben heard voices on that long approach, that he might want to flee the bird as soon as it was on deck... because something bad was about to go down.

He had no problem landing the jet and shut it down near four large hangars in the middle of the airfield. He exited first as the only hijacker who knew how to open the exterior door. The other hijackers stayed behind, blindfolding and handcuffing the surviving passengers... prepping them to disembark.

At Pier 39, they arrived at Gizmo to find a group of gawkers staring at the boat.

Swizzle raised a finger for her to wait.

One moment.

He disappeared into the cabin and returned a minute later with her figurine bag from the party. He opened it for her, revealing that on top of the figurines was a VHS tape in a plastic case.

"Something you should see," he whispered, "but—," looking around surreptitiously, "it can get you killed."

She lifted the tape.

"A VHS—really? You know these went out in the early 80s?"

His eyes smiled at the sublime dig, but he held fast.

"I mean it. Be careful."

Vyla set her cruise control bound for Palo Alto and sat back, still miffed at herself and what seemed to be her constant fight against her new reality.

The swirl of so much new information was daunting. The Screamshit phenomenon was simply tragic. On top of that, was all the new information she had learned with Yen on her latest trip to S-4. The incredible moments with Oppenheimer and Vannevar Bush and the reanimation of Setimus. She thought about James Forrestal and how he seemed so shocked in the movie, watching Setimus reanimate in front of him. She remembered Dan telling how Forrestal had been thrown out of a 16th floor window because he threatened to tell the world the truth.

Wow, she thought.

Thinking about the Cabal assassinating him, she wanted to exact revenge but knew it was a fleeting anger that had no proper direction due to the passage of time.

Revenge? she thought.

The members of the Cabal had undoubtedly changed many times over the years, and it would be impossible to bring those responsible for the initial cover-up to justice. Thinking of Truman and the scientific team back in 1947, it made sense to her that the administration would want a few answers before causing a chaotic jolt to the American public and the world. But she now understood there was never a plan to tell the public. If anything, the lie had grown more deadly.

She remembered Swizzle speaking of the Reptilians running the show. How the Draco were masters at conquering a planet in a velvet takeover. She realized it was the Reptilian agenda to keep the alien interactions completely sealed off from the regular human population. Because if humans knew there was an alien race controlling them from behind the curtain, humans would rebel and eventually figure out the game. But as yet, the Draco had brilliantly worked their magic. Humans were walking blindly into their own slavery.

And now, she was part of it too. S-4, the Widow, the footage, the actual amount of alien interaction that she was now aware of—and she knew she had only touched the surface of how much was actually happening on the planet. And outside the planet.

What level had it reached now? she thought. *Interstellar*, she guessed, and beyond.

She couldn't even imagine what must already be in motion, and for decades! She exhaled.

Where the fuck do you even start to tell the public—and what makes you think anyone would believe you? she thought.

She felt her frustration rising, staring out the window as she drove at the mass of humanity walking those sidewalks who didn't know that alien races from light years away were here among them, working deals with America's Cabal. And that the whole thing was in full operation all around them and right above them on their own moon! And for so many damn years!

She stared out at the humans. Her kind. Walking the streets from all over the globe... and none of them believed—really believed, that aliens even existed. The Cabal had become pristine that way, she thought. The hoodwink was so well done and continued without the threat of discovery. They already had human mind control in full command mode. The global populace was theirs to shape—and now she was on the inside, exasperated at what was available to humanity—and hating that she knew humans were just cattle. Happy, dumb, manipulated, and perpetuating the Cabal's narratives that kept them in that decades-long, life-stealing loop.

She pulled into the Stanford campus parking lot in complete darkness and crossed the campus in circuitous ways to fool the Twins, eventually sneaking up to Hoppy's house. She thought about the new blue car and how only one Twin was visible whenever she did catch a glimpse. But it really didn't matter that there was only one for the moment; she would still think of them as her boys; the Twins.

Marten told her that Hoppy kept vampire hours, often working very late, so they were meeting at 11 p.m. Marten answered the door when she knocked, and immediately, she could see his face was one of disbelief.

"Hey... what?" she inquired.

Marten shook his head and tersely whispered in her ear.

"Come on in; I don't even want to try explaining. And keep in mind Hoppy's tech assistant, Maggie, has no idea the footage is real. She thinks it's a sci-fi movie."

Vyla nodded. They entered a large living room, and there stood Dr. Jane Hoppensowski holding a cup of coffee. She offered her hand to Vyla with a smile.

"I've heard too many good things about you over the last year, and I hear you now have a great new job. Congratulations," Hoppy said.

Vyla looked her in the eyes.

"You are the venerable perfection Marten has alluded to for so long. I'm honored to meet you," Vyla said.

Hoppy smiled and motioned to Maggie Crawley, a twenty-two-year-old tech student, who sat at a desk with a computer and two VHS machines.

"Maggie is my assistant for all things technical," Hoppy said with a smile. "She knows how to make old footage look great with the help of an AI program."

"Nice to meet you, Maggie," Vyla said.

"Likewise," Maggie replied, smiling.

Marten patted the couch next to him, holding up a bottle of water for Vyla.

"Have a seat. The VHS is already loaded up, and we can take a look."

Vyla plopped down next to him and took a sip, glancing quickly at Hoppy, who stared grimly one last time at her before dimming the lights. All three watched as Maggie hit play. Within seconds, it became apparent that the footage was inside some form of medical facility.

A title card appeared:

DULCE DSD-3

Rhyolite/Majestic/Eyes only.

"Majestic-12 Alphacom team brief: Interrogation of Nebu Grey alien regarding the activities on alien levels four and below of Dulce facility."

The footage showed a group of American scientists and military personnel around a small Grey alien, its limbs strapped tightly to a dissection-style table as it was tortured for information. The Grey screamed like a shot jackrabbit. The high-pitched whine was continuous as it fought against its restraints. Maggie turned to Vyla.

"The special effects in this are amazing—look at that alien!"

Vyla nodded with her best-dumbfounded look.

"Wow."

Marten shot a quick glance at Hoppy, who stared transfixed, her tragic eyes saying it all. *This was no Hollywood sci-fi movie.*

A moment later, the footage of the alien being tortured ended, and the screen went completely black. But it was clear from the little white scratches that the footage was still rolling. Suddenly, the screen filled again with a 1980s-style film counting down from ten to zero, then a BEEP. Followed by several descriptive titles:

DULCE DSD-3/ Rhyolite.

Grey production of glandular drug Adrenochrome. Street name: *Screamshit.*

Dulce Level Green—Four.

The following captured footage shows the moments just before the DSD-3 special forces team, accompanied by dissident Grey aliens, descended into the Level IV medical/genetics lab in 1979.

The screen went black momentarily. From the black screen, audio rose—of humans being tortured. Horrific screams. Female and male. The footage faded-in to show a gymnasium-sized cave with mountain-style rock walls, which appeared to have been modified as a genetic medical lab. The lab was lined with one hundred stainless-steel tables, each surrounded by medical staff adorned in white lab coats.

But they were not human staff. They were Grey aliens wearing lab coats. The specimens on their tables were nude humans of all nationalities, being held down against their will by small Greys as the squirming humans screamed and writhed, attempting to escape. Towering over each tortured human at the head of each table was a Tall-Grey, also in a lab coat. The huge black eyes stared down at the terrified human as the Tall-Greys systematically raised the level of pain to induce secretion of more adrenochrome.

Suddenly, a dark shadow crossed the screen as someone ran into the frame, so close to the camera that their head momentarily blocked everything. Then, as the automatic focus adjusted, Vyla and the others could see the tortured eyes of a twenty-five-year-old woman screaming into the camera. She was bleeding profusely from the temple and clearly out of her mind as she yelled directly into the camera.

"Help me! Help me!"

She then looked to her left, off-screen, at someone or something approaching her. She defiantly raised both of her middle fingers, screaming,

"Fuck-youuuuuu!"

Then took off running away from camera, nude, racing between the medical tables, eluding capture. Blood and torture marks stained the lower part of her neck and down her spine. A moment later, in the distance, they saw she was suddenly subdued by a Tall-Grey who attacked her like a spider jumping on a fly and then held her immobilized—placing its face an inch in front of hers, its large black wrap-around eyes neurally engaging her.

She dropped to her knees and was immediately lifted by small Greys, who returned her to her table and held her down as she slowly regained consciousness and began screaming again. The Tall-Grey took its place at the head of the table. The long silver, blood-covered temple probe in its hand. In the background, large steel five-by-five-foot cages with steel bars lit up, all occupied by nude human test subjects. They stared out from their bars, dull-eyed, empty of emotion, watching the woman as she was recaptured.

Suddenly, the audio became that of shots being fired. Two Tall-Grey aliens were seen taking bullets to their torsos, hesitating, before falling. The screen went black as the audio continued for a moment, the sounds of a battle beginning to rage with shots, yells, and the muffled booms of hand grenades. Then it clicked off, and the living room fell silent.

Vyla inhaled and fell back on the couch. She wanted to scream but glanced at Maggie, who was enthralled.

"Unbelievable special effects, right?"

Vyla raised her eyebrows and nodded. Maggie turned back to her computer array and stared at her AI program while tweaking settings.

"This program is only going to make this footage look even cleaner. I just wish we knew what movie this is from?"

"Maggie," Hoppy said, "if you'll excuse us now, I've got to do a session with Vyla and Marten. Perhaps I can see you tomorrow?"

"No problem, Dr. H."

Maggie stood and grabbed her laptop.

"Well, it was nice meeting both of you!" she said as all pleasantries were exchanged, and she was gone a moment later. Vyla felt Marten's hand gently on her shoulder.

"I'm sorry."

Vyla looked at him, then up at the screen.

"Don't feel sorry for me."

Her face was a mask of determination. Marten and Hoppy both noticed the change. Vyla sniffled, still staring at the screen. She sucked her teeth as if contemplating revenge. Hoppy sat down beside her.

"Marten, let me know a little bit about your letter from your Papa, Colonel Steve

Wilson," Hoppy said.

Vyla watched her as she continued.

"I knew him. He was well-liked in the UFO community, but because of his wild stories, few believed him back then—and it was hard to swallow many of his claims at that time. The technology he was alluding to seemed way beyond possible—but now I know he was telling the complete truth."

Vyla nodded, amazed that anyone outside the military knew him, but then recalled that Papa's last days were spent on the UFO speaking circuit.

Hoppy touched her arm.

"I've had clients in the past who claimed to have been medically experimented on by Greys in lab situations, but their claims were always via hypnotic recall, so there was no way to verify their stories. Marten may have told you about my clients' videotaped sessions—they're awful to watch, with each torture they endure."

Vyla nodded, staring at the carpet.

"This tape has two more segments on it," Hoppy said, and Vyla looked up.

"More of the same?" Vyla asked.

Hoppy slowly shook her head, grim-faced and silent. Vyla felt Marten's hand on her shoulders. When she turned, tears were streaming down his face. He stared, beginning to sob.

"No..."

He lowered his head into his hands, whispering as he trembled and began to weep.

"No... it's fucking children... trapped in cages, being electrocuted, then taken out and harvested... creating that Screamshit."

Vyla stared with dull eyes. At this point, she simply had nothing left in the tank—just more disbelief. She had no energy for a plan, a solution, or even an angle on where to begin with this ongoing atrocity.

"Do you know more about the Dulce facility?" Hoppy asked.

Vyla slowly shook her head.

"Not much other than it's supposedly been down there for a thousand years."

Hoppy stared, perplexed.

"How can you know that?"

Vyla realized she was again attempting to communicate with humans who didn't have her newfound knowledge. But she also considered Hoppy's vast background in working with alien-abducted clients. Vyla took a deep breath and looked around, wondering if the Twins had figured her out and were listening now.

"Could you crank up some loud symphonic music?" she asked.

Hoppy knew exactly what that request meant and was up in seconds, cranking up Mahler's 5th Symphony.

Hoppy sat quickly again, and Vyla slowly put her arms around both their shoulders, gently pulling them into her, whispering.

"My friend, the one who gave me the VHS—he's an alien."

Hoppy looked up, and so did Marten. Both gave her questioning looks.

"I know it's hard to believe... but—"

"I believe you," Hoppy said.

"So do I," Marten chimed in.

Vyla looked at both of them.

"Okay... that was easy. Now, how do we get the rest of the world to believe as quickly as you two?"

A t daybreak on the Stanford campus, the sparsely lit parking lot had only a few vehicles at that early hour.

She approached her truck and noticed a piece of paper sticking out near her door handle. She glanced around, retrieved the note, unlocked the truck and climbed in, slamming the door behind her, and re-locked it. She unfolded the simple piece of notebook paper to see a few typed words that had clearly been written in a hurry, as they were not even on the lines of the notebook paper.

Knife found hanging in his stateroom. Tried to acquire his heads-up footage of the intercept. Not one to commit suicide. Jerry's been arrested. I'm on terminal leave. Hope you are okay. B safe. B quiet.

T-drive on top of back left tire.

She sat stunned. The cryptic message naming his buddy as Jerry... let her know it was Dan who had somehow tracked her to this parking lot. She looked around again. Nobody in sight. Dan had told her during their interlude that his Navy Lt. Commander friend, who had shot the surveillance videos of Flight 370, referred to himself as one of *Jerry's Kids*. Meaning he was part of a squadron called *Jerry's Kids* in the Navy because of their smarts. And Jerry's Kids got whatever they wanted as far as technology for their surveillance needs. So, this simple note meant Dan suddenly had three sad things happening at once.

His good friend and pilot, Frank "Knife" Jacobs, was dead. His VP-2 tracking buddy had been arrested for leaking the videos. And Dan himself was off the ship on terminal leave. But the final note about keeping her mouth shut was a terse warning.

Damn. she thought. *The Cabal executed Knife. Wow.*

That felt too close to home. She hopped out and found the thumb drive on top of the back left tire and pocketed it. Hopped back in and started the truck... immediately heading toward the freeway, feeling bewildered. She wanted to help Dan, knowing he was alone and scared. But he knew enough not to leave any clues as to his whereabouts or that it was even him. She pulled into the Moss Landing gravel parking lot in the early morning fog and was out of her truck in seconds, walking quickly to the fueling dock where Gizmo was just pulling in.

Peg stood ready with the fuel nozzle, and Swizzle tossed his stern line with one hand as he kept his other hand on the wheel. Before Vyla even reached the fueling area, and before Peg noticed her, Swizzle was in her head. Not looking up at her, but his message was rapid and thorough.

Turn now. Stay the fuck away!

And Vyla did just that. It had been her voice, deep inside, but unmistakably Swizzle's words.

Telepathy, she had learned, was communication in a complete wrapper. It was all at once imagery, consciousness, and emotional waves, mixed with an unmistakable through-line message. And it came instantaneously. Faster delivery, translation, and understanding than could ever be spoken. Like a bright red warning sign showing an explosion symbol mixed with the added depth of human terror and fear... telepathy was all of that... instantaneously.

And this morning's telepathy from Swizzle had the added urgency of real danger nearby and his parting shot:

All will be revealed. Drive to Monterey Beach and rent a kayak.

With that, Vyla slapped her forehead as if she'd forgotten something and turned around. Walking back to her truck, she lifted her cell and pretended to dial. She raised it as if listening to a voicemail and, as she did so, casually scanned the area. The white Impala had been switched out for a blue one, and she saw only one silhouette in the car. But Swizzle's energy was about something else, and then she knew.

She didn't look up to scan the sky... but she just knew. She fired up the truck, gunning it out of the gravel parking lot, kicking up a nice rooster tail of dust and gravel in the heavy fog. She figured she'd give whichever Twin was in the car a little rise in the dull tedium of always following her at the speed limit.

She hopped on Highway One South, curving the twenty minutes around the bay to Monterey Beach, and wondered what was up there...above her? Was it a drone? An alien ship? Or was she just thinking she felt him correctly, and there was nothing there?

No, there was something up there, she heard her inner voice whisper, but still didn't know for certain if it was monitoring her or Swizzle. She checked her rearview mirror, but the highway was packed behind her with cars and fog. Yet, she wondered why the Twins would switch car colors so often, as if somehow, they would be more inconspicuous? And then realized, of all the things she had to think about—perhaps the Twins should not rate a real worry?

Maybe... she thought, *I should worry about something a little more important, like what in the fucking hell is happening here?!*

There was far too much to process this quickly, and she knew, at a base level, to just breathe and hold the steering wheel. She was alive and communicating telepathically with aliens. She had witnessed a UAP doing antigravity moves beyond all known scientific laws... and had a job at S-4 with flying saucers that were alive and brainwave connected to their pilots, and was about to test-fly one in one week. And she now knew for certain that Oppenheimer, Einstein, and all her heroes were absolutely involved in this same alien realm clear back in the 40s.

Okay, there you are. No big! she told herself as she plowed through the dense white—heading into Monterey. And above her, somewhere up there, she was being monitored—or perhaps Swizzle was, and that's how she got the energy hit that there were eyes on her.

She pulled into the kayak rental shop and could hear the Monterey harbor foghorn howling its distant, ghostly warning. She entered the shop only to find the surprised young man stuck working on the worst weather day, not understanding why a person would want to go kayaking in zero visibility conditions.

After questioning her resolve, the young man realized that she was either a pro athlete or crazed, but she had produced a one-hundred-dollar bill on his second inquisition and was saying, *keep the change...* which he sheepishly did. This worked against her, though. He proceeded to give her his polished twenty-minute brief on how to properly wear a life vest and the different functions of the oar and kayak should an emergency arise, especially since she was choosing to kayak in such perilous conditions.

"There are boats out there that won't see you on radar and will unknowingly cruise right over you. And there are 1,200-pound sea lions which could flip you like a pancake."

Vyla had to fight the snicker on that one but swallowed it down with the terror-filled visual of it possibly occurring. She had never kayaked before.

But hell, how hard could it be?

The young man was obviously bound to a liability policy that allowed no exceptions on his full twenty-minute spiel. She was still wearing her cargo pants from the trip to Nellis and wished to hell she had a swimsuit or shorts.

Screw it—they're all I've got, she thought.

And wondered how long it would take the Gizmo to motor the roughly sixteen miles in heavy fog. Plus, Swizzle had just pulled into the fueling dock, so that had to add time as well. She figured, sixteen miles of foggy ocean from Moss Landing to Monterey... meant the best that Swizzle could do... would be around eight knots, which meant she would be stuck out there kayaking... for at least two hours.

Whatever, she told herself.

She figured she could make kayaking fun and maybe get a little workout in. She had Stanford friends who were avid river kayakers and had often coaxed her to come along. They were all fit and wild, so she figured this would be a good intro. She also enjoyed the thought of physical freedom, knowing it would be tough for the Twin to follow her in her kayak—especially since her phone was off and already in the dry bag for the coming excursion.

She endured another five-minute briefing on the beach, then realized she couldn't get on the damn kayak without getting soaked up to her knees. The young man was nice enough to help stabilize the kayak as she climbed aboard, and he gave her an aggressive push directly into the waves. As she paddled, settling on top, he watched her... just get over the first set of rolling waves... and then seemed to really enjoy her capsizing.

She climbed back onto the kayak, soaked from head to toe, and paddled furiously away from the shore until the smiling, waving, yelling young man disappeared in the fog behind her.

Bitch will get no tip! she thought, as the chill sank into her bones, and the realization hit her, that she had already paid his full damn junior college tuition!

Welcome to simple, easy sea-kayaking, Vyla! she told herself. *Really, how hard can it be?*

She gritted her teeth and paddled as fast as possible toward the pier she knew was just ahead in the fog. She needed a quick visual reference of direction and distance from the beach. Everything was soaked—from her bare feet, past her cargo pants and tank top with light sweater, right up to her blonde wet mop. She exhaled, shaking to her bones. Heading directly into the foggy wind. She just wanted to quit this whole endeavor and sit by a big roaring fire... hoisting her white flag of surrender.

She heard the sea lions howling on the far pier and knew she was close to the exit of the harbor. She had walked the Monterey pier many times with friends and knew the harbor pretty well.

The waves were already getting bigger as she passed a boat going the opposite way, just outside the pier. The wind was picking up, dropping her core temperature even more, and she decided right then that it was time to pull the plug. Even if she were dry and tied off to the pier, the quickest Swizzle could get over there would be at least two hours.

"Paddle away from the pier, quickly if possible," she heard in her head.

Her voice... but Swizzle's unmistakable words.

But telepathy doesn't work from a great distance? She thought, and she knew she was going crazy. She looked around, and all she could see was fog.

What the hell, he can't be here!

"Yes, but I am here. Will you paddle, please?"

And with that snarky response... even in her own voice, she followed orders, shaking and paddling, and looking around, knowing she was going nuts.

She heard the sea lions howling to her left side somewhere out there in the fog and had the momentary thought of pancakes flipping when suddenly, from below her... she felt something firm and rising! She screamed, imagining the damn sea lion lifting her, and could no longer stay upright with the rising. She felt herself falling sideways, letting go, onto the hard wooden deck of GIZMO!—rising silently, straight up, from the depths below her!

She looked up, and Swizzle was at the helm as she gasped,

"What-in-the—"

Swizzle put his finger to his lips, cutting her off, and pointed skyward into the cloud cover. He motioned for her to sit. As she did, he placed both hands in the silver handprints near the steering wheel. She saw him get a look, connecting, and a split second later, they were in the depths of Monterey Bay, hundreds of feet down, in a gravity bubble, cruising along at a magical six knots, with fish and sea life and wonder all around.

She stared out in utter bewilderment at the heart-stopping view. She momentarily forgot her shivering, forgot her worry, her sadness, herself—her mouth agape at what was all around her, the majesty—breathtaking. And that's when it hit her, literally. A heavy, soft material landed perfectly over her, and her frozen-to-the-bone world... suddenly became... cozy black.

A spelsin, Goldmeyer, and Teebeck were focused on the screen in front of them.

The sound of human screams filled the room. Suddenly, the *Fuck You!*... of the tortured woman from Swizzle's Dulce video echoed through the speakers. Aspelsin used the remote to lower the volume.

"The young woman with this footage," Aspelsin said, "uploaded it at Stanford University campus to an AI program to enhance it. Our best guess is that it's being prepared for release at some point online or to give it to the press."

"Well, do we know who she is with, sir?" Goldmeyer inquired.

Aspelsin tapped a remote, and the footage on-screen changed to a bird's-eye view from a drone over Moss Landing Harbor. The footage showed Vyla walking toward the Gizmo, where Swizzle and Peg were about to refuel the ship. It then captured the moment when Vyla suddenly tapped her head and turned around.

"That's Vyla Kells, our test pilot!" Goldmeyer said, looking over to Aspelsin, who nodded.

"There seems to be some connection between Dr. Kells and the man who owns the boat. We think the tape may have come from him. That he's a hybrid Grey, modified to appear completely human. He has been on the planet, off and on since 1948."

"Mr. Aspelsin, sir," Goldmeyer said, "I can have Vyla Kells placed in a wet room immediately if you would like to question her."

"That won't be necessary," Aspelsin whispered. "I believe she is slated to test-fly the Widow at the end of the week, and I'm certain that will take care of our little problem—at least with her."

Goldmeyer slowly nodded, thinking of how the Widow had made mincemeat of every test pilot so far.

"Well, yes, sir, that's a very interesting way of handling this issue with Vyla Kells," Goldmeyer said, then looked at Teebeck, raising his eyebrows.

Aspelsin stood and departed without a word as both men watched. Teebeck turned to Goldmeyer, who was still contemplating the Reptilian. He slowly turned to Teebeck.

"Well, he's certainly efficient. I would never have thought of disposing of a traitor that way."

Teebeck slowly nodded.

"Right, sir. We'll have all the cameras rolling when she's in the Widow for the test flight," he said with a slight smile.

T om stared at his hands as Hoppy watched him.

"It all came back over the last two days," he said.

She watched him, knowing that he was talking about the Malaysian flight.

Jane learned early on that the worst parts of trauma are sometimes withheld from an individual... only allowing what the person can handle to come through.

She remained silent and could feel his extreme sadness.

"I certainly terminated many of the disassembly crews over the next several weeks of the jet coming apart and being gutted." Tom said.

"Hans did," she whispered.

"Yeah, Hans did," Tom said, "and the rest came flooding through too."

Jane knew it then, that Tom now had the full recall... to fill in the gaps of what he had already seen. She had a really dark feeling about what was coming, but knew not to interrupt. Tom needed this... so Jane remained quiet as he sniffled and continued.

"So, it turns out I had been... I mean, Hans had been up there for all of it. He actually came to the surface as the jet was landing... not afterwards. He stood next to Chief One as the jet came to a stop and the stairs were rolled into place by other Black Navy operatives. The pilot opened the jet's front door and came down the steps alone, wearing a black tactical outfit, and he seemed very controlled as he descended the steps. He said nothing to anyone and just disappeared. That's when the maintenance crew arrived at the tail and began working.

"The other hijackers were yelling at the passengers inside the jet. Chief One ordered Hans to remove the maintenance crew... just as more yelling erupted from the jet. The hijackers started bringing them out. They were all blindfolded and handcuffed with nylon zip-tie cuffs. Each held the shoulder of the one in front of them. After the first set of passengers came down the staircase, the two lead hijackers got into an argument over the slow pace of the hostages.

"One hijacker then stormed down the steps and removed the blindfold of the front hostage so she could walk faster, since she was leading the whole long line. The other hijacker immediately executed the hijacker who had removed the blindfold."

Jane put her hand to her mouth, slowly shaking her head.

"Chief One was there, and since the maintenance crew had just started their disassembly on the tail, he ordered Hans into the hangar, where the remaining passengers were taken."

Tom hesitated and began crying silently. Jane handed him a box of tissues but remained quiet.

"We lined up the hostages in rows in that hangar, and all were on their knees, still blindfolded and handcuffed."

Tom burst into tears, and Jane could tell he was seeing it all again.

"And Goddamn there were over two-hundred of them... including teenagers, and children and babies."

He put both hands over his face and inhaled slowly.

"The twenty engineers were marched up front, and their blindfolds were removed."

He hesitated and looked at Jane, slowly shaking his head, his forehead twitching with the heavy stress.

"Chief One gave the order—and all five of the hijackers began firing."

Jane closed her eyes. Felt the tears come... and let them. She inhaled slowly, opening her eyes to see Tom staring at the wall, his lips quivering.

"It took a full two minutes... as the hijackers had to fucking reload."

Jane put her hand to her forehead in silence, eyes closed, tears streaming as Tom continued in a whisper.

"Then Chief One had the defecting engineers led away... as well as one of the Caucasian hostages... a middle-aged guy—Philip Wood—some kind of tech executive. Hans would later end him in a wet room after a long interrogation with Cabal interrogators.

"At that moment, there were five of us assassins... standing with Chief One. All five remaining hijackers were loaded into separate Humvees for a ride to the debriefing hangar. Hans rode in the backseat of the Humvee behind the lone female hijacker. Hans had never seen a female operative. She had blonde hair and didn't say a word to anyone. One minute into the ride, on orders from Chief One, Hans put a bullet in the back of her head."

Jane allowed herself to continue crying silently as Tom was in tears too... trying to speak, but the words were sparse.

"By the time Hans got back, the forklift driver was loading the construction dumpsters. Chief One ordered Hans to remove the assassins who had just executed the hijackers. As each assassin arrived back inside the hangar... Hans did as ordered. When those four had been executed... the Chief ordered him outside... and sent him toward the maintenance crew."

Tom leaned forward at that point, placing his head in both hands, and she could see his body rock in silent heaves.

She felt the grief coming... an inexorable wave of sadness... heavier than any she had ever known.

Chapter Forty-Four

"How about some dry clothes?"

Vyla heard Swizzle's raspy voice whispering outside the blanket. She slowly pulled the covering back and looked up to see Swizzle's soft, safe eyes looking at her. Standing next to him, waving shyly—was Peg. She felt it, knew she had to say it, and did so with a smile.

"What-the -fuck?" she said.

Lifting her hands to the bubble around them, a mile below the surface of the ocean. Swizzle and Peg snickered, watching as Vyla slowly stood, still dripping wet but adorned in the blanket. She checked her balance as she walked toward them, then realized that even when the ship leaned slightly on the whim of Swizzle's brain, she remained stable—locked in a consistent one-G environment.

Wow! was all her flooded mind could muster. As she approached Peg, she could see that her eyes were beaming, too.

"Did you know he was—" Vyla started to say.

"No, I didn't know he was a fucking alien," Peg interrupted. "And when he told me today that he was—I laughed and said, 'Yeah—prove it.' And here we are!" She smiled at Swizzle. "I mean, I knew he was weird and all. And I'd heard this ship could do some wild shit, but—DAMN!" she said, raising her hands upward.

Vyla nodded, smiling.

Peg patted the pile of clothes next to her. "These are Plato's, but Swizzle said she wouldn't mind if you borrowed them for today. At least they're dry."

Five minutes later, Vyla came back on deck, still draped in the blanket, but she opened it for Swizzle and Peg to see her see-through Plato outfit. It was clearly a Union Square showstopper. Everything but actual nipples could be seen on top, and the fishnets below were only slightly better than full nudity.

"Well, I'm dry and a lot warmer," she said as they snickered.

"Wow," Peg purred. "I'd listen to you lecture anytime!"

They all laughed as a manta ray with a ten-foot wingspan glided by, followed by a school of sparkly fish darting about. Bringing up the rear was a jellyfish that looked like a huge pink cloud, swirling and pulsing. Gismo made no sound whatsoever except for Bob Denver crooning from an old scratchy cassette player.

Swizzle lit a cigar as the ship slowed, but the engines were clearly not on. No vibrations of any sort could be felt. Vyla slowly shook her head.

"He's got a great style," she said to Peg as they stared at Swizzle. Then she noticed Peg sniffle slightly and saw them—tears.

Vyla remembered her first moment talking with an alien on Swizzle's boat. It had been overwhelming. She turned to him.

"We'll be in the cabin for a few minutes."

Swizzle nodded without looking up.

"Of course. Take your time."

Not knowing her that well, she figured Peg was still in complete shock. Upon learning that aliens not only existed, but were all around her... and they even owned boats!

She sat beside her on the small couch in the cabin. Almost immediately, Peg turned.

"Swizzle told me we're in some type of gravity bubble. That's how we're moving underwater and not affected by submersion."

Vyla slowly nodded, watching Peg closely.

"I'm a physicist by trade, and it appears to me that he's telling the truth. Somewhere aboard, there's a small nuclear reactor, and it creates the gravity bubble around the ship," Vyla said.

Peg watched her, then looked at her hands.

"I always hoped I'd meet an alien one day," she said.

Vyla nodded as Peg continued... explaining that her generation was much more open to the whole possibility that aliens were real. She joked that it was wild to realize her first contact had been with her old algebra tutor! They shared a laugh and discussed their new secret world.

Vyla sighed.

"I wish I could tell you it was all great and wonderful, that every alien race had the best of intentions for humanity—but unfortunately, they're much like humans. Each has his or her own agenda."

She assured Peg that Swizzle was one of the good ones, and Peg said she already had a fatherly impression of him from years ago.

"One of the kindest and funniest men I've ever met."

Vyla nodded.

"And now you know—"

"He's not a man!" they both said together, laughing.

"Holy shit," Peg exclaimed, shaking her head.

Vyla reminded her that, between the two of them, Peg was the first one to actually fly on an alien ship. And they both laughed again. Peg took a deep breath, looking around the cabin, and then told Vyla that the whole thing had come about because Swizzle had mentioned to her that he had an investigation she could do that might be interesting.

Vyla watched her, waiting for more.

"When I told him I was pursuing investigative journalism, Swizzle played me an old tape. It had a scene from a movie—a woman screaming while Grey aliens tortured her."

Vyla tensed. She knew exactly which horrific scene Peg was talking about.

"I mean, the damn movie was actually hard to watch—but I figured it was just good special effects."

Vyla nodded, remembering the poor woman.

"That's when our discussion turned to the Tall-Greys in the video doing all the bad stuff," Peg said, sniffling slightly.

"When Swizzle then told me they were real, I laughed and said, 'Right—they're fucking real aliens, bro.'"

"That's when he told me the place in the video was real. A place called Dulce. And that he—Swizzle—was actually an alien. We both laughed, and I told him he'd have to prove it. And that's when he said, 'If you can promise never to tell anyone, I'll prove it to you.' And I said, 'You're on!' He told me to meet him at his boat today, and we would go just outside the harbor, and he would prove that he was an alien. I wasn't scared, because we had spent so much time together. We had just cleared the harbor when he put his fingers in those silver impressions—and the next thing I know, I'm a thousand feet down, breathing in a bubble, with fucking fish everywhere! She said, exasperated.

"And literally a few moments later, we are rising and picking you up!"

Vyla snickered, smiling.

"God, was I glad to see you!" Peg said with a sigh. "I have to admit until you came along, I wasn't sure what was going to happen."

She paused, then turned.

"Shit! Are you an alien, too?"

Vyla shook her head.

"Nope," she smiled. "Just a human."

Peg exhaled.

"Oh, thank God."

She smiled, but her energy darkened slightly.

Vyla gently wrapped an arm around her shoulders.

"You gonna be okay?"

Peg gripped her arm and slowly nodded.

"Swizzle told me that if I wanted to, I could investigate that Dulce thing. He said it needs to be out to the world—and that's why he approached me with it. He thinks I'll make a really good investigative reporter."

Vyla nodded.

"I'm certain of it."

Then hesitated... concerned.

Peg sighed, shaking her head.

"I'm mad about that video, now that I know that poor woman is real... and what those Greys are doing to those humans—I mean fuck—damn assholes!"

Vyla watched her and knew that Swizzle had purposefully kept the kid's version hidden from her.

"We should really talk about it before you proceed, Peg. I know you'll be a stellar investigative journalist, but starting with content that nasty could..."

"Get me killed," Peg finished her sentence.

Vyla watched her for a moment.

"Or worse," Vyla whispered.

Peg turned, and then shrugged.

"Oh yeah, you mean they could torture me to death?"

Vyla almost snickered.

"You don't seem scared—I mean—you almost seem okay with it?"

"No, I'm not," Peg said. "But every investigative journalist that I admire... or admired, I should say. Usually died doing what they loved... exposing the bad people or groups."

Vyla slowly nodded.

"What if there was a way to expose them without putting your life on the line?"

Peg turned.

"How could you do it?"

Vyla looked out.

"Well, if you can get someone famous to step forward, like someone from the current administration, and give them enough evidence, then when they present it to the planet, they're too well-known to erase. That's one way to do it."

"I never thought about that," Peg said.

Vyla nodded.

"My friend does public policy work at the state level, and she would know how to get the right amount of visibility for something that nasty without you having to fear being murdered."

Peg got quiet.

"Right," she whispered, then looked up at Vyla.

"Are you like a big-time kayaker or something?"

Vyla stared at the amazing young woman.

"Well, if by *big-time* you mean willing to get wet and cold and miserable, then absolutely."

Peg laughed good-heartedly and noticed Vyla's bare feet. She motioned to the closet with a smile.

"You know there are stilettos over there, too?"

Vyla snickered.

"Yeah, I'd last about ten seconds and break my friggin' neck."

They both laughed.

"How about we rejoin the alien on his deck—since this is positively a once-in-a-lifetime moment?" Vyla offered.

They both stood, and Vyla gave her a big hug.

"Thank you," Peg whispered. "It's not often I get hugged by a hottie in fishnets and see-through everything!"

"Well, clearly, today is a banner day for you all around," Vyla said, and they both snickered their way back up to the deck. Both were awestruck again upon reaching the helm. Gizmo was now floating freely, ascending slowly without any forward momentum whatsoever. Breathtaking. The ship had clearly risen closer to the surface as tons of light streamed down.

The whole atmosphere was otherworldly. They could hear the water outside the gravity bubble—the deep gurgle of things, big things, moving within that realm.

Swizzle was enjoying his cigar in a lawn chair on the front deck near the kayak. Two more empty chairs sat nearby, and soon, all three were occupied. A sack of fish and chips had been placed on each chair, and Vyla and Peg scarfed down half their meals, sipping on cold beers provided from Swizzle's cooler.

"They must put Crack in these fish and chips," Vyla said, wolfing down a bite. "I could eat this every night."

"Here, here," Swizzle said, patting his beer belly. "Twenty years and counting."

The girls snickered.

"So," Vyla said, looking up. "Can the drone or whatever you're running from see you down here?"

Swizzle looked over, cigar in mouth, and shook his head.

"No, we're safe here. No way to monitor our discussions this far below."

Soon, the topic turned to alien questions, many of which came from Peg. It was a rehash of Vyla's questions from Mission Dolores Park. Swizzle asked Vyla to answer, testing if she had paid attention, and she fared pretty well. Then, the Dulce torture footage came up.

Swizzle shrugged.

"Well, I know, and you two know it's real, but I'm still stumped on how you would prove to the American people that there's a base below the surface of the earth. DUMBs and exposing their existence did not fare well for your miner guy, Phil Schneider."

"Who was he?" Peg asked.

"A tunnel engineer and geologist who tried to expose the Dulce complex," Vyla said. "He was strangled to death with his own catheter tube."

Peg nodded as if it was expected. Vyla was amazed by her matter-of-fact view of whistleblowing and the consequences it could bring.

"Well, it sounds like, on some level, he got the word out enough for them to want him terminated." Peg offered.

Swizzle and Vyla watched her.

"Disclosure of atrocities is usually most successful in stages," Peg said. "A little here, a little there. The groundswell for change can only occur when enough people believe it."

She gestured with her beer.

"You know that America first learned about the extermination camps in Nazi Germany three full years before they were liberated? But the public didn't believe any of it until the liberation was instigated and the films of those camps started hitting movie screens. Until they could see it for themselves, nothing was done."

She took a swig.

"So, I'm just saying, the footage is great—if you can back it up by getting into the actual facility, into the underground complex," she said, looking up.

Vyla looked at Swizzle, who pulled on his cigar, mulling it over.

"There's no way to get in there. It's under layers and layers of security, not to mention miles below the surface," he said.

Vyla watched a huge school of fish go by and had the oblique thought she was on an alien's World War II patrol boat, under the ocean, watching fish swim by... while discussing a conspiracy.

Swizzle abruptly giggled, reading her thoughts, and Peg looked at both of them.

"What—what just happened?"

"He was just being an alien," Vyla said. "I'll explain later about telepathy."

Peg nodded as Swizzle rocked his head back and forth, thinking. Suddenly, he became more sober and looked toward Peg as he exhaled his cigar.

"I'm certain that Dulce is not the only harvesting facility for Screamshit, as there are DUMBs all over the U.S. and the world. Every country has them now. I'll put dollars to doughnuts that if you follow the money trail, you'll get angles on who the dealers are and where they're getting supplied from. But the problem with following the money trail for DUMBs is that it's all above federal auditor clearance levels. All of that money is being moved below board, in ultra top-secret clearance categories—called USAPs. Unacknowledged Special Access Programs. Which are way above federal auditor clearance levels."

"So, you're saying there's no way to find the money trail to begin with?" Peg asked.

"Well, there is a reason that each year there are unaccounted-for trillions taken out of the American taxpayer account."

Peg nodded as Swizzle continued.

"And those trillions build and fund the DUMBs and the Mag-Lev shuttle that connects them all."

"Speaking of connections," Vyla said, turning to Peg.

"I think you should meet Maggie Crawley, a tech geek I know at Stanford who's enhancing the Dulce video. You two are about the same age, and she's really cool. If you two can enhance a copy of that footage... then you can get it to my girlfriend Charlotte, so she can give it to Senator Feinstein."

Peg was suddenly stoked.

"This Maggie knows how to enhance the footage? Cool! When can I meet her?"

"Right now," Vyla said, and then turned to Swizzle.

"I need an hour of your time alone, young man."

Swizzle turned, raising his eyebrows. Vyla had a look in her eyes that was all business, and he knew it was time to follow orders. Moments later, they surfaced in the dense fog outside Moss Landing. Swizzle switched on the regular engines, and they motored to the fueling dock. They off-loaded the kayak, giving Peg instructions to deliver it back to Monterey and then drive to Stanford, where Peg would meet Marten, who would introduce her to Maggie.

"Just get the enhanced footage to Charlotte by tonight," Vyla reminded her. "She leaves first thing in the morning for Washington with Senator Feinstein."

HUSH

Peg saluted them both, and Swizzle pulled Gizmo out of the harbor, using radar as the fog had thickened even more. Vyla watched Swizzle place his hands and connect again, and a moment later, they were hovering nearly a mile deep in the famous Monterey Bay canyon. It was completely dark all around them until Swizzle flipped a switch, illuminating the area within thirty yards with a soft glow.

"So those lights are powered by the reactor too?" Vyla asked.

Swizzle pointed at her, but before he could answer, a shadow half the size of the ship shot past them. A squid the size of a school bus suddenly glided into view, raised its long arm tentacles to its side, and shot away into the dark, leaving a cloud of inky blue where it had been.

"Ahh," Vyla whispered. "I could spend my life down here!"

Swizzle turned in his chair.

"Well, pretty soon, this will be the only place I can bring the ship. I can take you places quickly... but not to space."

Vyla turned.

"What, this old tub can't get up there or something?" She asked.

"Oh, be careful," Swizzle warned. "Gizmo heard that, and she could toss you overboard."

Vyla quickly bowed her head and raised her arms, pleading;

"Okay, sorry, Gizmo! I didn't mean that!" she shouted. "My bad!"

She looked up at Swizzle.

"Was that enough pandering to your ship?"

He snickered and adjusted his cigar.

"Oh, she'll go anywhere, and faster than most," he said. "But your government put Solar Warden in space years ago, and they have microscopic taglets that circle the planet. Any ship passing through those areas gets covered with the minuscule taglets, and then the ship is brought down seconds later by particle-beam weapons employed around the globe. I don't leave the atmosphere anymore. And most of my travel is underwater. But that's coming to a close soon, too, because your Underwater National Reconnaissance Office is now tracking ships below the oceans."

He exhaled.

"But fortunately not in Monterey Bay yet."

She nodded and then noticed the silver handprints near the wheel. No more words were needed. She looked at him, and he nodded with a smile. She positioned herself in front of them and placed her hands gently over the silvery impressions.

"Anything I need to know?" she asked, clearly tense but excited.

"Nope... go right ahead!"

The posh Alora restaurant at Pier 3, Hornblower landing on the San Francisco waterfront offered Andre and Hoppy a stunning view as they finished their five-course meal of fresh Mediterranean cuisine.

Andre had paid for the extra table for his security, and the maitre d' was nice enough to seat them several tables away.

"Wow, this has been such a treat," she said. "Thank you."

He smiled and took her in.

"I haven't been on a date in years, and it's so nice to enjoy this with someone I admire," he said, finishing his last bite of baba ghanoush.

Hoppy nodded at him.

"Well, when we first met, and I realized what you had created, I had a devilish agenda in my head, but then realized—for whatever reason—that I was also immediately attracted to you."

"Oh, that," he shrugged. "The girls all fall for the coke-bottle glasses and thinning gray hair."

She snickered.

"So," he leaned in. "Do tell, this devilish agenda?"

She laughed and casually looked around, tightening her lips. Andre knew she was torn about asking.

"Well, you can imagine the stories I hear about the dark stuff you mentioned that occurs in the DUMBs," she questioned.

Andre gave a much more serious look and nodded.

"Some of the atrocities I hear about that occur in DUMBs," she said, "I have no way of proving them. It's just a client's vivid retelling, and then several clients who don't know each other describe the same base or the same crimes against humanity. But there is no physical proof and no way to change public opinion that aliens not only exist but that there are malevolent ones in contractual obligations with our Cabal, who continue to hoodwink the damn planet."

Andre stared, and then slowly nodded. She watched as he took another bite and exhaled, calmly enjoying the view outside. He whispered as he spoke.

"I have pictures of many humans and aliens alike, strapped to tables in medical labs deep in the DUMBs, clearly being genetically tested, altered, and dissected, and cloned. DUMBs across the globe—but in the U.S. bases alone—Kirtland, Indian Springs, Diego Garcia, and all over the U.S. On the border of Missouri and Illinois, there is a massive DUMB below the Rock City National Archives and Records facility. And down there, humans and aliens alike are being subjected to absolutely horrific alterations and modifications. The Draco-Reptilians down there are huge and winged and, of all things, have white, almost transparent skin. Absolutely terrifying. Many of the humans being tested and modified, are..." He shook his head and exhaled. "Children."

She was stunned that Andre had jumped into the darkness with her so quickly.

"This is one reason I have not sold my patents to the U.S. government. I love this country, but it's the global elite that are fueling these atrocities. The Cabal is not aware that I can see all they are involved in. Only what I show them from the exact areas they want to see, but," he exhaled, "I'm pretty certain they know I can see much more than I'm letting on, hence the men at the other table."

She nodded and took a sip of wine, sitting back in her chair.

"Sounds like you've been trying to work this out as well?"

He exhaled a long sigh.

"I've spent too many hours wondering how to reveal the actual realm that exists without scaring too many."

He turned slightly away as if looking at the waterfront.

"So, you're the top psychologist. How... how do you change public opinion, as I know a video will not do this?"

"Correct," she said.

"I have a close friend who has direct access to a well-known senator from this state. They are traveling to Washington in two days' time. My friend knows the senator like a mother. She is positive that, with the right proof to back it up, the senator would step forward in front of TV cameras and demand an investigation into any atrocity committed by the Cabal."

Andre was heeding every word, knowing Hoppy was referring to the one and only Dianne Feinstein—the only female senator from California.

"And what would you prove?"

Hoppy looked up.

"All I need to prove to the world is that the DUMB at Diego Garcia exists. A photo of the actual DUMB, and then my senator could present that photo and demand an investigation. One that actually takes a team to the DUMB for a complete tour of the facility. Diego, as you've probably seen, is a huge spaceport, but it's also where the missing Malaysian flight was diverted to."

He stared.

"You have someone who saw it there?" he asked.

She nodded.

"One of my clients was cloned by the Cabal and worked there as an assassin, terminating many of the maintenance crew that disassembled that jet."

Andre got a look.

"I wasn't certain until now, but I have imagery of Diego Garcia, and in one of the topside hangers is clearly a commercial jet that has been taken apart. It is exactly two-hundred and nine-feet long."

Hoppy stared, perplexed.

"What does that mean?" she whispered.

"The only jet in the world that is that exact length is a Boeing 777," he said.

"You have a picture of MH370 disassembled in a hangar next to the runway at Diego Garcia?"

He nodded.

"Oh, shit!" she whispered

"But the picture wouldn't be enough. Your senator would have to show a picture of the DUMB to the world if she wanted to demand an investigation."

Hoppy nodded.

"The public will jump on board completely if we can get TV cameras inside a DUMB like Diego and also show the Mag-Lev train station there—verifying for the public that those Mag-Lev trains crisscross the planet."

He nodded.

"And to confirm the existence of the underwater spaceport. The Cabal would not have time to disassemble an entire DUMB. They could blow it up... before you arrive, but at some point, the public will know that this sinister group has been weaving its atrocities around them for decades."

She nodded, and he watched her as she whispered,

"There are Greys and Reptilians that work in and below the Diego DUMB. Humans are down there, too, being used as genetic test subjects by the Greys and the U.S. Black Navy. There's also a dungeon where the U.S. detains high-profile terrorists—where they can basically get away with extreme torture, disregarding all policies on basic human rights."

He stared.

"Your client, who worked there, told you all of this that I have already seen in my photos?"

She nodded. He stared and slowly turned toward the water. A huge exhale.

"I couldn't possibly deliver a photo of Diego Garcia to your friend."

Hoppy stared, then nodded, knowing that was the end of that. Her frustration at revealing this whole hidden realm was infuriating. The Cabal was just too good at hoodwinking the world—and had the clout to ensure people like Andre would never come forward. She exhaled, looking at her hands as he whispered,

"I'm so sorry, Hoppy—I just can't do it. But..."

She looked up as he turned to lock eyes with her in a confident and loving gaze.

"You could."

Inside Maggie Crawley's apartment, Peg could tell the girl was a complete geek.

She was amused by how intense Maggie was about tweaking the footage. Marten had warned Peg before introducing them that Maggie still wasn't aware the footage was non-fiction. Peg understood... she also had been a non-believer until her underwater excursion with Swizzle.

Peg had given her word never to reveal Swizzle's true nature, and nothing was going to alter that commitment to him.

Marten cooked for them in Maggie's kitchen while Peg and Maggie sat next to each other, tweaking the footage.

"You really eat Top Ramen three times a day?" Marten asked as he stirred the pot.

"About all I can afford," Maggie replied. "Shit, it's friggin' five bucks for a cuppa coffee on this damn campus, and I need that cash for all my geeky hobbies," she said, looking at Peg and winking.

Peg smiled back, amazed at how good the footage was looking as Maggie worked her magic.

"Let's try one more filter, and that's about it," Maggie said as Marten stepped over with the ramen.

"Bon appétit," he said, placing the steaming bowls in front of them.

Maggie made a grand gesture of hitting the final button for the movie to begin burning to disc.

"It's printing!"

"Awesome," Peg replied, and the three of them sat back for a bite.

"How long will it take?" Marten asked. "I'm heading right by Charlotte's—I could drop it off and save you two the trip."

Maggie gave a thumbs-up with her mouth full, then raised four fingers.

"I can wait four minutes," Marten said.

Maggie nodded and looked at Peg.

"Do you want to stick around... and hang out with a geek like me?" she asked. "Or are you gonna do the big drive back tonight?"

"If I could crash on your couch, that would be awesome," Peg said.

Maggie nodded, mouth full of food, as a computer tone sounded. Out popped a CD. Maggie placed it in a plastic hard case and handed it to Marten.

"I'll send you the file by email too."

Maggie said as Marten dropped the CD in his jacket pocket and hounded one last bite, placing his bowl in the kitchen.

"Cool, cool... thank you so much, Maggie. And Peg, it was great to meet you!"

Peg gave a thumbs-up with her mouth full, and Marten was out the door a moment later.

He looked back across the dark campus and could see them laughing through Maggie's living room window.

He didn't notice in that quick glance that there was a figure sitting on the dark bench below the oak tree, calmly smoking a cigarette. Marten kept walking... not looking back to see the Cabal's top assassin tilt a hand-sized vial of *Winking Wolf...* and then shake his head violently as the red drops—shot like kryptonite—into the depraved killer's stalking state.

Chapter Forty-Five

The Widow test flight would commence at 4 a.m.

Vyla had flown the Widow simulator every day for the entire week. Her time flying Gizmo in Monterey Bay with Swizzle had certainly helped her get used to the one-G environment, as she effortlessly flipped Gizmo upside down or sideways at high speed. Gizmo had in moments become her companion. The connection felt similar to what Vyla had shared with Banjo when he was young and healthy. Back then, they would play in the parks and go for walks, and Banjo was at her beck and call. Sometimes, their bond felt so strong it was as if she was part of *Team Banjo*.

She and Gizmo had bonded in that same way. Swizzle was amazed how quickly the ship was in step with her slightest whim on direction, speed, altitude, and lateral movement. If she could think it, the ship was already in that evolution. She was dumbfounded when she finally realized how much she and the ship co-created what transpired. But the Widow simulator at S-4 could not create an accurate feeling of what the pilot would experience in the Widow. By the third day, Vyla realized that Yen's team was overly optimistic about her chances of getting the Widow off the ground, much less flying her.

She had been allowed to enter the Widow twice just to have the seat morph around her, but still felt an edge of anger with the Widow. She decided that if the Widow would not bond with her, then that would have to be okay. She could not control what a living conveyance might prefer. She decided that tonight she would get really quiet in her stateroom at S-4, and allow herself to just enjoy some downtime prior to the test flight.

J ack Goldmeyer stared at Yen as she stood before him in his office at S-4.

"So, Miss Jee, the security breach in Japan a few weeks back?"

Yen stared.

"I'm sorry, sir—"

"Apparently," Goldmeyer whispered tersely, cutting her off. "Your young Asian thief had already been paid to deliver that hard drive to Beijing and to the worldwide press."

Yen stood dumbfounded.

"The young man spent his final moments in that wet room, Miss Jee."

Yen stared at the floor.

"His entire plan came out rather quickly when his fingers started coming off," Goldmeyer whispered. "Sang like a bird once the pliers came out."

Yen went silent.

"Under extreme torture, he divulged exactly where he had taken the hard drive from and who else had access to it."

Yen adjusted her diamond watchband, her fingers shaking.

"Fortunately for you, Miss Jee, he was a lone wolf, and we caught him before he exposed all your financials to the public, and you won't ever have to worry about him anymore."

Yen looked slightly up, her breathing labored.

"It only took a few minutes for my team to clean the wet room with fire hoses and disinfectant after he bled to death."

Yen went cold.

"Is there something on the carpet you're curious about, Miss Jee?"

"No, sir," she said, forcing herself to look up as he continued in a whisper,

"As you well know, we've always got your company's best interest in mind, Miss Jee, and perhaps that confirms for you what you always knew about wet rooms... and what they're for?"

Yen nodded nervously. Goldmeyer sucked his teeth, watching her. Yen looked slightly away from his icy eyes.

"Miss Jee, are you familiar with the missing Malaysian flight?"

She turned back, somewhat relieved that she had been given a regular question and was smart enough to milk it for some sympathy.

"Yes, sir, I am. I actually have a sister in Hong Kong who was on that flight with her family."

Goldmeyer stared, then gave a tight-lipped smile.

"Had a sister and her family."

Yen looked up.

"I beg your pardon, sir?"

"Well, unfortunately, Miss Jee, the hard drive that was stolen from your facility by your little Asian fucking thief just happened to be in his briefcase on that flight... to Beijing.

Yen hesitated. The implications starting to come through.

"Now, perhaps you understand, Miss Jee, that we employed extraordinary measures to get that hard drive back, not to mention... some American semiconductor technology, that was heading to Beijing as well. And that hard drive alone would have exposed your illegal USAPs. All the money your company has been paid below-board was on that hard drive. So, you understand what that means, Miss Jee?"

Yen stared anxiously as the implication seeped in.

"Unfortunately, Miss Jee, to liberate your financial hard drive, and all the semiconductor technology that was also on board the flight, with his twenty engineer friends, we had to redirect that aircraft to an area where we could apprehend your thief."

Yen was frozen, staring at the carpet.

"He was removed from the jet, and that's when his wet room ordeal began."

Yen didn't move.

"Yes—yes, sir, and the rest of the passengers?"

"Yes, well, the fate of the passengers and crew was also part of our extraordinary measures."

Yen gasped but caught herself as Goldmeyer gave no quarter of sympathy.

"Now, Miss Jee, perhaps you need to get down to the Widow and prepare for the test flight with Vyla Kells," he continued. "There will be many in attendance this morning, and you can rest assured, Miss Jee, that this is your final test. If she does not fly the ship, your contract will be voided and given to another contractor who is looking forward to the opportunity."

Yen was still frozen in place when Teebeck's clone placed a firm hand on her shoulder.

"Right this way," the muscular clone commanded.

behind her in the same watery fashion.

Despite the shock a moment ago, she couldn't help but gaze in astonishment at the dimensional transcendence before her. The cavernous cockpit just couldn't be—and yet, she was standing in it. *Magic.* She picked the left seat and marveled at its molecular morphing around her. Even though she had felt it before, the technology was still otherworldly.

Wow, she thought, as it wrapped around her.

Yen's team on the tarmac near the hangar began their procedures while up in the overview many watched.

"The pilot has boarded," came over the loudspeaker in the overview room.

Jack Goldmeyer and Chernal Teebeck sat with several military personnel, watching the screens. Goldmeyer leaned close to Teebeck, whispering,

"Teebeck, do we have recording devices rolling for this?"

"Sir, we do," Teebeck responded.

Next to the hangar door sat Yen's team of flight support personnel, who monitored video screens showing wide-angle views from inside the cockpit. They had watched as Vyla had been absorbed into her seat and the subsequent action of the interior walls of the saucer becoming transparent all around her.

In the Widow, Vyla looked out for the first time at the desert and the Papoose dry lakebed plateau in the moonlight. There was no light pollution anywhere, and she could see everything in all directions as if there were no windows in front of her.

Unbelievable, she thought.

On loudspeakers throughout the tarmac area, Vyla's voice could be heard going through the preflight sequence—a checklist of tasks she was supposed to do before she placed her hands in the metal imprints.

I n Washington D.C., it was already ninety-two degrees and climbing at The House Triangle press area, just outside the U.S. Capitol building.

It was only noon, but the enormous grass viewing area across from the podium was filling up with spectators as Charlotte and Hoppy answered questions of Senator Dianne Feinstein.

The Triangle had long been the favorite outdoor podium for press conferences of House and Senate members, and Dianne's team had put the world on notice about this morning's ultra-important news event. The rush of press and concerned parties toward the Capitol building was stopping traffic all around the famous location. Feinstein had opted for a noon press conference due to the heatwave crossing the nation, which had landed firmly on Washington, D.C. Many in the audience were already dousing themselves with water, and two fire trucks near the enormous grass circle were offering a simple spray into the grass that many in the crowd were walking through.

Dianne straightened her congressional-looking outfit and noted the vast throng awaiting her speech, along with the enormous press gaggle of trucks and reporters with TV cameras already rolling.

All around the podium, Dianne's team had placed enlarged images of Malaysian Flight 370 on wooden tripods and then combined those photos with the UAV and satellite video footage of the flight being tracked and teleported. Both angles of the jet being teleported were playing on continuous loops. Several TV stations had reporters viewing and discussing the astounding footage. Interspersed between those video feeds were Andre's ground-penetrating radar images showing the DUMB and spaceport extending below the Diego Garcia runway, deep into the ocean. In addition, there were images of the Malaysian jet sitting in pieces inside a hangar on the Diego Garcia tarmac. Next to those enlarged images were screenshots of Philip Wood's final SOS message on the 4chan website, as well as photos of the candlelight vigils held worldwide for missing passengers.

Senator Feinstein turned to Charlotte and Hoppy.

"Okay, remember, I'm not bringing up the Dulce footage... that's too much on day one."

Charlotte and Hoppy nodded.

Dianne took a deep breath and looked up at the audience.

"Alright, let's get to the bottom of this," she said to the two women and then stepped off, walking up the steps to the podium, to a loud, raucous crowd that was growing by the minute. She cleared her throat as the audience hushed. A somber stare as she began, her short hair blowing in the light breeze.

"Hello, America, and all of you watching from across the world!"

She held her stern gaze and gestured at the videos and images around her.

"As you can see on these enlarged images and videos, an atrocity is displayed... a cover-up, committed by elements of my own American government!"

The crowd suddenly tensed and focused.

Senator Feinstein gazed at them

"Those at the very top will now have to answer for crimes that have been ongoing for decades!"

The crowd erupted in applause and yells. Dianne watched them, holding her intense gaze. She aimed a laser pointer at the image of the Diego DUMB complex next to the podium.

"This underwater complex—is a United States, top-secret, Deep Underground Military Base, located at Diego Garcia in the Indian Ocean."

483

The crowd tense. Focused.

"It is a colossal facility going down many levels deep into the ocean."

She paused for effect.

"For those of you who don't know, a Deep Underground Military Base, or, more commonly called in the military...," indicating quotes with her fingers, "by its acronym—DUMB."

The crowd was quiet and intense. On point.

"This United States deep underground military base was tragically the final destination for Malaysian Flight 370 and its passengers and crew."

The throng murmured in tangible disbelief amid hushed, tense whispers. She pointed the laser at the looped video showing the jet being tracked.

"A rogue, elitist group of Americans, working covertly with access to sixth-generation warfare technology, hijacked that Malaysian jet and brought it to Diego Garcia."

The crowd was silent.

"At that U.S. Navy base is where units of our own military terminated the passengers and crew of that Malaysian flight for an agenda I won't name today."

She stared at the audience, some of whom were already in tears. She raised a finger to the sky.

"Because no military agenda is worth the lives of over two-hundred innocent civilians!"

The crowd erupted in anger as she nodded and continued.

"Those victims of MH370 were men, women, and children from all over the planet! They were YOU and ME!"

The crowd was now yelling their outrage.

"The video footage of that Boeing, triple-seven-jet—by two U.S. Air Force reaper drones—and stamped with our own National Reconnaissance Office geo-location stamp... on its final flight... is enough proof for me to demand a full investigation!"

The crowd raised fists and yelled their support.

"And let's be very clear. Our president, the one I campaigned for—and voted for—in the last two elections, was, and is, absolutely aware of America hijacking that jet!"

The crowd was suddenly astonished, booing.

"He and all the top intelligence agencies—of my own beloved country—have known since the day of the hijacking... that our own American military units had executed all those innocent passengers and crew!"

The crowd suddenly sobered, staring in shock.

HUSH

In the overview room at S-4, Jack Goldmeyer watched the TV showing Dianne Feinstein at the Capitol Triangle.

He hardly noticed all the dignitaries in the room around him, shooting glances his way as everyone checked his reaction to the shocking news happening outside the U.S. Capitol building.

Goldmeyer pressed a button on his cell phone and glanced quickly at the monitors showing Vyla in her preflight sequence. Outside the hangar, the team flight surgeon spoke into a microphone, calling out vital signs as the preflight checks were underway.

"Blood pressure normal, temperature normal, pulse slightly high but within SOP. Oxygen intake normal, and all other vital signs are green for go."

The team watched Vyla staring forward, and she shifted in her flight chair slightly. The ship's gravity envelope would not create itself until she connected with her hands in the imprints. She took a slow, deep breath and hovered her hands over the shiny indentations.

"Okay, connecting," she said.

The flight support team watched on an interior video camera showing the side of her face as her hands came down. The moment her hands were firmly placed in the imprints, a tiny round light above each of her ten fingers illuminated. Each light, a different color.

In that moment, even though she had entered with a wide-open heart, she felt a dark wave beginning to circle her, and she knew it was not her, but instead the Widow. A jolt of electricity surged momentarily, and she lost her breath.

"We have full connection," called out a technician monitoring her vitals. "Brain throughput is normal at twenty-two percent."

Vyla's body felt an abrasive jolt every few seconds now that there was a solid connection. And in that moment, amid the light shocks... she decided she was done and that this flight wasn't going to happen. She exhaled and lifted her hands. But the lifting didn't happen, and suddenly, she was terrified as she realized—the Widow—had her.

At the US Capitol, Dianne had the crowd on point, astounded at her every word.

"Furthermore, we have video testimony of an eyewitness who watched that jet being hastily disassembled at Diego Garcia on the day it went missing!"

The crowd tensed, yelling in outrage. She pointed her laser at the Philip Wood S.O.S. message.

"In addition, Philip Wood, an American I.B.M. employee on that flight, sent his last, tragic message from—of all places—a hangar at the Diego Garcia airfield!"

The crowd was in full outrage, yelling.

Dianne stared out, connecting with the tense stares and tear-filled eyes of her audience.

"The evidence you see behind me is the last straw in this absolutely ridiculous fight for transparency and justice within my own government and military!"

The crowd swelled with applause and volume as they became enraged and chaotic.

I n the overview, Jack Goldmeyer stared at the TV and whispered,

"Oh, goddamn," as Teebeck approached at a fast clip, weaving through the shocked dignitaries.

"Yes, sir?" Teebeck whispered.

"Teebeck, have the Malaysian jet parts that are stored in the hangar at Diego removed. I don't care how you do it; just make it happen."

"Yes, sir."

Teebeck departed as Goldmeyer turned off the TV showing the Washington problem. He exhaled and lit a cigarette, focusing on Vyla in the ship. He turned to see Aspelsin watching him from the alien partition next door.

"All vitals still green for go." Vyla heard the flight surgeon call out as if in some murky memory, and though frozen in fear, she could see the Widow's skin slowly coming to life with a deep red band of light that pulsed from top to bottom continuously. With each increase in voltage, the Widow seemed to emanate a thrumming sound, growing louder.

Vyla's chest heaved when the team first heard a loud hiss, like an electric substation might produce, and the Widow rose a few inches, slightly wobbling, her central axis tilting a few degrees from vertical.

Yen watched with her team and knew this was the moment in time where Captain Andle's flight became fatal. Just then, a technician called out.

"Throughput up to eighty-nine percent!"

A hint of anxiousness in his voice as he turned quizzically to the flight surgeon.

"We're still green," the flight surgeon said with his calloused calm.

There was an electric-blue glow of a corona discharge on the bottom of the Widow as the air below her was crushed and photons were emitted. Then the team heard Vyla breathing way too heavily—the first sounds since connecting. It came over the speakers in the overlook, and Jack Goldmeyer seemed almost amused. This would finally be the termination spectacle he and Aspelsin knew would solve a piece of the Dulce video issue. For Goldmeyer, he could hand this ship over to a new company, which he had already chosen.

Inside the Widow, Vyla was fighting an energy that had suddenly grown, and she looked out one last time onto the desert plateau. The final visual of her lifetime. She was completely frozen in pain and could do nothing—but let go.

She heard a muffled—*Throughput is 167 percent!*—that seemed to come from a faraway dream. At the flight console, the flight surgeon jumped forward, slamming his hand on the comms button.

"Disconnect Dr. Kells!"

But it was just another hollow echo... way too late.

In that moment, she heard them—and felt them all around her—and knew they were with her for this transition. She felt his feathers around her—the tribal headdress of Elu in starlight—comforting her. Looking out at the stars, she could see Waya pulling back his arrow and chanting with power. And Dah, dancing in her strongest stomping, her hands wide, heart open, singing her most powerful passing song.

And there too was Sam, strongly lifting his young daughters with Catherine, and Vyla could feel it—the echo of Gloria's whipping wind around her and Papa as they shot up vertically in their glorious bird, reaching the peak of Gloria's Hammerhead stall—and the beginning of their falling.

And in the falling too, she felt them all. Her dad and mom and brother Daniel all around her, and Charlotte, Marten, and Steph staring at her with a love infinite and breathtaking.

And Vyla was okay... okay with this... her own passing. She was spent and had nothing left to give... sitting there in the Widow's hovering cockpit.

She closed her eyes in her ending. And it was suddenly quiet, and there was nothing but black silence. A vast, expansive—nothing.

And then she heard...

Her.

The little one was not having it, was not giving up—the little one was rising and stepped suddenly forward in that blackness—forward in her unbridled power, and yelled with her little-girl, full-power abandon,

"Eyes closed, Sophia! Eyes closed!"

Raising her tiny fists, she slammed her eyes shut... and knew, without a doubt... in her little-girl gigantic heart... that this bond with Sophia was now happening, and there was no doubt about it—she was willing it—and in that power, Sophia heard her name called for the first time... *in years.*

Outside Sophia, all the watchers on the tarmac and in the overlook were transfixed as the ship suddenly hesitated and rose thirty feet. And as if showing off, extended the landing gear to their full extension and then retracted those three legs with hemispheric pads.

Inside the overlook, the dignitaries were thrilled and yelled their encouragement. "Wow!" "Yes!" "Damn!"

Jack Goldmeyer and Teebeck were drop-jawed.

On the tarmac, Yen raised both hands, looking up at the ship, now pulsing in a teal glow that had an urgency to it... and everyone yelled and applauded.

Sophia was a ship changed, one that had suddenly heard the sweetness of her name. And with that change, Sophia immediately adjusted to wanting a full bonding with the entity that had suddenly awakened her—calling out her name—which she had not heard for so... so long.

Her name... and this Vyla Kells—and the little one deep inside—and Sophia pulsed in a brilliant, shimmering dark teal. Everyone watching, held in a stupor as the new energy emanated... and a moment later, as Jack Goldmeyer realized too late what was about to happen, he screamed into his handheld radio:

"Shoot it down! Shoot-it-down!"

Watching as that ship, with Vyla Kells, the traitor, at the helm, pulsed again and—vanished!

Everywhere at S-4, on the tarmac and in the overlook, there was a deafening silence. Aspelsin, Goldmeyer, and Teebeck all silently looked out—toward the desert plateau, and up at the stars, and then at each other. Aspelsin and Goldmeyer knew at the same instant that it was not Vyla Kells who did this—to them. Both of them put it together at that infuriating moment. A taste of their own medicine—from an old-man alien none of them knew. And he had done it in a velvety, silky-smooth act of subtle perfection.

Each of them knew, without a word being said... that all of them had just experienced, without a doubt, the most monumental sting of simply epic proportions. And they knew, from doing it to others for so long, what had now been so easily done to them—an unforgettable—and absolutely infuriating... hoodwink.

Chapter Forty-Six

At the Capitol, Dianne had the crowd tense in front of her.

"I am hereby demanding a walkthrough of the entire Diego Garcia facility immediately!"

The crowd's applause was overwhelming as she continued.

"I will show you the DUMB that is there, even if they try to blow it up before I get there... I will show you the covert evil that has been ripping our country apart for decades!"

The crowd went ballistic.

"And I can assure you, this DUMB is one of hundreds below us worldwide that have been bought and paid for by you, without any presidential or congressional oversight!"

The crowd began to jeer in pandemonium.

"You own these DUMBs! All of them. Not the Cabal, not the Deep State... YOU own these DUMBs. And I intend to take full control of that which you and I have sweated and bled for!"

The crowd went berserk.

Vyla slowly lifted her hands from the console as Sophia settled onto the mesa at Hart Canyon, New Mexico.

She could see Swizzle standing outside Sophia as the ramp lowered. He ran up the ramp like a little kid, tapping the walls as Sophia pulsed and chirped to each loving tap. A reunion for the ages. Vyla could feel Sophia react as Swizzle yelled, running past her, sliding his hands all over the ship. Sophia responded wherever he was, with blinking lights, vibrations, and soft tones.

"Sophia, Sophia, Sophia, my sweet friend!" he yelled.

Vyla beamed, watching him.

"I take it you're friends," she said with a soft smile.

He slammed into her with a bear hug and then looked at everything around him. She saw them then, his face awash in them. They locked eyes.

"Oh, thank you so much!" he said, hardly able to speak.

She nodded.

"And you worked that whole thing back there at S-4, yes?"

He looked at her, wondering if she was okay with it all.

"I chose this, right?" she said. "Signed up for it—royalty?"

He smiled and pointed. She smiled back.

"I'm glad you didn't tell me the plan, as it would have never worked if you had told me in advance."

He slowly nodded.

"Thank you."

She nodded and looked out to see Gizmo hovering just a few meters away, with Plato at the controls, smiling and nodding at them. They waved. A moment later, Gizmo flickered in energy and vanished. Swizzle looked at Vyla.

"We're running late for an important show."

She stared.

"Washington?"

He pointed. She pointed back. She motioned to the cockpit seats.

"Why don't you show me how it's done?" she said.

He shook his head.

"No, I'm a ship's mechanic, and you, young lady, are a complete badass aerobatic pilot. Trust me, Sophia knows it... and she wants you to wring her out. Wants to know you—deeper."

He motioned, and they both sat, admiring the seats, wrapping them up in molecular perfection. She looked one last time at him as she placed her hands over the impressions on her side.

"You sure?" she asked.

He stared at her, nodding ever so slightly.

"Be the Top Gun you already are. Sophia wants to 'Rock and Roll!'"

"Okay, you asked for it," she whispered.

He slowly nodded and watched. And what he watched was breathtaking. She lowered her hands into the impressions and opened her heart wide. He suddenly felt Sophia gearing up as never before... as if she had reared up on unseen legs of infinite strength—and a split second later—he felt her leap into her warping of space-time.

A t the Capitol, Dianne stood infuriated, her finger pointed in the air, bringing that energy and determination for her audience's delight.

"I am coming to Diego Garcia!"

The crowd went berserk!

"I am bringing a contingent of my peers with me! The NRO can't stop me, the CIA can't stop me! The NSA can't stop me! DARPA can't stop me! The FBI, the Joint Chiefs of Staff, the United Nations, the NRO, the Majestic-12, or the pathetic Cabal!"

She allowed all this to sink in amid the crowd's pandemonium.

"None of them will stop this tidal wave of justice that is now free—and growing—and inexorably slamming into every wall of denial and deceit this world has put up with for too long!"

She lifted her finger one last time.

"I—am—coming!"

The crowd's roar swelled into utter pandemonium. She turned and walked off the stage. Charlotte had her cell to her ear and tapped Dianne on the shoulder as she went by, pointing up. Dianne looked up to see the glimmer high above and nodded. She turned and marched back up to the podium to even more crowd bedlam.

"People of the world she said, hesitating—to capture them. I just delivered dire news... news that many of you will find tough to believe. But to prove to you... that you have been lied to... I will now show you technology that the Cabal has been hiding from us... for decades!"

The crowd quieted. Tense. On point.

"Technology that could have changed all our lives for the better decades ago. I want to show you a real—she pointed to the ship high above—off-world ship!"

The crowd stood stunned, looking up, pointing at Sophia. Hovering at 20,000 feet... and gasped in astonishment.

"Know that we will deal with the darkness I mentioned moments ago, but in this new moment, right now, I have an unbelievably great surprise for the world. I want to present a friend of mine to you, as she is now arriving in that same off-world ship!"

Dianne pointed at the ship as the crowd quieted in hushed astonishment.

"Please do not be afraid! Arriving this minute, from high above, is an American patriot—and my dear friend, Dr. Vyla Kruvant Wolf!"

The crowd went nuts. And just like that—Sophia descended from 20,000 feet in one second flat—and was suddenly hovering silently, only a few feet from the Capitol itself. So close, it seemed impossible. The crowd was in hushed astonishment and then began to cheer even louder. Dianne raised her finger.

"If anyone in the military shoots at this stunning ship, I will have-your-head!"

The crowd roared! Inside Sophia, Swizzle raised his eyebrows at Vyla's flying ability. She had zoomed to within inches of the famous building. She turned to address his concern.

"This close to the Capitol, I don't think they'll attempt to shoot a missile at us, as it might destroy the Capitol."

He slowly nodded.

"Now say, 'Sophia, please land.'"

"What?" she said.

He stared until she heard him again in her head. She looked at the flight console next to her hands and realized that she had a new trick available to her. She then whispered,

"Sophia, please land."

The throng outside watched in hushed astonishment as three large hemispheric pads lowered from the ship in a tripod formation. Simultaneously, a mist of yellowish spray shot from the three hemispheric pads as they lowered, and the crowd reacted with oohs and ahhs. And then, magically, the ship descended the last few feet and landed. The crowd stood in full astonishment, staring at the magic many had only dreamed of. Sophia sat on her stunning landing gear and pulsed in her deep teal coloring. Then, like mercury flowing towards the crowd, the magical ramp extended from nowhere as the crowd watched in astonished whispers. With the ship sitting high on its legs, nine feet off the grass, everyone could see a soft light emanating from within the ship. The crowd waited in stunned, excited anticipation. Inside Sophia, Vyla shook her head, beaming at Swizzle.

"What was the yellow mist?"

"Disinfectant," he said matter-of-factly. "When you land on any given planet, Sophia ejects a disinfectant, assuring the crew that any harmful planetary molecules would be neutralized around the perimeter of the ship."

Vyla stared, astonished.

"I need a drink," she whispered.

"Perhaps you should greet your people first?"

She stared at him, noting the open ramp, and they could hear the crowd.

"Right," she said, and looked at him with soft eyes. "This one's for you—Setimus," she whispered.

He nodded in admiration.

A t Palo Alto Elementary School, near Dah's house, Stephanie was drawing at her desk in her sweltering fifth-grade art class.

Sweat rolled down her cheeks, and all around her, the other kids were attempting to cool themselves by waving paper fans as they worked with colored pencils. Steph's teacher was adjusting the two oscillating fans at the front of the room.

"Okay, kids, I want all of you to grab your waters right now and everyone take a big gulp."

The kids began to sip when suddenly they heard the principal's voice booming through the public address system.

"All teachers, please bring your students and report to the gymnasium for an important news announcement. Everyone should have a water bottle with them."

"Okay, kids, you heard the principal. Single file, hurry," the teacher said and opened the classroom door.

Stephanie whispered to her friend Anne as they filed out with the others.

"Oh good, maybe they're going to let us out early."

Anne nodded, clearly overheated, and took a sip from her water bottle as they filed out. All the classrooms flowed into the hallway and, moments later, into the large gymnasium. They filed into the bleachers as a huge viewing screen hanging in the center of the gymnasium showed CNN broadcasting from the Capitol in Washington, D.C. The principal stepped in front of the bleachers with a wireless microphone. Her long black hair flowed over her summer dress, and she was clearly sweating from head to toe.

"Okay, everybody, a special news bulletin just came out about this flying saucer landing at the Capitol, and I wanted all of us to watch."

Excited yells and whispers from the kids.

"Let's all remain quiet and listen, and I want to see everybody drinking their water, or we'll go back to our classes."

She turned up the audio on the big screen as Senator Dianne Feinstein spoke at the podium next to the landed ship.

"Ladies and gentlemen of our amazing planet Earth. I am delighted to inform you that the flying saucer you see behind me, which is not from this planet, has come in peace. The American physicist, Dr. Vyla Kruvant Wolf, just flew that ship here. Vyla, if you can hear me, we are ready for you!"

The crowd erupted as Vyla appeared, walking down the ramp and waving. Stephanie and her schoolmates stared at the screen, transfixed.

"That's Vyla!" Stephanie shouted, standing up and pointing to the big screen. "She's my mom's girlfriend!"

Everyone turned toward Steph as she quickly sat down, suddenly embarrassed.

O utside the ship, Vyla waved to the insane crowd as she approached the podium.

She heard another crowd roar and looked back in time to see the ramp close behind her, just as Swizzle raised the landing gear. The ship was again hovering silently next to the Capitol. *Stunning.* At the podium, Senator Feinstein continued as Vyla approached.

"And trust me, if this ship came to do us harm, with the technology you are now witnessing, it certainly could have. So, I am warning all U.S. military personnel: put your missiles and particle beam weapons down! We have all been waiting for this day. I'm telling you... do not shoot! You will only destroy our own Capitol and kill many innocent citizens in the process!"

Whoops and massive applause from the audience as she continued.

"And without further ado, let me welcome to the podium right now, Dr. Vyla Kruvant Wolf."

The crowd erupted into utter pandemonium as Vyla and Dianne shared a strong embrace, holding that hug and clearly exchanging whispers, while Charlotte and Hoppy stood just behind them, arm in arm. Dianne stepped back, holding Vyla at arm's length and beaming. She motioned for Vyla to take the podium, and as she did so, she snuck a wink to Charlotte and Hoppy on her way by.

She stood still in front of the microphone and allowed herself to breathe, staring out with her hair blowing back gently in that stunning moment. The atmosphere was electric as the crowd waited for her, with the world press corps in high gear, camera flashes strobing from every direction and behind the press mob, satellite trucks of every kind. She looked one last time at Senator Feinstein, who gave her a strong thumbs-up.

A t Stephanie's school, the students and teachers were locked on the big screen when suddenly, the entire gymnasium shifted—as an earthquake hit—and it wasn't a small one.

Screams echoed throughout the gym as everyone scrambled toward the exit, some stumbling in the stampede. The principal grabbed the microphone and yelled.

"Outside, quick... everybody, get outside!"

The ground shifted even more as the floor became a wave of boards. The huge rafters above began to fall. The big screen crashed down as teachers tried to help the stampeding students escape. Most made it out of the building as a huge ceiling rafter gave way and dropped, just missing a group of escaping students, who screamed! But there were stragglers still caught in the shaking building as the roof began coming apart in huge pieces, raining debris into the gym.

Dah ran through her house and burst through her screen door amid the violent shaking, only to find Banjo crushed under a beam from the porch.

She screamed and attempted to lift the beam, but it was no use during the continuous shaking, and he was clearly dead. Pieces of her porch rained down as she ran into the yard.

"Banjo!" she cried, falling to her hands and knees as the ground rolled in a wave fashion.

The shaking grew more violent, and the house next door... collapsed. She looked up as a nearby fire hydrant suddenly burst, gushing water, and she could hear transformers exploding down the street as sirens began wailing in the distance. The telephone poles on the street swayed like willows. The thick electrical line finally went taut and snapped in a blinding blue-white explosion. Then, as suddenly as it came, the shaking stopped. An eerie pause. The eye of the storm, Dah knew. She was on her hands and knees, in tears, whimpering. Suddenly, a realization.

"Stephanie!" she whispered, jumping to her feet and raising her cell phone.

But in that moment... it came. The aftershock! She dropped the phone as the yard began rolling again like a wave, sending her back to her hands and knees, reaching for her phone as she screamed.

At Stephanie's school, another volley of yells erupted as people ran in terror, the buildings around them shaking like card houses.

Full chaos everywhere. Weeping parents and kids who had reunited after the initial quake now cowered in groups in the parking lot. City sirens wailed, and an air-raid siren moaned in the distance. Fires raged at the far end of the school. Transformers in the neighborhood exploded as the principal staggered in her summer dress, yelling into a handheld megaphone, ordering students to stay together for a roll call. Stephanie and Anne were in tears, holding each other tightly in the parking lot, huddled with the other kids.

"My mom's not here! She's in Washington with Senator Feinstein!" Stephanie said to Anne through tears.

"You can come to my house," Anne replied in tears. "You can stay with us."

At the Capitol, Vyla leaned into the mic.

"Hello, America, and hello, all humans across the globe." She paused momentarily, looking back at the now-hovering saucer.

"My name is Vyla Kruvant Wolf. I am an American physicist who was born and raised on this beautiful planet. But the ship you see behind me is not from Earth. I repeat, not from this planet."

She shot a quick glance over her shoulder at the ship, hovering inches from the Capitol, and continued.

"That ship came here from beyond our solar system. As did the humanoid pilot who is hovering the saucer for you this moment…"

Three hundred yards due east of the Capitol press triangle, Case departed an elevator onto the 5th-floor roof of the Thomas Jefferson Congressional Library.

A building with a perfect overlook of the Capitol just to the west. Following him were Aspelsin and a two-man sniper unit—a shooter-spotter team. All four walked to the very edge of the roof.

Five floors below, crowds flocked to see the hovering saucer, and flowing into the melee were police and firefighters. Approaching the Capitol but keeping their distance were two Black Hawk helicopters, and further in the distance, news helicopters were arriving and circling on station. The area around the podium, for blocks in all directions, was quickly packing out as the word spread, and police and Capitol security moved through the throng.

Case stared at the huge flying saucer hovering near the Capitol. Even though he had read about them and wanted to believe in them, he had never seen a real one. He found himself in awe, blown away by the silence and the capability of what it was doing—hovering effortlessly, so close to the building. He took a breath and raised a pair of binoculars. He could see Vyla standing at the podium and knew that in a few more moments, she would be shot.

In a way, she was the final connection Case had to Will, and he felt a tinge of melancholy at how this whole evolution was coming down to its deadly conclusion. The shooter-spotter team quickly and efficiently set up their gear on the flat, three-foot-wide roof edge.

A perfect shot by any standards, Case thought.

Aspelsin had his cellphone out and was listening to Vyla speak on CNN as the sniper team got ready. Case watched as the tall, blonde sniper opened a long, thin box, which could have been a pool cue case, but instead contained a Barrett MRAD tactical sniper rifle. All around, from every radio and cellphone tuned to CNN, Vyla's speech could be heard. Case monitored the sniper team getting ready, then looked up toward Vyla at the podium, and the wild scene behind her of the hovering saucer.

Vyla stared out from the podium and continued speaking.

"For those of you who can't believe what you are seeing... the ship creates its own gravity wave." She turned slightly, glancing at Sophia as she continued.

"This allows it not only to hover but also to travel well beyond the speed of light."

Hushed amazement was followed by whistles. She shot a quick glance over her shoulder at the ship... hovering inches from the Capitol and continued.

"This craft is what we call a living conveyance, and she is actually alive and interacts with her pilot, not unlike when you ride a horse."

"Her name..." staring at the ship, before gesturing with her hand, "Is Sophia. Setimus, would you move Sophia from side to side, please?"

In a flash, the ship appeared to swoop left two hundred feet and then swoop back to the right, all in the blink of an eye! A loud roar of hushed amazement was followed by thunderous applause, cheers, and whistles. Vyla nodded, smiling, and leaned into the mic.

"I know... I still can't get over the magic," she said, staring at the ship before gesturing with her hand.

"And that bright future—is here now—for all of us!"

Loud whoops and applause.

On the library roof, the sniper calmly unfolded the gunstock, clipped his ten-round magazine into place, and knelt against the roof lip. The huge silencer on the rifle barrel was the only thing extending from the building's edge. Case watched as the sniper adjusted the parallax and mil settings on the scope knobs. The Spotter was set up next to him with a tripod, staring through his Leupold spotter scope. Within seconds, he had it dialed in. Case knew that from the time they began their sniper-speak, there would be only seconds before the first round would travel downrange. He knew these two would not miss on their first shot, especially under these optimal conditions—of almost no wind, a perfect view of their target, and a range of only three hundred meters.

"Shooter, lock and load," the Spotter whispered calmly, like he was buttering toast.

"Ready," the Sniper responded with the same nonchalance.

The Spotter watched.

"Shooter, by eye, go to the podium next to the Capitol... this side of the saucer."

"Contact," the Sniper replied.

"Go to glass," the Spotter said.

The Sniper moved his head closer to his scope and adjusted his body against the building's edge as he began describing Vyla... speaking to the crowd.

"Okay, target at the podium has blonde hair, female, leaning slightly to the right."

"That's your target," replied the Spotter. "Check parallax and mil."

The Sniper reached forward to his parallax knob and began focusing more closely, ensuring his vertical crosshair was dead center on Vyla's head and chest, which were above the podium.

"One-point-six," the Sniper whispered.

The Spotter looked at his handheld ballistics module and tapped in a number.

"Check level," the Spotter said, checking wind. "Holdover five-point-four."

Case watched as the Sniper began his firing sequence, breathing in and out more calmly, taking up slack in the trigger, and with that last bit of breath, he reached his natural respiratory pause.

"Ready," the Sniper calmly whispered.

The Spotter checked his glass.

"Left-point-two."

The finger pull that came next was smooth, sending the bullet down the barrel and through the silencer.

"PFFFT!" was all that could be heard of the bullet as the Sniper's head exploded in a bursting ball of blood and viscera, spraying onto the three-foot-wide ledge. The Spotter looked up, terrified, just in time to see the wrong end of Case's H&K P9S pistol with a Qual-A-Tech silencer pointed at him. The Spotter raised his hands, pleading.

"Bro—"

PFFFT! The Spotter's execution was just as quick. Case looked up at Aspelsin, who was startled but clearly not scared. Aspelsin glared at Case, and Case knew not to look directly into his eyes.

"Get on the ledge, or I'll shoot you," Case said calmly.

And before he could even think, Aspelsin put him into *a Hell-Realm.*

Case was suddenly frozen, his body softening. Imagery of humans mutilating each other flooded his mind. His body became slack as he dropped his pistol, falling to his knees. Aspelsin took a step, picked up the pistol, and fired immediately from two feet away, exploding Case's head. He stared down at the deadman momentarily, then calmly dropped the pistol and walked to the blonde sniper, or what was left of him, and rolled his body to the side, away from the sniper rifle. Aspelsin knew the gunsight was already zeroed-in on Vyla at the podium. He calmly picked up the rifle, knelt against the ledge, steadied himself, and placed the crosshairs on her.

V yla at the podium was speaking as she watched the ship.

"Setimus will now go to space and back in roughly two-point-five seconds. Camera people, this is your chance to go wide angle and point your cameras straight up, if you will."

On the library rooftop, Aspelsin had the crosshairs perfectly lined up on Vyla's chest. He let out a half-breath and put a gentle pull on the trigger.

PFFFT!

And suddenly what felt like a sledgehammer... hit his hip—as a bullet exploded into him—slamming him against the ledge. He dropped the rifle and looked up to see Chief Petty Officer Dan Day, pointing Case's pistol with the silencer directly at him.

"Move an inch, and you're dead," Dan said calmly.

"Who are you?" Aspelsin moaned as a strange, blood-like liquid was pumping from his hip wound and pooling near his feet.

"Doesn't matter who I am," Dan said. "Who the fuck are you?"

And instantly, the Hell-Realm began. But Dan had watched Case earlier. He had told Case he would help him take out the Sniper team, but traffic and crowds had delayed him. Case had warned him about Aspelsin, and Dan had watched through the glass door leading to the roof as Aspelsin had made Case fall to his knees before executing him. Dan had then waited, studying Aspelsin as the strange man picked up the rifle and began aiming. That's when Dan had come in with his best silent approach. But now, in this moment, as he felt it—the Hell-Realm—he switched to his energy training, of which he was a long-time master. He guided his mind before Aspelsin could get his hooks in. Dan slid into a field for fighting with energy, one that no human or even Reptilian could alter. He dropped his pistol and slammed into Aspelsin, driving himself into the Reptilian, lifting him in a bear hug as the wounded Aspelsin began twitching and morphing—shifting from human to Reptilian and back, in strength and visual. But it didn't matter.

Dan had come to protect Vyla, and he knew from Case's death moments before that he could only last seconds in his energy field before Aspelsin would get a second wind and perhaps break his field. He also knew another bullet might not kill the freakish Reptilian, and he wanted to be damn sure... this son of a bitch would not harm the amazing woman at the podium. A woman he had come to admire—and perhaps more.

In that instant, Dan looked Aspelsin in the eyes as he lifted the lizard and himself, pushing off with his powerful legs. Aspelsin screeched in fear, trapped in Dan's incredible grip as the tall martial-arts master... unbelievably, took both of them... over the ledge.

Chapter Forty-Seven

At the podium, Vyla was directing.

"The ship will now go side-to-side and up-and-down for you over the next five seconds... Setimus, take it away!"

The ship performed to oohs and ahhs.

"And now for a special treat, the tractor beam will be deployed, and you can watch me disappear as my molecules are scattered. But don't worry, I'll be back just after I disappear. Setimus, go ahead."

The crowd watched in astonishment as Vyla dematerialized and was completely gone... for three full seconds... then re-materialized. The crowd reacted with each change. Vyla then turned, gesturing to the ship, pointing to space. The crowd watched, stunned, as the ship shot vertically to 80,000 feet—hovered for a second—then returned! A hushed awe fell over the audience. And then applause and shouts of—

"Do it again! Do it again!"

Vyla nodded at the ship, which then extended its hemispheric legs and landed. A moment later, the ramp morphed down, and Swizzle departed the ship. Vyla approached, and the two exchanged a long hug to loud applause. She then walked him to the podium as they both waved at Senator Feinstein. The crowd was going wild, hyper-focused on the alien humanoid walking beside Vyla.

Swizzle greeted Dianne with a humble handshake and bow. She beamed and motioned him to the podium. He slowly stepped to the microphone. Then turned to watch Vyla walking toward the ship. The crowd waited with bated breath as Swizzle gazed out at them, giving a gentle nod to all.

"Hello, my name is Setimus, and I am from a race that exists outside the limits of your solar system," he began.

The crowd was transfixed, silent, spellbound.

"I was not born on your magnificent planet, but I have lived here all of my adult life. I donated my ship to your government, clear back in 1948. I had no idea they would never inform their own people about the existence of my ship. I taught school here, and I have friends here that I love and...," he looked quickly at Vyla. "That love me."

Vyla turned, smiling and gently tapped her fist on her chest, nodding sincerely, then proceeded up the ramp as it morphed closed behind her. A moment later, the ship's gear retracted, leaving it hovering. *Magic.* Swizzle continued.

"I taught Vyla how to fly Sophia, my ship there, and she's gotten pretty good!"

The crowd whooped.

"Vyla... liberated Sophia today from a rogue element within your own government—one that has kept the world ignorant of the existence of this incredible living conveyance—for over seventy years. My ship, Sophia, as you have now witnessed, is as alive as you and I. And I taught Vyla how to bond with her."

More applause and wonder.

"In exchange—Vyla has taught me—how to love."

Whoops and cheers from the audience as Sophia pulsed and let out a deep tone of acknowledgment behind him.

"My people, my kind, aliens... come in all forms. And just like you humans, there are those who mean well and want humanity to flourish, and then there are some who do not. Though my kind has been on your planet for over a thousand years, many of you, even seeing me here, will fight against the belief systems you grew up with. It's okay. Take your time and enjoy the ship today for all the technology it will show you. And certainly, those of you who need further proof that I am from somewhere else will, over time, understand that truth. I am as real as they come, and I want to welcome all of you on planet Earth to the Galactic Community. We have been waiting for you," he said, smiling.

Cheers erupted as he looked upon the audience, his face slowly taking on a more somber expression.

"I first came here in March of 1948 in the ship you see behind me. I landed in

Aztec, New Mexico, and after a short time meeting with your wonderful scientist J. Robert Oppenheimer at Los Alamos, I was awarded Ambassador status by your then-President, Harry Truman."

More applause.

"I stayed in America in complete secrecy—and that secrecy was not of my choice, but because your government did not think Americans, or the world, could handle the reality that the universe was teeming with life."

He paused, letting those words settle.

"Millions of races—large, small, odd, spiritual, physical, and multidimensional."

The audience was still hushed. Trying to grasp the overwhelming shift in their destiny.

"Your leaders at the time, who were part of Truman's administration and military, were terrified of losing control after the Great Depression. After one year of secret meetings and no genuine movement toward disclosure, I left your planet. And I knew then that your Cabal—would never tell you the truth about all the life teeming around you in the galaxy... and within your planet, and the many races who wanted to welcome you to the Galactic Community. Now, at this moment, I am here to announce that humanity is in a dire position. And you, as humans, are the only hope to save your own planet."

He paused again for effect.

"Understand that disclosure will never happen. There are trillions of dollars for private multinational companies willing to keep their mouths shut about the alien presence on your planet. A presence that has now been in effect for over seventy years. Those trillions continue to flow to military contractors willing to remain silent. So, you can't expect to suddenly have all those corporations apologize to you for keeping you in the dark for the past seventy years. In the dark about technology that could have saved millions in hospitals and technology that could have prevented countless wars."

The crowd was quiet, reflective.

"Finally, I'm glad to say that Vyla and I are here to help all of you understand that benevolent alien races, like your human race—are waiting in the wings to welcome you to your future."

Whoops and applause. He nodded, but again took a hard look at the crowd.

"We are in touch with Senator Feinstein and will return in a few days' time. Thank you."

He walked towards the ship to raucous applause around him as Sophia's legs suddenly extended; the ramp came down and absorbed him as he entered. The crowd went ballistic. Sophia pulsed for a few seconds, and a moment later, shot diagonally into the deep blue sky—and vanished!

The roar of the crowd in that moment, and the stunned, mystical faces staring at where the ship had disappeared into infinity, was, for the aged and venerable Dianne Feinstein, worth a lifetime she had given.

J ust beyond Steph's school, Anne and Stephanie were walking quickly along the neighborhood sidewalk.

The heat was crushing. All the houses had damage, and the occupants were in their yards, trying to reconcile their belongings. The two girls were constantly stepping over fallen tree parts and debris, and just ahead, they could see the downed power line near Dah's house. There were burning road flares near the downed lines, and two military men steered Steph and Anne around the still-sparking wires.

Another military man approached with ice-cold bottles of water. The girls thanked him and kept walking, opening the cool water and gulping. They both poured some over their heads as they moved along the sidewalk.

Ahead, they saw a military ambulance with a big red cross emblazoned on the green paint. Next to it, two military personnel were loading a stretcher with what appeared to be one of their classmates. They looked at each other, puzzled.

"Is that Tommy?" Stephanie said, and suddenly felt dizzy. She slowed.

"Are you okay?" Anne said, grabbing Steph's shoulder and attempting to hold her up. But Anne, too, was suddenly overwhelmed. Her dizziness growing, she released Steph, who collapsed on the sidewalk.

Anne dropped a moment later to her hands and knees, feeling like she was going to puke, but managed to look up one last time at her water bottle and finally at the two military men approaching with a stretcher. Her vision dimmed as she collapsed next to Stephanie, already knocked out, lying on the sidewalk.

D ah stood in tears, placing a blanket over Banjo's crushed body as she finished a passing song for him.

She slowly stepped off the porch, sniffling, walking the sidewalk towards Steph's school, and exhaled a sigh of relief when she saw the military had arrived. Small comforts in the chaos. Ahead, she saw the flares and was escorted past the wires by two soldiers guarding the electrical line.

She suddenly heard a siren fire up and watched a military ambulance pull away from the curb.

She walked fast, passing a soldier holding water bottles. He only half-looked her way, and she wished she had brought one with her as she picked up her pace towards the school just ahead. She had a sense to look back at the ambulance and turned, but it was long gone. She turned back towards the school and upped her pace, sweating, and placed a call to Charlotte.

I n the moonlight, Sophia was resting on her extended landing gear and hemispheric pads in the middle of a high school football stadium just outside Arlington, Virginia.

Pitch black in the empty stadium. Swizzle and Vyla stared out at the empty bleachers.

"The cloaking is on. If there is anyone out there, they simply won't see the ship," he said.

They shared a moment.

"I can't thank you enough for all of this," he said.

She nodded, and they embraced.

He gave her a look.

"If you need to run down the ramp to throw up, it's alright."

She shook her head at him, realizing he had read her thoughts—and then she ran. Racing down the ramp into the pitch-black night, she dropped to her hands and knees, purging on the football field's dewy wet grass. He was standing behind her when she finally came up for air.

"Would you like some water?" he said, holding out a bottled water.

She nodded and got to her feet, wiping her mouth with her hands and then wiping her hands on the wet grass. He was smiling quizzically at her when she took the water, popping the top to gulp.

"Yes," she said. "I'm pregnant."

He nodded slowly.

"And this is a good thing? He asked. "Expected?"

"Not expected, but a wonderful thing," she whispered.

He nodded.

"Well, as long as you are happy, I'm happy."

"I'm happy that we got your ship back and that the world knows a little more than they did yesterday." She whispered.

He nodded.

"Me too."

They shared a final hug, and she turned, walking toward the stadium exit as Swizzle walked up the ramp, which morphed, closing behind him. Vyla kept her pace up, turning around to see that the ship was, in fact, cloaked. She waved anyway and felt an energy shift as it departed. She looked up momentarily to see the ship become visible for one split second, high above her. A Swizzle *goodbye*. She pulled out her cell and dialed, listening for a moment.

"I'm on my way out. Just hold on, I'll be there in a minute."

She scampered around the bleachers and passed through the ticket turnstile, departing the small stadium to the street behind. Her thoughts were half on Charlotte ahead of her in the rental car, and half on the tiny magical one growing inside her. Too much to process around that in this moment. She approached Charlotte's rental car and could see her sitting behind the wheel in tears. She hopped in and pulled the passenger door closed, seeing that Charlotte was silently sobbing. Vyla touched her hand.

"Sweetie—what's happening?"

Charlotte reeled herself in.

"There's been an earthquake in the Bay Area. Massive."

Now fully crying as Vyla reached to grip her shoulder.

"Marten and Dah—they..." Charlotte said and stopped.

Vyla watched her as she tried to rein it in. Charlotte burst into tears again, yelling,

"My flight's not for seven more hours! And Dah and Marten are out looking—they can't find Steph or Anne!"

I n Palo Alto, near Steph's school, the military ambulance pulled into a secluded parking lot surrounded by trees.

The parking lot was secured by military types in black tactical uniforms. Immediately, the rear doors of the ambulance were opened, and three large operatives picked up the passed-out girls and little Tommy, carrying them towards a half-sized shipping container. The operators were a well-oiled machine.

A moment later, the door to the half-sized shipping container was opened as the three drugged kids were placed on the floor. They were the last to be loaded, as the container was now jammed full. Most of the other kids, of all races and ages, were prone, still knocked out. But a few could hear the big container door opening and were attempting to sit up when the gush of air hit them, but couldn't find control of their limbs.

The military operatives who carried Steph, Anne, and Tommy quickly stepped back as the huge steel door was closed and latched. The container was painted in tactical camouflage colors—army-style patterns of muted green. It was already mounted on a small trailer behind a Ford F-550, painted in the same military style.

HUSH

The F-550 pulled out and accelerated onto Highway 101 southbound.

Ricky Slepher smoked a cigarette as the five Ford F-550s arrived, towing their respective containers.

The large blimp hangar at Moffett Field, called *Hangar One*, was famous as one of the world's largest freestanding structures. Ricky looked down and realized he had a tiny bit of blood splatter on his arm from last night's executions of the two young Stanford students attempting to expose Dulce Base. He shook his head and puffed on his cig, realizing that nobody would notice the little blood splatters on his arm... or care. He looked up and nodded at the female operative next to the hangar door, wearing a black baseball hat that matched her tactical outfit. She flipped a switch, and a deep mechanical sound was heard, followed by the huge doors of Hangar One sliding open—just enough for his convoy of five F-550 trucks to pass.

He watched as all towed their shipping containers. The sky had grown dark, and many more of Ricky's operatives watched from inside the hangar as the line of trucks continued deep into the enormous facility. The huge doors then closed as the final truck passed. Ricky looked up inside the hangar, where a massive, rotating, antigravity ship, as big as a football field, hovered just forty feet off the hangar floor. The octagon-shaped craft had a pointy top and bottom, like a diamond. Silent, and colored in a deep-black hue from which no light escaped. He knew it as a Reptilian ship, and it was damn impressive. Far beyond the antigravity TR-3Bs of the American space fleet.

But hell, he thought, *the Reptilians had been spacefaring for eons. Made sense their ships were the big bad-asses in this realm.*

In two minutes flat, all the shipping containers from the trucks were placed onto the concrete, round ramp that somehow sat at ground level but also appeared to be attached to the ship, hovering just above the pad. When the final container was in place next to the others, all five F-550s departed out the far end of the hangar. Ricky nodded at several of his operatives as he stepped onto the platform near the shipping containers. He watched above him as the huge ship suddenly illuminated, flashing red, yellow, and blue lights flickering from each of the eight sides of the octagon.

A switch was thrown at the far end of the building, and the huge hangar doors opened again, just enough. The ship, rotating silently at first, then began to thrum louder, like a bass amp with a pulsing electrical hum as it geared up for its jump into space-time. The entire platform, carrying Ricky and all the containers, began rising into the huge hovering monstrosity. The operatives in Hangar One watched in fascination as the Draco ship pulsed once and then shot through the open hangar doors, dissolving in a black haze of soundless velocity, up into the arriving twilight.

S tanding in the enormous, Cabal-owned St. Louis hangar, only fifteen minutes after departing Moffett Federal Airfield in California, Ricky pulled on another cig, and thought about how fast they had just traveled.

He was now dressed in his civilian truck driver attire—red shirt, blue jeans, and boots. He double-checked that the rear doors of his semi were closed and latched. He looked up to see the same hovering octagonal ship and, just below it, sat the empty, open shipping containers. He pulled his P9S pistol, slid the action to put a round in the chamber, and then placed the sidearm back in the hidden holster below his loose t-shirt.

He boarded his semi, noting the nicely painted 'Little Rome's Pizza Delivery' on the side of his truck as he entered the cab. Then, cranked the engine, watching as the other semi drivers boarded their trucks, ready to follow him. He heard the ship's thrumming begin to rise and watched as the circular ramp rose and reattached to the circling black phantom. And then his favorite part... as the ship circled faster, the sound vibrated his huge semi-truck, and then—just like that—it vanished through the open hangar door.

He shook his head at the marvel that still got to him. He pulled out, sneaking his semi past the hangar doors into the pitch-black night at a crawl. He pulled on his cig and turned on the radio as he departed St. Louis Lambert International Airport, still at just a crawl. He settled in for the hour-long drive, turning the dial to his favorite alternative rock station. Checked his mirror to see that all six semis were in place behind him. He downshifted and lowered the pedal to the floor as the engine jumped the semi up to highway speed. He led the caravan onto the interstate and, in short order, took Highway 270 South, out of St. Louis toward Memphis. Checked again behind him to see the other semis right on his tail in the far-right lane. He set his cruise at fifty-five. No speeding tickets tonight for his drivers and their precious cargo.

It was only sixty easy miles south to the incline ramp at the Rock City facility. He pulled again on his cig and flicked the still-burning stub out the window. Took a deep breath and exhaled, passing a billboard advertising the new movie with Tom Cruise and Tom Hanks playing two down-and-out homeless guys who stumble upon a time machine. He snickered at the billboard and wondered how hard it must be to stay on top as an actor, always having to battle getting older. He caught a glimpse of himself in the mirror and then turned to look again.

Not bad. He thought. *Haven't aged at all since he began using his own product three years ago. This shit really does work!*

He smiled to himself and remembered his granddad warning him to stay clear of Screamshit. And he loved the old man, but the times were different now, and you had to really know your product—not to mention all the benefits of longevity. His granddad had passed fifteen years ago, but it was not for Ricky to grow old. He had found The Fountain of Youth. *Owned it.* He figured the old man would be proud of how Ricky was now the top distributor on the planet.

Forty minutes and three cigarettes later, he saw the exit sign for Rock City was only three miles ahead. He triggered his hazard lights. On that signal, all six trucks behind him passed as Ricky liked to be the last to arrive. He saddled in behind his flock and felt good that he was driving tonight. The earthquake in California had provided six hundred little ghosts from all over the Bay Area, and this haul would bring him closer to his goal of owning his own antigravity craft. He often went to the Draco base on the moon to deliver a batch of his little ones, but that required waiting for a ride—and he wanted his own transportation. He had worked out a deal with the Reptilians that if he delivered good numbers this month, he would be awarded a small ship for personal use.

That would be his crowning achievement. The very top of the food chain. It wouldn't be long now. He allowed the six trucks ahead of him to gain some distance, knowing they would have to unload first and then hit the ramp for their washout. So, he was in no hurry. He enjoyed pulling in last and getting through the process quickly, not having to wait for the other trucks. He popped open the center console and pulled out the beautiful vial. It was small and stunning and felt good in his hand. He lit another cig and stared at his little gem, smiling at his accomplishment.

These high-dollar ones only went to the global elite. The thick handmade glass, the gold tag hanging from the beautiful red string—just below the eyedropper top. He caught the tag on his thumb and admired it. That two-centimeter, shiny gold square had Ricky's emblem embossed in black. His *Winking Wolf* symbol meant you had the finest strain in the galaxy. He thought about those elite Reptilians bartering for his fucking Screamshit. He slowly unscrewed the eyedropper. This was a fresh bottle, and he took his time, driving with his knees so he wouldn't spill a drop. He leaned his head back slowly, keeping his eyes on the road. Steady as a rock on cruise control.

He sucked up a half-eyedropper-full and admired the stunning red magic. Took a deep breath and dropped eight drops all over his tongue. Replaced the top and ensured it was sealed nicely. He slowly closed his mouth, setting the vial down, savoring the good stuff now sliding like a powerful snake into his system. He felt the surge of its electricity starting to ignite his entire body. Howled his wolf howl at full volume, then shook his head to re-ground himself. *Wow!*

He still couldn't get over the kick. And the energy reminded him of being on the bench at Stanford, as he was about to move on those two girls who had the Dulce footage. And he thought about that evolution. How one just cried, and he had to snuff her out quick—because he hated that shit. But the other one, the black-haired one with the tattoos, she was a rare bird. One of the only ones he had ever encountered who wouldn't say shit while being tortured.

Not a goddamn thing.

And the fucking old man she was working for—she wouldn't even give his name. Not a word... hardly a whimper.

She even managed to chuckle at him after his slap knocked her head damn-near off her shoulders. Her sassy grin, through all that blood, made him want to slit her throat right then. But he had to make it all look like a murder-suicide, so he just strung her up. He couldn't get that look of hers out of his mind—her calm eyes staring at him as he hoisted her. And she held her eyes that way right to her end. Like she knew she had won.

Fucking bitch. He hoped she burned in hell.

He kept driving and thought about the Reptilians far below Rock City, down in the DUMB. He was always happy to do business with those winged bitches. And, by God, there were plenty of them, miles below where he would park his truck. Those Reps were huge, white-skinned, and as evil as evil could ever think to be. He had once witnessed them torturing two twin kids before devouring them alive.

That was some shit! Holy-fucking God!

That one took him a while to get past. He had never seen a human eaten alive until that night, years ago. Since then, he had seen way crazier stuff—the Cabal was doing wild experiments with huge-ass spiders way down there. Ones they imported from Mars or someplace.

And they altered those big-ass arachnids, feeding humans to those bitches just to see if the spiders would spin a stronger web material—one that would increase the strength of Cabal soldier uniforms used in off-world skirmishes.

Fuckin-A! Ricky thought.

And still, there was so much more that nobody would ever believe the Cabal could do—unless you were like him—and you guarded that shit. He heard a semi ahead of him blare its horn for a car going by, and he remembered it was only a few more miles to offload this new batch of his little ghosts.

Veal, as the Draco-Reptilians referred to his little ones in the back, would provide many more vials—and keep his coffers full.

He smacked his lips and savored it. He had come to enjoy the taste of his very top strain. And the magic of how he developed it. Taken from the youngest of each batch. *So be it.* He thought, as he reveled in the electricity of his perfected strain surging through him in that moment.

Delicious—with a hint of adrenaline.

Just a few more miles, and his team would begin it all again. The demand was only growing bigger. Two million taken worldwide per year was the last he heard.

Two million per year? he wondered.

Realizing there must be many distributors like him worldwide. *Competition.* He'd think about those fuckers later—and how he would absorb their operations. He still couldn't believe nobody had put it together?

But then again, nobody believed in aliens either!

He laughed aloud at that one, shaking his head at how easily the deception was maintained. Humans could be led to believe anything, he thought. Just put the shit right in front of them, and magically, they won't notice it.

He shook his head as cars with families flew by his caravan of pizza-delivery semis. Kids in the back seats even waved up at him, coaxing him to honk his big horn. But he knew the parents couldn't see him. Wouldn't see him. Didn't want to believe someone like him could exist.

He was *Ghostwalker.* And the ones in back were his *little ghosts,* and sometimes, he would honk his horn for those nice families passing by as the parents waved and smiled up at him. But they wouldn't see him... or aliens either. He chuckled again and shook his head, amused.

Minutes later he rounded the Limestone Lane turn in his semi and was at a crawl in the pitch black as he passed the brown *Rock City National Archives and Records* sign. He could see the other trucks parked in their spots, but with their engines still running.

Strange.

He could see his tactical team standing behind the first truck. He parked and quickly shut down.

What in the hell? he thought, looking over at the truck driver next to him, who just seemed to stare ahead, looking into the distance.

Ricky got out of the cab—pissed.

Heads are gonna fuckin' roll, he thought. *I don't give a goddamn what their excuse is—these trucks should be unloaded already!*

Then he noticed a muted drumming sound in the far distance. Like a whisper.

A friggin' drum corps is rehearsing at this hour? Whatever.

He rounded the corner behind his truck and approached the tactical team gathered there. He was astonished that every truck was still running!

These machines should have all been shut off minutes ago! he thought as he quickly approached his tactical team, and not one of them turned to acknowledge him!

He finally stepped into the circle, and that's when it hit him. They were all standing in a stupor, their eyes open, but they all seemed to be in limbo. And that's when *he saw it.* On the edge of the forest, in the distance. A one-hundred-foot silver ship. Incredible, and the perfect size for a personal ship!

Was this for him!? Holy shit! he thought. *The fucking Draco-Reptilians had come through!*

She was stunning! Sitting on three long legs with three huge hemispheric landing pads on the end of each leg. And the ramp was open, with a beautiful soft glow emanating from inside the ship. And on the outside, she glowed a dim, deep teal. Then—a sound. And a smell nearby.

A cigarette?

Ricky turned to see a vagrant smoking a cig—coming around the corner of his last truck. Shuffling, hunched over.

Homeless fuck, what was he doing here!?

Approaching with his cigarette in mouth and clearly no threat, but Ricky raised his pistol anyway until he could see the old man more clearly. He cocked the trigger. *I don't have time for this bitch!* he thought.

His mind was still tripping, with the ship in the distance and his team all weird-looking. He shook his head in utter disgust at the homeless fuck, relishing the thought of shooting that vagrant in the face, but he would wait—to see the old man's terror when he realized that it would be his last fucking breath!

"Have you got any spare change, young man?" the old man said, moving forward as if he couldn't see the barrel inches from his face.

Ricky snickered, shaking his head... staring the old man right in the eyes... and pulled the trigger.

But Ricky was just a hair too late.

He had already been ensnared by the vagrant, who now stared at Ricky with no quarter. All of Ricky's neural pathways to muscular action had been severed. And even though he had sent that last message from his brain to pull the goddamn trigger and blow that old man fuck away, his finger didn't react to his brain's command.

"Relax, you piss-ant, and put the gun back."

Swizzle pulled on his cig, watching as Ricky slowly lifted his red T-shirt and re-holstered the pistol. Ricky's angry face betrayed his last vengeful thought, but his actions now were almost robotic, slow—calm. And in his controlled state, Ricky heard the thundering of the drums growing in volume around him—coming from the forest. And Swizzle heard them too and wondered about them, knowing he didn't bring them—the ones now flickering in and out of space-time all around them.

Ancient Navajo and Apache, in full warpaint and adorned for battle, flittering through the trees—angry, dancing, chanting, and drumming. And now coming clear to Swizzle—standing before the throng of warriors, the two Swizzle almost couldn't look at because of their power.

Waya, the huge one, stood stone-faced, holding the reins of the horse next to him. And sitting on that horse, with his ancient stare, adorned in his full ceremonial dress with a hand on his vertical war lance, was Chief Elu.

Swizzle turned to catch sight of Vyla exiting the ship, the intensity of her gait as she approached—and he knew—she had brought them.

"Where are they?!" she said in a terse whisper, approaching with Charlotte just behind.

"Steph and Anne are in truck three. That's where I'm picking up her beacon," Swizzle said, still struck by the power Vyla was wielding, in a display the likes of which he had never seen.

She nodded, passing him with Charlotte just behind, and they went truck to truck quickly, reefing hard on the rear doors of the semis, opening them wide.

The thundering of the drums grew from those light beings in the forest. And the two ancient leaders stood in front with their intense stares. Swizzle watched as Vyla and Charlotte pulled each door, sending a gush of fresh air into each darkened trailer, waking many of the little ones.

Charlotte and Vyla were strong for all, as they reached and lifted the children, setting each one gently on the ground. Little girls and boys ranging from three to thirteen, each with the stench of too many packed together, with no place to relieve themselves.

Swizzle had those sweet ones sit in rows in the fresh night air, so each could be accounted for. And the children stared out at their protection in the forest and almost forgot their ordeal. Their eyes swept over the ancient ones all around them, and each felt the thundering of those drums.

The three adults walked among the kids, assuring each that they were being returned to their parents and their homes. Many were crying and certainly drugged, and fortunately, none had died on the journey. Steph and Anne were still drugged, but okay. Those two, Charlotte took to the ship, holding their hands, and disappeared up the ramp.

Swizzle noticed Vyla hesitate as she passed Ricky Slepher in his switched-off stance. She seemed to focus curiously on his forearm and then looked up to his menacing face, staring down at her, and Swizzle could see she was beyond fear now.

Vyla opened her pipeline as she looked at the man—to what she now understood, loitering there in his dark energy world. And that was all she needed. Swizzle watched in wonder as she stepped away from Ricky to the crying kids nearby. He understood the next level of her power then, as he watched her whisper, comforting the little ones. A moment later, she slowly turned to see Swizzle watching her. He nodded, and she raised her phone and placed the 911 call, telling them what they would find at the Rock City government facility behind the pizza delivery trucks.

He watched as she put the phone away and produced a small notepad and pen from her back pocket. She scribbled a note, sliding it into Ricky's shirt pocket as she passed. Then she walked among the children one last time and up the ramp into Sophia.

A moment later, the ship was cloaked, not visible, but he knew it was still there.

He stepped to Slepher and noted Vyla's rolled note extending from the large man's shirt pocket. Swizzle didn't have to read it. He looked Slepher directly in the eyes as he whispered to him.

"You won't remember me. You won't remember an old man disabling your tactical team, and all your truck drivers. You won't remember the two women with me unloading all the kids. You won't fight the sheriff's deputies that are on their way. You'll begin to wake up when they are putting handcuffs on you, and you won't remember seeing that ship in the distance."

He took one last look at Slepher and could hear sirens out on the highway, growing closer. He walked among the lines of children, comforting the ones who reached out to touch his legs as he passed by.

He had all of them look at him.

"Stay where you are and soon you'll be home—those in the forest are here to protect you."

And he knew that even if the kids wanted to move from that point forward, they would be incapacitated until the sheriffs arrived.

He walked slowly toward the ship and seemed to vanish as the ramp morphed around him.

Vyla, Charlotte, and Swizzle watched from the cloaked ship as the first sheriff's car came around the corner and quickly slowed, its headlights illuminating the many children sitting in rows.

Two deputies jumped out with guns drawn, staring around, seeing the tactical team with their guns, standing frozen in their circle, and Ricky standing nearby. Everywhere around the deputies were the bewildered kids on the ground, holding hands, as more law enforcement cars raced in, lights flashing.

The deputies didn't look toward the ship, because there was nothing to see in that direction. Nothing for the deputies to see but the scared little ones, staring up in tears, wanting to go home.

And yet, the deputies were curious—many of the children seemed to watch the forest. But there was nothing there the deputies could see.

Only the little ones could see them—and hear their thundering drums, and the stunning ship, pulsing softly. The deputies quickly had the tactical team and Ricky completely disarmed, as they remained frozen in place.

Swizzle sensed something then, standing just behind Vyla in the ship, as they watched the actual sheriff arrive and step out of her SUV. Something about that sheriff. And Swizzle knew—she could see.

The sheriff of Monroe County, Illinois, closed the door of her SUV and stood still, listening... feeling the thunder of the drums. She saw them all around her in the forest, and the ship too. She knew they were Navajo and Apache. She was conversant in both languages. A gift from her father, who had recently passed.

Vyla watched Sheriff Helen Elizabeth Boyd as she walked among the kids, and Swizzle could feel the profound connection between the two women as Helen glanced toward the ship, moving through the children.

"Sheriff Boyd, ma'am!" A female deputy guarding Ricky yelled. "Somethin' here for ya!"

Sheriff Boyd slowly approached Ricky Slepher, noting his still suspended, angry expression, as she looked up and down his large frame. She reached to Ricky's t-shirt, lifting the rolled paper. She noted Vyla in the ship and then looked down, slowly unrolling the note.

The blood specks on my right forearm will match the DNA of two women murdered at Stanford University yesterday evening.

Helen looked up at the frozen Ricky and raised the note high above her head. In the ship, Swizzle watched Vyla's steady gaze as Sheriff Helen Boyd held the note high in the starlight. They then watched her lower the note.

Sheriff Boyd turned away from Slepher, sliding the note in her pocket as she took in the forest all around her. The Warriors were everywhere, and she noted the two in front. The two that knew her father and shared their lives with him. Those two before her now. The huge one—the Navajo hunter standing next to the horse with the venerable chief sitting astride, holding his lance—as the night breeze blew the feathers of his ceremonial headdress.

She looked one last time toward the ship as it began to pulse. And the children could see it too. Each child held spellbound—and just for that moment, each felt time stop.

Sophia suddenly pulsing for the little ones, glowing her shimmering teal in the midst of the thundering drums of the dancing warriors. She silently lifted, ascending up and away, and the protection in the forest, all of them seemed to flicker—and dissolve.

Yet the sound of their thundering drums continued as the kids watched in wonder.

And then, a sight none of them would ever forget.

That deep teal ship, rising and pulsing—becoming more brilliant as it climbed higher—and then, suddenly, it was a biplane... spinning as it ascended... into the twinkling heavens, pulsing one-last-time, as if to say *goodbye*... finally shooting deep... into that speckled and shimmering Navajo blanket of stars.

EPILOGUE

Diego Garcia is asleep during the day but comes alive each night.

Darkness is when the cloaking of the base is activated so that satellites and space-based platforms can't monitor the spaceship activity at the facility. This nightly cloaking culminates with the 4:05 a.m. German *Dark-Fleet* space freighter arrival. The Nazi Mothership arrives from high orbit and descends—80,000 feet in one second—to a hover position over the Diego loading dock, one hundred feet off the deck. The huge space freighter never touches down.

All materials to and from the ship are loaded via tractor beam in complete silence. The rest of the surface base personnel (regular white uniform, U.S. Navy) are on lockdown in those early morning hours and cannot access or view the area where the space traffic is working in silence.

There are many regular Navy personnel who worked at Diego Garcia for years and had no idea the base was an operational spaceport below them and around them, due to the above lockdown protocols.

Diego's surface distribution works in combination with the DUMB, where submarines, spaceships, and mag-lev trains access the Diego facility via undersea and tunnel routes. These platforms distribute off-world materials and *traffic* as well as delivering goods to the facility that are bound for off-world destinations. From simple spices to weapons of mass destruction, it all goes both ways at the Diego spaceport.

Currently, the American Black Navy (Cabal created, but run by the CIA) controls the upper floors of the spaceport and DUMB. The CIA MK-ULTRA program is still in full swing at Diego as well as a large National Security Agency facility within the DUMB. Lower in the DUMB are the German *Dark-Fleet* levels working under a caste system, and below that are the city areas and then the sewers, to include the tunnel people mentioned in the story. Below the sewer level is the Grey alien genetic testing lab, and below that is the prison level often called *the Dungeon*. Further down still are the Reptilian areas, several of which can only be accessed via teleportation.

Weekly meetings with generals from various countries are helmed by a twelve-foot tall Reptilian who literally controls all commerce arriving to and departing from the planet. He is, in a nutshell, a completely AI-created entity and uploads his weekly information to a Reptilian mothership (also completely AI) that can be accessed by other malevolent alien races... hoping to trade with Earth through the Draco. The big AI Rep is currently being hacked by a country he loathes.

Mag-Lev shuttles, submarines, and spaceships arriving undersea are nightly visitors to the facility. Also housed at the Diego DUMB is the majority of the Vatican library, dealing with ancient alien artifacts. All the past reported Silk Road Gold is there as well. The facility is often used as a first meeting place for alien congregations arriving on the planet. The DUMB is themed in red velvet with many Greco-Roman artifacts and statues. Huge hangar-size spaces, used for facilitating large spaceships, are available when needed.

The base was created from Reptilian sound technology before Homo sapiens evolved on the planet. The base basically built itself and like current spacefaring ships that are molecularly alive... the Diego Base, deep below, is also alive, but currently in a sleeping state. Since the late 1970s, the expansion of the DUMB by the Nazis and the Cabal has been continuous.

Benjamin R. Waters hid in a military vehicle and escaped the slaughter of the hijackers, and though currently free—really isn't—and never will be.

Kill switch.

MEMORIAL

The symbol of MH370—a stolen monument of lost loved ones.

The disassembled MH370 jet still sits in a CIA hangar on the southwest end of the surface airbase, gathering dust. The hangar is a block from where Philip Wood's final text message was sent. The wings and tail pieces are stacked against the walls. The fuselage is still in one piece... but gutted. The paint is gone, and one would not see anything identifying the jet as being associated with Malaysia Airlines, but the fuselage measures exactly 209 feet long. A unique length. The Boeing 777 length.

Finally, to the most important—you, the survivors—the many loved ones of the massacred passengers and crew of MH370.

My hope is that, on some level, this story—that I know to be true—about your loved ones' final hours... will provide some closure.

My heart goes out to all of you.

M.D. Selig
September 19, 2025

M.D. Selig is a produced screenwriter and director with previous shows on Netflix, Showtime, and Amazon Prime. A decorated combat veteran and former Marine jet-attack pilot. He enjoys heavy research to place historical characters back within the covert evolutions they took part in. He lives and works in California and the Caribbean.

Acknowledgements

To the many who sacrificed everything to tell the truth.
This one's for you.

My sincere thanks to the following:

John and Helen Selig.

My dear friends and family.

Graphic artist and audiobook recording engineer, Nick Olivo.

Chris Baird and Debbi Dachinger for their invaluable help in growing the visibility of *HUSH*.

Editors Pam Murphy, Lincoln Molin, Pamela Minch.

Artist Gary Simmons for his stunning *Wolfrobe* sketch. (Inspiration for Chief Elu) Copyright © 1979 Gary Simmons, all rights reserved.

The many authors, researchers, and whistleblowers who provided foundation material for all the factual historical events in our covert history.

My gratitude to Laura Eisenhower, Barbara Lamb and Kaedrich Olsen for their endorsements and support.

Finally, a very special thanks to Rebecca Baron at *Find the Light RB*, for her otherworldly insights.

Websites about content in *HUSH*. MDSelig.com
Patreon.com/MDSeligAmazon.com/author/MDselig
Contact@QueenHelensRevenge.com

M.D. Selig A-6e Intruder Desert Storm 1991